CYANIDE WELLS

SHARON MCCONE MYSTERIES
BY MARCIA MULLER

DEAD MIDNIGHT
LISTEN TO THE SILENCE
A WALK THROUGH THE FIRE
WHILE OTHER PEOPLE SLEEP
BOTH ENDS OF THE NIGHT
THE BROKEN PROMISE LAND
A WILD AND LONELY PLACE
TILL THE BUTCHERS CUT HIM DOWN
WOLF IN THE SHADOWS
PENNIES ON A DEAD WOMAN'S EYES
WHERE ECHOES LIVE
TROPHIES AND DEAD THINGS
THE SHAPE OF DREAD
THERE'S SOMETHING IN A SUNDAY
EYE OF THE STORM
THERE'S NOTHING TO BE AFRAID OF
DOUBLE (*with Bill Pronzini*)
LEAVE A MESSAGE FOR WILLIE
GAMES TO KEEP THE DARK AWAY
THE CHESHIRE CAT'S EYE
ASK THE CARDS A QUESTION
EDWIN OF THE IRON SHOES

NONSERIES
POINT DECEPTION

CYANIDE WELLS

MARCIA MULLER

Published by Warner Books

An AOL Time Warner Company

Copyright © 2003 by Pronzini-Muller Family Trust
All rights reserved.

 Mysterious Press books are published by Warner Books, Inc.,
1271 Avenue of the Americas, New York, NY 10020.

Visit our Web site at www.twbookmark.com.

An AOL Time Warner Company

The Mysterious Press name and logo are registered trademarks of Warner Books, Inc.

Printed in the United States of America

First Printing: July 2003
10 9 8 7 6 5 4 3 2 1

Library of Congress Cataloging-in-Publication Data
Muller, Marcia.
    Cyanide Wells / Marcia Muller.
        p. cm.
    ISBN 0-89296-781-1
    1. California, Northern—Fiction. 2. Missing persons—Fiction. 3. Runaway wives—Fiction. 4. Lesbians—Fiction. I. Title.

PS3563.U397C93 2003
813'.54—dc21   2002045516

For Robin and John Reese—
members in good standing of the Top-of-the-Hill Gang

Thanks to:

Barbara Bibel, for aid in researching;
Victoria Brouillette, my Minnesota connection;
Joe Chernicoff, for information on antique firearms;
Charlie Lucke and John Pearson, for their
photographic expertise;
And Bill Pronzini, who makes me work much too hard!

CYANIDE WELLS

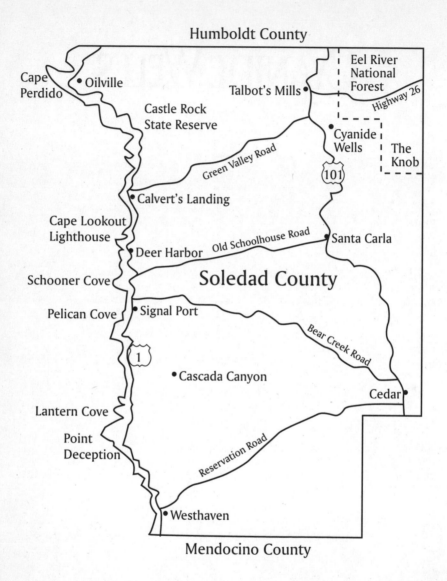

Humboldt County

Cape Perdido • Oilville

Talbot's Mills •

Eel River National Forest

Highway 26

Castle Rock State Reserve

Green Valley Road

Cyanide Wells

The Knob

101

• Calvert's Landing

Cape Lookout Lighthouse

Old Schoolhouse Road

Santa Carla

Deer Harbor

Schooner Cove

Soledad County

Pelican Cove • Signal Port

Bear Creek Road

1

• Cascada Canyon

Cedar •

Lantern Cove

Point Deception

Reservation Road

• Westhaven

Mendocino County

Saugatuck, Minnesota
Thursday, July 28, 1988

atthew Lindstrom?"

"Yes?"

"This is Sheriff Cliff Brandt of Sweetwater County, Wyoming. Are you married to a Gwen Lindstrom?"

". . . Yes, I am."

"And she drives a white Toyota Tercel, this year's model, Minnesota license number four-four-three-B-C-Y?"

"That's correct. What's this about, Sheriff?"

"Her car was found in my jurisdiction, parked by the side of County Road Eleven, eight miles from Reliance. That's a farming community north of Interstate Eighty. Nothing wrong with the vehicle, but there were bloodstains on the dash and other signs consistent with a struggle. A purse containing her identification and credit cards was on the passenger's seat."

"And Gwen? What about Gwen?"

"No sign of her. Tell me, Mr. Lindstrom, does she know anyone in Reliance? Or Sweetwater County?"

"As far as I know, she's never been to Wyoming."

"When did you last see Mrs. Lindstrom?"

"Two weeks ago, on the fourteenth."

"Two *weeks* ago? And you've got no idea where she's been since then?"

"We're separated. Have filed for divorce. We met on the fourteenth to go over the property settlement."

"I see. Messy divorce?"

"Amicable. We have no children and very little in the way of assets."

"There was a student ID from Saugatuck College in your wife's purse."

"Yes, she's a senior in the journalism department."

"And what do you do, Mr. Lindstrom?"

"I teach photography there, operate a small studio on the side. Mostly wedding portraits, that sort of— Why are you asking me these questions? And what are you doing to find Gwen?"

"Just familiarizing myself with the situation. I take it you can account for your whereabouts during the past two weeks?"

"Of course I can! I was here in Saugatuck, teaching summer courses. Now, what are you doing to find—"

"Don't get all exercised, Mr. Lindstrom. My last question was strictly routine. As for finding your wife, we plan to circularize her photograph, but we're hoping you can provide a better likeness than the one on her driver's license."

"I'll overnight several to you. If you find her, will you please ask her to call me? Or if . . ."

"*If* Mr. Lindstrom?"

"Well, if something's happened to her . . ."

"Don't worry. We'll be in touch."

Thousand Springs, Nevada
Thursday, July 28, 1988

hat's a bad place to hitchhike. Somebody could pick you off coming around the curve. Where're you headed?"

"West. Where're you going?"

"All the way to Soledad County, California."

"Good a place as any, I guess. If you'd like some company . . ."

"Hop in."

"Thanks, I really appreciate it. I was starting to get spooked, all alone here."

"Why were you alone, anyway?"

"My last ride dropped me off. I kind of . . . had trouble with him."

"That'll happen. Hitching's not the safest way for a woman to travel."

"I know, but it's the only way I've got."

"How long have you been on the road?"

"A couple of days."

"Coming from where?"

"East. What's this place—Soledad County—like?"

"Pretty. Coast, forest, foothills, small towns."

"Lots of people live there?"

"No. We're one of the most sparsely populated in the upper half of the state. Isolated, too; it's a four-hour drive to San Francisco, even longer to Sacramento because of bad roads."

"Sounds nice."

"Well, you've got to like the quiet life, and I do. I live in the country, near a little town called Cyanide Wells."

"So you think Soledad County is really a good place to live?"

"If you want, I'll sing its praises all the way there. By the way, my name's Carly McGuire."

"Mine's Ardis Coleman."

Port Regis, British Columbia
Sunday, April 21, 2002

atthew Lindstrom?"

"Yes?"

"I'm calling about your wife."

"I have no wife."

"Oh, yes, you do. Gwen Lindstrom—"

"My wife disappeared fourteen years ago. Our divorce went through shortly after that."

"I know, Mr. Lindstrom. And I know about your legal and professional difficulties surrounding the situation. They must have been very painful. Put an end to your life as you'd known it, didn't they?"

"Who is this?"

"A friend. My identity's not important. What's important is that your wife is very much alive. And very cognizant of what she put you through when she disappeared."

"Listen, whoever you are—"

"Aren't you curious? I'm sure I would be if I were you."

"All right, I'll go along with your game. Where is Gwen?"

"Soledad County, California. Has lived there for the past fourteen years near a place called Cyanide Wells, under the name of Ardis Coleman."

"Ardis Coleman? My God, that was Gwen's mother's maiden name."

"Well, there you go. Let me ask you this, Mr. Lindstrom: Will revenge taste good served up cold, after the passage of all those years?"

"Revenge?"

"Surely you must feel some impulse in that direction, considering . . ."

"What the hell are you trying to do to me? Who *are* you?"

"As I said, a friend."

"I don't believe a word of this!"

"Then I suggest you check it out, Mr. Lindstrom. Check it out."

Cyanide Wells, California
Sunday, April 21, 2002

ey, Ard, you're awfully quiet. Something wrong?"

"Nothing that I can pin down, but I feel . . . I didn't sleep well last night. Bad dreams, the kind you can't remember afterwards, but their aura lingers like a hangover."

"Maybe it's your book. It can't be easy reliving that time. And from what I've read, it's a much more personal account than what you wrote for the paper."

"It is, but that's how I want it, Carly. Besides, I don't think this is about the book—at least not completely."

"What, then?"

"Matt, maybe."

"After all these years?"

"I've been thinking of him a lot lately. Wondering . . ."

"And feeling guilty, I suppose."

"In a way. When I found out they suspected him of murdering me, I should've come forward."

"You found out way after the fact. And when you did try to contact him, he was gone, no forwarding."

"I know, but instead of trying to find out where he'd gone, I just felt relieved. I didn't want to hurt him any more than I already had."

"So he's better off."

"No, he'd've been better off if I'd been honest from the first. I could've—"

"As my aunt Nan used to say, '*Coulda*'s, *woulda*'s, and *shoulda*'s don't amount to a hill of beans.'"

"I guess. But I'm concerned for Natalie. My anxiety's obvious, and it upsets her."

"She hasn't said anything about it to me."

"You know her; she's a child who holds everything inside. Carly, d'you think I'm being irrational?"

". . . You're stressed. You'll get over it once the book is done."

"Will I? Sometimes I think that given all the terrible things I've done, I don't deserve another good night's sleep in this lifetime."

Matthew Lindstrom

Port Regis, British Columbia
Wednesday, April 24, 2002

att Lindstrom watched the tourists struggle along the pier, laden with extra jackets, blankets, tote bags, and coolers. City people, up from California on holiday and unaccustomed to the chill temperatures and pervasive damp that characterized the northern tip of Vancouver Island at this time of year. Americans were also unaccustomed to going anywhere without a considerable collection of unnecessary possessions.

Smiling ruefully, he turned around, his gaze rising to the pine-covered slopes across the small harbor. When had he stopped identifying with the few U.S. citizens who ventured this far up-island? At first he hadn't been conscious of his waning allegiance; it had simply crept up on him until one day he was no longer one of them, yet not a Canadian either. Stuck somewhere in between, perhaps permanently, and in an odd way his otherness pleased him. No, not pleased so much as contented him, and he'd remained contented until the past Sunday evening. Since then he'd felt only discontent, and a sense of unfinished business.

"Matt?" His deckhand, Johnny Crowe, stood by the transom of the *Queen Charlotte,* Matt's thirty-six-foot excursion trawler. A full-blooded Kootenay, Johnny was a recent transplant from the Columbia River Valley. He asked, "You want me to button her up?"

"Yeah, thanks." Matt gave him a half-salute and started along the dock, past fishing boats in their slips. The tourists he'd taken out for the morning's charter were bunched around their giant Ford Expedition, trying to fit their gear among the suitcases piled in its rear compartment. They'd spent the night at Port Regis Hotel at the foot of the pier—an establishment whose accommodations one guidebook had described as "spartan but clean," and from the grumblings he'd overheard, he gathered that spartan was not their first, or even second, preference.

When he reached the end of the pier, he gave the tourists a wide berth and a curt nod and headed for the hotel. It was of weathered clapboard, once white but now gone to gray, and not at all imposing, with three entrances off its covered front porch: restaurant, lobby, and bar. Matt pushed through the latter into an amber-lighted room with beer signs and animal heads on the walls and rickety, unmatched tables and chairs arranged haphazardly across the warped wooden floor. The room was empty now, but a few hours before, it would have been filled with fishermen returning at what was the end of their working day.

"Hey, Millie," Matt called to the woman behind the bar.

"Hey, yourself." Millie Bertram was a frizzy-haired blonde on the far side of fifty, dressed in denim coveralls over a tie-dyed shirt. The shirt and her long beaded earrings revealed her as one who had never quite made a clean break with the sixties. When Matt moved to Port Regis ten years ago, Millie and her husband, Jed, had co-owned and operated the hotel. Two years later Jed, who fancied himself a bass player of immense if unrecognized talent, ran off with a singer from Vancouver, never to be seen again. Millie became sole proprietor of the hotel, and if the prices had gone up, so had the quality of food and service.

Now she placed a mug of coffee in front of Matt. "Early charter?"

"Only charter. Those guests of yours from San Jose."

"Ah, yes, they mentioned something about a 'boat ride.'" The set of Millie's mouth indicated she was glad to have seen the last of them. "Fishing?"

"Not their thing. Bloody Marys, except for one woman who drank mimosas. Point-and-shoot cameras and a desire to see whales."

"On a day when there's not a whale in sight."

"I pointed out two." Matt sipped coffee, burned his tongue, and grimaced.

"Let me guess," Millie said. "Bull and Bear Rocks."

"You got it."

"You're a con man, Lindstrom."

"So they're leaving happy and will tell all their friends to look me up."

Millie went to the coffee urn, poured herself some, and leaned against the backbar, looking pensive. Probably contemplating the summer months that would bring more tourists with a desire for whales, who would become drunk in her bar, look askance at her chef's plain cooking, and leave her spartan guestrooms in a shambles.

Matt toyed with the ceramic container that held packets of

sugar and artificial sweetener. "Mil, you're from California, right?"

"Yeah."

"You know where Soledad County is?"

She closed her eyes, apparently conjuring a map. "Between Mendocino and Humboldt Counties, on the coast. Extends east beyond the edge of the Eel River National Forest."

"You ever hear of a place called Cyanide Wells?"

"Sure. Back when Jed-the-asshole and I were into our environmental phase, we protested at Talbot's Mills. Lumber town. Company town. Identical little houses, except for the mansions the thieving barons built on the labor of the loggers and millworkers they exploited."

Matt made motions as if he were playing a violin.

"Okay," Millie said, "so I'm still talking the talk even though I'm not walking the walk. Anyway, Cyanide Wells is maybe thirty miles southeast of there. Former gold-mining camp. Wide spot in the road back in the seventies, but I guess it's grown some by now. I do know it's got one hell of a newspaper, the *Soledad Spectrum*. Owned and edited by a woman, Carly McGuire. About three years ago they won the Pulitzer Prize for a series on the murders of a gay couple near there. How come you asked?"

"I just found out that somebody I used to know is living near Cyanide Wells."

"Somebody?" Now Millie's tone turned sly. She was, Matt knew, frustrated and puzzled by his lack of interest in a long-term relationship with any of the women she repeatedly shoved into his path.

"Somebody," he said in a tone that precluded further discussion.

Somebody who, fourteen years ago, had put an end to his life as he'd known it.

*　　*　　*

Matt sat on the deck of his cabin, looking out at the humped mass of Bear Rock, which was backlit by the setting sun. It *did* look like a whale, and he was glad he'd given the tourists their photo op this morning. Clouds were now gathering on the horizon, bleaching the sun's brilliant colors, and a cold breeze swayed the three tall pines that over the past ten years he'd watched grow from saplings. Feeling the chill, he got up and took his bottle of beer inside.

The cabin was snug: one room with a sleeping alcove on the far wall, and a stone fireplace and galley kitchen facing each other on the side walls. A picture window and glass door overlooked the sea. The small shingled building had been in bad shape when he'd first seen it, so he'd gotten it cheap, leaving enough of the money from the sale of the Saugatuck house for the down payment on the *Queen Charlotte.* During two years of drifting about, his life in ruins, he'd taken what odd jobs he found and scarcely touched the money.

He lighted the fire he'd earlier laid on the hearth, sat down, and watched the flames build. Dusk fell, then darkness, and he nursed his warmish beer without turning on a lamp.

Fourteen years. A way of life lost. A home gone. A career destroyed.

Then, finally, he'd found Port Regis and this cabin and the *Queen Charlotte,* and he'd created a new way of life, built another home and career. True, he was not the man he'd intended to be at thirty-nine, and this was not the life he'd expected to lead. But it was a life he'd handcrafted out of ruin and chaos. If it was as spartan as one of Millie's guestrooms, at least it was also clean. If his friends were little more than good acquaintances, so much the better; he'd learned the small worth of friendship those last two years in Minnesota. He was content here—or had been, until a late-night anonymous phone call destroyed all possibility of contentment. . . .

He wasn't aware of making a conscious decision, much less a plan. He simply turned on the table lamp and went to the closet off the sleeping alcove, where he began going through the cartons stacked in its recesses. When he located the one marked P EQUIP., he carried it to the braided rug in front of the hearth, sat down cross-legged, and opened it.

Memories rose with the dust from the carton's lid. He pushed them aside, burrowed into the bubble-wrapped contents. On top were the lenses: F2.8 wide angle, F1.8 and F2.8 telephotos, the F2.8 with 1.4x teleconverter, and even a fisheye, which he'd bought in a fit of longing but had seldom needed. Next the camera bag, tan canvas and well used. And inside it, the camera.

It was an old Nikon F, the first camera he'd ever bought and the only one he'd kept when he sold his once-profitable photography business. Heavy and old-fashioned next to the new single-lens reflexes or digital models, the markings were worn on the f-stop band, and the surfaces where he'd so often held it were polished smooth. He stared at it, afraid to take it into his hands because if he did, it would work its old magic, and then what he now realized he'd been subconsciously considering would become a reality. . . .

Don't be ridiculous. Picking it up isn't a commitment.

And just like that, he did.

His fingers curled around the Nikon, moving to long-accustomed positions. They caressed it as he removed the lens cap, adjusted speed, f-stop, and focus. He sighted on the flames in the fireplace, saw them clearly through the F3.5 micro lens with a skylight filter. Even though the camera contained no film, he thumbed the advance lever, depressed the shutter.

The mind may forget, but not the body.

She'd said that to him the last time they made love, in a sentimental moment after being separated for two months, but he sensed that her body had already forgotten, was ready for new memories, a new man. She'd told him she needed to be free— not to wound him, but with deep regret that proved the words hurt her as well. But now, after allowing him to think her dead for fourteen years, it seemed she was alive in California, near a place called Cyanide Wells. He had no reason to doubt his anonymous caller, who had taken the trouble to track him down for some unexplained reason.

"*. . . your wife is very much alive. And very cognizant of what she put you through when she disappeared. . . .*"

Matt's fingers tightened on the Nikon.

Picking it up had been a commitment after all.

Soledad County, California
Tuesday, May 7, 2002

ain clouds hovered over the heavily forested ridge-line that separated central Soledad County from the coastal region, reminding Matt of home. As the exit sign for Talbot's Mills appeared, he took his right hand off the wheel of the rented Jeep Cherokee and rubbed his neck. It had been a long drive north from the San Francisco Airport, and he was stiff and tired but keyed up in an unpleasant manner that twice had made him oversteer on Highway 101's sharp curves.

It had taken him two weeks to put the charter business in order so that it would run properly under Johnny Crowe's supervision, as well as to prepare his cabin should his absence be a long one. All the time he was going about his tasks, he felt as if he were saying good-bye: to Millie, to Johnny, to the woman at the bank where he arranged for payment of what few bills would come in, to the clerks at the marine supply he patronized, to the mechanic at the gas station where he had his truck serviced for the drive to Vancouver. Once there, he left the truck in the garage of a woman with whom he'd had an on-and-off affair for years, and she drove him to the airport. As his plane took off and his adopted country receded below him, he wondered what kind of man he'd be when he returned there.

Now he rounded a bend in the highway and sighted the lumber company town nestled at the base of the ridge. Clustered around the interchange were the ubiquitous motels and gas stations and fast-food outlets, and beyond them a bridge spanned a wide, slow-moving river. Two huge beige-and-green mills sprawled for acres along its banks, and small houses rose on the terraced slope above them. Higher on the hill were larger homes, including one whose gables cleared the tallest of the trees.

Matt exited on a ramp whose potholed surface threatened to jar the Jeep's wheel from his hands. Logging rigs lined the frontage road's shoulder on both sides, in front of a truck stop advertising HOT SHOWERS AND GOOD EATS. He'd pulled off for a burger hours ago in a place north of the Golden Gate Bridge called Los Alegres, but the keyed-up feeling had prevented him from eating most of it. He knew he should have a solid meal, but his stomach was still nervous, so he drove past the truck stop, looking for a motel.

There was a Quality Inn sandwiched between a Denny's and a Chevron station about fifty yards ahead. Grease and exhaust fumes were a potential hazard, but its sign advertised vacancies, and if he didn't like it, he could move. He pulled in, rented a surprisingly spacious room, and then set to work with the county phone book.

No listing for an Ardis Coleman. Listing for the *Soledad Spec-*

trum on Main Street in Cyanide Wells. No public library there, but Talbot's Mills had one, located in the Talbot Mansion on Alta Street. Best to make that his first stop, gather information, and map out strategy before visiting the smaller town.

He wasn't concerned that he'd run into Gwen and she'd recognize him. Immediately after making his decision to come to Soledad County, he had begun growing a mustache and beard, neither of which he'd ever worn before. The heavy growth rate of his facial hair, which he'd cursed his whole life, produced both quickly and respectably. The dark-brown dye he had applied to his naturally blond hair the night before he left Port Regis had further changed him, and as proof of the tepid quality of his relationship with the woman friend in Vancouver, her only comment on his new look was, "I don't like beards."

Even without these changes it was possible Gwen wouldn't know him should they come face-to-face. For one thing, she wouldn't expect to find him here. And he was older, his weathered skin a deep saltwater tan. His once-stocky body had been honed lean by his active life on the sea. He walked differently, with the catlike precision necessary to maintain balance on an often heaving deck. He spoke differently, with the slowness and economy of one who spends a great deal of time alone.

No, he was not the man Gwen used to know.

While he was crossing the bridge, the pretty picture of the old-fashioned company town that he'd formed from a distance deteriorated. One of the long mills was still in operation, a thick, steady stream of smoke rising from its tall stacks, but the other was in poor repair, surrounded by broken, weed-choked asphalt and twisted heaps of rubble. As he climbed higher on the slope, he found that the small, identical frame cottages on the terraced streets had peeling paint, sagging rooflines, and many boarded windows; their patches of yard were full of disabled vehicles, trash, cast-off furnishings. Still higher, a small business district contained mostly dead storefronts and empty sidewalks. Even the equipment in a playground had been vandalized.

Matt drove slowly through the business district, looking for Alta Street, found it at the very end, and turned uphill again. The homes there were of Victorian vintage—mostly modest, but larger and in better repair than the cottages below. At its end tall, black iron gates shielded a parklike area, and beyond rose the mansion he'd glimpsed from the freeway: three stories of forbidding gray, with iron railings, verdigrised copper gables, huge stained-glass windows, and balconies with trim as delicate as the icing on a wedding cake. Although it must have been built in the Victorian decades, it bore little resemblance to the recognizable styles of that era; if anything, it was a hodgepodge of architectural features that only a serious eccentric would incorporate into the same edifice. A sign on the gate identified it as the Talbot Mansion, now the Central Soledad County Public Library and Museum.

Matt studied it for a moment, wondering what kind of lunatics the Talbots had been to create such a place, then drove through the gate, parked in the small paved lot, and went inside. After an hour and a half he'd amassed a surprising amount of information about Gwen and her new life as Ardis Coleman.

He went to bed early that night but found he couldn't sleep, not even after the double shot of Wild Turkey he'd poured from the bottle he'd bought at a nearby liquor store. Finally he got up and dressed and drove back to Talbot's Mills. There he prowled the deserted streets, looking for . . .

What?

He didn't know, so he kept walking until he found an open tavern in the half-dead business district—a small place with a single pool table and a jukebox playing country songs. Only three old men hunched over their drinks at the bar, and the bartender stood at its end, staring up at a small, blurry television screen. Matt ordered a beer and took it to a corner table, where dim light shone down from a Canadian Club sign.

Canada . . .

Most people led one life. They might move from place to place, marry and divorce and remarry, change careers, but the progression was linear, and they basically remained the same persons from birth to death. Until fourteen years ago Matt, also, had been one person: He'd enjoyed an overprivileged childhood in Minnetonka, a suburb of Minneapolis; learned boating from his father, an accomplished sailor, at the family's cabin near Grand Marais, on Lake Superior; attended Northwestern University, majoring in prelaw while studying photography under a master of the art in nearby Chicago. When photography won out over the law, his teacher recommended him for a position at small but prestigious Saugatuck College in his home state. The pay was also small, so his parents offered to loan him the money to establish his own commercial studio. Two years later he married a journalism student who had taken a course from him, pretty Gwendolyn Standish. Life should have been good.

Yet it wasn't. After their marriage, Gwen's personality changed, so much that she seemed like two persons encased in one skin. Caring and passionate, withdrawn and cold. Cheerful and optimistic, depressed and pessimistic. Open and filled with confidence, closed and filled with self-doubt. Eventually the negative side overwhelmed the positive, and despite Matt's assurances that he would do anything to save the marriage— counseling, therapy, walking barefoot over hot coals—she insisted on a divorce.

Even the divorce hadn't ended what he now thought of as his

first life, though. That was brought on by her disappearance and its aftermath.

Suspicious minds . . .

The words echoing from the jukebox meshed with his thoughts. The first hint of suspicion had come during the call from the Wyoming sheriff, Cliff Brandt: "I take it you can account for your whereabouts during the past two weeks." And he'd too quickly replied, "Of course I can! I was here in Saugatuck, teaching summer classes." Too quickly and also dishonestly, because of an ingrained fear of the authorities that stemmed from his older brother Jeremy's arrest and eventual conviction for dealing cocaine in the mid-seventies; Matt was thirteen at the time and had watched the officers brutally subdue Jeremy when he attempted to resist them.

In truth, Matt had been nowhere near Saugatuck during those two weeks. The summer of 1988, a drought year, was the hottest and driest Minnesota had experienced since the 1930s. Matt's temper grew shorter with every July day, and he found it difficult to maintain focus on his work. So he closed down the studio, turned his summer classes over to a colleague, and went on a solo driving and camping trip designed both to escape the heat and help him put the failure of his marriage in perspective. It was his bad luck that the trip, which ended in Arches National Park, on Utah's Green River, took him home through Wyoming along Interstate 80 at approximately the same time Gwen's car was abandoned by the side of a county road north of there.

Sheriff Brandt found that out, of course, when he called the college to verify Matt's alibi and then checked the paper trail of credit card and gas station charges. His department lifted Matt's fingerprints from the abandoned Toyota (which he had occasionally driven) and inside Gwen's purse (where he had occasionally placed items of his own too large for his pockets).

The Lindstroms' property settlement showed that Matt had consented to pay Gwen half the value of his photography business. And, most damning, Matt had lied to the sheriff during their first conversation. Brandt, unable to produce any trace of Gwen, seemed determined to prove Matt a murderer.

Eventually, of course, Brandt had given up. Even in Sweetwater County, Wyoming, he had more pressing matters to attend to, and the district attorney convinced him that no-body cases were difficult to prove in any jurisdiction. But by then, the damage had been done.

The police in Saugatuck watched Matt's every move; he was repeatedly stopped for nonexistent traffic violations, and it became common for him to see squad cars cruising past his house and place of business. Gwen's disappearance and his possible involvement were worked and reworked by the media. Initially friends and neighbors were supportive, but after a while they stopped calling him. Halfway through the fall semester, a television show, which both described in sensational terms his romantic involvement and marriage to a sophomore and raised questions bordering on the libelous about her disappearance, prompted several students to withdraw from his classes. In the spring the college's governing board unanimously decided it would be advisable that he take a year's sabbatical without pay; if the "regrettable situation" was resolved before the year was up, his pay would become retroactive.

And yet there remained no trace of Gwen.

By the anniversary of her disappearance in July, Matt's former friends were crossing the street to avoid him. Requests for his services at weddings, anniversary parties, and bar mitzvahs dropped off sharply. New mothers no longer brought their babies to his studio for their first portraits. Engaged couples took their business to his competitor across town. At Christmastime he shot a photograph for only one customized card: an elderly

woman and her "family" of three toy poodles. The dogs yipped
and snarled and peed on the carpet, and when the woman was
leaving, she told him she'd only come there because she
couldn't get an appointment with the other photographer.

At least, Matt thought, his competitor had a clean rug.

He stubbornly hung on in Saugatuck, however, living off his
savings. It was his home; he'd done nothing wrong except stu-
pidly lie to a Wyoming sheriff. Sooner or later he would be vindicated.

When his savings were about to run out, he phoned home to
ask for a loan; his mother agreed but then called back the next
day.

"Your father and I have discussed the loan," she told him,
"and we have come to the conclusion that it's time we stopped
spoiling you. Look what happened to your brother because
of our indulgence: He's down in New Mexico, taking drugs
again." When Matt started to protest that Jeremy was in Albuquerque working as a counselor in a program for troubled
youth, she cut him off. "No, hear me out. Your father and I
know you couldn't have killed Gwendolyn. We didn't raise you
that way. But the negative publicity has made it very difficult
for us—"

Matt hung up on her.

Still, he remained in town, selling off cherished possessions
and then the photography business. With some of the proceeds
he hired a private investigator to look for Gwen; the man delivered sketchy reports for a month and then ceased communication; when Matt called his office, he found the phone service
had been discontinued.

Then, three weeks after the second anniversary of Gwen's
disappearance, a chance encounter in the supermarket ended
his first life.

He was in the produce section, filling his cart with the vegetables that had become staples of his diet now that he could no longer afford meat, when he looked up into the eyes of Gwen's best friend, Bonnie Vaughan, principal of the local high school, a heavy but attractive woman with long, silky hair and gray eyes. Eyes that now cut into him like surgical instruments.

"So you *are* still here, you bastard," she said in a low voice that was more unsettling than if she'd shouted.

"Bonnie, I—"

"Shut up, you murderer!"

The words and her tone rendered him speechless.

"We know what you did," she went on. "And we know why. You'd better get out of Saugatuck before somebody murders *you!*" Then she whirled and walked away.

Matt stared after her. Bonnie had always been a gentle, caring woman: She tended to her friends' homes and pets while they were out of town; she could always be counted on in an emergency; she brought thoughtful, handcrafted gifts when invited to dinner. The last time he'd seen her, eleven months after Gwen disappeared, she'd hugged him and said he had her full support. If the hatred that had infected the rest of the community could also infect a woman like Bonnie Vaughan, he wanted nothing more to do with Saugatuck—

"Hey, mister."

Matt started and focused on the woman who had spoken. He'd been so deeply mired in his memories that he hadn't noticed her come into the bar. She was in her early twenties, too thin, with long brown hair that could stand a washing, and an unhealthy grayish pallor to her skin.

"Buy me a drink?" she asked with a tentative smile.

He didn't want company, particularly her brand of company, and his expression must have said so, because her smile faded.

"Listen," she said in a different tone, "I'm not selling anything, if that's what you're thinking. I just need somebody to talk to."

Something in her voice convinced him she was telling the truth. Besides, her earnest, pleading expression made him feel sorry for her. Maybe listening to her troubles would help him keep his own pain at bay.

"Okay." He motioned at the chair opposite him. "What'll you have?"

"Whatever you're having."

He took his empty mug to the bar and ordered a round. As he was paying, the bartender said in a low voice, "Be nice to the kid. She's going through a bad time."

He nodded and went back to the table.

"Thanks, mister." She raised the mug in both hands and drank.

"You're welcome. I'm John." As in Johnny Crowe, the name that he'd borrowed for the journey, with his deckhand's blessing. "What's yours?"

"Sam. Short for Samantha. Thanks for not making me drink alone."

"Drinking alone's no good."

"But you were."

"Yes, I was. So tell me about yourself, Sam."

"What d'you want to know?"

"Anything you care to reveal. You said you needed somebody to talk to, and you seem upset."

"Yeah, I'm upset. Got every right to be. My father . . . died last week."

"I'm sorry, Sam."

"Not as sorry as I was for Dad. He had it rough there toward the end. Twenty-one years with the mill, and they laid him off. No severance pay, and then they told him we had to be out of the house in thirty days. Dad sweated all his life for the company, and that's how they repaid him. He worked his fingers to the bone for them—and us."

"Who's 'us'?"

"Me, my brother, and my mom. My brother got out, joined the army. I don't even know where he is now. Mom died two years ago, cancer. I was all Dad had left."

Matt took the empty mug from her hands and went to the bar for a refill. Sam was hurting, that was for sure, and a few beers seemed poor comfort. But he wasn't used to comforting others, especially strangers; that particular activity had never been a part of his life, except for the brief time he'd been married to Gwen.

When he went back to the table, Sam was sitting very still, eyes focused on a beer sign depicting a mountain meadow. The tilt of her nose was delicate, her cheekbones and forehead high. She'd've been pretty if she weren't in a disheveled, grief-stricken state. Matt set the beer in front of her, and she nodded thanks, keeping her gaze on the sign.

She said, "I'm thinking maybe I'll get out, too."

"And go where?"

"Anyplace there's a future. Everything's dying here—the mill, the town. Pretty soon it'll just be a wide spot on the freeway for people who want a cheap motel and the kind of crap I serve up at the Chicken Shack."

"I noticed one of the mills is closed."

"Yeah, and the other one'll close later this year."

"Environmental regulations causing that?"

"Not really. Talbot's never relied on old-growth forests, like Pacific Lumber up in Scotia did. No, what happened is, it got sold. Ronnie Talbot, the last of the family that owned it, he didn't give a rat's ass about the business. He was a faggot, and all he wanted was a lot of money so he could live high on the hog with his lover. This Portland company bought it, and they're letting it fail so they can get the tax write-off." Her lips curved up in a malicious smile. "At least Ronnie didn't get to enjoy the money. Three months after the sale was final, somebody shot him and his lover at their house over by the Knob. Killed them both, right there in their bed."

That afternoon at the library, Matt had read the *Soledad Spectrum*'s Pulitzer Prize–winning series on the murders in a secluded home east of Cyanide Wells with more than usual interest. Many of the accounts had borne Gwen's assumed name. In a way, it hadn't surprised him; she was a talented reporter, and it was the logical thing for her to be doing here.

Sam's use of the word "somebody" didn't jibe with the published accounts, though. "I thought they caught the guy who shot them."

"Well, Mack Travis confessed to it and hanged himself in his jail cell, but nobody here believes he did it. There was evidence that he'd been in Ronnie and Deke's house that night, but Mack was always a couple of cards short of a full deck, and he was the type who'd confess to anything if anybody gave him half a chance. He had a peculiar relationship with his momma, if you know what I mean. Confessed because he thought the cops had him dead to rights, then offed himself because he didn't want to shame her."

"That paper over in Cyanide Wells won a Pulitzer for their coverage of the murders, didn't they?"

"Uh-huh. Biggest thing that ever happened around here— of the good kind, I mean. I liked those articles. I'm no fan of faggots, but that Ardis Coleman, who wrote most of the stories, actually made me understand how lousy their situation is in a place like this."

"You ever meet her?"

"Me? Do I look like somebody who hangs with Pulitzer

Prize—winners? I've seen her in the supermarket, is all. And, of course, I used to read her."

"Used to?"

"She quit the paper right after they won the prize, is writing a book about the murders."

Evidently had been writing it for close to three years now. She'd probably never finish it, let alone get it published. Gwen had lacked the ability to handle large projects; she agonized over term papers but was able to knock off a good newspaper article under extreme time pressure. But if she wasn't working for the paper, how was she paying her bills?

"Mister . . . John, what d'you think I should do?"

The question startled him. "About what?"

"Should I stay here or just chuck everything and go? What would you do in my place?"

He thought for a moment, then imparted the sum total of his wisdom.

"I'd go, but I'd also keep it in mind that no matter where you are, you'll still be you. You'll still be carrying the same old baggage."

Wednesday, May 8, 2002

y the time Matt delivered Sam to the small company home that would soon cease to be hers—gently refusing her offer of a nightcap—it was after one. He drove back to his motel, stripped off his clothing, and got into the shower. After drying off, he wiped the steam from the mirror over the vanity and once again appraised his somewhat altered appearance.

Yes, he was definitely a different man. A man created out of pain.

After finally leaving Saugatuck, he thought he'd experienced enough pain for any one lifetime, but he hadn't counted on his brother, Jeremy, compounding it.

When in distress, Matt's first impulse had always been to turn to family, and even after being rebuffed by his mother and father, he had thought he could count on his big brother. So he set out on the long drive to Albuquerque, what few possessions he hadn't sold packed in his old Chevy Suburban. He didn't bother to write or call; the brothers had extended standing invitations to visit each other without advance notice.

Jeremy's house was on Vassar Drive, a stucco ranch-style with a yard filled with gravel instead of grass, cacti instead of flowers. Four years before, Matt and Gwen had visited there, and the spare key Jeremy had given him was still on his keychain. When Jeremy didn't answer his ring, Matt checked the garage, saw no car, and let himself inside. In the kitchen he helped himself to a beer and sat down at the table to leaf through the help-wanted ads in a copy of the *Journal* that had been left there. Although the Southwest had never particularly charmed him, it was a long way from Minnesota, and distance was what he now craved.

Some fifteen minutes later he heard the front door open. Footsteps came along the hallway, and Matt looked up in anticipation of seeing his brother's face. Instead a woman came into the room, carrying a sack of groceries. She was short, blond, and slightly overweight, with a bland, pleasant expression that changed radically when she saw him.

She gave a little cry, dropped the grocery bag, and shrank back against the doorjamb. Oranges rolled across the floor. Matt stood up, so quickly that he knocked over his chair.

"Hey," he said, holding his hands out. "Don't be frightened. I'm Jer's brother, Matt. I guess I should've phoned—"

The woman whirled and fled down the hallway, sobbing.

That was the end of Matt's hopes of making a new start in Albuquerque.

"She's damaged," Jeremy said later of his new wife, Marty. "I met her when I was doing volunteer work at a center for victims of violent crimes. Two years ago a man invaded her home, shot her husband, and held her captive for twenty-two hours.

Repeatedly raped her. Can you imagine what she thought when she found a total stranger in our kitchen?"

"I'm not a 'total stranger.' And how come you didn't let me know you'd gotten married?"

Jeremy's expression became remote, as it always did when he was preparing to lie. "We've only been married six weeks. I planned to tell you the next time we talked."

But when would that have been? During the past year and a half their phone conversations had tapered off to once every three months or so. "Do the folks know?"

"Why would I tell them? The last time I spoke with Mom was when I bought this house. I thought she'd be proud of me for getting my act together. Instead she all but accused me of making the down payment with profits from drug deals."

"I've tried to explain to them——"

"I know you have. But they're not going to listen to what they don't want to hear. They've always been good at labeling people, and my label was pasted on the day I was convicted of dealing."

"Well, you're not alone in that. They've labeled me, too. About Marty—is she gonna be okay?"

"She'll be fine. She's cooking her special spaghetti for dinner, in honor of your visit."

But Marty wasn't fine. That night at dinner she fidgeted and refused to make eye contact with Matt and finally excused herself before they were finished eating. As he and Jeremy loaded dishes in the washer, Matt said, "Something's still bothering her, and it's not because I scared her this afternoon."

"I don't know what you mean."

"I think you do. She's afraid of me, your wife-killer brother."

"Oh, Matt, don't go there."

"In spite of what you've told her, she believes I did it."

Jeremy began scrubbing a pot, steam clouding his glasses.

Matt said, "You *did* tell her I'm innocent?"

No reply.

"You *do* believe I'm innocent?"

Jeremy looked up, shut off the water. Steam coated his lenses, but through it Matt could see the fear in his eyes.

Give him an out. Don't let this turn ugly.

"Well, don't feel disloyal, brother," he said. "Maybe I did do it."

The next morning he left his brother's house for good.

After that, what he thought of as his wandering years began. From New Mexico he drove across Arizona and into Southern California. In San Diego he worked two months for a contractor, mainly doing demolition work, then moved on north. All the way up the coast to Oregon he camped out or stayed in cheap motels or hostels, spending frugally, then cut inland to Portland.

In the window of a Portland secondhand bookshop he saw a Help Wanted sign. He worked there as a clerk for six months while living at the YMCA. The city was nice enough, but he became restless and once again headed north, stopping in Seattle. He'd always been drawn to cities on the water, and he liked the hills and sweeping vistas, so he rented a room in a residential hotel and got on with another contractor; within two months he began scanning the want ads for more permanent quarters. But then a chance encounter near Pioneer Square changed his plans.

"Matt! Matt Lindstrom!" a man's voice had called out.

He turned and found himself face-to-face with Dave Kappel, one of his former students. Dave, ever the motormouth, grasped his hand and pumped it, chattering.

"So this is where you're living now. Guess you wanted to get away from that rotten town, and I sure don't blame you. Shitty, the way people treated you after your wife disappeared."

Matt opened his mouth to say that he wasn't living in Seattle, was merely a tourist, but Dave went on, oblivious. "I came out here last fall. I'm a staff photographer on the *Post-Intelligencer*. Married, too. Kid on the way. Fast work, huh? Why don't you give me your phone number? We'd love to have you to dinner."

Automatically Matt gave him the number of the phone that only rang for work-related calls.

"Great, man," Dave said as he scribbled it down. "You know what I'm thinking? I'll talk to a reporter I work with about doing a feature on the shit deal you got back in Saugatuck. Use photos I've got of the place, take others to show you in your new life. Unfounded rumor, innuendo, wrecking a life, but in the end you triumph. Way cool. People eat up that kind of thing."

Just his luck, Matt thought. The only person from Saugatuck who was on his side—and only for purposes of personal gain—had to be on the staff of the major newspaper in a city where he'd flirted with the idea of settling.

He was on the ferry to Vancouver, B.C., the next morning.

For the next year he traveled about British Columbia: east to the Rockies, up to the edge of the Northwest Territories, down to Prince Rupert, then back to Vancouver. He stayed mainly in small towns, picked up work when and where he could, and was charmed by the friendliness and courtesy of the people. By the time he boarded the B.C. Ferry for Vancouver island, he was seriously considering taking up permanent residence in the province.

Another chance encounter, this one more fortunate than the incident in Seattle, turned possibility into reality. While strolling along the pier in Port Regis the morning after he'd checked into the hotel, he met Ned Webster, owner and operator of the *Queen Charlotte*. A garrulous man in his mid-sixties,

Ned responded with pride and pleasure to Matt's questions
about his handsome craft and allowed him to pilot her during
a free harbor tour. Later, over drinks in the hotel bar, his interest in Matt became apparent: He was looking for a partner who
would buy the business when he decided to retire—but not
just any partner. The *Queen Charlotte*'s new captain would have
to be a man who would appreciate her and maintain her in the
style to which she was accustomed. Matt, Ned told him, had
passed the test.

By the next afternoon Matt had requested that his Minnesota
bank wire the funds necessary to buy into Webster Marine
Charters. The following morning the local real estate agent
took him to look at the run-down cabin with the view of the
sea and Bear Rock. By that afternoon he'd put in a second request to his bank for the funds to buy it.

His second life, the wandering years, was over, and his third
life had begun.

As he stood staring into the mirror in his motel room in Talbot's Mills, he reflected that by leaving British Columbia he'd
ended that life and embarked upon yet another. His fourth life
would not be nearly as pleasant as the last, but it would surely
make up for the pain that had ended his first.

Cyanide Wells lay in a wide meadow some twenty-five miles
southeast of Talbot's Mills, near the Eel River National Forest.
High grass, as yet unbrowned, rippled on either side of the
well-paved two-lane highway, and clusters of ranch buildings
appeared in the distance. Ahead, under a clear blue sky, lay the
rolling, pine- and aspen-covered foothills of the forest, and
above them towered a bald, rounded outcropping that Matt assumed was the formation called the Knob.

The previous afternoon in the library he'd read about the
town and learned it was a former gold-mining camp, once

called Seven Wells because of its abundant underground springs. In its heyday in the 1860s its population had numbered nearly ten thousand, and it had boasted of five hotels, three general stores, various shops, twenty boarding houses, twenty-seven saloons, seventeen brothels, and two churches. The rocky Knob contained one of the richest veins of ore in the northwestern part of California, but the mines were eventually played out and abandoned. Seven Wells was on the verge of becoming a ghost town when, in 1900, cyaniders, as they were known, from a Denver mining company arrived, equipped with knowledge of how to use the deadly poison to extract gold from the waste dumps, tailings, and what low-grade ore remained in the earth. A bitter rivalry between one of their engineering team and an old Cornish miner with a small, poor claim had resulted in the poisoning of the seven public wells for which the town was named—an incident so notorious that the popular appellation of Cyanide Wells took hold and was years later made official, even though the water supply had long since been cleansed. By now most of the wells had run dry.

The town and its contrast to Talbot's Mills took Matt by surprise. The business district consisted of two blocks of restored false-fronted buildings, and on the side streets tidy, Victorian-era cottages mingled with larger, more contemporary dwellings. Bed-and-breakfasts abounded. Although Starbuck's hadn't yet invaded, Aram's Coffee Shop was doing a turn-away business; Dead People's Stuff offered "fine antiques"; the Good Earth Bakery advertised fresh focaccia; Mamma Mia's featured lobster ravioli; the Main Street Diner looked to be a takeoff on the Hard Rock Cafe. Everything was freshly painted and too tidy and seemed a counterfeit of the real world. As he drove along, Matt began to feel nostalgia for Port Regis's rough edges.

He soon located the *Soledad Spectrum* in a white frame building with Wedgwood blue trim, sandwiched between M'Lady's

Boutique and the Thai Issan restaurant. Cars and trucks and campers lined the curbs, and there wasn't a parking space to be had, so he pulled off onto a side street and walked back, his camera slung around his neck. As he merged with the people on the sidewalk, he took in details with his photographer's eyes. For twelve years he'd shunned his true calling, but he'd never stopped looking at his surroundings as if through the lens.

Couples in shorts and T-shirts, holding hands the way they did when on their own in a strange place, took in the sights. Locals in casual or business attire entered and exited Bank of Soledad, First American Title, State Farm Insurance, Redwood Cleaners, and Tuttle Drugs. Children, on some sort of field trip from grade school, walked in line behind their teacher, clutching at a colorful braided rope like a litter of puppies on a lead. Old men lounged on a bench in a park by a stone-walled well—presumably one of the seven that had been poisoned over a century before. Several women in flowered dresses sipped cappuccino at a wrought-iron table in front of the Wells Mercantile. At the post office, newspaper racks were lined up on the sidewalk: everything from the *New York Times* to the *Soledad Spectrum.*

He bought a copy of the local paper and, at the Mercantile, an area map. Then he walked over to the park and sat down on a bench by the well to study both. The front section of the *Spectrum* was devoted to county news; national and world items off the wire services and syndicated material filled the second; the third covered the arts. Nowhere was Ardis Coleman's byline. He turned to the op-ed page, and immediately his eye was drawn to a boxed ad at its bottom.

Wanted: General assignment photographer for Soledad Spectrum. *Small paper experience, references required. See C. McGuire, 1101 Main Street.*

Sheer coincidence? Fate? He didn't believe in either, yet a chill was on his spine.

Photographer? Yes.

Small-paper experience, references? No.

But those he could acquire.

After half an hour on the phone to Port Regis, making explanations to Millie Bertram that were at best half-truths and giving instructions that she carefully wrote down and repeated, Matt stepped through the door of the *Soledad Spectrum.* An unmanned reception desk confronted him, flanked on its left by a gated railing barring access to the area behind. Four computer workstations, three of them unoccupied, filled the rest of the room, and a trio of closed doors led to the rear of the building. When Matt came in, a slender, dark-haired man who was pounding on a keyboard at the station farthest from the reception desk glanced up and snapped, "Help you?"

"I'm looking for C. McGuire."

"You're the only one, buddy. Carly's on a tear, and everybody but me has taken off early for a long lunch. I'd've gone to earth, too, if I didn't have to finish this goddamn story on the new logging regs." He lifted his hands from the keyboard, flopped them beside it in an exaggerated gesture of helplessness. "But my manners—where are they?"

"You tell me."

The man smiled and got up, came over to the rail, and extended a hand. "Severin Quill, police/political reporter. Don't laugh at the name. It's ridiculous, but few people forget it."

"John Crowe, wanna-be general assignment photographer."

"All right!" Severin Quill's mouth quirked up. He was no more than twenty-five, with a puckish face and, apparently, a sense of humor to match. "You just may be our salvation, Mr. Crowe. One—though by no means all—of the reasons for

Carly's bearish mood is the defection of our former photographer. He took off last week without a word of notice. Not that I blame him."

"Why don't you?"

"Because on her best of days Carly McGuire is a pain in the ass to work for. I feel duty-bound to warn you of that before you go back there"—he jerked his thumb at one of the closed doors—"into the harpy's nest."

"So why are you here?"

"Because to any newspaper person worth his or her salt, Carly's standards and expectations are challenges others only dream of."

"Then maybe I'll take my chances."

The first word Matt heard out of Carly McGuire's mouth was *"What!"*

Loud, even through the closed door, and very irritated. But also low-timbred and sultry—the kind they used to call a "whiskey voice." One that, whatever potential abuse lay behind that door, made him determined to see its owner.

"I'm here about the photographer's job," he called.

"So don't just stand there. Come in!"

He pushed through into a small, cluttered room. A huge weekly calendar scrawled with notations covered the far wall. Tearsheets and lists and photographs were tacked haphazardly to the others. The floor was mounded with books and papers; in its center sat a large, equally mounded metal desk. And in *its* center a woman in black jeans and a T-shirt sat cross-legged, glaring at him.

Carly McGuire was around forty, slender and long-limbed, with honey-colored hair that fell straight to her shoulders. Her skin glowed with what looked to be a year-round tan, and her oval face framed rather severe features. Or maybe they only appeared to be severe because of the horn-rimmed half-glasses that perched on the tip of her nose, and the frown lines etched between her eyebrows.

"Well?" she said.

"I saw your ad—"

"Of course you did. Get to the point."

"I want the job."

"And why do you think I should hire you?"

"Small-paper experience—eighteen years. A reference— from my editor and publisher. And I'm a damned good photographer."

She seemed to like his response. At least her scowl didn't deepen, and she took off the glasses, twirling them around as she studied him.

"Name?" she asked.

"John Crowe."

"From?"

"Port Regis, British Columbia."

"Here for?"

"A change of scene."

"Reason? Fired? Divorced?"

"Neither. Leave of absence for now, but it could become permanent."

She nodded. "Okay, none of my business and rightly so."

"I'm glad you realize that."

She compressed her lips and studied him some more. Then she unfolded her long legs and scooted over to the edge of the desk, knocking several files to the floor but sliding off gracefully. "Let's have you fill out an application, and then I'll put you to the test."

"What test?"

"You'll see."

*   *   *

Carly McGuire seated Matt with an application form at the still unmanned reception desk and disappeared into her office. Before he could get started, Severin Quill expelled a dramatic sigh and swiveled away from his workstation. "The piece is finished, and so am I," he announced. "Lunchtime—a long, liquid one. Sorry to leave you here to fend on your own, Mr. Crowe."

"If you hear screams, come running."

Matt waited till Quill had left the building, then scanned the desk where he sat. A Rolodex, fat with cards, stood on one corner. Quickly he turned it to the *C*'s, located Ardis Coleman's name, and copied the address and phone number onto a piece of scratch paper.

Easy, but things are if you think them through.

He then turned his attention to the job application.

Former employer: the—fictional—*Port Regis Register.* Contact: Millie Bertram, editor and publisher.

Position: chief photographer.

Employed: 1984–2002.

Education: BA, English and prelaw, Northwestern University. McGuire wouldn't check with the college, given the passage of time.

Address and phone number—

Damn! He'd registered at the motel under his own name. But . . .

He reached for his wallet, took out the slip of paper that Sam—last name D'Angelo—had written her phone number and address on when he'd delivered her there the night before. He'd phone, ask her to field his calls. If necessary, he'd take her to dinner as payment for the favor. No, he'd do it anyway; the kid could use a good meal.

He was signing the application with Johnny Crowe's name

when Carly McGuire emerged from her office, smiling fiendishly.

"What's this?" Matt asked, staring at the red Ford pickup with the white camper shell on its bed and a Save the Redwoods sticker on its bumper. It was pulled up against the wall in the alley behind the building.

"The test," she said.

"You want me to take pictures of a *truck*?"

"I don't want you to take pictures of anything." She seized the strap of his camera bag and relieved him of it, then slapped a key into his hand. "I want you to make it start."

"Huh?"

She tapped the toe of her cowboy boot on the gravel. "You said small-paper experience. I don't know about the *Port Royal Register*—"

"Port Regis."

"Whatever. But here at the *Spectrum* we all pitch in to do whatever it takes to get the paper out. And if I can't get this truck started, I can't get the week's issue to the printer down in Santa Carla by six o'clock tonight. In all the years I've owned the *Spectrum* we've never missed press time."

"So if everybody pitches in to get the paper out, why haven't any of them already gotten the truck started? Or offered you the use of their vehicles?"

McGuire's mouth drooped and she suddenly looked tired. "A couple of them tried and gave up. And I don't like to drive other people's vehicles."

Meaning other people didn't like to lend theirs to her. "How about calling a garage or Triple A?"

"I have a . . . problem with the local garage. And I accidentally let my Triple A membership lapse. Can you fix it or not?"

Fortunately, he'd spent most of his life poking his nose into various engine compartments. "I can fix it."

It wasn't an old truck—1999 Ford Ranger, and appeared to be well maintained. But when he eased himself into the driver's seat and tried to turn it over, the idiot lights flashed and bells rang, but there wasn't even a click, just the faintest of hums.

"It's not the battery," he said.

"I know that! It was the first thing the others checked."

He jiggled the gearshift lever, depressed the clutch, turned the key again. Nothing. "This an alarm system?" he asked, pointing to a unit with a blinking red light mounted beneath the dash.

McGuire came over and peered through the open door. "Yeah. The dealership put it on because there had been a lot of thefts off their used-car lot. I didn't want to pay for it, and they were supposed to make an appointment to have it taken off, but they never got back to me. I don't even know how it works."

"Raise the hood, will you?" While she did, he set the ignition to Start. When he went around to the front of the truck, he found McGuire staring at its innards with a bewildered frown.

"I hate mechanical things," she said.

"Maybe if you knew more about them, you'd like them better. D'you have some pliers?"

"There's a toolbox in the bed. I'll see." She went away, came back with a pair. "These okay?"

"Yep." He took them from her and went to work connecting the ignition wire directly to the solenoid. The engine roared, then began to purr.

McGuire smiled as if the sounds were the opening notes of a favorite symphony. "What was wrong with it?"

"Well, it could be a problem with your starter, but my guess is that the truck's paranoid."

"It's *what?*"

"The kind of alarm you have prevents theft by keeping the vehicle from starting. Apparently your truck decided somebody was trying to steal it and activated its own alarm."

She scowled. "Is this a joke?"

"Truck's running, isn't it?"

She transferred her scowl to the Ford. "Is it fixed for good?"

"No. I bypassed the alarm for now, but it should be disconnected."

"Can you do that?"

"It depends."

"On what?"

"On whether I have the photographer's job."

McGuire sighed. "You have the job, Mr. Crowe."

A difficult woman, Carly McGuire. Puzzling and contradictory, too. But Matt couldn't afford to dwell on her. After he spent half an hour disconnecting the Ford's alarm, he had more immediate matters to attend to.

First the call to Sam, who was so eager to help him that she hadn't asked why he needed to use her address and phone number, and so happy to be invited to dinner that she offered to cook for him. He didn't think it was a good idea, but when she insisted, he agreed.

Next he went to the Jeep, removed the standard lens from the Nikon, and attached the F2.8 telephoto with 1.4x teleconverter—a combination that afforded the equivalent of a 400 F4.0 lens without the bulk and length. On the area map he'd bought earlier, he located Drinkwater Road, northwest of the Knob, along the creek of the same name. Before he left town, he bought a sandwich and a Coke at a deli and ate while he drove.

Aspen Road led him across the eastern side of the meadow toward the Knob. To either side of the pavement, houses spread behind rustic split-rail fences: new, with much glass, yet weathered to blend in with their surroundings. An exclusive development to match the tricked-up little town, here in what he'd learned was a poor county where the economic bases of logging, mining, and commercial fishing were eroding. Perhaps luxury dwellings and services for retirees and second-homers would provide the answer to Soledad County's dilemma, but to Matt it seemed they would only create a dangerous gap between the haves and the have-nots.

Ahead, the Knob rose against the clear sky: tall, rounded on top, slightly atilt, eroded and polished by the elements. He couldn't help but smile. Perhaps it had resembled an upended doorknob to the settlers who named it, but to him it looked like a huge erect penis. God knew what the retirees in their expensive homes thought about spending their declining years in the shadow of an enormous dick!

Drinkwater Road appeared some two miles from town. He followed its curves as it meandered north along the creek bed. The stream was swollen with runoff from the mountain snowmelt, and its water rushed over rocks and foamed between them. To the road's left, wooden bridges led to dwellings on the creek's other side; eucalyptus and pine and newly leafed aspen blurred the buildings' outlines. To the right of the pavement rose a rocky slope, broken occasionally by dirt driveways with mailboxes. He didn't need to consult the slip of paper on which he'd written Gwen's—no, Ardis Coleman's—address; he'd already committed it and the phone number to memory.

He drove slowly for several miles, taking careful note of his surroundings: blind curves, sheltered places to turn off, areas where there were no houses or driveways. When he saw a wood-burned sign at the end of a bridge on the creek side, bearing the number 11708, he didn't stop. Instead he drove for another mile, still observing, then turned back.

The house where his ex-wife lived—possibly had lived for all of the fourteen years he'd presumed her dead—was set back from the creek and screened by trees and other vegetation; the plank bridge was not wide enough to accommodate a car or truck, but there was a paved parking area to its right, currently empty. Matt stopped there, took up the Nikon, and scanned the property.

One-story redwood-and-stone house with chimneys at either end and a number of large bubble-type skylights. Flagstone patio in front, equipped with a hot tub, table and chairs, chaise longues, and barbecue. Rope hammock in an iron stand under an oak tree to the other side of the walk.

Nothing at all like the modest home he and Gwen had shared in Saugatuck.

After a moment, he moved the Jeep to a different vantage point. There was a rose garden beyond the hammock, fenced off, probably against the incursions of deer. Gwen had always loved roses. And beyond that sat a child's swing set. Gwen, unlike him, had never wanted children. . . .

A car, coming along the road from the south, taking the curves swiftly and surely.

Matt started the Jeep, pulled away as the other vehicle crested a rise and sped past. Not Gwen, but it wasn't a good idea for anyone to see him here. There was a place about fifty yards to the south that he'd spotted earlier, where he and the Jeep would be concealed from all traffic—a place that commanded a view of Gwen's parking area.

That was where he'd wait for her.

*   *   *

By four-thirty he was cramped and tired and suffering from a severe tension headache. Best to pack it in and head back to the motel. After all, he'd waited fourteen years; another day or two wouldn't kill him. He was now gainfully employed—general assignment photographer and truck mechanic for the local paper. That gave him a bona fide reason for prowling the countryside.

But still he waited. Five minutes, ten, fifteen . . . Cars and trucks and SUVs passed—residents returning to their homes. He counted them, one through twenty, and then a white SUV appeared, slowed, and turned off into Gwen's parking area. One of those new Mercedeses he'd seen written up in the automotive section of the Vancouver paper; suggested retail price was in the neighborhood of seventy-three thousand U.S. dollars.

Doing well, Gwennie.

He took up the Nikon again as the driver's-side door opened. Leaned forward with the lens aimed through the Jeep's windshield. A woman came around the vehicle—tall and slim, with a model's erect posture and a dancer's graceful step. Gwen's posture. Gwen's step.

She went to the passenger-side door and opened it. Said something to someone inside and turned. Now he had a clear view of her face. Her once-smooth skin bore fine lines at the corners of her eyes and mouth, and her long dark-brown hair had been cut so that it curved in smooth wings to her jawbone, but he recognized her instantly. He gripped the Nikon hard, and his nervous finger depressed the shutter.

As Gwen moved to the rear of the SUV and opened the door, the passenger stepped down. A girl of nine or ten, dragging an enormous backpack of the sort all the kids seemed to favor these days. Her skin was honey-tan, and her features and curly black hair indicated African-American heritage. Had Gwen married a black man? Adopted a mixed-race child?

Gwen was taking a folded metal cart from the rear of the vehicle. As the child approached, smiling up at her, Matt took
another photograph. Gwen set up the cart and began filling it
with grocery bags. After she finished and shut the door, she
tried to take the backpack from the little girl, who resisted,
laughing. Gwen laughed, too, ruffling the child's hair; the love
in her eyes was reflected in her daughter's. The two started
across the footbridge, Gwen pulling the cart with one hand,
the other resting on the girl's shoulder.

Matt snapped a picture of them before they passed out of
sight behind an overhanging fringe of pine branches.

*Well, now you know, Lindstrom. She's got herself a nice home, nice
little girl, probably a nice husband. The good life that she somehow
couldn't find with you.*

Now you know. And you know what you have to do.

Back at his motel, he had one drink of Wild Turkey and then
another. They did nothing to take the edge off. Even though
he'd expected to see Gwen's image through the camera's lens,
its actual appearance had shocked him. Altered him, too, in
ways that he couldn't yet begin to guess at. His hands were
shaking as he poured another drink and the memories crowded
in, their former bittersweet flavor now charred by rage.

*"Let me help you. Gwennie. Whatever's wrong, I can help you
through this if you'll let me."*

"Nobody can help. Least of all you."

"Is it my fault? What's wrong with me?"

"It's not you. Just leave it."

"Gwen—"

"Just leave it. And leave me alone!"

* * *

"Why don't you want kids? Give me one good reason why."

"For God's sake, Matt, look at the world we're living in. Do you really want to bring children into it?"

"Ah, the standard line."

"What does that mean?"

"It's everybody's excuse when they're—"

"When they're what? Too selfish? Is that what you think of me?"

"No, but maybe you're afraid of the responsibility."

"Well, what if I am?"

"I'd share the responsibility. You wouldn't be alone."

"I don't know. I just don't know. Kids, they make everything so . . . permanent."

"The way you're looking at me, Gwen, it's as if you hate me."

"Matt, no . . ."

"Well, that sure isn't the way a woman looks at the man she loves."

"I do love you; that's not the problem."

"Then what is the problem?"

"Matt, I want a divorce."

"You say you love me, but you want a divorce?"

"I want a divorce because if I don't leave you, I will hate you."

"The mind may forget, but not the body."

"Then stay. Refresh your memory."

"It's not that simple, Matt."

"Why not?"

"Because it just isn't."

When he reached for the Wild Turkey again, he saw the bottle of wine that he'd bought along with his lunch at the deli in Cyanide Wells.

Sam! Jesus Christ . . .

He'd been due at her house at seven, but now his watch

showed eight-forty. *Better phone. No—go. Think of some plausible excuse on the way.* Poor kid, she'd been so excited; he couldn't brush her off with a call.

Sam's little frame house was dark when he stopped at the curb, and for a moment he felt relieved. He could just drive away, call her in the morning. But then he spotted a flicker of light on the porch, and a figure moved in the shadows. After he cut the Jeep's engine, Sam's voice called, "Well, John Crowe. The roast I spent my hard-earned money on this afternoon is as tough as beef jerky by now, and the fresh asparagus have turned gray. So what's your excuse?"

He got out of the Jeep and mounted the steps. The light he'd seen came from a candle in a glass globe on a small table between two broken-down wicker chairs. Extending the wine bottle to her, he said, "I'm sorry."

She took the bottle and turned toward the door. "It's my fault, for making a big deal out of having a guy I met in a bar over for dinner."

"No, it's my fault. I lost track of the time." The elaborate excuse he'd concocted about his new job and a time-consuming first assignment seemed a shabby lie now.

Sam said, "I'll open the wine and get us glasses. Maybe after we drink some, the beef jerky won't seem so tough, and I can probably get the asparagus up on their feet with some salad dressing."

In a couple of minutes she came back. Wordlessly she handed the open bottle to him, set down two glasses, and indicated he should pour. When she sat, the candle's light touched her face, and he saw her eyes were puffy and red.

"You've been crying."

"Crying's kind of my thing these days."

"Sam, I should've called. I was thoughtless, and I'm sorry."

"One 'sorry' is enough, thank you. How much bourbon have you drunk, anyway?"

"Too much."

"You shouldn't've driven in your condition. I don't like drunks behind the wheel. My girlfriend's little boy died because of somebody like you."

"I'm—"

"Yeah, I know—you're sorry. Give me your car keys."

"What?"

"Your car keys." She held out her hand, snapped her fingers. "You can stay here tonight, because I plan to drink this wine and then some more, so I won't be able to take you back to your motel."

"But—"

"It's not a proposition. My dad's bed is made up fresh."

He reached into his pocket, surrendered the keys.

She nodded in approval. "So why the communion with the bottle?"

He had an easy answer prepared. "Celebrating too much."

"Celebrating what?"

"My new job as general assignment photographer for the *Spectrum.*"

"Hey, that's great!"

"I'm pretty happy about it."

"That what you did up in Canada?"

"For a much smaller paper."

"Then you know about all the world-shattering events you'll be taking pictures of: the hog judging at the county fair, old folks celebrating their fiftieth wedding anniversaries, the groundbreaking for the new Denny's."

"Listen, in order to get the job I had to fix Carly McGuire's truck. After that, everything else'll seem exciting."

Sam laughed. "She bullied you into it, huh?"

"Sort of."

"I hear she's not easy to work for, but if you've got a good idea she'll turn you loose on it. That's what she did with Ardis Coleman on the series that won the Pulitzer. And she ran an arty shot by the last photographer every week. You give her something she likes, she'll print it."

"You sound as if you know her."

"I don't really know anybody in Cyanide Wells."

"What about Ardis Coleman?"

"I told you last night, the closest I've gotten to her is being in the next line at the supermarket."

"You must've heard something about her. She's a local celebrity."

"How come you're so interested?"

"I guess it's kind of like hero worship. This is the closest I've gotten to a Pulitzer winner—being in the same county with her."

"Well . . . They say she's reclusive. Lives out on Drinkwater Creek on a big piece of property. Doesn't give interviews or make public appearances. I think somebody told me she has a kid, but I don't remember whether it's a girl or a boy. She must have money, though; that's one expensive, snooty town. I don't know why that paper's there. They crusade for all the things rich people are against: financing decent health care and welfare programs through higher taxes, making big corporations pay their fair share. They're for preserving the environment, too, but they don't go overboard; they recognize that people like loggers and fishermen have to make a living. What they want is a reasonable balance, and I like that. I also like it that the paper's owned by a woman. It's the kind of thing I'd've wanted to do if I'd gotten a decent education and had the kind of money Carly McGuire must."

In the light from the candle Sam suddenly looked melancholy. She added, "Lots of *if*s, huh? But *if*s don't count. I'll be working at the Chicken Shack till I keel over serving a Supreme Combo with cole slaw and fries."

"You told me last night that you were thinking of getting out of here."

"I *think* about a lot of things. It's the doing that's hard." She sipped wine, more pensive. "So you'll be staying around. Got a place to live?"

"Not yet. On my salary I couldn't even afford a closet in Cyanide Wells, so I'm thinking of looking here. I like Talbot's Mills better, anyway."

"Why?"

"It's real."

Sam smiled grimly. "Oh, it's real, all right. My dad could've told you how real it is. But listen, I know of a room for rent, with kitchen privileges."

"Oh?"

"Yeah. Very cheap, if you volunteer for some chores, like fixing the drippy bathroom faucet and cleaning out the gutters."

"When can I look at it?"

"Right now, if you want." She stood and moved toward the door.

"I thought you had to be out of here next month."

Sam looked uncomfortable. "I didn't tell you the whole truth about my dad. He . . . shot himself. Just couldn't take being laid off at his age. After the funeral, one of the *Spectrum*'s reporters, that Donna Vail, interviewed me. I didn't exactly hold back about the way the mill treated him. The manager there found out they were printing the story, so he called this morning and said I can live here rent-free till the end of the year, and if I want to stay longer, they'll negotiate a fair price."

"And of course their P.R. department called the paper as soon as you agreed."

"Of course, but what the hell do I care? It's a roof over my head, and if you move in I might actually be able to save some money."

He considered. Sam struck him as both levelheaded and easy to get along with. She wasn't especially curious about either his prior or his present life and seemed disinclined to initiate a sexual relationship with him. Plus, she was an excellent source of information about the community. But best of all, he could get out of the motel, where he'd registered under his own name.

"I don't need to inspect the room," he said. "I'm sure it'll be fine. I'm good with plumbing, so the leak should be fixed by this time tomorrow. Give me a little longer on the gutters."

Thursday, May 9, 2002

A tour of the *Spectrum*'s offices, under the guidance of Severin Quill, was the first activity of the new day. Matt, nursing a hangover, suffered most of it in silence, saving his strength for Quill's introductions of their fellow staff members. He'd already been greeted at the reception desk by the office and subscription manager, Brandi Webster, a young woman with the good looks of a high school cheerleader and the mannerisms to match; normally he would have found them delightful, but today they just seemed wearisome.

As Quill got up from his desk and came to meet him, a heavyset woman in a purple straw hat and voluminous flowered clothing rushed past Matt, calling out, "Vera Craig, arts editor. Welcome aboard!" The scent of violet perfume trailed after her.

Quill smiled. "Appearances to the contrary, Vera's a damned

good reporter and an astute critic. This morning she's off to chronicle the opening of the new Thomas Kinkade gallery."

"Kinkade?"

"California's 'painter of light.' Mass-produced 'originals.'"

"Like Keane paintings?"

"No, more palatable. Idyllic scenes instead of glassy-eyed children. Very popular in the nineties; less so now, and his enterprises are overextended—hence a gallery in our provincial little community."

A woman came through one of the doors at the rear of the room, and Quill called, "Donna, meet John Crowe, our new photographer. John, Donna Vail, general assignment reporter. You'll be working closely with her."

Donna Vail was small, blonde, and attractive. She wore shorts and a tee, and her frizzy shoulder-length hair was topped by a baseball cap. Her blue eyes surveyed him with frank interest, and she said in a husky voice, "Good to meet you, John. I'm sure I'll enjoy working *closely* with you." Then, like Vera Craig, she was out the door.

Quill chuckled, and Matt realized his mouth had fallen open. "Don't mind Donna," Severin said. "She likes to project a bad-girl image. In reality, she's a dedicated soccer mom and wife of the golf pro at the Meadows."

"The Meadows?"

"A big planned community on the road east of town. The way to handle Donna is to serve back to her what she dishes up. She won't know if you're serious or not, so she'll back off and treat you like a buddy."

"Well, that's a relief."

The tour went on to a large back room full of cubicles, where Matt met the display ad manager, advertising sales representatives, and mail-room personnel. As they were passing through the front room again, Quill introduced him to the religious/

education and sports reporters. The door to Carly McGuire's office was closed, and a Do Not Disturb sign—courtesy of Ramada Inn—hung on its knob.

"She's hiding?" he asked.

Quill rolled his eyes. "Yes, thank God. She came in loaded for bear."

"Why?"

"Who knows, with Carly?"

"The truck got her to Santa Carla and back okay, didn't it?"

"If it hadn't, my friend, you wouldn't be alive."

Quill led him through another door, to a room where the production manager and chief of page makeup and their assistants congratulated him on joining the staff. Beyond their areas were a couple of desks, a bank of file cabinets, and a light table. A door labeled DARKROOM was set into the wall opposite them.

"Your bailiwick," Quill said, with a flourish of his hand. "Your assistant, Joe Maynard, is currently in the inner sanctum, printing what he claims are perfectly egregious photographs he took at the Calvert's Landing mayoral press conference this week."

"Calvert's Landing?"

"It's the largest town on the coast. An Alaskan company wants to float gigantic, ugly plastic bags at the outlet of the Deer River to collect water to sell to southern California. Mayor's all for the deal; he claims the water belongs to the state, not the municipality, so they can't stop it. Which means he's been paid off by the Alaskans. His constituency is concerned about environmental issues and visual pollution. The mayor's effort to convert them to his point of view ended up in an unfortunate egg-throwing incident, which Joe captured on film."

"Egregiously."

"He tends to underestimate his talents. Anyway, I'll leave you to await his emergence."

Matt had hoped, now that the tour of the facilities was at its final destination, to ask Quill about Ardis Coleman. But when he invited him to sit down and chat till Maynard was done, the reporter said he had an appointment in fifteen minutes. Maybe they could have a beer after work? Matt suggested. Sure, Quill said, if they finished at the same time. Hours at the *Spectrum* were irregular at best.

Joe Maynard was built like a linebacker, with a shock of unruly brown hair, a nose that looked as if it had been broken more than once, and almost no neck. His hands were so large and clumsy-looking that Matt wondered how he could manipulate the settings on his camera. As they began trading histories in the cautious manner of men who know they must get along in order to work together, he found that Joe had indeed been a linebacker, at UCLA, where he'd earned a degree in fine arts.

"So what brought you to Cyanide Wells?" Matt asked.

"A chance to work at a paper in a place where I could also hunt and fish. After college I played a couple of seasons on special teams for the Pittsburgh Steelers, but I hated the weather back there. And I wasn't really pro caliber, anyway. So I saved my money, came back to California, and worked for the *Long Beach Sentinel*. Then I heard about an opening here and applied. They'd just won the Pulitzer, and McGuire had an interesting reputation. Plus, I could live cheap."

"How come McGuire didn't promote you when the last guy left?"

"She tried to, but I turned her down. I don't want to work full-time. I invested well before the dot-com bubble popped, took my profits, and put them into conservative holdings. And a year ago my wife presented me with twin boys. I want to be as much a part of their lives as I can."

"Good for you." Matt proceeded to give him the same abbreviated details of his made-up life that he'd told Carly McGuire, then said, "Now, let's see how those shots of the egg-faced mayor have turned out."

Maynard's photographs were so good that Matt wondered what he might have accomplished had he had the desire to apply his talent. But talent alone, he knew, wasn't enough to ensure success; success took drive and dedication, which his new assistant plainly lacked.

"So," he said as they emerged from the darkroom, "you came to the paper before it won the Pulitzer?"

"Afterwards. That was one of the things that attracted me. I mean, how often do you get to work for a small country weekly that's achieved the granddaddy of journalistic honors? The only other one that comes to mind is the *Point Reyes Light,* for their exposé of Synanon, and that was decades ago."

"I understand the bulk of the *Spectrum*'s prize-winning articles were written by a reporter called Ardis Coleman. You know her?"

"I've met her."

"What's she like?"

"Quiet. Unassuming. Self-deprecating, actually. She once told me she didn't do anything special, she was just handed a great story. But under the circumstances, I'd say her coverage was extraordinary."

"What circumstances?"

"Ronnie Talbot and Deke Rutherford, the murder victims, were good friends of Coleman's, and she was the one who found their bodies. Yet she was able to separate herself from her emotions and write extremely balanced, well reasoned stories. I admire that kind of control."

And how had Gwen achieved such control? The picture that Maynard painted was not of the woman Matt had married.

"What's Coleman like personally? She married? Have kids?"

Maynard smiled. "What, you thinking of asking her for a date?"

"I'm just curious about how a woman like that balances work and family, if she has any."

Maynard seemed unconvinced of his reply. "Look," he said, "she's a good friend of McGuire's. Why don't you ask her?"

He'd have more success prying information out of the Great Sphinx. "I guess I'd better wait till she's having a better day."

"Good luck, buddy."

Within fifteen minutes, a memo from McGuire was delivered to his desk by a young man with magenta-and-green hair and multiple body piercings, who identified himself as the office gofer. "Name's Nile, like the river."

"No last name?"

"Don't need one. How many people're called Nile? Besides, Nile Schultz sounds just plain stupid." He gave him a little salute and walked away.

Matt picked up the memo and studied it. It was computer-generated, printed on the back of what looked to be copy for a story, which had a big black X through it. McGuire clearly didn't waste paper—or type very well, either.

John,I called your former editor this a.m.and she gave you a glowing recommendation.I hope youcan live up to it.Here's the schedule of your assignments fortoday.I want to meetwith you at 4:30 after you've completed them.11:30a--meet Vera Craig at the newKinkade gallery,MainSt.next to the Book nook.Vera will tell you what shots she needs.1:30p--Gundersons silver wedding anniversaryshoot,their home,111 Estes St.I assume youhave a map,if not purchase one.2:15p--Pooh's Corner, next toAram's,need shots of new line of anatomically correct dolls that are causing thecurrent

*flap. Avoid private parts, the parents are up in arms and we don't
want to further incite them. Thanks, Carly.*

It was now a little after ten; since his first assignment wasn't
until eleven-thirty, he had time to slip away and check out
Gwen's home more closely. Grabbing his camera bag, he left the
office and drove off toward Drinkwater Road.

The expensive SUV sat in the paved area by the footbridge
but in a different place than on the previous afternoon; probably Gwen had driven her little girl to school. Matt drove past,
turned, and zoomed in on it, snapping a photo showing its license plate number. Then he drove to where he'd parked before
and moved along the road, taking random shots to either side.
A casual observer would probably have assumed he was docu-
menting the regional plants and trees, but the true objects of his
shots were Gwen's mailbox, the footbridge, and the extent of
her property. When he finished the roll, he drove back toward
town and his first appointment, wondering whether he could
persuade Vera Craig to have lunch with him. The arts editor
seemed open and friendly, exactly the sort of person who might
be willing to answer his questions about the paper's prize-
winning former reporter.

"Hell, honey," Vera Craig said, "none of us see much of Ard
these days." She speared a lobster ravioli from the plate she and
Matt were sharing at Mamma Mia's, bit into it with her eyes
closed, and made a sound of pure sensual delight.

Matt tasted one. It was good, but not enough to nearly in-
duce an orgasm. "Why not?"

"I guess she's just holed up at home, working on her book. It's
giving her trouble. At least that's what Carly says."

"You know her well?"

"Nobody knows Ard well, except for Carly, and sometimes I wonder about that. I've been acquainted with her since she came to town, and after fourteen or fifteen years, I still don't know what makes her tick."

"She worked for the paper right from the first?"

"Yeah, as a gofer, then general assignment reporter. Good one, willing to take on anything. She just got better and better, till Carly finally promoted her to roving-reporter status, meaning she basically covered any story in the county that she found controversial or interesting. Then came the murders."

"I understand she was the one who found the bodies."

Vera Craig's face grew somber, and she set her fork tines on the edge of the plate. "Yeah. Bad for her in a couple of ways. Finding two men slaughtered in their bed was pretty horrific. And they weren't strangers; they were her friends. But besides her grief she had to deal with community reaction."

"I don't understand."

"Cyanide Wells and the county as a whole are pretty conservative. You've got your rich people, mostly retirees; you've got your religious people, your young families, your working-class people, and your assholes who like to drink and shoot their guns and would consider a good evening's fun burning a cross on somebody's front lawn—or blowing away a couple of 'faggots' in their own bed. And, like anyplace else, you've got your gays who mainly keep a low profile. Ronnie Talbot and Deke Rutherford didn't, and Ronnie compounded the general dislike by selling off the mill. When it came out that Ard was their friend, the dislike was transferred to her."

"That must've changed when the paper won the Pulitzer."

"It changed when people started reading her stories. They were so powerful, they made the readers understand—or at least think about—the problems of gays who live in this type of environment."

"So now she's writing a book."

"Has been for over two years. It's contracted for and is due to be turned in pretty soon, but like I said, she's having problems with it."

"It can't be easy, dealing with that kind of material."

"I guess not." Craig picked up her fork and attacked the ravioli with renewed vigor. "But enough about Ard. Tell me about yourself, honey. What brought you to our little village, anyway?"

Lying, Matt reflected as he packed up his gear and said goodbye to the proprietor of Pooh's Corner, could be an exhausting business. Today he'd given various versions of the life and times of John Crowe to at least five people. He was glad that his final encounter would be with Carly McGuire, Severin Quill having canceled their tentative plans for drinks—he had to go someplace called Signal Port on a story. McGuire, Matt assumed, knew everything about him that she wanted to know, and would be more interested in his work than his personal history.

He had roughly an hour and a half before their meeting, so he headed back to the darkroom to develop his films. The contact sheets showed he hadn't lost his eye, although there were certain technical skills that weren't as sharp as they'd once been. He particularly liked the last batch of photos: the inanely smiling girl and boy dolls that were causing such controversy among local parents. Innocence, if not downright stupidity, radiated from their faces, and the private parts—which he'd shot for his own amusement—were no more threatening and much less realistic than those that the children of Cyanide Wells surely witnessed while playing the time-honored game of "doctor."

Four-thirty on the dot. Armed with his contact sheets, Matt

went to McGuire's office. The door was slightly ajar, and before he could knock, he heard Carly's raised voice.

"Don't you threaten me, Gar!"

"That was a mere statement of fact, not a threat." The man's voice was deep and full-bodied—and vaguely familiar.

"Facts, I'm afraid, are open to personal interpretation."

"Perhaps, but you should realize that there are complex issues at work here, which you can't possibly begin to understand."

"Complex issues. Which I can't understand. I don't think so."

"You're not infallible, Carly. If you don't believe me, look to your own life."

There was a silence, and then McGuire spoke, her voice low and dangerous. "Get the fuck out of my office, Gar."

"You're being unreasonable—"

With a shock, Matt remembered where he'd heard that voice. "Out. Now!"

The door opened, grazing Matt's shoulder. The man who pushed through was tall and lean, with a thick mane of gray hair. The cut of his suit, and his even hothouse tan, spoke of money; an old, jagged scar on his right cheek and the iciness of his eyes were at odds with his gentlemanly appearance. His gaze barely registered Matt's presence as he strode from the building.

McGuire came to the door, her face pale, mouth rigid. She started when she saw Matt. "I suppose you heard that," she said.

"I heard you telling him"—he jerked his thumb at the door—"to get the fuck out of your office. Good for you. I don't like the look of him."

"What's to like?"

"Who is he?"

"Our mayor, the esteemed Garson Payne. An asshole who, in four years, hopes to be our district's representative to the state legislature."

At least now Matt had a name for the man who had made the

anonymous call to him in Port Regis. But why would an elected official do such a thing? And how had he found him?

He tried to ask more questions about Payne; McGuire declined to discuss him further. Instead she invited Matt into her office and went over the contact sheets intently, staring at them through her half-glasses, circling the shots she wanted him to print. When she came to the doll series, she said, "Oh, my God! *This* is what all the commotion's about?"

"Maybe you'd like to run one of them as your arty shot of the week?"

She grinned. "I've half a mind to. No, instead I think I'll run one with Sev's article. He said the same things you've captured here. This one." She circled it. "And also this, where their faces look like they're flirting with each other. The smug mommies and daddies of this county can use a shaking up."

"You like messing with people's heads."

"If it serves a purpose. That's what a good newspaper should do: Challenge the readership's opinions; make them think. I'll need these by tomorrow at one. Nice first day on the job, John."

"Thanks, I enjoyed it. The people I talked with really like and respect the paper. Of course, not every town of this size can boast of a Pulitzer-winning publication."

"True." She handed the sheets back to him and stood.

"I've read the series, and I liked it a lot, particularly the stories written by Ardis Coleman."

"Ard's a terrific writer. We'll never see the likes of her again."

"She quit to write a book on the murders?"

"Uh-huh."

"You still see her?"

McGuire had been gathering papers and putting them in her briefcase, but now her hands stilled. "Look, John, we'd better get one thing straight right off the bat. This is a small paper, and a small community. When you live at close quarters with your coworkers and fellow citizens, you've got to draw boundaries. The one I insist on is the separation of one's professional and personal life."

"I couldn't agree with you more. The only reason I asked about Ms. Coleman is that I'd like to meet her, talk with her about the articles."

"That's not possible. Ard's at a difficult place in her work right now, and she doesn't wish to be disturbed."

"Maybe later, when the book's finished?"

"Maybe, if you haven't moved on by then."

"Why would I move on?"

She busied herself with the papers again, avoiding his eyes. "You moved on after eighteen years with your former paper."

"Eighteen years is a long time."

"You're what—thirty-eight?"

"Thirty-nine."

"Well, in my experience, that's an age when men tend to get antsy. Move from woman to woman, job to job, place to place. Right now you could be at the beginning of a long journey."

As he worked on the leaky faucet in Sam's small bathroom early that evening—didn't the woman know that washers eventually wore out?—Matt thought about McGuire's comments. She'd sensed his restlessness but interpreted it in conventional terms—and wrongly. His was a condition born of a desire to wrap up old business rather than to seek out the new. And the long journey he'd undertaken was not geographical, but one that would take him deep inside himself to confront things that now were only shadowy and unsettling. The prospect of that confrontation made him turn such a vigorous hand to tightening the pipes under the sink that one joint began to spit water.

Just what he needed. Sam had no plumbing supplies on hand, and although he'd noticed an Ace Hardware in one of the strip malls near the freeway interchange, he hadn't planned to spend all his evening performing handyman's duties. He went to the kitchen, rummaged in the drawer where Sam kept her tools, and found a roll of duct tape. In his opinion, duct tape was one of the greatest inventions of the past century, a quick fix for everything; he'd used it for such diverse purposes as temporarily repairing a camera and hemming a pair of jeans. After he taped the pipe joint, he left a warning note for Sam, who was working till ten, and set out for Drinkwater Creek.

Gwen's house was wrapped in shadow when he arrived, its lighted windows a pale glow through the surrounding trees. He freed the Nikon from its bag, reattached the telephoto, adjusted the settings. It wasn't till he looked up that he noticed there were two vehicles in the paved area by the footbridge: Gwen's luxury SUV and a red Ford Ranger with a Save the Redwoods sticker on its rear bumper. Carly McGuire's truck.

Paranoia seized him. His explanation for his interest in Ardis Coleman hadn't rung true to McGuire, and she'd come here to discuss him with her friend. Somehow Gwen would figure out who he was, and . . .

Don't get ahead of yourself. McGuire's probably here for a perfectly normal visit.

He turned off the switch on the truck's dome light, slipped out, and ran lightly across the pavement. The footbridge was easily visible from the house, so he walked downstream until he found a narrow place where he could cross on stepping-stones. After scrambling up the opposite bank, he stopped to get his bearings. The house was on a forty-five-degree angle to his right, screened by a windbreak of eucalyptus. He moved toward them and stood in their shelter, sighting on one of the lighted windows with the telephoto.

Kitchen: granite tiles, wood cabinets, lots of stainless steel. Table with remains of a meal for three set in a cozy nook.

He moved to the next window. Living room: hearth with fire burning, white cat sleeping on the area rug in front of it, black leather furniture. Gwen sat at the end of the sofa, her feet propped on a coffee table, her head bowed as she went over some papers, probably manuscript pages. A half-full wineglass sat on the table beside her; she reached for it and sipped, looking up at the window. Involuntarily Matt stepped back, even though he knew she couldn't possibly see him. She set the glass down, turned her head, and spoke to someone outside his range of vision. Appeared to be waiting for an answer.

Still pretty, Gwennie, even after fourteen years. You've taken good care of yourself. Of course, with money, that's easy.

He began to snap photographs.

Gwen said something else, set down the papers, and curled her legs beneath her. She was wearing a long blue robe, and she pulled its hem over her bare feet—a gesture he remembered.

Now Carly McGuire came into view, moving around the sofa and setting a glass of wine on the coffee table before she sat. Gwen spoke again, and Carly shrugged, her mouth set. Gwen frowned, said something else to Carly. Even though he couldn't hear her words, Matt remembered that look and the tone that accompanied it. McGuire closed her eyes, shook her head.

God, it was like witnessing a scene from his marriage: Gwen angry, himself on the defensive.

Gwen's lips tightened, and she looked away from Carly. Matt could now see her face-on, and this, too, was familiar. For a moment her mouth remained in a firm line, but then it began to crumble at the corners; her teeth nipped at her lower lip as her eyes filled. She squeezed them shut, and the tears overflowed, coursing down her cheeks as she remained perfectly still. She was, he knew, making no sound. Her silent weeping had always unnerved him, made him want to flee.

Apparently it had the same effect on McGuire. As Matt moved the lens to her face, he saw panic. But just as his own panic had quickly dissolved, so did Carly's. She closed the space between them and took Gwen into her arms.

How many times had he done just that? He watched, fascinated, as a part of his first life was reenacted before the powerful lens of his camera.

Carly stroked Gwen's hair. Her lips murmured words that had belonged to him in years past: *"It's going to be all right. You'll see. It will be all right."*

Gwen's face was pressed into Carly's shoulder. Soon she would raise her head and ask in a little girl's voice, *"Do you mean that? Do you really mean it?"*

And Carly, like Matt, would be forced to lie: *"Yes, of course I do."*

As he watched the scene through his lens, a chill touched Matt's shoulders, took hold of his spine. He was years in the past, comforting his wife. He was here in the present, a voyeur. He was about to step into a future he wasn't sure he cared to visit. . . .

Gwen raised her head, asked her question. Carly gave her response. Gwen's face became suffused with hope.

Then, forcefully, the women's lips met and held.

And with a jolt, Matt realized the nature of the relationship between them.

Friday, May 10, 2002

e was halfway to Santa Carla, the county seat, driving blindly while trying to absorb what he'd learned about Gwen and Carly McGuire, when the Jeep ran out of gas. He coasted onto the shoulder, set the brake, and leaned forward, his arms resting on top of the steering wheel. The dashboard clock showed it was twelve-seventeen in the morning, and he hadn't seen another car for at least ten minutes.

Briefly he debated leaving the Jeep and walking south to find a service station, but decided against it. Some miles back the highway had narrowed to two sharply curving lanes, dangerous to walk along in the darkness. Besides, stations were practically nonexistent between towns, and the last sign he'd noticed said he was thirty-five miles from the county seat. Instead he set out an emergency flare, shut off the Jeep's head-lights, and settled in to wait for a Good Samaritan.

His thoughts kept turning to Gwen, picturing the look of hope on her face before she and Carly kissed. So his former wife had formed an intimate relationship with another woman after leaving him. A long-term, stable one from the looks of it. There was a child. Gwen's? Carly's? Natural? Adopted? Who had fathered her?

Had Gwen been involved with women before and during his marriage to her? He knew about the men she'd been with ear-lier, and up to now had felt reasonably certain she'd remained faithful to him until she disappeared. Surely he'd have known had it been otherwise. Or would he? The possibility of his wife having a lesbian affair is not the first to occur to a man, even when his marriage begins to deteriorate.

Did the trouble that had arisen so quickly in the marriage stem from Gwen's confusion about her sexual orientation? From her inability to discuss it with him? From her guilt over an affair?

How long after she left Saugatuck had she met Carly? Where and how? Did Carly know that Gwen's former husband had been suspected of murdering her? Gwen had known, according to his anonymous caller, now identified as Mayor Garson Payne.

And now to the big question: Would the current situation alter his feelings toward Gwen? His plans? Should it? He'd waited such a long time for . . .

Headlights flashed around the curve in front of him. The ve-hicle slowed, its driver spotting the flare. It U-turned and pulled onto the shoulder, beams blinding in the rearview and side mirrors. Matt stepped out of the Jeep.

A woman walked toward him, moving in a deliberate but cautious manner, as a cop does when approaching a stopped vehicle. When she came closer, he saw she had closely cropped black hair and a pretty, fine-boned face; she wore a dark suit and had her right hand thrust inside her shoulder bag, as if it might contain a gun.

"Need some help?" she asked in a guarded but friendly tone.

"I'm out of gas. Can you give me a lift to the nearest service station?"

"Sure can, but I'll have to ask to see your license and registration first. Detective Rhoda Swift, Soledad County Sheriff's Department." She flashed her identification at him.

He got the rental papers from the Jeep, removed his license from his wallet.

The detective examined them in the headlights' glare. "British Columbia, huh? Nice country up there. What brings you to Soledad County, Mr. Lindstrom?"

"I've taken a job here, as a photographer for the *Spectrum*." As soon as he spoke the words, he realized he'd made a bad mistake. John Crowe, not Matt Lindstrom, had taken the job.

"Good publication. How's Carly these days?"

"Prickly as ever, but fine."

Rhoda Swift smiled faintly and said, "Well, Mr. Lindstrom, let's get going before the sun comes up. I was headed north for Green Valley Road, but I can just as easily take Old Schoolhouse out of Santa Carla."

"I don't want to make you go out of your way—"

"Insuring the public's safety is what we're here for. Green Valley's a better road, but Old Schoolhouse is more direct to where I'm going. I'll deliver you to the service station there, and they'll give you a lift back."

Matt barely had time to get his seat belt fastened before Rhoda Swift accelerated onto the highway, clearing the Jeep's bumper by scant inches. He glanced at her, and she grinned wickedly—a good, fast driver who took pleasure in showing off for her passenger.

There was a police radio mounted beneath the dash, its mutterings indistinguishable to him. Swift turned down its volume, and he was about to ask her about her job when she reached for the mike, keyed it, and said, "Yeah, Valerie, what've you got for me?"

A pause, then a sigh. "I've told him my cell doesn't work on this side of the ridge. . . . Okay, patch him through to me." She rolled her eyes at Matt. "Men! Yes, Guy. . . . I told you— Oh, never mind. . . . The meeting ran longer than I thought it would, but I'm on my way. Just have to deliver a motorist in distress to a service station first. . . . Don't worry, I'll be careful. . . . Yes, *dear.*"

As she hung up the mike, Rhoda Swift laughed softly.

"Overprotective husband?" Matt asked.

"Overprotective gentleman friend. He's a New Yorker, spends part of the year at his vacation home near Deer Harbor. When he's in Manhattan, he thinks nothing of wandering the streets at two in the morning, but should I be driving one of our rural byways at night, his mind conjures up all sorts of peril."

"Men like to think we're fierce protectors even when we're not, I guess. Where's Deer Harbor?"

"On the coast, north of Signal Port."

"One of our reporters was covering a story in Signal Port today."

"That would be the Dawson case. Hugh Dawson, owner of the Sea Stacks Motel. Miserable cuss, and last night his wife finally decided she'd had enough of his abuse and shot him. I've just come from a meeting with the D.A. in Santa Carla; we're in agreement that it was justifiable homicide."

For the remainder of the trip into town Matt chatted with

Rhoda Swift about the county, learning more about the coastal area, which, by virtue of being cut off by the ridgeline, seemed a world unto itself. When she dropped him at the Chevron station at Old Schoolhouse Road, she said, "Welcome to Soledad County, Mr. Lindstrom. Take my advice, and fill up often from now on."

"I will. And thanks for the lift."

Her big eyes clouded. "No problem. A couple of years ago I didn't give a stranded motorist a lift, and I very much regret it. I try to make up for it every time I can."

The encounter with the sheriff's detective had calmed Matt. After the Chevron station attendant returned him, with a supply of gas, to the Jeep, he drove to a small motel near the county courthouse in Santa Carla and took a room. As soon as the government offices opened the next morning, he was there and, with the help of a kindly clerk, began researching the public records.

The house on Drinkwater Creek, it turned out, belonged to Carly McGuire. She'd bought it in 1983, the same year she bought the *Soledad Spectrum.* By his estimate, Carly couldn't be more than forty-five, which would put her in her twenties at the time of the purchases—large purchases for one that young. Money there. Perhaps she was a trust fund baby.

He had no name for the child he'd seen with Gwen, so he asked the clerk to show him how to access birth records by the parent's name. No child had been born to Ardis Coleman or Carly McGuire in Soledad County during the four-year period when he assumed the birth would have taken place. Adopted, perhaps?

One question answered. More raised.

He headed back to Cyanide Wells.

*   *   *

"So you think you can just show up at your leisure, do you, Crowe?" McGuire stood outside her office door, arms folded, expression severe.

"Car trouble," Matt said. "Sorry."

Boss trouble, he thought. Big time.

"You can fix my piece-of-shit truck in half an hour, but something goes wrong with that fancy Grand Cherokee that keeps you away all morning?"

"I said I'm sorry."

"Your assignment sheet's on your desk. Get cracking."

God, what did Gwen see in the woman?

"Got time for that drink this evening?" Matt asked Severin Quill.

The reporter looked up from his keyboard. "You could probably use one right now, after the contretemps with Attila the Hun." He looked at his watch. "I have to attend a press conference in Santa Carla at two. Why don't we meet at Rob's Recovery Room at five-thirty. You know where that is?"

"Uh-uh."

"Just south of the Talbot's Mills exit on the east side of the freeway."

"Kind of far from here."

"Yes, but it's on my way back. Plus, it's seedy enough that Attila wouldn't deign to set foot there."

"Are we hiding from her?"

"Not exactly, but her policy of separation of work and private life makes for uneasy encounters here in town."

"I'll see you at five-thirty, then."

Rob's Recovery Room was a country tavern, and fully as seedy as Quill claimed. The bar was gouged with initials and other penknife graffiti; the upholstery of the black leatherette booths had been eviscerated in places. The customers were mainly men with work-hardened hands and weathered faces, wearing faded clothing and baseball caps with logos. Whiskey and something called Knob Ale seemed to be the drinks of choice. After Matt shouldered through the knots of patrons by the bar, he asked for a Knob, no glass, and took a booth from which he could survey the crowd.

On the surface, the atmosphere was convivial. The men laughed and joked and made suggestive remarks to the lone busy waitress; a trio of women occupied the booth next to him, and their conversation was punctuated by shrill giggles. But soon he began to detect a curious hollowness to the sounds and noticed that the smiles stretched people's lips but didn't reach their eyes. When voices rose in anger near the door, the thin, sallow-faced woman to Matt's left winced and said to her companions, "Doug's gonna be a handful tonight; I just know it."

"Got his notice, did he?"

"Yeah."

"What're you guys gonna do?"

"My brother thinks he might be able to get him on at the mill where he works up in Washington. But things're bad there, too."

"Fuckin' tree-huggers."

"Yeah, but they're not the only ones to blame for what's happenin' here. Maybe if the mill had a better manager it wouldn't be failing."

"Wrong, honey. The manager follows orders from the top, and what they're orderin' him to do is shut the place down. They'll make more money that way than if they ran it proper. Ain't that always how it is? The people who've got money get more, and the rest of us . . . Well, that's how it is."

*   *   *

By six-thirty Severin Quill had not appeared, and Matt was growing weary of the bar scene. He had decided to give him another fifteen minutes, then pack it in, when he heard the bartender call, "Is there a Matt Lindstrom here?" Automatically he rose and went to take the receiver the man held out to him.

"Well, Mr. *Lindstrom*, what do you have to say for yourself?" Carly McGuire's voice, low and furious.

"How did you . . . ?"

"Find out your real name? Funny story. Sev Quill went down to the county seat for a press conference at the sheriff's department about a murder case he's covering in Signal Port. He got to talking with the investigating officer, and she told him she gave a lift last night to a Matt Lindstrom, who claimed he'd taken a job as a photographer for this paper. Sev knew something was wrong, so he came to me and told me where I could find you. I know who you are and who you've come here to hurt."

Damn! He hadn't had any choice but to reveal his true name to a law enforcement officer, given his lack of identification as John Crowe.

McGuire went on, "I don't know how you found Ardis or what your plans are, but I'm putting you on notice: You are to stay away from her, our child, this newspaper, and me. If necessary, we'll get a restraining order against you, and if that doesn't work, I own a handgun and I'm not afraid to use it."

Anger of the sort he hadn't felt since Saugatuck flared. "What does Gwen have to say about that?"

"*Ardis* doesn't know you're here yet. I plan to tell her, but she's fragile, and I'll have to handle it carefully. My first order of business is to protect her and our little girl. And that means keeping you away from them."

"This is none of your business. It's between Gwen and me."

"What is it I said that you don't understand? Perhaps you've never heard of a restraining order?"

"I wonder if a judge would look favorably upon a woman who deliberately disappeared and left her husband under suspicion of murdering her. A woman who sat back and allowed his life to be ruined."

"You're not listening to me, Mr. Lindstrom. I will do anything to protect Ardis and our daughter. Is that clear?"

"Is that clear? You bet. Am I going to roll over for you? No way."

McGuire hung up on him.

He slammed down the receiver and went outside. Leaned against the Jeep, shaking with rage. Gwen had a fierce protector in Carly McGuire, but not fierce enough. No one had been there to protect *him* fourteen years ago. No reason it should be any different for Gwen.

The house on Drinkwater Creek looked much as it had the night before—windows lighted, but only Gwen's SUV in the parking area. He entered the property by the same route, clutching his Nikon. Again he sighted on the windows, but this time he saw no sign of Gwen or the child.

Around him the shadows were deepening. Springtime scents drifted on the warmish air—freshly growing things, pungent eucalyptus, and something sweet that he had always associated with his first love. Behind him he heard the rush of the creek, the hum of tires on the pavement. Before him the house's windows glowed, but without motion. As he waited, staring through the telephoto, unease stole over him. The house seemed too quiet. . . .

He slipped out from the trees' shelter and sprinted across the open ground between them and the kitchen window. A half-full glass of red wine sat next to a cutting board; a knife and a heap of green beans lay on the board, some of them trimmed. The table was set with three placemats and napkins, but the cutlery was scattered across it.

His unease was full-bown now. He moved to the living room window. No one there.

After a moment he went around the corner to the front door. It was ajar. He stepped inside, waited until he could make out lines among the shadows. A small table lay on its side, a broken lamp beside it. A rug was bunched against one wall.

A chill took hold of him. He stood very still, listening. No sound except the rush of the creek in the distance. No one moved here. No one breathed.

After a moment he felt beside the door for a light switch, flipped it on. He was in a hallway, rooms opening to either side. Terra-cotta tiled floor, puddled with red. Red on the bunched-up rug. Red smears on the beige wall . . .

Sound of a vehicle on the road. Engine cutting out by the footbridge. Quick steps on the path.

He reached for the light switch, but his arm felt leaden, and his hand fell to his side. He was about to step into the doorway behind him when a voice exclaimed, "Oh, my God!"

He whirled and stared into Carly McGuire's eyes. Their pupils were huge black holes, and the blood was draining from her face. Her gaze jumped from him to the puddles on the floor, to the stains on the rug, to the smear on the wall, and back again.

"You bastard!" she screamed. "What have you done to her?"

Carly McGuire

Friday, May 10, 2002

rdis's former husband stood in a circle of light in her front hallway, staring at her as if he couldn't comprehend the meaning of her words. Her eyes again moved to the bloody smears on the wall, and she felt a growl rising from deep in her throat. She launched herself at him, pushing off on the balls of her feet, intent on doing him serious damage, but at the last second he feinted to the left, caught her from behind, and pinned her arms between them. His rough, strong hand covered her mouth.

He's killed Ard, and now he's going to kill me!

"Be quiet," he whispered. "Whoever did this may still be in the house."

She struggled against him, but he tightened his grip and dragged her into the living room. In the mirror above the mantelpiece she saw his face: pale under its tan, its planes honed sharp by tension. And his eyes . . .

He was afraid, too.

Without taking his hand from her mouth, he said, "I did not do this, Carly. You've got to believe me. I did not do . . . whatever was done here tonight."

Of course you'd deny it, you bastard.

"Think," he added. "You called me at Rod's at—what? Six thirty-five? There wasn't enough time for me to drive here and cause this kind of damage before you arrived."

She calculated. Thirty minutes max. Thirty minutes to drive here and kill a woman. Her woman. And what about Natalie? Where was she?

Slowly Lindstrom took his hand from her mouth, turned her so she faced him. "Look at me," he said. "Do you see any blood? Whoever did this would be covered in blood."

She shook her head, stepped away from him, sank, weak-kneed, on the edge of the sofa. Lindstrom moved toward her, and she snapped, "Get away from me."

He backed off, his expression watchful.

She perched on the cushion's edge, poised to spring should he make another move toward her. "If you didn't cause that"— she motioned at the hall—"what're you doing here?"

"I wanted to talk with Gwen."

"Talk?"

He looked down at his feet. "All right, confront her."

"And?"

"The house seemed unnaturally still when I got here. The door was partway open. So I came inside. A minute or so before you arrived."

"And you think whoever's responsible might still be in the house. So why didn't you stay outside and call nine-one-one? And why are you talking in a normal voice?"

"I just said that to make you stop fighting me. There's no-body here but us. I can feel it. So can you."

Nobody alive, anyway . . .

"Carly," he added, "we ought to search the house."

For a body. Or bodies.

She took several deep breaths and pushed up from the sofa. "You go first, so I can keep an eye on you."

Ard's office, across from the living room: compulsively neat, as always.

Kitchen: no sign of a struggle except for the flatware strewn across the table. Setting the table was Natalie's responsibil-ity. . . .

Don't go there.

Formal dining room, seldom used, but Ard loved the cherry-wood table and silver candlesticks. . . .

All in order.

"Bedrooms?" Lindstrom asked.

"That way." She pointed him toward the hall that led to the house's other wing, motioned for him to precede her.

Guest room: tidy, waiting for visitors who seldom came.

Her at-home office: as chaotic as the one at work.

Back in the hall he asked, "Where does this door lead to?"

"Natalie's room. Our little girl." She steeled herself, pushed it open, stepped inside.

No girlish pink or yellow for Nat. Instead, bright-green walls with stencils of jungle animals, and a dark-blue ceiling with her favorite constellations painted in silver Day-Glo.

"She could be hiding," Lindstrom said.

Carly nodded, crossed to the closet while he checked under the bed. Together they searched the few nooks and crannies but found no trace of Nat.

Finally they moved along to the last door. Beyond it was the master suite with two baths and a fireplace. It had seemed too large when she'd bought the house, a lone and lonely young woman, but now it often seemed too crowded. . . .

"Carly?"

Even though she knew she must, she did not want to go into that room. What if Ard was lying dead there and Lindstrom had lured her on this search with the intention . . . ?

She looked up at him, met his gaze.

No, there was no danger in him. One of her assets as a journalist was the ability to see into people through their eyes. And what she saw within Matt Lindstrom was what she felt within herself: fear of what he might find there.

She said, "Let's go."

The spacious blue-and-white room was much as she'd last seen it that morning: bed linens rumpled, comforter askew, yesterday's cast-off clothing tossed over the armchairs by the fireplace. Ard, a late riser, usually tidied up, but today she hadn't. The *Sacramento Bee,* which she liked to read in front of the fireplace with her morning coffee, sat unopened in plastic wrap on the big table between the chairs, her Mr. Peanut mug—a birthday gift from Nat—resting beside it. She'd apparently relighted last night's fire; the smell of wood smoke was strong. On the padded window seat overlooking the meadow lay Gracie, the little white cat that had wandered in during a rainstorm eleven years ago—a flighty but endearing creature they'd named after the comedienne Gracie Allen.

Surely nothing horrible could have happened in this room.

Carly crossed to Ard's bathroom. All was in order there. The same was true of the room containing the shower and oversize tub that connected Ard's bath with hers. Her bath was in its usual state—one that frequently made the cleaning woman roll her eyes in despair.

Lindstrom was holding Gracie when she returned to the bedroom. He set her down, said apologetically, "She crawled up my leg, yowling."

"It's her only trick."

"So what happened here, McGuire?"

". . . I don't know."

But an unpleasant suspicion was forming in her mind, and much as she tried to push it away, it took hold and grew.

Lindstrom said, "We ought to call the sheriff's department."

"Not just yet."

"Why not? It looks as if they've been attacked and abducted. Every minute you hesitate in calling the sheriff puts them at greater risk. I read someplace that the first two hours are critical to recovering kidnap victims alive."

"There's something I need to check first." Something she'd earlier glimpsed, but not fully registered, in the kitchen. She turned and hurried down there.

In the brushed-chrome sink sat a freezer bag containing a steak. Its top was open, but there was none of the blood that usually drained out of defrosted meat. A mixing bowl, stained red, sat beside it.

A horrible certainty took hold of her as she crossed to the refrigerator, looked into the freezer. A few bags of vegetables and fruit, some fish, but no meat. She went back to the sink and opened the cabinet beside it, where two trash receptacles were mounted on a pullout rack. Empty. With Lindstrom's voice at her back she went outside to the garbage and recycle bins in their enclosure next to the kitchen door. They were full of freezer bags containing spoiling steaks and roasts and ground beef and chicken parts—but no blood.

Ard had planned this in advance, then. Carly pictured her coming downstairs this morning, in such a hurry that she hadn't put the bedroom to rights. She'd removed all the meat from the freezer, left it to defrost, and later, maybe after she'd picked Nat up from the school where Carly had dropped her in the morning, she'd poured the blood into the bowl and created the scene in the hallway. Created the scene in the kitchen, too.

Where had Natalie been while Ard was doing that? In her room or outside, Carly hoped. Still, she must've known something was wrong. . . .

And then Ard hadn't even hidden the evidence of what she'd done. The bowl and bag in the sink, the meat in the garbage—they were a tip-off to one who knew her well.

Or did she want me to know what she'd done? Did she want to hurt me yet another time?

"Carly?" Lindstrom had come up behind her. "Do you want to check around out here before we call the sheriff?"

"There's no need to make a call. The blood is animal, not human." She swept her hand at the garbage bins.

"I don't understand."

"Ard did this. She set up a violent disappearance. She staged the whole thing."

Of course Lindstrom couldn't understand, not without knowing the history of their relationship. He didn't press for an explanation, though, just followed along silently as she checked Natalie's room and the master suite for items Ard might have taken with them. There were telling gaps in the clothing in both closets, and Nat's prescription medication for asthma was gone. The largest travel bag in Ard's matched set was also missing, as were Natalie's duffel and backpack.

Carly picked up the bedside phone and called the town's taxi service: Had Ardis Coleman been picked up on time that afternoon? No, the dispatcher said, she hadn't called them. A similar inquiry of the local car rental agency produced the same result: Ms. Coleman had not reserved a vehicle with them.

Of course not; her partner was clever—and devious. Most

likely she'd rented a vehicle in another town, or even bought one. Long-range planning, then.

As she hung up the receiver, she saw that Lindstrom had grown impatient. He said, "Will you please tell me what's going on here?"

Could she trust him with this? Could she trust him at all? But who else could she turn to?

"We need to talk," she said.

They returned to the living room. As Lindstrom sat on the sofa, she studied him. He didn't look like the man whom Ard had described as "handsome in a pretty-boy way. A typical Minnesota Swede." This man's face was weathered, with lines etched by hard experience; his hands were work-roughened, his body lean and muscular; he'd dyed his blond hair an unbecoming shade of brown. No more pretty boy, but character and presence made him attractive in a rough-hewn way.

"Tell me," she said, "what is it you actually do up there in British Columbia? You're not a newspaper photographer, are you?"

"No, I run a small charter business—one boat, one deckhand. Tourists, mostly wanting excursion cruises. Some fishermen. Now, what do we need to talk about?"

She sat on the opposite end of the sofa, tucking one foot under her. "Ardis. I don't know if she was this way while she was married to you, but as long as I've known her she's exhibited a pattern of behavior that I call cut-and-run. Whenever things get unpleasant or she's overwhelmed by a situation, she just takes off."

"Has she done this often?"

"Often enough. The first time was when we'd been together less than a year."

"And you've been together how long?"

"Nearly fourteen years."

"Since right after she disappeared, then. D'you mind if I ask how you met?"

"She was hitchhiking in a dangerous place outside of Thousand Springs, Nevada. I picked her up."

She remembered Ard, standing bedraggled by the side of a two-lane highway in northeastern Nevada. She was wearing dirty jeans and a tee with a ripped-out shoulder seam and was sitting on a big blue duffel bag. Her face was sunburned and peeling, her long dark hair straggling down from a ponytail.

Normally Carly wouldn't have stopped for any hitchhiker without the sense to wear a hat in the glaring sun, or one too lazy to stand up when a vehicle approached. In fact, she seldom picked up hitchhikers at all. But the way Ard's face had suddenly filled with hope made her put her foot to the brake pedal. . . .

"Did she tell you her true name?" Lindstrom asked. "Or why she left home?"

"Not at first. She just said she was going west and asked if Soledad County was a good place to live. I brought her here, gave her a job as a gofer, found her a cheap place to live. It wasn't till months later, after we became lovers, that she told me her story."

Lindstrom flinched at the word "lovers" but quickly recovered. Was he homophobic? Disgusted at the images that came to mind? Or was he simply wounded, even at fourteen years' remove, that his wife could so easily make a new life for herself?

"Why did she up and disappear from Saugatuck?" he asked.

"Her business," she said. Then, more gently, "It had nothing to do with you—at least, not directly. She loved you."

"I wish I could believe that." He was silent for a moment. "Okay, the first time she took off . . . ?"

"I'd promoted her to general assignment reporter. She'd covered the trial of a woman who had killed her abusive boyfriend, and I criticized her stories for lack of objectivity. She insisted that we owed it to our readers to take a firm stance against abuse of any sort, and I said that was what the editorial page was for, and if anybody took a stance it would be me. We fought, and the next morning she was gone. Two weeks later she showed up, contrite, saying she'd gone away to get her head together."

"And you took her back."

"Yes. She disappeared a few other times for varying periods over the next couple of years. Then, in the fall of ninety-one, she left and stayed away for fifteen months."

"What precipitated that?"

I'm not going there—not with you.

"That's private. Anyway, she returned with Natalie, who was under a year old. Seems Ard had gone to San Francisco, taken up with a black musician who played at a jazz club where she was waitressing. Nat is the result of their union." A familiar bitterness welled up, clogging her throat.

"But you still took her back."

"You criticizing me, Lindstrom?"

He shook his head. "I'd've probably done the same. There's a quality to Gwen—Ardis—that makes you want to help her no matter what she's done."

Yes, she knew that quality well—had for years tried to analyze it. Often she'd thought that if she could pin it down, she would become immune to it, gain control over her situation, but its exact essence remained elusive.

"Well, then you know," she said. "I not only took her back but welcomed her. I'd never wanted children and was concerned about what kind of mother Ard would make, but I thought Natalie might settle her down, bring stability to our relationship. And by and large she's done that. Ard's a good mother, and I've found I enjoy having a kid around."

Lindstrom eyed her keenly. "But?"

"Did I say 'but'?"

"You didn't have to."

"All right!" Her irritation gave way to relief. It felt good to unburden herself, even though the recipient of her confidences couldn't have been more unlikely. "I love Natalie, but sometimes she's a reminder of how much Ard has hurt me."

"I understand. This running off—has it stopped since she had Natalie?"

"No. But it's not as frequent, and of shorter duration—usually only a day or two."

"It's enough of a pattern, though, that you think this"—he nodded toward the hallway—"might be more of the same."

"I'm sure it is. Ard's been under a lot of pressure lately. I think I told you the book she's writing is due at the publisher soon, but it's not going well." She hesitated. "And we haven't been getting along."

"Why not?"

"My business, Lindstrom."

He held up his hands, palms toward her. "Sorry, I didn't mean to pry. Has she ever done anything like this in the past? Staged a violent scene?"

"No, and she's never taken Natalie along, either. Frankly, I'm worried about her mental health. She claims somebody's been watching her, that somebody's been in the house while we were gone."

"You don't believe it?"

"No. There's no evidence of forced entry, and I haven't noticed any prowlers. Besides, she's always been a little paranoid."

"When did she first mention this?"

"Yesterday."

"Well, that explains it. I was out here then, and today, taking pictures with a telephoto lens. Maybe she sensed my presence. But I never got any closer than that grove of trees to the south. Tonight's the first time I've been in the house."

She studied him thoughtfully. He was either an honest man or an adept con artist.

He added, "If you're worried about her mental health, you really ought to call the sheriff's department."

"No." she shook her head. "I can't do that to Ard. The department didn't like her coverage of the 'faggot murders,' as they privately called them. God knows how they'd handle this, what they'd say to the media. And I'll admit to more than a little self-interest—my newspaper is the one voice of reason in this county, and I don't want it discredited because its editor couldn't control her personal life."

He nodded in understanding. "That detective who gave me a lift last night—Rhoda Swift—she seems nice, a sympathetic person. Nonjudgmental, too. Maybe you could ask for her."

"No, I couldn't. Rho only works cases in the coastal area."

"But as a favor?"

"Rho's all the things you say she is, but she's also a by-the-book cop. She'd have to bring the local deputies in on it. I know how she operates because I did a special interview with her a couple of years back about an old murder case that she cracked. Besides, she's romantically involved with a best-selling journalist; if he got wind of this, Ard and I might end up as the subjects of his next book."

"Which neither of you needs." Lindstrom frowned. "Me, either."

For the first time she considered how the situation might affect him. "Let me ask you this," she said. "What did you plan to do about Ard? Obviously you came here with an agenda."

He looked away from her. "I guess you could say so."

"And that was . . . ?"

"To take pictures."

"Pictures of her?"

"Right. I wanted to make an identification. Document her new life. Then I was going to take the photographs to the Sweetwater County, Wyoming, Sheriff's Department—where there's still an open file on her disappearance naming me as the prime suspect—and vindicate myself. Vindicate myself in the eyes of my family and former friends. Vindicate myself in the national media as well."

He paused, gaze turned inward. "And," he added, "I wanted a confrontation with her. Wanted to wring out of her the reason she disappeared and left me to face a possible murder charge. Wanted to make sure she knew what a despicable human being I think she is."

Despicable? Carly turned the word over in her mind. From his point of view, she supposed it was appropriate. But from hers, *damaged* was the better choice.

"If it's any consolation," she said, "she abandoned her car and purse hoping you'd think she'd been killed and not look for her. She had no idea you'd be suspected—or that you had been, until long after you'd left Saugatuck. When she found out, she tried to call you, but you'd vanished as completely as she had."

"She could've set the record straight with the authorities."

"Maybe, but by then the case had received major publicity. She was afraid of more."

"Why?"

". . . She had her reasons."

"And again, they're none of my business."

Carly was silent, thinking bitterly of those reasons. Had she cut Ard entirely too much slack all these years? Probably. But wasn't that what you did when you loved someone?

Lindstrom said, "Well, never mind. That's long past, and

what's happened today changes the situation. I've got my photographs, and if I can get a statement from you—"

"You're not thinking of leaving?"

"Of course I am. There's nothing to hold me here."

"Oh, yeah? You can't just walk away from this mess. After
all, you admitted she probably took off because of your sneaking around here."

"So what am I supposed to do about that?"

"Help me find her. You and I are in this thing together,
Lindstrom, and together we are going to see it through."

Once Lindstrom's astonishment at her pronouncement had
faded, he smiled mockingly. "Ready to take her back again, are
you?"

She glared at him.

"My advice is to embrace her philosophy: Cut your losses
and run."

"You forget, there's another factor in the equation: Natalie.
She's a delicate child, has asthma. If Ard's become unbalanced,
she may neglect Nat's health. I need to find them, bring them
home, or at least to someplace safe. Afterwards I'll decide about
the relationship."

"And you think I can help you find her?"

"Maybe. You could have some knowledge about her that I
don't. Something that will suggest what she might've done."

*But do I really believe that, or do I just want him here so I won't
feel alone?*

He smiled, gently this time, as if he intuited her thoughts.
"Okay, I'll stay and try to help you—for a while. Where do we
start?"

"Well, the major problem in Ard's life recently—except for
you showing up—is the trouble she's having with the book. I
think we should both go over the manuscript and her notes."

He looked at his watch. "How long will that take?"

"Hours, probably."

"Then I'd better make a phone call."

Carly showed him to the cordless unit in the kitchen, listened as she ground beans and brewed a pot of coffee.

"Hi it's— Yeah, I should've called. Don't be upset. Something— No, not some*one*. I spent last night in Santa Carla— What d'you mean, the duct tape's not holding? It's a miracle fix. . . . Well, just slap some more on, then. I'll buy the joint I need on the way home tomorrow. . . . No, I'm working on a major assignment and likely to be out all night. . . . Assignment, not *ass*ignment! I'll see you in the morning, and don't forget about that tape."

As he replaced the receiver, Carly folded her arms and regarded him with mock severity. "You don't waste any time when you hit a new town, Lindstrom."

"That was my landlady. I fix things in exchange for cheap rent."

"Uh-huh."

"Well, it *was*."

"And just what did you put the duct tape on?"

"The pipe under the bathroom sink. It leaks, and I didn't have the right— What's so funny?"

"You. And believe me, Lindstrom, right about now I could use a laugh, however feeble." She paused. "By the way, I think I should continue to call you John Crowe in public. People here know you as that. A change could complicate things."

"Sev Quill knows I'm Matt Lindstrom."

"I asked him not to tell anyone, and he won't. Where'd you come up with your alias, anyhow?"

"Johnny Crowe's the deckhand I mentioned. I figured if anybody here wanted to check on whether such a person used to live in Port Regis, he's in the directory. And he said he'd cover, claim to be subletting his place from me."

"This Millie Bertram, your alleged publisher—who's she?"

"Owner of the Port Regis Hotel."

"She was well coached."

He was as clever and devious in his own way as Ard was in hers. And Carly herself had her moments. Perhaps together she and Lindstrom could outwit her missing partner.

"Okay, Matt," she said, "grab a cup of coffee and let's get started on Ard's papers."

Saturday, May 11, 2002

he stood naked on the threshold of the gold-and-cream ballroom, and one by one the beautiful, formally attired people turned to stare. Silence fell, punctuated only by the tinkling of the crystal chandeliers. She turned to flee, but the doors had become a solid wall, barring exit. As she searched frantically for a way out, a woman behind her said, "She is not one of us," and a man agreed, "Definitely not one of us." Then the others began chanting, "Not one of us, not one of us—"

Carly jerked up from where she was slumped on the wide armrest of the chair. Her shoulder throbbed, and her neck was stiff. She blinked, looked around, saw sunlight streaming through the windows of Ard's office. Looked down and saw she was swaddled in one of the afghans from the living room. Her reading glasses hung over one ear.

The dream . . .

She hadn't had it in more than two decades, since she willfully banished it during her senior year in college. But now it was back in vivid detail, reminding her of her humiliation. . . .

Don't go there. Not today. You have to stay focused.

Focused on what?

Oh . . .

The events of the previous night returned to her in a painful rush of memory. She groaned, put her hands to her face, winced at the tenderness in her neck. After a moment she looked around, saw a note propped on the keyboard of Ard's computer, extricated herself from the afghan, and went to read it.

Carly:

I've finished the manuscript and gone to fix my landlady's leaky pipe. (I really do fix stuff in exchange for cheap rent!) Didn't want to wake you. I'll call or come by as soon as I can.

"Johnny"

She crumpled the note and tossed it in the wastebasket, anchored her glasses atop her head, and went to the kitchen for coffee. The maker was still on, and the dregs of the carafe she'd brewed last night had distilled to sludge. She ran water into it and, while it soaked, got out the cleaning supplies that she'd need to remove the evidence of Ard's latest betrayal.

An hour later—after purging the hallway, taking a quick shower, and dressing—she was back in Ard's office looking for the manuscript Crowe had been reading while she'd examined the legal pads and index cards full of notes. It was neatly stacked in a tray on the workstation. When she picked it up, its slenderness surprised her, and she flipped to the last page, numbered 130. Less than half the amount of pages Ard had led her to believe she'd written, and even at twice that number she'd've had trouble meeting her July first deadline.

At what page had Ard told her she'd rather she didn't read any more until the book was done? One hundred, and that had been over six months ago. Yet nearly every night she proofed her day's work after dinner. Where had those pages gone?

Carly moved to the file cabinet and scanned the disks in their holder: financial records, copies of stories going back to when she worked for the paper, correspondence, idea files—but nothing beyond page 130 on the manuscript, working title *Cyanide Wells*. Strange. Ard was paranoid about losing her work in case of a crash; she put it on disk every day.

My God, has she been sitting here for six months, staring at a blank screen? Proofing the same pages night after night? Are those one hundred thirty pages all she has to show for two years' efforts? Granted, she had to do a lot of research, but . . .

Ard must've been hopelessly blocked and afraid to admit it. But why? Because she was afraid of botching her first book—one that she considered a memorial to their murdered friends? Because it meant so much to her? What was it she'd said a few weeks ago?

"Reality's starting to interfere with the writing. I have nightmares about that morning."

And Carly had replied, somewhat unsympathetically, "You're bound to come face-to-face with reality. The book's a fact-based account."

Ard had given her a look whose meaning she couldn't decipher and had gone back to proofing what she claimed was the current batch of pages.

Now Carly returned to the armchair and located the stack of legal pads containing Ard's handwritten notes. Some had slipped to the floor; another was mashed down the side between the cushion and the arm. She smoothed out its rumpled pages and—

"Carly?"

She started, looked around. Lindstrom, back from the plumbing wars.

"Sorry for just walking in on you," he said. "I left the door unlocked in case you were still asleep when I got back. Hope that was okay."

"That's fine. We always left our doors unlocked before Ronnie Talbot and Deke Rutherford were killed. Our friends felt free to just walk in."

"But that changed."

"Yeah, it did. Everything changed."

"In what way?"

"You really want to know?"

"I do."

"Why? Ard's your ex-wife; I'd assume it would be painful to hear about her new life, particularly because . . ."

"Because she made that new life with a woman?"

She nodded.

He went over to the computer, examined the screen saver. "Roses," he said, "she's always loved them."

Biding his time, because whatever he wants to say has to be said just right, or we'll lose the connection that's growing between us. And he wants that connection because he's still unsatisfied with what he's found out about Ard's disappearance.

He turned the desk chair around, sat facing her. "You know, I was thinking about her new life the whole time I worked on the plumbing. And I concluded that Ardis Coleman is no longer Gwen Lindstrom. She's someone else entirely, the evolution of a woman I once loved but probably didn't know. In a sense we reinvent the people we love to our own specifications, and that's what I did with Gwen."

"Then why're you here now? Having realized that, you could've walked away."

"To tell you the truth, I'm not sure. Maybe it's because I like you. Or I feel for your little girl. And even though I didn't know Gwen, I loved her very much. I suppose I care about the woman she became."

"Or maybe you still want that confrontation. To tell her what a despicable woman she is."

He shook his head. "Doesn't seem important now. The woman you describe is troubled, needs help. It occurred to me while reading her manuscript that what she did yesterday may be less related to me than to a disturbance brought on by having to relive your friends' murders. Maybe if you tell me more about the circumstances surrounding them, we can figure out what's happening with her."

A good man. A kind, thoughtful man. Possibly better than his Gwen, my Ardis, deserved.

"Thank you," she said. "Where would you like me to begin?"

"Wherever you care to."

"Well, Ronnie and Deke were closer to Ard than me, although we were friends, too. Deke was a painter, very innovative and talented. Ard met him when she interviewed him about a big show he was having at a San Francisco gallery. Ronnie inherited the mill before he met Deke, and put its management into Gar Payne's hands, claiming he didn't have a good head for business, but I think that was just an excuse to get out, because a few years later he took over as Deke's manager and did a great job. He dealt with the galleries, arranged for the shipping of the canvases, handled their finances and investments."

"Gar Payne—that's the mayor?"

"Right. The mayor's job is only part-time. Of course, when

Ronnie sold the mill, Gar had to go back to trying to peddle the unsold lots in the Meadows. As you witnessed on Thursday, he's been cranky ever since."

"Is he just a salesman there or the developer?"

"The developer, along with a partner, Milt Rawson. Only about half the lots have been sold in the ten years since they bought and subdivided the land, and there've been problems with the homeowners' association over how the place should be run." Lindstrom gave her a questioning look, and she added, "Don't ask. The Meadows is a hotbed of petty intrigue. Too many affluent people with too much time on their hands. But why're you so interested in Payne?"

"When the two of you were arguing at the paper, I recognized his voice. He's the man who made an anonymous phone call to me and told me where to find Gwen."

"Gar? Why would he do that? And how did he know about you in the first place?"

"That's what I've wondered. Is it common knowledge that Ardis was married before she came here?"

"Only her close friends are aware of that, and most of them don't know your name."

"And Payne's not one of those friends?"

"Hardly."

"Then how . . . ? Well, no use speculating on it now. You were telling me about Ronnie and Deke."

"Right. Ard hit it off with both of them, and pretty soon they were in and out of here all the time, as we were at their house near the Knob."

"I thought the Knob was in the Eel River National Forest."

"It is. Ronnie and Deke's house backs up on the forest—very secluded, on nearly a hundred acres that Ronnie inherited from his father."

"Ardis's newspaper accounts made the two of them sound like special people."

"They were." She pictured Ronnie delicately removing a painful foxtail from the nose of Gracie the cat. Deke, doing his campy Toulouse-Lautrec impersonation. Ronnie, picking up and comforting Natalie after she took a tumble from the pony he kept for the enjoyment of friends' children. Deke, producing with a flourish his "world infamous" chorizo enchiladas. Ronnie, in a ridiculous pink bunny suit at their annual Easter egg hunt. Deke, clumping the seven miles from his house to theirs on snowshoes to bring them a sackful of candles and emergency rations during an unusually severe winter storm.

She said, "They were caring. Loyal. They'd go out of their way to help a friend—or a stranger. In all the time I knew them, I never heard them exchange a harsh word." She paused. "Of course, we all know appearances can be deceiving. Ard and I have never exchanged a harsh word in public, but at home they fly."

Lindstrom seemed to prefer to let the comment slip by. He said, "Okay, the murders. I've read both the newspaper accounts and the account in Ardis's manuscript. They're quite different."

"Well, the facts are the same, but the newspaper accounts are controlled; she let her professionalism take over. But she deliberately made the book's version emotional. Too much so, in my opinion. I suspect she was working something out through the writing."

The morning she discovered their friends' bodies, Ard had called her, gasping for breath, her words practically unintelligible. Carly wouldn't have been able to figure out where she was, except she'd mentioned at breakfast that she planned to stop by to deliver a load of the zucchini she'd overplanted. "Even if Deke and Ronnie aren't crazy about the stuff, I'd rather share the bounty with friends than be forced to sneak around leaving it in strangers' parked cars and mailboxes," she'd joked.

When Carly arrived at the spacious redwood-and-glass home in the shadow of the Knob, she found Ard lying on the front lawn beside a pool of vomit. Ard was more coherent than before, but her words were punctuated by sobs and dry heaves. "The house was . . . too quiet. It felt . . . weird. I called out to them, then . . . went looking. They're in the bedroom, both shot in the head, and the blood . . ."

Carly went inside, verified what Ard had told her, and—when her hands stopped trembling enough to dial—called the sheriff's department.

By the time the first deputies arrived, however, Ard was on her feet and had pulled herself together. When they emerged from the house, grim-faced and shaken, she had her notebook and tape recorder in hand and set about covering the biggest story in the history of the *Soledad Spectrum.* Carly watched in awe; she'd always been aware of a core of strength in her partner, but Ard's erratic behavior and emotionalism usually eclipsed it. That day Ard proved the often-cited principle that extreme circumstances often force a person to call upon the better side of his or her nature.

"Carly?" Lindstrom said.

"Oh. Just remembering. Anyway, after that day everything changed. The gay and lesbian communities here had always kept a low profile, but suddenly we felt targeted. Those of us who never locked our doors installed deadbolts and alarms. We were even more circumspect than usual in public places. Our hetero friends felt the need to shield us. I even found I was self-censoring my editorials about the crime. The only bright light was Ard, who'd been the most traumatized by the killings. She wanted our readers to understand Ronnie and Deke's situation, the situation of every gay person in this county. And she illuminated it beautifully in her stories, by making the reader see the two of them as human beings rather than just gay victims."

"My landlady says she's 'no fan of faggots,' but that the series gave her some understanding of their problems."

"Well, that's progress of a small sort, isn't it?"

"I guess. How did the paper winning the Pulitzer affect things?"

"Well, the prize brought a lot of attention to the county and made some people proud. But it pissed off the small-minded folk who thought it branded the place as a hotbed of homosexuality. And the gay community still locks its deadbolts and sets its alarms."

"Is it common knowledge you and Ardis are partners?"

"You can't hide something like that in a place like this."

"People sure hid it from me. The staff members at the paper brushed off my inquiries about her, and Sev Quill cited your dictum that employees' professional and personal lives are to be kept separate."

She smiled. "Well, sure. That's because of the memo from me that they all found on their desks the morning you started work. From the first I felt something wasn't quite right with you, so I warned them to be on their guard. Even after I spoke with your Millie Bertram I had my reservations."

"And here I thought I was such a good actor."

"Well, you aren't all that bad. And you're good-looking, even if you do seem to be having a permanent bad-hair day."

Carly customarily worked in her office at the paper on Saturday afternoons, and she decided, in the interest of keeping Ard's flight a secret, that today should be no different. She and Lindstrom could continue their conversation there behind a closed door, so she told him to follow her into town.

When she was passing the Mercantile, however, her plan abruptly derailed. A crowd clustered around the old well in the park across the street, and two men were leaning over its high stone wall. Her newswoman's instincts kicked in, and she pulled her truck to the curb. Lindstrom pulled in behind her. Without waiting for him, she hurried across the street and into the park, asked a man on the fringes of the group what was going on.

"Looks like some kid's fallen into the well and drowned."

Natalie!

The response was irrational because by now Natalie was probably far away from here, and there wasn't enough water in the well to drown a mouse. Still, adrenaline coursed through her as she pushed forward. One of the men at the well straightened and turned. Timothy Mortimer, an old drunk who frequented the park's benches. She recognized the other man by the green-and-blue wool stocking cap whose tassled tip hung over his face as he stared downward: a shabbily dressed newcomer who had moved into the town eyesore, the Golden State Hotel, a few weeks ago. He'd taken to hanging out with Timothy, who also lived there.

Now Timothy's red, bleary eyes focused on her. "You all right, Ms. McGuire?"

"What's happened here?"

"Looks like there's a dead kid in the well. Me and Cappy're tryin' to—"

"Let me look," Lindstrom said. He shouldered Timothy aside and leaned over the wall. The man called Cappy straightened and glared at him.

"That's not a child down there," Lindstrom said, his voice echoing. "It's a backpack. Green, I think."

Like Nat's backpack. Why . . . ?

Lindstrom turned, and his eyes met hers. She nodded

slightly. He frowned, unsure of her meaning, but said, "If somebody's got a heavy rope, I can get the pack out."

"There's one in my van." Will Begley, owner of the Mercantile, said.

Matt peered up at the peaked roof that sheltered the well. There was, Carly knew, an iron bar anchored between its supports, which was once used to lower and raise a bucket. He reached up, tested it, then came over to her.

In a low voice he asked, "What is it?"

"Natalie's backpack is green with purple trim."

"I see. Well, if this one is hers, you've got to tell the sheriff's deputies."

"But then I'll have to tell them what Ard did. And that I destroyed the evidence of it. I don't know why she would've put the pack in the well, but I sense it's part of a plan."

He considered, eyes moving from side to side. "Okay, I'll deal with it."

Will Begley returned with the rope, helped Lindstrom secure it to the bar, held it fast as he climbed down the thirty-some feet to the well's bottom. He was there some time before he climbed back up and heaved the pack over the wall. Carly knelt to examine it.

Definitely Natalie's. It had purple trim, and she recognized a tear in one of the outside pockets. Her hands trembled as she opened it and looked inside.

Pencils. Colored Magic Markers. Drawing pad. Packet of decorative stickers. Gym socks. Apple. Kit-Kat bar. Half an egg-salad sandwich.

Carly had placed the sandwich Ard made on Thursday night, plus the apple and a small bag of potato chips, in the pack on Friday morning. She couldn't positively identify the other items as Nat's, but the little girl liked to draw and had a great fondness for Kit-Kat bars, which could be purchased in the school cafeteria. The backpack had also typically contained textbooks, various spare items of clothing, and a Palm Pilot that Ard had insisted on buying for Nat the previous Christmas, all of which would show—by bookplate, name label, or user—who their owner was.

Carly looked up at Lindstrom. He winked, indicating that he'd been responsible for the disappearance of those things.

And then, just as she was feeling relief, a male voice behind her said, "I'll take that, Carly."

Deputy Shawn Stengel was, in Carly's opinion, the biggest asshole in the sheriff's department. Someone must have phoned the substation at Talbot's Mills, and he'd rushed over here, intent on being first on the scene of what he thought could turn into a major case. Unfortunately, while Stengel was short on interpersonal skills, he wasn't stupid; and he had three young children, so he knew how much stuff kids carried in their heavy backpacks. How long before he realized this one was suspiciously light and checked the well, where Lindstrom must've dumped the items that would identify it as Natalie's?

She glanced at Matt, but he seemed unconcerned.

Stengel ran his hand over his neatly cropped blond hair. "I hope nobody moved the kid's body."

Carly said, "There's no one in the well."

"The call that came in said there was a dead kid down there."

"The men who spotted the backpack only thought it was a child."

"Where are they?"

She looked around. With the arrival of the law, Timothy and Cappy had vanished. She told Stengel who they were, and that they lived at the Golden State.

The deputy grimaced. "Somebody oughta torch that place, get rid of it and the vermin that stay there."

"Shawn, are you advocating that one of our citizens commit arson?"

His jaw knotted. "You know damn well I'm not! And if you dare print anything of the kind, I'll haul your ass in for obstructing an investigation."

The threat was too absurd to warrant a response.

Stengel scowled down at the backpack. "Doesn't surprise me that those two thought that was a kid. They're both probably boiled." He hefted the pack, shook his head. "Not much stuff in here, is there? My kids're always toting at least half a ton of crap. I worry it'll ruin their spines."

She said, "Maybe somebody got a new pack, thought it would be fun to toss the old one down the well."

Stengel squatted, went through the contents. "That doesn't seem right. I can see them getting rid of a dried-up sandwich and socks with holes in them, but Kit-Kat bars and this other stuff? I don't think so."

"So what *do* you think?"

He straightened, looked self-importantly at the bystanders. "At the moment I'm not at liberty to say. Especially to a member of the press."

Carly closed her office door and leaned against it, expelling a long sigh. Matt went over to her desk and began unloading objects from the pockets of his jeans, shirt, and jacket.

He said, "The books are wedged under a pile of debris at the bottom of the well, and I ripped out the bookplates. Everything else that could identify Natalie as the pack's owner is here."

"Thank you, Matt." She examined what lay there. Gym shorts and blouse, with labels. Bead necklace spelling out "Natalie." Graded papers, art club membership card, soccer team uniform shirt with her name and number embroidered across the back. No Palm Pilot.

Ard let her keep her favorite thing.

Lindstrom leaned against the desk, arms folded, frowning. "I tell you, McGuire, I don't feel comfortable hiding things from the authorities—even though Stengel's an idiot."

"He's not an idiot; he's an asshole. There's a difference."

"He didn't seem too bright to me."

"You'd be surprised. Even though he was the deputy who coined the term 'the faggot murders,' he worked damned hard on the case. In fact, he brought in the lead on Mack Travis."

"I've heard that some people don't think Travis killed your friends."

She sat down on her desk chair. "Isn't that always the way when there's no trial or resolution? But to be fair, Ard didn't think so, either. When she started working on her book, she told me she hoped her research would shed light on what really happened."

"And you—what do you think?"

"I think Ard and the others who believe in the killer-who-got-away theory have been taking the Mystery Channel much too seriously."

"Well, to get back to what I was saying, I don't like with-holding information from the cops."

"Even after what the cops did to you when Ard—Gwen—disappeared?"

"Even after that. Lying to a Wyoming deputy was what got me into trouble in the first place."

"No, Gwen's actions were what got you into trouble."

"I don't care to debate the point. And since when have you taken to calling her Gwen?"

"Since when have you taken to calling her Ardis?"

". . . I guess we're each trying to reconcile who she was with us with who she was with the other. Calling her by the name she used at the time we're talking about helps. But frankly, it's not an easy job, and it's giving me a headache."

His words made her aware of a dull throb above her eyebrows. "Me, too. Let's get out of here."

"And go where?"

"Someplace that will cure our headaches and allow us to speak in total privacy."

"This is beautiful," Matt said in slightly winded voice.

"Isn't it?" Carly sat down on the outcropping on the western side of the Knob, feet dangling over the precipitous drop. "More than a hundred and eighty degrees visibility from here. The first time I climbed up, I thought I could see all of California."

"How'd you ever find the trail?"

"Ronnie Talbot showed it to Ard and me. Not too many people know about it. Ronnie did a lot of hiking and exploring here in the forest."

"You must do a lot, too. You're less winded than I am, and I lead a very active life. Don't tell me Ardis hiked with you."

"Only the one time." She realized she sounded curt, as she tended to when anyone strayed too close, however innocently, to the aspects of her life she chose to keep private. Such as the discord at home that drove her to solitary hiking.

In a gentler voice she added, "Ard's thing is gardening. It doesn't seem like much exercise, but when you're hauling around huge bags of fertilizer and peat moss . . . Anyway, she keeps in shape that way, and I hike. Newspapering's a pretty sedentary occupation."

"Gardening. She always loved it." He came over and sat beside her. "Point out some landmarks to me. Except for being able to see the Pacific out there, I'm disoriented."

Glad he'd settled on a neutral topic, she swept her hand to the south. "The coastal ridge, the valley between it, and these foothills run down through Mendocino County. We're not talking very high elevations on the ridge—maybe eleven hundred to fifteen hundred feet. But look around to the east, and you'll see peaks in the national forest of up to seven thousand feet. And to the northwest"—she moved her hand again—"that's the King Range, below Eureka and Humboldt Bay. People who don't know the state always think of California as Los Angeles or San Francisco or urban sprawl. They have no idea of the vast wilderness and agricultural and ranch lands. There's endless territory to explore."

"You love it here, don't you?"

"Absolutely."

"Are you a native?"

"No. I grew up in a suburb of Cleveland, Ohio—Ellenberg. Studied journalism at Columbia, worked for a time as a reporter on the *Denver Post,* then on the *Los Angeles Times.* At the point when L.A. started to wear on me, my aunt died and left me a lot of money; I'd heard about this small-town weekly that was up for sale, and thought, Why not? So here I am."

"Quite a history. Never had any desire to return to Ellenburg, Ohio?"

"About as much as you have to return to Saugatuck, Minnesota. You and I, Lindstrom, are brother and sister under the skin."

"Meaning?"

"You left Saugatuck because everybody thought you were a murderer. I left Ellenburg because everybody knew I was a lesbian."

The corner of Matt's mouth twitched, and for a moment he didn't speak. Then he asked, "You want to tell me about it?"

"No. Not now."

"Why?"

Because for all our common suffering, I don't know you that well. May never know you that well.

"This isn't the right time. I brought you here so we could both clear our heads and have the privacy to talk about some things I found in Ard's notes."

She pulled from her daypack the legal pad on which she'd highlighted certain entries. "When Natalie was small, she had an odd conversational style. We'd be driving along in the car, for instance, and she'd be talking about something that had happened to her in school. Then all of a sudden she'd interrupt herself and exclaim, 'Oh, look—horses!' And next thing, without breaking stride, she'd go right back to whatever she'd been saying before. Some of Ard's notes remind me of that."

"Read them to me."

She flipped to the first of the pages she'd marked. " 'Ronnie Talbot had made the decision to sell the mill a year before the deal was Meryl Travis finalized. . . .' "

"Huh?"

"Exactly my reaction. The name Meryl Travis is circled."

"Who is that?"

"The mother of Mack Travis, the man who confessed to the killings and hanged himself in his jail cell."

"Odd. What else?"

" 'Members of both the gay and straight communities came to the support of the friends of the victims as Ronnie Talbot and Deke Rutherford were laid to rest, but then the Andy D'Angelo process of fragmentation began.' "

"D'Angelo? That's my landlady's last name. Her father . . ."

"Killed himself recently. That's Andy. How'd you meet the daughter?"

"In a bar in Talbot's Mills. But it wasn't the way you think. She's a nice woman."

"Did I say anything, Lindstrom?"

"No."

"I flat-out hate people telling me what I do or don't think."

"Sorry."

"I mean, how can anybody assume—"

"Sorry."

"Oh, hell, I'm—"

"Sorry."

"We sound like a bad comedy routine."

"Maybe we should work on it, take it on the road. So is Andy D'Angelo's name circled?"

"Yes. And there's another reference of the same kind. 'Guns are common in this county, but the sheriff's department ballistics expert maintains the markings on the fatal bullets are distinctive and Rawson or Payne the missing weapon has never been found.'"

"Rawson or Payne—the developers of the Meadows."

"Right."

Lindstrom's blue eyes grew intense; they locked on hers and held. "Is she naming them as the killers?"

"I don't know."

"Are these references some kind of code?"

"I doubt it. Ard's mind doesn't work that way. She runs out of patience with crossword puzzles or rebuses. She hates mystery novels because she can never figure out their solutions. Natalie loves to do jigsaws, spreads them out on the dining room table, but Ard doesn't have the vision to fit the pieces together."

"Then what *do* these things represent?"

"Possibly reminders to herself to check something out."

"She'd break in the middle of a sentence to note them?"

"Given how distracted she's been lately, it wouldn't surprise me. Here's something else I found on the last page of this pad." Carly flipped to her marker. "It's a list: Wells Mining. They owned the Knob mine in its heyday—the eighteen-sixties. Denver Precious Metals. That's the firm that bought it around the turn of the twentieth century and used a cyanide-based process to extract the remaining gold from the waste dumps and low-grade ore. They donated the land to the national parks system in the nineteen fifties. Neither company had anything to do with Ronnie or Deke. The next item is CR ninety-two. I have no idea what that is. And then there's Moratorium ten-slash-zero-zero. Again, I haven't a clue."

"Anything else?"

"Just a name—Noah Estes. And a date—nineteen seventy-four. Estes is a fairly common name in this county; the manager of the mine under Denver Precious Metals was John Estes, and he and his wife had a number of descendants. I don't recall a Noah, however."

Lindstrom nodded but remained silent. A breeze started up out of the northwest, blowing about the branches of the newly leafed aspen trees in a declivity below. Carly studied the play of light and shadow on them. She loved this time of year, when spring crept up into the foothills; its arrival always invigorated her, gave hope. But this year she felt sluggish and despondent—had felt that way even before Ard pulled her latest disappearing act.

Matt said, "Andy D'Angelo—did he have any connection to you, Ardis, or your friends?"

"I wasn't aware the man existed till he committed suicide."

"As owner of the mill, could Ronnie Talbot have known him?"

"I doubt it. He never took an active role in its management."

"Well, why don't I talk with Sam D'Angelo? See if she knows of a connection."

"Good idea. In the meantime, I'll check on the items on Ard's list."

He stood. "You coming?"

"Not yet." They'd driven there separately. "I want to stay for a while."

"I'll call you later, then, after my talk with Sam."

After Matt's footfalls faded on the other side of the Knob, she moved to a more sheltered spot and propped her back against the smooth rock wall. Tried to empty herself of thoughts and emotions—a bastardized Zen technique that she'd developed after attending a couple of weekend retreats. It worked about forty percent of the time, but not today. Finally she abandoned it and fell back on the mantra often quoted by her brother, Alan, during their troubled teenage years: "Everything ends. Everything ends."

The mantra had helped both of them survive their parents' deteriorating marriage and their increasingly disturbed mother's unreasonable restrictions and unfounded accusations. ("I saw you with that Watkins kid. You've been smoking, haven't you?" "I caught you smiling at that boy on the street. You've been messing around, haven't you? You tramp!") It got them through long periods of punishment for the most minor of transgressions. ("You didn't make your bed right. No TV for thirty days." "You fed the cat five minutes late. No desserts this month.") And it helped them endure the long, chilly silences that were somehow more disturbing than the spates of verbal abuse.

Today the mantra didn't work at all. Instead it reminded her that, for Alan, everything had indeed ended: twenty years ago on an icy country road in upstate New York, when he'd been trying to outrun a storm to get home to his wife and baby son. A year later his wife had died of breast cancer, and the son had been spirited away by his maternal grandparents, who didn't want him exposed to the "evil influences" of the family their daughter had married into.

The foremost of the evil influences they cited being his lesbian aunt.

My brother, my best friend, the only family member besides Aunt Nan who accepted me for who I am—lost to me forever. My sister-in-law, also my friend, who understood the pain I'd been through—also lost. My nephew—I didn't know him, will never know him.

And now what if Ard and Nat are lost, too?

Old grief welled up, choking her; fresh grief made her eyes sting. She stood, hefted her pack, began climbing down the steep trail. She'd go home, get on the computer, tackle the problem.

But then, when she was in her truck, another old grief made her turn in the opposite direction.

The redwood-and-glass house stood in the shadow of pines and live oaks; the rose garden that Ard had helped Deke plant showed robust new foliage. Carly got out of her truck and breathed in the mentholated scent of the eucalyptus that lined the long driveway. Everything here was well tended, courtesy of the Talbot estate, of which Ardis was executor; in the years since the residents had been murdered, no one, not even the most pragmatic of potential buyers, had made an offer on the property.

She still had a spare key to the house on her ring; she and Ard and Ronnie and Deke had traded plant-watering and pet-caring duties during the times they traveled. She fingered the key, studying the windows whose closed blinds had blocked out the stares of the curious in the days after the killings. She hadn't been back here since Ard's frantic summons, and she found she couldn't get past the memories of her partner lying on the lawn next to a pool of vomit, her friends lying dead in their bloodstained bedroom, the impersonal bustle of the officials' activity. She would have given anything to envision Ronnie coming through the front door to envelop her in a welcoming hug, Deke following close behind to offer a glass of excellent cabernet. But while she knew such moments had occurred many times, it was as if they had happened in a film she'd seen and half forgotten. Here, in this peaceful place, she could only feel pain and the remnants of horror.

Still, she felt drawn to the house.

Don't do it, McGuire. It's not healthy.

She went up the walk, slid the key into the lock, opened the door.

The tiled hallway whose big window overlooked the swimming pool at the opposite side of the house was cool and shadowy. The living plants that Deke had cultivated under the skylights had been replaced by silk imitations, but otherwise nothing was significantly altered. She moved along, glancing into the living room, the library, the den, the exercise room, the dining room, the kitchen . . .

Something unexpected there. An odor. She sniffed, recognized it as bacon. An aroma she encountered frequently in her own kitchen on Saturdays and Sundays. One of the household bonds was a love of bacon, the crisper the better.

She moved slowly into the room, taking in small details. Stove: clean, but some streaks showing where it had recently been wiped. Scattering of crumbs on the edge of the pullout breadboard. Purple smudge on the handle of the double sink's faucet. She touched it, smelled her fingers. Blueberry jam.

Ard was a neat freak in her office, but seldom in the kitchen.

Carly went to the refrigerator and looked inside. Only a box of baking soda. But in the adjoining laundry room she found a damp and stained dishtowel inside the hamper.

She started upstairs to the bedrooms. Stopped, remembering what she'd found there the last time, then steeled herself and went on.

Guest rooms, three of them. Those who came to dinner parties here at the end of the long, winding road preferred to stay over, and Ronnie and Deke had provided accommodations. The first room showed no signs of occupancy; in the second the blinds on the two windows were closed in different directions—a mistake the realty people wouldn't have made. And in the third the comforter on the bed hung lopsided—exactly as the one on Nat's bed at home always did.

Carly didn't have the heart to search further. It was clear that Ard and Natalie had stayed here last night. Slept in a place where Ard knew no one would ever look for them, while Carly agonized and spent the night trying to find clues to their whereabouts.

They'd gotten up this morning, and Ard had prepared their traditional Saturday breakfast: orange juice, bacon, eggs over easy, toast with blueberry jam from a mail-order house in Montana. Had Nat asked why they were staying at Uncle Ronnie and Uncle Deke's house? Asked why Carly wasn't with them? How had Ard explained that?

And how had she summoned the courage to spend the night in this place where their friends were brutally murdered? Or had she visited here many times without Carly's knowledge?

Her breath came ragged and fast; then black spots danced across her field of vision. As dizziness overcame her, she sank to the floor, pressed her face into the comforter.

After a few moments her physical reactions subsided, but her emotions swung wildly—from rage to despair to rage and back to despair. She pounded the mattress with her fists, twisted the comforter with vicious fingers, and finally wept.

Why, Ard? Why?

It was after seven when she left the house. Pink and gold streaks lingered in the sky over the coastal ridgeline, but shadows enveloped the valley, and to the east the foothills were dark. The temperature had dropped sharply, and a chill was on the air, along with the scent of damp earth and growing things. . . .

Movement in the underbrush—slow, stealthy.

She stopped, listening.

"Who's there?"

No reply.

"Who's there?"

Nothing.

She must've imagined it. Probably had caught Ard's paranoia. Feeling foolish, she ran for the truck.

Once inside she turned on the dome light and twisted the rearview mirror so she could see her face. It was blotchy, her eyes red and swollen. She looked, in short, like shit. But her emotional fit—something she hadn't permitted herself in years—had proved cathartic: She was in control once more and hungry as a wolf.

At home she fixed a huge sandwich from a leftover roasted chicken, took it and a glass of Fume blanc to the table by the windows, shutting the blinds before sitting down. She ate the sandwich, drank the wine, went back to the fridge for potato salad and more wine. She was back again, in hot pursuit of ice cream, when the blinking light on the answering machine caught her attention.

Lindstrom: "Carly, I talked with Sam, and now you and I need to talk." He gave a number.

Mayor Garson Payne: "Have you given any more thought to what we were discussing the other day? Call me. You have my numbers."

Arts reporter Vera Craig: "Hey, honey. You looked kinda peaked when you and Johnny Crowe rushed in and out this afternoon. Need some of Aunt Vera's TLC?"

Sev Quill: "Hi, boss woman. What's happening with Crowe, a.k.a., well, you know? I'll be home till six, not back till morning, if I get lucky. Redheaded tourist, and she's just fascinated with newspaper reporters."

She listened to Matt's message again, then dialed the number he'd left. The phone rang ten times—no answer, no machine. The mayor's message she deleted; she was not open to further discussion with him—now or ever. Vera's message she'd ignore; if the big-hearted woman caught the slightest hint of something gone amiss, she'd be over in a flash to smother her with affection and eventually glean all the details. Sev, of course, was now busy charming the redheaded tourist.

She went to her home office and—after stepping over a stack of environmental-impact reports, a paint-stained sweatshirt, three pair of athletic shoes, and an unabridged dictionary that Nat had been perusing last week—logged on to lii.org, a site created by librarians, which listed other sites to go to for a wide variety of reliable information. An hour later she had amassed a considerable amount of printout on Wells Mining and Denver Precious Metals, none of which appeared to be relevant to anything but the dim past.

CR-92 continued to baffle her. A county road she'd never heard of, perhaps? She hurried through the still night to her truck, consulted her local map. No numbered roads; Soledad County preferred more colorful appellations. A road in another county? Another state? A search would take hours, maybe days.

She returned to the house, consulted the list. Moratorium 10/00 puzzled her as much as CR-92.

Noah Estes? A glance through the phone book showed plenty of Esteses in the county, but no Noahs. This was something on which she could turn loose her best researcher of local matters, Donna Vail, but it was now close to eleven, so that call would have to wait till morning.

Again she went to lii.org and scrolled through the categories listed there. A few that she hadn't yet tried seemed relevant to her search, so she clicked on them and visited a couple of sites, then followed links to other sites. And as she did, a feeling stole over her. . . .

She sat up straighter, listening. Nothing but a tree branch tapping against the house's wall. She glanced at the window, saw only her own reflection. Her face bore the expression of a deer caught in the glare of oncoming headlights.

Imagining a watcher again, McGuire? You're getting as bad as Ard.

She turned back to the computer, clicked on yet another link, but the feeling persisted. Finally she left the office, went to the darkened bedroom, and peered out at the fringe of oak trees at the meadow's edge. Motion there, but it could merely have been caused by the wind or an animal. Raccoons, deer, opossum, even kit foxes coexisted with humans here in the country.

She went back to her office and drew the curtains, then sat, propping her feet on a broken-down desk chair she'd been meaning to get rid of for more than a year now, and contemplated the framed movie poster on the opposite wall. *The Last Picture Show,* a film based on a novel that had had a profound effect on her as a teenager. Larry McMurtry's vivid portrait of life in a poor, windswept West Texas town mirrored the emotional poverty of her youth and had elevated that condition to the universal. She'd taken comfort in the story's bleakness, because after reading it she no longer felt so alone.

Loneliness had been the hallmark of her childhood. When her brother, Alan, was nine and she five, their father, a successful insurance agent, had accepted an executive position with his company's home office in Cleveland and moved the family north from a small town in Georgia. While their new home in suburban Ellenburg was lovely and the neighbors hospitable, their mother refused to adapt and instead turned to the tenets of the fundamentalist church in which she was raised—a faith so out of the mainstream that even the most conservative of Christian sects viewed it with skepticism. While Stanley McGuire's job took him farther and farther afield, his wife, Mona, attempted to keep the outside world at bay; her restrictions on Alan and Carly quickly isolated them from the community, made them freaks in the eyes of their schoolmates. Even the well-meaning teachers who asked Mona to come in to discuss the children's poor socialization eventually gave up in the face of her refusals.

Alan was four years older and soon figured out how to circumvent his mother's strictures, but Carly was at her mercy. She couldn't understand why she had to return home for lunch rather than eat in the school cafeteria. She was repeatedly disappointed when her mother refused to sign permission slips for field trips. There were no after-school sports for her, no extracurricular activities; no sleepovers, birthday parties, ballet lessons, or trips to the mall. In sixth grade, when her mother tore up the permission slip for a class trip she desperately wanted to make, she complained to her father. The bitter quarrel that ensued between her parents made her vow never to do so again, but even without complaints on her part, the dissension between Stanley and Mona escalated.

A few days before she was to start junior high school, Alan sat her down and taught her his mantra: "Everything ends. Everything ends. When things get really bad, like when they're screaming and throwing stuff at each other, you say it over and over. But when he's gone and Mom's not looking, you slip and slide."

"What do you mean?"

"Say you want to go to the mall with some of the kids—"

"Nobody wants me along."

"That'll change, once you're in junior high—if you stop being Mama's baby girl. The other kids'll like you if they think you're getting away with something."

"So how do I do that?"

"Okay, Mom has her rule about being home fifteen minutes after school lets out. But you tell her, 'Mrs. Smith asked me to stay to help her set up a display. Nobody else got picked, just me. Can I?' "

"She'll say no."

"Uh-uh. She'll think it's an honor, so she'll say yes."

"What if she calls the teacher to check up?"

"She won't. Here's the key to Mom: She's afraid of people, especially people like teachers, who she thinks are better than her. Why d'you think she's never gone to PTA or Parents' Night?"

"Mom, afraid?"

"She's one of the most afraid people I know."

Carly thought about that for a moment. "Your science project, the one you have to work on after school in the chemistry lab, it isn't for real?"

"Nope. Same with the math study group on Saturday mornings."

A new world was opening up before Carly's eyes.

Alan added, "When you start high school and want to slip out at night, I'll show you my escape route."

"You go out at night, and Mom hasn't caught you?"

"Not once."

"But what if she checks your room?"

"I'm good at bunching up pillows under the covers to make them look like me. I can show you how to do that, too."

"But she might come in, to straighten the covers or kiss you good night."

"When was the last time she did that to you?"

". . . When I was really little."

"Here's another thing you should know about Mom, Carly: She liked us when we were little kids, but she doesn't like us now that we're growing up and turning into real people. That makes us just another thing in her life that she can't control. Trust me, she won't ever come into your room."

All of a sudden Alan sounded angry. Carly asked, "D'you hate her?"

He shook his head. "No. She's my mom, and I love her, and I suppose in her weird way she loves me. If I hate anybody, it's Dad, for not standing up to her. I don't feel good about the stuff I'm doing, but I've got to have a halfway normal life, and so do you."

Alan had placed a gently worded farewell note on the kitchen table and left home the day he turned eighteen. He attended college at Cornell University, took a job with an accounting firm, married, and had a child. He had created a completely normal life for himself, until it was abruptly cut off on that icy road.

Carly, on the other hand, had left home under far more dramatic circumstances and had never striven toward normalcy—at least not of the sort Alan achieved. Her definition of normalcy was self-acceptance, satisfying work, and love—and for a while she believed she'd found all three.

That belief had been an illusion, of course, but sometimes our illusions sustain us.

What, she wondered, was going to sustain her now?

Sunday, May 12, 2002

Not one of us . . . not one of us . . . not one of us . . .

Carly jerked upright in bed, hands gripping the edge of the comforter. She was sweating, her heart pounding. Someone moved close by in the darkness—

And thumped on the bed. A voice said, "Ur? Ur?"

"Oh my God, Gracie!" She fumbled for the switch on the lamp. She and the little white cat squinted at each other in the sudden glare. Carly gathered the animal in her arms, lay back against the pillows. Gracie resisted at first but quickly settled down.

Cats were such habitual creatures, sensitive to every change in their daily routine, and Gracie's had been altered big-time. She usually slept with Natalie, but Nat had been gone two nights, and by now the cat had also noticed Ard's absence. Her questioning sounds amounted to "Where are my people, and will you go away and leave me, too?"

Carly stroked Gracie absently, still in the grip of the dream. Dammit, why was she having it again, after all these years? She'd thought last night's appearance an anomaly, but apparently it was not.

Unlike many of her dreams, this one required little interpretation; it was a symbolic reenactment of the most humiliating experience of her life—one that had caused her to sever her ties to Ellenberg, Ohio, forever.

As her brother, Alan, had predicted, once Carly devised ways to circumvent her mother's restrictions, she attracted a circle of friends, and in high school hung with a wild crowd who gathered late at night to drink beer and smoke grass at a secluded spot by the Chagrin River. She had a reputation as clever and crazy, a girl who'd try anything. Wily C. McGuire, her crowd called her. Other, more elite cliques were not so kind; they called her a slut.

By now Carly was used to being different, so she ignored their taunts and did her best to live up to the reputation; if they were going to call her a slut, she'd be the best the town had ever known. But a series of less-than-successful heterosexual experiences undermined her confidence and finally forced her to face what it was that really set her apart from the others.

It was 1976. The sexual revolution had transformed American society; gays and lesbians were openly holding hands on the streets of the cities—but not in Ellenberg, Ohio. There, homosexuality was usually the subject of smutty jokes, and teachers of the high school's euphemistically titled Practical Living Course branded it an aberration that could and should be cured by counseling. Carly kept her secret, withdrew from her friends, and developed a case of depression so severe that her homeroom teacher insisted she talk with the school district's staff psychologist.

Victoria Sherwood was a wise woman who quickly intuited Carly's problem; through their sessions she enabled her to accept her sexual orientation, while cautioning her against coming out while she was still living in Ellenberg. Given Carly's family situation and the conservative views of the community, Ms. Sherwood felt such a move would prove disastrous. Instead she put Carly in touch with a support group, and before Mona McGuire put a stop to that and all other forms of counseling, Carly had met her first female lover, a woman from a nearby town, Dierdre Paul. Soon she was slipping out at night to meet Dierdre, and though they tried to be discreet, eventually a classmate of Carly's spotted them together and figured out the nature of the relationship.

As the rumors began to circulate, the situation turned ugly.

The veiled glances and sudden silences as she passed groups in the hallways were nothing new; they'd started long ago and increased along with her bad reputation. But graffiti in the women's lounge—*McGuire is a lesbo*—was harder to take, and a note stuffed inside her locker—*We know what you're doing and who you're doing it with*—brought on a panic attack. The boys who considered themselves studs set up a betting pool to see who could score first with "the dyke," and reacted angrily when she rebuffed them; the girls who had been catty before were now downright cruel. Some of her friends stood by her, but passively, never directly confronting her tormentors, and the school's faculty looked the other way.

Victoria Sherwood had by then transferred to a district in another part of the state, and Carly had no way of getting hold of her. She called Alan several times, thinking to confide in him, but found she didn't have the nerve. Finally she broke off the relationship with Dierdre, sank once more into depression, and went back to hanging with her old crowd. But nothing was the same; even with them she felt like an outsider.

When Eric Baer, a popular member of the student council who had always treated her kindly, asked her to their senior prom at the last minute, she saw accepting the invitation as a way to lay the rumors to rest. And it was important that they die, because, much to her disappointment, she would be forced to stay in Ellenberg for another four years; her mother had decreed that the family would pay for her college education only if she attended Case-Western Reserve University in Cleveland and lived at home. The week before the prom Mona was in Georgia, caring for her ailing mother, and Stanley was easily persuaded to allow Carly to go on the date—factors she mistakenly took as good omens.

The evening began well enough, with dinner at a pricey restaurant with two other couples, and a limo to ferry them to the country club where the prom was being held. She was a good dancer and actually enjoyed herself. When the band took a break, she and Eric went with a number of couples onto the golf course, where they shared wine and joints; as she laughed along with the others at their own wickedness, she felt they accepted her. The remainder of the evening might present problems, given the way Eric was already pawing her, but as she sailed along on a grass-and-alcohol high, Carly felt confident she could handle him.

The group returned to the ballroom as the band struck up a fanfare. Tom Clifford, class president, and Shannon Michaels, vice president, were preparing to announce the prom king and queen. Shannon, her face flushed and animated, took the microphone and, after the usual screeches and groans of the audio system subsided, spoke into it, her voice high-pitched with excitement.

"Before we announce Ellenberg High's royal couple of nineteen seventy-six, we have a special award to present. One that's well deserved. It goes to Carly McGuire, our own lesbian princess. Come on up and claim your trophy, Carly!"

She went ice-cold, her limbs numb. For a moment her vision blurred. When it cleared, she was looking at Eric, who wore a triumphant smile. The boys who had been in the group on the golf course were exchanging high-fives, and the girls were laughing and smirking. Her gaze swung to the bandstand, where Tom Clifford had produced a female mannequin with crewcut hair, dressed in overalls and a plaid shirt. A sign pinned to the overalls' bib read DIERDRE DYKE. He extended it toward her, grinning.

Not everyone was laughing, however. Some of her classmates stared at her in horror, others with startled recognition. Mr. Andrade, the principal, was white-faced and tight-lipped as he strode up to the bandstand and snatched the mannequin from Tom's hands. The chaperones, also outraged, were close behind him.

Carly whirled and ran.

Out of the ballroom, down the hallway, across the lobby, through the front door. She smacked into the valet parking attendant, pushed him away as he tried to steady her.

"Hey, you okay?"

She started to cry, kept going.

They set me up—Eric, the whole rotten bunch of them. Why would they do that? Why? And now what am I gonna do, where am I gonna go, can't go home, that's for sure. The school will call Dad and he'll kill me, and Mom, oh, my God, Mom, can't ever go home again. . . . Dierdre—no, she said she didn't want to see me anymore after I broke it off. . . . Ms. Sherwood—I don't even have a phone number for her. . . . Alan . . .

The thought of her brother calmed her. Although she hadn't been able to tell him she was gay, she knew he wouldn't condemn her. At the end of the club's long driveway she slowed, turned right, began walking down the dark sidewalk. A few blocks ahead at Price Street was a convenience store with a phone booth. She had only a small amount of change in the little silk purse that matched the little silk dress that was de rigueur at high school proms that year, but enough to make a collect call. Alan would tell her what to do. . . .

"Call Aunt Nancy," he said.

Her mother's sister, the crazy one, who lived in New York City. "She's nuts. She can't help me."

"Nan's not nuts. She's a very well-respected partner in a major stock brokerage, is about to set up her own firm, and is on the board of a half-dozen corporations. She also feels terrible about what Mom's done to you and me."

"But Mom says she's been in and out of institutions—"

"The only institutions Nan's been in are financial ones."

"Mom lied about her own sister?"

"She lies about a lot of things, but she probably believes what she's saying. When're you gonna get it through your head that Mom's a very sick person?"

". . . You don't think I'm sick because I'm—"

"Carly, you're not. Who's sick are the assholes who did that stuff to you tonight. Call Nan; she'll help."

"Are you sure? She hardly knows me."

"Of course I'm sure! Who d'you think sent me my one-way ticket out of that hellhole four years ago? Who d'you think's been paying my tuition?"

After Aunt Nancy accepted Carly's collect call, her husky smoker's voice said, "I've been waiting years to hear from you, honey. What's wrong?"

It was difficult to tell her story to a relative stranger, and she kept breaking down, but Nan gently led her through it.

"Okay, honey," her aunt said when she'd finished, "here's the

way I see it. The school's already reported what happened to
your dad, and all hell's about to break loose. I love your mother,
but she's never been emotionally stable, and your father . . .
he's a nice man, but he's weak. I think you should come here to
me."

"Come to New York? How?"

"Planes fly east from Cleveland several times a day. I can
have a ticket for the next flight waiting for you at the airport.
Just go home, pack your things, and leave."

A spark of possibility warmed her. "Mom's down in Georgia
with Grandma, but Dad—"

"How long will it take you to get home?"

"Maybe fifteen minutes."

"Okay, I'll call him, keep him on the phone. While I'm talking to him, you sneak in and out. Do you have enough money
to get to the airport?"

She had over a hundred dollars hidden in her sweater box.
"Yes."

"Good. Hurry, now."

She hesitated.

"What?" Nan asked.

"If I leave now, I won't graduate."

"Oh, yes, you will. A school district that allows a student's
classmates to continually torment her—let alone do what they
did tonight—owes her. And I'll see to it that they pay."

Could Aunt Nan really do that? "Mom and Dad will come
after me."

"Their treatment of you for all these years is the equivalent
of child abuse—or neglect, on your father's part. If they come
after you, I've got a team of very good lawyers, and frankly, I'd
enjoy watching them go up against Mona and Stan."

Someone wanted her. Someone cared. But . . . "Why're you
willing go to all this trouble? You don't really know me."

"I know you well enough. And you forget, your mom and I were raised in the exact same kind of household as you. There was nobody to help me when I got out, and I wouldn't wish that kind of experience on my own flesh and blood. Life's tough enough as it is. You deserve a chance to make the most that you can of yours. But I do want something in exchange."

At the moment, Carly would have sold her soul to her. "What?"

"The same thing I asked of Alan: Be strong; do your best; contribute something; be your own person."

"Even if that person's a lesbian?"

"You know what? I don't give a rat's ass if you love a woman or a wildebeest. There're bigger issues in this world than who you sleep with, and I sense you're a person who can tackle them."

And over the next four years, under Nan's expert tutelage, she had learned the art of tackling—

The phone rang, loud in the silence. Gracie levitated as Carly lunged for the receiver, her heart pounding with the alarm that a postmidnight call always provoked. She fumbled with the talk button, answered curtly.

"Carly?"

"Lindstrom, d'you know what time it is?"

"Sorry. After I left my message on your machine, I had to go out."

"So why didn't you turn yours on—your landlady's, I mean?"

"Sam doesn't have a machine. She can barely afford a phone."

"Okay, I shouldn't've snapped at you. You said we need to talk."

"Yeah. I found out some interesting things from Sam, and we followed up on our conversation with a visit to Meryl

Travis. That led us to— Well, it's too complicated to go into on the phone. Can we come over?"

She glanced at the clock radio. Two thirty-eight, but who was sleeping? "I'll make some coffee."

"Try opening a bottle of brandy instead."

Sam D'Angelo, the woman Matt called his landlady, surprised Carly. She was twenty-five at most, thin to the point of anorexia, and her long dark hair fell limply to her shoulderblades. She wore a cheap cotton sweater and ragged jeans that were several sizes too large, and the toes that protruded from her flimsy sandals must have been freezing on this chilly night. As Lindstrom made introductions, Sam regarded her warily, clasping her hands behind her back as if to avoid a handshake. Lindstrom looked tired but keyed up—the way Carly had often felt when working on an important story. He prodded Sam forward, and they went to the kitchen, where Carly had already set out a bottle of brandy and three glasses.

"So what have you got?" she asked as she poured.

"Let us relax a little before we get into it," he said.

"I'll go first, then." She related what she'd discovered at the Talbot house.

Sam's eyes grew wide, while Matt's narrowed. When Carly finished, he said, "I can't believe she went there, let alone spent the night."

"It's occurred to me that she may have been going there all along."

"Why, for God's sake?"

"To get inspiration for her book, soak up atmosphere, commune with the dead."

"That's morbid."

"To you and me, it is. To Ard—who knows?" Carly glanced

at Sam, who had leaned forward and was listening intently to the conversation.

Matt said, "That house is up for sale, right? I wonder how Ard would've explained her presence to a real estate agent."

"She had good reason for being there; she's executor of Ronnie's estate."

"You didn't mention that before."

"It didn't seem relevant. So what did you and Sam find out?"

"It's pretty confusing. Sam, why don't you tell Carly about your father?"

Sam flushed and looked down at her hands. "No, you go ahead."

Carly said to her, "If you don't mind, I'd rather hear it in your own words. I don't know what . . . John's told you, but this isn't for the newspaper. It has to do with people I love who may be in trouble."

Sam raised her eyes; they were a gold-flecked gray and very disturbed. "What I've got to say, it has to do with somebody I love, too."

"Of course."

"I . . . Dad's memory, it's all I've got. When I told John, I didn't understand that Dad might've done something wrong. . . . Oh, hell, if it's really all that bad, it'll probably come out anyway." She took a deep breath, clasped her hands on the table. "Okay, John asked if Dad had anything to do with your friends who were killed. He didn't. But he was connected with Mr. Payne, from back when he managed the mill."

"In what way?"

"He fixed things."

"At the mill? Payne's house?"

"No, it wasn't like repairing machinery or . . ." Sam shrugged and glanced at Lindstrom.

He nodded encouragingly.

"Okay. I never knew about this till two days before Dad killed himself. After he got his layoff notice, he started drinking real heavy. Didn't report to work, even though he knew we'd be needing the money. The second night, he told me that he didn't like fixing things for Mr. Payne, because it sometimes got messy, but he guessed he'd have to keep on doing it, just like Mack Travis, because where else was he going to get a job at his age? When I asked him what kind of things he fixed, he yelled at me, told me to leave him the hell alone. And the next day he shot himself."

Sam's pained, bewildered voice made Carly feel for her. She said, "I'm sorry. I know it's been rough for you."

"Thanks."

Carly turned to Matt. "So after you and Sam talked, you went to see Meryl Travis. What did she tell you?"

"That her son was a good boy who never harmed anybody. He worked hard on construction and sometimes he 'made deliveries' for Payne and Milt Rawson. Often he had to drive as far as Sacramento and be home in time for his early-morning shift."

"She say what kind of deliveries?"

"She claimed she didn't know."

"Political payoffs?"

"I suspect so."

"Well, maybe if I visit Mrs. Travis I can get more information out of her." But she doubted it. The Travis woman had been widowed in her early thirties and never remarried; when Ard had interviewed her for her book, she'd said her home in Talbot's Mills resembled a shrine to the dead husband and son. Surely she'd be averse to revealing anything negative about Mack.

Matt said, "She also mentioned a Janet Tremaine, Mack's former girlfriend. Claimed Janet could've given him an alibi for the time of the killings, but somebody 'got to her first.' So we decided to track her down. D'you know the Spyglass Road-house?"

"Yes." It was north, in the foothills off Spyglass Trail: a rambling log structure that featured country bands, hearty meals, and cheap drinks. Carly had only been there once, but she recalled stuffed animal heads, barstools shaped like saddles, and sawdust on the floor.

"Janet Tremaine waitresses there, so we decided to stop in for a beer. I told her I was an old army buddy of Mack's. Tremaine joined us on her break."

"What's she like?"

"Good-looking, except for her hair; it's an unnatural shade of red and chopped off like she cuts it herself without the aid of a mirror. Initially she was willing enough to talk about Mack, was surprised when I told her what his mother said about her having been gotten to before she could alibi him. Tremaine maintains she didn't see Mack the entire week before your friends were murdered."

"You believe her?"

"No. At that point she got very jumpy. So I mentioned Mack's deliveries for Payne and Rawson, to see what kind of a reaction that would provoke. Tremaine blew up at me, told me I'd better be careful about repeating what I'd just said. Claimed it could get me into bad trouble. I asked her why, and she said, 'Obviously you don't know who and what you're dealing with.' Then she got up and disappeared into the crowd on the dance floor."

"So she was angry?"

"More afraid, and using her anger to cover it."

"She said, 'who and what you're dealing with.'"

"Right."

"So we have Sam's father 'fixing things.' Mack Travis 'making deliveries.' And a warning from his former girlfriend. I'd say the *what* is something major, and Ard stumbled onto it in the course of her researching. As for the who, Rawson and Payne are the obvious choices."

Lindstrom said, "What were you arguing about with Payne at the newspaper the other day?"

"He and his partner want to buy the Talbot property by the Knob. God knows why; the Meadows hasn't turned out so well, and I hear another project on the sea north of Calvert's Landing is stalled. But they've been after Ard to sell to them, and she doesn't want to. Payne was trying to persuade me to get her to change her mind."

"Why doesn't she want to sell? I'd think she'd be glad to get that place off the estate's hands."

"She dislikes both Payne and Rawson, to put it mildly. They're homophobes and have gone out of their way to be unpleasant to both of us. Payne even went so far as to talk about asking the district attorney's office to investigate improprieties in Ard's handling of the Talbot estate. I suppose he thought that if he could have her removed, the bank's trust department would be more reasonable about selling the property."

"But he didn't act on the threat?"

"He may have talked to the D.A., but his claims are groundless. Ard's handling of the disposition of assets has been strictly accounted for."

"So then he had to come up with another game plan."

Carly's eyes met Matt's, and she could tell he was thinking the same thing she was: that the new game plan had involved an anonymous phone call to British Columbia. As she opened her mouth to speak, he shook his head and glanced warningly at Sam, who still knew him as John Crowe.

Sam had been silent, her eyes remote, since she related what her father had told her, and Carly assumed her thoughts were far away, but now she spoke. "My mother used to do house-cleaning for Mr. Payne's wife. She liked Mrs. Payne, but she said he was one mean son of a bitch. Mom could be pretty mean herself, but Mr. Payne actually scared her. Maybe he scared Ms. Coleman into running away."

Carly looked at Matt. "Maybe it wasn't you after all. Maybe Payne and Rawson were the ones watching her. To tell the truth, I felt like somebody was watching me tonight. Maybe one of them, or somebody they hired, really did break into the house."

She closed her eyes, thinking back to Thursday night. At the dinner table, in front of Natalie, Ard had made her claims, and Carly had cut her off because she could see they were scaring the little girl. Later, in the living room, she and Ard had argued.

"Carly, we've got to talk about what's going on."

"No, we do not. And I never want you to mention it in front of Nat again. You frightened her."

"If something's going on, isn't it good for her to be aware of it?"

"If the something's real, yes. But I think you're on edge and over-reacting."

"It is real, I tell you—"

"I don't want to discuss it!"

"But I have a plan—"

"I don't want to discuss it. What part of that sentence don't you understand?"

Ard's face had crumpled at the harsh words, and she began to weep in her eerie, silent way. God, it was unnerving when she did that! Carly would do most anything to get her to stop. So she'd comforted her, and they'd gone up to bed early.

Why didn't you listen to her, McGuire? Why didn't you pick up on that single word—"plan"?

Because you stopped really listening to her years ago, when she came home with Natalie, offering excuses for the inexcusable.

"Carly?" Matt said.

She shook her head, returned to the present. "Sorry. I was trying to remember anything that would point to Payne and Rawson as the trigger for Ard's disappearance. I'm too tired to think logically, I guess."

"Me, too." He yawned, glanced at Sam, and asked, "What say we pack it in and grab a few hours of sleep, kiddo?"

Sam looked at her watch. "We better. I'm due at the Chicken Shack at seven. Would you believe that people actually eat Cluck 'n Egg, hash browns, and milkshakes at that hour?"

After Matt and Sam left, Carly shut off the lights and went back up to bed, where she repeatedly shifted position and punched the pillows into ever more uncomfortable shapes. Gracie had disappeared, probably into Nat's room, so she didn't even have the cat for company. Finally she got up, thinking to make a fire to warm the chill dawn, but when she set some kindling on the grate, she saw there was an unusual amount of ash, as well as a scrap of paper caught between the grate and the rear wall. She fished it out with the tongs.

It was only a fragment, burned around the edges, bearing a single handwritten line: *mine and I got the right . . .*

What? Whose? And what right?

The penmanship was crude and childlike, which went with the incorrect grammar. But that didn't necessarily mean the writer was poorly educated; for a variety of reasons, many people had bad handwriting, and she herself, editor of a Pulitzer-winning newspaper, said "I got" upon occasion.

Perhaps this was part of a letter to Ard from Matt, asking her to reconcile. Something to the effect of "You're mine and I got the right to be with you." No. That wasn't his style, and besides, she remembered his bold, well-developed handwriting from his job application.

She set the scrap on the table, curled up in her chair. So much information flooded her mind, and none of it meshed. She'd done some investigative reporting while with the L.A. *Times,* but she'd had a good deal of assistance on those stories, and none had posed such complex—or personal—questions.

Well, she'd just have to tackle them one by one.

Tackling.

It was a word that she'd heard often during the years she lived with her aunt Nancy. Nan's method of dealing with the world—and she'd elevated it to an art form. No subtlety in her game plan; she merely advanced down whatever field of endeavor she currently was playing on, knocking over all those who opposed her. But like a good lineman, she earned respect from her opponents.

During the four years Carly lived in her aunt's fashionable Sutton Place apartment while attending Columbia at Nan's expense, she'd learned quite a bit about tackling.

Business dinners for the rich and occasionally famous, during which Nan overran their objections to investing in lucrative but risky schemes. Elaborate parties designed to separate the elite from large amounts of cash for her favorite charities and political candidates. Long discussions on quiet evenings, when Carly learned that the way most people thought the world operated and the way it actually did were polar opposites. Abrasive arguments between Nan and her many lovers, which she heard through the walls; none of them, even the most powerful, was strong enough to oppose her. Nan tackled constantly: her clients, her friends, her men, Carly herself. And Alan . . .

On the night that he died during the ice storm, Alan had been in the city visiting Nan—as was Carly, on vacation between her old job in Denver and her new one in Los Angeles. At a dinner party at the apartment, Nan had announced Alan's appointment to a full partnership in her investment firm. Although visibly stunned, he reacted graciously in the company of the guests, but later that evening, in the privacy of Nan's study, he turned the position down, berating her for announcing it without consulting him. He had the life he wanted upstate: his family, friends, good work, respect within his small community. Nan railed at him, saying he owed it to her to help carry on the firm while Carly tackled the big issues through her journalistic career. Finally Alan departed in a rage that had surely affected his judgment and led to a fatal mistake while driving.

Even in the depths of her grief, Carly couldn't completely blame Nan for Alan's death. But the circumstances under which he died made her question her aunt's desire to take control of everything and everyone. The move to L.A. proved positive, putting the necessary distance between them, and it wasn't until a year later, when Nan died of colon cancer, that Carly realized why she'd been so insistent with Alan: She'd known she had limited time left, and was afraid her firm—her own piece of immortality—would die with her unless she positioned her nephew to take over. As, of course, it had. In her will, Nan had stated that she was leaving Carly the bulk of her estate so she might "have the enjoyment in her adult life that was denied her in her childhood."

Remembering, Carly laughed, the sound loud and bitter in the empty house.

Enjoyment, Nan? Look at your little protégé now. Against her best efforts she's turned into you. She bullies her employees, buries herself in her work, ignores her friends, gives short shrift to a little girl who needs her attention. But worst of all, she can't forgive the woman she loves for a mistake she made ten years ago.

I'm you, Nan.
God help me.

A shower and a full carafe of coffee jump-started her day. Nothing to eat—her nervous stomach wouldn't permit it. She tried not to think of the leisurely weekend breakfasts she, Ard, and Nat had enjoyed. If she were to accomplish anything, she'd have to banish her memories. And tackle.

First, a call to Donna Vail, her foremost staff researcher. For a while before coming to the paper, Donna had worked for Good Connections, a service that put people in touch with those they were looking for: birth parents, adoptees, lost relatives, old loves, school classmates. As a result she had access to various databases the firm had developed. If anybody could identify Noah Estes and pinpoint his current whereabouts, Donna was the one.

"Carly!" Her employee's voice was warm. "I was just thinking about you guys. We're having a salmon roast over on the beach near Castle Rock this afternoon, and we'd love it if you could join us."

"I—we'd love to, but I'm backed up on work. I'm having trouble with a story idea I want to assign to Sev, and I thought you might be able to help me, but if you're having a party . . ."

"A potluck, and Dan's in charge of the salmon. All I have to do is show up. What d'you need?"

"An identification, but all I have is a name—Noah Estes. There're a lot of Esteses in the county, but the phone book doesn't list a Noah."

"So this would be a local guy?"

"I think so."

"Give me twenty minutes, and I'll get back to you."

Twenty minutes dragged by like hours. Carly considered making more coffee but decided her nerves were bad enough as it was. When the phone finally rang, she snatched it up and heard Vera Craig's voice.

"Honey, you never called me back. Is everything okay?"

"I . . . yes, everything's fine."

"You sound kinda edgy."

"I'm expecting a call and—"

"Working on Sunday again? I'm gonna have to talk to you about that. It isn't good for your relationship or for Natalie."

"Vera, I've got to keep the line open." She pressed the disconnect button.

Two minutes later the phone rang again. Donna.

"Okay," she said, "I ran two searches through International Locator. First, a national name sweep. The database contains info on eighty-five to ninety percent of people in the country. There're two Noah Esteses, one in Vermont, the other in Alabama."

"Does the database give addresses and phone numbers?"

"It does, but I don't think you'll be needing those particular ones. My second search was a national death sweep. Eight Noah Esteses turned up, and one sounds like the guy you're looking for. Social Security number was issued in California. Born March sixth, eighteen eighty-three. Died November thirtieth, nineteen eighty-one. Zip code for the place he died is Santa Carla's."

"That's probably my man."

"You need anything else?"

"Your potluck . . ."

"It's hours before we have to leave. Here's a thought: Why don't you and Ard and Nat join us at the beach? See if you can't entice that sexy John Crowe to come along, too; I've got a single girlfriend I'd like him to meet. If you come, I'll give you the skinny on Noah Estes then."

". . . Ard and Nat are away this weekend. And, like I said, I'm swamped with work."

"Well, if you change your mind we'll be at Schooner Cove. Meantime, I'll get going on this."

Carly thanked Donna and ended the call. There was no way she could face a crowd of the Vails' friends today, many of whom she knew well, and who would be sure to ask after Ard and Nat. But what was she going to do for the rest of the day? Normally on weekends her time was filled with activities, but today stretched endlessly before her.

She could visit Meryl Travis and attempt to draw her out about Mack's "deliveries." She could track down Janet Tremaine and question her. She could return Sev Quill's call and enlist his help. She could run upstairs and pull the covers over her head and scream. . . .

No, McGuire. Tackle.

The doorbell rang. Lindstrom, probably, back to rehash what they'd talked about in the early morning hours. She moved along the hall, grateful that she'd no longer be alone. Opened the door and stared up at Garson Payne.

Payne loomed over her, eyes stony. The scar on his right cheek—a souvenir of a hunting accident, he claimed—stood out in relief against his tan, as it always did when he was angry. He said, "You didn't return my call, Carly."

"I didn't see any reason to."

He tried to move into the house, but she blocked him, her hip against the doorjamb.

"Inhospitable this morning, aren't we?"

"My home is not open to you—now or ever."

"Perhaps you'll reconsider when you hear what I have to say."

"Then say it and leave."

"Very well. Milt Rawson and I have come up with some very disturbing information about Ardis. Old but damaging information. If you'll allow me to come inside and discuss it with the two of you, I believe it will persuade her to be more reasonable in the matter of the Talbot property."

In spite of the morning sun washing over her, Carly felt a chill. It could only be one thing. How had they found out?

"Neither Ardis nor I have anything to discuss with you."

Someone was crossing the footbridge. Payne's bulk blocked her view.

He said, "Milt and I realize that you and your partner have no reason to like us, but our offer is a good one."

The footsteps slowed at the end of the bridge. Then they resumed, their sound muted as if their owner had moved off the path and onto the grass.

Carly said, "And since Ardis has rejected your offer numerous times, you've now decided to resort to blackmail."

"That's a nasty accusation, Carly."

"And you have a nasty way of doing business."

"Let's not trade insults. If we can sit down and discuss the situation rationally—"

Lindstrom's voice said, "Yes, let's do that."

Payne whirled, scowling. "Who the hell are you?"

"A friend of the family. Why are you harassing Ms. McGuire on such a lovely Sunday morning?"

"I was not harassing—"

"Was he?" Matt asked her.

"Yes, he was."

"Seems to me he'd be better off in church."

Payne said, "This doesn't concern you, whoever you are."

"He's my new staff photographer, John Crowe," Carly said. "And a good shot—both with a camera and a forty-five."

The mayor took a step backward. "Is that supposed to be funny?"

"Depends on your point of view. I find it hilarious."

"Then we'll continue this discussion later, when you're in a more serious mood." He turned and set off at a measured pace.

Matt watched him, eyes narrowed. "Was that about the Talbot property again?"

"Yes."

"What's this I overheard about blackmail?"

Oh, God. Now is the time to go upstairs, pull the covers over my head, and scream.

"Carly?"

"I'm okay."

"No, you're not."

"Dammit, Lindstrom, I hate being told how I am, how I feel!"

"Hey, I'm not the enemy."

"Why did you have to turn up when the shit's about to rain down all over me?"

"What kind of shit?"

"None of your business."

"I'm making it my business."

"Jesus, I hate you!"

"You don't know me well enough to hate me."

"Stop being reasonable!"

"One of us has to be."

"Fuck you!"

"Carly, where's all this anger coming from?"

From years back. From the day before yesterday. From five minutes ago.

Time's up. Got to face it.

Got to tackle . . .

Matthew Lindstrom

Sunday, May 12, 2002

Matt followed Carly inside her house. In the days since he'd entered her office and found her sitting on her desk, she'd changed perceptibly: Her tan had faded to sallowness, and her facial skin pulled tight against the bone; her eyes were sunk in shadow.

A skull, he thought, topped by brittle, dead hair. He shook his head, pushed the image away, but he couldn't rid himself of the notion that some essential part of her was dying.

Without a word she went to the living room window. Matt followed and looked over her shoulder. Gar Payne sat behind the wheel of a green Jaguar that blocked Carly's truck, a cell phone to his ear.

"Get off my property, Payne!" she exclaimed.

As if he'd heard her, the mayor set down the phone, started the car, and drove off.

Carly expelled a long sigh. "Let's go outside, huh? It's stuffy in here. I need some air."

She led him to the patio in front of the house. It was in full sun, so she raised the umbrella between two chaise longues and they sat side by side. Matt waited for her to speak and, when she didn't, asked, "Are you ready to tell me about it?"

"I don't think you want to know. It's about Ard, and it's bad."

He didn't think he wanted to know, either. Every revelation had been bad, only to be topped by something worse. But he sensed in Carly's tone a need to tell it, as if she'd already made the decision to place it in his hands.

He said, "You may as well get on with it."

She sighed again and rested her head against the chaise's high cushion. "Payne is pushing hard now to get his hands on the Talbot property. This morning he wanted to sit down and talk about an offer with Ard and me. When I wouldn't let him in the house, he made reference to some damaging information he and Rawson have about her."

"He say what it was?"

"Didn't have to. I know."

He waited, letting her tell it in her own way.

"I told you that Ard took off for fifteen months and came back with Natalie."

"Right. She went to San Francisco."

"Well, I didn't tell you why she left. I came home one night and found her in bed—our bed—with a man. Gar Payne. He's one of those macho homophobes who can't believe a woman can resist him. So he set out to prove it with Ard and then rub my nose in it. Apparently he hasn't grasped the concept of bi-sexuality."

Somehow it didn't surprise him. Maybe nothing would have the capacity to surprise him again.

Carly went on: "After I chased Gar out of here, Ard and I fought. She said she felt smothered by a monogamous relationship. She said she needed to be with both men and women. She said I was the flip side of the coin from you, but that in essence we were both the same."

"Meaning?"

"We were trying to control her, confine her to one way of life."

"She never accused me of that."

"No. Because she loved you and didn't want to hurt you. With me she always seemed to want a confrontation."

And because she'd avoided a confrontation, he'd never suspected. . . .

Or had he, on some level?

There was the night, a month or so before Gwen began talking about divorce, when he'd come home early from a wedding shoot and called out to her from the front hall. She'd come running down the stairs in her bathrobe, expressing surprise at his return. She and her friend Bonnie Vaughan had been about to color her hair.

Except Gwen never colored her hair, and Bonnie came downstairs a few minutes later, clearly uncomfortable. The dyeing project was abandoned, and after a glass of wine, Bonnie went home.

Bonnie Vaughan, Gwen's best friend. The woman who had ended his first life with her harsh words: "You better get out of Saugatuck before somebody murders *you!*"

In light of what he'd recently learned about Gwen, it all made sense: She and Bonnie had been lovers. Whether there had been other women before Bonnie didn't matter. Gwen had loved her; Gwen had loved him. To a woman of the conservative upbringing she'd described to him, that was an untenable situation, even in the freewheeling eighties, so she'd run from both of them. And though Bonnie had initially supported Matt, eventually she'd turned her grief over losing Gwen to hatred for him—everybody's favorite scapegoat.

"Matt?" Carly said.

He didn't respond.

"Earth to Lindstrom."

"Sorry. Just remembering. So Ardis ran away, and . . . ?"

"Came back with Natalie. Came back with all her usual excuses for returning. Her love for me, her love for our home, which would be the ideal place to raise our child. She actually said that: 'our' child, as if we'd created her. But then she came to the main one, and it was a biggie."

Carly's voice had gone hard and flat.

I don't want to know. I don't.

"The man Ard was involved with in San Francisco was an abusive alcoholic and a drug user who did not want a child. One night, when they were both high and he was trying to persuade her to get an abortion, they fought. Physically. Ard grabbed a kitchen knife and stabbed him. And then she ran. After she had the baby, she came home to me.

"So that's what Gar Payne is holding over my head. Somehow he found out that Ard stabbed Natalie's father, and that I helped cover it up."

Impossible.

Or was it?

No. Nothing his former wife had done was impossible anymore.

"You say she stabbed him," he said, his own voice sounding foreign to him. "Fatally?"

"No. If that had been the case, there would've been something in the San Francisco papers. She monitored them for weeks."

"Why wouldn't the boyfriend have gone to the police?"

"Probably because he had a long arrest record, didn't want to have anything to do with the law."

"Okay, Ardis stabbed him and ran. Where?"

"Los Angeles."

"And Natalie was born there?"

"Yes."

"And when they came here, Natalie was how old?"

"Four months."

"And Ardis never heard from the boyfriend—what's his name?"

"Chase Lewis. No, she never heard from him again."

"I'm surprised he didn't appear to claim his share of the glory when the paper won the Pulitzer."

Her lips twisted in a wry smile. "I don't think drugged-out trombonists follow the news all that closely."

"Still, he must've made some effort to find her."

"Ard's theory is that it was too much trouble for him. Of course, she said the same of me because I didn't hire a private detective every time she disappeared." Carly closed her eyes, shook her head. "God, when I look back on the past fourteen years, I wonder how I got into such a messy relationship, much less remained in it. I never considered myself the kind of woman who lets herself be victimized, but that's exactly what happened. And now I'm really in a mess."

"Well, in order to extricate yourself from said mess, first you need to find out how serious it is. Find out how much damage Gar Payne and his partner can inflict on you. While you stay here and keep working on leads to Ardis and Natalie's whereabouts, I'm going to find out what happened to Chase Lewis."

Within two hours he left for San Francisco. Highway 101 narrowed some four miles south of Talbot's Mills, widened to a freeway at Santa Carla, then narrowed again to a two-lane arterial that meandered along the bank of the Eel River. The expanse of water was swollen from the spring runoff; across it Matt glimpsed small cabins among the tall, newly leafed trees. They made him think of his own cabin overlooking Bear Rock, and he felt the strong pull of home. He was tempted to drive straight through San Francisco, turn in the Jeep at the rental car company, and use his open ticket to Vancouver. He had his camera on the seat beside him, its bag containing the films of Gwen; they would vindicate him. Let Carly McGuire solve her own problems.

But he didn't go on to the airport. Instead he took the Lombard Street exit from Doyle Drive and checked into the first motel with a vacancy sign. In the lobby he bought a city map, then went up to his room to study it.

He'd visited San Francisco once during his wandering years, but found it too dreary and expensive. In the few days he'd spent there, he'd learned it was difficult to navigate—full of one-way streets and natural obstacles that made it impossible to travel in a straight line from one point to another. After he'd refamiliarized himself with the map, he pulled the phone book from the nightstand and looked up Wild Parrots, the jazz club where Carly said Ardis had waitressed. It was still in existence, on Grant Avenue in the bohemian North Beach district. It was not the starting point he would have chosen—that was the now-closed library, with its files of old newspapers—but he decided to drive over there anyway.

Traffic in North Beach was heavy and parking spaces at a premium. Wild Parrots, shabby-looking in the early-evening light, didn't have valet service. Many blocks away he found a lot with hourly rates so high it would have been more economical merely to trade them the Jeep; then he joined the crowds on the sidewalks. The district seemed seedier than he remembered it: Barkers outside the topless clubs were more aggressive; trash littered the gutters; homeless people reclined in doorways. It was a relief to turn uphill, onto the lower slope of Telegraph Hill, where Italian bakeries and delis and esoteric shops replaced the rough-and-tumble commercialism.

The club was small, with a raised bandstand at one end and round tables scattered across the floor. A bar ran along the righthand wall, the smoky glass mirror behind it etched with a flock of colorful parrots. He recalled reading in a guidebook during his first visit to the city that such birds, once escapees from their cages but now generations in the wild, frequented Telegraph Hill.

It was early, only a little after six. A couple sat at the far end of the bar in earnest discussion, but otherwise the club was deserted. Matt took a stool at the other end and waited until a bald man in a vest whose colors matched the parrots' plumage emerged from a curtained doorway, carrying a case of Scotch. After setting it down, he approached Matt, slapping a paper cocktail napkin in front of him.

"What'll it be?"

"Sierra Nevada."

When the bartender set the bottle and glass in front of him and started to turn away, Matt added, "And some information."

"About?"

"Chase Lewis."

"What about him?"

"He used to play here."

"Yeah."

"You know him?"

"Was before my time. I know of him. They say he could've been one of the greats, but he didn't get the breaks."

"You know what happened to him?"

He shrugged. "What happens to any of them that've got the talent but don't make it? They booze, they do drugs. They're in rehab, they're outta rehab. Some of them do time. Chase Lewis, I don't know. It's been years since anybody here has seen him." He gestured at the wall beside the mirror. "That's him, the middle picture."

Matt squinted through the gloom but could make out very few details. "Would you have an address on file for him?"

The bartender's eyes narrowed. "You a cop?"

"No. I'm trying to locate a woman he was once involved with. A family member."

The suspicion in the man's eyes turned to greed. "I don't know. I'd have to check a long ways back."

"It's worth twenty bucks to me."

"I shouldn't leave the bar. Business'll be picking up pretty quick."

To Matt, it didn't look as if business would ever pick up. "Thirty bucks. Final offer."

After the bartender disappeared through the curtain, Matt got up and went to examine the photograph of Chase Lewis. It showed a slender, light-skinned black man with a small mustache and conservative Afro, smiling and cradling his trombone. A standard publicity still, and it told him nothing about the man who had fathered Ardis's child.

The man whom Ardis had stabbed and run from.

He returned to the bar, sipped his beer, waited. The couple at the far end left, and no other patrons materialized. It was nearly ten minutes before the bartender returned and slid a piece of scratch paper across to him.

"Had to get it from one of the file boxes in the storage room," he said. "Why's it that the box you want is always on the bottom of the stack?"

Matt placed thirty dollars on the bar as he read the address. "Hugo Street. Where's that?"

"Inner Sunset, a block from Golden Gate Park. Nowhere place. You'd think a guy like Chase Lewis would've lived in a more lively neighborhood."

Yeah, but I bet it was plenty lively the night Ardis stabbed him.

The apartment house was on a corner: three stories of beige stucco with bay windows, and fire escapes scaling its walls. In the arched entryway was a bank of mailboxes with buzzers beneath them, Number five was labeled with the name C. Lewis. His good luck that the man hadn't moved.

He pressed the buzzer twice but got no response. Then he rang number six, which by his reckoning would be on the same floor. No response either, but seven gave an immediate answering buzz. Matt pushed through the door into a dimly lighted lobby that smelled faintly of cat urine.

There was no elevator, so he started up the narrow staircase. A woman's voice called down, "Hey, how much do I owe you?" Her face appeared over the railing, round and eager, but it quickly turned wary. "You're not the pizza guy," she said.

"Sorry. I rang you at random. I'm looking for Chase Lewis. He doesn't answer his bell."

"The guy in five? He's not here very much. I don't really know him."

"Is there anybody else in the building who does?"

"Uh . . . Mrs. Matthews, maybe. She kind of functions as the manager—at least she's the one who calls the owners when something in the common areas needs fixing. She's lived here forever. Number two."

Matt thanked her and located the apartment at the rear of the first floor. Mrs. Matthews looked to be in her sixties, a petite blonde-haired woman in jeans and a blue sweater. "Of course I know Chase," she said. "What's he done now?"

"To tell you the truth, I've never met the man. I'm trying to locate him on behalf of a family member who was involved with him about ten years ago—Ardis Coleman."

"Ardis. Of course. Lovely girl. She didn't deserve the way Chase treated her. I was happy when she left him."

"How did he treat her?"

"Abused her, both verbally and physically. Threatened their little girl, too, and she was only a baby when they moved here."

"When was that?"

"September of ninety two."

"And Ardis left him when?"

"In November."

"What were the circumstances of her leaving?"

Mrs. Matthews looked uncomfortable. "You say Ardis is a family member. I'd think you'd know."

"She doesn't like to talk about that part of her life, but I understand there was some unpleasantness. If I'm to deal with Lewis, I think I should be prepared, don't you?"

"Well, yes. On the night Ardis left, I heard a lot of yelling and screaming up there." She motioned toward the ceiling. "More than the usual. Then it got very quiet, and someone ran out of the building. An hour later Chase came to my door reeking of alcohol, with his shoulder wrapped in a bloody towel, and asked me to drive him to the emergency service at S.F. General. He said Ardis had left him and taken the baby, and he got so upset he stabbed himself accidentally."

"Did you believe him?"

"Of course not. To me it was obvious what had happened, but it was no business of mine. And he managed to convince the emergency room personnel of his story."

"Did Chase ever try to find Ardis and the baby?"

"No. He drank even more afterwards, and I think he was using drugs as well. He kept getting fired from his jobs, but somehow he managed to support himself and keep the apartment. Then, a few years ago he got himself into a program and has been clean and sober ever since." Mrs. Matthews frowned. "Of course, he's as mean as ever, although he controls himself better. Why do you want to see him?"

"A legal matter involving the little girl. Do you have any idea when he might be coming home?"

"No, I don't. Last month he mentioned that he'd landed a long-term gig at Lake Tahoe."

"Where?"

"He didn't say." She hesitated. "When you talk to Ardis, will you tell her hello for me? She may not remember me after all these years, but just say I wish her well."

Back at the motel he paced nervously, contemplating his next move. A drink from the bottle he'd brought along failed to calm him, so finally he sat down and dialed directory assistance in the 612 area code, copied down the number he received, and called it. Seconds later, Bonnie Vaughan's soft voice answered.

"Bonnie, it's Matt Lindstrom. Don't hang up. I have good news."

"You've got a lot of nerve, calling me."

"Gwen's alive, Bonnie. She's been living in a small town in California since shortly after she disappeared. I've seen her, photographed her."

A long silence. "I don't believe you."

"It's the truth. Let me tell you how I found her." The story spilled out of him like water rushing through a sluiceway. He ended by asking, "The two of you were lovers, right?"

". . . Oh, Matt, what difference does it make?"

"It's important to me. It explains a great deal."

"All right, yes. You must've suspected. That time you nearly caught us at your house . . . She was so afraid you'd figure it out and hate her. Hate me, too. The thing was, she loved both of us, but she loved you more."

"Why d'you think that?"

"Because she stopped sleeping with me after that night. In a way, I was relieved. If there had been a scandal, I'd've lost my job. A high school principal having a lesbian affair with a married woman . . . Well, you know."

"She broke it off with you, but she still asked me for a divorce."

"Because she was afraid if she stayed with you, she'd end up really hurting you. She planned to wait till the divorce was final and then leave town, claiming she'd gotten a job in another state."

"If you knew her plans, how could you think I murdered her?"

She sighed. "I didn't at first, although I thought it was strange that she disappeared before the divorce was final, without saying good-bye to either of us. But Gwen was impulsive and didn't always act rationally, so I decided something had happened to make her run. But then two years went by, and she never got in touch with me. Everybody else thought you were guilty, and I started believing it, too."

"And now?"

"It all makes sense. These disappearing acts, they're part of a lifelong pattern."

Her phrasing gave him pause. "Lifelong?"

"Well, she did run away from home in her teens. She spent a couple of years in Chicago before she came to Saugatuck. Where she got the money to attend college, I'm not sure. She didn't volunteer the information, and I guess I really didn't want to know."

"She told me her parents had died in a plane crash and that she was using their life insurance money for school. And she told me a lot about being raised by an ultraconservative grandmother in Muskegon, Michigan."

"She was raised in Muskegon, yes, but her parents are very much alive."

Yet another revelation. Why had Gwen lied to him about a thing like that? "Did she give a reason for running away from home? Was she neglected? Abused?"

"No. She said her parents and Muskegon were boring. She wanted more from life than they could offer."

"I suppose she also found Saugatuck boring. And me."

"Matt? Are you okay?"

"Yeah. I just need some time to take all this in. We'll talk again soon, Bonnie, I promise."

Carly sounded depressed when he called her an hour later, and he hated to relate news that would further deflate her spirits. As he told her the things he'd found out that evening, she listened silently.

Finally she said, "I lived with her all those years and never knew any of this. I accepted everything she told me without question. How could I be so stupid?"

"You had no reason to doubt her. Neither did I."

"She told me she stabbed Chase Lewis because he was pressuring her to have an abortion. Now it turns out she'd already had Nat. What's the sense in a lie like that? Or the lie about her parents being dead and her awful childhood with her grandmother?"

He'd thought about that as he'd nursed a drink in his dark motel room after talking with Bonnie. "I think there's some deficiency in her that makes her need drama in her life. The running away, the lies—they're all a part of that. When we were married, she would create situations that would throw our lives into chaos: a fire in the kitchen, ramming the car into the garage door. Nothing major, but it got her a lot of attention."

"The same's been true with us, now that you mention it." Carly hesitated. "So are you coming back now?"

"No. I still want to find out the details of the night Ardis stabbed Chase Lewis. I think I'll make a run up to Lake Tahoe in the morning."

Monday, May 13, 2002
Stateline, Nevada

xpensive-looking hotels that Matt didn't recall
from a previous visit to Lake Tahoe hugged the
shoreline, blocking views of the water. A major
building boom was under way on both sides of the Nevada bor-
der; cranes rose high against the sky, the noise of piledrivers
was deafening, and scaffolding covered the sidewalks. Traffic
on the boulevard linking the two states crept.

By contrast, the interiors of the casinos seemed curiously deserted, even for early afternoon. The stools at the long banks of
slot machines were largely empty, and many of the gaming tables were covered. The brightly lighted rooms were too quiet,
too chill, too cheerless. Even the newest and most opulent of
the gambling establishments seemed shabby and fouled by
stale smoke. A paradox, given the near-frantic construction

going on outside. Although the casinos were the victims of an economy that had never recovered from the aftermath of the horrific events of the past September 11, the developers would eventually fall victim to their own false optimism and greed.

He tried to canvass the casinos quickly but became frustrated by layouts designed to force a person to pass through most of the moneymaking attractions before arriving at a place where information could be had. Finally, while stopping for a badly needed drink at one of the bars in Caesar's Palace, he encountered a waitress who knew Chase Lewis and had heard that a group he frequently played with, the Fillmore Five, was currently engaged at the Hyatt Regency at Incline Village.

He drove north past pleasant-looking enclaves called Zephyr Cove, Cave Rock, and Glenbrook, bypassed the road to Carson City. Incline Village was near the tip of the lake, on the Nevada side, and the Hyatt Regency, some dozen stories tall, dominated the shoreline. He left the Jeep with the valet, went inside to speak with the concierge, and was directed to a smaller building on the beach, which housed a restaurant. When he stepped into its dim interior, it took a minute for his vision to adjust; then he saw wood beams, massive iron chandeliers, and a huge stone fireplace. At the far end, in a bar area, a slender black man with a receding hairline was adjusting sound equipment on a platform. Not Chase Lewis.

The man straightened and turned as Matt approached. "Sorry, man, they're not open yet."

"I'm looking for someone with the Fillmore Five."

"You found him. Dave Rand's the name."

"Can you put me in touch with Chase Lewis?"

He frowned and stepped down from the platform. "Wish I could. We'd be sounding a whole lot better if he was with us on this gig, but he pulled out at the last minute. Guy we got to replace him's pretty lame."

"Why'd he pull out?"

"Something came up. With Chase, something always comes up. He called last Monday, said we'd have to do without him."

"He say why?"

"Nope. Chase doesn't let other people know his business, especially when he's got a mad on. And from the sound of his voice I could tell he was pissed off. I'll tell you, he's a good trombone man, but as a human being"—he shook his head—"mean as a rattlesnake, and then some. Why you lookin' for him?"

"I need to settle a legal matter with him, for a family member." The lie came easily; he half believed it himself.

"Huh. You a lawyer?"

"No, just helping out."

"This family member suing him?"

"Nothing like that. I just need for him to sign some papers."

"This wouldn't have to do with Ardis?"

"Ardis Coleman? Yes."

"She and the little girl all right?"

"They're fine."

"Good. It's a goddamn shame the way Chase treated her. She was one sweet thing. Nobody was surprised when she split and took the kid—except for Chase. He's had a mad on for the whole world ever since."

"He must've loved her."

"Nope. Chase doesn't give a rat's ass for anybody but himself, but no woman's supposed to turn her back on him. Or take something from him."

Matt spotted a stack of cocktail napkins on the bar, took out a pen, and wrote Sam's phone number on one. "If you hear from Chase, will you call me?"

"Sure, but I doubt I'll be hearing. When he canceled out, I told him he'd never get another gig with us, and he knew I meant it." His eyes clouded. "You might warn Ardis that he's still gunning for her."

"You think he'd go after her if he found out where she is?"

"Damn straight he would. And she'd be one sorry mess by the time he was through with her."

Tuesday, May 14, 2002
Talbot's Mills, California

s he approached the exit, Matt yawned widely. It was nearly one in the morning. There had been no easy way to get to Soledad County from Lake Tahoe, so he'd been forced to detour south to Sacramento and Highway 5, then take a secondary road east to Highway 101. A long trip, and he drove without pleasure, his thoughts on the puzzle that was Gwen.

A lifelong pattern of lies and running away. Parents who had presumably loved her living in limbo, never knowing what had become of their daughter. Two years as a runaway in Chicago. God knows who she'd conned there in order to get the money for college—or how she'd cast them aside after collecting. And then she'd abandoned him and Bonnie Vaughan. Abandoned Carly numerous times. Even as vile a person as Chase Lewis probably didn't deserve to be stabbed and left bleeding. God knew how many other lives she'd poisoned. . . .

The personal history that he'd learned didn't square with the woman he'd married: gentle, vulnerable, dependent, needing constant reassurance. But neither did the scene Carly had described: Ardis efficiently taking her notes at the Talbot house after she'd discovered their friends' bodies. Could such opposite components exist within one person? Apparently so.

A deer appeared in the wash of his headlights, standing by the side of the road. For a moment he feared it would leap into his path, but then it whirled and plunged into the underbrush. After that he emptied his mind and simply concentrated on driving.

Now as he pulled up to Sam's house, he saw lights in the front room. He'd phoned her from Willits and told her he'd be very late, but apparently the call hadn't kept her from worrying. But why should she worry? And why should he care if she did? She rented him a room, nothing more, although he had to admit he'd grown fond of her in a big-brotherly way.

He got out of the Jeep and mounted the porch steps. Sam must have heard him, because she had the door open before he could find his key. Carly stood in the hallway behind her, and from the look on her face, he knew something very bad had happened.

Without preamble, she said, "Chase Lewis is dead. He was shot sometime over the weekend in a motel in Westport."

"Jesus." When the initial shock had subsided, he moved past the women, into the front room. Sank onto a butt-sprung recliner and ran his hands over his face, as if he could wash the moment away. He looked up, saw that Sam had disappeared. Carly came into the room and sat down on the sofa.

She said, "Sev Quill was routinely monitoring the sheriff's calls this morning when he heard a one-eighty-seven, code two. Homicide, urgent. He rushed over to Westport to get the story, and phoned me from there so I could tell Production to hold space on the front page. As soon as I heard the victim's name, I decided to drive over there, too."

"And?"

"I talked with Rho Swift, who's handling the investigation. Lewis checked in on Thursday night. He pretty much stayed in his room, with the Do Not Disturb sign out. Yesterday morning, Monday, the maid got concerned because she hadn't seen him, and used her passkey. Lewis was lying on the floor, fully clothed, with a gunshot wound to the head. The autopsy's not scheduled till tomorrow morning, but Rho thinks he was killed sometime on Saturday."

"Did anybody at the motel hear the shot?"

"No. He was at the far end of an isolated wing—a room he requested after looking at two others—and there weren't many other guests."

"Does Rhoda know what kind of gun he was shot with?"

"I suppose, but she didn't tell me. I do know they dug a wild-shot bullet out of the wall above the bed."

"What kind of handgun do you own?"

"Handgun?"

"When you warned me off Ardis after you found out who I was, you said you owned a handgun and weren't afraid to use it."

She looked down at the floor. "I lied."

"You don't own a gun?"

"I hate the things. I just said that to scare you."

"Does Ardis own one?"

"No."

"Are you sure?"

"It's the one thing about her I *am* sure of. She's even more afraid of guns than I am. Ronnie Talbot had a weapons collection that he inherited from his father, and she was always after him to get rid of it, even though it was stored inside locked cabinets in the library, where nobody could see it."

"Okay, did you tell Rhoda Swift about Lewis's relationship to Ardis and Natalie?"

"No."

"Carly, that's obstructing a homicide investigation."

She looked up at him, eyes agonized. "I know that. But Ard could not have done this. She could *not.*"

He let it go for the moment. "So you came over here to tell me about the murder."

"I called, and Sam said you'd be back late. I decided to wait for you."

Wait for him, further involve him. He'd've been better off driving straight through San Francisco to the airport on Sunday.

He asked, "Does Sam know any of this?"

"She knows about the murder, and that I'm upset, but she thinks this is newspaper business."

He closed his eyes. Secrecy, lies, threats, fear—and now murder. What had become of the life he'd built for himself—the life that was clean, and his alone?

He said, "I think you should tell Rhoda Swift everything. Put it in her hands and let the sheriff's department deal with it."

No reply. When he looked at Carly, she had drawn her knees up to her chest and was hugging them, her face conflicted. "I found something," she said in a small voice. "In the ashes in our bedroom fireplace." She reached into the pocket of her corduroy shirt and extended a small, charred piece of paper to him.

He studied the words that were scrawled there: . . . *mine, and I got the right* . . .

"So what do you think this means?" he asked.

"I think Lewis somehow found out where Ard was and wrote her, making a claim on Natalie. She probably didn't respond, so he came up here. I think he was the person who was watching her, who had been in the house."

"But he was staying in Westport, south on the coast."

"Yes, because as a black man, he wouldn't stand out so much there. He could've been a tourist, or one of the people working in the service industry. Cyanide Wells, even Talbot's Mills, is too lily-white for him to escape notice. But Westport's not all that far from here. He must've called Ard, demanding to see their daughter, so she ran. She was probably far away when he was killed."

She wanted to believe. As he had once wanted to believe. Gently he said, "She was at the Talbot house on Friday night."

"But that was only a stopover. It was empty when I went there on Saturday."

"Yes, and Saturday's when they think Lewis was shot."

Carly stood and turned away from him. He saw her arm move as she brushed at her eyes. From behind she looked fragile, a stick figure. "Why are you doing this?" she asked.

"Because we have to face the possibility that she killed Lewis. We won't know what she did or didn't do until she chooses to come forward."

"Cold comfort to help me through the night, Lindstrom."

"I doubt I'll get through very well myself. Why don't you grab that blanket, and I'll come sit with you. We'll weather this together."

She hesitated, then took up the brightly colored throw that was folded on the back of the sofa. He moved over beside her, propping his feet on the coffee table while she turned off the overhead light. She sat, her body rigid; the throw barely covered both of them, so he gave her the larger part. Although she didn't speak, he could feel the swirl of her emotions.

"Not long till morning," he said. "Then we can do something."

"What?" Her voice was flat, bleak.

"Something," he said firmly, and tucked the throw around her shoulders.

Gradually the tension seeped out of her, and her breathing became deeper. Her head tipped to the side and rested against his upper arm. The in-and-out rhythms of her sleep soothed him, but they also brought an odd, measured clarity to his thoughts.

Bad as the aftermath of Gwen's disappearance had been, over the past years he'd built a foundation of certain things he relied upon and took to be true. He'd thought it a foundation more solid than what had sustained his previous, largely unexamined life, but apparently he'd been wrong; in the space of one anonymous phone call it had been undermined, as surely as the sea undermines a badly constructed bulkhead, and the events of the subsequent weeks had battered at it with the force of a severe winter storm.

Now it, and he, were poised to crumble.

Carly McGuire

Tuesday, May 14, 2002

arly looked down at the stack of notes in Donna Vail's neat handwriting and sighed. That morning she'd asked Vail to drop her other work and look up two items for her, but now, at close to five, she was disinclined to deal with the reporter's findings. Instead of reading them, she pushed her chair away from the desk and leaned against its high back, closed her eyes, and listened to the day winding down at the *Spectrum.*

Voices calling good-bye. Car doors slamming in the alley. Engines starting, tires crunching. The gradual cessation of phones ringing. And then . . . peace. The building, a former assay office, was solid; back here in her office, normal street noise didn't carry. Only the creaks and groans that were evidence of age intruded, and they were reassuring, reminding her that some things lasted.

She'd spent most of the day in Santa Carla—when, at twenty-four hours before press time, she should have been here tending to her newspaper—following up on the scant information Donna had found on Noah Estes. The task had been an easy one: Make contact with people; ask the right questions; give them her full attention. A good reporter's technique, and one particularly suited to a person who disliked having the focus on her. But it had also taken its toll, and now she was tired.

The information Donna had gathered about Noah Estes was bare bones: He'd died of pneumonia in a Santa Carla nursing home, Willow Creek, in 1981, his ninety-eighth year. Carly had called the home and made an appointment with the administrator, a Mr. Tompkins, claiming the paper was interested in doing an article on the Estes clan. The facility was an attractive low-rise complex on extensive landscaped grounds where a line of willow trees bordered a small stream. Inside, the usual unpleasant odors of such institutions were masked by some substance that must have been added to the air filtration system; the staff were courteous, and what few residents she saw seemed well cared for. Carly had always been biased against nursing homes, and she couldn't help but react with cynicism to Willow Creek; it was targeted to the well off—no Medi-Cal or Medicare patients need apply. But she found herself liking Mr. Tompkins, a small man with neatly manicured hands, whose puppy-dog brown eyes radiated compassion.

Instead of taking her to his office, Tompkins led her outside to a teak bench by the side of the stream. "I knew Mr. Estes well," he told her. "His father—stepfather, actually—was one of the original cyaniders up at the Knob."

"That would be John Estes?"

"Yes. He came out from Denver at the turn of the twentieth century and later married a widow, Dora Collins. Noah was her only child by her first husband, who was killed in an accident at the mine. John was manager there until they shut down operations in the early thirties. He adopted Noah, and he and Dora had four more children of their own. They raised the family in a big house that they built out near the Knob. People who knew them claimed Noah was always John's favorite child, and possibly that's true, because his stepfather left him the Knob property when he died."

"You're something of a local historian, Mr. Tompkins."

He smiled, lines crinkling at the corners of his eyes. "Many of the people who reside here are descendants of old county families. I like to listen to and tape-record their stories; you can learn a lot from the elderly. Someday I plan to publish a volume of oral history."

"I'd enjoy reading it. This property near the Knob—is it now part of the national forest?"

Tompkins looked surprised. "You don't know? It's . . . Well, I'm getting ahead of my story. Noah Estes went to the Colorado School of Mines, like his adoptive father, and also became an engineer. He worked all over the world—South America, Australia, South Africa—but he made periodic trips back here and eventually returned for good, a wealthy man with an Australian wife and five children. They settled on the land John left him. Noah had a reputation as a gentle person with a concern for the environment—unusual in one who made his fortune in mining—and I can attest that it lasted throughout his final years."

"When did he come to Willow Creek?"

"In nineteen seventy-five, the year I started here."

"He was ninety-two then. Why didn't one of those five children, or grandchildren, take him in?"

"He wouldn't permit it. Mr. Estes was fiercely independent. He'd had a good life and didn't want to get in the way of his children and grandchildren enjoying theirs in turn. Living here didn't curtail his enthusiasms, though; he was quite active until his last two months and took great pleasure in reading— mostly about the environment—and in advising our landscapers. Much of what you see around us is due to his input."

"D'you know where I might find any close relatives of Mr. Estes?"

"They're scattered all over the county. I have an address for a granddaughter, Sadie Carpenter. She's the relative who visited him most regularly. I'll ask the receptionist to give you the information."

"One more question, Mr. Tompkins: You seem to think I should know the Estes property near the Knob. Why?"

"Well, my dear, what happened there was the basis for your paper's Pulitzer-winning series. Shortly before he moved into our facility, Noah Estes sold the land to Ronald Talbot. His son, Ronald Junior, inherited it. He, of course, was one of the men who died there."

Sadie Carpenter lived on Second Street, in the old part of the county seat, several blocks before the inevitable sprawl of tracts began. When Carly called to ask for an appointment, using the same excuse for wanting to talk about Noah Estes that she had with Mr. Tompkins, Mrs. Carpenter expressed pleasure at the possibility of an article on her family but said she could only see her between one-thirty and two.

"I'm a confectioner," she explained, "and my assistant and I have to turn out three large batches of chocolates today."

The house, pink clapboard with frothy white trim, was perfectly suited to a candy-making operation, but the thin, angular woman who greeted Carly didn't look as if she'd sampled many of her wares. In the fragrantly scented living room a tea service was set out, its centerpiece a two-tiered plate of chocolates. Mrs. Carpenter poured and urged Carly to partake, selecting a large nougat for herself. So much for appearances.

After sampling a truffle and pronouncing it wonderful, Carly said, "Mr. Tompkins at Willow Creek says you're the family member who visited Noah Estes most often."

"That's correct. Granddad outlived all his children—a few of his grandchildren, too. I was the only relative living here in town, although the others visited when they could. We all loved him; he was a remarkable man."

"Tell me about him."

"Well, he knew more about horticulture than anyone. He'd studied the geology and ecosystems of the area and until his mid-eighties sat on the boards of a number of environmentally concerned nonprofits. In a way, those seem strange interests for him; after all, his career was in mining. But after he retired, he regretted the destruction that most of his projects had caused, and was determined to make up for it. And living in the shadow of the Knob must have been a constant reminder of how people lay waste to the land."

"The Knob was turned over to the National Parks Service when?"

"In the fifties. Denver Precious Metals had been carrying the land as a tax write-off up to then."

"Why didn't your grandfather follow suit and donate the adjacent property, rather than sell it to Ronald Talbot?"

"Primarily because he was afraid of what might become of it, given the Nixon administration's record on the environment. And then there was Watergate and Nixon's resignation, the uncertainty of what our political climate would evolve into. Granddad felt the land was better off in the hands of an individual whose stewardship he could trust."

"And he trusted Ronald Talbot, a lumberman?"

"Definitely. Ronald Talbot was never a proponent of aggressive, destructive logging, or any logging of old-growth forests. He and my grandfather had worked for decades to promote responsible management of our natural resources. And Mr. Talbot was not interested in mining."

"Why was that important? I thought the veins of ore in that area were played out long ago."

Mrs. Carpenter looked at her watch, then poured more tea. "Oh, no, dear. There's a rich vein of gold in that land, one that Wells Mining never discovered and Denver Precious Metals never searched for, since their focus was only on the slag heaps and low-grade veins at the Knob. My grandfather found out about it after he moved onto the property, and he decided it would never be mined—not by him, his descendants, or future owners. Mr. Talbot agreed, and that stipulation was made one of the terms of purchase."

My God, that's what Hayward and Rawson are after. That's what Ard found out.

During a stop at the county hall of records to view the probated wills of the Talbots, Carly learned that while Ronald Senior had stipulated in his bequest to his son that the mineral rights to the Knob property were not to be sold, transferred, or otherwise exploited, Ronnie's will contained no such provision. Had he ignored or forgotten his father's agreement with Noah Estes? Had he even known about the gold under the new house he'd built there? And if he had known, would he have cared?

Ronnie had struck Carly as one who, because he'd always had enough money, didn't give it much thought. And Deke had been so deep into his art that he was oblivious to their finances. The two had lived well, but not extravagantly, and she doubted that knowing they were literally sitting on a potential gold mine would have impressed either of them.

Thoughts of her friends occupied Carly on the drive back to

Cyanide Wells. She tried to remember the last time she'd seen them alive. Their annual Fourth of July barbecue? No, it had been canceled the year they were killed—something to do with having to go out of town to attend to Deke's seriously ill uncle. A dinner party? Perhaps, but there had been so many of them that they all blurred together. Their Memorial Day celebration had also been canceled, but she did remember Ronnie coming over for lunch on a Saturday early in May; Ard had fixed a crab salad, his favorite, but he had a hangover and didn't eat much. Deke had begged off, saying he needed to finish a painting.

There was one other time, in July, when she'd seen Ronnie alone. He'd appeared at her office unexpectedly on a Wednesday afternoon, when Sev Quill had offered to deliver that week's issue to the printer, leaving her at unaccustomed leisure. She and Ronnie went to Aram's Cafe and sat at a table in the backyard garden, drinking wine and talking of small things.

Natalie's getting so tall. . . . Ard's roses are wonderful this year, even if the wisteria was disappointing. . . . The rhodos out at the preserve near Deer Harbor were terrific, too. . . . We'll have to go see them next year. . . . I found a great recipe for Santa Maria barbecue. . . . That would go well with my recipe for pinto beans. . . . Last week's issue looked good, especially the photo of the mayor that made him look bloated. . . .

At one point Ronnie had held his glass up and squinted at the sunlight playing on the deep red of the merlot. "This is so nice," he said. "I wish it could go on forever."

Now she put on her glasses and reached for the notes Donna Vail had left on her desk. She'd asked the reporter to look up two of the items on Ard's list: CR-92 and moratorium 10/00. Each had continued to elude her, but as a researcher she was easily discouraged; Donna, on the other hand, was tenacious when it came to digging up information. It seemed her efforts had paid off.

Carly—there are hundreds of things that these notations could mean, but the following are the only ones that apply locally.

CR-92: Soledad County Regulation 92, enacted November 11, 1997. Stipulates that new mining may be permitted on privately held property abutting the Eel River National Forest only if mining is currently being conducted on the adjacent 20 square acres within the forest itself. The regulation was designed to prevent blasting and dredging on privately held lands that would harm the ecosystem of the forest. A bill was introduced in the legislature in October 1999 that would have made the regulation invalid, but it was defeated.

Moratorium 10/25/00: moratorium imposed by the Clinton administration on new mining in the Eel River National Forest, to prevent further damage to the ecosystem. Cancelled by Bush administration, 3/20/02. Enviro groups have major concerns about this, as there is renewed interest in the Knob area from two large mining companies. And, of course, it would open up a hell of a lot of privately held acreage abutting it to mining as well.

We really need to do a series on this, Carly. And we really need to designate someone as a reporter on environmental issues. I'm volunteering. This is scary stuff, and I don't know how we've missed it.

Donna

I know how we missed it. I've been so busy dealing with my personal problems that I've failed to pay attention to the larger issues.

Payne and Rawson started the serious pressure on Ard in March, right after the moratorium was canceled. Did Ard know or suspect their reason?

And if she did, why didn't she tell me?

"Excuse me, Carly."

Deputy Shawn Stengel filled up the doorway of her office. The armpits of his brown uniform shirt were sweat-stained, and there was a streak of dirt across his shiny forehead. Not the immaculate image he liked to project.

"Yes, what is it?" She shuffled some papers on the desk, trying to look as if he were interrupting her at an important task.

"I wonder if you'd take a ride over to the substation with me. There's something I'd like you to see."

"I'm busy, Shawn. Can't you just describe it?"

"This won't take long; I'll bring you right back."

Foreboding settled on her as she got to her feet.

She stood by the table in the interview room at the substation, staring down at Natalie's backpack.

"You dragged me over here to look at this?"

"You recognize it?"

"Of course, from the other day at the well."

"Not from before?"

"What's this about?"

"It belongs to Ms. Coleman's daughter, Natalie. We took it to the school, asked the kids if they knew whose it was. Three of her friends recognized it from this." He fingered the tear in the outside zipper compartment. "They remembered she was upset when it happened, while she was crawling under a barb-wire fence to take a shortcut."

Damn.

"You sure you don't recognize it?"

"I don't know. I guess it could be Nat's. I don't pay all that much attention to her stuff. Something's in fashion, she's got it; then it's out of fashion, and she gets rid of it. Kids . . ."

"I hear you." Stengel propped a hip on the table and folded his arms across his barrel chest. "The teacher says Natalie hasn't been to school this week, and when I stopped by the house, nobody was home."

"She and Ard . . . went out of town."

"During the school year?"

"It's an educational trip."

Stengel looked skeptical but didn't ask where they'd gone. "One other thing, Carly." He reached for a paper sack he'd carried in from his cruiser and placed it on the table next to the pack. "When I couldn't reach Ms. Coleman, I decided to search the well where the backpack was found. There were some textbooks buried under the rubble at the bottom. No name in them, but I noticed something in this math workbook." He flipped its pages and held it out.

A heart with an arrow through it. *Natalie loves Duane.*

Well, now we know the kid's straight.

An absurd thought to pop into her mind at a time like this. She fought off the urge to laugh, knowing she'd sound hysterical. "I don't understand why those things were buried."

"Me, either. You going to be talking with Ms. Coleman?"

"Eventually."

"Will you ask her to ask Natalie about the pack?"

"Of course. I'm as curious as you are."

"Another thing: the fellow who dragged this up from the well. You know him?"

"Yes, he's an employee at the paper. John Crowe, my staff photographer. Why?"

"I'd like to talk with him. You have his address?"

"I can give it to you when you take me back to the office. Is that all, Shawn?"

"For now." He stood. "One thing occurred to me—that this is a prank Natalie's friends have pulled. You know, steal the pack, throw it down the well."

"That's probably what happened."

"What doesn't fit, though, is, I asked the kids what kind of stuff Natalie kept in the pack. They mentioned a Palm Pilot. Why wasn't it there?"

"She was using it when they took the pack? One of them stole it? I don't have a clue."

"And why didn't she report the missing pack to her teacher? Or her mother?"

"Maybe she did."

"Not the teacher, anyway. I asked."

"Well, she could have told Ardis. I haven't been paying much attention to what goes on with Nat lately—work pressures, you know."

Stengel nodded in understanding. "Well, I'll run you back now. Let me know when you talk with Ms. Coleman."

If I ever talk with her again . . .

Matthew Lindstrom

Salt Point Estates, Western Soledad County
Tuesday, May 14, 2002

att had spent the morning taking photographs for next week's issue—an overturned truck at the Talbot's Mills off-ramp, and the town's most senior citizen—and then spent the rest of the day trying to track down Gar Payne. The trail led from the Meadows to the office Payne shared with Milt Rawson in Cyanide Wells, to a tract of land his secretary said he was checking out on the ridge, and finally to a new seaside housing development some twelve miles north of Calvert's Landing.

As he followed the sinuous curves of a secondary road from the ridgeline to the coast highway, he felt the temperature drop in steady increments. The afternoon was brilliantly clear, and through the redwoods he caught glimpses of the placid water. Cabins were tucked under the trees at the ends of dirt driveways;

satellite TV dishes stood in clearings; dead cars, old tires, and cast-off appliances lurked under low-hanging branches. A poor section of a relatively poor county, where existence was hand-to-mouth and people wasted minimal effort on beautifying their surroundings.

At the coast road, all that changed. A wood-and-stone hotel hugged the clifftop, its grounds landscaped in purple-blossomed ice plant and twisted cypress trees, its parking lot filled with expensive vehicles. Redwood Cove Inn, obviously a popular place. He turned north past a Victorian bed-and-breakfast, a gallery, a tricked-up country store. A few miles farther, and he spotted the split-rail fence that marked the boundary of Payne and Rawson's newest development.

For the first mile and a half the land was wild and overgrown; a weathered barn stood as a monument to the tract's days as a working ranch. He turned in at the main entrance toward the lodge and restaurant, where he'd been told he could find Payne; both buildings were in the earliest stages of construction. An earthmover stood idle beside a double-wide trailer, and only one vehicle, Payne's Jag, was parked there. Matt pulled up beside it, got out of the Jeep, and knocked on the trailer's door.

"Around here," Payne's voice called.

He skirted the trailer, through knee-high weeds to the side that faced the sea. Payne was seated in a green plastic chair, a can of beer in hand. When he saw Matt, his mouth drew down in displeasure.

"What the hell're you doing here?"

"Looking to have a talk with you."

"We talked enough at Carly's on Sunday."

"I don't think so."

Payne looked at his watch. "You've got thirty seconds to get off my property."

"Or you'll . . . ?"

"Get the goddamned sheriff on your ass." He patted a cell phone clipped to his belt.

"Aren't you interested in what I have to say? I would be, if I were you." Perversely he parroted the words Payne had used in the anonymous phone call that had lured him to Soledad County.

"Okay, so say it, and get off my land."

"Fair enough. Carly McGuire asked me to deliver a message."

"Oh?" A glimmering of interest now.

"She doesn't appreciate you pressuring her partner to sell you the Talbot property. Or that you called Matt Lindstrom, Ardis's former husband, and told him where she is."

Payne was caught off guard. "Shit, how'd she find out about that? Lindstrom never showed."

"Yes, he did. He came to their house a few days after you called him. What exactly did you hope to accomplish?"

"I figured if he went public with who Ardis was, she'd be discredited. Then the bank would take over the administration of the Talbot estate, and I could deal with someone rational."

"Or maybe you hoped Lindstrom was a violent man who would do what they said he did to her all those years ago."

Payne sipped beer and looked at the sea, but a tic at the corner of his mouth gave him away.

Matt asked, "How'd you find out about Lindstrom?"

"By accident. One of those true-life TV shows when I was in the Midwest visiting relatives. You know—'This woman disappeared. Do you know where she is now?' I recognized Ardis right off. Lindstrom was harder to find, but even people who want to get lost permanently leave traces that a good private detective can follow."

Especially since he hadn't really tried to get lost. He'd simply walked away.

Payne asked, "So where's Lindstrom now?"

"Home, I suppose. They got things straightened out, and then he left. He didn't appreciate what you did, either."

"Wait a minute—how'd he know I was the one who called him?"

"Ardis and Carly suspected you because of your interest in the Talbot property. So they arranged for him to listen to your voice, and he made a positive identification. Not smart, Payne. If Carly decides to publish an account of your shenanigans, it might make people think twice about contributing to your campaign fund. And if Mack Travis and Andy D'Angelo weren't both dead, they'd be in a position to scuttle all your political aspirations."

Payne flushed, his scar turning livid. He hurled his beer can into the weeds. "For somebody who's been around—what? A week?—you've sure gotten cozy with McGuire and Coleman. You into dykes, Crowe?"

"I'm into good people, Payne. And I hate to see them pushed around by scumbags like you."

Payne growled, then struggled from his chair, staggering before he gained footing. He loomed over Matt, thrust his index finger into his face. "I want you off my property *now!* The clock is ticking."

Matt backed off, slowly. "I've delivered Carly's message. I'm going."

It wasn't more than five minutes before Payne's Jag exited the development and turned south, moving fast. Matt pulled out from under the low branches of a cypress tree and followed it to the Redwood Cove Inn. Payne left his car in a far corner of the lot and went into the lobby. Matt waited half a minute before he approached.

Inside the double glass doors he could see a large timbered room with a huge stone fireplace at one end and a bar to the right side. Leather chairs and high-backed sofas were arranged in groupings across its floor, screened from one another by bamboo in planter boxes. Payne was disappearing around one of the stands of canes, and Matt saw the outline of his tall body fold as he sat. A waiter in a white jacket moved toward him.

Two armchairs, both empty, backed up on this side of the bamboo screen, only feet from where Payne had settled.

Take a chance, Matt told himself. What're the odds he'll see me there? And if he does, so what? Man's got a right to stop in for a drink. Even the sheriff would agree with me on that point.

He walked over, sank onto the soft leather. Another waiter materialized; Matt waved him away. Behind him Payne was speaking, just loudly enough to be heard. To the waiter? No, on his phone.

"He left yet? . . . Damn! You think he'll call in? . . . Good. When he does, tell him I'm at Redwood Cove, not the development. . . . In the bar. . . . Thanks, Cheryl."

Cheryl, the secretary at Payne and Rawson's Cyanide Wells office. The partner must be on his way to the coast.

Matt sat back, looked around the lobby. A number of handsome, well-fed cats lounged on the furnishings. Outside a window wall across from the bar was a courtyard with a lily pond; a woman sat at the pond's edge, feeding kibble from a bucket to a family of raccoons. The mother and two babies were so tame, they ate from her hand. Guests wandered in and out, took seats at the bar, lounged in front of the fireplace. After a short period of silence, Payne began to make other calls.

"Jenny, I'm out at the cove. Something's come up, and I'll probably stay the night. See you tomorrow."

"Ben, what the hell's the story on our interim financing? . . . Yeah, I know. . . . Okay, we'll talk in the morning."

"Sandra, we got your Visa bill this week, and your mother and I are seriously upset with your spending. Hold the plastic, will you?"

"Cheryl, did he call in? . . . He wants what? . . . A double, two olives. Got it."

Next came a discussion with the waiter about a Bombay gin martini to be delivered as soon as his partner arrived. Then Payne made several other calls, none of consequence. Obviously he was an individual who couldn't bear to be disconnected.

Fifteen minutes later a rotund, red-faced man in chinos and a hideous lime-green shirt waddled through the entrance, paused to look around, then crossed the room toward the sofa where Payne sat. He didn't even glance at Matt as he went by.

"So where's my drink?" he demanded.

"David's bringing it. Sit down. We've got a problem."

"The financing . . ."

"Is the least of our worries. That photographer Carly McGuire hired, John Crowe, showed up at Salt Point this afternoon. She knows about my call to Matthew Lindstrom and sent Crowe to inform me of her displeasure."

Matt listened as Payne related the gist of their conversation. "I'm afraid she's going to use it against me, ruin my political career before it gets off the ground, plus make sure we never get our hands on that property."

"Yeah, that's the sort of thing the bitch would do. The . . . other, does she know about that, too?"

"I don't think so."

"Well, even if she does, she wouldn't dare use it. Not after—"

"Here's David with your martini."

Silence. Then, "Thanks, David."

After a pause during which, Matt assumed, he was partaking of his long-awaited drink, Rawson said, "We never should've brought the second husband here. What if McGuire figures it out? We could be implicated in—"

"Get a grip, Milt. There's no way they can connect us to it. Besides, McGuire wants to protect Coleman and the kid. She's not going to make their relationship to him public."

"Speaking of them, where are they? I keep watching the house, following McGuire, and there's no sign of them."

"Maybe she sent them out of town. That's what I'd do. And stop following McGuire. You said she almost caught you a couple of times."

"Well, I never said I trained as a private eye!"

"Dammit, keep your voice down. I don't want to broadcast our business to the entire north coast."

More silence. Then Payne stood, saying he needed the restroom.

Matt was off his chair and on the way to the door.

At a service station in Calvert's Landing he shut himself in a phone booth and got the number of the Incline Village Hyatt Regency from directory assistance. The Hyatt's operator located Dave Rand, the musician with whom he'd talked yesterday, in the restaurant. Yes, Rand said, he had time to answer a few more questions.

"Was Ardis Coleman married to Chase Lewis or just living with him?"

"They got married in September of ninety-two. Down in San Fran. I stood up for him."

"When was their baby born?"

"Their baby?"

"Natalie."

"Oh, guess I didn't make that clear. The kid wasn't Ardis's. She was Chase's, with a woman he'd been seeing a while back. I never knew that one."

So Ardis was not a mother after all, any more than Carly was. This was certainly going to surprise her.

"How'd he end up with the baby?"

"Bitch dropped her off with him right after he and Ardis got married. Was supposed to be just for the weekend, but she didn't show on Sunday like she said she would. They called the number they had for her, but it was disconnected. Nice wedding present, huh? Chase was pissed, but Ardis said she'd raise the kid as her own. But hey, how come you're askin' these things, when you're a family member?"

"It seems Ardis hasn't been completely honest with me. Did she legally adopt the baby?"

"Nope. Couldn't find the mother to get her consent."

"So when Ardis took off with the child, technically she kidnapped her."

"I suppose."

"But Chase didn't go to the police."

"Chase didn't want *nothing* to do with the cops in those days, if you know what I mean. And what the hell was he gonna do with a baby, anyway? He didn't even try to find them, just stepped up his intake of controlled substances."

Matt thanked Rand and headed across the ridgeline to Cyanide Wells.

It was clear to him what Payne and Rawson had been talking about: After their attempt to disrupt Ardis's life by summoning him hadn't worked immediately, they—or more likely their detective—had found the record of her marriage to Chase Lewis. Probably he'd also unearthed the record of Natalie's birth and pieced together what had subsequently happened. Payne and Rawson, realizing they had their hands on very damaging information, had reasoned that bringing Ardis face-to-face with Chase Lewis would make her more willing to deal.

Unfortunately, they hadn't counted on murder entering the equation.

Carly McGuire

Tuesday, May 14, 2002

he didn't know why the house near the Knob continued to draw her, but as she stood in its central hallway, door open to the cool evening breeze, she realized it no longer had the power to haunt her. It was simply a house where happy times had been lived out and a tragedy had occurred. A house that had been cleansed of all signs of that tragedy and rendered bland for sale.

She walked along the central hallway, looking into the silent rooms she knew so well. What struck her now was the lack of clutter. Ronnie had inherited a great many things from his father, a consummate collector, and all of it—books, a model railroad, stamps, coins, firearms, sculptures, animal heads, Indian artifacts, old typewriters—had found its way from the architecturally overwrought mansion where he had grown up to this new, simpler house on the land that once had belonged to

Noah Estes. The things Ronnie didn't care for, such as the animal heads and firearms, were kept out of sight, but most of it
had been on display. Carly supposed the real estate agent had
packed it up so that the house would show better, but its absence made the house seem ordinary. The decor was nice, the
curve of the staircase graceful, but the kitchen was badly designed and the rooms were too small.

No, the house—even if two people hadn't been murdered in
it—was not what made this property desirable; it was the
beauty of the land, the privacy. The house could be razed and
another, more attractive one built. A prospective buyer would
be a fool not to realize that.

So why hadn't there been offers?

Maybe there had. Maybe Ard, as executor of the Talbot estate, had turned them down. Because she knew about the vein
of gold running under the property? Because she was holding
out for a better offer than those, or Payne and Rawson's? An
offer that would allow her to pocket some of the money?

*I'm really starting to doubt her now. Whatever shreds of trust in the
relationship that remained are gone.*

She took hold of the banister and started up the stairs. Going
to the bedroom where Ronnie and Deke died. Going to face her
demons a final time.

Of course, it was no longer the room where she'd viewed
their bloodied and ruined bodies. New paint, wallpaper, and
carpeting had made it innocuous. But when she closed her
eyes, she could picture the bodies on the bed, clad in Japanese
silk robes, their features shattered by the gunshots to their
heads. Blood on the pale-green sheets, the dark-green headboard, the nightstand . . .

What, McGuire? What is it?

She'd lost the image.

She moved to the center of the room, looked around. It was

easily the most attractive in the house: French doors led to a balcony overlooking the pool area; window seats were tucked into alcoves on either side of them; bookcases flanked a stone fireplace. There was a large bath with a Jacuzzi tub, a huge walk-in closet.

The door to the closet was open, and out of idle curiosity she looked inside. Cardboard cartons were stacked there—probably containing the collections that had formerly cluttered the main floor. They would fetch a good price at an auction house, but apparently Ard had yet to get around to arranging for their sale. She stepped inside and followed a path through them, confirming their contents from their labels. Felt a thump on her head as it connected with the long, heavy chain that lowered the folding stairs to the attic.

Deke's studio—the one prospective buyers and the occasional interviewer or photographer were invited into—was in an outbuilding beyond the garage and greenhouse, but he'd done his actual work in the attic, under several big skylights. When Ronnie built the house, he hadn't yet met Deke, and by the time his partner declared his fondness for the attic space and had the skylights installed, it would have been prohibitively expensive to create easier access. Deke didn't mind—he was the only one who went up there, even barring Ronnie from the place where he entertained his muse. In fact, he liked to joke about entering his work space by way of a "secret passageway."

But Deke was dead, and now Carly wanted to see the studio where he'd created his paintings. She'd neglected to turn on the overhead fixture, though, and she couldn't see all that well. Craning her neck, she looked up to gauge if there was enough clearance to pull the stairs down, and saw something striped suspended from the framework of the trapdoor. A bag? Odd place to hang something—

A man's voice called out to her from downstairs.

*   *   *

"Detective Grossman. What are you doing here?" Nervously she ran her hand over her hair, brushing at a spiderweb that must have caught there while she'd been poking around in the closet.

"So formal, Carly." The tall gray-haired man smiled thinly. In his conservative blue suit, the recently appointed head of the Soledad County Sheriff's Department Investigations Bureau looked out of place for the countryside.

"Sorry, Ned. You startled me. Why're you here?"

"I could ask you the same."

"I, uh, received a message that the property is being shown tomorrow. Ardis is out of town, so I decided to make sure everything's in shape."

"Isn't that the real estate agent's job?"

"Well, yes, but we can't always count on her. Did you follow me here? It's not a place that you'd be driving by and decide to stop in."

"Actually, Deputy Stengel followed you and reported your whereabouts to me. I ordered him to maintain a surveillance on you."

"For what reason?"

"We'll discuss that at headquarters in Santa Carla."

When she entered the interview room, the first person she saw was Rhoda Swift.

"Carly." Swift nodded and motioned for her to sit. Grossman shut the door and sat next to Rhoda.

Carly said, "What's this about, Rho?"

"It's come to our attention that your interest in our West-haven homicide is more than professional."

It was what she'd feared. "I don't understand."

"I think you do. But let me fill you in on our investigation so far. In the absence of witnesses, fingerprints, and the murder weapon, we began by building a profile of the victim, Chase Lewis. Born, San Francisco. Only child—both parents deceased. Graduate, Balboa High School. Two semesters, City College. Talented trombonist, played with pickup bands while working as a security guard, and eventually turned professional musician. The lifestyle caught up with him; he was arrested several times for drug-and-alcohol-related offenses but served no serious jail time. Known to become violent when high, particularly against women. In September of nineteen ninety-two he married one Ardis Lynette Coleman in a civil ceremony at City Hall."

"*Married?*"

Rhoda nodded. "Apparently they were still married when he died."

She felt as if she'd been punched in the stomach. This news made Ard's betrayal of her complete.

"You didn't know?" Rhoda asked.

She shook her head.

"Well, there's no record of a divorce, either in California or Nevada. And another interesting thing: There's no record of Natalie's birth, at least not to Ardis. But Chase Lewis did father a child, by a woman named Marisa Wilson, in July of 'ninety-two. And the child was called Natalie."

"My God." She pressed her fingers to her lips. After a moment she asked, "This Marisa Wilson—where is she now?"

"She died of a drug overdose in San Diego eight years ago."

"Did Ardis adopt Natalie?"

"There's no record of it."

"So she has no legal right to her?"

"We'd like to question her about that—among other things."

Meaning Chase Lewis's murder.

Rhoda went on, "I understand you told Deputy Stengel that Ardis has taken Natalie out of town on an educational trip."

Carly ignored Rhoda's words and asked, "If it turns out that Ardis has no legal right to Natalie, what'll become of her?"

"She'll be made a ward of the court and placed in a foster home while Social Services searches for blood relatives. If there aren't any, or they don't want her, she'll be put up for adoption."

"An older mixed-race child? She's not a very likely candidate. Why would they take her from a perfectly viable home, one where she's loved and cared for?"

"The decision as to the viability of that home would be up to the individual judge. But to get back to the original subject: Do you know where we can reach Ardis?"

Make up something to buy time. Camping in Yosemite, maybe.

No, you've lied enough, McGuire. Don't put yourself at further risk. They think Ard—or maybe even you—killed Chase Lewis.

She said, "I want to speak to my attorney."

Matthew Lindstrom

Wednesday, May 15, 2002

att leaned across the Jeep's passenger seat and opened the door for Carly as she stepped from her attorney's car in the alley behind the *Spectrum*'s offices. She slumped in the seat, slammed the door, and stared straight ahead.

"You okay?" he asked.

A shrug.

"Talk to me, Carly."

She sighed, and then the words came—haltingly at first, but soon tumbling out so fast that it was difficult for him to understand her; several times he had to ask her to speak more slowly. When she got to the part about Rhoda Swift telling her Ardis had married Chase Lewis and later taken his child, her voice broke.

Quickly he said, "I know about that. Doesn't matter how I found out. Go on."

"They suspect either Ard or me of killing Lewis. After my attorney got there, they asked if I owned a gun, had been to the motel in Westhaven prior to the time I showed up there on Monday. Kept pressuring me to tell them where Ard is. Wanted to know if there was trouble in the relationship. That's when my attorney cut off the interview. They've got no evidence, so they can't hold me, but I'm sure they'll continue the surveillance. A car followed us from Santa Carla, and it's probably parked at the end of the alley."

"How long d'you suppose they've been watching you?"

She shook her head. "Don't know. I need you to do something for me."

"What?"

"Drive me to the house by the Knob to get my truck."

"No problem." He reached for the ignition.

She stayed his hand with her fingertips. "There's more. When I was there this afternoon, I went to the master bedroom, and I had an impression—one of those half-memories that won't quite come to the surface. Something related to what I saw the morning after the murders. I think it's important, and I need to get at it."

"Carly, under the circumstances I don't think it's wise for you to go back to that house."

"I don't, either. But you could. Do you have your camera with you?"

"My camera? Why . . . ?"

"Good. After I drive away, take it and photograph the master bedroom from a lot of different angles. Maybe when I study the prints they'll trigger—"

"No."

"The deputies aren't interested in you. They'll follow me."

"No, Carly. I'm not breaking and entering."

"I have a key to the house. And you have my permission."

"The key was given to you by Ronnie Talbot?"

"Yes."

"He's dead, and Ardis is executor of the estate."

"So?"

"Then only she or the real estate agent, acting on her instructions, can give me permission."

"Since when're you a lawyer?"

The familiar testiness in her voice relieved rather than annoyed him; at least some measure of the old Carly remained. "I was prelaw in college and have done extensive reading in the field."

"Well, aren't you the renaissance man!"

Now she *was* pissing him off. "Look, I know you're upset, but—"

"Okay, sorry. Maybe I'd be handling the situation better if it only involved Ard and me. At this point I'd probably have no trouble saying fuck it and cooperating fully with the sheriff's department. But it also involves Nat."

"No matter what, Ardis would never hurt her."

"She's not the one I'm worried about. It's the sheriff's department." She twisted to face him, her back against the door. "In spite of people like Rho Swift and Ned Grossman, it's one of the worst in the state. The county doesn't have enough money to attract many good people, and there's still a stigma attached to the department."

"What kind of stigma?"

"You remember I said Rho Swift cracked an old case a few years back? It was a mass murder that had gone unsolved for thirteen years. Eight people, two of them children, shot to death in an isolated canyon south of Signal Port. The department mishandled it, but you can scarcely blame them; they'd simply never encountered a crime of that magnitude. By the time the feds stepped in, much of the evidence had been lost or tainted, so they weren't able to solve it, either. In the aftermath, a lot of the departmental personnel moved to other jurisdictions or got out of law enforcement entirely. The rest just became more and more demoralized."

"But you said the case was solved."

"Yes, but it takes more than a few years to build up a good department. It's getting better, but recently there have been some disturbing incidents."

"Such as?"

Carly sat up straighter, ran her fingers through her hair. "An overzealous pursuit of a speeding tourist in an SUV by a new deputy—it rolled, and the driver, his wife, and two young children were killed. A hostage situation during which an estranged husband and his five-year-old daughter were fatally shot by deputies who wouldn't wait for trained negotiators to be brought in. Another fatal shooting, this time of a ten-year-old boy whose father was using him as a decoy while stealing at a convenience store."

"Jesus."

"What I'm saying, Lindstrom, is that our deputies are not well enough trained to evaluate a situation and protect the innocents who are involved in it. Too often they shoot first and make excuses afterwards. If for some reason Ard and Nat are still in the county . . ."

"Okay, I understand. But I don't see the connection between what you half remembered in the Talbot house and the current situation."

"I just have a feeling there is one. Call it woman's intuition, if you will, but it's very strong."

Carly's expression was close to pleading; asking for this favor must be costing her a great deal. And what would it cost him to do as she asked?

Taking photographs in an empty house wasn't like knocking over a liquor store.

"Okay," he said, "I'll do it."

After the truck's taillights disappeared down the long eucalyptus-lined driveway, Matt waited, fingering the key Carly had slipped from her ring and pressed into his hand. He was sure they'd been followed here, having glimpsed a pair of headlights in the distance behind them, and a car moving slowly past after they'd turned in. Now he wanted to make sure it tailed Carly back home. After an interval of no more than thirty seconds it drove by again, more swiftly—a nondescript dark sedan. Soon the sound of its engine faded into the distance.

Matt continued to wait, listening in case another car arrived. There was no logical reason for the sheriff's department to maintain a surveillance on him; they must not yet know he was Ardis's former husband, since they hadn't mentioned him during their interview with Carly. But he decided to play it safe anyway.

Rustlings in the underbrush. Tree branches soughing. A distant howl: coyote. The wind picked up, warm, bringing with it a familiar scent. He breathed in deeply, felt a tug of emotion. Gardenias . . .

A formal affair at the faculty club in Saugatuck, in honor of some visiting dignitary whose name and field he'd long since forgotten. Near the end of the spring semester, a warm, balmy night. Men ill at ease in dinner jackets, many of them rented; women in long dresses, purchased at great strain to the academic family's budget. He and Gwen in their first public appearance as a couple, she in dark blue silk, his gardenia corsage on her wrist. An appearance of professor and student made possible by the diamond ring on her left hand.

Unsettling rumors about Matt Lindstrom and Gwen Standish had circulated through the tightly knit college community for months, so his colleagues' reactions were more relieved than surprised when he presented her as his wife-to-be. Better to marry, even unsuitably, than to burn in academic hell. The chairman of his department told her how lovely she looked and how fortunate Matt was; the president of the college took her hands and held them longer than was proper, saying she'd make a fine faculty wife.

As the party was winding down, they walked across the wide lawn to the lakeshore, where other couples stood admiring the play of the Japanese lanterns on the water. "That wasn't so bad," Gwen, who had been dreading the evening, said. "Not bad at all," Matt, who had been looking forward to showing her off, replied. "They loved you," he added. "*I* love you." As he kissed her, she put her hand on the back of his neck, the gardenias brushing his cheek, their scent becoming one that would forever take him back to that night. . . .

His face was wet. He put a hand to his eyes. Crying, for all the lost nights and lost days. For the woman he'd only imagined Gwen was.

Angrily he brushed the tears away and got out of the Jeep, turning on its headlights so he could navigate without stumbling, grabbing his camera bag. He was furious that he could still allow Gwen's memory to wound him, and fury made him careless. When a car's engine roared to life nearby, he froze, looking around.

Headlights bore down on him from the rear of the property, where Carly had said the stables, studio, and garage stood.

Boxy vehicle, a van gathering speed. He threw himself to the side, sprawled down. As he tried to pull himself up, scramble out of the way, he saw Gwen behind the wheel, mouth set in a grim line, face pale in the wash of his own headlights.

She wrenched the wheel—too late. Their gazes were still locked when the van smashed into his lunging body. . . .

A hand touched his forehead, light and cool.

He tried to open his eyes. Couldn't.

Couldn't move, either.

Footsteps hurried away.

Pain. His chest, his hip, his arm.

Something draped over him. Warm.

Sleep . . .

Motion. Flashing light in his eyes.

"Get him stabilized."

"What the hell happened here?"

"Who called it in?"

"Medevac chopper's on its way."

Pricking in his arm.

Darkness . . .

"Matt?"

Carly's voice.

He opened his eyes. Winced and shut them. His head hurt like hell.

"Matt?"

"Don't shout." The words came out a croak.

"I'm not. Here, let me give you some water."

When he opened his eyes this time, he saw her face. Strained, tired. She looked almost as bad as he felt. She raised his head, made him sip through a straw, but most of the water dribbled into his beard and onto his chest. She took the cup away, swiped at him. "Is that better?"

"Some. Feel smithereened."

"I don't think that's a word."

"Don't care. How I feel."

"You'll mend. Nothing serious was broken in the accident."

"Accident?"

"We'll talk about it later."

"Now." He tried to grab her arm, but it hurt too much to raise his hand.

"Later. You need your rest."

Thursday, May 16, 2002
Santa Carla, California

he did this to you? That bitch! I'd like to—"

"Carly, stop."

"I will not stop! This is the absolute last straw!"

"Keep your voice down."

She compressed her lips, glancing back at the door to his hospital room and frowning.

He said, "She didn't know it was me. When she realized who I was, she tried to turn the van away, but it was too late. She covered me with a blanket, called for help."

"And cut and ran again, accepting no responsibility. Left you lying there. You could've been dying, for all she knew."

"Well, I wasn't."

"And where was Nat while Ard was running you down? Did she see the whole thing happen?"

"I don't know."

"What the hell does Ard think she's doing, skulking around the Talbot place like some demented ghost?"

"Carly, please stop. The pain medication finally kicked in, and you're making my head hurt all over again."

"This pain medication—it doesn't make you woozy?"

"I don't think so. Why?"

"Because Ned Grossman's out in the hall, waiting to speak with you. I think you should tell him the whole story."

"That I was struck by an unknown driver."

"It's too late to play these games."

"This is not a game." He grasped her arm. "There is unfinished business here. Our business, yours and mine. I want us to be the ones who conclude it."

"If the doc hadn't told me differently, I'd say you sustained brain damage along with the cracked ribs, concussion, and sprained ankle."

"Don't forget the assorted scrapes and bruises."

She glared at him.

"Lighten up, McGuire," he told her. "And get ready—we've got a job to do."

"You didn't get a look at the van's driver, and you can't identify the make or model," Detective Grossman said.

"It was dark, and the headlights blinded me."

"Perhaps we could start from the beginning. What were you doing at the Talbot property?"

He closed his eyes, took a moment to frame his reply. "My employer, Ms. McGuire, phoned me and asked that I drive her there to retrieve her truck."

"Why you and not her attorney? He drove her back to Cyanide Wells."

"I assume because he charges by the hour. Besides, she's been having difficulty with the truck—something wrong with the starter. I fixed it for her the other day, and she wanted me there in case it acted up again." An easily verifiable explanation—the story of his getting his job because of his mechanic's skills had made the rounds.

"So you drove her there. Then what?"

"The truck started right up. She drove off and . . ." Jesus, where was he going with this hastily improvised scenario?

"Mr. Crowe?"

"Could I have some water, please?"

Grossman picked up the cup on the nightstand, handed it to him. Matt thought furiously as he sipped through the straw.

"Okay," he said. "I was going to follow her, but as I started to leave, I noticed another vehicle tucked away in the shadows. Ms. McGuire had told me the property is vacant and up for sale, so I decided to investigate. I guess I frightened the occupants, because the driver started the engine and peeled off. I didn't get out of the way in time."

Grossman frowned. "Previously you said you didn't see the driver, but now you say occupants, plural."

"I had the impression of two people. Teenagers, I suppose, parking in a place where they didn't think they'd be interrupted."

"Possibly." Grossman paused, studying his fingernails. "There was an anonymous call about you to nine-one-one. Came from a pay phone at the entrance to the national forest. A woman. And someone covered you with a handwoven blanket."

"So the doctor told me."

"Do you have any recollection of them covering you?"

"No. I guess it was the people in the van."

"That was our original assumption. But one of my men found the door of the house ajar; he entered to see if anyone was hiding inside, and found a matching blanket on the back of the sofa in the living room. Then he searched the premises. There were signs of recent occupancy."

"Maybe the people in the van were using the house for a tryst?"

"If so, they had a key. There were no signs of forced entry. Is it possible that someone with access to a key had reason to lie in wait and run you down?"

"I don't know who would have a key, detective. And I've only been in Soledad County ten days. I haven't had time to offend anyone to that degree."

"Are you sure of that . . . Mr. Lindstrom?"

Hearing his real name sent shock waves along his spine; he couldn't think of a reply.

Grossman added, "When Detective Swift heard that John Crowe, the newspaper's new photographer, had been injured in a hit-and-run, she contacted me and told me about her encounter with Matthew Lindstrom on the highway last weekend. One of the names had to be false, so we ran a check. The real John Crowe is running Matthew Lindstrom's charter business in Port Regis, British Columbia, in Lindstrom's absence.

"Matthew Lindstrom is not listed in this state's criminal files, and the FBI has no record of him. He hasn't committed a crime—that we know of. But a man doesn't leave a profitable business and a community where he's liked and respected to live elsewhere under an assumed name. Unless, of course, there is something that draws him to that community. Something that he wants to keep secret."

Now, Grossman, who had been standing the whole time, pulled a chair uncomfortably close to Matt's bed, sat, and placed his hand on the mattress. In a confidential tone he said, "I'm no world-beater, Mr. Lindstrom. I don't make much money, have terrible luck with women, worse luck at poker, and even my dog doesn't much like me. But I am a good cop, and to me that means being impartial until all the facts are in. You help me, and I guarantee I'll do my best to help you out of whatever trouble currently has you by the short hairs."

In the absence of a viable alternative Matt told Grossman his story—part of it, anyway. Gwen's disappearance. The suspicion that had destroyed his life. The anonymous phone call. His decision to come to Cyanide Wells, photograph and confront her.

"She must've seen me somewhere," he concluded, "and was afraid I'd come here to harm her, because she's taken her little girl out of town. Even Carly McGuire doesn't know where they've gone."

"And did you intend to harm her?"

"Emotionally, maybe. But not physically."

"Strange, you and the other husband appearing at around the same time."

"I guess one of us was to be backup, in case the other didn't show."

"And you've got no idea who your caller was?"

"I'm working on that."

"Care to share your thoughts with me?"

"Not yet."

"Fair enough. When you came here, did you know Ardis Coleman had married again?"

"No."

"Or that she was living in a lesbian relationship?"

"No."

"Do you own a gun?"

"I have a flare gun aboard my charter boat."

"No handguns? Rifles? Shotguns?"

"No. I don't care for firearms."

"Have you ever been to Westport?"

"No."

"Okay, let's talk about Carly McGuire: Did she know who you were when she hired you?"

"No."

"Does she know now?"

"Yes."

"How'd she find out?"

"Detective Swift mentioned rescuing me on the highway to Severin Quill, the police reporter. He told Carly."

"And what was Carly's reaction?"

"I'm lucky to still be alive."

Grossman smiled thinly. "Obviously the two of you have gotten past that, since she's paying your hospital bill." He got to his feet. "Okay, Mr. Lindstrom, I'll get back to you."

After the door closed behind the detective, Matt expelled his breath in a long sigh. Then he reached for the phone on the nightstand, called Carly's number, and left a detailed message about the talk with Grossman on her machine. Finally he phoned Sam at the Chicken Shack.

"John!" she exclaimed. "I went to the hospital, but you were sedated and they wouldn't let me see you. How are—"

"The doctor says they'll release me this afternoon. Can you pick me up? There's something I need to do."

Carly McGuire

Thursday, May 16, 2002

n the time it took to drive from the hospital in Santa Carla to Cyanide Wells, Carly formulated a plan. Not the best of plans, perhaps, but one that would make her feel she was doing something, plus keep her mind off what Ard had done to Matt.

When she'd been admitted to his hospital room the first time—a privilege extended to her because she was his employer and paying his bill—he'd seemed diminished, more a hurt boy than a man. His groggy confusion and the scrapes and bruises that covered his face and arms wrenched at her, and she regretted every caustic word she'd spoken to him over the past week and a half. But today she'd witnessed the return of his steadiness and strength—his quiet determination, too, as he'd insisted that the two of them would see this matter through to its conclusion. Alone she might not have attempted that, but

Matt was a person she could lean on. She'd come to respect this man who had been far too good for Ardis.

Just as I was far too good for her.

Giving mental voice to the concept failed to surprise her, as it might have yesterday or the day before. For years she'd been accustomed to making excuses for Ard's actions and failings, had taken her back and forgiven her. But when Matt had said, "Ardis was driving the van that hit me," the past fourteen years' worth of abuse from her partner had become inexcusable, unforgiveable. And she'd allowed herself to see the relationship for exactly what it was.

Just like that. In an instant. Truth.

As she drove through town and headed east toward the Knob, she noticed an old brown station wagon following at a discreet distance and smiled wryly. Deputy Shawn Stengel's family car. He couldn't have maintained surveillance on her in his cruiser, but did he really think she hadn't seen him toting his brood around in that oversized machine? Either Shawn wasn't as smart as she'd thought, or he underestimated her powers of observation.

She drove past her own turnoff at Drinkwater Road and, after three quarters of a mile, signaled left onto Spyglass Trail. The two-lane blacktop snaked north into the hills, between rocky outcroppings where stubborn vegetation clung, passed through a grove of aspen, then hooked in a series of switchbacks to the west. After a mile or so, the Spyglass Roadhouse appeared.

Its central portion resembled a log cabin with a peaked roof, and jutting off it were long rough-board wings, windowless with flat roofs. On one of them sat an enormous satellite TV dish. A few cars were in the unpaved parking lot, but now, at two in the afternoon, the place had a lifeless look. Carly pulled up near the entrance and went inside, momentarily blinded by the darkness.

Two men in workshirts and jeans sat at the near end of the bar, watching a soap opera on the big screen, where a couple were cuddling in bed—the woman with perfect makeup, the man with impeccably groomed hair. The woman exclaimed, "I've never experienced anything as wonderful as last night!"

One of the watchers said to the screen, "Yeah, so where'd you and lover-boy spend it? The beauty parlor?"

Carly spotted a red-haired woman who resembled the description Matt had given her of Janet Tremaine at the far end of the bar, sitting on one of the stools, a solitaire game spread before her. As she started toward her, the waitress looked up and smiled.

"Ms. McGuire, why're you here? Nobody's shot up the place in maybe two weeks."

Carly slipped onto the stool next to her. The goddamn saddle seats were sized for men and hurt in all the wrong places. "You know who I am?" she asked.

"Sure, everybody does. Newspaper editor, important person."

"The editor of the *New York Times* is important. I'm not. Business is light today, huh?"

"Yeah." Tremaine went back to her solitaire game.

"Black ten on the red jack," Carly said.

"Huh?"

"That'll win it for you. Then I'll buy you a beer."

"I shouldn't—"

"Nonsense, it's not like you're a cop on duty. I'm having an IPA."

Tremaine swept the cards into a pile. "Well, okay. Thanks." She went behind the bar, drew drafts, and slid Carly's over to her.

Carly stood. "Let's go sit in a booth."

Tremaine's eyes grew wary.

"Come on." Carly walked toward the far side of the room.

After telling the bartender she was taking a break, Tremaine followed.

"What's this about?" she asked as she sat down opposite Carly.

"Mack Travis."

"Not you, too? A so-called army buddy of his was in here asking about him the other night. Was he one of your people?"

"Uh-huh."

"I *told* him to lay off—"

"Janet, don't you think the cover-up's gone on long enough?"

"What cover-up?"

"You know. It's time you told the whole story."

"There's nothing to tell."

"Yes, there is, and you need to get it out in the open. Keeping secrets like that can damage a person."

"Secrets? What secrets?"

"You know."

"I don't!" She glanced around the room, lowered her voice. "Really, I don't."

"You told my employee that he didn't know who and what he was dealing with. You know what that says to me? It says you've been silenced by powerful people. Who are they?"

Tremaine's shoulders slumped, and she leaned forward. "Listen, I'm scared."

"Well, I'm not. And I can help you."

Silence.

"Tell me what you know, Janet."

"So you can publish it in your newspaper?"

"No, so you won't have to be afraid anymore."

". . . Oh, hell. What've I got to lose? I'll tell you."

*   *   *

Carly spun the truck's tires as she left the Roadhouse parking lot, sending up a spray of gravel. She vented her anger by taking the switchbacks of Spyglass Trail at a dangerous speed. Behind her, Shawn Stengel struggled to keep up in his clumsy station wagon.

Halfway down, somewhat calmer, she found a wide spot, pulled off, and waited for the deputy. Stengel was driving so fast that he almost missed seeing her. When he did, he slammed on the brakes, fishtailed to a stop, then put the car in reverse and backed onto the shoulder. As he got out and walked toward her, she called, "Hey, Shawn."

"Carly."

"Anybody ever tell you that you stick out in that big boat?"

"Anybody ever tell you it's dangerous driving like that in a truck?"

"So how come you're following me?"

"Grossman's orders. What were you doing at the Roadhouse?"

"I felt the need of a cold one." Before he could speak, she held up her hand. "That's *one,* Shawn, over more than an hour. My blood alcohol level's legal."

"I don't doubt that. But why the Roadhouse? I've never known you to go slumming."

"There're lots of things you've never known me to do. Doesn't mean I haven't done them. You planning on following me around forever?"

"Till Grossman lifts the surveillance." The deputy leaned against the truck's tailgate, arms folded across his chest. "Hell, Carly, you think I like spying on you? If you'd just tell Grossman what you know about the murder—"

"You mean tell Grossman what he wants to hear."

Stengel shrugged. "He's a good cop. If he senses he's onto

something, he probably is. It's damned suspicious, Ms. Coleman disappearing at the same time her husband got killed."

"She didn't disappear. She went out of town. Before Chase Lewis was murdered."

"And without telling you where she was going?"

"That's right."

He sighed. "So where're we headed next?"

"My house. You can wait out front all night if you like. I'll even bring you a sandwich and some coffee."

"You know, I think I'll take you up on that. And do me a favor? Take it easy the rest of the way down."

With Stengel close behind, she drove carefully toward the flatlands, thinking over what Janet Tremaine had told her.

On the morning after Ronnie Talbot's and Deke Rutherford's murders, Janet was awakened by a banging on the door of her trailer, in a mobile home park outside of Talbot's Mills. She opened it to Mack Travis. Mack was a mess: rumpled, babbling, shaky, and drunk. Afraid her mostly old and retired neighbors would report his visit to the park manager—there had been previous complaints about him—she quickly pulled him inside. He was unsteady on his feet, so she shoved him into the armchair in front of the TV and, at his request, brought him her bottle of Southern Comfort—a liquor he hated but which he sucked down as he began talking.

Talking of bodies and blood. Of a gun and the smell of burnt powder. Of how Gar Payne and Milt Rawson would kill him. Of how he wished he were dead, too.

Over and over he mumbled and whimpered and eventually cried. Finally he passed out in the chair, and Janet, unsure whether what he'd said was real or an alcoholic delusion, left him there to sleep it off while she went to her noon-to-eight shift at the Roadhouse. But as the day wore on, every patron who came in was talking of the murders of Ronnie Talbot and Deke Rutherford.

Janet was afraid to go home. Afraid to call the sheriff's department, too, because she might be accused of harboring a killer. She solved her problem by remaining at the Roadhouse after her shift ended, drinking one shot of Southern Comfort after another, and finally spending the night on the cot in the employees' lounge. When she returned to her trailer the next morning, Mack was gone; two days later he was arrested and confessed to the murders.

The night after Mack hanged himself in his jail cell, Gar Payne appeared at Janet's door. He knew, he said, that Mack had come there after killing Talbot and Rutherford, and wanted to know what he'd told her. Janet gave him an account of Mack's drunken ravings. Then Payne asked if Mack had left anything with her. Papers, perhaps, in a manila envelope. Janet hadn't seen any, but she offered to look and found the envelope stuffed between the chair's side and seat cushion. Payne took them, saying something about Mack's having been supposed to make a delivery for him. Then Janet made her first mistake.

Was it a delivery to Ronnie Talbot and Deke Rutherford? she asked.

Payne turned steely eyes on her. Had Mack told her that?

No, she just thought it might've been.

Payne didn't believe her. After a long pause he issued an ultimatum: She was to tell no one Mack had been there. She was to tell no one he had been there. And under no circumstances was she to tell anyone about the envelope.

And if she did?

He'd see to it that she lost her job. He'd make sure she never got another in the county. She could do jail time for harboring Travis. Or maybe her neighbors would want to testify as to her loose morals. Women who sold themselves weren't welcome in Soledad County.

Tremaine had a temper. It flared at the accusation.

Oh, no? she asked. Then what kind of women did he visit at Foxxy's up in Oilville?

Payne had a temper, too.

Women like her disappeared all the time, he said. No one would miss her if she did.

Just thinking about what Tremaine had told her made Carly's blood race. She stomped on the accelerator, leaving Shawn Stengel far behind, then eased up and told herself to think logically rather than indulge in rage. The logical conclusion, of course, was that Payne and Rawson had been after the Talbot property for quite some time; they'd probably sent Mack Travis there to deliver an offer, but somehow things had gotten out of hand and he'd killed them. Then he'd killed himself in order to escape Payne and Rawson's retaliation.

Again she stomped on the accelerator.

God, I hate people like them! Mack Travis wasn't much, but they shouldn't've used him the way they did. Janet's not much—in their eyes—but she shouldn't have had to live in fear of them for three years.

Payne and Rawson have got to be stopped. And I'm the woman to do it.

After she made Shawn the promised sandwich and delivered it to his car along with a thermos of coffee, she checked her phone messages. Calls from the office—plaintive voices begging for direction—and one from Matt. It was close to five, so newspaper business took precedence. After she'd finished with her employees, she replayed Matt's message. He'd handled Grossman well, but she knew the detective would want her to verify his story. How long before Ned came knocking on her door?

She dialed the hospital in Santa Carla, found that Matt had been discharged late that afternoon. No answer at Sam's house. Damn! Where was he? Had Grossman put a deputy on him, also?

Six-seventeen now. It wouldn't be dusk till around eight-thirty, and until then her movements would be restricted. She paced the kitchen floor, considered having a glass of wine, decided against it. A clear head was a necessity tonight. Stamina, too, so she made a sandwich and ate it standing at the counter. It tasted like cardboard, but in her present state anything would. Finally she went to her office and ran some Internet searches that turned up nothing of interest.

At eight-fifteen she went to her bedroom and changed into black jeans and a black sweater. Thick socks, a knit hat, and hiking boots completed her ensemble. From the crisper in the refrigerator she took one of the point-and-shoot flash cameras that she and Ard kept there—Ard's contention being that film lasted longer if kept cold. She put it, a small bottle of water, and a flashlight into her daypack.

In her dark living room she looked out the window. Stengel's station wagon was still parked beside her truck. She turned on a table lamp and the TV, moved conspicuously about the room for a few minutes, then drew the curtains. Slipped down the hall to the dining room, where French doors opened onto the backyard. She opened one and listened.

Night sounds. Rustling in the brush, the cries of birds, a dog barking, a car passing on the road. From somewhere nearby came the smell of a barbecue. It was so quiet, she could hear the rush and babble of the creek.

After a careful look around she stepped outside, set the lock on the door, and shut it behind her. Ran across the backyard to the shelter of an aspen grove.

Seven miles as the crow flies.

Deke had told her that the night of the big storm, when he appeared on snowshoes with candles and emergency rations. But he had known the crow's route. In her ignorance of the off-road terrain she might have to walk considerably farther.

You can do it. You have to do it.

She set out through the grove.

The houses here were on large tracts, spaced far apart, creating little light pollution. The night was dark, the moon a mere crescent. Carly took out her flashlight and aimed its beam at the ground, walking swiftly but carefully. When she came out of the trees and into the open meadow, she sighted on the towering mass of the Knob and headed toward it. Crickets fell silent as she passed, then again took up their chorus.

After about ten minutes she entered forest land. The trees were mainly pines, and their resinous smell filled her nostrils. She zigzagged through them, hands sticky where she touched their branches, and eventually realized she'd lost her bearings.

Sheer madness to think I'd find my way. I could be walking around in circles till morning.

She dug her cell phone from her pack and punched in Sam D'Angelo's number. No answer. Next she tried the newspaper on the odd chance Matt might have gone there, but only reached the machine.

Well, what would I have said to him, anyway? "I'm lost in the woods; come and rescue me?"

She put the phone away and resumed walking. After a while the trees thinned and she found herself in a clearing. Craning her neck, she located the Knob—dead ahead and closer than before. She wasn't lost after all.

She angled to the south, across the clearing, with renewed

vigor. Plunged into underbrush where dead blackberry vines ripped at her clothing, and came out on a dirt road. Quickly she conjured up her mental map of the area: Drinkwater Creek, Spyglass Trail, the Knob, the Talbot house. This, then, would be the unpaved end of the trail. If she followed it to the right, it would lead her to its intersection with Highway 26, which passed through the national forest. Turn right, and within fifteen minutes or so she'd be at her destination.

She hadn't been hiking much lately, and her calf and thigh muscles ached. The boots, which weren't thoroughly broken in, pinched her toes. She ignored her discomfort and kept going. Then the growl of an engine came out of the distance. She stopped, listening to get a sense of its direction. Hazy headlights appeared behind her.

Grossman. He went to the house, found me gone, is looking for me.

The detective looking for her in this particular place made no sense, but still she ducked down and scrambled into the ditch by the roadside. It was muddy, and her boots sank deep into the muck. Moments later the vehicle passed at high speed; she raised her head, trying to glimpse it, but it was already around the bend.

Going where? Nothing out here for miles but the national forest. And Ronnie and Deke's house . . .

Ten minutes later she stood in the shelter of a stand of pines, looking at the house. No light showed. She ran across the road and angled toward it. The driveway and front parking area were clearly visible now, and vacant. The vehicle that had passed her was probably heading through the national forest toward the intersection of Highway 26 with Interstate 5 at Redding. Still, she studied the house for a few minutes more before she went over and let herself inside.

In the entry she shone the flashlight's beam around. She lis-

tened, heard only the sound of a tree branch tapping on the
front window. After removing her hiking boots she climbed to
the second story and went to the master bedroom. Took out her
point-and-shoot, and—

"I'll do that," Lindstrom's voice said.

She whirled. His face was pale against the darkness.

"Jesus! You scared me!"

"Sorry. I didn't want to show myself till I was sure it was
you."

"Where've you been since you got discharged from the hospital? I've called a couple of times."

"Sam and I had dinner in Santa Carla. After we got back to
Talbot's Mills, she went to her shift at the Chicken Shack and
I drove here. Pulled my Jeep around back and came inside. Was
setting up to take pictures when I heard you arrive."

Carly sat on the bed, took off her cap, and let her tangled
hair fall to her shoulders. Her eyes had now acclimated to the
darkness, and she looked around, taking in the room's shadowy
outlines. When her gaze rested on the nightstand beside her,
she frowned, then shone her flash on it.

"What?" Matt asked.

"That's it. I saw something there."

"When? The other day?"

"No. The morning after the murders. That was the only
other time I've been in this room. But why can't I remember?
Dammit!"

"Don't force it. It'll come eventually."

"Eventually isn't good enough." She closed her eyes, began
employing a technique a Denver hypnotherapist whom she'd
interviewed for a feature article had explained to her.

Go back to that morning. You're outside Ronnie and Deke's house.
What's the weather like?

Warm. It'll get hot later.

What do you smell?

Ard's vomit. Dry grass and eucalyptus. Cape jasmine from the blue urns by the front door.

What do you hear?

Ard—she's crying. Bluejays screeching in the oak tree. A crow caw-ing.

Look at the house. What do you see?

Door's open.

"Carly?"

"Not now!"

Go inside the house. What's the first thing you notice?

It's cooler in here. But the temperature rises as I climb the stairs.

Go to the master bedroom. What do you see there?

I don't want to—

Look!

Ronnie and Deke are on the bed. Their heads . . . There's blood on the sheets, on the headboard. . . . I can't do this anymore.

Yes, you can. Look at the nightstand.

Okay. The nightstand. There's nothing on it, not even much blood.

Look more closely.

Well, some blood. But it's in a pattern. There're circles and a rect-angle, clear and polished wood. Three small circles and a bigger one. And the rectangle's about the size of a paperback book.

She opened her eyes. "Maybe."

"Maybe what?" Matt asked.

"Come on." She stood. "It's getting late and there's some-body I need to talk with."

Dr. Arlene Hazelwood was in her sixties—a slender but strong woman with a long patrician nose, relatively unlined skin, and hair the color of old ivory. She was Carly's personal physician and one of her role models. Arlene walked in marathons to raise money for medical research, ran a program that arranged for children and pets to visit elderly patients in county nursing homes, mentored troubled teenagers, and still managed to maintain an active medical practice. An Aunt Nan without the controlling edge.

The doctor seemed unsurprised when Carly, having parted with Matt at the *Spectrum*, appeared at her door at ten-thirty that evening. She invited her into the parlor of her white Victorian on a quiet side street not far from the newspaper offices and prepared mugs of herbal tea. Then she settled into her armchair and said, "I assume this is not a social call. Are you on the trail of a hot medical story?"

"Actually I'm not. I need some information from you for personal reasons."

Arlene's blue eyes assessed her keenly. "You're not ill, although you do appear to be under considerable stress."

"I am, and it relates to the reason I'm here. You were Ronnie Talbot's and Deke Rutherford's primary care physician?"

"Yes."

"Does doctor-patient confidentiality extend beyond death?"

"It does."

"Even if the death is a homicide, and the victim's medical condition might have bearing on the reason he died?"

"What is this leading up to, Carly?"

"All right. Ronnie and Deke were close friends of Ard and me, as you probably know. A group of us—a dozen or so—celebrated various holidays together, usually at their place. Yet for at least seven months before they were killed, none of us saw Deke and seldom saw Ronnie. They didn't schedule the customary events and were frequently out of town—tending to a sick uncle of Deke's, they claimed. But in retrospect, I remember that Deke had no family."

Arlene set down her tea and folded her hands, waiting.

Carly went on, "I suspect the reason they broke off contact

was because Deke had AIDS. He was a proud man—vain, too. He wouldn't have wanted his friends to watch him waste away from the disease, so he withdrew from us at the time when he needed us most—perhaps went out of town for treatment."

"If that was true, then we should respect his wish for privacy."

"I would, except I think there's a connection between Deke's medical condition and the murders. I'm not sure what it is, but I strongly feel it exists."

"Mere intuition is a flimsy reason for you to ask me to violate my ethics."

"Would you be violating your ethics if you helped me uncover the real reason they were killed?" She leaned forward, fixing an earnest gaze on the doctor. "Recently I've learned things that indicate the murders were more than the act of a deranged individual working alone. People manipulated Mack Travis—powerful people. And tonight I remembered something significant."

Arlene cocked her head and raised her eyebrows.

"After Ard found Ronnie's and Deke's bodies, she called me, hysterical. When I got to their house, I went to their bedroom to confirm what she'd told me. There was a good deal of blood; it had sprayed on the sheets, the headboard, and a nightstand—the one on the side of the bed where Deke lay. And the pattern on that nightstand was odd. To me, it looked as if four pill bottles and a paperback book had been set there. But they must've been moved after Ronnie and Deke were shot."

"Why? And by whom?"

"I don't know why. Probably they were moved by Mack Travis. But I do know Travis was there under someone else's orders."

"Whose?"

"It's better if I don't say."

The doctor pursed her lips thoughtfully. "I've lived in Cyanide Wells my whole life, except for college and my medical training. I've observed the transitions and shifts of power. We have our good people, our worthless people, and our ruthless people. The lines are fairly well drawn, so you don't have to name names."

Carly waited as Arlene considered.

"Very well," she said, "I'll confirm what you've already figured out. Deke was dying of AIDS. After the initial diagnosis he failed at an accelerated rate. I sent him to a specialist in San Francisco, but there was little he could do for him; it was as if Deke had made up his mind not to fight. He would most likely have been dead by Christmas."

"So it was medicine bottles that made the pattern on the nightstand."

"Yes. The paperback book was probably an inspirational volume that I give to terminal patients. The last time I saw Deke, he told me he cherished it and read from it every day."

"So the presence of it and the medicines would have indicated he had AIDS?"

"Most likely."

Carly paused, full of fresh grief for her friend. "How did Ronnie handle Deke's illness?"

"Admirably. He was a rock, even when I had to tell him his own blood test was HIV-positive."

Oh, Ronnie . . . "When was that?"

"July twenty-second, shortly before they were killed."

July twenty-second. Wednesday afternoon.

"This is so nice. I wish it could go on forever."

Ronnie had said that to her as they sat drinking wine in the backyard garden of Aram's Cafe. But he hadn't been talking about the moment, as she'd assumed. He'd been talking about his life. And Deke's.

"Carly?"

"I'm sorry. I was just . . . missing them."

"I miss them, too. Miss all the patients I've lost. I've dealt with death my whole career, but I've never been able to inure myself to it." Arlene looked away for a moment, then said briskly, "Now, is there anything else you need to know?"

"One thing: Why wasn't AIDS mentioned in the autopsy reports?"

"There was no need to mention it; it had no bearing on the way they died. And the county medical examiner is a dear friend of mine."

"You asked him to suppress information?"

"It was a mutual decision. I warned him of their condition so he would take extra precautions while performing the autopsies. He, in turn, urged the investigating officers and EMTs to be tested yearly—just routine, he told them, since the victims were homosexual. So far, none has come up HIV-positive."

"What if they hadn't bothered to be tested?"

"Then he and I would have gone to the authorities and divulged everything. Doctor-patient confidentiality is sacred to us, but nothing is more sacred than protecting innocent lives."

"So why did Mack Travis think he needed to conceal Deke's illness?"

Carly looked at Matt and shrugged, lowered her head, and stared at her crossed ankles. They were in her office at the *Spectrum,* where he'd been waiting for her while she talked with Dr. Hazlewood. She was sitting in the center of her desk, he in her chair with his feet propped up in front of her.

"Tired?" he asked.

"Yeah. I didn't tell you before, but on my hike to Ronnie and Deke's house I got lost. In a pine forest. I tried to call you on my cell phone."

"And what did you expect me to do?"

"That's what I wondered after you didn't answer."

"Well, if I had answered, I'd've done something."

"Like?"

"Send out a carrier pigeon with a map. Set the Talbot house on fire to guide you. Steal the sheriff's department helicopter and fly low over all the pine trees in the county, bellowing for you on a bullhorn."

She looked up, smiling. "You know, Matt, you almost make me wish I was hetero."

"Oh, yeah?"

"I said *almost.*"

"Just as well. I'm not sure this simple boy from Minnesota could handle becoming romantically involved with his ex-wife's former lover."

"Probably not, but I doubt there's anything simple about you."

"You, either. Maybe that's why we're friends."

Friends.

It wasn't a word—or a concept—she took lightly. But they had become just that.

"Maybe," she said. "We both know what it's like to be outcasts. We both know how it feels to be unfairly attacked. And"—she raised her hand dramatically—"we have both suffered the slings and arrows of outrageous Ardis."

He rolled his eyes, took his feet off the desk, and stood. "That declaration tells me you need at least twelve hours' sleep."

"I do, but where? I'm too damned tired to slink through the countryside to my back door. And if you deliver me to the front, that damn Shawn Stengel—"

"I know a place in Talbot's Mills where there's a lumpy sofa. I might even trade you my bed for it."

Matthew Lindstrom

Friday, May 17, 2002

t ten in the morning Carly was still asleep in Matt's room. He stole in for some clothes, showered and dressed, left her a note on the kitchen table, and departed quietly, heading for Cyanide Wells and the *Spectrum*.

Shortly before he was discharged from the hospital the previous afternoon, he'd received a call from the paper's production manager, asking somewhat wistfully if he'd be able to develop the film he'd shot on Tuesday in time for next week's issue. Matt felt he ought to fulfill his obligations to the paper while Carly was unable to fulfill hers, so he told the manager he'd have the photos on his desk this afternoon.

The newsroom was empty when he arrived, but Brandi Webster sat at the reception desk, glaring at her computer screen. Her usually perky features were drawn, her voice curiously flat as she expressed dismay over his accident and asked how he was mending.

"I'm not too bad, if I don't make any sudden moves. At least I'm not muddleheaded anymore."

"Well, I'm glad it wasn't any worse. What kind of a person does a thing like that, anyway? The sheriff's people have been working overtime to find them. They were in here yesterday asking a lot of questions."

"Oh? About?"

"Stuff like how well do we know you and do you have any enemies. Nobody could tell them much, since you just started." She turned back to her computer. "This damn thing's so slow. I wish I had a better one."

"What're you doing?"

"Updating the subscriber lists, and I'm way behind. I haven't gotten much done this week, and neither has anybody else, because Carly hasn't been around. We all complain when she is, because she can be such a bitch, but her bitchiness kind of puts an edge on that energizes us. What's with her, anyway?"

"I don't know, Brandi." He made a hasty exit before she could ask him anything else.

In the darkroom he wound film onto the spool for developing and, after a few minutes, found himself enjoying the quiet, dim atmosphere under the glow of the safelight. As he busied himself with the exacting processes of drying, enlarging, shading, and printing, he realized how wrong he'd been to give up photography. Although it wasn't a viable way to make a living in Port Regis, it could again be a pleasurable pursuit, maybe even a sideline. When he went back, he'd set up a darkroom.

The pictures of the overturned hopper truck, its load of artichokes spilling down the slope at the Talbot's Mills off-ramp, appeared ordinary at first, but when he examined them more closely, he saw a man and a woman who had pulled up their sweatshirts to form baskets and were filling them with the bounty. He made another print, emphasizing the enterprising couple. His portrait of Cyanide Wells's most senior citizen— 101-year-old Elsa Turner, who still tended a vegetable garden, canned, and had recently published a first volume of poetry— had turned out well, speaking of vital old age and indomitable spirit. When all the prints were out of the dryer and on the production manager's desk, Matt found himself reluctant to put the darkroom in order and leave.

Well, what about his personal films, the ones he'd taken in order to vindicate himself? He dug the canisters out of his camera bag and set to work.

Ardis and Natalie arriving after grocery shopping. The images created an ache under his breastbone. Ardis—once his Gwen—so lovely in spite of the years' passage. Sunlight caught in the wind-tangled strands of her hair; love glowed in her eyes as she smiled down at the little girl. And Natalie: laughing, innocent, trusting. A child taking pleasure in something as small as Ardis's hand on her shoulder as they crossed the footbridge.

For a moment thoughts of what might have been had he and Gwen had a child threatened to take hold of him. Then reality pushed them aside.

The pictures that he'd taken the next morning of the property and its surroundings were pedestrian—mere documentation. The SUV in the parking area, its license plate, the mailbox, footbridge, trees to either side.

But what was that?

He picked up a loup, peered at the contact sheet. Took it outside the darkroom and examined it under the neon light. Went back inside and put the negative in the enlarger. Studied the image again.

A man was standing in the trees to the left of the footbridge.

No, not standing—he was walking toward it. A slender man with dark, curly hair.

He went back into the darkroom, positioned the negative, and enlarged it. The man's features were dappled by sunlight but recognizable from the publicity still Matt had seen at Wild Parrots.

Chase Lewis, about to pay a call on the woman who had left him and taken his child.

"I don't understand." Carly was sitting on Sam's sofa, a mug of coffee clutched in both hands. Matt noticed that she'd appropriated one of his T-shirts.

Although he knew she wasn't fully functional—she'd gotten up only half an hour before he returned—he had little patience with her. "Look at the print." He waved the eight-by-ten at her. "Look at the man in the trees by your footbridge."

"I see him. Are you sure it's Chase Lewis?"

"Positive. I took this shot on the morning of Thursday, the ninth, around ten-thirty. Ardis was home; her SUV was there. Lewis paid her a visit the day before she staged her disappearance."

Carly frowned at the photographs. "But why didn't she tell me he'd been there? That night all she said was that she thought someone was watching her and had been in the house."

"She didn't tell you, because she didn't want you to find out she'd married him and stolen his child. My guess is, she was setting you up to take her disappearance seriously."

Carly's fingers gripped the mug harder, and coffee sloshed onto her bare thighs. Matt took the mug from her and set it on the table.

"Scenario," he said. "Gar Payne calls Lewis, tells him where to find Ardis and Natalie. First Lewis writes to her; that scrap of paper that you found in the fireplace—'. . . mine and I got the right . . .'—was what was left of the letter. Then, when he doesn't get a reply, he drives up to Cyanide Wells and goes to the house, demands his daughter. What would Ardis have done?"

"She wouldn't have argued with him. He'd been violent with her before. And she knew she was in an indefensible position. Lewis could've gone to the sheriff's department, had her arrested for kidnapping. But she wouldn't have agreed to let him have Nat."

"So what alternative did she have?"

"I think she probably agreed to bring Nat to him, set a date and a time. Sent him to the motel in Westport, since she couldn't chance them being seen together here, and staged the disappearance, including the backpack in the well. She thought I'd report it, and Lewis would be afraid he'd be blamed and go back where he came from. Then, after a while she'd surface and reclaim her life."

"Or begin a new life elsewhere."

Carly compressed her lips, looked away from him.

Quickly he went on, "The plan was hastily conceived; she only had from Thursday morning to Friday evening. And she made mistakes, like leaving the bloody bowl in the sink and the meat in the garbage cans. When there were no reports on TV or radio about their disappearance, she knew she'd screwed up."

Carly closed her eyes. Matt knew she was fighting the inevitable conclusion, searching inside herself for some shred of doubt. He'd done similar soul-searching in the darkroom after he'd recognized Lewis in his photographs.

After a moment she said, "I don't know where she stashed Nat after they left the Talbot house, but I do know she went to Lewis's motel on Saturday. I don't know where she got the gun;

maybe it was his. He might've threatened her with it, and somehow she got it away from him. But I do know she killed him."

When she opened her eyes, they were bleak and lusterless. Seldom in his life had he seen such sadness.

While Carly showered and dressed, Matt paced the small living room. Perhaps now that she accepted the idea that Ardis had killed Chase Lewis, he could persuade her to tell the sheriff's investigators what they knew. Because of Natalie, the department could call in the FBI, and with their resources she'd soon be delivered to safety. It would be Ardis's business to explain herself to the authorities, and he and Carly could free themselves from this mess and get on with their lives.

Carly returned, looking fresher but red-eyed, as if she'd been crying in the shower. He didn't comment, simply outlined his thoughts to her. She listened quietly but surprised him with her reaction.

"What makes you think this is a matter for the FBI?"

"A kidnapped child who's probably been taken across the state line by now? I'd say that qualifies."

"I don't know if there's a statute of limitations on kidnapping, but Ard took Nat a long time ago, and she's been happy with us. Besides, I'm not so sure they've even left the county."

"If you'd murdered someone, wouldn't you put as much distance as possible between yourself and the crime scene?"

"I would, but . . ." She sat on the sofa, drew her legs up, wrapped her arms around them. "Ard knows a fair amount about police work and what kinds of information the authorities can access, but she doesn't respect our sheriff's department. And she can be naive. She probably thinks she's covered her past well; maybe she thinks Lewis finding her was a fluke. She was at the Talbot house two days ago; something kept her here."

"What? What's so important that she'd risk arrest for it?"

"Natalie, of course."

"But wouldn't she think it best for Natalie if they went far away?"

"I can't fathom what she would or wouldn't think anymore. I feel as if you and I are operating in a vacuum. I wish we knew what the sheriff's investigators have found out so far."

"Well, since they suspect you of being an accessory, if not a murderer, I don't think they'll be forthcoming if you ask."

She studied him thoughtfully. "No, they're not about to share with me. But you . . ."

"Oh, no. Don't go there."

"From what you told me about your talk with Grossman yesterday, you handled him very well. You could go see him."

"On what pretext?"

"You could tell him you need to go home to B.C. Ask his permission; then get him talking about the case."

"He doesn't strike me as the garrulous type."

"But he is—at times. I've heard rumors about him: He's a lonely man and likes his Scotch. He's particularly fond of single-malt."

"Oh, yeah, I'm supposed to walk into the station carrying a fifth—"

"I happen to have his home address."

"You're insane. It'd never work."

"It might. I think Ned cares more about the truth than his clearance rate. He's one of the good guys. So are you, Matt."

He stared at her face, which wore a pleading little look. Noted the slyness underlying it. "Did you learn this from Ardis?"

Wide-eyed innocence now. "Learn what?"

"The art of getting your own way."

She laughed—hooted, actually—stripped of her guileless mask. "I learned at the knee of my late aunt Nancy. Compared to her, Ard is a mere novice."

"Then your aunt must've been a truly frightening woman." He fell silent, considering the situation. The detective hadn't believed he'd told him his full story during their interview at the hospital; perhaps his distrust could be worked to an advantage.

"Okay," he said, "I'll go try to bond with Grossman."

The detective lived in Santa Carla on a narrow, tree-lined street whose small stucco bungalows differed only in their colors. In that area, however, diversity ruled: standard white, cream, gray, and beige intermixed with garish turquoise, orange, lime, and fuchsia. What was it about stucco, Matt wondered, that inspired some people to excess?

Grossman's house was in the more subdued camp: cream, with a tidy patch of grass inside a chain-link fence. An enormously fat black-and-white spotted dog of indeterminate breed sprawled on the concrete path; at first Matt hesitated to open the gate, but then the animal looked up and yawned, revealing a largely toothless mouth. Matt entered, said, "Hi, dog," and went up to the door. The dog heaved itself to its feet and followed, snuffling at his shoes as if it thought they might be good to eat.

Grossman, clad in a pullover, jeans, and moccasins, opened the door and raised his eyebrows. "Mr. Lindstrom, what brings you here?"

"I'd like to talk with you." He held up the bottle he carried. "And I've brought refreshment."

The detective smiled thinly. "Attempting to bribe an officer of the law, are you?"

"Not really, but I heard you like single-malt. It's also a personal favorite of mine, and I don't like to drink alone."

"Neither do I, Mr. Lindstrom."

"Matt, please."

"Ned." He opened the door wider and admitted Matt to a small room where a TV was turned to a golf game, the sound muted. The dog entered, too, wheezing.

"That's Everett," Grossman said, switching off the TV. "The critter who I told you doesn't much like me. Frankly, the feeling's mutual. He's a canine garbage can. Scarfs down stuff even I wouldn't eat. Take a seat; I'll get us glasses. No ice, right?"

"No ice."

"Good man."

He sat on the sofa, and Everett followed on his owner's heels, probably hoping for a snack. In their absence Matt studied the room. A diploma from Humboldt State University and a number of framed certificates hung on the wall behind the TV. A couple of bowling trophies sat atop a bookcase full of thick volumes, most of them dealing with police science. No personal photographs, nothing that revealed the inner man. The room smelled stale, as if it were uninhabited a great deal of the time, and a thin film of dust overlay everything.

Grossman returned, shadowed closely by Everett, whose hopes of a snack apparently had been fulfilled, since he was licking his chops in an extremely satisfied manner. After pouring a round, the detective settled into an armchair that faced the TV. As he swiveled it toward Matt, the dog sat at his feet and rested its head on his knee; Grossman began rubbing the floppy ears.

Sure the two of you don't much like each other. Matt raised his glass in a toast, sipped.

Grossman followed suit, smiling in appreciation. "Whatever

you want to talk about must be damned important. This is quite a bribe."

"It's important, all right. I need to get back to British Columbia. I'm concerned about my charter business. You didn't tell me not to leave the county, but I thought I should ask your permission."

"A problem up there?"

"Nothing serious, but we're getting into our peak season now, and my deckhand's not going to be able to handle the volume of business."

"I understand. My grandfather was a commercial fisherman, out of Calvert's Landing. When the fish were running, he needed all the hands he could get—mine included. I imagine it's the same with tourists."

Everett farted noisily. Grossman wrinkled his nose and glared at him but went on rubbing his ears. "How close are you to Carly McGuire, Matt?"

"Carly? Why?"

"Just wondering. You do have something in common—Ardis Coleman."

"Does she strike you as a good reason for closeness?"

Grossman shrugged. "You were with Carly when Natalie's backpack turned up in the well—retrieved it, in fact. You drove her to the Talbot house Tuesday night, even though her attorney could just as easily have done so."

"I told you she was having trouble with her truck—"

"Yes, she was, until you disarmed the alarm the week before. She's had no problems with it since, according to the folks at the paper. And in addition, she paid your hospital bill."

"She felt she ought to, since I was injured while doing her a favor. My health insurance—"

"And after she eluded our surveillance last night, she slept at Sam D'Angleo's house, where you rent a room."

"How d'you know that?"

"Deputy Stengel went to the door around two-thirty this morning to ask her to refill the thermos of coffee she'd given him. The lights and TV were on in the living room, but Carly didn't answer the bell. He was mightily disgruntled about that when he reported in this morning—Shawn likes his creature comforts—and it made me wonder if she'd slipped out on him, and if so, where she'd gone. So I asked myself, 'Who's she been hanging around with lately?' Your name came up high on the list."

"That doesn't prove—"

"Later I talked with a neighbor of Ms. D'Angelo's, who said she'd looked out her bathroom window and seen the two of you arriving. She recognized Carly because she used to houseclean for her and Ardis."

"So what is it you think? That I'm having an affair with Carly?"

"Hardly. But I'm curious as to what the involvement between the two of you is."

"We're friends, that's all."

"And where does Ardis Coleman fit in?"

"She doesn't. She's left Carly."

"Then this story of the educational trip . . . ?"

"Face-saving on Carly's part."

"Face-saving, in spite of the fact that Ardis's husband was just murdered?"

"Carly's confused and fragile right now. And naturally she doesn't want to believe that her partner—former partner— could murder someone."

Grossman stood and poured them another round, sat down, and fixed Matt with a flat, knowing stare.

"Okay, Matt," he said, "you want to go back to British Columbia? Well, I've got a proposition for you."

*   *   *

As he drove north from Santa Carla, Matt felt like a double
agent. Or maybe a triple agent. Which one, he wasn't sure.
He'd read spy novels with pleasure but had never been fully
able to comprehend the twists and turns of their plots. Who
was on which side? Who was on both? Who was acting strictly
on his own? And now he couldn't fully comprehend his present situation. Whose side was he on? Carly's? Grossman's?
Both? His own?

The proposition the detective had offered him was simple:
The surveillance on Carly would be lifted, and over the course
of the next few days Grossman would feed Matt bits of information about the Lewis investigation. He, in turn, would pass
them along to Carly and observe her reactions, which he would
then report to Grossman.

"You're going to have to let go of this misplaced loyalty to
Carly, unless you want to be charged as an accessory in the
Lewis murder," the detective had told him. "She knows a great
deal more than she's letting on, and the information I give you
may trigger a telling response that will help us solve it."

What he offered Matt in exchange for his cooperation was
also simple: He would be allowed to leave the country by the
following weekend. In addition, Grossman would personally
inform the authorities in Sweetwater County, Nebraska, and
Saugatuck, Minnesota, that Gwen Lindstrom was alive and had
been living in his jurisdiction for the past fourteen years. And
when the Lewis investigation was closed, he would make sure
that the solution to her disappearance received national publicity.

"Maybe then," Grossman said, "you'll feel free to return to
your home and your people."

Matt shook his head. "Port Regis is my home. I have no people."

No people. No real friends, either.

Except for Carly.

When she let him into her house at a little before ten that evening, he stepped into chaos. A heap of clothing lay in the entry, and cardboard cartons filled with cosmetics, underwear, shoes, and books stood by the door. Gracie, the little white cat, cowered just inside the living room. Carly held a black-and-red lacquered jewelry box, which she dumped on the floor.

"What's all this?" he asked.

"Housecleaning. I'm getting rid of Ard's shit." She swept her arm at the accumulation. "She's dead to me. When people're dead, you clear out their stuff."

He was silent, staring at the things his former wife had left behind.

"Why're you pulling that long face?" Carly demanded. "Isn't this what you did when she disappeared?"

"Not exactly. When the lease ran out on her apartment, I asked a friend to do it." Bonnie Vaughan. Later she'd told him she cried the whole time.

"Not nearly as satisfying." Carly started for the hallway to the bedrooms.

"Don't you find it sad?"

"No. I'm too pissed off."

"Maybe you should wait till you can feel something other than anger."

She paused, turning. "Why?"

"Because I didn't, and I regret it. Before our friend cleaned out Gwen's apartment, I went over there. Tore it up in a rage, looking for clues to what happened to her. And all I came away with was a bitter taste and the realization of how completely she'd banished me from her life. There were photograph albums, you see. Pictures of the two of us. Our wedding photos.

She'd spent a lot of time putting the albums together, so when we split, it was natural she should have them. But apparently the only reason she wanted them was to destroy them."

"Oh, Matt, no." Carly shook her head. "Go into the kitchen; pour us some wine. There's a bottle next to the cooktop. I'll be right back."

He did as she told him. Apparently household items belonging to Ardis were also being ousted: dishes and vases and a pasta maker sat on the floor; the table by the window was covered with pots, pans, and small appliances. A calendar of famous rose gardens that he'd seen on the wall lay beside them. But Natalie's drawings remained on the refrigerator door.

He poured wine from the open bottle of merlot. Carly entered, carrying a manila envelope, and held it out to him.

"I found this at the back of her closet," she said. "I never knew it was there."

The envelope was stuffed full of photographs: their wedding, holidays, the two of them on his father's boat. Gwen stood in front of him, and he had his arms wrapped around her, his chin resting on the top of her head. A happy young couple, their whole lives ahead of them . . .

"I can't deal with this, Carly. Get rid of them."

"No, I'll put them away for you. Just like I'll keep her stuff—for now."

He was sitting at the table when she came back, his eyes closed. Her hand touched his shoulder briefly; then she sat and picked up her glass. "How did it go with Grossman?"

On the drive back he'd realized he could hold nothing back from her. She was his friend, and besides, he was the one who had insisted that they, and they alone, should bring the situation to its conclusion.

"He wants me to spy on you. Here's the deal."

*   *   *

"Okay," Carly said when he'd finished, "I don't blame him for using whatever means he can to work his case. In fact, I think it's damned clever of him. What information did he feed you?"

"Ballistics. And you're not going to like what you hear. The bullets they took out of Chase Lewis and his motel room wall were unusual. Short thirty-two caliber, copper-jacketed, of a type not manufactured in this country. The lab technician thought he'd encountered something similar before, so he accessed past records for county homicides. The bullets were a match for those that killed Ronnie and Deke."

"I never heard anything about the bullets that killed them being unusual."

"It was never revealed by the department, even after Mack Travis killed himself and they closed out the case. Grossman said the sheriff never believed in Travis's guilt."

"Then Ard didn't kill Lewis, after all. Whoever killed Ronnie and Deke did."

"Possibly."

"Gar Payne? Milt Rawson?"

He shrugged.

"I'm afraid I don't know much about ballistics. Could they tell what kind of gun the bullets were fired from?"

"Not the exact make, but from the bullet, the tech thinks it's an older gun, perhaps a collector's item."

Carly swirled her wine, stared into its depths. Matt could tell that the information had disturbed her.

"The technician couldn't be wrong?" she asked.

"Grossman said that kind of evidence, like fingerprints or DNA, doesn't lie."

She nodded, still staring down. When she finally looked up, her face was pale.

She said, "Let's go, Matt. There's something I need to check out."

He shut off the Jeep's engine and lights. The night was oppressively dark, the Talbot house a black hole before him. Carly slid out and slammed her door, then looked back through the open window and said, "You coming?"

"Yeah." He unlatched his seat belt, took his time. Easing into it. All the way here she'd been silent, refusing to answer his questions, her tension palpable. He knew without a doubt that whatever her reason for coming back to the house, it would lead to yet another unpleasant revelation—perhaps the most unpleasant of all.

By the time he caught up with her, she was through the door and taking a flashlight from her daypack. He followed as she switched it on and moved along the hallway to an open door about halfway down. Inside was an office with a row of file cabinets and a computer workstation that was at odds with a handsome rolltop desk. She went to the desk, opened it, shone the light around.

"Carly, what . . . ?"

"In a minute." Her voice was grim. She fumbled with an ornately carved panel, pressing it in several places till it popped open, then took out a set of keys that were its only contents. "Come on." She led him across the hall to a facing door.

The room was a library, furnished in leather, with bookcases built into the walls. Below the heavily laden shelves were carved wooden doors with brass fittings. Carly went to one of them, squatted down, and slipped a key into the lock. It wouldn't turn, so she tried another and then another until one did.

Matt moved closer. She was removing a glass-fronted display

tray, one of several that were stacked inside the cabinet. "Help me with this, would you?" she asked.

He grasped one end, and they lowered it to the floor. She turned the flashlight's beam on it.

Handguns. Sunk into velvet-lined indentations specially contoured for them. Each depression had an engraved brass plate positioned below it.

And one was vacant.

Carly made a sound close to a sob.

Matt read the label: "Austrian Rast and Gasser Army Revolver, Manufactured eighteen ninety-eight."

Carly said, "Ronnie's father's collection. The missing gun is probably the one Ard used to kill Chase Lewis. And Ronnie. And Deke." Her voice shook.

"Not them, too! My God, Carly. Killing off a man who abused her and was threatening to take Natalie away is one thing, but Ronnie and Deke were her friends."

She was silent.

Still not believing it, he asked, "Where would she get ammunition for that kind of gun?"

"The collection includes it." She motioned at spaces for cartridges—eight of them, all empty.

He took the flashlight from her hand, shone it upward at her face, and had a sudden vision of how she would look as an old woman.

She shaded her eyes and said, "Ard has known for years that these guns are here. And she's also known where the keys to the cabinets are kept."

"But so do you. And probably any number of people. Mack Travis—"

"Would have had no way of knowing about them. Ronnie didn't like the guns, locked them up, but kept them out of sentiment—or guilt. He couldn't get rid of any of his father's stuff, because while he loved him, they didn't get along. His father was always after him to give up on the lifestyle he'd 'chosen.' As if he'd gotten up one morning and said, 'I think I'll turn gay now.' "

"What about Gar Payne? Or Milt Rawson? They might've known."

"No, I'm sure neither of them has ever been in this house."

"Other friends of yours?"

"Some of them may have known about the collection, although not many. Ronnie didn't talk about it much; that would've been dangerous. Burglars go after firearms, particularly old and valuable ones. And I seriously doubt that anybody knew where the keys were kept. The only reason Ard and I found out was that during the last Christmas party here we were wrapping gifts in the office. Ronnie came in to get the keys because an old friend of his father's had stopped by and wanted to look at the collection, thinking he might buy it."

"Was the friend with him?"

"No. Ronnie was even uncomfortable that Ard and I saw him get the keys."

Though it was cool in the library, Matt's face was filmed with sweat. He got up, felt his way across the room, and sank into one of the leather chairs. When he spoke, he barely recognized his own voice.

"Why would Ardis kill Ronnie and Deke?"

"Well, she did get a great series of stories out of their deaths."

"No one kills a friend to score a journalistic coup."

"Try this one, then: a rich vein of gold running under a house whose owner has just made you executor of his will."

All the way back to Carly's house they argued about taking what they knew to Grossman.

"Her killing Chase Lewis I can somewhat understand," he said. "But this other—you can't be willing to risk her getting away with it."

"I need time—just overnight, that's all."

"Christ, Carly, you don't know what else she's done. Or what she might do next."

"Will ten or twelve hours make a difference?"

"It might."

"She's not some crazed serial killer. Besides, they issued a be-on-lookout order for her days ago. What more can they do in the middle of the night?"

She had a point. "All right, but we're going to see Grossman first thing tomorrow."

"Agreed, Why don't you come over at eight? We'll drive down to Santa Carla together."

After he dropped Carly at her footbridge, he sped off, turning on the Jeep's radio in the hope that some music would calm him. The only station that came in clearly was KSOL, easy listening out of the county seat. Not his first choice, but in his present frame of mind, anything would do. He'd just arrived at Sam's when the announcer's voice broke in; he left the Jeep running and turned up the volume.

"This just in: Acting on an anonymous tip, Soledad County sheriff's deputies stopped a car driven by Cyanide Wells Mayor Garson Payne and, in the process of investigating a routine traffic violation, seized a handgun from the glove box. Although ballistics experts have yet to confirm it, a department spokesman says they are 'ninety-nine percent certain' that the weapon, an old Austrian army revolver, was used to kill San Francisco musician Chase Lewis in his Westport motel room last weekend. In a related development, the spokesman said that technicians have

matched the bullet that killed Lewis with those used in the three-year-old fatal shootings of prominent Cyanide Wells residents Ronald Talbot Junior and Deke Rutherford. Interviewed outside the Talbot's Mills sheriff's department substation, where Payne is being held pending arraignment, the mayor's attorney, James Griffin, stated that his client has no idea how the gun came to be in his car. The case against the mayor will be thrown out of court upon arraignment, Griffin contends, because of the 'illegal nature' of the search . . ."

Matt put the Jeep into a fast U-turn.

Carly McGuire

Saturday, May 18, 2002

hen she'd entered the house after Matt dropped her off, Carly had taken grim satisfaction at the sight of Ard's stacked and strewn possessions. Earlier she'd allowed him to sway her about immediately disposing of them, but on Monday they were headed for the Salvation Army. Or maybe the county dump. She didn't want to saddle anyone, no matter how needy, with the accumulation of Ard's lying, cheating, murderous life.

In the postmidnight hour she moved through the empty house. It felt as it had the night she'd moved in, a lonely twenty-eight-year-old who feared she'd made the biggest mistake of her life. How could she, who had lived in crowded, noisy cities since her late teens, adapt to such isolation and silence? What had possessed her to think she could grasp the reins of a failing country weekly and guide it to success?

Well, you adapted, grasped, and guided. You created a successful life for yourself. You would've been fine if Ard hadn't come into it. Moral: Never pick up hitchhikers.

But for years the hitchhiker, and later her daughter, had brought joy to this house. In spite of the fights and Ard's penchant for fleeing, there had been many good times.

All behind you now, McGuire, the good and the bad.

But can you ever really put that big a part of your life behind you?

She tried to reconcile the woman she'd thought she knew with the woman who had killed their friends, but couldn't. She thought back to the night they'd died, trying to find a shred of evidence that would prove Ard innocent. The coroner had put the time of death at around three in the morning. Ard was supposedly in bed beside her at that hour. But they'd had an argument, and Carly had taken a sleeping pill. Still, wouldn't she have noticed if Ard had left for any appreciable length of time? Maybe, maybe not. And Ard was the only person besides her who had access to Ronnie's gun collection. . . .

Suicide.

The word loomed suddenly in her mind. Odd that the two men who had fixed things for Payne and Rawson had killed themselves. Could there be a connection . . . ?

The phone rang, shrill in the silence. She started, then rushed to the kitchen to pick up.

"Carly?"

The sound of her name, spoken in the old familiar way, jolted her. She drew in her breath, a combination of surprise and anger threatening to choke her. It was a moment before she could respond.

"Ard. Where are you? Where's Natalie?"

"Carly, I need your help. Chase . . . It's been on the news. Everybody thinks I did it."

Get her back here, McGuire. Make her turn Nat over to you.

"Look, Ard, why don't you and Nat come home? I'll hire a good attorney; we'll get through this together."

"I can't. It's over between you and me. It's been over for a long time. But Nat . . . she's sick. She caught cold and then her asthma flared up, and now she's out of medication, but I don't dare go to the pharmacy for a refill. And I think the cold's turning into pneumonia. I want her to be with you, where she belongs. Our . . . your place is the only home she's ever known."

"Of course I'll take her. I'll see she gets what she needs."

"Thank you. I can't be responsible for her anymore. She's been sick for a week—so sick I haven't been able to move her—and it's all my fault."

"Then bring her here right away."

"No, I can't come there. It's the first place the sheriff's department will expect me to show up. They're probably watching the house."

"They were, but not anymore."

"Look, will you quit talking and come get her?"

"Okay—where?"

"At the Knob. We've been camping out in my rental van near that lookout point—the one Ronnie showed us."

"I can be there in half an hour."

"Good. And one other thing . . . could you bring me some money? My credit cards're maxed out, and I've run through all my cash."

Demanding a ransom, are you?

"How much do you need?"

"A few thousand. Whatever's in your emergency stash."

Nearly three thousand dollars in a Jiffy bag in the office-supply cabinet. Ard must've snooped. She'd never respected anyone's privacy.

"I'll bring it."

"Oh, Carly, thank you. I know you'll take good care of my little girl."

Chase Lewis's little girl, who has now become excess baggage.

"Half an hour," she said, and replaced the receiver.

Carly pulled her truck into the parking area at the trailhead and got out. The national forest was an eerie place at night: chill even after the hottest of days; silent but full of dangerous, prowling life. She took out her flashlight and began walking along a familiar path that was altered by darkness, keeping a wary ear out for sounds in the underbrush. A dry winter had brought mountain lions and bears down from the higher elevations in search of food and water; coyotes and wild pigs also inhabited these foothills.

She followed the trail slowly and cautiously, but her thoughts moved at a furious pace. Something had occurred to her before Ard's call, and she was now linking previously unrelated bits and pieces of information, discarding others. If she could only make the final connections—

A thrashing overhead, then a scurrying in the underbrush. The scream of a small victim.

Owl, probably a great horned, catching his dinner. I hate that sound.

She was nearing the Knob now, but still there was no sign of Ard's rented van. She'd probably driven in on the fire trail to the far side. How she'd eluded the forest rangers while camping in territory that was closed to all but official vehicles, Carly couldn't imagine. Or why, after Nat fell ill a week ago, she'd continued to stay here, where nighttime temperatures were always frigid. Her treatment of the child had become criminally negligent.

The trail began angling uphill, around boulders and over rocky ledges. Soon she spotted the ramshackle building that had once held the cyaniders' equipment. Slag heaps rose to either side, and where the trail split, her flashlight picked out the boarded-up entrance to the old mine, now covered in a wild pattern of graffiti. She turned to the left and started around toward the lookout point.

The terrain was rougher now, and bulky shapes lurked in the darkness—a dumping ground of broken equipment and metal drums that had once contained cyanide, abandoned by the mining company and allowed to remain by the forest service as a memorial to the place's history. Some people thought the area should be cleared, but Carly preferred it this way; to beautify and sanitize it would be denying the reality of what had occurred here. . . .

She stopped, staring at the shapes without really seeing them.

As a memorial . . .

Reality's starting to interfere with the writing. . . .

He was a proud man . . .

This is so nice. I wish it could go on forever. . . .

Suicide . . .

The connections were made.

She began walking faster.

"You're ten minutes late. I thought you weren't coming or had called the cops. So I hid up here."

Ard's voice came from a ledge above her. Carly shone the flashlight upward; she stood with her arms folded, legs planted wide, wearing jeans and a sweatshirt that were insubstantial for the chill night. Even at a distance she looked tired and unkempt. There was no sign of Natalie.

"You know I wouldn't do that to you."

"Did you bring the money?"

"Yes. Where's Nat?"

"In the van. Leave the money there on the ground where I can see it. Drive back to the entrance, and I'll deliver her to you."

"You're not getting the money till Nat's safe with me."

Ard was silent for a moment. "Well, it seems we're at an impasse. If I don't get the money, you don't get the kid. If you don't get the kid, I don't get the money. How're we going to work this out?"

"Maybe we can strike a deal."

"What?"

"You answer a few of my questions—truthfully, for a change—then the money is yours."

"Done."

"First question: When you got to Ronnie and Deke's that morning"—no need to explain which—"what did you find?"

"Jesus, Carly, can't you think of anything better to ask? You know what I found: our friends murdered in their bed."

"I don't think so. You found Deke murdered in their bed, but not Ronnie. He killed himself. It was a murder-suicide pact."

Ard was silent.

"Second question: What did you do then?"

No reply.

"All right, let me tell you what you did. You removed the gun from wherever it was and replaced it in its case in the library cabinet—where it stayed until you took it out to kill Chase. You removed Deke's medications and inspirational book from the nightstand so no one would know he had AIDS. And you probably removed their suicide note from wherever they'd left it."

"There wasn't any note—" She broke off, realizing her mistake.

"Is that a yes?"

Silence.

"A *yes?*"

"All right! It's a yes!"

Carly crossed her arms, gripped her elbows with iron fingers. "And then what did you do?"

More silence.

"What did you do to their bodies, Ard?"

Ard continued to hesitate. Carly sensed what was going on with her: the trembling lips, the filling eyes, the silent weeping.

After all she's done, she still thinks that will work with me.

"What did you do to their bodies?"

"Carly, it was awful. They were wearing their fancy Japanese kimonos, and they'd been drinking champagne, and I guess they thought they'd look peaceful and released from all of it, but they didn't. Neither of them knew what gunshot wounds to the head can do, but Ronnie found out and— God, I don't even want to think about how it must've been for him. Still, even our inept sheriff's deputies would've been able to figure out it was a suicide pact, so I had to kind of . . . rearrange things. That was the really horrible part—touching them."

Carly was shaking now—sickened and enraged both by how Ard had desecrated their friends' deathbed scene and by her self-pitying whine. She said, "Last question: Why? Why did you do those things?"

"I didn't want anyone to know about the AIDS. Ronnie only told me about it when he gave me my copy of his will. He and Deke were so private—"

"Bullshit. You wanted a story. The murder-suicide of a gay couple was good but not great copy. An unsolved murder of a gay couple was. You did those horrible things for a *story.*"

In the flashlight's beam Carly saw Ard's eyes narrow and her mouth firm. "All right, so what if I did? You're a newspaperwoman. You ought to understand. Besides, why should you complain? It was your paper that got the Pulitzer, not me!"

"And you resent me for that?"

"For that and a whole lot of other things. You ordered me around at work from day one; you were so convinced you were the better journalist. And at home it was always *your* house that we lived in, *your* money that put food on the table. You even tried to tell me how to raise Natalie. It's always been about you, you, you. That morning I saw my chance to have something of my own, make a name for myself—but then *your* paper won the Pulitzer."

Carly stared up at her, unable to believe the depth of the woman's anger. Had she really treated her so badly? And if so, why hadn't Ard confronted her at the time rather than let her resentment fester?

"Then I got my book deal," Ard went on, "but I couldn't write the damn thing. That morning at Ronnie and Deke's had finally caught up with me, and I just couldn't get past it. And then Chase showed up, claiming he wanted Natalie, even though he didn't give a shit about her. All he wanted was money to keep him from going to the cops about me kidnapping her. Kidnapping! I saved her life. At best she'd've become his punching bag; at worst . . . But I didn't have any money; I'd spent the whole advance for the book."

"You could've come to me for the money. You didn't have to kill him."

"Oh, sure, I could've come to you. And spent the rest of my life enduring your holier-than-thou attitude."

Am I really that bad a person?

No, I'm not perfect, but I'm not the monster she makes me out to be. I've taken measure of myself in the past ten days, and I can live with what I've seen.

I can do good things—especially for Natalie.

She said, "That's enough, Ard. Come down from there and take me to Nat."

"Look, this stalemate isn't doing Nat or me any good. She's sick, she needs help. And I've bought some time, but not much."

"What do you mean?"

"Gar Payne was arrested tonight. Seems the gun that killed Chase, Ronnie, and Deke was in the glovebox of his car."

"You planted it there. And made an anonymous call to the sheriff's department."

"What if I did? It'll keep them busy till I can get out of the county."

Was there no end to what Ard would do? "Maybe the charge against Payne will stick. Then you could stay here. You'd still have control of the Talbot estate—and the gold."

"Gold? What gold? The mine's not part of the estate. Anyway, there hadn't been any gold there since the thirties."

Faking, or does she really not know?

Carly said, "Gold is the reason Payne and Rawson want that land. A rich vein of it runs through there."

" . . . You're lying. They want it for a development."

She doesn't *know. But what about her notes on Noah Estes, Denver Precious Metals. Wells Mining?*

Of course—simple reminders to research the history of the area where the murders took place. She's always been big on history.

"I'm not lying. If you'd done your homework, you'd've known."

Ard stood, hands loose at her sides, perplexed. Then she shook her head. "Well, gold, whatever—none of that matters now. Payne will wriggle out of the charges, and then they'll be looking for me again. I've got to get out of here. Just give me the money, will you?"

"No."

"But you said if I answered your questions—"

"I'm not the only one who can lie."

Ard's fists balled, and her face twisted with rage. "Then you won't get Nat! I never intended for you to have her, anyway. She's not in the van. You'll never see her again!"

She whirled and disappeared from the ledge.

For a moment Carly stood stunned; then she began to run—around the Knob toward its northeast side, where the fire trail ended. She had a head start on Ard, who would have to make the long climb down. If she could find the van, she might also find Natalie; not having her along was probably another of Ard's lies.

The ground was steep and treacherous. She skidded on stones, tripped over unseen obstacles. Fell once to her knees and dropped the flashlight, pawed for it, got up, and ran again. The terrain finally leveled off, and she caught a glimpse of the fire trail dead ahead of her. At its end she stopped and shone her light in a circle. Walked on a ways, and shone it around again.

A boxy shape was wedged into a stand of aspens to her right. The van. She moved cautiously toward it, tried the door. Locked. She aimed the flashlight through the windows. Empty. Dammit, Ard hadn't been lying after all.

Circling, she tried all the doors. Also locked. She pressed the hood release, thinking to disable the engine, but it wouldn't move. Finally she shut off her light and listened for Ard's foot-steps, but heard nothing.

Hiding. Staying still. But she knows where I am. The slightest sound carries for miles out here. No way I'll find her.

She circled the van again, shining her light through the win-dows one more time. Its rear compartment was loaded with

Ard's and Nat's luggage, a collapsed air mattress, a cooler, a familiar-looking Indian-weave blanket, a striped bag . . .

She went up on her tiptoes, staring intently. She'd seen that bag before, suspended from the ceiling of the walk-in closet off Ronnie and Deke's bedroom. Caught in the pull-down stairs to Deke's attic studio. It wasn't a bag at all. It was a pillowcase, now stuffed with matching sheets from a set that fit Nat's bed at home. And the blanket—it used to lie on a hassock in Ronnie and Deke's living room.

Now she knew where Natalie was.

As she sped along in her truck, Carly used her cell phone to call the sheriff's department central dispatch and ask them to send cruisers to the Talbot house. As she disconnected, she lost control and skidded on loose gravel. Stones flew up and bounced off the undercarriage; the truck pulled to the right, as if one of its tires was going flat.

Not now, dammit!

She wrenched the truck to the left, glanced in the rearview mirror. No headlights behind her. No taillights ahead. She slowed for the last curve and the turn into the Talbot driveway.

No van, and the house was dark.

She stopped the truck near the front door, stalled the engine, and jumped out, almost forgetting her key ring. When she got to the door her trembling fingers wouldn't connect the key with the lock. She took a calming breath, then let herself in.

Her flashlight's batteries were dying. When she tried the wall switch, nothing happened. The power was off. What a horror it must've been for Nat, who feared total darkness and always slept with a nightlight, to camp out here. She trained the flash's fading beam on the stairs and moved quickly toward them.

"Stop, Carly," Ard's voice said.

Astonished, she froze. Ard was behind her, near the exercise room. She'd beaten her here somehow, hid the van out back.

She turned slowly, bringing the light around on her. Ard stood several feet away, pointing a small handgun at her—another from the collection, she supposed.

Ard said, "I saw you at the van. I wasn't far behind. There's a shortcut from the fire trail to the main road, so I got here first."

Fear was making Carly's mouth dry, her palms wet. "Ard, I'll give you the money if you let Nat come home with me."

"You can't buy my child."

Carly made an involuntary move, and Ard brought the gun higher. "Stay where you are," she told her.

"All right. What happens now?"

"You give me the money."

"And then?"

In the silence that followed her question, she stared at Ard's face. The flash's dim light showed it was composed, devoid of emotion.

She's going to kill me. And it'll be easy for her. She's like an animal that, once it's tasted first blood, is compelled to kill again and again.

"I've called the sheriff's department, Ard. They're coming here. Even if you get away before they arrive, they have a description and the license plate number of the van."

"Give me the keys to your truck, then."

"They're in the ignition."

"Bullshit! The key to this house is on your ring, and you used it to let yourself in."

"I haven't carried that key on my ring since—"

The sound of a car's engine. Headlights turning into the drive, washing over the house.

"That's the law now," Carly said.

Ard turned her head but kept the gun aimed at her.

In that instant Carly snapped off the flashlight, sidestepped, and ducked down by the wall.

Ard fired, but the shot went wild, smashing into the wall above Carly's head. Carly crouched lower, ears ringing, as Ard ran toward the door.

Before she reached it, the door opened and Matt's dark form, backlit by the headlight glare, came running through. Ard fired wildly again, and he grabbed her; then Carly heard the gun clatter on the floor. Ard fought him, screaming. Before he was able to spin her around and pin her arms behind her, she bit his shoulder. Then she doubled over and suddenly went limp.

Carly rose on wobbly legs. The hallway was silent except for Matt's and Ard's labored breathing.

Then Ard said in a small, trembly voice, "I didn't mean for any of this to happen, Carly. Please tell him to let me go. You can have Natalie. I don't even want the money."

Carly turned on the flash and moved its beam to Ard's face. It was twisted, tear-streaked, and her eyes blinked at the sudden light.

"Please!" she said.

She's pleading for her life, and I don't feel anything.

She looked from Ard to Matt. He nodded, face grim.

He doesn't feel anything either.

We're both free.

"Mom?" the voice that came from Deke's attic studio was weak and frightened.

"No, honey, it's Carly. Your mom . . . sent me to bring you home." She scrambled up the steep pull-down stairs at the back of the master bedroom closet.

"What was that noise that woke me up?"

"Just my truck backfiring."

In the moonlight shining through the skylights she saw Natalie sitting up in a bed improvised from blankets, a sleeping bag, and an air mattress. She went over, squatted, and enfolded her in her arms. Even though it was cold in the room, Nat felt hot and sweaty.

"I can't go home," she said. "There's this man. . . ."

"Don't worry about him. He's . . . gone away."

"Are you sure? Mom said he never would. . . ."

"She was wrong."

From outside, Carly heard the rumble of sheriff's department cruisers, the chatter of their radios.

"Where is Mom? Why didn't she come for me, too?"

"She . . . She had something she had to do, so I volunteered to bring you home."

"I don't feel good."

"I know. We'll get you to a doctor."

Nat tensed suddenly, staring over Carly's shoulder. She glanced behind her and saw that Matt had come up the stairs and was standing at their top. "It's okay," she told Nat. "This is my friend Matthew."

The little girl relaxed some but continued to look suspiciously at Matt. He stayed where he was and said, "Hello, Natalie. Carly's told me a lot about you."

Nat didn't reply.

Carly said, "Have you been staying here the whole time since you and your mom left home?"

"Except for the night we went to Westhaven. We stayed in a cruddy motel, and that's when I got sick. Mom decided we should come back here till I got better, but we had to be very quiet and hide from that man. Mom said he was here in the house. A couple of times I heard him."

She heard me. I could've found her, brought her home sooner.

Carly stood and eased Nat to her feet. She was fully clothed in jeans and a heavy wool sweater. "Can you walk?"

"I don't know." As she spoke, she swayed and stumbled.

"Matt," Carly said, "maybe you could carry her downstairs."

"Is that okay, Natalie? May I carry you?"

"I guess."

He scooped her up, and they descended the steep staircase. In the bedroom Carly motioned for him to hold back and went to look down into the hallway. No one was there, but garish red-and-blue lights bounced off its walls.

She ran down the stairs and outside. Ard was being guided by a deputy into the backseat of one of the cruisers, her head sagging on her long neck like a flower on a broken stalk.

Carly turned away and went back to Matt and Natalie.

After the doctor at the emergency room in Santa Carla assured them that Nat would fully recover and was resting comfortably, Carly led Matt outside. The sky over the mountains to the east was tinged with pink and gold, but above them it was still midnight blue. She raised her face to it, breathed in the scents of the springtime dawn.

"So how'd you find me?" she asked.

"I went to your house after I heard a bulletin about Gar Payne's arrest on the radio. I figured Ardis had planted the gun. When I found your lights on and the door unlocked, I got alarmed and called Grossman. He called me back after you alerted the dispatcher, and told me where you were headed. I was close by, so . . . Well, that's me: Lindstrom to the rescue. Some rescue. I almost got myself shot."

"Thank God she missed you, too."

He glanced back at the hospital. "What d'you suppose will happen to Natalie?"

"I don't know, but she wants to come home. The courts usually take the wishes of a child her age into consideration. And Ard won't have any say in it; she's admitted to child stealing and murder."

"But it's your word against hers. Once she gets a lawyer, she'll probably manipulate her way out of it."

"Nope. Not this time." Carly reached into her pocket and took out her small voice-activated tape recorder. "It's all on here. Old reporter's trick: Never leave home without it."

Matthew Lindstrom

Friday, May 24, 2002

hen Matt crossed the footbridge, he saw Carly sitting on one of the chaise longues on her patio, and Natalie at the nearby table, drawing on a sketch pad. Carly set aside the book she was reading, pushed her glasses atop her head, and came to meet him.

"I just dropped by to say good-bye." He waved at Natalie, who had looked up and was regarding him solemnly. She nodded and went back to her drawing. "We're heading out now," he added.

"We?" Carly looked past him to where Sam sat in the Jeep, examining her image in the mirror on the visor. "Hmmm."

"Not what you think, McGuire. The kid needs to get away from here, so I've signed her on as a deckhand. Johnny Crowe says business is booming, but I want to spend more time on my photography. Sam's a hard worker, and I think she and John-ny'll hit it off."

"And what about you?"

"I don't understand."

"Are you going to open up and hit it off with somebody?"

He smiled. "Maybe. I'm sure there'll be no shortage of pos-sibilities. Millie Bertram is always throwing eligible women at me."

"So catch one, why don't you?"

"I just might do that, now that I'm no longer haunted by a ghost." His gaze moved to Natalie. "How is she?"

"Subdued. She hasn't fully comprehended what's happened to Ard. Thinks she's ill—which she is, at least according to her lawyer. The psychologist I took Nat to agrees she doesn't need to know everything till she's made significant progress. I re-ceived temporary custody yesterday, and after a family court evaluation, that may become permanent. I like the judge; she says better the home where Nat's been living than foster care.

"Are you going to be okay with that—raising a little girl alone?"

"It's more likely to be a case of Nat and I raising each other."

He stepped forward and hugged her. Then he broke away and strode across the footbridge toward the Jeep. At its end he turned and called, "Keep in touch. The two of you come see me, okay?"

She nodded and waved.

He slid into the Jeep and said to Sam, "Quit staring at your-self. You're a pretty woman, and you'll sweep the Port Regis guys off their feet."

Then he started the engine and drove on, into his fifth and final life.

Carly McGuire

Friday, May 24, 2002

armed by her brief talk with Matt, Carly returned
to the patio. Nat was still drawing, the tip of her
tongue caught between her teeth.

"May I see?" Carly asked.

Nat hesitated, then handed over the sketch pad.

The delicate, precise pencil strokes depicted a garden scene,
and at the center of it, working the soil beneath a rose bush,
was a surprisingly realistic portrait of Ard.

In a low voice Nat said, "She's never coming back, is she?"

*Point number one from the psychologist: Don't lie to her. If she asks,
she's ready to hear.*

"No, she's not."

"I didn't think so. She was so weird all the time we were hiding in Uncle Deke's studio. I mean, she didn't talk or read or

anything like she used to. She just sat, staring at me or the wall. It was really scary."

"And you'll always remember that. I'm sorry to say, bad memories don't go away. But after a while they fade. Try to remember your mom like she is in your drawing."

Nat nodded and reached for it.

"You know," Carly said, "you're really a good artist, honey. Maybe we should sign you up for some lessons."

"That'd be great. But will you stop calling me 'honey'? You've been doing that all week, and I hate it. It sounds like you feel sorry for me. I don't like *anybody* to feel sorry for me—not even you."

This child has just captured my heart.

"I promise I will never feel sorry for you or call you 'honey' again. So what *shall* I call you?"

"Natalie or Nat, like you used to. Those're my names."

"Okay, Nat. I'll check into those art lessons."

We've got a long road ahead of us, kid, but we'll tough it out—the two of us, together.

MAN AND HIS NATURE

MAN
AND HIS NATURE
A Philosophical Psychology

JAMES E. ROYCE, S.J.

SEATTLE UNIVERSITY

McGRAW-HILL BOOK COMPANY, INC.

New York   Toronto   London

1961

MAN AND HIS NATURE

ACKNOWLEDGMENTS

The following publishers deserve thanks for kind permission to quote from copyrighted material: Appleton-Century-Crofts, Inc., Barnes & Noble, Inc., Harcourt, Brace & Company, Harper & Brothers, Henry Holt-Dryden Press, Alfred A. Knopf, Inc., McGraw-Hill Book Company, Inc., and World Book Company.

PREFACE

This book is primarily a text for the philosophical psychology or philosophy of man course, but it should also be of interest to the general reader who has some knowledge of the biosocial sciences. It does not presume to teach introductory psychology; the philosophy of human nature is in itself a full task for one term. Nor does it presuppose a knowledge of psychology, as will be clear from the discussion of the independent nature of philosophy in Chapter 1.

Scholastic philosophers often deplore the tendency of textbook authors to copy from one another; they want a fresh approach. On the other hand, in symposia, presidential addresses, and other official activities, the members of the American Psychological Association disagree more and more often with the narrow empiricism of early twentieth-century psychology; they frankly recognize that scientific psychology is "replete with metaphysical commitments" (Berenda, 1957, p. 726).[1]

[1] For easy reading, only the briefest identification of sources is given in the text of this book. Full identification of each reference will be found in the General Bibliography at the end of the book. There the above citation, for example, will be seen to refer to page 726 of an article by Carlton W. Berenda, "Is Clinical Psychology a Science?" in The American Psychologist for 1957, Volume 12, pages 725–729. If there is more than one book or article by the same author published during the same year, they are listed as 1957a, 1957b, etc.

This book is an attempt to present the traditional Scholastic philosophy of man's nature in a fresh light, from a point of view that may make it more acceptable to the modern scientific mind. This should please the philosopher looking for a new presentation, and the psychologist looking for philosophical orientation. The object is not to dispense with either psychology or philosophy: marriage is never the reduction of one to the other—*vive la difference!* That the two are compatible is the theme of this book. It is up to the reader to decide whether the result is a happy mating or a mismatch.

In this kind of matchmaking, there is always the danger of pleasing neither prospective partner. The philosopher will note some shifts in terminology (e.g., "special senses" for "external senses") and the elimination of the words "faculty" and "instincts." These changes have been made for the sole purpose of enabling the student to speak the language of his peers from other philosophical climes, or even of his professors of scientific psychology within the same institution. If the philosopher talks about man and his operations without some awareness of what modern psychology is saying, he is open to exactly the charge he most bitterly resents, that of working in a vacuum. We cannot afford to prepare students for life in a hypothetical English-speaking thirteenth century.

The psychologist may not be pleased by an apparently cavalier disregard for the details of his science. Respect for its findings he will see. It will be harder for him to understand how philosophical conclusions can be valid independently of his scientific theories. Yet here is precisely why a sound philosophical background can serve as a framework on which to arrange the myriad facts that psychologists are so industriously trying to fit into theories. Philosophy is not scientific theory; nor should it be despised because it is easier. It cannot answer the problems of science as science, but it can make the scientist's task easier. Because philosophy is not enmeshed in the intricacies of scientific hypothesis and verification, it can help by eliminating blind alleys, clarifying the subject matter of experiment, and giving meaning to the finished product.

Dorwin Cartwright of the University of Michigan indicates the need for such help when he reviews the conclusions of a symposium of outstanding psychologists attempting to work "Toward a Unified Theory of Human Behavior" (*Contemp. Psychol.*, 1957, 2:122).

It should come as no surprise, then, to find the same ancient problems causing trouble. They were rarely taken on deliberately; they just had a way of slipping into the conference room. The mind-body problem was there in all of its manifestations, for the conference was trying to arrange a compatible marriage between soma and psyche. Teleology reared its ugly head, and much time was consumed worrying about the propriety of using the word "goal" in polite scientific society. Reductionism insisted on being heard, but there never was agreement on what was to be reduced to what. For a time it did appear, though, that psychology might be dispensed with as long as biology and sociology were kept. And meaning persisted in sneaking in. . . . And yet a gnawing uneasiness remained to the end. Do these concepts provide mere analogies? Has a unity of science been achieved? Is the result really a monism, or a socio-psychophysical parallelism? What is actually accomplished by noting that cells and societies both have boundaries and steady states? What is the proper role of analogy in science?

These are all philosophical questions, whose answers deserve a philosophical competence few psychologists even strive to attain.

At least the psychologist will find in this book no Cartesian dualism, no "little man in the head" who chooses or guides, no straw man of psychoanalysis pictured as mere pan-sexualism, no need to abandon any established fact about human physiology or psychology. In a review of an earlier work of mine, *Personality and Mental Health*, a president of the American Psychiatric Association could say that it contained nothing in conflict with modern scientific teaching on the subject. It is hoped that my fellow members of the American Psychological Association can say the same about the present offering.

The widely used introductory texts by Professor Ernest R. Hilgard of Stanford, former president of the American Psychological Association, are frequently referred to as representing the viewpoint of current scientific psychology. Like the writings of Robert S. Woodworth of Columbia, which are equally representative but slightly older, they show no overt influence of Scholastic philosophy, although they are quite compatible with it.

Long experience in teaching this subject matter has dictated certain practical features in the organization of the present book. The immateriality of the intellect, freedom of choice, and the nature of the human soul are deemed the three pivotal problems for the undergraduate, and space is allotted accordingly. Philosophical orientation is given for the study of topics important to modern social science, such as emotion and motivation, habit, and the subjective factors in perception. Some traditional questions of little interest and use to modern students have been dropped in favor of more recent problems. Certain topics are lifted out of their logical order and placed where students are best prepared to take them up.

My debt to many sources will be acknowledged in the proper places. Here I should like to express gratitude to all the professors, critics, and students from whom I have learned, and for many opportunities to do advanced work in both philosophy and psychology. Aware of his inadequacies in both fields, the author, like the optimist who views the glass as half full rather than half empty, would like to feel that at least he has had better than average training in philosophy for a psychologist, and better training in psychology than many philosophers.

James E. Royce, S.J.

CONTENTS

Acknowledgments iv

Preface v

Supplementary Readings xi

Part One. INTRODUCTORY

1. Philosophy and Psychology 3
2. The Whole Man 24

Part Two. HUMAN KNOWLEDGE

3. Knower and Object 41
4. The Special Senses 58
5. The Internal Senses 70
6. The Intellect 88
7. Intellectual Activity 115
8. The Nature of Knowledge 131

Part Three. HUMAN DYNAMICS

9. Motivation 155
10. Emotion 165
11. Volition 175
12. Free Choice and Its Limits 186

Part Four. HUMAN POWERS AND HABITS

13. Operative Powers 227
14. Habits 238

Part Five. HUMAN SUBSTANCE

15. Man a Living Being 257
16. The Soul as Form 279
17. Nature of the Human Soul 307
18. Immortality of the Human Soul 321
19. The Origin of Man 337

    Appendix   Do Animals Have Intellect? 355

General Bibliography 365

Index 391

SUPPLEMENTARY READINGS

Below are listed a few books which will be helpful throughout the treatise. They will usually not be repeated in the lists of readings which follow each chapter.

AQUINAS, ST. THOMAS. His works are probably most readily available in Anton C. Pegis (Ed.), *Basic Writings of St. Thomas Aquinas*. New York: Random House, 1945. His treatise on man is in Vol. I, pp. 682–862; Vol. II, pp. 225–411. Much of this is contained in Anton C. Pegis (Ed.), *Introduction to St. Thomas Aquinas*. New York: Modern Library, 1948. Pp. 280–608.

AQUINAS, ST. THOMAS. *The Summa Theologica*. Trans. by the fathers of the English Dominican Province. New York: Benziger, 1947. The most readily available Latin text is *Summa Theologiae*. Ottawa: Studium Generale, O.P., 1941–1944. References to *S. T.* can be located by question number in the Pegis or other editions. Questions 75–90 of Part I (Ia) are especially pertinent.

AQUINAS, ST. THOMAS. *On the Truth of the Catholic Faith (Summa Contra Gentiles*, abbreviated *C. G.*) Trans. by James F. Anderson. Garden City, N.Y.: Doubleday (Image), 1955. Book II, Chaps. 46–90. Note that although the wording of the title of each *Summa* indicates theological content, we shall refer to them only as sources of philosophical argument.

AQUINAS, ST. THOMAS. *The Soul*. Trans. by John P. Rowan. St. Louis: Herder, 1949.

AQUINAS, ST. THOMAS. *Truth* (*De Veritate*). Trans. by R. W. Mulligan, S.J., J. V. McGlynn, S.J., & R. W. Schmidt, S.J. Chicago: Regnery, 1952–1954. 3 vols.

ARISTOTLE. *On the Soul* (*De Anima*) may be found in *Basic Works of Aristotle* (Ed. by Richard McKeon). New York: Random House, 1941; Modern Library, 1947.

ARISTOTLE. *De Anima* (in the version of William of Moerbeke and the commentary of St. Thomas Aquinas). Trans. by K. Foster & Silvester Humphries, with an introduction by Ivo Thomas, O.P. New Haven: Yale University Press, 1951.

Manuals

ANABLE, R. J., S.J. *Philosophical Psychology*. New York: Fordham University Press, 1941.

BRENNAN, R. E., O.P. *Thomistic Psychology*. New York: Macmillan, 1941.

DONCEEL, JOSEPH F., S.J. *Philosophical Psychology*. New York: Sheed, 1955.

GARDEIL, H. D., O.P. *Introduction to the Philosophy of St. Thomas*. Vol. III. *Psychology*. Trans. by J. A. Otto. St. Louis: Herder, 1956.

KLUBERTANZ, GEORGE P., S.J. *Philosophy of Human Nature*. New York: Appleton-Century-Crofts, 1953. Very thorough treatment.

KOREN, HENRY J., C.S.Sp. *An Introduction to the Philosophy of Animate Nature*. St. Louis: Herder, 1955.

MAHER, MICHAEL, S.J. *Psychology: Empirical and Rational*. (9th Ed.) London: Longmans, 1921. Old but thorough.

REITH, HERMAN, C.S.C. *An Introduction to Philosophical Psychology*. Englewood Cliffs, N.J.: Prentice-Hall, 1956. Includes many texts from Aristotle and St. Thomas.

RENARD, HENRI, S.J., & MARTIN O. VASKE, S.J. *The Philosophy of Man*. (2d Ed.) Milwaukee: Bruce, 1956.

Studies

COPLESTON, F. C. *Aquinas*. Baltimore: Penguin, 1955. Pp. 151–234.

FARRELL, WALTER, O.P. *Companion to the Summa*. New York: Sheed, 1942. Vol. I, Chaps. 12–15; Vol. II, Chaps. 2–3. Popular treatment.

GERRITY, BRO. BENIGNUS, F.S.C. *Nature, Knowledge, and God*. Milwaukee: Bruce, 1947. Pp. 145–287 treat of human nature in a synthesis of Scholastic philosophy.

GILSON, ETIENNE. *The Christian Philosophy of St. Thomas Aquinas*. New York: Random House, 1956. Pp. 147–264. This is a revision of his *The Philosophy of St. Thomas* (St. Louis: Herder, 1925) now out of print. Chaps. 10–15.

GILSON, ETIENNE. *The Spirit of Medieval Philosophy.* New York: Scribner, 1936. This is a classic work by perhaps the greatest Scholastic philosopher of this century. The treatise on human nature is in Chapters 9–15.

MEYER, HANS. *The Philosophy of St. Thomas Aquinas.* Trans. by Rev. F. Eckhoff. Part II. Sec. II. St. Louis: Herder, 1944. Chaps. 8–15.

OLGIATI, FRANCESCO. *The Key to the Study of St. Thomas.* Trans. by J. S. Zybura. St. Louis: Herder, 1925. Chaps. 2, 5.

PHILLIPS, R. P., O.P. *Modern Thomistic Philosophy.* Vol. I. Westminster, Md.: Newman, 1950. Pp. 173–346.

SERTILLANGES, A. D., O.P. *Foundations of Thomistic Philosophy.* Trans. by G. Anstruther. Springfield, Ill.: Templegate, 1956. Chaps. 2, 6, 7.

SULLIVAN, DANIEL J. *An Introduction to Philosophy.* Milwaukee: Bruce, 1957. Chaps. 8–16.

A useful bibliographical source is Mortimer J. Adler (Ed.), *The Great Ideas: A Syntopicon of the Great Books of the Western World.* Vol. II. Chicago: Encyclopaedia Britannica, Inc., 1952. Chap. 51.

PART ONE

INTRODUCTORY

1

PHILOSOPHY AND PSYCHOLOGY

What is man? Scientific theories and models contrasted with the methods and conclusions of philosophy. Aristotle's essentialism and mere correlationism both naïve. The peculiar nature of the subject matter of psychology as a science involves a special relation to philosophy. History and present status of the question.

What is the nature of man? And how can we come to know it? These two questions are vital not only to any complete philosophy, but also to some of the most basic problems that the human mind confronts. What is the true reason for our existence? Where did we come from? Why are we here? And where are we going? Is there a discoverable nature of man as a person with rights and dignity, which can serve as a foundation for our cherished democratic concepts? What is the basis of law? of human responsibility? of human rights? Is the notion of freedom compatible with the laws of nature? Does man have a nature which includes the spiritual, and how can this be known? In what does man's ultimate happiness consist? Questions of what man *should* do can be based only on what man *is*.

3

These are questions fundamental to that democratic way of life which we like to think is the core of western civilization, but we do not find universal agreement on how they can be answered. At first glance, it would appear that the brute animals are more competent than men in almost every area. We use bloodhounds instead of deputy sheriffs because dogs can smell and discriminate between odors better than man. Eagles can see farther, deer can run faster, elephants are more powerful physically, bats have their own built-in radar, cats can solve puzzle boxes, rats can learn to run a maze perfectly, and chimpanzees seem to solve problems in mechanical engineering. And now we have computing machines which calculate more reliably than brains and faster than scores of statisticians working frantically. Where do these facts leave man?

These questions must be answered with certainty if our present ideals are to have any meaning. With all due respect to the engineers, if our civilization breaks down it will not be because our bridges collapse, but because we have not formulated an adequate and satisfactory concept of the nature of man.

Vercors (1953)[1] wrote an interesting bit of science fiction about the discovery of a whole tribe of "missing links." The problem in the novel was to decide whether these creatures were to be regarded as human or not. The plot involved even the deliberate killing of one of them to precipitate a trial and force a court to make the decision. The solution is not very satisfactory, but the story points up the problem of this book: How can you tell whether a being is human or not?

SCIENCE, PHILOSOPHY, AND THEOLOGY

There are many ways of seeking the answer to such a question. Many sciences study man: psychology, anthropology, sociology, biochemistry. Can they give us the answers we seek? No, our questions do not fall within the scope of the natural sciences. Are we, then, to jump to the supernatural? Is an answer based on hope or belief

[1] To be found in the General Bibliography at the end of the book. The manner of identifying references used in this book is explained in footnote 1 of the Preface, p. v.

the only alternative to science? Theology may have its place, but it is not philosophy. An intelligent man needs to feel that his faith is reasonable, based on facts and an intelligent interpretation of those facts which will stand up under questioning by those who will not accept faith or divine revelation as a source of knowledge. We want satisfying answers that are not mere sentimentalism or fuzzy thinking. We must know for sure whether or not we are different from the brute animals if we are to have adequate reason for not acting like them. This knowledge must be more than theoretical, for it is hard to be reassuring if we are not sure.

That type of knowledge which is not religion or theology on the one hand, nor science on the other, is called *philosophy*. Occupying the middle ground between science and theology, philosophy has, until recently, not been fully appreciated. The last several centuries have seen first theological controversies and then the progress of science to a dominant position in our culture. Philosophy, meanwhile, has been belittled as mere empty speculation from a pre-scientific era. (Philosophy can be called a science in one sense of the term, but as with the word "psychology," we prefer to conform with current usage and equate the word "science" with the positive or empirical sciences, physical and behavioral.)

The average college student thinks of philosophy as some very abstruse, mysterious, and difficult study which is far beyond his powers. Actually it is much simpler and much easier than the physical sciences. The basic conclusions of this course can be reached much more easily than the molecular structure of a polymer or a sulfa drug.

Whereas science today is characterized by theory and approximation to truth, philosophy is concerned with certitudes and demonstrable fact. The trite stereotype of the armchair philosopher idly speculating about how many angels can dance on the point of a pin, or the metaphysician with "both feet firmly planted in the clouds," are not pictures obtained by a scientific investigation of the facts.

It is paradoxical that many scientists who have this conception of philosophy have never actually bothered to read what the philosophers say. When the scientist comes to discuss philosophy, he too often tends to abandon his concern for facts and indulge in the very type of unfounded speculation he deplores. Some psychologists, for example, have alluded derisively to an anecdote about medieval friars disputing the number of teeth a horse has, instead of going out and examining a horse.[2] These psychologists would not publish the slightest reference to scientific literature without footnoting and careful documentation, yet they make no attempt to substantiate this story by scholarly investigation of the primary sources.

A study of the writing of the medieval philosophers in the original Latin reveals that St. Thomas Aquinas, for instance, dismissed as absurd the question about angels dancing on the point of a pin, was amazingly insistent on observable facts, and spent many volumes discussing seriously and sensibly some practical problems very pertinent to human nature both then and now. If the decadent Scholastic philosophers of a later era lost sight of his approach, so much the worse for them. Historically it is they, not the medievals, whose failure to keep in touch with science brought philosophy into disrepute.

PHILOSOPHY CONTRASTED WITH PSYCHOLOGY

How then does philosophy differ from science, and specifically, how does the philosophy of human nature differ from modern scientific psychology? To begin with, it should be noted that the word "psychology" had for many centuries been used to designate that part of philosophy which deals with man and his ultimate nature. The Greek word "psyche" means soul, and it was used because the philosopher found the ultimate characteristic of man to be that he was a be-souled organism. (Aristotle's De Anima is really περὶ ψυχῆς.) Ironically enough, the Greek symbol for the psyche (Ψ) is still used by the American Psychological Association on all its publications, although they contain no discussion of the soul. The reason is that after the modern biosocial science which we now know as psychol-

[2] Morgan (1956, p. 7) mentions it without citing any source. Munn (1956, p. 4) and Buxton et al. (1952, p. 59) quote it second-hand.

ogy was born, about 1879, it took over this word for itself. The philosopher, who might have argued his right to the word on the grounds of "who was there first," has had to search out a new term for that part of philosophy now called philosophy of man or philosophy of human nature. Modern science neither asserts nor denies the existence of the soul, since the whole question of ultimates is outside the scope of scientific investigation. There can be no collision here, since the two trains of thought are running on different tracks.

Aside from the name, scientific psychology differs from the philosophy of man in three chief ways: the kind of facts used as a starting point; the method of procedure; and the type of conclusions it seeks, that is, its formal object.

Kind of Facts Used

First, let us be clear that both the philosopher and the scientist start with facts. Any philosophy which is not grounded on facts is not worth considering. It must also be broad enough to be compatible with all the facts, physical or otherwise. Not only that, but the facts used as a starting point must be certain, or one can never reach certainty in one's conclusions. At this point the student will ask how any of Aristotle's philosophy could be valid today, since he was unaware of the many facts which have been uncovered by the modern techniques of experimental psychology. The answer is that the philosopher and the scientist work from different kinds of facts.

The *scientist* uses complex experimental facts whose discovery may involve highly elaborate technological equipment, experimental laboratories, or refined statistical procedures. He usually makes exact measurements and presents his data quantitatively. For instance, the scientist may want to measure precisely the relation between the intensity of a stimulus and the intensity of a resulting sensation, or how a certain manner of learning affects the quantity of the result. He must control variable conditions and take many readings.

The *philosopher* begins with simple, primary facts which are commonly observable and which require no technology to discover. Of these he can be absolutely certain, and he need not worry about the precision of his measurements. He bases his conclusions on general facts which are directly observable in the common experience and behavior of all mankind: the facts that people live and die, think, feel, digest their dinners, see and hear. St. Thomas Aquinas, when discussing the important problem of the unity of man, comes back time and time again to two easily observable facts: this man understands, this man dies. The fact that people know or people die need not be learned in a laboratory or through elaborate statistical investigation. There is nothing closer to us than the experience of knowing, and we are all quite certain that man is the sort of being that dies.

These general facts, so readily observable, are quite different from so-called "common sense" notions which are often mere folklore. Most psychology books begin with a list of such common impressions, which they rightly show to be unwarranted: purported differences between men and women, misconceptions about the influence of heredity, and the like. These are not observed facts, but theories illogically inferred from haphazard observation. They demand critical, scientific investigation. We are talking about facts so directly observable that they are not a matter of inference—facts that are admittedly broad and general, leaving details to the scientist—but that are so incontestably evident that they need no further verification and are universally admitted. For example, it is unscientific to say that people with red hair get more angry than others, but it is a commonly admitted fact that people do get angry. This is the type of general fact which the philosopher uses.

The experimental psychologist carries such certitude about commonly observable facts with him when he enters his laboratory. He could not even begin to set up an experiment on hearing or vision if he did not first know the difference between seeing and hearing, or that there were such processes. As Prof. A. A. Maslow asserts in the *Nebraska Symposium on Motivation* (1955, p. 2), ". . . experimentation is generally the *last* step in the acquisition of knowledge rather than the first. Much theorizing and naturalistic observing has to be done before worthwhile experiments are possible. The experimenter is the last member of a relay team."

Morgan says (1956, p. 11), ". . . the experimental method is not the only method for establishing facts." It is important to note that this is the reason why we are not called upon to revise our philosophical conclusions every time a new article refuting the claims of a previous article is published in one of the scientific journals. Facts of the type that the philosopher uses simply do not change. Scientists now realize this, whereas, at the turn of the century, they often asked religious people to renounce their faith in the name of some purported scientific discovery which has since been abandoned by the scientists themselves.

Method of Procedure

Besides this difference in kind of facts used, philosophy and science differ in method. The scientist uses his elaborate techniques of observation and his laboratory instruments to gather a very wide and valid sampling of detailed facts. He is concerned about the adequacy of his coverage of cases, and from them he develops an explanatory hypothesis, which he then proceeds to verify through experiments. The philosopher does not proceed in this way, but his method must be, if possible, even more certain. Beginning with commonly observable facts about man's behavior and experience, he reasons according to rigorous logic, proceeding from the fact that man has the power to perform certain operations to the conclusion that he is the kind of being which can do these things. Thus we proceed from activities or operations to powers, and from powers to nature.

From the fact that man lives, we conclude he is an organism. Be-

Figure 1

Method of the Philosophy of Human Nature

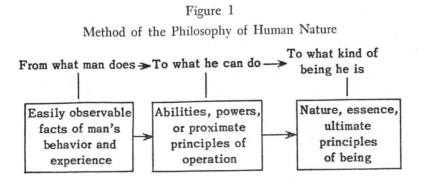

From what man does ➤ To what he can do ⟶ To what kind of being he is

Easily observable facts of man's behavior and experience	Abilities, powers, or proximate principles of operation	Nature, essence, ultimate principles of being

cause this organism is observed to see and hear, we know it is sentient organism, or animal. And since it also exhibits evidence of thought and choice, we call it a rational animal, or an organism that thinks. (This is merely an illustration of the process: we do not pretend to have proved anything at this point.)

It is now clear that we cannot begin with the essence or nature of man. Likewise, we do not deduce the existence of the soul from its definition, but rather we begin with the facts of man's operations and see if these facts lead logically to the existence of the soul as a necessary ultimate explanation. In doing so we shall often avail ourselves of data discovered in experimental psychology in so far as they clarify, confirm, and enrich common experience. It may be that on a few points the refined details of science may give us factual basis for modifying some minor philosophical conclusions but they cannot alter the general lines of our argument. This is because the commonly observable facts of which we spoke above are prior to both science and philosophy.

The philosopher will not and cannot afford to have his conclusions couched in approximations with a margin of error, such as those with which the scientist emerges from his laboratory. We may take an example from geometry to illustrate the difference (while noting that mathematics is not philosophy). A boy trained exclusively in the methods of the physical sciences would try to "prove" theorems by laying out lines and triangles carefully on gold foil, measuring them with a micrometer caliper for uniform thickness, weighing them on a delicate scale, or measuring them many times with precise instruments. At best he would emerge with the conclusion that angle A equalled angle B $\pm$ 0.0018°, or that the sum of the squares of the sides of a right triangle equaled the square of the hypotenuse plus or minus some respectable margin of error. In contrast, by some simple algebra or orderly reasoning about the congruence of triangles, we conclude that these angles or triangles are equal exactly and certainly, with no "plus or minus."

It should be obvious that the philosophy of human nature is not just "applied metaphysics." The philosopher does not take some preconceived metaphysical principles and from them deduce conclusions about the nature of man. Rather, he begins with the facts of man's experience and behavior, and from these he discovers what kind of a being man is. Since man is a being, it is clear that many of the conclusions will be intelligible in terms of metaphysical principles of being, such as potency and act, essence and existence, substance and accident, and so forth. These concepts are obviously analogous, not univocal. Neither can the philosopher begin with blind assumptions; however, he may legitimately accept as true some things which have been established elsewhere, e.g., in logic or metaphysics, just as the professor of biochemistry may assume the facts of general chemistry and anatomy.

Both Catholic and non-Catholic sources will be used throughout this book, for the simple reason that philosophy is not a matter of faith or religion, and consequently the authority of the source is not considered. The truth of the facts and the logic of the conclusions must be judged on their own merits, irrespective of who asserts them. It will thus be seen that the position taken is a purely rational one, independent of religious belief.

When we say that the philosopher argues from operations to nature, this does not imply that he attempts to decide whether a given trait or need is "natural" in a sense of being inherited or acquired. This is a problem for the scientific psychologist. The philosopher is content with the fact that man exhibits the trait, that his nature is clearly capable of this activity, whether because he is born with the capability or is the kind of being which can learn or acquire it. Much controversy among psychologists is thus irrelevant to the philosopher if he properly understands the limits of his investigation. This will be clear from the section below on the broad nature of philosophical knowledge.

Thus the method of the philosopher is simpler and more straightforward than the hypothetical-deductive-verification method which the scientist must use. Is there then no verification for the philosopher's conclusions? Besides the tests of consistency with the rest of his philosophy and confirmation by other facts, there is the further test of time. The importance of the history of philosophy will be considered shortly.

Type of Knowledge Sought

Philosophy also differs from science in its formal object, which indicates the type of conclusion to be sought. The material object, or subject matter, is the same, namely, man. The difference is in the formal object, or the formality under which man is studied. Thus sociology deals with man under the group aspect, biochemistry deals with him from the formal viewpoint of chemistry, the psychologist is interested in the laws of human behavior and experience. These sciences consider man socially, chemically, and psychologically.

The philosopher wishes to understand the very being of man *as man*. The philosopher may know only general truths about the nature of space, time, motion, and substance, without knowing specific essences. In the case of man the philosopher wishes to achieve a true, if limited, understanding of man's being or nature. This means an understanding of what man *is*, in terms of his ultimate causes: final and efficient, material and formal.

But how much can the philosopher know? Here we need a happy medium between the extreme of logical positivism, which would give us mere correlations, mere descriptions of the laws of man's operations couched in alternative possible theories or equally acceptable models, and the naïve essentialism of many Aristotelians, which implies that the philosopher can know the essences of all things. The scientist may have the more difficult task, for, at least in the case of man, the philosopher can use the facts of human operations to find out what a man is. Lawrence E. Cole of Oberlin College concludes his rather lengthy book *Human Behavior: Psychology as a Bio-Social Science* (1953, p. 822, italics his), with a summary restatement of Erich Fromm's position as follows: "There is an *essential Homo sapiens*. The essence is discoverable. . . . In a sense this is a kind of neo-Thomism, a neo-Aristotelian affirmation of an essential nature of man, an affirmation of the worthwhileness of the quest for a kind of *absolute* psychology, a super-cultural understanding on whose groundwork we could draw up a new *rights of man* that would form the charter for right living. . . ."

This type of statement would not be found in a textbook of psychology written before the middle of this century, but there is a growing awareness among psychologists of the need for philosophy. This was mentioned in the Preface and will be referred to again when we begin the study of the soul in Chapter 16. American psychologists are coming more and more to recognize explicitly the relation of their science to philosophy and the distinctly philosophical nature of some of the problems which have plagued them in the construction of their theories. One reason for this new point of view is the recent breakdown of logical positivism, which dominated so much of the philosophy of science during the 1920s and 1930s. Since 1950, P. Bridgman, R. Carnap (1956), and other leaders have reversed their position and recognized that at the level of theory and model we must go beyond mere correlationism. Some of the reasons given for this change are the increasing recognition of the role of analogy in science, the fertility of theory beyond expectation, the prediction of new kinds of events, and the convergence of theories. All of these indicate that the scientist in his theories is actually getting at reality, not merely correlating data (McMullin, 1955).

It is precisely because the scientist in his theory or model goes beyond data that he can never be sure of *exact* correspondence of his theory with reality, even though the theory provides more than the mere correlations to which the logical positivist limited him. Hence the value of a sound philosophy of human nature. While not productive of scientific theory as such, it can aid the scientist in formulating theory and protect him from the sterility which comes from a faulty perspective in the search for both phenomena and interpretation. Paradoxically, science is more dialectical than is philosophy: the more specialized a scientific investigation becomes, the more it involves hypothesis and deduction. The scientist invents intriguing theories and laboriously tries to substantiate them by analogy with ingenious models. The danger, of course, is of "not being able to see the forest for the trees," of getting lost in a realm of minute details or theoretical constructs.

The philosopher, because he observes only the most general facts, can move more easily from the existential order (particulars) to universal conclusion (essence). But his conclusions are also going to be more general and less specific than those of the scientist. He must humbly go about the sublime task of investigating man's fundamental nature, his essential properties. What he seeks is understanding in terms of basic principles: a viewpoint from which he can see all the facts in a balanced and meaningful relationship. A microscope is useful, but the bacteriologist cannot use it to tell whether his child has a smile or frown for daddy; he can see meaning in the arrangement of face muscles only by getting away from individual cells and looking at the pattern as a whole. Using only the most common and accessible facts, the philosopher misses much of the richness of detail uncovered by science. He must be content to paint with broad strokes a picture substantially correct in its bold outline, which can then be filled in by the psychologist's researches. His picture will not be exhaustive, nor does he naïvely expect an exact replica of man's nature; but it will be existential in the best sense of that word, for he moves directly from his experience of what man actually does to what man is.[3] His picture will not be stagnant, for he will be constantly at work to make it represent reality more and more perfectly; yet it will in a sense be unalterable, for it is based on facts and principles which cannot change.

IMPORTANCE OF THE HISTORY OF PHILOSOPHY

As Gilson points out (1937), the history of philosophy is to the philosopher what the experimental laboratory is to the scientist. When the scientist wishes to know what would happen if two chemicals are mixed, he takes a beaker and mixes them. When the philosopher wishes to know what will happen when this theory is proposed or that line of reasoning pursued, he does not have to speculate. He can delve into the history of philosophy and find

---

[3] In fact, the Jewish and Thomistic conception is more existential than Aristotle's, for Judaeo-Christian (not merely Catholic) thought is more concerned with the existing individual rather than with abstract essences. This does not mean that religious belief is invoked as philosophical proof: we simply call attention to the admitted fact that a given tradition is bound to influence one's way of looking at things.

recorded there the accumulated experiences of the human mind in dealing with these problems over the centuries.

The psychologist's disdain for philosophy has often robbed him of the fruits of over 2,300 years of human experience with the very problems to which his science almost always leads. The result is sometimes almost amusing. One quite competent American psychologist, in discussing a basic problem which occurs perennially, tried to show his awareness of history by stating that the problem was not a new one, for its history "goes as far back as Spinoza." What he seemed to be unaware of is that the problem was raised and solved by the ancient Greeks and thoroughly discussed in the Middle Ages. To go back only as far as Spinoza (A.D. 1677) shows a woeful lack of historical perspective and an ignorance of over 2,000 years of earlier philosophy. Bernard of Chartres says, "We are dwarfs, but standing on the shoulders of giants," the attitude we prefer to assume. The giants of the past give us a vision superior to the limited perspective we would have, were we unwilling to profit from previous experimenting.

This indifference of the psychologist toward the history of ideas is in striking contrast to his attitude toward the history of his own science. He does not simply lead the beginning psychology student into a well-equipped laboratory and tell him, "Now go ahead and discover the laws of learning," or perception, as the case may be, any more than the chemistry professor would turn his neophyte chemists loose in a laboratory full of reagents and have them "discover" oxygen, blissfully ignorant of the fact that Lavoisier ever lived. If, in the sciences, we have lecturers and textbooks to give the beginning student the benefit of the accumulated experiences and achievements of the past, why should we naïvely hope to start from scratch in philosophy and ignore what has gone before?

Professor Charles Spearman of the University of London spent much of his two-volume *Psychology Down the Ages* showing how often the psychologists of a later generation brought in the back door under a new name what had previously been thrown out the front door. The facts are there; rejection of a name usually means correcting a faulty conception with which the facts have become entangled.

Thus we have "faculty" thrown out and *ability* brought in a decade later; "instinct" goes out and *drives* come in; "intellect" falls into disrepute and fifty years later we have a great revival of interest in *thinking*; "free will" was rejected as unscientific nonsense and now we hear talk of *selective inhibition, client-responsibility*, and *choice-behavior*. And J. McV. Hunt, after surveying the past history and present status of psychology, concluded his presidential address to the American Psychological Association (1952) with a prediction that psychology would rediscover the soul. These cycles should reassure the student who worries lest what is contained here be soon outdated: truth is perennial, and if he just hangs on, it will eventually be in style again.

Intelligent men can never stray too far from the truth for very long, although their ways of conceiving of and expressing it may vary with the times and the language. If being is intelligible and man has the power of knowing it, sooner or later they are bound to get together. This is the basic assumption behind all progress in science. The reason why the "progress" of philosophy often takes a circular route (as does science in its pursuit of the intelligibility of the universe) is that philosophy deals with such fundamental problems. The eventual outcome of a line of reasoning is not easily foreseen; as a result, men cannot control the trend of a thought developed over several generations. (Nor do they always feel comfortable with truths which bridle pleasure; unconscious unwillingness to accept truth may start them off in another direction, as any clinical psychologist knows.)

Knowledge of history here will help the beginning student over one of his biggest hurdles: "How can I be right and very intelligent men be wrong?" If he has sentimentally distorted ideas of democracy or lives in a childish dream world, he may feel squeamish about facing the fact that contradictory opinions cannot both be right. He fails to distinguish between a person's right to an opinion and the opinion itself. The stand that "everything is just a matter of opinion" is itself merely an opinion, and it opens up the possibility that the opposite is true. If he tries to settle his bank balance on the basis of an opinion that two plus two equals five, he will find the teller tolerant of him as a person, but the truth quite intolerant.

Great tolerance for the divergent opinions found among even good minds flows from an awareness of "how they got that way." Students can find great help with this problem through a knowledge of the history of psychology based on Spearman's cycles. Behaviorism becomes intelligible when seen as a reaction against the abuses of introspection; psychoanalysis is understandable in its historical setting of sterile structuralism and puritan Victorianism; and determinism can be seen as flowing from the devotion to classic physics which characterized the scientism of 150 years ago. It is a painful and laborious process to sort through the mixture of truth and error which each great work contains, rather than characterize it as all black or all white, but history will often explain how the two became mixed in brilliant minds. Thus the student, though a dwarf intellectually, can have a vantage point that is denied those who, for a variety of historical and emotional reasons, do not share his perspective.

SPECIAL RELATION OF PSYCHOLOGY TO PHILOSOPHY

The peculiar nature of the subject matter of psychology, namely, man, seems to place it in a very special relation to philosophy, even though now it is a distinct science. This seems to be true not only of psychology as an applied art (clinical), but even as a pure or theoretical science. The existence of this special relation is evidenced by (1) the nature of psychology and (2) the writings of psychologists.

1. One fact peculiar to psychology is that the scientist is his own data: his nature is too close to the facts concerning his study to escape notice. Whereas the chemist can be proficient in his subject matter without elaborating a cosmology, the same does not seem to be true of the psychologist and a philosophy of man. The chemist can study structures and valences without asking why they should be that way, what is their purpose or goal. But goals and purposes are so

much a part of every man's experience that the psychologist is led inevitably to philosophical considerations.

Moreover, the concepts used in the empirical approach (the terms of the induction) usually have meaning only within a philosophical structure. Because of the complexity of man, you can hardly control all the variables or know when you have an adequate induction unless you have as a guide a basic understanding of the nature of man. Again, philosophical presuppositions determine our choice of the phenomena to be studied. The queer mixture of facts about man, namely, his mental or conscious experience and his externally observable behavior, lead at least to suspicions that his nature must be involved in two realms, the material and the immaterial.

2. This special relationship is confirmed by the history and present status of scientific psychology, as seen in statements by the psychologists themselves. The rejection of a philosophical orientation is surely a factor in the situation described by Frank W. Finger of the University of Virginia in a special review of general psychology textbooks in the *Psychological Bulletin* (1954, 51:90), "No great perspicacity is required to sense the restlessness that pervades instruction in general psychology. We can't quite agree on what we should be doing, or how."

J. L. McCary in *Psychology of Personality: Six Modern Approaches* (1956, pp. xiii–xiv) points out how modern psychology, which has never been able to stomach Cartesian dualism, has had to wrestle constantly with the apparent dichotomy between organic and mental, a split which is only now disappearing in favor of integration. These problems are inescapably philosophical. Likewise, the fact that man has some control and direction of his drives or responses to stimuli suggests that other laws of nature must apply to his behavior than those which control the activity of beings which do not have this inner regulation.

As a matter of fact, psychologists rarely succeed in avoiding at least an implicit reliance on philosophy, in spite of professing to stay in the realm of pure science. (See the quotation from Cartwright in the Preface of this book.) Psychologists often forget that the denial of metaphysics is itself a metaphysical position, and materialism is every bit as much a philosophy as is an attitude that goes beyond matter. Now that psychology has dropped the adolescent defensiveness which characterized its earlier struggle to emancipate itself from philosophy, it is time to acknowledge its awareness of interdisciplinary relations. As E. G. Boring of Harvard editorializes in *Contemporary Psychology* (1958, 3:362), ". . . the psychologists resist the humanizing deviations that would bring their science over toward scholarship and wisdom and understanding, resist them sometimes because they are dedicated to a narrow empiricism."

Although it would be quite legitimate to *prescind* from philosophy as many a good scientist does, most psychologists of the first half of the twentieth century were not entirely nonphilosophical. Rather, in their desire to avoid philosophy, they failed to take it seriously enough to achieve the competence necessary to develop any explicit philosophy, and simply indulged in some implicit and often lamentable philosophizing of their own.

Various schools of psychology in the first half of this century were inclined to imply that we can know nothing but external behavior, or nothing but operations. Now the denial of other kinds of knowledge is an epistemology, a philosophical position rather than a scientific one. Again, some tended to imply that man and indeed all reality is composed of nothing but matter. But any assertion or denial of the ultimate principles of being is a metaphysics. Hence the "nothing but" positions of these schools of psychology were really philosophical. Moreover, they were assumptions that were not based on data. There is always danger that the prestige merited in one field will be thought a proof of competence in all: neither the Pope nor a Beethoven are authorities on baseball, nor is the scientist as scientist an expert on philosophy. The present endeavor differs at least in being frankly philosophical instead of surreptitiously so. Even were this study of little aid to the scientific psychologist, it has in itself the value of all philosophy: Pursuit of that simpler truth which is wisdom.

REVIEW QUESTIONS

A summary of each chapter might tempt the student not to think through the material for himself. On the other hand, the following questions should help him to get the most from his reading.

1. Why is the philosophy of human nature the basis for political science and ethics? What are the political consequences of denying the special nature of man?
2. Is there any legitimate knowledge besides science and theology? What is the nature of this knowledge?
3. How does philosophy differ from theology?
4. Show how the difference in the kind of facts used explains how philosophy is independent of scientific advance.
5. What events in the history of the last 400 years would explain why many scientists are unwilling to look toward Aristotle and St. Thomas as sources of valid knowledge?
6. Are philosophy and psychology distinct? Have they always been kept separate?
7. What is logical positivism? If the logical positivists were right, could philosophy be true knowledge? Is logical positivism a scientific or a philosophical position?
8. Does modern psychology *as a science* take a position with regard to the existence of the soul?
9. Can we establish the existence of the soul from its definition?
10. How do we come to know a nature? Are essences as such directly observable?

FOR FURTHER READING

See also, for this and each subsequent chapter, the pertinent parts of the works listed immediately following the Table of Contents. To identify references in the text, consult the General Bibliography at the end of the book.

The student is to understand that inclusion of a book in these lists does not necessarily mean full agreement with everything it contains; as a philosopher he must decide whether there is any real disagreement and, if so, choose on the basis of evidence and logic. These lists at the ends of the chapters do not pretend to be exhaustive but merely suggest some of the possibilities for further information or alternative presentation.

Science and Human Nature

BARUK, H. "Personality: Psychological and Metaphysical Problem," *Phil. Today*, 1957, 1:122–127.

CALDIN, E. F. *The Power and Limits of Science.* London: Chapman & Hall, 1949.

DONCEEL, JOSEPH F., S.J. "What Kind of Science is Psychology?" *The New Scholasticism*, 1945, 19:117–135.

FEIGL, HERBERT. "Philosophical Embarrassments of Psychology" (invited address to the 1958 convention of the American Psychological Association), *Amer. Psychologist*, 1959, 14:115–128.

GILL, HENRY V., S.J. *Fact and Fiction in Modern Science.* New York: Fordham University Press, 1944.

KANE, WILLIAM H., O.P., and others. *Science in Synthesis: A Dialectical Approach to the Integration of the Physical and Natural Sciences.* River Forest, Ill.: Dominican College, 1953.

LEE, OTIS. *Existence and Inquiry.* Chicago: University of Chicago Press, 1949. Pp. 307–309 contain a clear statement by a non-Catholic on the difference between philosophy and science.

McCALL, RAYMOND J. *Preface to Psychology.* Milwaukee: Bruce, 1959. A clear explanation of the nature of scientific psychology.

MARTIN, OLIVER. *The Order and Integration of Knowledge.* Ann Arbor, Mich.: University of Michigan Press, 1956. Chap. 9.

WELLMUTH, JOHN J. *The Nature and Origins of Scientism.* Milwaukee: Marquette University Press, 1944.

WHITEHEAD, ALFRED N. *Science and the Modern World.* New York: Macmillan, 1925. Pp. 80–81, 214.

WILD, JOHN (Ed.) *The Return to Reason: Essays in Realistic Philosophy.* Chicago: Regnery, 1953.

For Historical Perspective

BOUTROUX, EMILE. *Historical Studies in Philosophy.* Trans. by Fred Rothwell. London: Macmillan, 1912. Boutroux deserves much of the credit often given to Bergson for stemming materialism in France.

BRACELAND, F. J. (Ed.) *Faith, Reason and Modern Psychiatry: Sources for a Synthesis.* New York: P. J. Kenedy & Sons, 1955. Edited by a recent president of the American Psychiatric Association who is also a Catholic.

BRENNAN, R. E., O.P. *History of Psychology from the Standpoint of a Thomist.* New York: Macmillan, 1945.

BRENNAN, R. E., O.P. *Thomistic Psychology.* New York: Macmillan,

1941. Part III, "The Moderns," shows relationships between scientific psychology and traditional philosophy.

CHANT, S. N. F., & SIGNORI, E. I. *Interpretive Psychology*. New York: McGraw-Hill, 1957. An introductory text which uses contributions from such Catholic psychologists as Moore, Schneiders, Arnold & Gasson, Herr, and Kobler.

GANNON, T. J. *Psychology: The Unity of Human Behavior*. Boston: Ginn, 1954. An excellent textbook of scientific psychology, with an introductory chapter which orients the whole in the context of history and scholastic philosophy. Gannon is a recent president of the American Catholic Psychological Association.

GILSON, ETIENNE. *The Unity of Philosophical Experience*. New York: Scribner, 1937.

MERCIER, D. J. CARDINAL. *The Origins of Contemporary Psychology*. (2d Ed.) London: R. & T. Washbourne, 1918.

MISIAK, HENRYK, & STAUDT, VIRGINIA M. *Catholics in Psychology*. New York: McGraw-Hill, 1954. Detailed account of the activities and contributions in modern scientific psychology by persons with a background of Scholastic philosophy, in both America and Europe.

MÜLLER-FREIENFELS, RICHARD. *The Evolution of Modern Psychology*. Trans. by W. B. Wolfe. New Haven: Yale University Press, 1935.

MURPHY, GARDNER. *An Historical Introduction to Modern Psychology*. (Rev. Ed.) New York: Harcourt, Brace, 1949.

SMITH, VINCENT EDWARD. *Idea-Men of Today*. Milwaukee: Bruce, 1950.

SPEARMAN, CHARLES. *Psychology Down the Ages*. New York: St. Martin's, 1937. 2 vols.

WOODWORTH, R. S. *Contemporary Schools of Psychology*. (Rev. Ed.) New York: Ronald, 1948.

Psychologists Examine Their Science

ADLER, MORTIMER J. "Introduction," in R. E. Brennan, O.P. *Thomistic Psychology*. New York: Macmillan, 1941, Pp. vii–xiv. Tells how a Ph.D. in psychology from Columbia University discovered Aristotle and St. Thomas.

BERENDA, C. W. "Is Clinical Psychology a Science?" *Amer. Psychologist*, 1957, 12:725–729.

CARTWRIGHT, DORWIN. Review of Roy R. Grinker (Ed.), *Toward a Unified Theory of Human Behavior*, *Contemp. Psychol.*, 1957, 2:121–123.

DAVIS, R. C. Review of Warner Brown & H. C. Gilhousen, *College Psychology*, *Psychol. Bull.*, 1951, 48:366–367.

FINGER, F. W. "Textbooks and General Psychology: A Special Review," *Psychol. Bull.*, 1954, 51:82–90.

HOOK, SIDNEY (Ed.) *Psychoanalysis, Scientific Method and Philosophy.* New York: New York University Press, 1959.

LUND, F. H., & GLOSSER, H. J. "The Nature of Mental Illness: Diversity of Psychiatric Opinion," *Education*, 1957, 78:154–166.

MOWRER, O. H. "Some Philosophical Problems in Mental Disorder and Its Treatment," *Harvard Educ. Rev.*, 1953, 23:117–127.

See also the presidential addresses of J. McV. Hunt, O. H. Mowrer, J. P. Guilford, and K. S. Lashley listed in the General Bibliography.

2

THE WHOLE MAN

Parts versus whole. Method of investigation: operations to powers to nature. Notion of operative powers: abilities distinct but not separate. Human experience and behavior. Preliminary view of man.

Every poet, philosopher, and psychologist has described in his own terms the warring factions within man: Plato, St. Paul, Shakespeare, Freud, Sartre. If man had only one operation, it would be clear that he is one being. Or if he only had one *kind* of operation, he would only be one kind of being. But in view of the complexity of human operation, the unity of man's nature presents a real problem. Gardner Murphy, in the closing pages of his *An Historical Introduction to Modern Psychology* (1949, pp. 444–445), states:

> But the most acute of all issues in contemporary psychology seems to be the issue of *wholes and parts*; the quest for patterned structure or for the definition and functional analysis of component elements. It is in a sense the old issue of Aristotle's forms versus Democritus's atoms, but it is stated today in terms of evolutionary holism, the indivisibility of the "living system," or in terms of

24

laboratory analysis of behavior into identifiable and measurable units. There are so many facts that call for the one approach, so many that call for the other, that at first sight one might hesitate to make a final choice between them. . . .

One may begin to suspect that the basic temperamental or emotional incompatibility of the promachine and antimachine theorists has changed rather little in recent decades. One might even point out that the issue drawn by La Mettrie two hundred years ago still stands approximately as he defined it. More and more technical research gives more and more weapons to each school. The history of biology and that of psychology give no reason for believing that the question of mechanism is soluble by the mere accumulation of more and more data . . . it cannot be resolved by any present type of evidence, or by any evidence of which we can conceive. . . .

This passage tells us that the question of the unity of man is perennial and acute. Murphy's further assertion, that the question is not to be answered by amassing more factual evidence, suggests that for a solution we look toward the methods of philosophy. Is man a machine, a conglomeration of parts? or is he a single unified organism? Heated as this question is in psychology, it is an even more crucial problem for the philosopher. If man is not one being, there is no need for the soul as the principle of oneness. The question must be asked the right way, or we will be guilty of presuming the very fact we pretend to prove. There is obvious multiplicity in man's operations; the question of oneness is not in regard to his activities but to his very being.

Method of Investigation

But how can we know anything about man as a being? We saw in the previous chapter that the nature of a being as such is not directly observable. We must observe its operations and then draw conclusions about its nature. The question now is, does man operate as many beings or as one being?

Operation Shows Nature. Our procedure, then, is from operations to nature, or from effect to cause. The justification for this procedure is simply the principle of causality expressed in the old adage, "Nothing gives what it hasn't got," or "Operation follows being" (*operatio sequitur esse*). This means that a thing acts in accordance with its nature, and consequently we can infer its nature from the way it acts. If it does this or that, it obviously must be the kind of being which can do so.

As St. Thomas Aquinas says, there are two ways of knowing that we have an intellectual soul. Our awareness of ourselves as a particular thinking subject is immediate and is implicit in the very act of knowing. But to make this awareness an explicit part of the general knowledge about the nature of the thinker requires a "diligent and subtle investigation." [1]

The precise nature of the inference involved in this investigation is now being reexamined.[2] Although making this inference is hard work, it seems to be less a matter of rationalistic deduction than older textbooks might suggest. The student must be warned that a syllogistic "proof" is often not a description of how knowledge was actually obtained, but analysis of what was perhaps grasped intuitively at first.

Since there is no knowledge of the existence of man apart from some knowledge of his nature (as will be evident later from our insistence on the perceptual judgment as the characteristic form of human knowledge), this procedure from-operation-to-power-to-nature might be described as a sort of experiential induction, a fuller realization of facts we already knew, implicitly and confusedly, about man from observing his actions.

Thus we have had some insight into substance and accident, or into potency and act, long before we ever opened a metaphysics book. Being analogous concepts, they are never grasped by pure abstraction: to predicate existence is not to impose a univocal form

---

[1] S. T., Ia, 87, 1.

[2] See Armand Maurer, C.S.B., "Introduction" to *St. Thomas Aquinas, The Division and Methods of the Sciences* (2d rev. ed. Toronto: Pontifical Institute, 1958); Peter Hoenen, S.J., *Reality and Judgment According to St. Thomas* (Trans. by H. F. Tiblier, S.J., Chicago: Regnery, 1952); John E. Gurr, S.J., *The Principle of Sufficient Reason in Some Scholastic Systems, 1750–1900* (Milwaukee: Marquette University Press, 1959); "Genesis and Function of Principles in Philosophy," *Proc. Amer. Cath. Phil. Asso.*, 1955, 29:131–133; "Some Historical Origins of Rationalism in Catholic Philosophy Manuals," *ibid.*, 1956, 30:170–180.

on something. Similarly, the existence of an operative power is unintelligible apart from some vague awareness of the subject which operates on the one hand and its operation on the other, as well as the relations between the three. But what is explicitly observed is the operation, and this naturally implies power and substance. We do not directly observe power as such. That ours is no wall-and-paint theory of substance and accident will be quite clear from the discussion of the nature of operative power in Chapter 13.

Whole or Parts? Man is too complex to study all at once, so it seems logical to take him part by part. This is the method used in such approaches to the study of man as psychophysics, structuralism, behaviorism, operationism, and in most testing. Painstaking work in these fields has contributed much to our knowledge of human activity, through the measurement of individual responses.

But how can we understand the parts except in view of the whole? A partial view could give us a false knowledge, which is worse than no knowledge at all. Moreover, there are many facts about man's operations which are total, that is, of their very nature they involve the whole man and we see them incorrectly when we try to take them apart. This has been the argument of the personalistic, holistic, and Gestalt psychologists, who insist that the whole is more than the sum of the parts. Their experiments on perception and theories of personality are quite at variance with the part by part approach. Even the operationalists, who want to define the "intervening variables" between stimulus and response purely in terms of the operations by which we try to study them, soon find that this approach involves a leap in the dark from observed data to concepts intelligible only in the light of the total personality or total organism. The same heat which melts the butter hardens the egg: response is rarely explainable by stimulus alone.

Which side shall we take in this perennial debate? We shall try to maintain balance by looking at the facts on both sides. We shall study man as a whole composed of many parts and try to look at the parts without losing sight of the whole. Here is a man who trembles with anger at the thought of some outrageous injustice. His trembling, his anger, his thoughts about injustice are all different, yet all are the acts of the same one man. To isolate them from one another or from the man is to make them not only meaningless but nonexistent. They can only exist in the man who is angry. There is a totality here which is undeniable, yet thinking about injustice is not the same as trembling.

Procedure. We shall begin with a preliminary view of the whole man, before we descend to the parts. (In so doing we may raise more questions than we can answer in this chapter. This should not disconcert us; the philosopher is a seeker after truth and he expects that the search will take time.) Then, in Parts 2, 3, and 4 (Chapters 3 through 14), we shall examine the various operations of man, always in the light of his total being. In Chapter 15 at the beginning of Part 5 we shall return to the question of the unity of man's being, for we must survey all of his acts and powers before we are in a position to draw definitive conclusions about his nature.

Both Objective and Subjective Data

Man has many activities, and they are of many different kinds. It would be begging the question at this point to determine which are specifically human and which are not. At least it is obvious that man's operations include some which are distinctly physical, for his body obeys the laws of gravity and motion, and some which are distinctively psychological, for man has conscious experiences of various kinds. If it is a fact that he has conscious experiences, it would be most unscientific to ignore them (Hilgard, 1957, p. 4). Consequently both the philosopher and the scientist must take into account man's external behavior as well as his inner experience.[3]

As a matter of fact, man can observe his own conscious experiences, though ordinarily he does not explicitly reflect on them. This act of reflection on the experience itself is what "consciousness"

---

[3] For this reason, the term "rational psychology" seems an inappropriate title for the philosophy of human nature. It has two unfortunate implications. It implies that scientific psychology does not study man's rational operations; yet thinking and behavior due to choice are unavoidable psychological facts, as we shall see in the next chapter. And it implies that philosophy studies *only* the rational operations; yet the sensory and organic aspect must be included or a false picture of man will result.

meant in the older philosophical sense, and it must be distinguished from simple awareness. The latter term is what consciousness usually means in common usage. "Simple awareness" includes "consciousness" only implicitly, to the extent that we can be aware of nothing without concurrently being at least dimly aware of ourselves as knowers. It is I who see, I who think, I who feel and digest and move.

Human Experience. This *I* is called ego[4] in psychology, and is becoming again the focal point of psychological investigation. It seems very appropriate to our psychological era to begin our discussion of the philosophy of man with the ego or self. Throughout this treatise the student should frequently ask himself, does this square with my experience? Is this what I experience happening to me?

Man is neither a disembodied mind nor a mere biological object, but a living, thinking organism. Man has traditionally been defined as a rational animal, though he often appears to be the only irrational animal. He does, however, have many experiences which he does not share with other animals: the fact that he cares, and is very bothered by the "care-less" man, means that he is committed to his fellow beings in a special relationship. He has emotions which are closely connected with his role as artist, as poet, as hero; yet neither artistry nor heroism is experienced as the result of mere emotion. Whatever we may know about animals by conjecture and analogy, we know that man has a sense of history: he is aware of the heritage of the past, and he knows that his own acts transcend the present and leave some footprints on the sands of time. He is conscious of his own mortality, yet because of his awareness of it he reaches out for relationships beyond himself: he wants to be remembered, to have relations with others that surpass his own contingent existence.

These facts of human experience are studied by modern existentialists and phenomenological philosophers such as Cassirer, Sartre, Husserl, Heidegger, Oliver Martin, and psychologists such as Ausubel,

---

[4] Psychologists distinguish between ego and self, usually attaching to the latter term a connotation of more subjective evaluation. For the philosopher, it is more important to distinguish between the empirical or conscious realm of accidents and the substance of man in which these accidents ultimately inhere.

Allport, and Nuttin. They give a personalistic subjectivity to philosophy without any epistemological subjectivism.[5]

Objective Data Important. We wish to avoid a mere phenomenology which could easily lead us into the unfortunate difficulties of pure introspectionism. The facts of experience to which we appeal are the common and repeatable observations of all men. Moreover, we constantly check our experience against observable behavior, as for instance Young does in his study of affective factors (1955, pp. 193–238), or the better Gestalt experimenters do.

These findings may be supplemented by observations of animals other than man, but we must insist that the data thus obtained are not in our direct experience and can give us information about human activities only by analogy. These remain our primary source of knowledge. Even the "tough-minded" experimentalist finds himself interpreting his data with reference to his own experience: operational definitions are really aimed at what is measured, though seemingly aimed at how we measure it (see Hilgard, 1953, pp. 567–568). Again, human physiology is more pertinent than zoology but sometimes it is expedient to use other animals in experiments and then try to draw parallels to human activity or verify findings in the more complex setting of man's body.

OPERATIVE POWERS OR ABILITIES

It will become clear that the same ego or self has many abilities and many operations. That he has many operations is obvious. That these flow from different abilities is clear from the fact that they are different *kinds* of operations: we do not think by means of our power of digestion, or walk by the power of vision. Therefore man must have abilities such as those of thinking, digestion, imagining, and seeing.

Now it would seem quite obvious that the power by which I digest is not the same as that by which I imagine. But unfortunately,

[5] See Joseph de Finance, S.J., "Being and Subjectivity," trans. by W. Norris Clarke, S.J., *Cross Currents*, 1956, 6:163–178; Robert O. Johann, S.J., "Toward a Philosophy of Subjectivity," *Proc. Jesuit Phil. Ass.*, 1958, pp. 35–75; F. J. Diemert, S.J., "Thomistic Psychology and the Social Dimension of Man," *ibid.*, 1959, pp. 11–64.

this simple notion became badly distorted in the eighteenth century by the introduction of the word "faculty" to designate these various abilities, with the implication that faculties were separate little things or substances within man. Thus we have the caricature of the will as a little man inside us pulling levers, the intellect as a little man inside us who thinks or guides.

Modern psychologists quite rightly rejected this preposterous conception, pointing out that it was impossible to discover any such entities within man. Unfortunately, they confused the concept of faculty with the common-sense notion of ability which we have described above and to which they would all consent. St. Thomas Aquinas in the thirteenth century, at once more medieval and more modern than the eighteenth century philosophers, hardly ever used the word "faculty" in this connection, although it was in his vocabulary. He preferred the terms "operative power" or "ability," as do moderns like Spearman and Thurstone. St. Thomas's approach is an operational one at this point. Observing what man does he naturally concludes that man has the ability to do so. But it is *man* who performs the operation, not some mythical entity. The power is not *that which* acts, but that *by which* man acts.

We shall return to a more philosophical analysis of this concept in Part 4, where we shall see that abilities are permanent proper accidents (or properties), as opposed to contingent accidents such as operations which can begin and cease. Abilities have not been offered as an explanation of behavior or to cover up our scientific ignorance. To say that a cat sees because he has the power of sight is no explanation; rather, we know he has the power of sight because he sees. The philosopher makes the obvious inference; the scientist makes the detailed investigation.

Distinct but Not Separate. The student must discern the difference between being distinct and being separate. It is important to understand that although we recognize the operations, the abilities, and the man as distinct, we insist that they are not separate. It is true that separation is often one sign of distinction; and thus the fact that the man can cease thinking, i.e., that man and his thought can be separated, is clear proof that they are distinct. But even if two things are never separated (and we still see this to be true of the man and his abilities) they may still be distinct. Distinct means not identical: that one is not the other. Two things may be distinct even though they are inseparable. Thus the man is not his thinking or his digestion, even if these operations were never separated from the man. An understanding of this difference between distinct and separate will prevent the student from becoming a victim of the fallacy that because two things are inseparable they are therefore identical: for instance, because certain mental operations cannot exist without an organ, we need not necessarily conclude that they *are* the organ.

One Substance, Many Accidents. The distinction between substance and accident may, but need not, be presumed from metaphysics. The distinction is also obvious in man's own experience, for his thoughts and actions come and go, yet he is conscious of being the same self who has the various thoughts and actions. At this point we do not presume anything about the nature of this self except that it must be substantial, since activities cannot exist independently of the one acting. Nature is simply substance considered as the source of operations, which are accidents. As we shall see, this distinction between substance and accident makes it possible to understand the unity of man as a being in spite of the multiplicity of his operations.

The unity of composition of substantial principles forming one being is a concept more difficult to grasp, but equally important, for on this point are reconciled the material and immaterial properties of man. Confining ourselves here to a phenomenological and operational approach (accidents), we shall return to the notion of substantial principles in Part 5 of this book. We are mentioning the subject now simply to warn against the error which has plagued the investigation of man's nature throughout history: the false dualism of Plato and Descartes, which considers that man is two beings because he shows evidence of two kinds of activity. Notice that this is a question of kinds of being, in the realm of ultimates. It is not the same as the parts versus wholes issue, which is in the order of operation and proximate principles.

PRELIMINARY VIEW OF MAN

Before descending to the details of man's various activities and supplying proofs as needed, it will be well to take an over-all view. Without their losing the commonly observable character as noted in Chapter 1, we see that these facts could be encompassed in the findings of a variety of approaches: physiology, psychology, anthropology, sociology, linguistics, semantics, and biochemistry.

How shall we arrange these facts? Any order would seem somewhat arbitrary in view of what we have said about the totality and complexity of man. For convenience we shall divide them first into the general categories of knowledge and dynamics. The distinction be-

Figure 2

The Activities of Man

Cognitive (knowing)	Appetitive (dynamic)
Intellection (thinking)	Volition (will acts)
Sensory knowledge: Sensation Perception Imagination etc.	Sensory appetition: Drives Impulses Feelings etc.
Vegetative functions	

tween knowing and wanting, between cognition and appetition, seems fairly obvious.

Cognition. Knowing is a complex activity involving sense organs, perceptual powers, and intellectual judgments. While recognizing that all these elements may be at work simultaneously in the same process, we shall study them in an ascending order from simple sensation to the process of thinking. Here we try to analyze what is involved when man acts as observer, dreamer, and thinker, namely, sense perception, imagination, intellect.

Dynamics. But man is not only a knower: he tends to act on his knowledge. This type of operation, tending as opposed to knowing, is called appetition. Approach-avoidance, attraction-aversion, and similar names are used to indicate that the tending is either toward or away from an object known, depending on whether it is "good to have" or "good to avoid." The term used is *elicited appetition,* because the appetite is elicited or stimulated by some awareness, to distinguish it from *natural* tendencies such as gravity, chemical valence, tropisms, or vegetative functions. Such tendencies are called "natural appetites" only by an extension of the term "appetite."

A study of human dynamics or appetition reveals a wide range of processes, from organic drives to self-directed activity. Desiring can become very intense, and emotion involves marked changes in the endocrine and sympathetic nervous systems. We range dynamic forces from the simplest biological need to the most intricate act of choice.

Again we remind ourselves that although we distinguish cognition from appetition for purposes of study, in reality knowledge and dynamics are intimately interwoven and usually inseparable, just as the sensory and intellectual levels are distinct but not separate.

Organism. All the processes connected with cognition and appetition involve physiological functioning in one way or another, using the nervous system as organ and connector. Endocrine glands and body structure exert important influence on human activity, and must be considered if we are to have a complete knowledge of man's nature. Man is animal and even vegetable, as St. Thomas repeatedly points out.

Another reason why the philosopher must consider the physiological side of man is so that he will know when a biological explanation is sufficient and will not appeal unnecessarily to more exalted interpretations. Likewise, he should be aware of the limitations of organism: Hilgard (1953, p. 110) says, "It is a general rule that human motives can never be fully explained on the basis of physiological influences alone."

Powers and Habits: Learning. A simple outline of the broad divisions mentioned thus far is given in Figure 2. But this chart lists only activities or operations, grouped according to kind and therefore suggesting different abilities or operative powers. Now if we are to take into account the subtleties of human behavior, we must recognize that such activities do not spring full-blown from the mere possession of said powers: *learning* takes place at every level, and many of our tendencies are elicited by stimuli of which we are not explicitly aware. To account for these facts our chart must indicate the distinction between operation, power, and habit. For learning, in the broadest sense of the term, means the modification or perfection of operative powers by the acquisition of *habits*.

Since only acts are known directly by our consciousness, and since habits as perfections of powers are in the realm of potency and not act, we are not directly aware of the existence of habits and powers, nor are we aware of how the results of learning may be influencing a given action. Experimental psychologists are busy studying the learning processes; clinical psychologists and psychiatrists try to uncover the results of ill-adaptive learning. These two approaches are gradually beginning to be integrated, and in time we shall have a better understanding of just how previous learning unconsciously influences our present behavior. Meanwhile the philosopher is content to indicate the general scheme of things as in Figure 3.

Note that only acts (shown in italics in Figure 3) can be conscious experience; all else can be explicitly known only by inference from the facts. Learning can be cognitive or appetitive, sensory or rational; any human learning is probably a combination of all these and is largely unknown to the learner. We shall return to the notion of habit as a perfectant of operative power in Part 4 of this book.

Figure 3
Powers, Habits, and Acts

Knowing (cognitive)			Dynamic (appetitive)		
POWER	Habits	Acts	POWER	Habits	Acts
INTELLECT	Science	*Ideas*	WILL	Virtues	*Rational de-*
	Wisdom	*Judgments*		and	*sire*
	Prudence	*Reasoning*		Vices	*Compla-*
					cency
					Choice
(Example of internal sense power)					
IMAGINATION	Habitual	*Images*			
	associa-				*Sense desire*
	tions				*Feelings*
			SENSORY	Affective	
			APPETI-	habits	
			TIVE		*Impulses*
			POWERS		*Drives*
(Example of special sense power)					
SENSE OF	Perceptual	*Seeing*			
SIGHT	habits				
(Examples of vegetative powers and functions)					
NUTRITION: Metabolism					
GROWTH: Cell proliferation					

NOTE: Only what is in *italic* is conscious; all else is unconscious. POWERS are in capital letters. Enumeration of powers is not complete. Observe the relatively large proportion devoted to the level of sensory or animal life.

Meanwhile we shall discuss cognitive operations in Part 2, and dynamic processes in Part 3.

The student would do well to remember that the schematic charts of Figures 2 and 3 are simply attempts to indicate in orderly fashion the facts of human behavior and experience. Other schemes can be used to portray alternative descriptions of the same facts; for example, the categories id, ego, and superego emphasize complex activity rather than basic powers. The present charts do not pretend to indicate the interrelation and organization of the various acts listed. But they suggest that a great deal of man's psychic structure is unconscious and much of it is animal, although the powers of rational control are preeminent. Emotion is not listed, since we shall see that it is a complex activity involving practically all man's powers.

Moreover, these charts avoid completely the question of man's being: the order of essence would demand a third dimension, indicating that all these operations and powers imply a substance in which they inhere. All we can say now is that man's essence must be such that it is capable of being the source of all these various kinds of activities: vegetative, sensory, and rational.[6]

REVIEW QUESTIONS

1. Is the problem of the unity of man a question of (a) whether he has only one operation or one kind of operation, or (b) whether he operates as one being or many? Why?
2. Does the philosopher argue that because man has a soul as a principle of unity, therefore man is one being? Why? Show the connection between this question and your answer to question 10 in Chapter 1.
3. Are accidents distinct from the substance which they modify? Are they separate? What is the difference between distinct and separate?
4. If "faculties" were separate, would they be substances or accidents?
5. Is it contradictory to assert the unity of man and then say that he has several distinct abilities? Show how your answer to question 4 answers this question.
6. Why do we begin the study of man with distinctively human experience instead of something simpler and more basic like biological functioning or animal behavior?
7. How are the dangers of pure phenomenology or introspectionism encountered in your answer to question 6 eliminated by making a distinction between philosophy and science in regard to the type of facts used? (Chapter 1, "Kind of Facts Used")
8. Would it be correct to say that philosophy studies man's soul, whereas science studies his body?
9. List all the reasons you can why the philosophy of human nature should include man's organic functioning.
10. Explain in your own words the difference between cognition and appetition.
11. Why does Figure 2 show this difference only at the sensory and rational levels, not at the vegetative?
12. Why is it not enough to enumerate powers and operations?
13. Why does not emotion appear on Figure 2?
14. Why does not the soul appear on Figure 3?

[*] Chap. 13, "Operative Powers," may be taken up in connection with this and the next chapter, if desired.

FOR FURTHER READING *

ALLPORT, GORDON W. *Becoming: Basic Considerations for a Psychology of Personality.* New Haven: Yale University Press, 1955.

ARNOLD, MAGDA B., & GASSON, JOHN A. *The Human Person: An Approach to an Integral Theory of Personality.* New York: Ronald, 1954.

CANNON, WALTER B. *The Wisdom of the Body.* (2d Ed.) New York: Norton, 1939.

CASSIRER, ERNST. *An Essay on Man.* New Haven: Yale University Press, 1944.

GILBY, THOMAS, O.P. "Vienne and Vienna," *Thought,* 1946, 21:63–82.

GILBY, THOMAS, O.P. "Thought, Volition and the Organism," *The Thomist,* 1940, 2:1–13.

GOLDSTEIN, KURT. *The Organism.* New York: American Book, 1939.

HOBAN, JAMES H. *The Thomistic Concept of Person and Some of Its Social Implications.* Washington: The Catholic University of America Press, 1939.

KLUBERTANZ, G. P., S.J. "The Unity of Human Operation," *The Modern Schoolman,* 1950, 27:75–103.

LILLIE, RALPH S. *General Biology and the Philosophy of Organism.* Chicago: University of Chicago Press, 1945. Chaps. 1–3, 14.

MARITAIN, JACQUES. *True Humanism.* New York: Scribner, 1938.

MOUNIER, EMMANUEL. *The Character of Man.* Trans. by Cynthia Rowland. New York: Harper, 1956.

Mouroux, J. *The Meaning of Man.* Trans. by A. H. C. Downes. New York: Sheed, 1948.

MURPHY, GARDNER. *Human Potentialities.* New York: Basic Books, 1958.

SIWEK, PAUL, S.J. *La Psychophysique humaine d'après Aristote.* Paris: Alcan, 1930.

TOURNIER, PAUL. *The Meaning of Persons.* New York: Harper, 1957.

WEISS, PAUL. *Nature and Man.* New York: Holt, 1947.

For readings on the notion of operative powers and their bearing on the unity of man, see Chap. 13 and the items listed at the end of that chapter.

* See also the pertinent parts of the books listed for general reference prior to Chapter 1.

PART TWO

HUMAN KNOWLEDGE

3

KNOWER AND OBJECT

Consciousness and modern psychology. Objective and subjective methods combined. Mind an ambiguous term. Knowing a total experience: the perceptual judgment. Proper and common objects of knowledge. Preview of Part 2.

A fundamental fact about man is his ability to know, to be aware of things, of himself, and even of his own awareness. We could not even begin to discuss the whole question of knowledge if we were not already aware by direct experience of what it means to know. All science presumes this ability, for science is simply one kind of knowledge.

But whereas the scientist may concentrate on the objects he knows, the philosopher must penetrate into this mysterious realm of knowing itself and try to understand what the process involves. The marvel of radar is nothing without the power of sight we take for granted as we examine the screen or read about the usefulness of this discovery. We may only infer that other animals know; but in the case of man the fact that he knows is clear, however we may explain it or whether we are able to explain it at all.

41

We shall begin by examining the facts concerning human knowledge, leaving to Chapter 8 the philosophical explanation of its nature. In the investigation of the knowing processes themselves we shall again rely largely on facts known by common or general observation, and supplement them with the findings of experimental psychology when useful.

KNOWERS VERSUS NON-KNOWERS

To begin with, knowing differs from non-knowing qualitatively, not merely in degree. If we analyze the activity of plants or the physiological level of operation which men and other animals share with the vegetable kingdom, we see that the quantity of the response is the important factor. There is always a direct relation or correspondence between the quantity of stimulus and the quantity of the response. There may be qualities which distinguish these reactions from those of nonliving things, but measurement is always possible. In psychological activity it is the quality of the response that is most important. There need not be any correspondence between the quantity of the stimulus and the quantity of the response, e.g., a dog reacts in the same way whether he sees his master 100 yards away or 10 feet away.

The amoeba can learn by experience that it can entrap living prey by putting out its pseudopod in a circular way instead of directly, whereas the fly-catcher plant never achieves this qualitative modification of response.

The fly-catcher plant (*mimosa pudica*) has leaves which will curl up at a slight touch and thus trap insects, but there is no more evidence for its being aware than there is for the morning glory or the heliotrope being aware of the sun; these reactions are in the category of vegetative tropisms. The mere fact of response is not evidence of consciousness. "How does the fly-catcher plant know that the fly is there?" can be answered by asking, "How does the rat trap know that the rat is there?"

The difference in quality between a knowing and a non-knowing being may be clear enough in theory, but we do not pretend that it is always easy to apply the theory in all instances. The details of the application are the work of the scientists. Our present knowledge does not enable us to tell for sure whether certain organisms are vegetative or animal. This does not prove that there is no difference between a vegetable and an animal. There might never be agreement on the precise point at which green shades into blue on the spectrum, yet no one would argue that therefore green is blue. The essential difference between plant and higher forms of life is not the possession of a nervous system or locomotion, nor is it a matter of photosynthesis, chlorophyll, or the direction of carbon dioxide interchange. Nor is it simply a matter of irritability or adaptive response. The difference lies in the possession of that unique and qualitative experience we call conscious awareness or knowing. Either a being has at least the elemental sense of touch or taste, or it does not. We have no right to assert the existence of such powers when there is no evidence of their operation.

CONSCIOUSNESS AND MODERN PSYCHOLOGY

The present attitude of modern psychology toward the experience of knowing can only be understood in the light of its history. As we shall see later, Descartes (died 1650) split man into two beings, a mind and a body. In the next century or two mind became a substance, and ideas were little bits of this substance associated by some sort of mental chemistry. Consciousness, instead of being an operation of the whole man, became some mysterious "mind stuff." Thus the philosophical stage was badly set before modern psychology made its entrance. The early experimental psychologists at the end of the nineteenth century began to study this "mind" experimentally in their laboratories, by a process called introspection.

Introspection simply means to look within oneself, to view the contents of one's own consciousness. It is the reflective observation of our own mental states and activities and the report on this observation. Now introspection is legitimate enough. Every scientist must trust his ability to report on his own conscious impressions. Even when he reads his thermometers and dials or looks into his microscope, what he records is really the result of his knowing process. If it is argued that he can always check his observations against those of others, the answer is obvious: since he knows the reports of others only through his conscious experience of hearing or reading them, he is again assuming the trustworthiness of his own experience as well as that of others.

More than that, introspection is the primary source of those data which are distinctively psychological: without it we would not have firsthand knowledge of the processes which are the peculiar domain of the psychologist. Many facts cannot be known directly except by introspection: the fact, for instance, that two railroad tracks seem to converge in the distance, the difference between red and green, the feeling of sadness. To convince yourself of this, try to imagine how you would explain the difference between red and green to a man totally blind from birth. Or explain what it means to have an idea to a being which never had one. Yet this knowledge is undeniably in our own conscious experience.

Like all good things, introspection can be abused. Its abuse began with the Cartesian notion of mind, and since then further abuses have crept in. Around the turn of the century, the materialistic bias of the structuralists under Titchener led them to absurd interpretations in their attempt to reduce thought processes to sensory experiences. Woodworth, Binet, the Würzburg group (Külpe, Bühler), and most other psychologists said that analysis of the content of consciousness revealed thinking as an irreducible component. On top of this quibbling about consciousness, Freud's followers were offering conjectures about unconscious motivation which raised doubt about whether consciousness was very significant after all. Finally Watson, quite understandably disgusted with the abuses and wild theorizing, decided to throw out consciousness entirely and make psychology merely a study of external behavior. During the 1920s it was fashionable to think of psychology as scientific only if it dealt exclusively with externally observable behavior and ignored consciousness entirely (behaviorism).

But it soon became obvious that it is not scientific to ignore a very large body of psychological facts. Within two decades[1] the extreme views of behaviorism were being abandoned, although its vocabulary still flavors the terminology of American psychology. (Behaviorism was never accepted widely in Europe.) It is said that at one time engineers were unable to explain how the heavy body of the bumblebee could be kept in flight, according to their principles of aerodynamics. Yet they could hardly conclude that the bumblebee, therefore, does not fly. It may have seemed that excluding consciousness from psychology was the easy way out, but it is no solution for the investigator who faces facts.

Objective and Subjective Methods Combined

It is now recognized generally that we must use both introspection and observation of external behavior. Neither method is sufficient by itself; one must be checked against the other. Since introspection is the only direct way of approaching certain facts, this method must be used as scientifically as possible.

If properly used, introspection is of unique value as a primary source of information about subjective states: our thoughts, perceptions, feelings. Since the report of subjective experiences is always liable to error, it must be used with care and constantly supplemented with other knowledge. To verify our own experiences, we must search outside ourselves and appeal to evidence in the external world, as apprehended by the senses. We examine the experiences of others during various periods of life from infancy to old age, in different races and different levels of civilization, in both normal and abnormal conditions, and in the light of the functioning of the brain, the nervous system, and the other physiological organs that mediate these processes.

But the mere fact that introspection is difficult does not justify abandoning it. Watching a white rat may be almost as easy as watching a ball roll down an inclined plane; but psychology is not physics,

[1] W. Harrell & J. R. Harrison, "The Rise and Fall of Behaviorism," *J. Gen. Psychol.*, 1938, 18:401–402; Marvin M. Black, *The Pendulum Swings Back* (London: Cokesbury Press, 1937).

however much the early psychologists wished to pattern their science after physics. Objective must not be made synonymous with true, for this implies that subjective experiences are not also facts. Try to describe a morning's activity purely in terms of "sciousness" without any reference to your conscious awareness of yourself. You will soon see that the consciousness cannot be ignored.

[Modern psychology has outgrown] the widespread feeling in some quarters that the admission of human feelings, attitudes, and perceptions as behavioral data flirts with the mystical and runs the risk of being "unscientific." No real science, however, can afford to ignore data relevant to its purposes simply because they are difficult to measure or do not lend themselves to treatment by orthodox means. If behavior is a function of perception, then a science of human relationships must concern itself with the meaning of events for the behaver as well as for the observer. Human feelings, attitudes, fears, hopes, wants, likes and aversions cannot be set aside while we deal with objective events. The subjective aspects of human experience cannot be suspended from operation. Perceptions are the very fabric of which human relationships are made. (Combs & Snygg, 1959, p. 308).

J. P. Guilford's presidential address to the American Psychological Association (1950, p. 445) exemplifies this trend away from the extreme behavioristic position: "What I am saying is that the quest for easily objectifiable testing and scoring has directed us away from the attempt to measure some of the most precious qualities of individuals and hence to ignore those qualities." And Cantril, in a presidential address to the Eastern Psychological Association (1950a, pp. 494-495), is even more explicit:

Explanation by means of variables as crude as reflexes, instincts, or physiological tensions are hopeless. . . . [We note] two characteristics of man as essential problems for any descriptive or explanatory system. One of these is man's capacity to sense the value in the quality of his experience . . . and another characteristic is fundamental and that is what may be called the enhancement of the valued attributes of experience. This can be regarded as the top standard of human experience, a standard in its own right. It is the capacity man has to sense added value in his experience that accounts for his ceaseless striving, his search for a direction to his activities, for his characteristic unwillingness to have things as they are.

Here Cantril is saying that the psychologist is concerned with what we would call intellect and will—ability to recognize values and the ability to enhance, or select action on the basis of, those values; namely, to make choices.

It is true that behaviorism as such is no longer defended, but an approach designated as "behavioristics" is sometimes still advocated. This approach holds that a quantitative, purely objective approach is the only scientific one. In contrast, E. G. Boring (1951, pp. 360–363) in a review of Gibson's book on perception, which he considers very valuable and scholarly although it is not quantitative, remarks that there are many facts of experience which are undeniable and as such should be the property of some science. He asks the question, what science takes account of these facts if psychology does not? He says that Gibson, to suit the behavioristic operationists, should have removed all doubt about his position by describing the operations by which it is verified of chimpanzees. But "How can we be sure that Zeitgeist is set eventually to make behavioristics the indisputable scientific truth? All in all the reviewer finds this book a remarkably keen, clear and wise description of just how it is that people see things. The chimpanzee phenomenology of vision, moreover, may need to wait until we have trained a chimpanzee to write it."

This shift away from extreme behaviorism is reflected in the current use of the expression "behavior and experience" in the definition of psychology in introductory texts (e.g., Ruch, Hilgard, Munn). Psychologists are unwilling to use words like consciousness, mind, mental, and introspection, which lost scientific respectability during the era of behaviorism. However they still wish to recognize that these psychological facts must be included in any description of human activity, so they now use such expressions as experience, covert behavior, inner behavior, or intimate behavior.

The important thing is that both sets of data must be taken into account. The preceding discussion on the way that psychology has now broadened the definition of its subject matter to include both behavior and experience simply confirms the necessity of using commonly observable facts, as the philosopher has always done.

The student should note that introspection is not psychoanalysis, i.e., it is not an attempt to understand or delve into the why and wherefore of our experiences, but simply a description of the experience itself. Again, we must not confuse consciousness, which is the simple fact of awareness, with conscience, which is one very small and restricted part of consciousness, namely, awareness of moral right and wrong. Finally, introspection tells us nothing of brain activity, since we are aware of what is going on in the brain only from a study of physiology and not from our own consciousness.

MIND

The word "mind," with its adjective "mental," is a very ambiguous term and the source of many difficulties in both philosophy and psychology. Webster's dictionary gives eight primary and five secondary meanings for a total of thirteen different meanings for the word. This deplorable ambiguity is largely the result of the confusion in philosophy since Descartes. We can distinguish at least four distinct meanings which the word might have:

1. *Act.* Mind may mean consciousness, the sum or stream of psychological activities going on, awareness, or experience. This is the meaning intended when one says, "What is on your mind?" i.e., what is in your consciousness or awareness? When used this way, "mind and body" refers to mental and physical processes, considering strictly the realm of operation, not substance.

2. *Habits.* But mind can also refer, not to the actual contents of consciousness at any given time, but to the habits which perfect our abilities, even though we may not be acting upon them. Thus if I say, "I know his mind on the question," I am not referring to what he may be actually thinking, since he may be asleep and not thinking at all. I refer rather to his habitual attitude about the matter, namely, the habits which dispose him to think about it in a certain way if he were to think about the topic.

3. *Powers.* But the word mind can also mean, not act, nor habit, but the sheer ability to perform psychological operations. Thus when one says, "He has a sharp mind," one is referring to his ability to think. Mind in this sense can refer to any or all of our mental powers but especially to the power of thinking, or intellect.

4. *Soul.* The word mind has even been extended into the realm of substance and is sometimes used as synonymous with the ultimate formal principle of mental operations, namely, the soul. Since Descartes, the use of the word in this sense usually suggests a gross dualism and is better avoided. As we shall see, the concept of the soul as form is quite different from the Cartesian idea of mind as substance.

Because of the frequent mention of the term unconscious in modern psychology, it is well to note here that only the first meaning (1) above pertains to the realm of consciousness. The other three meanings can be learned only from inference, not from direct conscious experience. Consequently the term unconscious could rightly include all three of the latter. However this term usually refers only to (3) the habits which modify our operations in subtle and powerful ways often quite unknown to us. Besides the unrecognized influence of habits, the term unconscious also covers many pertinent facts of physiology.[2]

Since the term mind is so ambiguous, we will generally avoid it in this treatise. Its adjective, mental, will be used only in a general way to refer to all cognitive and appetitive experiences. It is to be noted that the restriction of the word mind to the realm of operations is by no means a denial of soul, but simply a prescinding from it, which is quite legitimate.

HOW WE EXPERIENCE REALITY

Knowing is a total, unified experience, involving subject and object in a most unique relation. (If I see a house, I am the subject and the

[2] See James E. Royce, S.J., *Personality and Mental Health* (Milwaukee: Bruce, 1955), pp. 163–170, and the references on pp. 172–173, for a fuller discussion of the unconscious. "Subconscious" is perhaps best used to refer to states of marginal or subliminal consciousness.

house is the object.) The subject, man, is very aware that he is not just some disembodied mind, but a living organism. He is also quite aware of the reality of what he knows, as well as of his own knowing.

The Perceptual Judgment   *

Man knows existence not as some abstract concept but concretely, in the existing objects he perceives by his senses. He is implicitly aware of both his own existence and that of objects distinct from himself, in the very act of knowing at all.[3] Thus intellect, the power of knowing being as such, combines with sense perception, the act of knowing material objects, to produce the distinctive act of human knowledge, the perceptual judgment.

As Gilson[4] has shown, it is this basic fact, the sensory-intellectual nature of human knowledge, which is the answer to the epistemological problems of modern philosophy. We do not begin with a subjectivism which proceeds from subject to object. Nor do we subscribe to an Augustinian theory of illumination which would explain knowledge by some divine influence. Nor do we hold a naïve rationalism which begins with objects and then deduces man's knowledge of them. But we begin with the basic fact that if this man understands, his knowledge immediately involves the subject-object relation. This intellectivo-sensitive awareness is involved in any full act of human knowledge and puts one immediately into a relationship with the object which is not purely phenomenological because one is primarily aware of oneself and the object, not one's knowledge.

Moderate Realism

Three general lines of theory might be indicated with regard to man's relation to known objects. The first is what Hilgard (1953, p.

[3] John D. McKian, "The Metaphysics of Introspection According to St. Thomas Aquinas," *The New Scholasticism*, 1941, 15:89–117.

[4] Etienne Gilson, *Réalisme Thomiste et Critique de la Connaissance* (Paris: Vrin, 1939), a work which unfortunately has not been translated. Chaps. 7, 8, pp. 184–239, give the basic argument here, esp. pp. 207–209. On the importance of this work, see Gerard Smith, S.J., "A Date in the History of Epistemology," *The Thomist* (Maritain Volume), 1943, 5:246–255, in which he suggests that Gilson thereby puts an end to the epistemological haggling of the past three centuries.

292) has called the *copy theory*. In this naïve theory knowledge is an exact representation of the object as it is. This theory of course runs into great difficulties when faced with the facts of illusion, distortion, emotional and other subjective factors. At the opposite extreme, and perhaps growing out of despair in the copy theory, is the theory of operationism which makes no attempt to describe perception as the representation of reality. This approach is content to describe the operations by which we arrive at a piece of knowledge instead of the knowledge itself. It thus has the obvious disadvantage of never telling us anything about either knowledge itself or its real object, but only about our own methodological procedures.[5]

The third, and the one which seems to fit both the facts of experimental psychology and the demands of a sound epistemology, is that which holds that our perceptions are a true, though limited and imperfect, representation of things as they are. Such facts as constancy (to be discussed in Chapter 5), which have been verified by experiment, would seem to bear this out. There we will see that even the distortions and subjective factors that enter into our perceptions, although apparently aimed at untruth, actually result in the long run in a more accurate representation of the object than we would have if perception were a purely mechanical copying process.

What is to be emphasized here is that even our most exalted metaphysical conceptions, such as that of being itself, are discovered by the experience of direct contact with physical objects through the senses. The way I know existence is through my perception of existing things and through the awareness of the difference between myself and something else. The subject-object relationship is in one sense subtle and almost defies analysis (see Chapter 8 below), but on the other hand is so immediate and direct that it needs no analysis. It is the primary experience itself. So true is this that if a person claimed he did not know what existence was, it would be impossible to explain it to him, for there is nothing more immediate to which it can be reduced. Likewise, although we have the fact of

---

[5] Though grounded in scientific caution, operationism can rapidly approach the absurd point where "aptitude is how one performs on this test" or "love is two people kissing."

dreams and hallucinations, the basic distinction between knower and thing known is something which is absolutely irreducible to simpler terms. (If we did not know the difference, we could never even raise the question as to whether something was a dream or real.)

THE OBJECTS OF KNOWLEDGE

Since the power is known by its activities, and the activities in turn are known by their objects, we must distinguish different meanings of the word "object." Object in general means that with which any operation deals or with which an operation is concerned. Note that in this context the word object does *not* mean end or purpose, as it does in the expression, "what was his object in going downtown?" Rather, it simply refers to that in which the activity terminates. Thus the object of knowledge is that which is known, the object of desire is that which is desired.

Material object is simply the thing in its whole reality (whether this reality be physical or spiritual; the term is therefore somewhat misleading).

Formal object is the precise formality or aspect under which the material object is attained. Thus we saw in Chapter 1 that man is the material object of many different sciences: the same material object, man, is known under the different formal aspects of biochemistry, anthropology, philosophy of man, and so forth. It is clear then that the same material object can have many different formal objects, that is, it can be attained or operated upon in many different ways or under different aspects. Thus the material food on my plate can be considered under the formality of color, desirability, or calorie content, depending upon whether I am discussing visual perception, appetite, or nutrition.

Formal object is subdivided into proper, common, and incidental.

Proper object is that formality in the object which a particular activity reaches directly and by itself (per se), or toward which a particular operative power is essentially ordered. For example, color is the proper formal object of the sense of sight: it is directly and properly known in no other way and by no other power. The color-blind physicist may describe red in terms of wave lengths but he cannot have the unique sensory experience of this particular sensible quality.

Common object is that which is attainable by two or more different powers. For example, I may know the round shape of this object by either looking at it, pressing it against my skin, or running my finger around its edges. Thus shape is not proper to sight alone, but common to sight, touch, and kinesthesis (sense of motion).

Incidental (or accidental, or *per accidens*) object of a power is that which the power in question cannot directly attain either as proper or common. It just happens to be in the same material object toward which the power is ordered. Thus substance and causality are known by the intellect and flavor by the sense of taste; but all these just happen to be in the colored object known by the sense of sight; hence they are only incidentally objects of sight.

POWERS SPECIFIED BY THEIR OBJECTS

Man's operative powers and activities are said to be *specified* (recognized, identified as to species) by their proper formal objects. This simply means that we know what our different powers are by observing how many different *kinds* of operation we have, and these in turn depend upon different formal objects. We may see houses, trees, cars; but this does not give three powers of sight, since all these material objects are seen by the same kind of operation (seeing) and under the same formality, color. But color and odor, even in the same material object, are not attainable in the same way: smelling is a different kind of operation from vision. It has a different formal object and is therefore the act of a different power. Figure 4 on the following page lists all the powers by which man knows.

PREVIEW OF PART 2

In the next chapter, on sensation, we shall distinguish the various special senses by their proper formal objects. In Chapter 5 we shall discuss the more complex processes of sensory perception, imagina-

Figure 4

Human Knowledge: Summary of Man's Cognitive Powers

Power	Act	Organ	Proper object
INTELLECT	Idea Judgment Reasoning	None	(a) Essence of material beings (b) Being itself
INTERNAL SENSES:			
Central (synthetic)	Perceive, combine, distinguish sensations	End organ plus cerebral cortex	Sensed qualities of present material object
Imagination	Image	Cortex	Object not present
Sense memory	Recall and recognition	Cortex	Object *as past*
Estimative power	Instinctive estimate	Cortex	Suitability of behavior regarding sensed object
SPECIAL SENSES: Distance:	SENSATION:	RECEPTOR (end organ):	SENSIBLE QUALITY:
Visual	Seeing	Rods and cones in retina	Color { chromatic / black-white
Auditory	Hearing	Organ of Corti in cochlea	Sound { tone / noise
Chemical: Olfactory	Smell	Olfactory bulbs	Odor
Gustatory	Taste	Taste buds	Flavor
Somesthetic: Cutaneous	Tactual sensations	Nerve endings in skin	Pressure, warmth, cold, hardness, smoothness, etc.
Kinesthetic	Kinesthesis	Nerves in muscles, tendons, joints	Motion of parts of the body
Vestibular	Sensations of equilibrium, etc.	Vestibules, semi-circular canals	Motion, position, and balance of whole body
Intraorganic (visceral)	Nausea, ache, thirst, etc.	Nerve endings within body	Pressure, tension, heat, etc., within body

tion, and memory, and see that, since these activities have distinct formal objects, they indicate the presence of four internal sense powers in addition to the special senses. In Chapter 6 we take up still another kind of human knowledge, thinking or understanding. We are then in a position to survey in Chapter 7 the whole process of forming ideas, and in Chapter 8 to investigate the nature of knowledge as such.

The student is reminded that these processes, which must be spread over several chapters for the purpose of study, do not take place in isolation. Except in highly artificial laboratory situations created by the experimental psychologist, or in certain abnormal states (Moore, 1939, pp. 239–271), one never has just sensation alone, but always the total perceptual experience involving the activity of several cognitive powers acting at once. Thus I know red (sensation), apple (perception), and existing (intellection) all in the same instant.

REVIEW QUESTIONS

1. What is introspection? How does it differ from psychoanalysis? from philosophical analysis? from physiology?
2. Why was behaviorism a healthy influence in psychology?
3. Could an observation of objective behavior be false? Could an observation of subjective experience be true? What do you conclude from this as to whether objective and true are synonymous?
4. If the word "mind" refers to the facts of conscious experience, does it mean accidents or substance?
5. "Unconscious" is an adjective. If a noun must be supplied, what do you suggest? If you suggest "mind," which meaning or meanings must the word have?
6. What is epistemology?
7. What implications for the nature of man does a theory of knowledge based on the perceptual judgment have?
8. What is the difference between material and formal object? Give your own examples.
9. What is the difference between proper and common object? Give your own examples.
10. Is odor a common, proper, or incidental object of hearing?
11. How do we know how many different operative powers man has?
12. Does he have as many powers as he has acts?

FOR FURTHER READING

COMBS, ARTHUR W., & SNYGG, DONALD. *Individual Behavior: A Perceptual Approach to Behavior.* (Rev. Ed.) New York: Harper, 1959. Chapters 1, 2, and p. 308, state the authors' basic position.

LONERGAN, BERNARD. *Insight.* New York: Philosophical Library, 1956.

McKIAN, J. D. "The Metaphysics of Introspection according to St. Thomas Aquinas," *The New Scholasticism*, 1941, 15:89–117.

MARITAIN, JACQUES. *Distinguish to Unite: The Degrees of Knowledge.* New York: Scribner, 1959.

MARITAIN, JACQUES. *The Range of Reason.* New York: Scribner, 1952.

MICHEL, VIRGIL. "Psychological Data," *The New Scholasticism*, 1929, 3:185–188.

MONAGHAN, EDWARD A. "Major Factors in Cognition," *Catholic Univ. Stud. in Psychol. and Psychiat.*, 1935, Vol. III, No. 5.

Realism

DE FINANCE, JOSEPH, S.J. "Cogita cartesien et reflexion thomiste," *Arch. de Phil.* 1946, Vol. XVI, No. 2.

FOREST, AIMÉ. *La Structure métaphysique du concret selon Saint Thomas d'Aquin.* Paris: Vrin, 1931.

GILSON, ETIENNE. *Réalisme thomiste et critique de la connaissance.* Paris: Vrin, 1939. A classic treatise.

KEELER, LEO W., S.J. *The Problem of Error from Plato to Kant.* Rome: Gregorian University, 1934.

O'NEILL, REGINALD F., S.J. *Theories of Knowledge.* Englewood Cliffs, N.J.: Prentice-Hall, 1960.

RÉGIS, L. M., O.P. *Epistemology.* Trans. by I. C. Byrne. New York: Macmillan, 1959.

RÉGIS, L. M., O.P. *St. Thomas and Epistemology.* Milwaukee: Marquette University Press, 1946.

REINHARDT, KURT F. *A Realistic Philosophy.* Milwaukee: Bruce, 1944.

SMITH, GERARD B., S.J. "A Date in the History of Epistemology," *The Thomist* (Maritain Volume), 1943, 5:246–255.

DE TONQUÉDEC, JOSEPH. *La Critique de la connaissance.* Paris: Beauchesne, 1929.

WILHELMSEN, FREDERICK D. *Man's Knowledge of Reality.* Englewood Cliffs, N.J.: Prentice-Hall, 1956. Chapter 3 presents, in brief form, the author's point of view.

Critique of Positivism

ADLER, MORTIMER J. *God and the Professors.* New York: Conference of Science, Philosophy, and Religion, 1940.

ADLER, MORTIMER J. *What Man Has Made of Man.* New York: Longmans, 1937. Note 16a, p. 158; n. 17, p. 161; n. 36b, p. 191.

COPLESTON, FREDERICK, S.J. *Contemporary Philosophy: Studies of Logical Positivism and Existentialism.* Westminster, Md.: Newman, 1956.

FEIGL, HERBERT, and others (Eds.) "The Foundations of Science and the Concepts of Psychology and Psychoanalysis," in *Minnesota Studies in the Philosophy of Science.* Vol. I. Minneapolis: University of Minnesota Press, 1956. A symposium expressing many points of view, but note Carnap's shift away from logical positivism, pp. 38–76.

JOAD, C. E. M. *A Critique of Logical Positivism.* Chicago: University of Chicago Press, 1950.

McMULLIN, ERNAN. "Realism in Modern Cosmology," *Proc. Amer. Cath. Phil. Ass.,* 1955, 29:137–150.

MacPARTLAND, JOHN. *The March Toward Matter.* New York: Philosophical Library, 1952.

MARTIN, OLIVER. "An Examination of Contemporary Naturalism and Materialism," in John Wild (Ed.), *The Return to Reason.* Chicago: Regnery, 1953. Pp. 68–91.

WALKER, LESLIE J., S.J. *Theories of Knowledge.* (2d Ed.) New York: Longmans, 1924.

WELLMUTH, JOHN J., *The Nature and Origins of Scientism.* Milwaukee: Marquette University Press, 1944.

WILD, JOHN. *Introduction to Realistic Philosophy.* New York: Harper, 1948.

Among outstanding physical scientists who have rejected positivism should be listed the names of Percy Bridgman, Louis de Broglie, D. Bohm, and L. Janossy; Professor A. C. Crombie of the University of London, world authority on the Galileo question; and Alfred North Whitehead, whose *Science and the Modern World* was already, in 1925, pointing out abuses of the scientific method.

4

THE SPECIAL SENSES

Distance senses
  Visual
  Auditory
Chemical senses
  Taste
  Smell
Somesthetic (body) senses
  Cutaneous (skin)
    Pressure or touch
    Warmth
    Cold
    Pain
  Kinesthetic (active movement)
  Vestibular (body motion and position)
  Organic

All man's knowledge begins in some way with the senses. Consequently we begin our study of human knowledge by an analysis of sensation, the simplest form of awareness. Information is brought in to man through the special senses and elaborated by the internal senses into a total sensory perception. What is distinctive about the special senses is that each has its own receptor organ and has as its proper object some particular material quality.

A special sense is one which attains its object directly, in contrast to the internal sense powers which know only through the special senses. The special senses were originally called the external senses, but because many of the sensations arise within the body itself, the name was unfortunate. Kinesthetic, vestibular, and organic sensations all arise from within the body. Hence the modern term "special" seems more precise than the older term "external."

DEFINITION

A special sense may be defined as *a power by which we experience the quality of a material object stimulating a receptor organ.* Let us examine this definition.

"Power"—the sense is the power, sensation is its act. (Avoid the wider connotations of the word "sensation," which imply urge or excitement.) Obviously we are not aware of the power directly but make the easy inference that if we experience the sensations we certainly have the ability to do so; that is all that is meant by sense power. The power, then, is a property of the organism by means of which it is able to perform this particular operation.

"By which"—note that the power is not *that which* knows, but only that *by* which *man* knows.

"Experience"—this experience is an awareness, the simplest form of knowledge. Again we insist that this experience practically never occurs in isolation, but as part of a total perceptual process which involves the activity of the internal senses and perhaps also of the intellect.

"Quality"—the proper object of a sensation is the color, flavor, odor, or similar quality of a material object in question. This object is called a *sensible,* or sensible quality. It may be proper or common, as noted in the previous chapter. (The total awareness of the substance which has these qualities is called perception.)

"Material object"—sensory knowledge is organic, animal. By it we can only be aware of material objects and in a material way.

"Stimulating"—sensation is always a matter of present stimulation, the action of the object on the receptor organ at the present time. It is by means of the internal senses, such as imagination, that we can be aware of objects even in their absence.

"Receptor organ"—the receptor or end organ is the particular part of the body which is designed to receive the stimulation and is the instrument of sensory consciousness.

From the above definition it is clear that we can distinguish three aspects of the process of sensation: physical, physiological, and psychological.

1. The *physical* phase consists of the object with its material qualities of size, shape, color, odor, temperature, and the manner in which the quality is put into contact with the sense organ, usually through some medium. This aspect is the proper domain of the physicist, with his investigation of wave lengths and other physical properties. Note that in sensation the object is present and actually stimulating the sense organ here and now.

2. The *physiological* stage includes the activity of the receptor organ, the sensory nerves, and usually certain areas of the cerebral cortex or gray matter of the brain. The word organ means instrument, and many facts illustrate that the physiological processes themselves are not the sensation, but only the instruments of the sense power. The sensory organs may be active and still no consciousness result. This will be seen more clearly in the next chapter.

Figure 5

The Three Phases of Sensation

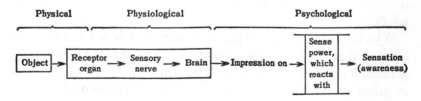

3. The *psychological* stage is that of actual awareness, when the sense power vitally reacts to the stimulation and issues knowledge or awareness. This will be discussed more fully in Chapter 8, on the nature of knowledge.

These three phases may be summarized by saying that in sensation an object through an organ impresses a sense power, which reacts with awareness of sensible qualities. This is schematically represented in Figure 5.

The sensory experience (3) will usually have attributes which correspond to the attributes of the physical stimulus: quality, intensity, and duration.

a. Quality. There is something in a green object which makes us see it as green rather than red, unless the medium (light) or organ is defective (color blindness).

b. Intensity. Bright, loud, very sour, correspond in general to the intensity of the stimulus. The correspondence is not exact, and we now know that it does not follow fully even the geometric proportion or law of diminishing returns expressed in the Weber-Fechner Law (Graham, 1950, p. 117).

c. Duration. Conscious experience usually lasts as long as the stimulation, but again with variations. Thus, sensation can continue after stimulus has ceased (after-image), or cease even though stimulation is still present (negative adaptation). The fact that we see a star which may be already burned out by the time its light reaches us simply indicates that the stimulation takes time to pass through the medium; this is not the effect of an after-image.

THE SPECIAL SENSES IN DETAIL

Detailed investigation of the operation of the special senses belongs to the field of experimental psychology. The philosopher is interested in the nature of sensation and its relation to the rest of knowledge, and what its analysis can tell us about the nature of man. Although cognitive powers are known by their formal objects, and consequently the number of senses is deduced from the number of qualities there are, each of which is knowable only by a particular power, in the case of the special senses we have additional help because we are able to distinguish the various receptor organs.

There are many different divisions of the special senses. The one given at the head of this chapter is fairly common and represents our present knowledge. It is interesting to note that Aristotle, centuries before Christ, knew that there were more than five senses. The tendency to restrict the number to five and group all of the somesthetic senses under the name touch is not only unfortunate but also contrary to Aristotle's conception. Philosophically, the number is unimportant.

Vision. The most well-known of our special senses is probably vision. Its proper object is color, which the psychologists usually divide into chromatic (the colors of the spectrum) and achromatic (the black-gray-white tones). Although, according to the physicist, black is the absence of wave length, the psychologists recognize a certain sensation designated as black. The specific receptor or end organ for vision is the rods and cones which form the endings of the optic nerve in the retina at the back of the eyeball. The organ also includes the optic nerve itself and the occipital areas of the cerebral cortex which form the visual center in the brain. Note that many extended things are not visible at all, including light itself under certain conditions. The object, then, is color, which is light as reflected or refracted by a surface, rather than light itself.

Hearing. The object of hearing is either tone or noise, the difference being largely a matter of the regularity of vibration in the air waves. The specific receptor is the organ of Corti in the inner ear, where the endings of the auditory nerve are arranged along the inner windings of a small bony structure called the cochlea, because it is shaped something like a snail shell. The marvel of hearing is perhaps less appreciated than that of seeing; actually, the ear is capable of extremely fine discriminations of pitch, intensity, and timbre or quality, and in some ways surpasses the eye.

Taste. Gustatory sensations have as their object the flavors usually designated under the categories of sweet, salt, sour, and bitter. The taste receptors are found on the taste buds, chiefly on the edges and around the surface of the tongue.

Smell. The formal object of olfactory sensations is odor. Attempts to standardize the terminology and classify odors have so far been only moderately successful. The receptor is the olfactory nerve endings high in the nose which are directly connected to the olfactory bulbs of the brain, lying just below the frontal lobes. Although smell has less importance in the life of man than in that of the lower animals, it does play a very important part in warning us of dangers and helping to identify objects. A great deal of what is mistakenly thought to be taste is actually a matter of odor. The common evidence for this is the lack of taste when one holds one's nose.

Cutaneous. The skin senses generally inform us of objects having the qualities of warmth, cold, smoothness, hardness and others which may affect us by exerting pressure on the skin. This pressure may even become painful. It is a matter of indifference whether pain be considered a special category of sensation or a quality of all sensations, since it seems that any of them can become painful if the stimulus is too intense. The receptors for the skin senses have been very carefully studied. Different types of nerve endings in the skin have been identified anatomically, and some success has been achieved in relating these to different sensory qualities. But the results of these investigations are by no means certain and adequate. As Morgan says (1956, p. 503), "Seldom have scientists worked so assiduously at a problem with so little success." Recent experiments have indicated that sensations of both pressure and temperature are the result not so much of the contact itself but rather of a change in contact. Thus pressure and temperature become relative to the previous stimulus rather than absolute, as far as sensation is concerned.

Kinesthesis. The word "kinesthesis," from the Greek words meaning feeling and motion, refers to the active movement of the parts of our body. The receptors are nerve endings in the muscles, tendons, and joints, which report the movement. The importance of this sense quality is readily seen when we consider the conditions in which it is absent: when our foot has gone to sleep, or when some disease makes us unable to feel the position and movement of our limbs, we find such movements as walking very difficult, even though the motor nerves are intact.

Vestibular. The sense of equilibrium has to do with body position in relation to gravity and passive motion of the body as a whole. It is concerned with starting or stopping movements, balance, position, and turning. The receptors are the semicircular canals and the vestibules of the inner ear. Although anatomically very closely related to the auditory nerves, these organs are not a part of hearing. They consist of bony cavities which contain liquids and otoliths, tiny particles of calcium. The equilibratory nerves end in tiny hair cells on the inner surface of the cavities and pick up stimulations from these liquids and particles.

Organic. Lastly, there are sensations of ache, pressure, nausea, thirst, and so forth, which seem to arise from within the body. These sensations are called intraorganic or visceral or interoceptive. Their origin and function is rather obscure in some details as yet.

Study of the Special Senses

Some of these bodily senses might be reducible to others; for instance pressure might include the kinesthetic and some aspects of the organic. Other divisions, such as extroceptive, proprioceptive, and interoceptive have been suggested, but these categorize the senses by material rather than formal object. At least it is obvious that there are several clearly distinct sensible qualities.

Not all animals have all the special senses, but the somesthetic senses seem to be basic, as all animals seem to have at least some elementary awareness of touch or pressure. Smell is also quite fundamental. The higher animals, those vertebrates with well-developed nervous systems (dogs, cats, apes, etc.), appear to have the same number of special and internal senses as man.

A shift has taken place in the manner in which the special senses are being approached by experimental psychology. Once its main preoccupation, they were neglected later when the emphasis turned to more dynamic processes. Since World War II there has been renewed interest, but from a different viewpoint. Their connection with adjustment and learning is emphasized more, and there is added interest in the subjective and emotional factors which modify our perceptions. Second, although the physics and physiology of sensation are inseparable from the total process, there is increased emphasis on the distinctly psychological or conscious aspects of the process in the new approach. Third, psychologists now seem to be more aware of the dynamic and self-actualizing nature of the sense power. Sensation is looked upon less as a purely mechanical or passive impression. This of course accords with the conception of Aristotle and Aquinas, for they realized that the cognitive power is not purely mechanical, but the ability to react vitally and consciously to a stimulus.

Fourth, where the earlier psychologists, in their anxiety to ape pure classical physics, concentrated exclusively on efficient causality and ignored final cause or purpose, the recent approach to the special senses has been quite teleological. Hilgard (1956, pp. 332–335) stresses the adaptive or purposeful approach, mentioning four functions of the senses: information, protection, orientation, and appreciation. He also notes that the knowledge of the workings of the special senses has been utilized by both the military and industrial psychologists to make working conditions more efficient and safe.

Lastly, the senses have recently been approached from the viewpoint of the whole, rather than from the aspect of the part. Even though the older psychologists tried to distinguish psychology from physiology on the basis of their concern with wholes and not with parts, they seemed to contradict this distinction by trying to explain sensation in terms of units of the nervous system, making conditioned reflexes the building blocks or atoms of psychology. It is now recognized that this molecular view is inadequate. The molar view considers sensation psychologically, as a total response even though concerned with a specific receptor, whereas metabolism may take place in the entire body but is still physiological.

Threshold or limen refers to the minimum amount of stimulation required for an awareness to occur. The term derives from the metaphor of consciousness as a room and the threshold as the doorstep over which the stimulus must pass in order to gain entrance. The higher the threshold, the bigger the stimulus must be before it can register. *Subliminal* stimuli are those just at the threshold, usually unnoticed except because of sudden change.

Adaptation refers to a change in the required threshold. Negative adaptation means that the threshold is raised, so that a greater amount of stimulus is required to produce awareness. For example when we move in next to a pickle factory, the odor at first is very noticeable. But after a few weeks we are not even aware of it. Our threshold has been raised, or we have become negatively adapted. Positive adaptation is the opposite. Threshold is lowered, so that very little stimulation is required. For instance, a mother may be sensitive to the slightest sound or change of breathing in her baby.

Spatial Relations

Those sensible qualities such as time, motion, and tridimensional space which are the common and incidental objects of sense arouse some interesting problems. They are often treated under the heading "complex sensation" because they are not like the simple awareness of proper sensibles, nor are they the same as perception of total material objects. Apparent movement (Phi phenomenon) must be distinguished from real motion. Awareness of time involves many physiological factors. Depth is a function of both binocular retinal disparity and more subtle perceptual cues. Ingenious experimentation has been done with binaural cues for perceiving the location and motion of sound, with sounds from the right being funneled to the left ear and vice versa (Young's pseudophone) or transmitted electrically to separate earphones on the opposite sides from the pickup.[1] Motion is shown to be an incidental object for hearing, as tridimensional space is for vision. Again, psychologists have worn glasses with

[1] P. T. Young, "Auditory Localization with Acoustical Transposition of the Ears," *J. Exp. Psychol.*, 1928, 11:399–429.

prisms which rectified from its normal inverted position the physical image projected on the retina of the eye.[2]

The upshot of these and hundreds of other experiments has been essentially the confirmation of the traditional Scholastic position. Sensation is neither a purely mechanical or neurophysiological process, nor are these "judgments" of distance, etc., a matter of intellectual deduction from sensory cues. Rather, a middle course seems indicated which places these operations definitely in the realm of animal knowledge, between the rational and the purely physiological. Likewise, the basic powers are inborn, but learning plays a large part in the development of their use. It is not purely a matter of inborn responses nor entirely a matter of learning (Hilgard, 1957, p. 383). A good summary of the results of the experimentation is given by Krech and Crutchfield (1958, p. 140):

> On the basis of all the available evidence the following generalizations may be made:
> (1) Primitive tri-dimensional space perception is a product of the way the nervous system works—no learning is necessary.
> (2) Perception of space is not necessarily fully present at the organism's birth, but may develop gradually with the physiological *maturation* of the nervous system.
> (3) The complex differentiation and organization of perceived space is a product both of primitive, inherent tendencies and of the learning of the relationships and meaning of cues through past experience.

REVIEW QUESTIONS

1. Why do we prefer the term "special senses" to "external senses"?
2. Which words of the definition of special sense refer to the physical, physiological, and psychological stages of sensation respectively?
3. Does the designation of these three phases imply that sensation is three activities?
4. What do we mean by saying that the receptor is the organ of the sense power? i.e., what is the relation of the receptor organ and the sense power? Are they identical?

[2] G. M. Stratton, "Vision without Inversion of the Retinal Image," *Psychol. Rev.*, 1897, 4:341–360; 463–481.

5. If I strike the closed eyelid, I may see a flash of light. Does this response fulfill the definition of sensation?
6. Philosophically, does it make any difference whether there are five senses or fifty?
7. Is the enumeration of special senses and their proper objects as in Figure 4 (end of previous chapter) complete?
8. Would you guess that a dog has the same special senses as yourself? does a fish? does a worm?
9. When we see, do we see images on the retina, or sensations, or visible objects? How does the experiment of wearing prisms which rectify the normally inverted images verify your answer?

FOR FURTHER READING

ADRIAN, EDGAR D. *The Physical Background of Perception.* New York: Oxford, 1947.

AQUINAS, ST. THOMAS. *Summa Theol.*, Ia, 78, 3.

ARISTOTLE. *On the Soul.* Book II, Chap. 5, to Book III, Chap. 2.

BORING, E. G. *Sensation and Perception in the History of Experimental Psychology.* New York: Appleton-Century-Crofts, 1942.

BOULOGNE, CHARLES-DAMIAN, O.P. *My Friends the Senses.* New York: P. J. Kenedy & Sons, 1953.

BRENNAN, ROBERT E., O.P. *General Psychology.* (Rev. Ed.) New York: Macmillan, 1952. Chaps. 9–13.

BUDDENBROCK, WOLFGANG VON. *The Senses.* Ann Arbor: University of Michigan Press, 1958.

GELDARD, F. A. *The Human Senses.* New York: Wiley, 1953.

GRAHAM, C. H. "Behavior, Perception, and the Psychophysical Methods," *Psychol. Rev.*, 1950, 57:108–120.

HARMON, FRANCIS L. *Principles of Psychology.* (Rev. Ed.) Milwaukee: Bruce, 1951. Chaps. 8–10.

LEDVINA, J. P. *Philosophy and Psychology of Sensation.* Washington: The Catholic University of America Press, 1941.

MOORE, THOMAS VERNER. *Cognitive Psychology.* Philadelphia: Lippincott, 1939. Pp. 93–130, 209–271.

PIRENNE, M. H. *Vision and the Eye.* London: Chapman & Hall, 1949.

SIMON, YVES, & PEGHAIRE, JULIEN. "The Philosophical Study of Sensation," *The Modern Schoolman*, 1945, 23:111–119.

SIWEK, PAUL, S.J. *Experimental Psychology.* New York: J. F. Wagner, 1959.

STEVENS, S.S. (Ed.) *Handbook of Experimental Psychology.* New York: Wiley, 1951.

STEVENS, S. S., & DAVIS, H. *Hearing: Its Psychology and Physiology.* New York: Wiley, 1938.
WEVER, E. G. *Theory of Hearing.* New York: Wiley, 1949.
WOODWORTH, R. S., & SCHLOSBERG, H. *Experimental Psychology.* (Rev. Ed.) New York: Holt, 1954.

5

THE INTERNAL SENSES

Sensation versus perception. Total sensory impression involves internal senses: central sense, Gestalt, secondary cues, and other perceptual factors; imagination; memory; sense estimation. The problem of "instinctive" behavior.

Our sensory experience is not limited to awareness of colors, sounds, odors, and other qualities but includes many operations which cannot be the activities of the special senses. Daydreaming, remembering, and the perception of a round, red, sweet, smooth apple are obviously impossible to any one special sense. It is a basic fact of human behavior that we react not to a single stimulus but to patterns of stimuli. Our perception of the world as composed of objects (tree) rather than mere sensory qualities (green, large) demands further investigation.

INTERNAL SENSES

How do we know that we have internal senses? In the same way we know the existence of any power: from its operation. If as a matter of fact we put together the impressions of red, smooth, firm, savory, and round and get apple, we certainly have the ability or power to do so. What power is this? Evidently not that of vision, since it knows nothing of firmness or taste. Again, can the sense of touch combine odor and color? Yet we do combine and compare these various sensible qualities and discriminate between them. Animals, too, show evidence of combining and discriminating between various sensory experiences: the dog pricks up his ears and looks, associates a sign or word with a trick, remembers where he buried the bone.

From all this it should be clear that there are inner or internal sense powers distinct from the special senses. They are not called internal only because they have no organ on the surface of the body, for, as we saw, that is true of certain special senses. They are called internal because they are not immediately impressed by their object but are impressed indirectly, through one or more of the special senses.

An *internal sense* might be defined as *the power of knowing concrete objects in a material way from sensible qualities experienced through the special senses.* Being sensory, they are organic and probably have as their organ large areas of the brain (cerebral cortex). Their object is always concrete and their manner of knowing is material, in contrast to intellection, which we shall examine later. Their object may be absent or present, real or imaginary, but it is always known with its sensible qualities. Their acts and proper objects are summarized in Figure 4 at the end of Chapter 3.

Usually, we enumerate four internal sense powers. There is some dispute among philosophers as to whether each of the four is really distinct. Certainly their operations are closely interwoven. St. Thomas and many of his followers feel that they have sufficiently different formal objects to prove that they are distinct. While inclining to this position, we leave it an open question. The four are the central or synthetic sense, the imagination, the memory, and the estimative power. Although we have good evidence for all four types of activity in the higher vertebrates, we do not say that all animals have this complete sensory equipment: one could hardly assert much evidence for imagination in an oyster.

THE CENTRAL SENSE

The first of the internal sense powers is called the *central sense,* or synthetic or unifying sense. It has sometimes been called the common sense, from its Latin name, but this is very misleading in English: we do not refer to good judgment, which is implied by the English term "common sense." Synthetic suggests its combining power, but not its function as a discriminator between sensations.

The *central* sense might be defined as *the power by which we perceive, distinguish, and combine sensations into total awareness of a present object.* By "present object," we mean one that is actually stimulating the sense organs here and now. The evidence for the existence of such a power is clear.

1. All animals, including men, show evidence that they are aware of their sensations. Now a special sense cannot sense that it is sensing; the object of a special sense is a material quality, not sensation itself. Sight is not visible; only color or colored objects can be seen. And yet I am aware that I am seeing. Moreover, for the special sense to be aware of its own operation it would have to have the power of perfect reflection; but being organic and extended, a sense finds this impossible, for an extended being can never bend back perfectly upon itself.

2. We can distinguish between the proper objects of the various special senses: between color and sound, for instance. This distinction obviously cannot be made by either the special sense of sight or that of hearing, since neither can know the proper object of the other. Since as a matter of fact we do make the distinction, our ability to do so must lie somewhere other than in either of these special senses. This is clear in the case of man, and can easily be inferred from the actions of the higher animals, as when the dog turns its head and looks in the direction of a sound.

3. Also, we are able to combine the sensations of the special senses. But to combine them requires a power of knowing all of

them, and each sense only knows its own. Otherwise we would only know a number of unrelated sensations of color, sound, and feel. (We speak here of combining the qualities of one object; association of one object with another is a function of imagination.) A. Galli has shown that Phi phenomenon or apparent movement is possible using two different special senses: e.g., a bell seen in one position and heard in another seems to have moved (Allers, 1942b, pp. 46–47). Neither vision nor hearing alone could account for this, but only a central sense.

Consciousness could be called in a very special way the function of the central sense, for it is by this power that we know concretely that we are actually awake and sensing. Being sensory, this power is organic and its organ is probably located in the brain; a knockout blow produces a mild temporary concussion which interferes with the organ of the central sense. Sleep, on the other hand, is not the cessation of all conscious functioning but is a state of partial consciousness in which chiefly the imagination is at work and the central sense is not.

Note that the proper object of the central sense is not the common sensible qualities, which are objects of the special senses. We can now see another reason for avoiding the confusing term "common sense." The common sensibles are known by the special senses through the proper sensibles; for example, shape is known through color.

Perception

We have already noted that we do not normally experience simple sensation in isolation. How then do sensation and perception differ? Both are sensory, animal types of knowledge. Both are psychological experiences, not mere physiological phenomena. Both are concerned with a present object. They differ in the same way that seeing the parts of the jigsaw puzzle differs from awareness of the whole picture they make up, or in the way that seeing daubs of paint on canvas differs from awareness of the scene they portray. Note here that there is not necessarily a question of intellectual awareness of the nature or essence of the object, but merely of a total awareness of the material object in a sensory way, as opposed to an awareness of the individual sensible quality known in simple sensation.

Perception may be defined as *the total sensory awareness of a material object present to the sense organs*. It is a function of the central sense plus one or more of the special senses and usually also shows influence of the imagination and the other internal senses. In practice it is impossible to know how much intellectual influence might also be there, but at least the term always refers to our total impression of a *sensed* object.

In modern times, Gestalt psychology, by its studies on perception, has experimentally rediscovered and further investigated the functioning of the internal senses. Beginning with the fact that we perceive not isolated notes but the pattern which makes a melody, not isolated bits of color but the pattern which makes a picture or a sunset, not individual still pictures but apparent movement in the moving pictures, these psychologists went on to investigate in great detail how the pattern of stimuli gives a total impression which is more than the sum of the parts. The parts may even be entirely replaced and the total impression still remain, as when a tune played in another key is recognizable as the same melody, even though not a single note would be the same.

The Gestaltists themselves assert (Katz, 1950, pp. 163–164) and many experiments make it clear that these total impressions are not the result of intellectual deduction from data given by the special senses: the process of forming the impressions is a sensory one. It is not a question of *knowing* the nature of the object, but rather of organizing simple sensations into perceptual wholes.

Both to illustrate the functioning of the internal senses, thus experimentally rediscovered, and to enrich our appreciation of the subjective factors in perception, it may be useful to review briefly some facts from experimental psychology which illustrate how perception molds, elaborates, and even distorts the data of the special senses.

Ambiguity. Ambiguous figures are those which give exactly the same stimulus to the special senses and yet can be perceived as two

Figure 6
Jastrow's Rabbit-Duck

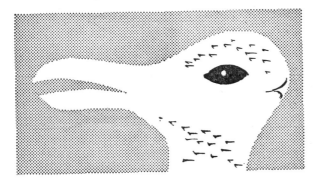

entirely different objects. Jastrow's rabbit-duck figure (Figure 6) is a common example. Whether we see it as a rabbit facing one direction or a duck facing the other cannot be due to the special sense of vision; it must be due to internal factors. Often the ambiguity flows from a reversal of figure and ground: the same stimulus is seen as the main figure at one time and as background at another. Thus we have either a vase or two faces in Figure 7.

Contrast. If a piece of gray paper is cut in half and one half is pasted on a large sheet of black paper, the other on a large sheet of white paper, it will be seen that the same gray no longer produces an equal shade in our total impression. By contrast, the gray on the white will seem darker, that on the black will seem whiter. Yet the one gray is hardly giving off a different physical stimulus. This is called simultaneous contrast; the same can be observed in successive contrast where the same pickle, for instance, tastes more sour after eating candy than it would otherwise.

Illusion. We are all familiar with the optical illusions which make straight lines seem crooked and equal lines

Figure 7
Another Ambiguous Figure

Figure 8

Some Illusions

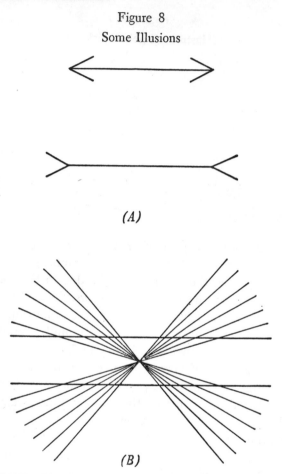

(A) is called the Müller-Lyer illusion: draw two lines of exactly equal length, then add the extra lines and see if they still appear equal. Do the same with (B): draw the two parallel lines first, then see if they appear to change when you add the diagonal lines. In either case, is the original stimulus different after the other lines are added?

seem unequal, and so forth. Whereas in the case of ambiguity the same stimulus could give rise to two percepts, each equally true, in an illusion we get a false impression due to the distortion of the sense data by the internal senses (Figure 8). Here again the addition of other lines or background does not change the physical or physiological nature of the original stimulus and its impression on the special senses; the distortion must come from internal psychological processes.

Illusion is distinguished from hallucination in that the former has a real object which is distorted, whereas hallucination mistakes an image for reality when there is no object present at all. Thus if I see a man as larger than an elephant because of distorted perspective, this is an illusion; if I see pink elephants on the ceiling where there is nothing, that is an hallucination. Both of these processes are sensory and thus are distinguished from delusion, which is an erroneous intellectual conviction; for instance, delusions of persecution or delusions of grandeur. Phi phenomenon or the perception of apparent movement in a series of still pictures, such as in the movies or on an electric display sign, is an example of normal illusion.

Secondary Perceptual Cues. Color-blind people distinguish colors only by the texture or grain of the various shades of gray which they see; this fact was utilized in World War II when color-blind men were employed to read aerial photographs to distinguish a brown plowed field from a green pasture or stand of grain. The Ames experiments in perception[1] are based largely on the importance of secondary cues and background. Relative position is a cue to size, but we can be fooled, as in these experiments where the distorted trapezoidal room gives a false perspective or where cards actually all of the same size are arranged so as to suggest relative difference of position, making some seem larger. Stage scenery does not represent objects, but gives us perceptual cues from which we construct the impression of objects. Three-dimensional movies and stereoscopic pictures involve the utilization of secondary perceptual cues of depth.

Constancy. An object tends to give a fairly consistent perceptual

[1] See A. Ames, Jr., "Visual Perception and the Rotating Trapezoidal Window," *Psychol. Monogr.*, 1951, 65, No. 7 (Whole No. 324), and many current psychology texts.

impression in spite of very divergent stimulations: for instance, the image striking the retina from a man close up is immense in comparison with the image on the retina from a man three blocks away, yet the former is not seen as a giant and the latter as a midget (size constancy). A red rose or a piece of white paper will actually give off highly different physical stimulations in bright sunshine and at dusk, yet we see them as having about the same color under either condition (color constancy). Likewise, a ring is seen as round even when the image striking the eye from an angle is really elliptical (shape constancy).

Selectivity. We tend to see what we want to see, rather than all that is there. Witnesses to an auto accident usually give highly different versions, depending upon their personal interest in the plaintiff or defendant.

Set. We tend to see what we expect to see. Experiments in which a black six-of-hearts or a red ten-of-spades is shown betray that we often report not what is actually there but what we assume or expect to see.

Motivation. Lastly, experiments have shown that our needs and the value we set on things can influence greatly how we perceive objects. Poor children who are asked to estimate the size of a dime according to carefully controlled measures were found to make it much larger than rich children did in the same experiment. Adult subjects in another experiment were shown vague pictures on a screen which they interpreted as food twice as often when hungry as when they had just finished a meal, and estimated the size of hamburgers shown on the screen to be 50 to 75 per cent larger when they had not eaten recently.

That all or many of these subjective factors can influence and distort our impression of what we hear as well as what we see is well illustrated by the old parlor game in which a story is told to the first person in a circle, who whispers it to the second, who repeats it to the next in turn, all around the room, and then the story is told aloud by the last person; often it is an unrecognizable version of the original. This is not deliberate or conscious distortion.

Does the influence of these various perceptual factors help or hinder our perception of reality? Hilgard (1953, p. 306) sums up by saying, "Ordinarily the result is so satisfactory as to provide a useful guide to action; in fact, it is only because cues are so commonly dependable that we trust them on occasions when they should not be trusted and so sometimes are led to error." These factors tend to correct real discrepancies between stimulus received and object, and thus make us see things more nearly as they really are than as they might seem to be. Images on the retina are inverted, yet we see objects upright. Images move on the retina as we walk, yet we see buildings as standing still. Even when we try to fool the senses, as by wearing inverted prisms for glasses which turn images up the other way or by the pseudophone, somehow our sensory apparatus adjusts to this reversal of stimulation and after a while we see and hear things in their right position. Morgan (1956, pp. 177–178) says,

> Our perceptions of objects correspond more closely to the true object, however, than to the sizes of images on the retina or to the sensory stimulus in general.
> As human beings, we enjoy several advantages from perceptual constancy. It would be exceedingly difficult to move about or operate in a world where sounds changed their location when we moved our heads, and where objects changed their shapes and sizes when we viewed them from different positions and distances. Imagine what it would be like if your friends and associates had a multitude of sizes and shapes that depended upon how far away they were and from what angle you viewed them. Or imagine how difficult it would be to live in our society if the colors of things varied markedly with changes in sunlight and weather. It would be impossible to identify anything by color or whiteness, since the color of an object would depend not only on what time of the day it was but also on such things as cloudiness and shadows.

He concludes that though our eyes do sometimes trick us, they do so only in the line of duty. They operate in a way which is more than a matter of physical efficiency; they give us impressions of the outside world which are basically correct, even though they are by no means perfect.

IMAGINATION

Both the special senses and the central sense function only in the presence of an object actually stimulating a receptor. *Imagination is the power of sensory representation of objects not present to the receptor organs.* Its product is called an *image.* This power can either simply reproduce the previous perceptions or it can combine them (or elements of them) into new images; for instance, a flying cow. Although the former function is sometimes referred to as reproductive imagination and the latter as creative imagination, these are not different powers but simply different functions of the same power. When a person says he has no imagination, he does not really mean that he lacks this power entirely, but rather that his imagination has a low degree of creativity.

Images may be evoked by physiological causes, by motivational urges, or by associations which vary from the apparently random to those which are directly the result of choice. Fantasy or daydreams as well as dreams during sleep will often reflect our wishes and fears; hence the distinction between the manifest and the latent content of our minds. But there is no proof that all dreams are symbolic, much less that all dream symbols are sexual or that the symbolism all follows one pattern. One of the interests of psychologists is to study the various ways and laws by which images may be associated.

It is to be noted that the imagination can reproduce not only visual perceptions, as is suggested by the word image, but any previous sensory experience. Hence we have not only visual images, but also auditory, olfactory, gustatory, kinesthetic, tactual, and so forth. Individuals vary greatly in their power of auditory imagination, for instance; some can hear very clearly in their imagination, while others find it difficult to imagine the simplest tune.

Because the imagination makes us independent of present sensory stimulation and allows us to soar beyond reality, it is a great tool of the intellect and is usually found well developed in poets, scientists, inventors, and other creative thinkers. But imagination can also contribute to illusion, neurosis, and overemotionalism, and is the explanation for much of the purported success of fortunetelling, telepathy, and similar phenomena.

MEMORY

The proper object of *memory* is past experience identified and recognized precisely as past, in contrast to the object of imagination, which is simply not present. Both powers reproduce past sensory impressions, and their functions are so similar and interwoven that some philosophers do not consider them as distinct powers; however the assertion that they are distinct seems justified by their difference in respect to the formal aspect of pastness, i.e., the actual identification and recognition of this experience in relation to me. Actually the word "memory" usually refers to the activity not only of this sense power but also of the imagination. Memory may also mean the retention of ideas, and this is simply another function of the intellect.

The organic nature of the memorative power is clear from the sensory manner in which it represents objects clothed with material qualities, and also from the relationships between memory function and brain injury.[2]

Since both imagination and memory store impressions by way of habit and play such a large role in learning, they are also pertinent to the discussion in Chapter 14 on habit and learning. As memory differs from imagination precisely in the aspect of recognizing a concrete relation to the past experience of the individual rather than a mere representation of an object, we might say that memory is to the estimative power what imagination is to the central sense. At least memory has a special relation to this estimative power which we take up next.

[2] Wilder Penfield, "The Permanent Record of the Stream of Consciousness," *Proc. 14th Intern. Congr. Psychol.*, Montreal, 1954. Although questionable in some of his philosophical implications, his account brings out the organic yet psychological nature of memory.

ESTIMATIVE POWER

The estimative power is the fourth internal sense, defined as *the power by which an animal recognizes, prior to learning and without understanding, suitable behavior regarding a sensed object.* It is the cognitive element of what can be called instinctive behavior, which also involves physiological, appetitive, and motor factors. "Suitable" in this definition does not imply moral rightness, but merely what is to be done: by this power the animal knows whether to eat, build a nest out of, run from, or mate with the object it perceives.

In man the estimative power is called by other names such as the *cogitative power,* the discursive power, the comparative sense, or even particular reason. Some of these names were coined by the Arabian commentators on Aristotle, whose development of the notion of this sense power in man greatly influenced St. Thomas. The reason for using these names is to emphasize the fact that in man this sense power works very intimately with the intellect and to that extent differs from the sense powers of other animals. Man's senses, especially the internal, show much greater flexibility and scope because of their cooperation with intellect,[3] but this does not change the essentially animal or sensory nature of the powers themselves. (Similarly, the word reminiscence is sometimes used to refer to the activity of memory when under the guidance and direction of intellect.)

Instinctive Behavior

The word "instinct" unfortunately has been associated with certain theories of the past two centuries in which behavior was ascribed to hypothetical entities such as an "instinct of mother love," or a "food-gathering instinct." To appeal to such an entity as an explanation of behavior, as when people say, "This happened by instinct," is of course meaningless. For this reason we prefer not to use the noun.

[3] Thomas Aquinas, *Truth,* q. I, a. 11; q. X, a. 5. See R. Allers, "The Intellectual Cognition of Particulars," *The Thomist,* 1941, 3:95–163; "The Vis Cogitativa and Evaluation," *The New Scholasticism,* 1941, 15:195–221.

But there is clear evidence that there are certain activities, especially in insects and lower animals but also to some extent in higher vertebrates and even in man, which seem to merit the adjective "instinctive" because of characteristics now well established by experimentation. Animals raised in complete isolation from all others will, at maturity, display distinctive patterns of behavior in mating, nest-building, and other actvities, which are peculiar to their own species and which could not possibly have been learned by imitation or trial and error. Although the word "instinct" was rejected in the first half of the twentieth century because it had been used to cloak our ignorance of just how animals function, recently the term has come into use again (Hilgard, Munn, Morgan) but in a more cautious and scientific way. We prefer the adjective "instinctive" to designate the behavior, without implying that instinct is a substance. This behavior is unlearned, impulsive, useful, complex, and modifiable by conditioning although basic to a given species.

Because instinctive tendencies are modifiable by learning and circumstances, it is absurd to look for examples of purely instinctive behavior at least among higher vertebrates, including man. But there must be something there to modify. Instincts cannot be classified and enumerated as if they were things, but we do have tendencies to act in accordance with our recognition of the usefulness or harmfulness of certain objects, without intellectual understanding or previous experience. The classic examples are the instinctive activities of ants, bees, and other insects.

These activities cannot be explained merely as a reaction to pleasant or unpleasant sensation caused by the object, since the animal often continues activity even though unpleasant. Again, this activity can hardly be a mere chain of reflexes,[4] since it is not mechanical but clearly psychological in origin. There is much evidence of at least sensory cognition, awareness of *what* is to be done, if not *why*. The activity is not automatic and stereotyped like reflex, but highly modifiable, irregular, and impulsive.

Ingenious experiments have shown that animals respond to certain

[4] Karl S. Lashley shows the inadequacy of the reflex theory in "Experimental Analysis of Instinctive Behavior," *Psych. Rev.*, 1938, 45:453.

internal stimuli such as changes in their blood chemistry with the gradual lengthening of the days in spring. But rather than being an explanation, these facts need to be explained. Why does the bird fly north rather than south when the days grow longer? Such responses are beyond any reflexes known to physiology. Some are so impressed by the nonmechanical nature of these responses that they go to the opposite extreme and ascribe to the brute animal possession of intelligence in the strict sense, not merely some ability to learn or know. This question is treated in the Appendix.

If this activity is neither merely reflex nor truly intellectual, the explanation must be at the sensory level. But the special senses cannot account for it, nor can any of the other internal senses. The evidence points to the existence of a power at work which is different from all of these, whose formal object is the usefulness (or harm) of a perceived object. This power is only one factor in a complex process, but is necessary to account for the unlearned, cognitive aspects. We conclude by stressing again the great interdependence among the various internal senses and their special relation to the intellect in the case of man.

REVIEW QUESTIONS

1. Explain each important word of the definition of internal sense in the same way as was done in the text in the previous chapter with the definition of special sense.
2. List all the ways in which the internal senses differ from the special senses. (See also Figure 4 at the end of Chapter 3 for function, organ, and proper object.)
3. List all the ways in which they are similar.
4. Describe the evidence for the existence of the central sense as a distinct power.
5. When one has "a song on the brain" what power is operating? Is this experience sensory, even though we cannot visualize it?
6. How does imagination differ from central sense?
7. Why would there be a tendency for intelligence to correspond with degree of imagination?
8. How does memory differ from imagination? Give examples.
9. Explain in your own words each element in the definition of estimative power.

10. Is an animal born with knowledge or only with the power of knowing?
11. Is estimative power the only factor in instinctive behavior?
12. St. Thomas calls the action of the estimative power a sense-judgment. Does this mean that the animal understands? Is judgment here a univocal or analogous term?
13. Explain how sensation and perception differ.
14. Does the enumeration of subjective factors in perception square with the epistemological position of moderate realism assumed in Chapter 3? Explain. Were Scholastic philosophers aware of such perceptual phenomena before the advent of experimental psychology?
15. Are these perceptual phenomena due only to the influence of central sense? If not, what other powers are involved?
16. If other powers are involved, what basic characteristic of perception indicates that it be discussed under the section on the central sense?

FOR FURTHER READING

AQUINAS, ST. THOMAS. Summa Theol., Ia, 78, 4. The Soul, a, 13. Truth, 15, 2.
BRENNAN, ROBERT E., O.P. Thomistic Psychology. New York: Macmillan, 1941. Pp. 121–146.
GAFFNEY, MARK A., S.J. Psychology of the Interior Senses. St. Louis: Herder, 1942.
EBBINGHAUS, H. Memory. Providence: Brown University Press, 1955. (Reprint of first 52 pages.)
KASNER, E., & NEWMAN, J. Mathematics and the Imagination. New York: Simon and Schuster, 1940.
RAPAPORT, DAVID. Emotions and Memory. New York: International Universities Press, 1957.

Perception

ALLPORT, FLOYD H. Theories of Perception and the Concept of Structure. New York: Wiley, 1955.
AMES, A., JR. "Reconsideration of the Origin and Nature of Perception," in S. Ratner (Ed.), Vision and Action. New Brunswick, N.J.: Rutgers University Press, 1953. Pp. 251–274.
BARTLEY, J. HOWARD. Principles of Perception. New York: Harper, 1958.
BEARDSLEE, DAVID C., & WERTHEIMER, M. (Eds.) Readings in Perception. New York: Van Nostrand, 1958.
BIER, W. C., S.J. (Ed.) Perception in Present-day Psychology: A Sym-

posium. New York: American Catholic Psychological Association (Fordham University), 1956. Good presentation of current experimental research in Europe and America. Includes discussions of implications for epistemology and for clinical, experimental, and social psychology.

BLAKE, ROBERT R., & RAMSEY, GLENN V. (Eds.) *Perception: An Approach to Personality.* New York: Ronald, 1950.

BRUNNER, J. S., & GOODMAN, C. D. "Value and Need as Organizing Factors in Perception," *J. Abnorm. Soc. Psychol.,* 1947, 42:33–44.

COMBS, ARTHUR W., & SNYGG, DONALD. *Individual Behavior: A Perceptual Approach to Behavior.* (Rev. Ed.) New York: Harper, 1959.

GIBSON, J. J. *The Perception of the Visual World.* Boston: Houghton Mifflin, 1940.

ITTLESON, W. H., & CANTRIL, H. *Perception: A Transactional Approach.* New York: Doubleday, 1954.

MCCLELLAND, D. C., & ATKINSON, J. W. "The Projective Expression of Needs: The Effect of Different Intensities of the Hunger Drive on Perception," *J. Psychol.,* 1948, 25:205–222.

MOORE, THOMAS VERNER. "A Scholastic Theory of Perception," *The New Scholasticism,* 1933, 7:222–238.

POSTMAN, L., BRUNER, J. S., & MCGINNIES, E. "Personal Values as Selective Factors in Perception," *J. Abnorm. Soc. Psychol.,* 1948, 43:142–154.

RYAN, EDMUND J., C.Pp.S. *The Role of the Sensus Communis in the Philosophy of St. Thomas Aquinas.* Carthagena, Ohio: Messenger Press, 1951.

SANFORD, R. N. "The Effects of Abstinence from Food upon Imaginal Processes: A Preliminary Experiment," *J. Psychol.,* 1936, 2:129–136.

WITKIN, H. A., and others. *Personality Through Perception: An Experimental and Clinical Study.* New York: Harper, 1954.

Gestalt Psychology

ANGYAL, ANDERS. *Foundations for a Science of Personality.* New York: Commonwealth Fund, 1941.

BRUNSWIK, EGON. *The Concept and Framework of Psychology.* Chicago: University of Chicago Press, 1952.

HAMLYN, D. W. *The Psychology of Perception: A Philosophical Examination of Gestalt Theory and Derivative Theories of Perception.* New York: Humanities Press, 1957.

HELSON, H. (Ed.) *Theoretical Foundations of Psychology.* New York: Van Nostrand, 1951.

HERR, VINCENT V., S.J. "Gestalt Psychology: Empirical or Rational?" in Anton C. Pegis (Ed.), *Essays in Modern Scholasticism*. Westminster, Md.: Newman, 1944. Pp. 222–243.

KATZ, DAVID. *Gestalt Psychology*. New York: Ronald, 1950.

KOFFKA, KURT. *Principles of Gestalt Psychology*. New York: Harcourt, Brace, 1935.

KOHLER, WOLFGANG. *Gestalt Psychology*. New York: Liveright, 1929.

LEWIN, KURT. *A Dynamic Theory of Personality: Selected Papers*. New York: McGraw-Hill, 1935.

Estimative or Cogitative Power

ALLERS, RUDOLF. "The Vis Cogitativa and Evaluation," *The New Scholasticism*, 1941, 15:195–221.

BERNARD, L. L. *Instinct: A Study in Social Psychology*. New York: Holt, 1924. Good presentation of the behavioristic viewpoint opposing instinct, though it is given some restricted place. Unfortunately uses uniformity of action-pattern as the criterion of instinctive behavior, which of course cannot apply to human beings because of social and learning factors.

CATTELL, RAYMOND B. "The Discovery of Ergic Structures in Man in Terms of Common Attitudes," *J. Abnorm. Soc. Psychol.*, 1950, 45:598–618.

FLETCHER, RONALD. *Instinct in Man: In the Light of Recent Work in Comparative Psychology*. New York: International Universities Press, 1957. Good criticism of behavioristic position.

FLYNN, THOMAS V., S.J. "The Cogitative Power," *The Thomist*, 1953, 16:542–563.

KLUBERTANZ, GEORGE P., S.J. *The Discursive Power*. St. Louis: *The Modern Schoolman*, 1952.

MOORE, THOMAS VERNER. *The Driving Forces of Human Nature and Their Adjustment*. New York: Grune & Stratton, 1948. Pp. 231–242.

PEGHAIRE, JULIEN. "A Forgotten Sense, the Cogitative, According to St. Thomas Aquinas," *The Modern Schoolman*, 1943, 20:123–140, 210–229.

WILM, E. C. *Theories of Instinct*. New Haven: Yale University Press, 1925.

For additional data on the activity of the estimative power in animals, see the further readings listed for the Appendix.

6

THE INTELLECT

Thinking: the difference between intellectual and sensory cognition. Conceptual language. Intelligence.

Man has traditionally been defined as a rational animal. Now a definition proves nothing; it just formulates the result of investigation. Moreover, we find many instances in which man is not nearly as rational as he would like to think himself. Yet his achievements in literature, art, poetry, engineering, science, government, and other areas of civilization clearly mark him off from the other animals, even from those among whom some apparent similarities to human traits have been found. The difference between intellectual and sensory knowledge is further suggested by the fact that a moron can store up a great fund of useless factual information, while a genius may not even know his own telephone number or may be ignorant of the facts of history. Mere sensory knowledge is not necessarily wisdom.

IS THOUGHT SENSORY?

Up to this point our analysis of human knowledge has been largely uncontroversial. Now there arises a fundamental question: is the difference between intellectual and sensory knowledge merely a matter of degree, or are they of essentially different kinds? Upon the answer to this question depends our solution to many crucial problems affecting law, society, and our own destiny. Man's responsibility as a free agent, the spirituality and immortality of the soul, and human rights and dignity, all hinge on the immaterial nature of intellectual operations.

Since even the most ardent materialist would hardly insist that he has never had an idea or that he cannot think, the problem is to analyze what thinking is. Is an idea the same kind of knowing as an image? Is thinking a matter of muscle twitches in the throat or neurological activity in the brain? Are attempts to reduce all knowledge to sense based on psychological facts or on philosophical preconceptions?

Here for perhaps the first time in this book we have a real issue. Some materialistic philosophers called sensists try to reduce all thinking processes to the sensory level. Note that a sensist is not one who merely asserts the existence of sense knowledge; rather he is one who denies that there is any knowledge beyond the senses. Opposed are those who claim that the thought processes involve operation of a distinctively different nature, going beyond sensory experience. For them, intellectual processes do not possess any material qualities, such as color, shape, sound, or extension, which we discovered even in the operations of the internal senses. They hold thought to be abstract, universal, immaterial.

Twentieth-century American students are often under the impression that a philosophy of materialism dominates the major portion of human thought, opposed only by a religious minority. Now truth is not decided by majority vote, nor does the philosopher argue from the weight of authority. But it is well to correct this impression by pointing out that the spiritual nature of the intellect is upheld by philosophers of widely different schools of thought, varied cultures, and all degrees of faith: pagan Greeks like Plato and Aristotle, Arabians like Averroës, most Oriental philosophers, divergent and even opposed European philosophers like Descartes, Kant, Hegel, Spinoza, and Bergson, and contemporary non-Catholic American psychologists and philosophers scattered across the country. Although the last are admittedly a minority, it is probably true that the majority of philosophers, except in our particular time and culture, oppose the materialistic view. After all if the facts are there and the mind is made for seeking truth, it would be surprising if the immateriality of intellection escaped very many people for very long.

False Issues

To sharpen the issue we should make clear that to claim that man is rational is not to deny the sensory, animal aspects of his nature or the fact that he often acts in a very irrational way. Infancy and early childhood, severe mental disorder, and the spontaneous actions of normal adults give ample evidence that much of our activity is animal. Since "He who proves too much proves nothing," we do not appeal to the intellect when animal powers will explain behavior.

Again, we must avoid the ambiguity which has accrued to many terms in current psychology because of the philosophical backgrounds of the people using them. Such terms as intelligence, meaning, insight, trial and error, and learning are all analogical and can be applied both to the operations of the internal senses and to those of the intellect. Professor Spearman (1950, p. 67) went so far as to say that the term intelligence had become so vague as to lose all usefulness. Even the term concept-formation is now used to refer to the association of images of a general type with certain words or arbitrary symbols, which is within the power of at least the higher brute animals. Similarly, the term problem-solving can refer to a great variety of activities, some involving intellect and some explainable by perceptual awareness of a total pattern of concrete relations (internal senses). We wish to examine thought in the strict sense of rational or intellectual processes. The essentially different nature of the intellectual process and the activity of the internal senses will be manifested by the following proofs better than by any definition.

PROOFS OF THE IMMATERIALITY OF THE INTELLECT

Universal Ideas. Let us begin with the process of abstraction. This operation may not be typical of how ideas are formed, but it brings out their nature very well. I observe a series of triangles of varying sizes, shapes and colors. They may be isosceles, equilateral, obtuse or acute. They may be large or small, red, green, purple, black, or white. I can reproduce each of these percepts as an image, seeing the various sizes, shapes and colors in my mind's eye. But I may do something else. I may prescind from color, size and shape (the negative phase of abstraction). Leaving aside these material qualities, I become aware of a common note (the positive phase). A note is simply anything intellectually knowable about an object; it may be the essence or nature, some essential property, or even an accidental quality. Thus I may abstract out the essence of triangularity, the essential property of having angles equal to 180 degrees, or the accidental fact that these triangles are all drawn with very thin lines. In any case I experience awareness of some attribute common to all the triangles, yet unable to be represented by any one percept or image. Take the essence of triangularity itself: my percept or image of the tall, obtuse, purple triangle hardly applies equally well to the short, acute, green triangle; yet my awareness of what a triangle is applies equally well to both.

This awareness of an essence is called an *idea.* It is the mental representation or awareness of what a thing is, without its material qualities, and is applicable to all objects of that class. It is also called the concept, understanding, notion, or simple apprehension. It is the result of abstracting out just the whatness or quiddity (Latin *quid,* meaning "what") of a thing, leaving aside other qualities. Later it will also be called the expressed intelligible species and the mental word, not to be confused with the words of language.

A *concrete* idea is the result of this generalizing kind of abstraction: thus my idea of man represents what is found in existing men. Beyond this concrete universal idea the intellect can, by a process of isolating abstraction, prescind even from the concrete objects (men) in which the notion is verified and treat a given note (humanity) independently of any object. The result of this process is the *abstract idea*: motion, energy, justice, circularity, are abstract ideas. They exist only in the mind, not as such in things. Men exist, but humanity is not something which exists in itself as such. However, God is real and concrete, not an abstraction in the mind, like relativity.

It is to be noted that all ideas are of their very nature universal.[1] Thus my understanding of what a triangle is is quite applicable to all triangles. I can think of a particular triangle only by relating the concept to some sensory experience. The exception is an idea whose object is of its very nature unique, so that if I correctly understand the essence I know that it is necessarily singular, e.g., the idea of God.

Note that the difference between intellect and sense is not a matter of whether the object is present or absent, real or unreal. Thus I can have an idea of the nature of a present object and a sensory representation (image) of an absent object. I can understand real objects such as horses, or imagine a nonexistent object like a flying horse.

Again, the unpicturable nature of an idea means not only the lack of *visible* qualities, but of *any* material qualities. We cannot *see* sounds or odors, but this does not make them immaterial. I can hear or imagine (auditory image) a particular tune, but the idea of opera or ballad has no melody and cannot be heard any more than seen. The universal idea of ballad applies to all ballads; the tune of "Danny Boy" does not.

The immateriality of thought is clear from its universal nature. Sense cannot soar beyond the particular, individual object represented with its material qualities. Sensists have tried to explain my universal idea of a horse, for instance, as a vague, general, neutral-

---

[1] This universality is aptitudinal, not formal or reflex. See pp. 125–126 below. Beware of thinking that "universal" means common to all men rather than common to all objects. If only one man existed, his universal idea of tree would still apply to all trees.

gray image which would apply equally well to white, brown and black horses. It certainly does not apply as well to horses of other colors as it does to gray horses. Much less can a single sensory representation apply equally well to every horse, whether standing or running, neighing or silent, etc.; but my idea does. Outside of the fact that my idea of a horse is not neutral-gray, the theory breaks down completely if I push the generalization a step further. I understand clearly what a mammal is, yet I have no vague image which would apply equally well to elephant, cow, rabbit and mouse. No sensory experience can provide such an image.

Immateriality of Object. Since we said that operative powers are known or specified by their objects, we can examine the intellect by noting its object. Whereas sense experience must always have some concrete object clothed in sensible qualities, whether real or imaginary, the object of the intellect need not be material at all. Justice and rights cannot be experienced in any sensory way, yet our courts are very busy defending these realities, clearly the objects of intellect. Man can know the abstract, whether it be a simple concept like circularity or an abstruse one like Einstein's theory of relativity. The object of a geometrician's calculations is not a line drawn on a piece of paper, which actually has not only length but breadth and even infinitesimal thickness. The line is merely a sensory representation drawn for his convenience. Man can know God and angels, and they are immaterial objects. Hilgard (1953, p. 327-328) puts it well:

> *Thinking may deal with contents and relationships not perceptible.* A second difference between perception and thinking is that thinking goes beyond perception by dealing with relationships that cannot be perceived, that lie outside the field of perception entirely. A relationship like the square root of minus one is commonly symbolized by the small letter "i." This letter can, of course, be perceived, but the thought content involved is beyond perception. A concept like "justice" is too abstract to be perceived, even though it, too, may be symbolized by something perceptible, e.g., a blind goddess holding a pair of scales and a sword.
> Perception, then, does not tell the whole story of thinking, even though there is an intimacy between thinking and perception.

Thinking may conflict with and correct perception; it may deal with contents that are not perceptible at all.

Because he can think, man has opened before him vast possibilities that perception and habit alone would never have yielded. Through thought man can transcend space and time and pry into the mysteries of a universe measured in millions of light years. He can depart from reality into a fanciful world of his own making; he can become a creator as well as a discoverer. Because he can use and understand symbols (words, formulas, etc.), he can treasure up knowledge from the past. The monuments of ancient and contemporary civilizations—old aqueducts and modern hydroelectric dams, medieval cathedrals and modern skyscrapers, great libraries and museums—are at the same time monuments to man as a thinker.

To claim that an immaterial object, independent of space, time, and individual material qualities, could be grasped by a material organic power is to contradict the principle of causality. A material power cannot cause an immaterial operation.

In using this argument the student is warned that he must avoid giving the impression that only abstract or spiritual realities prove the immaterial nature of the intellect. Even in its grasp of concrete material objects such as horses and trees the intellect shows its immateriality, since it represents these objects in a universal and immaterial way, as is shown above under the section "Universal Ideas."

Self-reflection. Another proof of the immateriality of the intellect is the fact that it is able to reflect or bend back perfectly upon itself. I can think about my thinking. No extended material being can bend back perfectly upon itself but only upon some other part or power at best; for instance, the central sense can know the activity of the special senses. But the intellect can know itself and its own act by a process of proper and perfect reflection which is beyond the limitations of material being.[2]

Unlimited Capacity of Intellect. A favorite proof of St. Thomas Aquinas[3] for the immateriality of the intellect is the fact that it can

[2] M. Maher develops this argument more fully in his *Psychology: Empirical and Rational.*
[3] *S. T.,* Ia, 75, 2.

know all bodies. The eye, he says, is limited to color, the ear to sound. But the intellect is not limited to any class of beings; it is in potency to know whatever is intelligible. We know from metaphysics that whatever exists is potentially knowable. In this lies the fascination of scientific research: man reaching out to discover the intelligibility of the universe.

If the sense of sight were already green, it would not be indifferent to color, and hence it would be incapable of knowing all other colors. To be in potency to all colors, it cannot be actually any one. Likewise, if the intellect were already a material body, it could not be in potency to know all bodies.

Several objections can be raised against this proof, which therefore needs further investigation. First, one might argue that the intellect could be organic yet in potency to the intentional or representative form of other bodies. We reply that if organic, the intellect would have to be actuated by these other bodies through its organ, and since the organ would be the first actuation of the intellect, it would no longer be in potency to reception of other forms, but would know only its own organ.

The objector might continue that the senses are organic, and therefore it would follow by analogy that the senses can know only their organs. We answer that the object of the senses is not the nature of any organ but of qualities which exist in objects and not in the organs. Thus the sense of sight is colorless, as stated above; the recent research on thermal sensations confirms the theory that the organs know only what is different from themselves, for the organs do have a certain temperature, and sensation has been shown to result from changes in temperature, or stimulation other than that of the original temperature, so that what we actually sense are the qualities of "hotter" and "colder." But the object of intellect is the natures of things.

Since we argue that if the intellect were bodily it could not know all bodies, the objector might say that if the intellect were being, it could not know all beings. Therefore the intellect would have to be nonbeing, which is absurd. The answer is that the argument does not assert that the intellect has no definite nature, but only that it has no organic nature. Matter is the principle of limitation, and therefore whatever is material or corporeal cannot be actuated by more than one form of the same kind; if the intellect is immaterial, this limitation does not apply. We may further admit that our intellect has no direct knowledge of spiritual beings as such, but knows only through and by analogy with material beings.

Lastly, we do not claim that the intellect is infinite, or that we have unlimited knowledge by the mere possession of an intellect. The intellect is subjectively finite but objectively unlimited because in potency to receive the representative form of any material being. Unlimited potency to finite forms is not the same as an infinite mind.

This unlimited capacity of the intellect is further confirmed by the fact that there is no limit to the amount of knowledge we can acquire: our intellect never becomes full like a box. If sound becomes too loud, it becomes painful; if light becomes too intense, we cannot bear it. But no one complains of understanding too clearly, nor does the learned man complain of knowing too much—rather, he is especially aware of how much more he wants to know.

That the object of thinking supersedes that of perception is brought out by Hilgard where he notes that when perception and thought disagree, the perception may persist even when thought has corrected it. For instance, I know that the railroad tracks remain parallel, yet they continue to seem to converge in the distance. He continues (1953, p. 327):

> The statistical nature of perception leads to a kind of stupid irreversibility in perception. The unconscious computations that go on lead to definiteness and clarity in the resulting perception even though the resulting perception is a false representation of reality. Thus, perception is less objective and less rational than thought.

Another way of seeing how intellect goes beyond sense is to imagine a square, hexagon, octagon, and so forth, until the imagination finally is incapable of getting clear pictures. But the intellect is still quite capable of understanding clearly the difference between a polygon of 3,897 sides as opposed to one of 3,896 sides. Sensory perception could not distinguish a polygon of 3 million sides from a circle, yet the intellect clearly knows the difference.

My sensory experiences may actually become more sharp as my ideas become more vague, and vice versa. My images of cow versus horse are clear; my ideas on the difference are hazy. But my idea of mammal versus nonmammal is clear, whereas the images become vague and inadequate here. Understanding is different from picturing.

Voluntary Attention. Another argument for the immateriality of intellection can be made from the fact that we can voluntarily direct our attention, within limits, to what we will. Attention of this kind must be suprasensuous in character, since any purely sensory process is determined by the causal stimulus and follows the material conditions of organic functioning. Voluntary attention, being self-initiated and self-controlled, enjoys a certain independence from physical stimuli and organic factors.

This is illustrated by what Piaget (1950, pp. 40–41) calls the *reversibility* of thought. I can easily *understand* the alphabet as the same sequence of letters starting from either end, ABC . . . or ZYX. . . . But I find it almost impossible to reverse the chain of sensory symbols and recite them backwards, without considerable new learning (Dollard & Miller, 1950, p. 111). Thought is free from sequences in time and space; I can arbitrarily view relationships from opposite approaches, choose alternative correct solutions to the same problem, substitute algebraic for arithmetical symbols for the same content, or substitute different contents for the same set of symbols, as I choose. Sensory knowledge manifests none of this openness to choice.

Judgment. Ach and Marbe, experimental psychologists of the Würzburg school, bring out the unpicturable nature of intellectual activity in their studies of the judgment. If one says, "No man is a stone," it is easy to have a sensory picture of a man and a stone and even of the word symbols "no" and "is." But the understanding of the fact that a man is not a stone has itself no material qualities knowable in a sensory way. This is especially clear if we consider the truth of a necessary judgment: the necessity is clearly grasped but impossible to reduce to sensory content. Even our judgment that the half-immersed oar is not bent is not expressed in a sensory way: we *know* it is straight, but we do not *see* it as straight.

Alfred Binet, founder of intelligence testing, experimented with thought processes involving analogy and the reconciliation of opposites, and came to the conclusion that these experiences are irreducible to sense. This is all the more significant because Binet, like the Würzburgers, began his investigations convinced of the truth of sensism.

The "Imageless Thought" Controversy. The expression "imageless thought" can have three distinct meanings.

1. It can mean *thought which is not derived from imagery or sense knowledge,* even in some indirect way. In this sense modern psychologists and Scholastic philosophers agree that there is no imageless thought, since all knowledge begins in some way in the senses. Aristotle rejected the theory of innate ideas put forth by Plato, his teacher, and took a very empirical approach to human knowledge.

2. The second meaning of the expression would be *thought which is unaccompanied by images.* This was avidly debated in the imageless thought controversy and it is still an open question. Ironically, St. Thomas tends to insist, because of the close relation between intellect and sense, that thought is always accompanied by *some[4]* imagery, whereas it was the modern experimental psychologists like Woodworth, Binet, Külpe, and K. Bühler who maintained that they had experience of thought unaccompanied by image. This position, if correct, would confirm the immaterial nature of intellection, but the question is irrelevant because even in St. Thomas's view correla-

[4] There is probably no real disagreement between Aquinas and these psychologists. He is willing to admit that the images which accompany ideas need not be those from which the ideas were originally derived nor do the images need to correspond with the ideas. The psychologists in turn were speaking principally of judgment (see previous section "Judgment"), which he would agree can have no corresponding image. Both hold the irreducibility of thought to image and would probably agree that no thinking occurs without *any* sensory experience whatsoever.

tion between image and thought does not mean identity. Even if the man is always accompanied by the clothing and the clothing by the man, it is still possible to analyze each and see that the nature of one differs from the nature of the other. Thus with the idea and its sensory clothing.

3. The crucial meaning of the expression is: *thought which is not image*, i.e., is not reducible to any sensory experience, regardless of whether it may be derived from sense (the first meaning given above) and accompanied by sense (the second meaning). The evidence seems clear that imageless thought in this third sense does occur.

The whole history of the imageless thought controversy, in which the Würzburg school took such an active part, confirms the impossibility of reducing thought processes to sense.[5] Not only K. Bühler, Külpe, and the other members of the Würzburg school, but also Alfred Binet and others in France, Watt and Spearman in England, R. S. Woodworth, Betts, and many others in this country, all agreed on the evidence. Their conclusion would seem to be the more objective because all these men started with a theoretical bias against this interpretation of the facts discovered. Titchener, who takes the contrary position, very frankly admits approaching the facts with a preconceived bias in favor of his interpretation. His Cornell observers were constantly running into the same facts upon which the Würzburg people base their claims; the argument depends wholly on the interpretation of the facts or the value placed on them as scientific evidence.

Titchener at best offered only negative evidence, inability to discover thought beyond images. Actually, it was his absurd distortion

[5] T. V. Moore, *The Process of Abstraction* (University of California Press, 1910) gives probably the most complete account of the controversy, based on original German sources and firsthand laboratory experimentation. Unfortunately out of print, it remains a most valuable historical record, even if Moore's own experiments were later criticized as not really involving abstraction but intellectual memory associated with images (Sister M. Coady, 1932).

H. Gruender, *Problems of Psychology*, Chaps. 1, 2, and *Experimental Psychology* (not his "Introduction"), Chaps. 14, 15, 16, gives a very full and lucid analysis of the arguments and counterarguments of Titchener and his opponents.

of consciousness that brought introspection into disrepute and precipitated behaviorism. He attempted to avoid recognizing the suprasensory nature of an idea by reporting that it was a "grey patch of fog in the northeast corner of consciousness" or by reducing meaning to "the blue-grey tip of a scoop" and saying that this image not only accompanied the thought but actually constituted the thought itself. Since others could have exactly the same thought without these images, it is clear that the imagery he reported was not the thought. When Morgan (1956, p. 139) says that the controversy showed that thought is not conscious, what he really means is that thought is not sensory. If you look for material pictures, you will never discover that you have an idea; but you are quite *conscious* of "what a triangle is." Your idea is a conscious act, but not one of *sensory* consciousness.

It was noted above that some proponents of imageless thought actually claimed evidence for thoughts existing without any accompanying image. While not going this far, the Scholastic assertion of the difference between thought and image is based on this type of positive evidence, not on negative (absence of imagery). Thought is more than some unknown intervening variable between stimulus and response. Ideas can be analyzed, discussed, communicated, and compared, as well as contrasted with object, word, and percept or image. They are not mystical, mythical, or supernatural, but part of the everyday experience of one whose nature includes the ability to think.

Superiority of Man. Another argument for the existence of the intellectual order of knowledge is the fact that we cannot account for man's superiority by any appeal to the sensory order. Brute animals can surpass man in every category of sense experience. The superiority must come from some other source.

Moreover, there are instances where human beings have been gravely deficient in the realm of the senses and yet have achieved remarkable superiority. The case of Helen Keller comes to mind, and there are many other similar examples of handicapped persons. A man completely paralyzed can still manage to communicate thought somehow, whereas the most glib parrot never does (Mowrer, 1954, p. 675). People surpass animals far better endowed. Monkeys are far more agile and can manipulate better than many cripples; man's superiority can hardly be explained purely because he has an apposable thumb. Attempts to explain human personality, responsibility, and dignity by appeals to a more refined nervous system do not seem to square with the facts. (See the Appendix.)

The same is true when man is compared with the machine. We now have calculators which compute much faster and more accurately than a staff of mathematicians and which have far better memories. Yet the men who work with these machines do not talk of their superiority but rather of their stupidity: the machine "knows" only what it is programmed to perform; it is helpless without a man to feed information in and interpret what is taken out. Such machines can be "taught" to play chess so well that they can beat most good players, but only because the mechanical brain has the statistical advantage of being able to run through all the possible answers to all possible moves instantaneously and without missing one. And it cannot design either games or machines.

Disproportion of Thought and Brain. If the brain produces thought as the liver secretes bile, one would expect some direct one-to-one ratio between brain and thought. Yet all attempts to establish such a relation have proved fruitless. Size of brain, either absolute or relative to the body, does not correlate with intelligence. The value of fish as a "brain food" because of its chemical content has long since been disproved, as has phrenology which tries to correlate mental powers with "bumps" on the head. In spite of rather accurate localization of centers in the brain for the various sensory and motor processes, all attempts to localize thought have failed, except the vague designation of "association areas" which are apparently the organs of the internal senses so closely associated with thought.

Particularly fascinating here is the history of the association of mental disfunction with brain injury. It was the evidence with regard to this association which apparently impressed such non-Scholastic philosophers at Bergson, Driesch, C. E. M. Joad, and others with the inadequacy of materialism. T. V. Moore, M.D., in his *Cognitive Psychology* (pp. 45–73) tells how the medical literature successively abandoned attempts to locate intelligence as a function of the right hemisphere, left hemisphere, frontal lobes, or any other part of the brain when war injuries or brain tumor operations showed that these parts could be removed and the person still think. Loss of speech and memory are connected with brain injury according to complex patterns involving degree of abstractness or concreteness of thought in a way hardly explainable if thought is a physiological mechanism.

Leaving aside psychogenic or purely mental disorder, the abnormal psychology of even brain-injured patients shows clearly that their mental symptoms cannot be explained purely in terms of the area or amount of brain damage.[6] The discrepancy between brain lesions and impairment of mental performance is too great to square with the theory that the brain is the principal cause of thought, rather than an extrinsic instrument (see the last section of Chapter 8, on relation of thought to brain).

Thought must not be confused with its physiological accompaniments. In the 1920s the behaviorists tried to reduce thinking to subvocal speech, namely, to electrically measurable muscular contractions in the throat which are the beginnings of the formation of words which would express thought. No one will deny the existence of these action currents or "implicit speech" any more than he will deny the evidence from the EEG (electroencephalograph) for brain waves during thought. But their existence does not prove whether they are cause or effect. The real question is whether these physical activities constitute the essence of thought as the behaviorists claim, or are merely its concomitants.[7] Every car makes noise, but this does not prove that the noise moves the car.

[6] N. Cameron, M.D., devotes Chap. 17 of his *Psychology of Behavior Disorders* (1947) to a detailed elaboration of this position, in spite of his behavioristic approach.

[7] Ruch (1953), p. 309; Hilgard, *Theories of Learning* (1956), p. 477, and *Introduction to Psychology* (1957), p. 314.

Brain waves may tell us how a man is thinking, but they never tell us what he is thinking. They give no clue as to the content of thought, but simply some indication of its emotional and imaginal mode. One confirmation of this theory seems to be the fact that there are two times when the brain wave pattern is strikingly similar: when there is no thought going on at all and when one is indulging in pure abstract thought (Travis, 1937). These two states are poles apart at the level of thought itself, but at the sensory level could easily have the same physiological pattern of low imagery and emotion.

Even Hilgard does not always carefully distinguish between what thought itself consists of and the vehicles by which it is expressed or accompanied. Thus he suggests (1953, p. 320) the old experiment of trying to *think* the word "bubble" with your mouth open. You will feel a catch in your throat, as if something were going on there. Because this happens, he concludes that *some* thinking does "consist of" talking to yourself. Now we do not think words, but thoughts. In our discussion of nominalism later in this chapter we shall see that Hilgard agrees that the *word* bubble is not the thought, or understanding of what a bubble is. When he suggests that you "think" the word, what he really means is that you get a verbal image. This word-image, being concrete and sensory, has not only a physiological component in itself but an obvious connection with throat movement. A synonym for bubble in another language might not produce the same reaction, and I might have the idea with no word imagery at all.

This tendency of thought to express itself spontaneously in action has also caused some psychologists to mistake muscular contraction in the right forearm for the act of choice itself. "I choose this one" would quite naturally be accompanied or followed by such infinitesimal arm movement, but this does not prove that the choice and the movement are identical. These hardly perceptible movements sometimes account for the success of the "mind reader" who finds hidden objects in a room, and they also explain the Ouija board, on which people unwittingly betray their thoughts or wishes.

Values and Recent Psychology. Finally, a practical argument for the immateriality of the intellect might be deduced from the fact that man acts because of motives other than organic drives or physical stimuli. If values can make a real difference to his conduct, man must have the power of knowing such values, and this power can only be the intellect.

It might be well to note the number of prominent American psychologists who now speak very frankly on the matter of the immateriality of their intellect; we do this not in order to argue on the basis of their authority but simply to indicate the trend of contemporary scientific psychology as it gains independence from the materialistic philosophy out of which it emerged.

Hadley Cantril of Princeton stated his position in 1950 in *The "Why" of Man's Experience*, even using terms like "immaterial" and "freedom of choice." Percival M. Symonds of Columbia University (1951, 1956) notes that the swing in emphasis is away from purely emotional factors in adjustment, toward rational control. The work of Spearman, Thurstone, and Guilford on factorial analysis constantly comes back to the notion of intellect as distinct but not separate, whether it be called G, super-G, or a second-order factor. (See Gannon, *Psychology: The Unity of Human Behavior*, 1954, pp. 347–362, for a full discussion of this, and for other examples from modern psychology.)

L. Terman, father of intelligence testing in the United States, toward the end of a long career stated that in his opinion intelligence could still best be defined as "the ability to do abstract thinking." Krech and Crutchfield (1958, p. 392) cite experimental evidence that knowledge of concrete facts in "pupil-oriented" learning may actually hinder problem solving if abstract principles are neglected. Abraham Maslow, Gardner Murphy, David McClelland, and others have recently emphasized that maturity is characterized by goal-seeking and by other activities which are rational rather than emotional, or at any rate are distinct from animal activity and mere need-reduction. Hilgard in his *Theories of Learning* (1956) indicates the swing back toward values and the responsibility of those who speak vaguely of intervening variables to face the question of their precise nature:

> An important aspect of motivation long neglected in learning theories . . . is that motives are organized in some sort of hierarchy within the individual, resulting in a value-system expressed in behavior. (p. 469) Stimulus-response psychologists . . . have assigned as little as possible to ideation, but they have usually recognized that some behavior is controlled by ideas . . . Tolman, in Behavioristic spirit, makes of ideation a "mere behavior-feint at running-back-and-forth" without specifying the precise nature of the feint. (p. 476)

CONCEPTUAL LANGUAGE

Since the use of conceptual language is often asserted to be a characteristic difference between men and the other animals, it is important to analyze the relation of language to thought. Whether or not animals communicate, with each other or with man, is a false issue. One reindeer communicates a sense of danger to the whole herd; one bee informs the others of the location of a find of sugar. The dog indicates to his master that he is hungry and to the delivery boy that he is angry. But all these manifestations are by natural signs and always communicating concrete sensory messages. The same is true when the dog "understands" a verbal command, as is clear from the fact that he will do the same thing in response to a meaningless word that *sounds* very similar, but he fails to recognize a synonym where meaning is identical but sensory experience differs. Parrots and other animals have all the mechanical equipment for language; the difference must be in whether they have anything to say, not in whether they can talk.

What we mean by conceptual language is a system of arbitrary symbols which can be the outward expression of ideas or concepts. Language may have its origin in natural signs, such as gestures or mimicry of certain sounds that suggest objects or movements. But it is not true language until these signs become conventional and are recognized as signs. No sensory power can recognize an arbitrary relationship as such. Bees and parrots do not discuss the functions of language, nor use metaphor. This is important, because a figure of speech always involves the separation of the sign from its natural or concrete significance. It requires the recognition of sign as sign, not merely as significant. It goes beyond mimicry and concrete association to meaning, in the strict sense of that term.

Language is at once of tremendous importance as the means of communicating thought and of relative insignificance compared with thought itself. The extent to which we can use our thinking process is almost entirely dependent upon the degree to which we can express or record our thoughts for ourselves or others. Yet the language in which we do so is a purely arbitrary, conventional set of symbols with no value in themselves, whose whole meaning is the concept or idea we have associated with them. Exceptions are a few onomatopoetic words like "whoosh" and "boom," where the form of the symbol itself expresses the idea. Except for the musical pleasure of the sounds, the most sublime literature of a completely foreign language has no more meaning for us than the babble of an idiot. A truth is equally true regardless of what language it is expressed in or whether we have an expression for it at all. Yet it is undeniable that the language in which we formulate our ideas to ourselves, or through which others communicate their ideas to us, has an important and subtle influence on the way we think as well as on the content of our thought.

The relationships between symbol or sign, object, and idea are subject to many interpretations. One theory is that there is a natural or magical relation between the symbol and the object. Some psychoanalytic psychologists have made much of this theory, and there is some evidence for certain instances of such a relation. It is not surprising that symbols and their objects can be very intimately related, especially in childhood and among primitive peoples. But analysis of conventional language among adults, especially those who can use several languages, shows the inadequacy of this as a comprehensive theory.

Behavioral psychologists have been inclined to explain the relation of symbol and object by saying that they produce a common response. The psychologists correctly infer that thought is a mediation process between symbol and response, but the issue is confused because the word "meaning" is applied to various types of response, some of which involve thought and some of which do not. Thus the sound of the dinner bell "means" food for both dog and man by concrete association of images; but whereas man can understand this meaning independently of any behavioral response, the dog apparently cannot. Osgood's (1957) work on semantic differentials as measures of the difference between denotation and connotation proves, or at least confirms, the distinction between thought and both its symbols and responses. The fact that his work could hardly apply to brute animals bears out our position.

An interesting theory of the relation between language and thought has been proposed by Benjamin Whorf (1956) from his study of comparative languages. Eskimos were found to have many different words for different kinds of snow but only one word for many objects for which we have separate terms. Whorf showed that these differences in language largely reflect the different ways in which people conceive of reality. The structure of a language parallels the pattern of the people's thinking. Few would agree, however, with Whorf's conclusion that the structure of language *causes* the manner of thinking; most would assert that the facts are equally well explained by the theory that the structure of language is caused by the manner of conceiving reality.

Nominalism

Much discussion in contemporary psychology on the relation of object, concept, and word is confused by the old error of nominalism. This is the philosophical position which claims that the word *is* the idea, rather than merely a symbol of it. In effect, nominalists deny that true ideas exist; the universal representation is simply the name (*nomen*) of the object. For them thinking becomes merely the manipulation of symbols. Language *constitutes* thought; it is not simply the vehicle for expressing it.

The distinction between the word and its meaning has been further confused by attempts to reduce meaning to the sensory clothing of thought or the behavioral responses associated with stimuli. Strictly speaking, meaning is neither of these, but is the idea or concept symbolized by the word: my understanding or mental representation or awareness of what the symbol stands for. Now obviously the word *food* does not stand for an image nor does it stand for the response of eating. My concept of what is edible need not involve either of these.

To understand the difference between word and concept it is only necessary to analyze the difference between a word whose meaning I understand and one whose meaning I do not. The word *fish* has meaning for me because I know what a fish is, or have some awareness of the nature of fish. On the other hand, the word *cabezon* is meaningless for me, even though I see and hear it perfectly, until someone explains that it is a certain type of large fish. Both words are equally visible and audible; one evokes an idea, the other does not. This would be impossible if the word were the idea, as the nominalists claim. According to them, I should have the idea from the mere fact of hearing the words of a foreign tongue. Try repeating a familiar word like *cat* several hundred times: its arbitrary nature becomes appallingly clear as the word becomes vapid and meaningless.

Again, we may have a very clear idea for which there is no word in our vocabulary, as Helen Keller's autobiography or a simple experiment shows. It is not the theoretical impossibility of this situation which prompts the teacher to refuse an answer such as "I know it, but I can't express it," but only the practical consideration that knowledge which cannot be expressed is of little use to the student and impossible for the teacher to grade. The parrot, on the other hand, has many words but lacks the corresponding ideas.

We can have many words for a single idea, or many ideas may be expressed by a single word; both these situations would be impossible if the word was the idea. Thus the words horse, *pferd, caballo,* and *equus* look and sound quite different, yet they represent but one idea, not four. Conversely, the word "bat" can have a great variety of unconnected meanings, from a flying animal to an instrument for hitting a baseball, which shows that the ideas must be different from the word which stands for them. Again, we do not group bat, hat, and cat together. We conclude with Hilgard (1953, p. 329) that "there is little doubt that language and thought are closely related but not identical."

MEASUREMENT OF INTELLIGENCE

One last obstacle to establishing the immaterial nature of the intellect is the fact that intelligence can be tested and graded according to the IQ or Intelligence Quotient. Quantity or extension is the hallmark of matter; mathematical measurability would seem incompatible with what is more than matter. Let us first review some definitions.

Intellect is the power or ability to think and simply refers to the fact that man is able to do so. Strictly speaking, it is not correct to say that the intellect knows; rather, man knows by means of his intellect.

Thinking or intellection is the act of this power and includes ideas, judgments, and reasoning. These are the operations for which the intellect is the basic natural potency.

Intelligence is the degree to which intellect is operative. It thus differs from intellect because it refers to the amount of measurable operation we can expect from this potency. But we say operative, not operating, since a man is equally intelligent whether he is think- ing at the moment or not. Intelligence thus differs from both root potentiality and actual operation. Intellect is a qualitative term, de- scribing the kind of being man is. Intelligence is a quantitative term, expressing the degree to which he can exercise this power.

Since a power is known by its act, there is no difficulty in ex- pressing mathematically the external effects of its operation.[8] The psychologist does not pretend to measure intellect directly, but only its functioning in comparison with the performance of others of the same age or other grouping. This relative performance can be ex-

[8] Thomas Aquinas, *S. T.*, Ia. 42, 1 ad lum, seems to have given the philosophi- cal foundation for the modern notion of intelligence testing. See P. Hoenen, S.J., "De Mensura Qualitatum," in his *Cosmologia* (Rome: Gregorian University, 1949), pp. 184–203, for copious references to St. Thomas.

pressed quantitatively without implying extension in the intellect itself.

When we say that all men are created equal we obviously do not refer to degree of intelligence any more than to amount of musical talent or color of eyes; we refer to the fact that, they are qualitatively similar; they have the same basic powers and rational nature, which gives them equal rights before the law.

The inheritance of IQ is explainable because of the dependence of thought upon sense. Any direct influence of parental intellect on that of the child through heredity is impossible, since procreation is a biological process and the intellects are immaterial. (Expressions such as "cultural heritage" refer to environment, not heredity.) But the parents' genes carry determiners for a brain and nervous system somehow similar to their own, causing the child's intellect to have similar sensory equipment with which to work. Greater perfection of nervous system means better preceptions, memories, and images for the intellect to abstract and manipulate. The extent of correlation between parental and child intelligence is for the psychologist to measure; they certainly do not correspond perfectly and even if they did it would not be wholly a matter of heredity. Psychologists are busy now trying to assess the relative influence of parental environment, as well as nonhereditary biological factors such as faulty embryological development.

REVIEW QUESTIONS

1. Why is the distinction between intellect and sense important?
2. Formulate a definition of intellect on the basis of this chapter and explain each element of your definition.
3. Define idea and explain your definition.
4. List all the ways in which an idea differs from an image or percept.
5. Which proof or proofs of the difference between intellect and sense do you feel are most conclusive?
6. Present this proof in syllogistic form.
7. In what way would an argument based on concrete universal ideas be even more telling against the sensists than the more obvious argument from abstract ideas?

8. Answer the following objections:
   a. We prove the immateriality of the intellect from its object, since every power is specified by its object. But I can have intellectual knowledge of a tree, which is a material object. Therefore the intellect is material.
   b. If all ideas are universal, man could not have any intellectual knowledge of singulars. But we do know singulars. Therefore ideas are not universal.
   c. I know the essence of trees only by examining trees. But this is a sensory experience. Therefore my knowledge of essences is sensory.
   d. Great thinkers report that they always think in words and symbols. But these are sensory. Therefore thought is sensory.
   e. Abstraction is just a special type of attention. But animals can direct their attention to one thing or another. Therefore abstraction could be just a sensory process.
   f. All ideas are derived directly or indirectly from sense experience. Therefore sensism is right.
   g. The proper object of the human intellect is essences of material objects. But God is not a material object. Therefore no human knowledge of God is possible.
   h. All thinking involves motor activity. But motor activity is organic. Therefore thought is organic.
   i. By the central sense we are aware that we are sensing. Therefore reflection does not require a suprasensory power.
9. Is the difference between sense and intellect one of degree or of kind?
10. Is the notion of man as a rational animal negated by his acting irrationally?
11. Is the difference between intellect and sense a matter of distinction or of separation?
12. Show how the difference in meanings of "imageless thought" is pertinent to the above question.
13. Show how the facts of brain waves and subvocal speech also exemplify the same problem as in question 11.
14. Why is the act of judgment an especially effective argument against the sensist position? Can you account for our awareness of abstract or universal relationships in sensist terms?
15. How true is it that we think in words? Even if we always formulated our thoughts to ourselves in words, would this prove that thought is merely words?
16. Do sense and intellect always cooperate in such a way that it would

be impossible for man to perceive reality through his senses as if he were an animal without intellect? Could he understand reality intellectually as if he had no senses?
17. Explain the difference between intellect and intelligence.
18. Does IQ express absolute measurement of intellectual operation or comparison relative to others?
19. Are all men created equal? How is the distinction between potency and act pertinent here?

FOR FURTHER READING

ADLER, MORTIMER J. *What Man Has Made of Man.* New York: Longmans, 1937. Notes 3, 17, 19.

AQUINAS, ST. THOMAS. *Summa Theol.* Ia, 75, 2, 3, 5; 84; 85, 1, 3.

GANNON, TIMOTHY J. *Psychology: The Unity of Human Behavior.* Boston: Ginn, 1954. Chap. 13.

GILSON, ETIENNE. *The Unity of Philosophical Experience.* New York: Scribner, 1937. Parts I and IV can be read as a complete treatise.

GRUENDER, HUBERT, S.J. *Problems of Psychology.* Milwaukee: Bruce, 1937.

HARMON, FRANCIS L. *Principles of Psychology.* (Rev. Ed.) Milwaukee: Bruce, 1951. Chap. 12.

KATZ, DAVID. *Gestalt Psychology.* New York: Ronald, 1950. This authoritative presentation rejects sensism and shows that Kohler did not claim that animal Gestalten were intellectual processes.

KELLER, HELEN. *The Story of My Life.* New York: Grosset & Dunlap, 1904.

LINDWORSKY, JOHANNES, S.J. *Experimental Psychology.* Trans. by Harry DeSilva. London: G. Allen, 1930. Pp. 250–270.

MARC, ANDRÉ, S.J. *Psychologie réflexive.* Brussels: L'Edition Universelle, 1949. Analysis of the use of words in Vol. I, pp. 1–57, exemplifies commonly observable facts as basis for philosophical conclusion; refutes sensism.

PIAGET, JEAN. *Logic and Psychology.* New York: Basic Books, 1957.

SPEARMAN, CHARLES. *The Nature of "Intelligence" and the Principles of Cognition.* (2d Ed.) New York: St. Martin's, 1927.

WHORF, B. L. *Language, Thought, and Reality: Selected Writings of Benjamin Lee Whorf.* Ed. by John B. Carroll. Cambridge, Mass.: Massachusetts Institute of Technology Press, 1956.

WILD, JOHN (ED.) *The Return to Reason: Essays in Realistic Philosophy.* Chicago: Regnery, 1953.

The "*Imageless Thought*" Controversy

Sensist:

CHAPIN, MARY V., & WASHBURN, MARGARET FLOY. "A Study of the Images Representing the Concept of Meaning," *Amer. J. Psychol.*, 1912, 23:109–114.

TITCHENER, EDWARD B. "Description versus Statement of Meaning," *Am. J. Psychol.*, 1912, 23:164–182.

TITCHENER, EDWARD B. *Experimental Psychology*. Part I. *Qualitative Experiments*. Part II. *Teacher's Manual*. New York: Macmillan, 1918.

TITCHENER, EDWARD B. *Lectures on the Experimental Psychology of the Thought Processes*. New York: Macmillan, 1927.

TITCHENER, EDWARD B. *Systematic Psychology: Prolegomena*. New York: Macmillan, 1929.

TITCHENER, EDWARD B. *A Text-book of Psychology*. New York: Macmillan, 1912.

WUNDT, WILHELM. *Introduction to Psychology*. Trans. by R. Pitner. London: G. Allen, 1912.

Anti-Sensist:

BINET, ALFRED. *L'Étude expérimentale de l'intelligence*. Paris: Schleicher frères, 1903.

BINET, ALFRED, & SIMON, TH. "Langage et Pensé," *Anneé Psycho.*, 1908, 14:284–339.

GRUENDER, HUBERT, S.J. *Experimental Psychology*. Milwaukee: Bruce, 1932. Pp. 286–300, 245–252.

MOORE, THOMAS VERNER. "Image and Meaning in Memory and Perception," *Psychol. Monogr.*, 1919, 27(119):67–296.

MOORE, THOMAS VERNER. "The Process of Abstraction," *Univ. of California Publ. in Psychol.*, 1910, I:73–197. Perhaps the most valuable source in English on the Würzburg school.

MOORE, THOMAS VERNER. "The Temporal Relations of Meaning and Imagery," *Psychol. Rev.*, 1915, 22:177–225.

WOODWORTH, ROBERT S. "Non-sensory Components of Sense Perception," in *Psychological Issues*. New York: Columbia University Press, 1939. Pp. 80–88.

WOODWORTH, ROBERT S. "A Revision of Imageless Thought," *Psychol. Rev.*, 1915, 22:1–27.

The chapters in Gannon and Harmon noted above contain copious references to experimental psychologists, Würzburg school and otherwise, whose data favor the intellectualist position.

Thought Not a Function of Brain

AQUINAS, ST. THOMAS. *Summa Theol.*, Ia, 84, 7 and 8.

BERGSON, HENRI. *Matter and Memory.* Trans. by N. M. Paul & W. S. Palmer. New York: Macmillan, 1950.

CAMERON, NORMAN. *The Psychology of Behavior Disorders.* Boston: Houghton Mifflin, 1947. Chap. 17.

DRESSLER, ALWIN. "Can One Live without a Brain?" *Magazine Digest,* 1934, 8:18–19. (Condensed from *Illustrierte Beobachter,* Sept. 9, 1933.)

ESTABROOKS, G. H. "Your Brain," *Sci. Amer.*, 155:20–22, July, 1936.

GOLDSTEIN, KURT. *Human Nature in the Light of Psychopathology.* Cambridge: Harvard University Press, 1940. Chaps. 2, 3, esp. p. 60, where the author insists that abstract and concrete mental processes differ in kind and not merely in degree.

JOAD, C. E. M. *How Our Minds Work.* London: Westhouse, 1946.

LASHLEY, KARL S. "Basic Neural Mechanisms in Behavior," *Psychol. Rev.*, 1930, 37:1–24.

LASHLEY, KARL S. *Brain Mechanisms and Intelligence.* Chicago: University of Chicago Press, 1929.

MOORE, THOMAS VERNER. *Cognitive Psychology.* Philadelphia: Lippincott, 1939. Pp. 45–73.

MOORE, THOMAS VERNER. "Consciousness and the Nervous System," *Catholic Univ. Stud. in Psychol. and Psychiat.*, 1938, Vol. IV, No. 3.

SHERRINGTON, CHARLES. *Man on His Nature.* New York: Cambridge, 1940. Chaps. 9, 10, 11. Unfortunately ends in dualism.

SOLOMON, HARRY C., COBB, STANLEY, & PENFIELD, WILDER (Eds.) *The Brain and Human Behavior.* Baltimore: Williams & Wilkins, 1958. Penfield favors the idea of a spiritual soul.

TRAVIS, L. E. "Brain Potentials and the Temporal Course of Consciousness," *J. Exp. Psychol.*, 1937, 21:302–309.

7

INTELLECTUAL ACTIVITY

The origin of ideas: sensism, idealism, senso-intellectualism.
Abstraction of ideas from sense data; need of an agent intel-
lect. The acts of the intellect. Object of the intellect.

To explain the origin of ideas has been one of the central problems
of philosophy through the ages. From the time of the ancient
Greeks there have been three main traditions with regard to this
problem.[1] The first is known as *sensism*. Democritus tried to explain
cognition by describing it as a tiny image caused by a stream of
particles emanating from material objects. This materialistic view
has been revived in various forms in the past few centuries: by the
associationists (who attempt to explain thinking as the association of
images), the empiricists, the positivists, and such modern psychologists as the behaviorists, some structuralists (Titchener and his followers), and many Gestaltists. In general their solution to the
problem is to deny one of the elements, i.e., intellect: there is no
problem in explaining the origin of knowledge from sense if it never
gets beyond sense.

[1] Thomas Aquinas, *S. T.*, Ia, 84, 6.

115

The other horn of the dilemma was taken by Plato and others who were so impressed by the evidence *for* the spiritual nature of ideas that they neglected the role of sense. This is called *idealism*, exaggerated intellectualism, or conceptualism, and has appeared in one form or another in almost every century. Although maintaining the spirituality of the human soul, it does great violence to man's nature by divorcing intellect from sense, thus splitting man into two beings. From exaggerated intellectualism flows the exaggerated dualism which has plagued philosophy and psychology especially since the time of Descartes. Aligned with this position are *ontologism*, which explains our knowledge as a direct intuition of God, and *innatism*, which says that ideas are innate (inborn). The men who take these positions seem all to have been impressed with the theory that the abstract and universal cannot come from what is singular and material.

As a biologist, Aristotle was too empirical to accept the idealism of his master Plato; but the evidence for the spiritual nature of our thought processes convinced him that the sensism of Democritus was not the answer either. Instead of trying to minimize either line of evidence Aristotle boldly seized both horns of the dilemma and solved the problem by proposing that the idea is derived from sense experience by the action of the spiritual intellect. Thus ideas are neither innate nor sensory. In this solution he has been followed by early philosophers, by the whole stream of Scholastic philosophy from the Middle Ages to the present, including some non-Catholics, by many existentialists, and by other followers of moderate realism such as John Wild.

This view, which does not deny either the true nature of an idea nor its derivation from sense, seems to be confirmed by our everyday experience. Every student is all too aware how right Shakespeare was in saying that "knowledge maketh a bloody entrance," and we might long for the ease of inborn knowledge. Learning would be unnecessary and psychotherapy impossible if our ideas were all innate. We always begin by examining sensible reality, even in building up our most abstract theories. We communicate such abstractions by means of sensory symbols and try to picture them to ourselves in concrete images. We always develop ideas of material objects prior to those of the spiritual realm, which are then built upon analogy with what we know first. The man born blind has no proper idea of color. People who are born blind and subsequently have gained their sight through an operation describe how they build up ideas from sensory experience.

THE PROCESS OF ABSTRACTION

Although this explanation of the origin of ideas seems to square with the facts, it leaves a serious problem. We have seen that the intellect is in potency to know, like a blackboard upon which nothing has yet been written. St. Thomas compares it figuratively with prime matter; the analogy suggests how the intellect is quite indeterminate in the realm of knowledge. In order to know, it must be actuated and determined by the impression of some form.

But we have seen that this form and therefore the power into which it is received are strictly immaterial. The impression can only be the effect of an immaterial cause. But sense knowledge is organic and has material qualities. Hence we are faced with the problem of how the spiritual intellect can be actuated by an impression received from the senses, for a material cause cannot produce a spiritual effect.

The Agent Intellect

Scholastic philosophers have solved this problem by asserting that sense knowledge is not the sole cause of intellection. They feel that the facts demand that we postulate another cause, one which is spiritual, to account for the spiritual effect. This cause they call the *agent intellect*. The term is slightly misleading because the agent intellect is not an intellect in which there is knowledge; it only causes knowledge in the intellect proper, which is called, in contrast, the possible or *potential intellect*. (The ideal term for intellect itself would seem to be passive intellect, but unfortunately this term has been otherwise used [2] and must be avoided.) It is in the potential

---

[2] Aristotle (*De Anima*, III, 5, 430a 22–25) used νοῦς παθητικός in a very ambiguous way, taken by ancient, Arabian, and medieval commentators in-

intellect that intellection formally takes place. The agent intellect is called such only because it is the efficient cause (along with sense knowledge) of the impression on the intellect proper. It is active, not passive. It does not need to be determined; it determines.

Since it is man's nature to have ideas, it is clear that the agent intellect is not God or something supernatural. Thinking is not a continuous succession of miracles but something within man's power.

Because of a different interpretation of a difficult and ambiguous passage in Aristotle (De Anima, III, 5, 430a 17), some Arabian philosophers thought that there was only one agent intellect, a separate spiritual substance, for all men. This theory seems to deny the control each man has over his acts of abstracting and understanding, and to contradict other evidence which points to the conclusion that each man has his own power of thought independently.

Agent Intellect and Phantasm

"Phantasm" is a word used in traditional Scholastic philosophy to refer to any sensory knowledge from which the intellect can abstract an idea. It does not have any specific reference to fantasy. Although a phantasm is usually elaborated upon by the imagination and other internal senses, it is here taken to mean a sensory awareness produced by the combining of any of the special and internal senses. Phantasm is conceived of in Scholastic theory as the subordinate and instrumental[3] efficient cause of the idea, the principal efficient cause being the agent intellect.

Two things need to be accounted for in the origin of ideas. Being spiritual and universal, they need a spiritual cause which can strip

---

cluding St. Thomas as imagination or estimative power, and translated as passive intellect. Potential or possible intellect proper is νοῦς δυνάμει.

For agent intellect, Aristotle used expressions like ποῖεν πάντα, "to make [become] all things," but never νοῦς ποιητικος which is the term of Alexander Aphrodisius and quite in accord with Aristotle's thought.

[3] The instrumental causality here seems to be of a unique kind. It is natural, not artificial; conjoined, not separate from the principal cause. St. Thomas calls the phantasm a "quasi-instrument" (Quodl. 8, q. 2, art. 3), and elsewhere speaks with similar caution (Q. Un. De Anima, art. 5 ad 8um; Truth, q. 10, art. 6 ad 8um).

the phantasm of its material qualities and can abstract just the intelligible note or quiddity common to all the objects which the idea represents, rather than merely perceiving the concrete individual as the sense does. This is the role of the agent intellect; being active, it is always in act and abstracts whenever there is something to work on.

We need also to explain why I have the idea of horse rather than tree; and if this determination had to be in the active intellect, the same problem of what determines a spiritual power would arise all over again. It is the phantasm which supplies the object from which the agent intellect can abstract the idea of this rather than that. Agent intellect can never provide the object, phantasm can never provide the spirituality.

This doctrine of an agent intellect thus seems to be a clear deduction from the facts of the case. At least it appears to be the most satisfactory solution yet proposed to the problem of the origin of ideas. It is not a psychological description of the process of abstraction, but an analysis of the causality involved. Again, we remind ourselves that neither this abstracting power nor the potential (or true) intellect are substances. To say that "this power causes" and "that power receives" is only a substitute for the more clumsy expression "Man by means of this power causes. . . ."

The action of the agent intellect has been compared to that of an X ray tube and the potential intellect to a blank X ray film which could not be used for ordinary photographic work. In this analogy, the level of X ray symbolizes the spiritual level of intellectual knowledge, in contrast to ordinary light and film which represent the level of sense knowledge. The action of the agent intellect in abstracting quiddity is compared to the action of the X ray tube in getting at bone structure hidden by flesh. Just as the X ray film will not be impressed in spite of the presence of objects unless the tube is on, so the potential intellect remains in potency unless there is a spiritual agent to impress it.

Radar suggests a superior simile in that it sends out the beam (agent) from the radar unit itself (intellect). St. Thomas anticipated this parallel (C. G., II, 76) by comparing the intellect to an eye which itself would emit the light whereby it sees. The agent intellect is thus likened to a radar transmitter which is always turned on and ready to impress; the potential intellect is like the screen. We are born with this equipment, so to speak. But just as there would never be a picture unless some object came across the path of the radar beam, so we would never have an idea unless sensory experience gave the intellect something from which to abstract. The object in either case specifies and determines what the idea or picture is to be of. Conversely, just as the object by itself cannot impress the radar screen without the special beam sent out by the transmitter, so the phantasm cannot impress the spiritual potential intellect without the help of the agent intellect. Like the comparison to X ray, this one also limps because transmitter and screen and object are all substances, whereas intellect and phantasm are only powers and operation, accidents inhering in the one substance, man. The formation of the idea would correspond to the reaction of the receiver and the resulting picture; but in radar there is only dead representation, not the vital cognitive union to be discussed in the next chapter.

THE ACTS OF THE INTELLECT

So far we have spoken principally of the *idea* or simple apprehension which is the most elementary operation of the intellect. In real life the idea never exists in isolation but as a part of much more elaborate processes. Since the formal object of the intellect is being itself, it is clear that each of the various acts of the intellect is under this one all-inclusive formal object. Now diversity of powers is required only by diverse formal objects; hence it is clear that these various functions do not require a multiplicity of operative potencies. Let us examine briefly these other functions of intellect.

Judgment. In logic we analyze the reasoning process into elements for the purpose of checking on its correctness. The terms of a proposition express the concepts which make up the judgment. The form of a proposition is somewhat artificial, and since being is known in a perceptual judgment (see Chapter 3 above), we must not think of the concepts which make it up as isolated acts or elements glued together by some sort of mental chemistry. St. Thomas (Geach, 1957) was quite aware that concept formation is not always a simple matter of abstracting a common element out of repeated experiences.

Reasoning. Similarly, the reduction of a line of reasoning to syllogistic form to study its logical correctness must not be mistaken for a psychological description of how we think. In practice we may skip many of the steps, as in hunches or intuitions. Or we may wander, with or without guiding principle, through many unnecessary steps.

The discrepancy between logic and our actual intellectual processes is bothersome only if we assume that our thinking is always formal reasoning. Maritain, Chevalier, Bergson, and others are probably right in stressing the intuitive aspects of intellection, which perhaps St. Thomas neglected in his emphasis on reasoning. According to Kapp (1942), Aristotle on this point was closer to Plato, who insisted on the superiority of νοῦς (*intellectus*, understanding) over διανοία (*ratio*, reasoning). But St. Thomas would agree that the actual contemplation or understanding of a truth excels the reasoning process by which we may have arrived at it.

An important factor in reasoning is that of *set*, which we mentioned among the subjective factors in perception in Chapter 5. The course of our thinking can be determined ahead of time. Given the numbers 2 and 3, we can instantaneously give an answer, but whether it is 5, 6, or 1 depends upon whether we have previously set ourselves to add, multiply or subtract.

Conscience. One function of the intellect often misunderstood is conscience. We noted above that Scholastic philosophy followed Aristotle in rejecting Plato's theory of innate ideas. It would be surprising, then, if the Christian concept of conscience implied that we are born with a ready-made set of ethical conclusions. We are born only with the power of reaching such conclusions, once we have experienced facts from which they can be deduced. We are not born with the concepts of "whole" and "part" but only with the power of recognizing their relation; once we understand what the concepts really mean, we cannot judge otherwise than that the whole is greater than the part. So we are not born with the ideas of "murder" and "bad" but only with an intellect whose nature is such that it joins these two concepts, once learned, in the appropriate judgment. Judging is an act; what is inborn is the power. Conscience is simply the functioning of the intellect in making moral judgments.

We are not surprised that human intellects do not always function correctly and uniformly: errors and conceptions based on diverse cultural viewpoints are to be expected. If we make errors in something as cold and objective as arithmetic, it is surely not surprising that all human beings do not judge alike on moral matters, in which emotional and social pressures can be so strong. An added reason for erroneous conscience is the variety of customs and cultures which influence the experiences from which we derive our concepts. Even a properly functioning machine will not give correct answers if fed with faulty data.

Emotion, self-interest, and cultural diversity do not alter the nature of the intellect with which we are born but they can and do interfere with the function of it which we call conscience, affecting either the process itself or the ideas with which it works. But since the object of intellect is the being of things, the intellect is able to judge moral issues and even correct its own errors by adverting to whether an act is in conformity with nature, independently of customs or mores. Because of this ability, conscience differs from Freud's superego, to which it is sometimes compared; for the latter is largely the irrational and unconscious influence of habits acquired from parental admonition and social approval during childhood, rather than intellect judging on the basis of the nature of things. (The strength of such influence is not denied, only its identity with conscience.)

Intellectual Memory. We shall see that knowledge does not consist in a purely passive possession of forms, as in wax or modeling clay. It is only when the knowing power vitally reacts to the impression received and entertains it in consciousness that we have that intentional union which is the act of knowing. But when this ceases, does the knowing power return to its original state of pure potency? The answer to this is suggested by the fact that the next time the intellect wishes to have this knowledge it need not start from zero or pure potency and go through the whole process again. To say nothing of the enormous funds of knowledge stored in the minds of certain geniuses, we have all had the experience of recalling things of which we have not been conscious for years, without having to learn them again.

This capacity to retain intellectual knowledge parallels the functions of imagination and memory at the sensory level. Once the knowing power has been actuated by an impression, it is evidently capable of retaining this impression and reviving it for future use. Theoretically, it would seem that any impression ever received would be capable of recall if only the right stimulus were hit upon. This seems to be confirmed by the use of hypnosis and sodium pentothal to recall stored experiences beyond the reach of ordinary means.

This *habitual knowledge* is halfway between actual knowing and merely being in potency to acquire knowledge. This is the state of habit which will be discussed in Chapter 14. We obviously are not always aware of all the things we know, so these forms, whether sensible or intelligible, are not evoking cognitive reaction. But they are in the knowing power, which therefore does not need to receive the impression anew but only to reactivate what has been there all along. The adequate stimulus seems to be some act of knowing or appetition which is associated with—or symbolic of, or motivationally related to—the original impression. Thus the familiar word "tree" causes me to have the idea, without needing a percept or even an object-image of a tree. Precisely how the knowing power selects this particular stored impression to be reactivated, rather than some other, is a difficult question. Neurophysiology of the cerebral cortex offers little help and philosophers can only emphasize the substantial unity of all man's powers on the one hand, and the very subordinate, instrumental role of phantasm on the other. The instrumental causality here is not like a chisel, which is a separate substance in the hands of the artificer; it is natural and conjoined to the principal cause. Once received, the impression is not subject to corruption since it is immaterial. Unlike the Freshman trying to juggle the fruits of his last cramming period, the experienced college student does not expect to carry all his knowledge around in a state of actual consciousness. He knows that if he has learned his material well he can recall it as needed from its state of habitual knowledge.

OBJECT OF THE INTELLECT

Material Object

The material object of a knowing power is what it knows. The material object of the intellect is all beings, actual and potential. We can think about objects which are material and those which are spiritual; we can think about substances and accidents, essences, principles, relationships, and negations. We can talk about the existential order of real beings, or we can understand and compute the area of a hypothetical nonexistent triangle, or consider other purely logical entities which have no existence outside our own mind. Since these beings do not have a common nature, they can be designated only by the broadest and most analogical term: they are all beings.

The magnificent scope of human intellection covering this all-inclusive range of objects is truly breath-taking. Meaning is discoverable throughout the universe. Wisdom seeks to understand man and all things in relation to Supreme Being, God Himself. Analogy does not weaken intelligibility but enriches and orders our knowledge by unifying it under the broad concepts of being [see Olgiati (1925), Rousselot (1935), and Sertillanges (1956)].

Formal Object of Intellect

The formal object is the particular aspect or formality or note by which the cognitive power attains its material object, as color is the formal object of sight. Here we must distinguish between (1) the adequate formal object of intellect as such, common to all intellects, and (2) that which is proper and specific to man's intellect.

1. *Common or adequate object of intellect.* Any intellect, be it man's, God's, or an angel's, can know an object only in so far as it is being or has relation to existence. We know it *as being*.

This concept is perhaps best understood by considering the opposite: what is absolutely impossible is also unintelligible. Try to get a good, clear idea of what a square circle is. There is no intelligible essence here which I can conceive as having a relation to existence, either actual or potential. In general metaphysics or the philosophy of being it is stated that being as related to intellect is said to have ontological truth. Hence the formal object of any intellect is *being* as intelligible, or being as true. Whatever is intelligible is known precisely as being. (Truth as truth is the proper object of the judgment and hence is not the formal object of intellect as such.) We might define intellect as the power of knowing being as being.

2. *Proper object of human intellect.* The proper object of a power is that toward which it is primarily and essentially ordered and in relation to which it knows all other objects. The power of sight knows extension and shape only by way of its proper object, color. What is the proper object of the human intellect precisely as human? Now what is distinctive of the human intellect in this life, as opposed to other intellects, is the fact that it must get its knowledge from sensory experience. Yet as intellect it knows not merely the sensory qualities but the very being of sensible things. Hence the proper object of the human intellect, as human, is the *abstracted essence or being of sensible things.* This does not mean that man has full or adequate knowledge of essences—this would take prodigious research. St. Thomas illustrates our gradual understanding of being by the example of a man seen on a distant hill: at first we know only that he is material being, then that he is walking and living, then that he is human, and lastly we recognize that he is John Jones. Similarly, St. Thomas notes that tiny children call all men Father and only later make distinctions, as their knowledge becomes more precise. The first thing we know about anything is being, the difference between existence and nonexistence. It is proper to man's intellect to know this formal aspect of being, from and in sensed objects.

Intellectual Knowledge of Singulars. We say the "abstracted essence" of sensible things because what the intellect properly knows is not the individual, sensible being but its universal nature. The individual being must be known by relating its universal nature to its particular set of accidents through sensory experience. The intelligible essence of a sensible thing is restricted to a singular, material object by a complex act of intellect and senses which combines their activities into a unified act of knowing.

We have seen that the idea itself represents what a thing is. This idea is consciously neither universal nor particular. We may reflexly advert to its universality, or we may recognize its applicability to a particular instance. But since what is represented in my concept is equally applicable to any individual in that class, the idea of *this* singular individual can only be obtained by relating the idea to a sensory experience which localizes it in time and space. St. Thomas says (Ia, 84, 7) that intellect does this by converting to the sensory experience or phantasm—by "convert" he does not mean "change into," but "turn back toward." This conversion is necessary because of the abstractive nature of human intellection, not because the singular is in itself unintelligible; otherwise God could not know the singular.

Suprasensible being, abstract and spiritual realities, are not the proper object of the human intellect because its knowledge is derived from sensory experience and mediated through sensory images and symbols. Hence we know these immaterial realities only by analogy with material things. Our knowledge of the spiritual is at best indirect and imperfect. We can abstract out such concepts as cause and substance, and apply them to God by negating the imperfections and limitations of materiality. Our inability to form proper ideas of immaterial reality is not because of any unintelligibility there. As being, immaterial reality is perfectly intelligible in itself, but not readily accessible to the human intellect which in this life must know in and through the senses.

This is the correct interpretation of the old Scholastic adage, "There is nothing in the intellect which was not previously in some way in the senses." Even spiritual realities such as God are knowable by the human intellect only because the foundations for such concepts existed already in what is in the senses and could be derived from sense knowledge by a process of reasoning and analogy.

ESP

At this point the question of ESP or extrasensory perception arises. Can we acquire or communicate ideas without going through the ordinary channels of sensory perception? This is still an open question, with perhaps the majority of experimental psychologists still maintaining that ESP is not a proven fact, and that apparent instances can be explained away as the results of secondary perceptual cues, suggestion, coincidence, or mere variations from statistical probability. Even those who claim that ESP is established fact do not pretend to have an explanation as to how it would work.

Although ESP is an activity apparently different from the ordinary way in which our minds are observed to operate, the notion contains nothing contradictory to the immaterial nature of the intellect itself. J. B. Rhine of Duke University claims that his researches on ESP give basis for a proof of the spiritual nature. We prefer to base our case for the spirituality of the soul on less contestable evidence but would welcome the confirmation from this source if it is established. If proven, it would cause no embarrassment to those who hold the essentially immaterial nature of the intellect; it would only prove an exception to the ordinary way in which our intellects operate. Its establishment would be most embarrassing to those whose philosophy does not admit reality beyond the material.

CONCLUSION

From this chapter and its analysis of human intellectual knowledge we can see how operations serve as a clue to the nature of a thing. An old axiom in philosophy says that whatever is received is received according to the manner or nature of the recipient. Now what is characteristic of human knowledge is precisely the fact that material being is known in a universal and immaterial way by abstraction from sense. Therefore man's nature must be constituted somehow of both material and immaterial principles, to make him capable of both aspects of this operation.

The need for the joint activity of intellect and sense in man's knowledge of singulars is another instance of how man's operations indicate the nature of his being. His manner of knowing singulars indicates his admixture of the spiritual and the material, and his unity as one knowing subject.

REVIEW QUESTIONS

1. In what way do we agree with the sensists?
2. In what way do we agree with the idealists?
3. What implications for the nature of man does the theory of innate ideas have?
4. What reasons would you give against the theory of innatism?
5. Would evidence (if established) of learning during the latter months of pregnancy, so that the child was born with some ideas, support Plato against Aristotle?
6. Is the agent intellect known by factual observation or by deductive reasoning?
7. If the sense power is also passive and needs to be determined, why is there no need for an "agent sense" as there is for an agent intellect?
8. Is the agent intellect really an intellect?
9. List all the differences you can between the agent and the potential intellect.
10. If the agent intellect needed to be determined or activated by phantasms, would the problem of the origin of ideas be solved? Why?
11. What is meant by phantasm in the discussion of the relations of intellect and sense? What is the relation of phantasm to the agent intellect? to ideas?
12. Compare the functions of conscience and of the estimative sense. How are they similar? How do they differ? Does either involve innate knowledge?
13. How does the intellect know the past as past? How does it know singulars?
14. What implications for the nature of man do you see in the position of senso-intellectualism?
15. If abstraction separates what is together in reality, is it not false knowledge?
16. Are all ideas formed by abstraction or are some ideas formed from other ideas?
17. Is truth in the idea or in the judgment? Do ideas exist which are not in judgments?

18. How does the formal object of intellect suggest the scope of its material object?
19. How is the proper object of man's intellect different from that of God or an angel?
20. Does this difference contradict the assertion that all intellects have being as their formal object?
21. How do we know suprasensible being?
22. Is any true science possible if there are no abstractions or universal ideas?

FOR FURTHER READING

ALLERS, RUDOLF. "The Intellectual Cognition of Particulars," *The Thomist*, 1941, 3:95–163.

ALLERS, RUDOLF. "Intellectual Cognition," in R. E. Brennan (Ed.), *Essays in Thomism*. New York: Sheed, 1942. Pp. 41–62.

AQUINAS, ST. THOMAS. *Summa Theol.*, Ia, 12, 4; 14, 6 ad 1um; 79; 84–88. Ia IIae, 92, 2; 94, 2.

ARISTOTLE. *On the Soul*, III, 4–8.

COADY, SR. MARY ANASTASIA. *The Phantasm according to the Teaching of St. Thomas*. Washington: The Catholic University of America Press, 1932.

DAY, SEBASTIAN J., O.F.M. *Intuitive Cognition: A Key to the Significance of the Later Scholastics*. St. Bonaventure, N.Y.: Franciscan Institute, 1947.

DUNNE, PETER. "The Production of the Intelligible Species," *The New Scholasticism*, 1953, 27:176–197.

GILSON, ETIENNE. *The Spirit of Medieval Philosophy*. New York: Scribner, 1936. Chap. 13.

KAPP, ERNEST. *The Greek Foundations of Traditional Logic*. New York: Columbia University Press, 1942.

KLUBERTANZ, GEORGE P., S.J. "St. Thomas and the Knowledge of the Singular," *The New Scholasticism*, 1952, 26:135–166.

PORKES, A. S., and others. *Ciba Foundation Symposium on Extrasensory Perception*. Boston: Little, Brown, 1956.

RENARD, HENRI, S.J., & VASKE, MARTIN O., S.J. *The Philosophy of Man*. (Rev. Ed.) Milwaukee: Bruce, 1956. Chap. IV. Contains extensive quotations from St. Thomas.

ROUSSELOT, PIERRE, S.J. *The Intellectualism of St. Thomas*. Trans. by James E. O'Mahony, O.M.Cap. London: Sheed, 1935.

Experimental Psychology of Concept-formation:

BARTLETT, SIR FREDERIC. *Thinking: An Experimental and Social Study.* London: G. Allen, 1958. Thinking is "the extension of evidence in accord with that evidence so as to fill up gaps in the evidence." (p. 75)

BATESON, G. "Cultural Determinants of Personality," in J. McV. Hunt (Ed.), *Personality and the Behavior Disorders.* Vol. II. New York: Ronald, 1944. Pp. 714–735.

BROWN, ROGER. *Words and Things.* Glencoe, Ill.: Free Press, 1958.

BRUNER, J. S., GOODNOW, J. J., & AUSTIN, GEORGE A. *A Study of Thinking.* New York: Wiley, 1956.

DUNCKER, KARL. "On Problem Solving," *Psychol. Monogr.,* 1945, No. 270.

DUNN, MIRIAM F. "The Psychology of Reasoning," *Catholic Univer. Stud. in Psychol. and Psychiat.,* 1926, Vol. I, No. 1.

GEACH, PETER. *Mental Acts: Their Content and Their Objects.* New York: Humanities Press, 1957. Shows the inadequacy of defining abstraction as merely recognition of common element in repeated experiences.

HUMPHREY, G. *Thinking: An Introduction to its Experimental Psychology.* New York: Wiley, 1951.

JOHNSON, DONALD M. *The Psychology of Thought and Judgment.* New York: Harper, 1955.

McANDREW, SR. M. BERNARDINA. "An Experimental Investigation of Young Children's Ideas of Causality," *Catholic Univer. Stud. in Psychol. and Psychiat.* 1943, Vol. VI, No. 2.

MOORE, THOMAS VERNER. "Reasoning Ability of Children in the First Years of School Life," *Catholic Univer. Stud. in Psychol. and Psychol. and Psychiat.,* 1943, Vol. VI, No. 2.

OSGOOD, CHARLES E., and others. *The Measurement of Meaning.* Urbana, Ill.: University of Illinois Press, 1957.

OSGOOD, CHARLES E. Review of J. P. van de Geer, A *Psychological Study of Problem Solving* (Haarlem: Uitgeverij de Toorts, 1957), *Contemporary Psychol.,* 1958, 3:197–198.

PIAGET, JEAN. *The Moral Judgment of the Child.* Glencoe, Ill.: Free Press, 1948.

PIAGET, JEAN. *The Origins of Intelligence in Children.* New York: International Universities Press, 1953.

PIAGET, JEAN. *The Psychology of Intelligence.* New York: Harcourt, Brace, 1950.

VINACKE, W. EDGAR. *The Psychology of Thinking.* New York: McGraw-Hill, 1952.

8

THE NATURE OF KNOWLEDGE

Intentional being and intentional union. The degrees of immateriality. The causes of knowledge. Is cognition active or passive? The role of the species. Summary of the process of intellection. Knowledge not merely physiological. Relation of thought to brain.

We have described the facts of human knowledge and analyzed the distinction between the two essentially different kinds of knowledge in man, sensory and rational. This description, though less technical than a psychological analysis, has had much in common with it. But philosophy is not content merely to describe these processes; it tries to understand their nature. What does it mean to know?

The nature of knowledge is elusive partly because it is so close to us. We describe it largely in terms of what we know and how we know, without directing our attention to the nature of knowledge itself. Another difficulty is that there is nothing simpler and more immediate to which we can reduce knowledge, or in terms of which we can understand it. Either I have had the experience of knowing or I have not. Any communication, explanation, or attempt to understand already presupposes the experience under investigation. Nevertheless the philosopher cannot be content with a merely behavioral or operational description but must seek to understand the nature of knowing.

UNION OF KNOWER AND OBJECT

When we enter the realm of knowledge we must be prepared to deal with a new order of things, a unique reality to which there is no precise equivalent in the world of physical reality. The first thing that we notice about cognition or knowledge is a certain openness, the ability to acquire something other than oneself. This other may be a real object or merely a fanciful image or abstraction, but in any case it is something outside the nature of the knower. The knower is not limited simply to what he is.

Intentional Being and Intentional Union. But how does the knower add this *other* to his own being? We have already distinguished cognition from appetition in that the latter is a tendency toward actual physical union with the object, in order to enjoy it or possess it. Cognitive union is different. Instead of tending to go out toward physical union with the object, cognitive union receives the object into the knower. But since the object continues to exist physically in the same way after it is known, it must be received into the knower and have existence there in another manner than that of physical or natural existence in reality. This existence of the object as other in the knower is called intentional being.

The word intentional is perhaps unfortunate because it suggests purpose or resolve. The original Latin did not have this meaning and could perhaps better be translated as "attentional." It is the kind of being that the object has in me when I direct my attention toward it so that it exists in my consciousness. "Representative" might do, except that it suggests that I know primarily the representation rather than the object. As we have seen, my idea of a horse does not look like a horse; we must not think of knowledge as pictures. It simply means that "what a horse is" somehow is now within me.

KNOWING INVOLVES IMMATERIALITY

Physical Change. It will help to understand the nature of this intentional existence which the object has in me if we contrast it with physical change. Suppose I take a cube of wax and impress it with the seal of the State of Washington, which happens to have the face of George Washington on it. The wax loses its form as cube and acquires the form of George Washington's face. In a sense it has become George Washington, so that we can point to the wax and say, "Look, there is George Washington." But we would not even suggest that the wax becomes aware or knows what George Washington looks like. The change has been a purely physical one: the loss of one accidental form or shape and the acquisition of another. The subject (wax) has become the object (Washington), but physically, not intentionally or attentionally. Take another example of material change. When a cow eats hay or a plant takes in other materials and makes them into its own substance, there is also a loss of form. This time the loss is in the object, not in the subject. The hay loses its form and is now united with the form of the cow (see Chapter 16). Again, there is no awareness on the part of the cow in this action as such. The ingested matter now exists within the cow physically, not representatively.

Intentional Change. Let us now see what happens when the cow *sees* the hay. The hay keeps its form, the cow keeps its form. Neither is physically changed, but the hay begins also to exist in the cow intentionally. The cow, without losing its form, acquires the form of hay, but without the matter of the hay.

What is characteristic of cognitive union is the fact that the knower acquires the form of the object without its matter. Instead of the loss of form there is an enrichment of form. When I know something, that object begins to have intentional being in me so that in a sense I have "become" that object without ceasing to be myself.

Form without Matter. We say that the knower becomes the thing known, not physically but intentionally. The reason is that form is what makes a thing to be what it is; matter is undifferentiated except by the form with which it is united. If union with a form is what makes something become what it is physically, the philosopher says that union with intentional forms makes the knower "become" other things intentionally. For this reason Aristotle says that by the intellect man can become all things.

It is thus clear that the hallmark of cognition is a certain freedom from the limitation of matter. Matter of itself is limited to only one form at a time. The knower must be able to possess not only his own form but other forms also. These forms must be capable of existing in the knower intentionally, without ceasing to exist physically in the object known. For this reason we speak of a "well-informed man," because he contains many forms besides his own, or much information. Similarly, we define truth as the conformity of knower and object, because the knower has acquired the same form as the thing known.

Degrees of Immateriality

Although some sort of immateriality is necessary for all knowing, the different kinds of knowledge will demand different degrees of independence from matter. Cognition is an analogous term; it has partly the same meaning and partly different meanings when applied to different kinds of knowers. Some students are impatient with such gradations and would like to simplify reality to the point of falsification by saying that it is either material or immaterial. But the philosopher must take things as he finds them, not impose upon them his own scheme of things. We must distinguish three senses of the term immateriality as related to cognition.

1. The lowest degree of immateriality is that found in sensory cognition: form without matter but with material qualities. As we saw above, the animal is not limited like the wax to a purely passive reception of form in a physical way but is capable of entertaining the intentional forms of other beings along with its own. But the object of sensory knowledge always exists in the knower clothed with the sensible qualities of a concrete individual thing. This retention

of the sensible qualities is true of any sensory knowledge, be it percept, image, sense memory, or instinctive estimate.

These sensible qualities are accidental forms and although they exist in the knower without the matter of the object known, being material they must exist in some matter, for material qualities cannot exist outside a material substance. This substance is probably the cerebral cortex of the brain. When I say that I have a lake in mind, I do not have water on the brain. But if this is a sensory image, I do see the lake as a certain size, shape, color, and from a certain direction. Because this lowest degree of intentional being is but one step removed from the limitations of matter and is still bound up with these material qualities, St. Thomas referred to it as "quasi-immaterial," meaning to a degree or "sort of" immaterial.

2. The second degree of immateriality is that proper to human intellection: spiritual, but related to matter. When the cow *sees* the hay, the cow has the form of hay with a particular set of material qualities of size, shape, color, etc. When man *understands* hay, he has the form of the hay, regardless of the appearance of any individual sample. Here he has acquired the form of hay without its material qualities, which St. Thomas calls the conditions of matter. Note that we only say that the intellectual knowledge itself has no material qualities; being human knowledge, it may be accompanied by the material qualities in the senses. "Without material qualities or the conditions of matter" refers to the intrinsic nature of thought itself, regardless of its sensory concomitants and origins. For this reason intellection is called *strictly immaterial* or *spiritual* because matter does not enter into its internal constitution. It is said to be *intrinsically* independent of matter.

But although the human intellect has this intrinsic or essential independence of matter, all our ideas in this life must be derived in some way from sensory experience. The senses are extrinsic to the intellect itself and its operations, though intrinsic to man. Hence we say that the intellect has only *extrinsic* dependence on matter. This is in contrast to sensory knowledge with its material qualities which demand intrinsic dependence on matter, since matter enters into the very nature of the process.

Spiritual, therefore, means strictly immaterial or intrinsically independent of matter. It may or may not involve extrinsic dependence on matter: this is the difference between the second and the third degrees of immateriality. Spiritual does not mean supernatural. If it is part of man's nature to think, then such power is not above man's nature. The use of the term "spiritual life" is misleading when applied to the supernatural life of grace, because any truly intellectual operation is spiritual, even though very secular.

3. Immateriality can also be *absolute*: intrinsic independence of matter without even extrinsic dependence on matter. This is the manner of operation in the case of God and the angels, since their intellects do not even need to abstract knowledge from sensory experience.

The mention of God and angels at this point should not be misunderstood. They are introduced purely for the purpose of contrast with man's intellect, not as a proof of anything. Although some ancient pagan philosophers seem to have concluded by natural reason alone that pure created spirits exist, we might grant that certain knowledge about the angels can be learned only in theology. Since they are introduced here only for purposes of explanation and not as the premise of a proof, we can leave the question of their existence open and simply say that if there are such things as angels their intellects would differ from man's, inasmuch as their manner of cognition is absolutely immaterial. In dealing with analogical notions such as knowledge, life, being, substance, and so forth, it is often useful to see how they apply over a wide range of instances; St. Thomas frequently does this to orient his reader.

From this we can get a better appreciation of precisely what the adjective "rational" means when applied to the human intellect. We usually think of man's rationality as putting him at the top of the visible universe, and so it does. But in the realm of intellect, a rational intellect is the lowest and most imperfect type. God knows by means of one infinite and exhaustive act of knowledge; the angels, by intuitive judgments. Man's rational intellect must get its knowledge piecemeal through the process of abstraction from sense experience, then laboriously combining and distinguishing these ideas in judgments and reasoning—what St. Thomas calls compounding and dividing.

Defining Knowledge

Cognition might thus be summarily described as union with the form of an object immaterially. More fully, it is the act by which the knower becomes the known intentionally by possessing, in addition to his own form, that of the object, but without its matter. This intentional being of the object in the knower is not to be taken too lightly. The poorest art student looking at a cheap copy may really know and thus possess, or become intentionally, a masterpiece much more fully than the millionaire who possesses the original canvas in his safe. Using the other meaning of the word intentional, if I am resolved to commit murder, I am already guilty of committing murder, not physically but intentionally. For just as a block of marble becomes the statue by taking on the form of the statue, so I become that which I know when I take on its form.

It will be noted that we say cognition may be "described" rather than "defined," for it should be clear by now that knowledge cannot be strictly defined for many reasons. Being an analogous term, it does not admit of a univocal definition. There are degrees and kinds of knowledge. Secondly, definition requires genus and species, and knowledge fits under no genus which is common to knowledge and other things. Lastly, definition should be in terms of what is more known than the defined; but knowledge is the most basic and immediate experience we can have, so there is nothing simpler or more fundamental to which we can reduce it. It is a unique type of being, not explainable in terms of any other type of being. Hence all attempts to define knowledge in terms of behavioral response are doomed to miss its unique essential nature.

THE CAUSE OF KNOWLEDGE

Is Cognition Active or Passive? Knowledge is the act of possessing another by having its intentional form. It is not in itself change, although we compared intentional with physical change to try to understand its nature. But it is clear that we can pass from a state of not-knowing to a state of knowing, a change which must be explained. The following analysis holds for both sensory and intellectual cognition.

Does knowing change its object (active), or is the knowing subject changed by the object (passive)? Let us return to our examples. If the cow eats the hay, the object, hay, is changed. But if the cow sees the hay, there is no change in the hay—only in the cow. An object is no different for having been known. The change is in the cow as it passes from the state of potentially knowing to a state of actually knowing. From this it seems clear that the intentional change involved in becoming a knower is *essentially passive*, the knowing subject being acted upon by the object. Grammar could play us false here: "see" is an active verb, but the cow is not acting on the hay.

But is knowledge therefore *purely* passive? The wax and the modeling clay are capable only of purely passive reception of forms. An object such as a seal impresses its form upon them, but they do not know; their reception is purely passive. Even the photographic film, which might be said in some way to react to the impression, is really only passive; we do not say that the camera knows. Knowledge is a characteristic of living things which have the power to react to the impression of forms in such a way that they are able to entertain these forms precisely as other, in contrast to their own.[1] "Con" in

---

[1] Curiously enough, St. Thomas does not mention examples of immanent activity like cognition in explaining his definition of an active power. Perhaps it is because he took the definition bodily from the text of Aristotle as then known: ". . . an active potency is a principle of acting on another as other," which of course would not apply. But several variant codices consistently read ἢ ᾖ instead of simply ᾖ, as the text St. Thomas had reads. This gives "on another or on the same *as* other," justifying W. D. Ross's translation. Since the knower becomes "other," the cognitive powers could then fall under the second alternative in this version of the definition. One can only speculate whether St. Thomas would have spoken of cognitive powers as also active in connection with his definition of active potency if he had known of this other version in the manuscripts of Aristotle.

See James E. Royce, S.J., "St. Thomas and the Definition of Active Potency," *The New Scholasticism*, 1960, 34(4):431–437.

the word "consciousness" means "with," and it is this relationship of knower getting together "with" object known which is distinctive of knowledge. It is the difference between the purely passive possession of form by the wax and the copenetration of being by which a knower is capable of soaring beyond the limitation of matter to only one form. Intentional change is thus essentially passive, but also *vitally reactive* and therefore not purely passive.

Two Causes. Knowledge is thus both active and passive. If it were purely passive, then the wax or modeling clay would know. If it were essentially active, then knowledge would create its object and we would have no way of telling whether things were real or the product of our knowing processes.

The answer to the question of what causes knowledge can be brought out by asking the trite old question, "If a tree falls in a forest and there is no man or animal around to hear it, is there a sound?" The answer, of course, is to define the word "sound." If by sound you mean the purely objective physical stimulus for hearing, its presence could easily be verified with a tape recorder and it is absurd to imagine the laws of physics do not operate simply because we are not there to observe the results. But if by sound you mean auditory sensation, it is equally obvious that there is none unless there is a being present equipped with the power of experiencing such sensation.

Knowledge, then, is the joint product of two causes: the object and the knowing power. Without an object impressing it, the knowing power would remain in sheer potency to know. Without this peculiar potency to receive it, the impression would never result in this knowledge.[2]

ROLE OF THE SPECIES

The cognitive power is in potency to know. The fact that it begins to know actually here and now, and to know horse rather than battleship, cannot be explained by the power which is potency but

[2] Thomas Aquinas, *S. T.*, Ia, 84, 6; 78, 3.

only by the object which is in act. But it is not sufficient for the object to have its own actual existence; it must somehow begin to exist in the knower. We have seen that it does so by impressing upon the knowing power its intentional form.

In Scholastic philosophy, the technical term for this intentional form is *species*.[3] The term is perhaps unfortunate, for it is not to be confused with species in logic which is a division of genus, nor with species as in zoology where it means a class of animals. Nor is it an image or picture which we know. It is simply a means or intermediary by which we know objects. It is the actuation of the cognitive power whereby its indeterminacy is removed and by which we are made to be actually aware of this rather than that.

It is not the object of knowledge, for we know things and not *species*.[4] These we only know by a process of reasoning from the facts. The *species* is not knowledge itself, for it is a part cause of knowledge and a cause cannot be identical with its effect. The *species* is not a miniature object. The *species* is not the physical or physiological changes which take place in the organs of sense. These changes are the cause of the *species* in the knowing power. It is an intentional form, not a physical one. Moreover, the mere reception of the impressed *species* is not yet knowledge. For this reception is purely passive, and cognition is act. The *species* is the means by which the object is made present in the knower.

The *species* is necessary both from the standpoint of the knower and from that of the object known. The knower, being in potency, is indifferent to what it will know, and needs to have this indeterminacy removed by being actuated and specified. The object needs to be able to be present in the knower in a manner proportionate to the degree of immateriality involved in knowledge. But since no material object can be immaterial in its physical being, it needs this *species* or intentional form to give it immaterial existence in the knowing power.

[3] Following Klubertanz, we shall always print the word *species* in italics when used in this special meaning.

[4] Thomas Aquinas, S. T., Ia, 85, 2; 54, 1 ad 3um. Regarding the texts of St. Thomas on this point, see the summary in Gardeil (1956), pp. 148–152.

Kinds of Species

Impressed. Since sensory and intellectual cognition are different kinds of knowledge, they will have correspondingly different kinds of *species.* (1) The material object is present in the sense power with its material qualities by way of an *impressed sensible species* (quasi-immaterial). (2) The same material object when present in the intellect is there without its material qualities and individuating notes, and therefore in strictly immaterial form, by an *impressed intelligible species.* This difference exists because everything which is received is received according to the nature of the receiver.

Expressed. We said that the purely passive reception of *species* was not in itself knowledge, for knowledge consists in the act by which the knower is united with the object.[5] The wax does not know; teachers cannot impart knowledge to nonthinking students. The union of knower and object demands some activity on the part of the knower.

If the object is present, as in the case of sensory perception, the knower can unite directly with the object known and the act of knowing terminates in the object present.[6] But when the object is not present, as in imagining, or when it is not present in a way proportionate to the act of knowing, as in the case of a universal idea of even a present material object, the act of knowing cannot terminate directly in the object.

But the cognitive union must have a terminus, and we have already analyzed the products of the cognitive activity when we discussed the difference between image and idea. These are called the *expressed sensible species* and the *expressed intelligible species* re-

[5] See Thomas Aquinas, S. T., Ia, 54, 11 ad 3um; *De Veritate* 8, 1 ad 7um. The term *expressed species* originated with Scholastics after the time of St. Thomas, who used other phraseology (Gardeil, 1956, p. 144).

[6] For this reason the central sense apparently forms no expressed *species* (Brennan, *Thomistic Psychology*, 1941, p. 136). This would seem to be confirmed by the fact that although we *know* that the oar half in the water is straight, we do not form an image of a straight oar but continue to perceive it as bent. Theologians tell us that the same is true of the beatific vision, in which the immortal soul after death knows God intuitively and directly. The parentheses in Fig. 9 are dictated by these exceptions.

spectively. (1) An image is an expressed sensible *species*, the picture I have in mind, with which the act of imagination unites in the absence of any real object. (2) Similarly, the idea or concept is the expressed intelligible *species*, the content of thought, which is what I possess when I say that I understand what a thing is or what a word means.

Note that we can be aware of images and concepts, or expressed *species*, and can analyze and compare them. They are not usually what we know, but only that by which we know. But being expressed knowledge they can be in our consciousness if we choose to reflect upon them, whereas the impressed *species* is only known by reasoning from the necessity for some actualization of a potency.

The impressed and expressed *species* are always really distinct. The impressed *species* belongs to the cause of cognition, whereas the expressed *species* is a product; but cause and effect are always really distinct.

The expressed *species* is not in itself the essence of knowledge, nor is the purpose of cognition to produce the expressed *species*. For we can have cognition without any expressed *species*, as in the case of direct perception (and also the beatific vision). And if cognition existed only for the sake of producing an expressed *species*, it would cease when the *species* had been produced. Rather, the expressed *species* exists for the sake of cognition, as a means of union with the object when the knower cannot unite with it immediately. Cognition is not an action, in the sense of something which produces an effect. It is essentially the act or state of intentional union. It is not representation, nor similitude, but simultaneous possession of one's own form as well as another's form without its matter. To make cognition consist essentially of representation is to raise the old question of how do we know that the representation conforms to reality if we only know the representation and not the thing.

SUMMARY OF INTELLECTUAL PROCESS

The process of forming an idea may be instantaneous. Only by analysis and reasoning may we discover that several powers are operative in the process, whereas the product is a matter of clear experience and was examined in Chapter 6 when we contrasted idea with sense knowledge. Without suggesting that there is any actual separation or even time interval between the parts of the process, the accompanying diagram depicts the various stages in the formation of an idea.

We start with an object, since even the phantasms of imaginary beings like the flying horse have their foundation in our sensory experience of birds and horses. The object impresses itself through a medium physically upon the receptor organ and brain. This physiological activity is the means or instrument by which the object actuates the sensory power which is in potency to know. The resulting impression is called the impressed sensible *species*. The sense power vitally reacts, uniting with the object intentionally, either directly if the object is present in a percept, or through an expressed sensible *species* if the object is imagined or remembered.

In any case, the object is now present in the knower as form without matter, but with material qualities, and hence in only a quasi-immaterial state (phantasm). The light of the agent intellect now causes this intentional form to be impressed upon the potential or true intellect in a strictly immaterial or spiritual way, without individual material qualities. The form thus received in the intellect by the joint action of agent and phantasm is called the impressed intelligible *species*. Since knowledge does not consist in a purely passive reception of forms, the intellect in turn vitally reacts and produces the expressed intelligible *species*, also known as idea, notion, understanding, concept, simple apprehension, or "mental word." Lastly, unless the object which started the whole process was a spoken, written, or imagined word symbol, language completes the

Figure 9

The Process of Intellection

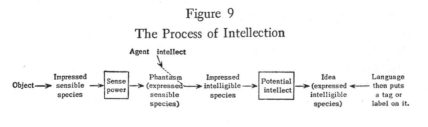

process by hanging a tag or label on the finished product, so that we now have a means of expressing our idea in conventional terms. Before understanding (idea), the word would be useless because meaningless.

When knowing ceases, the impressed *species* are usually stored in the knowing power as habitual knowledge. Under proper stimulation, as we have seen, they can again actuate the power and result in the production of expressed *species* in consciousness.

"Mental Word" and Language Words. The conventional symbols which are the words of language must be clearly distinguished from the technical term "mental word," used in philosophy to mean idea or concept. As we saw when discussing nominalism in Chapter 6, the same idea can be expressed by an unlimited number of synonyms or widely different equivalent words in various foreign languages. In many languages, although rarely in German, the same word may be a symbol for several different ideas.

The mental word is the representation or awareness or understanding of the meaning of the language word. As the product of intellection, the mental word is the *logos* in Greek which is the combining form in such terms as bio-logy. Although often translated as "the study of," it really means not the process but the product of such a study, the knowledge or understanding we have. (In the beginning of St. John's gospel the second person of the Trinity is spoken of as the *Logos*, or Word, which was in the beginning and is identified with God as the product of divine intellection, the eternal Word spoken by the Father.)

KNOWLEDGE NOT MERELY PHYSIOLOGICAL

Finally, it should be clear that both the impressed and expressed *species* are psychological qualities, accidental forms existing in the cognitive power. They are not physical or physiological forms; although their production may require these in the case of the senses. The distinctively psychological nature of these processes can be shown both (*a*) deductively and (*b*) empirically.

a) Since any cognition demands a certain degree of immateriality, it is clear from the principle of causality that the form which removes the indeterminacy of even a sense power cannot be merely physiological. Since the knowing power is in itself indifferent to objects and undetermined, and since the knowledge is intrinsic to the power, it needs an intrinsic determination. This determination or form can only be of the same order as the power of which it is a form. This will always be true, regardless of how future research on cortical field and feedback theories may supplant the present inadequate theories of memory trace and lowered synaptic resistance.

b) This philosophical conclusion would seem to be confirmed by evidence from physiology and experimental psychology. Illusion, ambiguity, constancy, and other perceptual phenomena described in Chapter 5 show instances in which stimulus or physiological activity remain constant and the psychological or conscious response varies, or vice versa. Blindness induced by hypnosis or emotional shock leaves the optic nerve intact. Another confirmation would seem to be the case of excessive physical stimulation of the physiological organ, which may produce less or even no psychic activity instead of more, as would be expected if psychic and physiological were identical. The same conclusion is suggested by the abandonment of the theory of specific nerve energies for the different types of sensation. Nerve energies certainly do not explain everything: compare hypnotically induced color blindness with that due to a physiological defect. The testing and training of pilots as well as the correction of certain visual defects indicates that what and how we see appears to be as much a matter of perceptual habits as of physiological functioning. In all of these examples there is a discrepancy between the physiological pattern and the resulting conscious impression which is incompatible with any theory which would identify them.

Current texts in psychology are frank in admitting that in spite of extensive experimentation we still have no factual basis for claiming to explain psychic activity in physiological terms. Substitution of "central" or cerebral theories for peripheral does not alter the basic issue. Physiologists admit that they cannot observe any change in synapse or neuron which will explain learning (Hilgard, 1957, p. 290). After decades of talking about engrams or memory traces in the brain, we now admit that we have no factual evidence of their existence or nature. Such theories seem incompatible with the facts of habit formation, to say nothing of either the extreme case of the hysterical blindness produced by a single traumatic experience, or the ordinary instance of a lifelong recollection from a single perception. We have no evidence that such single events wear a groove or alter a nerve. Sir Charles Sherrington, the eminent neurophysiologist, repeatedly notes in Chapters 9 to 11 of his *Man on His Nature* that mind is irreducible to biochemistry or neurology. Even a physiologically oriented psychologist such as Hebb[7] confesses:

> Until neurological theory is much more adequate, the psychologist has to take it with a grain of salt. But we must go further. It seems that some aspects of behavior can never be dealt with in neurological terms alone. . . . Psychology cannot become a branch of physiology. . . .
> It seems on occasion to be thought that the neurological entity is somehow more substantial, more "real," than psychological entities; that the study of nerve impulses is a more scientific affair than the study of anxiety or motivation. This is entirely mistaken.

Thought and the Brain

The above rejection of materialism applies even to animal or sensory knowledge, which is only quasi-immaterial. Being spiritual, intellectual knowledge is even more impossible to explain in terms of brain function, as has already been discussed in Chapter 6.

There is obviously some dependence of thought upon the nervous system, since all our knowledge is derived in some way from the senses and they are organic. The fact that understanding requires to be fed by sense does not prove that understanding itself is sensory any more than the fact that an automobile needs gasoline proves that the automobile is the fuel. The dependence is real but it is extrinsic and instrumental. If I continuously knock the brush out of the painter's hand, he does not get much painting done. The brush is not the painter, only an instrument. There is a real de-

[7] D. O. Hebb, A *Textbook of Psychology* (Philadelphia: Saunders, 1958), pp. 262–264. Further documentation on this point, especially from Hilgard and Lashley, will be found in the section "Habits and Learning" in Chap. 14.

pendence, but that the brush is only extrinsic is clear from the fact that the artist can get another brush or even finish the painting with his finger. Contrast this extrinsic interference with the essential change which takes place if I alter the intrinsic nature of the painter by killing him.

Lashley's work on equipotentiality of brain areas, and the history of brain injury mentioned in Chapter 6 (pp. 101–102), both seem very compatible with these facts. Whereas sensory and motor functions, being organic, can be assigned to quite definite areas in the cerebral cortex, the higher thought processes seem to defy all such localization, and have only been vaguely assigned to the so-called association areas. These latter are obviously the organ of the internal senses from which the intellect must abstract its ideas.

There is not only a lack of a definite place for thought in the brain but also a notable lack of the one-to-one correspondence and proportion between brain damage and rationality which one would expect if the brain were the principal cause of thought and not serving merely a subordinate and instrumental role. While slight damage in a certain area may cause death or paralysis, the medical literature attests to many cases of continued rationality in spite of very wide destruction of cortical areas. Brain injury may interfere with mental functioning, but thinking can take place as long as there is any nervous tissue left which can provide sensory materials upon which the intellect could work. Brain cannot be the proper and immediate organ of the intellect, but only indirectly, through the mediation of sense.

Such facts are quite compatible with the explanation proposed here of an essential or intrinsic dependence upon matter for sensory and vegetative activities, but only an extrinsic and instrumental relation for the processes of thought. Conversely, a materialistic philosophy seems hard pressed to explain cases where thinking continues in spite of widespread destruction of large masses of the brain. Note that we do not adduce these cases as the principal evidence for the spirituality of the intellect, but rather to point up the inadequacy of the materialistic theory.

St. Thomas was so aware of the relation of thought to brain that he even seems to have anticipated recent theorizing as to the organic factors in functional psychosis, though he certainly insisted on the spirituality of intellect. When he speaks of organic disturbances causing *lethargici* and *phrenetici*, the modern man wonders if he meant schizophrenia and manic-depressive mental disorders respectively (Ia, 84, 7; cf. also C. G., III, 84). Although a spiritual power cannot be touched by a blow on the head or poisoned by alcohol or noxious gases, these things can and do interfere with thought. This shows a real, even if extrinsic, dependence of intellect upon the internal senses whose organ is the brain.

The question of mental fatigue would seem to be best explained in this way also. The weariness of the individual doing continuous mental work has been shown experimentally to be muscular fatigue, which in turn can affect activity measured in time and errors, but there is no evidence that the intellect itself wearies like the muscles (Adler, 1937, p. 162, note 19). We seem to tire readily when studying metaphysics because of the strain involved in trying to picture the unpicturable, to conjure up helpful concrete images for abstract ideas and universal principles such as potency and act, which cannot be pictured. (See Thomas Aquinas, S. T., Ia, 84, 7).

Recall what was said previously about the meaning of rational as opposed to other kinds of intellect. Aristotle compares our human intellect in its present state with the night owl. Just as this bird cannot bear direct sunlight, so our human intellect receives the light of pure intelligibility only when softened by reflection through matter. Both St. Thomas (S. T., Ia, 76, 5) and Aristotle (De Anima, II, 9, 421a 20–26) discuss the intimate relationship between intellect and sense organs, and even mention a correlation between intelligence and sensitivity to pressure and pain which has been verified experimentally in modern times. (Slavin, 1936, pp. 129–131 and references therein.)

It is really incorrect to talk about intrinsic and extrinsic dependence, as if there were question of dependence of one thing upon another thing. Man is only one thing. Intellect and sense are principles of operation. Aristotle and St. Thomas preferred to talk about a substantial form which was human but virtually animal and vegetative, so that these various powers were encompassed in the same nature. Brain may be extrinsic to thought, but it is intrinsic to man. (See footnote 3 in Chapter 7 on the unique, natural, conjoined instrumentality of sense knowledge.)

REVIEW QUESTIONS

1. Is knowledge a univocal or analogous term? Explain.
2. Why is the analysis of knowledge difficult?
3. Can knowledge be defined simply as response to stimulus? Why?
4. "Scientists cannot tell whether certain organisms have sensation or not. Hence they could be either plant or animal. But if they could be either, then there is no real difference." Evaluate this argument (see beginning of Chapter 3).
5. Can the difference between physical union and intentional union be explained in terms common to both? to some other union?
6. Why does all awareness involve *some* immateriality? Explain what you mean by this immateriality.
7. Is it contradictory to say that sensory knowledge is organic and yet say that all knowledge involves immateriality? Why?
8. Describe fully the precise degree of immateriality proper to sense knowledge.
9. a) Define "spiritual."
   b) Describe precisely what spiritual means in the case of human intellection.
10. If all cognition involves immateriality, then how can we say in Chapter 6 that intellect differs from sense by being immaterial?
11. If human and angelic intellection are both spiritual, do they differ? Why?
12. What do you mean by "rational" intellect as opposed to other intellects? What practical import does this distinction have for education?
13. Can knowledge be defined by strict logical definition? Why?
14. Is knowing active or passive? Explain.
15. What would be the epistemological consequence of saying that knowledge is purely active?
16. Is there any contradiction in saying that knowledge entails vital activity and yet is essentially passive?
17. What is the connection between the essential passivity of knowledge and the need for *species*? What is an impressed *species*?
18. Why do we need both sensible and intelligible *species*? Would not one suffice for all knowledge of the same object?

19. Is the *species* that which we know? Why is there no need for an expressed *species* in the case of direct sensory perception and in the beatific vision?
20. Is it possible to observe the expressed *species* in our experience? the impressed *species*?
21. Show how the facts of illusion, ambiguity, and constancy indicate that cognition is not merely a physical and physiological process.
22. Is memory trace in the brain an observed fact or a theory?
23. Will the psychological nature of sensory knowledge be disproven by more fruitful research on central (or cerebral) factors in the brain? Why?
24. Is matter extrinsic to thought? to man? to sense knowledge?
25. Is there any contradiction in saying that the intellect is extrinsically dependent on the brain and yet intrinsically independent of it?
26. If the intellect is spiritual, explain how brain injury can interfere with thought.
27. If heredity is biological and thought is immaterial, how can you explain that there is some real correlation between IQ of parents and children? Is it simply a matter of parental environment? (See last section of Chapter 6.)
28. Explain the entire process of getting an idea, naming all the steps.
29. Do these steps indicate a sequence in time?
30. List all the differences you can between the idea or "mental word" and the verbal or language word.
31. If the intellect retains impressed *species*, why is it not actually knowing all the time? (See the section "Intellectual Memory" in Chapter 7.)

FOR FURTHER READING

AQUINAS, ST. THOMAS. *Summa Theol.*, Ia, 14, 1 (Since St. Thomas includes sense knowledge under *cognoscitivus*, "knowing" seems a better translation of the word than "intelligent," which appears in some English versions.); 17, 1 and 2; 77, 3; 78, 3; 79, 2; 84, 2 and 6; 85, 1 and 2; *Truth (De Veritate)*, I.

ARISTOTLE. *On the Soul*, II, 12; III, 4.

BRENNAN, ROBERT E., O.P. *Thomistic Psychology*. New York: Macmillan, 1941. Pp. 111–117, 135–137, 169–209.

GILSON, ETIENNE. *The Spirit of Medieval Philosophy*. New York: Scribner, 1936. Chap. 12.

HILGARD, ERNEST R. *Theories of Learning*. (2d Ed.) New York: Appleton-Century-Crofts, 1956. Pp. 452–485.

KLUBERTANZ, GEORGE P., S.J. *Philosophy of Human Nature.* New York: Appleton-Century-Crofts, 1953. Chap. IV.

KOREN, HENRY J., C.S.Sp. *An Introduction to the Philosophy of Animate Nature.* St. Louis: Herder, 1955. Chap. 6.

MARITAIN, JACQUES. *Distinguish to Unite: The Degrees of Knowledge.* New York: Scribner, 1959.

MARTIN, OLIVER. *The Order and Integration of Knowledge.* Ann Arbor: University of Michigan Press, 1956.

MAYER, MARY HELEN. *The Philosophy of Teaching of St. Thomas Aquinas.* Milwaukee: Bruce, 1929.

MOORE, THOMAS VERNER. *Cognitive Psychology.* Philadelphia: Lippincott, 1939. Since he is both a psychiatrist (M.D.) and a psychologist (Ph.D.), Dom Moore is able to give much fascinating medical and experimental data, which reputes a purely materialistic explanation of cognition.

MOWRER, O. H. "On the Dual Nature of Learning: A Reinterpretation of 'Conditioning' and 'Problem-solving'," *Harv. Educ. Rev.,* 1947, 17:102–148.

OLGIATI, FRANCESCO. *The Key to the Study of St. Thomas.* Trans. by J. S. Zybura. St. Louis: Herder, 1925. Chaps. II, V.

RENARD, HENRI, S.J. "The Problem of Knowledge in General," *The Modern Schoolman,* 1946, 24:1–11. (Chap. IV in his book, *The Philosophy of Man,* Milwaukee: Bruce, 1956.)

SERTILLANGES, A. D., O.P. *Foundations of Thomistic Philosophy.* Trans. by G. Anstruther. Springfield, Ill.: Templegate, 1956. Chap. II.

DE TONQUÉDEC, Jos. *La Critique de la connaissance.* Paris: Beauchesne, 1929.

PART THREE

HUMAN DYNAMICS

9

MOTIVATION

Appetite in general. Appetition follows cognition. Motives and motivating factors. Kinds of motivated activities.

Why man acts has always been of great concern to the student of human nature, whether philosopher or psychologist. We are rarely satisfied with knowing merely what man does, without knowing why he does it. Dynamics are so central in the study of human personality that when contemporary psychology speaks of theories of personality it usually means theories of motivation.

When studying knowledge in Part 2, we made practically no mention of the use of that knowledge. But man does not merely know; he tends to act in accordance with that knowledge. To be aware of a situation is a different kind of activity from being inclined to do something about it.

Appetition (or appetency) is the name traditionally given in Scholastic philosophy to this tending, the ability or power being called *appetite*. Modern psychology uses a great variety of terms to describe this activity: motivation, orexis, conation, dynamics. Since the tending may be either toward or away from the object known,

155

paired terms are sometimes used, such as attraction-aversion or approach-avoidance.

None of these terms is perfectly satisfactory because the notion is analogous rather than univocal and refers to many different types and powers of tending. The analogy must include the divine will in which there is no motion or imperfection, as well as those acts of the human will which regard a good toward which there is no longer tendency or motion but which is already possessed and enjoyed: certain acts of love, enjoyment, complacency, continued consent, etc. (*S. T.*, Ia IIae, 12, 1–16).

Appetite is likewise not a wholly satisfactory term, since it also connotes striving or tending toward. Aristotle's word "orexis" is suggested by Spearman (1937, I, 303) and this is Brennan's choice too (1941, 148, 210). But this word in Greek has the same connotation of motion and imperfection, though it otherwise has a very broad meaning. St. Thomas (*C. G.*, IV, 19) uses the expression "to be affected." The root notion of our word "affection," as implied there, without a connotation of sentimentality, brings out the idea. This suggests that the basic notion of appetite is how this knowledge affects me, what it makes me feel like doing about the object.

It is clear that the powers of cognition and appetition are distinct, since they have different formal objects. The object of the cognitive potency is the being as knowable, whereas the object of the appetitive potency is the being as good or desirable.

Appetition Follows Cognition

We can see both from experience and from analytic reasoning that appetition is a tendency consequent upon knowledge. From experience (*a posteriori*), it is obvious that advertising, salesmanship, politics, and all forms of persuasion exemplify this fact. Objects are presented in such a way that they evoke desire. The same conclusion seems readily inferred from the actions of animals whose behavior is so largely dependent upon what appears good, or good to avoid.

It can also be revealed by reasoned analysis (*a priori*). We have seen that any cognition is a form possessed by the knower. Now from the principle of finality in general metaphysics we know that any form must have a purpose or reason for being the way it is. But since nothing except God is its own sufficient reason this form must be for the sake of something else. Consequently if knowledge were not followed by appetition, it would be utterly sterile. Knowledge would be useless if it did not evoke a tendency to act upon it. Even a normal man would starve to death without appetite.

KINDS OF APPETITE

This close relation between cognition and appetition gives us the basis for a division of the appetites. Since every knowledge has its corresponding tendency, there are as many kinds of appetition as there are kinds of cognition. The object of the sensory appetite is good known in a sensory way, while the power of volition or rational appetency has as its object an intellectually known good. For instance, the sight of a mountain stream may evoke thirst, whether I really need water just then or not. I may know intellectually that this unpleasant medication will save my life, even though I experience a sensory repugnance toward it.

Natural and Elicited Appetite

The appetition which we are considering is called elicited, to distinguish it from what the Scholastic philosophers call natural appetite. If I let go of this piece of chalk, it "tends" toward the center of the earth; but no one would imagine that this tending is the result of any knowledge or conscious desire on the part of the chalk. Its tending toward the center of the earth is called natural appetition, by an analogous use of the term. Chemical affinity, magnetism, the natural tendency of the eye to see or the stomach to digest, are called *natural* appetites because these inclinations are not elicited or evoked by any knowledge. Much of what falls under the psychological term "need" is a matter of natural appetite.

Elicited appetition is tendency which is evoked or brought forth by some knowledge or awareness. It is to be noted that there may not be a very explicit awareness of the precise goal or object, so that the appetition may be a vague, hardly conscious craving. But appetition as we shall discuss it here is always evoked by some knowledge and corresponds to the type of knowledge possessed.

Hierarchy of Tendencies

Man thus has different appetitive powers, distinct from one another and from his substance. These again are not substances or separate from the man, but simply his abilities.

In this context, the dictum of some psychologists that "all behavior is a matter of stimulus and response" is perfectly acceptable if we remember that there are many different kinds of stimuli and hence a corresponding number of different responses. Beyond the tap of a rubber hammer on the patellar tendon giving a simple natural reflex, the stimulus can be anything from a sensory awareness eliciting an act of the sense appetite up to a sublime ideal or principle apprehended by the intellect and eliciting a response of the will such as choice.

Throughout this range of variety in response runs the basic principle that these activities do not "just happen" but are always the result of some cause. But cause is an analogous term. Let us survey briefly the different kinds of causality involved here.

Ordered operation supposes a goal; goals suggest ontological good, that which has value in itself and is perfective of that which seeks it. All operation in some way involves tendency toward the good. The perfection of this tending will be measured by the value or excellence of the good itself and the perfection of the manner in which it is sought. The most imperfect kind of seeking is that in which there is no awareness on the part of the seeker, and the highest is that in which there is fullest knowledge of the excellence of the good in itself as well as of its perfectiveness to the seeker. Thus we have in nature a hierarchy of tendencies with their corresponding objects or goods. The atom has its chemical affinities and the plant its thermotropisms and selective osmosis. To say that a plant "loves" water is a very broad analogy, because it is not even aware that water is good for it, and much less aware of the excellence of water in itself. The more perfect form of tending is that in which the seeker is aware of the object, and experiences a conscious tendency, such as happens in sensory appetition. At this level man and the other animals may be aware of the object and *that* it is good, but the precise reason *why* it is good is not recognized. Highest on the scale is intellectual appetition, in which the knower is not only aware of the object but also of its goodness and why it is perfective of the seeker.

As we ascend this scale of tendential forces in nature, we see an increasing disproportion between stimulus and response. At the lowest level of physical causality, there is a direct proportion between the efficient cause exerted and the magnitude of the effect. In the realm of living things we see that at the vegetative or physiological level a very slight stimulus can produce a remarkably powerful and complex effect, as in the case of fertilization or reflex response to a stimulus. Ascending still higher on the scale, we see that there is an even greater disparity between the external stimulus and the end result, still more being due to the activity of the organism. Thus, the slightest menacing gesture on the part of the postman or even his mere appearance may throw the watchdog who has been kicked by him into rather violent defensive reaction. Still higher is the case in which the simple word or sentence may set in motion the whole machinery of human warfare, and lastly there is the instance where the activity seems initiated entirely within the man himself or at least is under his control.

These facts have led some investigators to worry about whether there is some violation of the law of cause and effect in higher human activity. Actually, there is no question of this but simply of a shift in proportion between the amount of causality exercised by the stimulus and that exercised by the responding organism. Moreover, such activity involves not only greater efficient causality on the part of the agent rather than the stimulus, but also and especially a higher degree of participation by him in the final causality involved. We have seen that the nature of cognition is such that it makes the knower capable of possessing the object known somehow within himself; this makes it possible for the goodness or perfectiveness of the object to exercise a higher degree of final causality. There is no violation of the principle of causality, but simply a shift from outside forces to the agent himself.

The concept of final cause is established elsewhere, in general metaphysics. ("Final" here does not mean last or ultimate, but purpose or goal.) "How can a thing act as a cause when it does not even exist?" is a question which only serves to bring out the difference between efficient and final causality. If the final cause or goal exists only in the mind of the one desiring it, it can hardly exert efficient causality. It causes precisely by being desirable, by attracting, by stimulating the efficient cause to take means to make it a reality.

The study of final causes is called teleology, from the Greek *telos* meaning end or goal. Because psychology in its earlier days was anxious to attain scientific status by patterning itself after classic physics, which ignored finality, psychologists once tended to decry teleology. But motivation is impossible to ignore in studying the determinants of human behavior, so the notion crept back in. At first it was controversial, but Hall and Lindzey in their work on theories of personality affirm that opposition to teleology in psychology has waned (1957, p. 539).

MOTIVES AND MOTIVATING FACTORS

Motive, from the Latin word for "move," means whatever moves one to act. The term was restricted by the medieval philosophers to a reason for action of which one is aware at the rational level, an intellectually known good serving as the object of the will. Modern psychology has considerably broadened the meaning of this term and brought it back closer to the original Latin root. We think it practical to conform more to the current English usage and use the term motive to refer to any specific goal or object which, on a conscious level, directs conduct, regardless of whether it is sensory or rational. Thus used, the term is more or less synonymous with incentive, and runs through a wide range of psychological dynamics.

A cognitive act, whether sensory perception, image, or idea, is not precisely a motive until it serves as a stimulating force to our appetitive powers. Knowledge is not virtue, principles are not character, daydreams are not meritorious, temptation is not sin. It is only when these things lead to action or at least to deliberate resolve or intention that they merit praise or blame.

One reason why there is confusion in modern psychological discussion of motivation is that everyday terms are frequently taken over without distinguishing between final and efficient causality. Strictly speaking, the terms motive, incentive, goal, purpose, stimulus, and even need, all refer to the realm of final cause. Drive, urge impulse, desire, emotion, and choice refer to appetitive responses with regard to such motives and are in the realm of efficient causality. Knowledge gives us the goal, and appetite gives the inclination towards it.

Motivating factors is a term sometimes used to designate other influences which initiate or sustain activity and which are not incentives or motives even in the broadened sense used above. These include needs and drives, physiological conditions of the organism, the unconscious influence of previous experience, and a host of other factors which may be only vaguely conscious or completely beyond our awareness. Motive refers to the object of a power; motivating factors can refer to the power, its natural tendency to action, habits which can modify its action, and even the appetitive act itself. Modern psychologists often use the word motive as a general term referring to both motives and motivating factors: anything which contributes toward need-satisfying and goal-seeking behavior, including the avoidance of undesirable objects.

A *need* is a lack of something either suitable or necessary: food, information, social acceptance. *Drive* is a tension or tendency to act caused by an unfilled need: hunger for food, curiosity for knowledge, loneliness for acceptance. The philosopher need not be concerned that modern psychologists are not wholly consistent in their use of these terms.[1] Philosophically, a need is an objective fact, the actual lack. The drive is an appetitive state consequent upon that need.

---

[1] The confusion and inconsistency of psychologists in the use of these terms is noted by E. T. Prothro & P. T. Teska, *Psychology: A Biosocial Study of Behavior* (Boston: Ginn, 1950), p. 77. For further clarification see the discussion of needs and drives in James E. Royce, S.J., *Personality and Mental Health* (Milwaukee: Bruce, 1955), pp. 24–28.

It is usually rather indeterminate until directed by a specific incentive or goal. Thus the drive of hunger may be a vague craving which causes Junior to wander aimlessly in the general direction of the kitchen, but action becomes specific once the cookie jar comes into view.

Motivated Activities

Impulse is a "tendency we experience, in the presence of actual opportunity, to exercise any one of our human abilities" (Moore, 1926, p. 140). Here the motive is present and activity is called for at once upon its apprehension. The incentive or deterrent may be instinctual, learned, or intellectual, but in any case it calls for indeliberate and immediate response, which makes control difficult. Impulse differs from reflex in being conscious, less mechanical, more complex, and more dynamic. It differs from drive in being called forth by a specific incentive.

There is no point in trying to enumerate or classify our impulses; we have as many impulses as there are things we can feel impelled to do. This view also obviates useless attempts to name "instincts," as if such a set of entities existed. Evidence merely indicates that some tendencies are unlearned, that often there is at least a partially instinctive impulse impelling us to exercise our natural abilities.

Desire is a similar tendency, but regarding an *absent* object or situation. (The word "appetite" is often used in common speech to refer to this act, instead of in the traditional sense of any tending power.) Again, desire may involve our lowest animal needs or our highest human aspirations. Moore (1926, p. 152) defines desire as "a craving we experience to seek or produce a situation in which impulsive tendencies may be satisfied or natural wants supplied."

Such desires may have *goals* which are clearly defined, or vague. They may be necessary, or mere "wants" acquired beyond nature's demands. They may be insightful, or without an understanding of their true motivation ("repressed"). Normal desires are usually more controllable than impulses, and less dependent on the present situation or organic conditions. They are modifiable by education and training, as opposed to impulse which is usually modified only by satisfaction or by the passage of time.

Affective states are more general in their reference to action, but powerfully dynamic. They include feeling, mood, sentiment, and emotion, all defined in the next chapter.

Choice has as its stimulus a motive in the old Scholastic sense of an intellectually known good which serves as an object of rational appetite. The object may be only apparently good, or it may be seen as "good to avoid." It may be material or immaterial, means or end, fleeting or habitual. The motive can be an attitude, a principle, an ideal, or some sentiment based more on feeling than on intellect and perhaps involving bias or prejudice.

Motivation is complex. All these motivated tendencies except the last, choice, may be either sensory or rational or both. Usually in the human adult there is such a combination and mixture of the sensory and rational in motivation that it is practically impossible to identify a given tendency as purely animal or purely rational. We must turn to infants, the mentally abnormal, or brute animals to find clear-cut cases of unmixed sensory appetency. And even the act of choice, although elicited by awareness of an intellectually known good, usually occurs with an admixture of sensory motivation. As in the case of knowledge, we distinguish for purposes of study what is not separate in reality.

We shall devote the next chapter to the affective states, especially emotion, which is the most important and involves principally our sensory appetites. Then in the following two chapters we shall take up the rational appetite and the question of free choice.

REVIEW QUESTIONS

1. Distinguish between cognitive and appetitive operations, using examples.
2. Distinguish between natural and elicited appetition.
3. Do acts of natural appetite have a stimulus?
4. Is it logical to divide appetite into elicited and sensory?
5. At the turn of the century scientific psychology tended to reject teleology. We have noted that recently this rejection has been withdrawn. What reasons can you give for this?
6. Show in two ways that appetition follows cognition.
7. (*a*) Why is the notion of an unmotivated appetition absurd?

164   HUMAN DYNAMICS

(b) Does this mean that we are always aware of the specific motive for our actions?
8. Distinguish impulse from desire.
9. Distinguish several different meanings of the word motive.
10. "All man's activity is a matter of stimulus and response." List at least four different kinds of response and their corresponding stimuli which this statement must include to be true.

FOR FURTHER READING

AQUINAS, ST. THOMAS. Summa Theol., Ia, 80, 1 and 2; 81, 1; Ia IIae, 26; 27, 1 and 2.
EYMIEU, ANTONIN, S.J. Le Gouvernement de soi-même. Vol. IV. La Loi de la vie. Paris: Perrin, 1936.
GILSON, ETIENNE. The Spirit of Medieval Philosophy. New York: Scribner, 1936. Chap. XIV.
HARMON, FRANCIS L. Principles of Psychology. (Rev. Ed.) Milwaukee: Bruce, 1951. "Motivation," Chap. 16.
McCLELLAND, DAVID C. (Ed.) Studies in Motivation. New York: Appleton-Century-Crofts, 1955.
McDOUGALL, WILLIAM. The Energies of Men. (4th Ed.) London: Methuen, 1939.
MASLOW, ABRAHAM A. Motivation and Personality. New York: Harper, 1954.
MOORE, THOMAS VERNER. The Driving Forces of Human Nature and Their Adjustment. New York: Grune & Stratton, 1948. Pp. 231–250.
MOORE, THOMAS VERNER. Dynamic Psychology. Philadelphia: Lippincott, 1926. Pp. 132–133.
Nebraska Symposium on Motivation. Lincoln: University of Nebraska Press. Published annually since 1953.
NUTTIN, JOSEPH. Psychoanalysis and Personality: A Dynamic Theory of Normal Personality. New York: Sheed, 1953.
WOODWORTH, ROBERT S. Dynamics of Behavior. New York: Holt, 1957.
WOODWORTH, ROBERT S. Experimental Psychology. (1st Ed.) New York: Holt, 1938. Pp. 234–241.
WOODWORTH, ROBERT S., & SCHLOSBERG, H. Experimental Psychology. (Rev. Ed.) New York: Holt, 1954. Pp. 655–694 are pertinent, but omit the clear basic statement on appetition in the first edition cited above.
WUELLNER, BERNARD, S.J. A Christian Philosophy of Life. Milwaukee: Bruce, 1957.

10

EMOTION

Affective states: feeling, sentiment, mood, emotion. Concupiscible and irascible appetites. Nature of emotion itself: physiological changes, spontaneity, complexity.

Emotion is an important part of human nature. Man's actual achievements are ordinarily in direct proportion to the extent that he is emotionally involved. We usually do well what we feel like doing, and it is important to enlist emotion on the side of principle. How we feel is of primary importance in what we actually do, though our feelings cannot be relied upon to indicate what we should do.

Contrary to the stand of puritanism by whatever name, it is a fact that feelings are an integral part of human nature. Man is not an angel, and his rational operations cannot be studied in isolation from his animal appetites and affections. These need to be controlled, but they cannot be eliminated or ignored.

AFFECTIVE STATES

Affective states is the general term used in psychology to comprise this intriguing area of dynamics. It includes the following:

Feeling: the most elemental states of pleasure or displeasure.

Mood: an affective state more acute and more prolonged, but still rather vague.

Sentiment: a group of emotional tendencies concerning some object or person. More specific in its object and associations than feeling or mood, it is like them in being weaker and longer lasting than emotion.

Emotion: a spontaneous, intense feeling state, aroused by a meaningful stimulus and characterized by peculiar bodily changes. It is more complex and more intense than any of the aforementioned, as well as more specific in its relation to the meaning of the situation. It involves therefore more perception, and in addition has a characteristic bodily resonance.

Temperament: one's habitual emotional disposition—habits, as opposed to the actual emotions.

Although these are all complex processes involving cognitive, appetitive, and physiological activity, they are primarily movements of the sensory appetites. Psychologists once distinguished more sharply between the mild feeling states of pleasantness and unpleasantness and the intense state of emotion, but the tendency now is to consider them a continuum ranging in intensity and specificity, without attempting to delineate the precise point at which the feeling becomes so intense and meaningful as to be called an emotion. They are called affective states because they refer to the way in which some stimulus affects us, that is, how it makes us feel.

DIVISIONS OF SENSORY APPETITION

There are many different divisions of emotions. Perhaps the most obvious is that of pleasant and unpleasant, namely, those aroused by a desirable stimulus and those aroused by an undesirable one.

This obviously is on a different axis than the division in terms of intensity or duration given above.

From Aristotle to John B. Watson, various attempts have been made to reduce emotions to a certain basic few. Psychologists have largely abandoned such attempts at identifying primary emotions and prefer a developmental approach, studying the gradual growth from the simplest excitement of the infant to the variegated shades of adult emotional response. The generalized excitement first observable in infants becomes differentiated fairly early into fear, rage, and love. Later we can observe desire, joy, hatred, sorrow, hope, despair, courage, and still later further refinements. Love, in the general sense of a tendency to seek the good and avoid what threatens its loss, can be said to be primary and basic to all other appetency. (*S. T.,* Ia IIae, 26–28).

St. Thomas asserts that sensory appetitive power itself is twofold: concupiscible and irascible. The distinction is based on whether the good desired (or evil to be avoided) is considered simple to attain (or avoid) or as involving some difficulty. Concupiscible or pleasure-pain appetite refers to unqualified attraction and avoidance: desire, joy, aversion, sorrow. Irascible or aggressive appetite is aroused when there is some threat or difficulty in the attainment or avoidance of the object. Thus hope, despair, courage, fear, and anger would be considered acts of the irascible appetite.

This distinction seems to be well founded in the fact that these two tendencies can oppose one another, and hence could not be acts of the same power. We know that hunger or sex desire (concupiscible) can be diminished or temporarily wiped out by anger or fear (irascible). This fact has recently been used by a Dutch psychiatrist to explain repression: pleasure-drive is overcome by fear or strengthened by boldness, rather than by volitional control. This would explain the irrational and unconscious nature of anxiety and other neuroses, which are then due largely to habits of the irascible appetite (Terruwe, 1958).

One can also see some vague parallel between this distinction and the mutually antagonistic activities of the two divisions of the autonomic nervous system. Concupiscible appetite seems to involve the parasympathetic (craniosacral) functions which mediate routine behavior. Irascible partakes more of the sympathetic (thoracolumbar) division and adrenal glands which activate the body to an emergency state. However, oversimplification here is dangerous since both divisions of the autonomic, as well as the central nervous system, are involved in many emotional states.

Psychologists and physiologists have tried for many years to distinguish emotions on the basis of different bodily reactions. External reactions, such as facial expression and gestures, seem to be largely stylized by convention. Even parents were unable to tell from observing silent motion pictures of their own infant whether the child was joyful or sad. The internal physiological changes, which are really the more important aspect of the bodily reaction, likewise fail as an adequate basis for distinguishing emotions. Blood pressure and pulse rate may go up equally high without telling us whether the presence of a newcomer arouses love or fear. Since the discovery of noradrenalin (another secretion of the adrenal medulla), some slight success has been attained in distinguishing physiologically between fear and anger. But we must still depend largely upon our conscious experience of the appetitive impulse itself to determine whether we love or hate a person, whether we are happy or sad at a bit of news.

NATURE OF EMOTION

We all know from direct experience what it means to be angry or afraid, joyous or hating. It is not so easy to analyze the nature of these states, especially because while we are experiencing them we are in no mood for analysis. Emotion is also difficult to grasp or define because it is a highly complex activity. Yet an understanding of its nature is important not only as a basis for any intelligent discussion of its development and control, but also because it is a good indicator of the ultimate nature of man.

Although centered in intense movements of the sensory appetites, emotion involves practically all of man: sensory cognition and especially imagination and sense-estimate, intellect and some spontaneous volition, and striking physiological changes. In general, it is more complex and more intense than feelings or moods, and has a more direct relation to a meaningful stimulus-situation. It therefore involves more perception. Another very important difference is the characteristic bodily resonance, a set of physiological changes peculiar to emotion.

Of course, when we actually have an emotion we are not aware of all of this complexity; we only feel very strongly in a certain way. Nevertheless we can distinguish three elements upon analyzing emotion: (1) the apprehension of the stimulus, (2) an appetitive response, and (3) bodily resonance reinforcing this response.

1. *Meaningful stimulus.* It is not enough that I see a situation or hear a word to be aroused emotionally. Whether I so react depends on whether I recognize the situation as pleasant, desirable, or threatening to me. A meaningless stimulation would cause no emotion. The object may be present or absent, remembered or imagined. But it must be not only perceived but also appraised as affecting me personally in some way. Even habitual emotional response which is the result of conditioning or learning presumes this initial appraisal in the past experience.

It is important to note that I need not be conscious of the connection between the stimulus and the emotion, or know why it has this emotional meaning for me. Abnormal emotional states are often due to a failure of the individual to recognize the emotional meaning which a situation or object has acquired for him.

The manner in which the meaning is grasped serves to distinguish a truly human emotion from a purely animal one. In an analogous sense we can say the lamb fears the lion, or a dog loves its master; but the fear and love here result from mere sensory cognition, whether it be an instinctive appraisal by inner estimative power or the result of stored-up associations in imagination and memory. In contrast, a love proper to a human being should include some intellectual appreciation of the goodness of the beloved, and even my fear of a tiger may involve some rational as well as sensory cognition, although in neither case is the emotion a purely Platonic affair existing only at the rational level.

2. *Appetitive response.* The heart of emotion is the impulsive,

almost explosive movement of the appetitive powers, especially at the animal or sensory level. It is an affective or feeling state, not a cognitive act. That is why the Scholastic philosophers divide emotion according to the divisions of the sense appetites (concupiscible and irascible).

It is with this connotation in mind that the medieval philosophers described or called emotion by the name of passion. Now *passio* has some six different meanings in Scholastic philosophy, as Klubertanz points out (1953, p. 73, n. 17). On the other hand, in modern English the word passion or passionate is often restricted to just one appetitive response, that of carnal love. This is unfortunate because puritanical thinking then goes on to imply that all emotion is bad, whereas the truth of the matter is that emotion as a natural response is essentially good. It is also unfortunate because passion might suggest passivity, although the adjective passionate does not imply this.

One notable characteristic of emotion is the fact that it is spontaneous. This does not mean inborn, for we have already noted that the power of a stimulus to elicit an emotional response is largely acquired through previous learning experience. Spontaneous is the opposite of deliberate, and refers to the automaticity which is proper both to our sense appetites and to the autonomic division of the nervous system which enters so intimately into emotional response. Even the volition which may be involved in a truly human emotion is not the deliberate act of choice, but the first spontaneous tending of the will which usually precedes (and sometimes overrules) the act of free choice.[1]

This spontaneity means that emotions are not subject to our control directly, but only indirectly. Aristotle (*Pol.* I, 5, 1254b2) and St. Thomas (*S. T.*, Ia, 81, 3 ad 2um) distinguish between those acts over which we have despotic or dictatorial power and those acts over which we have only political or persuasive power. Spontaneous appetition and autonomic responses obviously fall in the latter class.

[1] See Thomas Aquinas, *S. T.*, Ia, IIae, qq. 8–16; or *C. G.*, IV, 19.

They are to be distinguished from emotional behavior, the external behavior which may be dictated by emotion: this is usually within our direct or despotic control. Thus I am usually able to refrain by direct control from hitting someone, but the fact that I feel like hitting him is not so easily handled.

3. *Body resonance.* Certain notable physiological changes are characteristic of emotion. They constitute an integral part of emotion, being closely bound up with any intense activity of our animal appetites. Some progress has been made in identifying specific physiological responses for the different emotions, and at least a general pattern of organic activity is seen to be characteristic: heartbeat, blood coagulative power, perspiration, digestive processes, and adrenal secretion all undergo marked changes commonly recognized as integral to emotional experience.

These mobilize the body for the action or protection usually called for in an emotional situation. We say usually, for although in other animals emotion prompted by the unreasoned estimate of a situation may be an adequate guide for action, in human beings action depends also on reasoned evaluation of the goal. Since this goal may be a distant one and the means to it unpleasant, emotion may hinder rather than help.

Note that *awareness* of these physiological changes may or may not accompany the emotional experience; this is irrelevant to the nature of emotion itself.

Facial changes and other external expressions of emotion are likewise of little import. For one thing, they are more separable from emotion. Moreover, they lack the spontaneity which typifies emotional response. A good poker player can control the emotion on his face because this is a matter of voluntary musculature; but he can do little, except indirectly, about the autonomic physiological changes which we have enumerated and which the polygraph or so-called lie detector measures. The latter, incidentally, does not measure truth and falsity, but simply the spontaneous physiological aspects of embarrassment which are beyond our control.

ORGANIC NATURE OF SENSE APPETITE

From all of this it is clear that sensory appetition is by no means immaterial. This should be equally obvious from the fact that cognition and appetition are at the same level, and we have already seen that sensory knowledge is at best only quasi-immaterial. Emotion especially is very important in modern psychosomatic medicine, which is the study of those physical ills and symptoms due largely to psychological and especially emotional causes. But a clear grasp of the organic nature of sensory appetition itself precludes any possibility of separating psyche from soma as if they were two different beings. The psychic and somatic aspects of emotional experience do not constitute the acts of two separate beings, since they constitute one affective experience.

REVIEW QUESTIONS

1. Is the ideal man one who has no emotions? Why?
2. Why is emotion treated in the chapter devoted to the sense appetites?
3. Why is immaturity often characterized as a predominantly emotional condition?
4. Distinguish feeling as used in this chapter from feeling as a tactual sensation.
5. What is the relation between temperament and emotion?
6. In S. T., Ia, 81 (2 ad 2, and 3 ad 2) does St. Thomas confuse two different bases for division of sense appetite, [sic] "unqualified versus difficult to obtain" and "known by instinctive estimate versus known by perception and imagination"?
7. Why are there different and overlapping bases for divisions of the emotions?
8. Are they contradictory to one another?
9. What reasons can you give why the classification of emotions must take into account subjective factors?
10. Why is the way one defines emotion an index to one's concept of the nature of man?
11. Is there any contradiction in saying emotion is spontaneous and yet is largely developed? Explain.

12. In what sense is emotion learned?
13. Which of the three elements of emotion is involved when we say that a truly human emotion should have a rational aspect?
14. What is meant by saying that emotion is more adrenal than cortical?
15. Why is emotion the key to understanding the unity of man in the face of psychosomatic phenomena?

FOR FURTHER READING

AQUINAS, ST. THOMAS. *Summa Theol.*, Ia, 81, 2 and 3; Ia IIae, 22 and 23.

ARNOLD, MAGDA B. "The Status of Emotion in Contemporary Psychology," in A. A. Roback (Ed.), *Present-day Psychology*. New York: Philosophical Library, 1955. Pp. 135–188.

ARNOLD, MAGDA B., & GASSON, J. A. "Feelings and Emotions as Dynamic Factors in Personality Integration," in M. B. Arnold & J. A. Gasson (Eds.), *The Human Person*. New York: Ronald, 1954.

BAKER, RICHARD D. *The Thomistic Theory of the Passions and Their Influence on the Will*. South Bend, Ind.: Notre Dame University, 1941.

BRIDGES, KATHERINE M. "A Genetic Theory of Emotions," *J. Genet. Psychol.*, 1930, 37:514–527.

CANNON, WALTER B. *Bodily Changes in Pain, Hunger, Fear and Rage.* (2d Ed.) New York: Appleton-Century-Crofts, 1929.

CANNON, WALTER B. *The Wisdom of the Body.* (2d Ed.) New York: Norton, 1939.

DUNBAR, H. FLANDERS. *Emotions and Bodily Changes.* (4th Ed.) New York: Columbia University Press, 1954.

EYMIEU, ANTONIN, S.J. *Le Gouvernement de soi-même.* Vol. I. *Les Grandes lois.* Paris: Perrin, 1925.

FEIFEL, HERMAN, and others. "Symposium on Relationships Between Religion and Mental Health," *Amer. Psychologist*, 1958, 13:565–579.

FRANK, LAWRENCE K. *Feelings and Emotions.* New York: Doubleday, 1953.

GEMELLI, AGOSTINO. "Orienting Concepts in the Study of Affective States," *J. Nerv. Ment. Dis.*, 1949, 110:198–214, 299–314.

MICHOTTE, ALBERT E. "The Emotions Regarded as Functional Connections," in Martin L. Reymert (Ed.), *Feelings and Emotions*. New York: McGraw-Hill, 1950.

MOORE, THOMAS VERNER. *The Driving Forces of Human Nature and*

Their Adjustment. New York: Grune & Stratton, 1948. Pp. 107–164.

RAPAPORT, DAVID. *Emotions and Memory.* New York: International Universities Press, 1957.

REYMERT, MARTIN L. (Ed.) *Feelings and Emotions: The Wittenburg Symposium.* Worcester: Clark University Press, 1928.

REYMERT, MARTIN L. (Ed.) *Feelings and Emotions: The Mooseheart Symposium.* New York: McGraw-Hill, 1950.

ROYCE, JAMES E., S.J. *Personality and Mental Health.* Milwaukee: Bruce, 1955. Pp. 63–69.

TERRUWE, A. A. A. *Psychopathic Personality and Neurosis.* New York: P. J. Kenedy & Sons, 1958.

WOODWORTH, ROBERT S., & SCHLOSBERG, H. *Experimental Psychology.* (Rev. Ed.) New York: Holt, 1954. Pp. 107–191.

11

VOLITION

Existence and place of the will. Nature of volition. Role of motive. Object of the will. Elicited and commanded acts. Actual, virtual, and habitual voluntariness. The will and other powers of man.

Men have proposed many different theories of motivation to explain human conduct. As in most complex problems which the human mind attacks, there is a grain of truth in every one, for each discovers some one facet of the total picture. They are usually correct in what they assert, and wrong in their denial of other aspects of reality. Thus they are not so much errors as part-truths.

One such theory is the naïve stimulus-response formula of classic *behaviorism*, which would ignore our mental experiences and pattern all human activity after the simple reflex. As an exclusive view, it has long since succumbed to the criticisms of psychologists. The *instinct* theory suffered a similar fate as an exclusive view, since to claim that the sources of all activity are innate is to ignore the importance of learning or conditioning, as well as other factors. *Hedonism* is the theory which holds that all human activity is

175

governed by sensory pleasure. It ignores activity prompted by utility, generosity, and many needs of both self and species, as well as higher goals and motivations. Those versed in clinical or depth psychology are likely to stress very much *unconscious motivation*, and certainly we are unaware of many of the influences within us. The *extreme voluntarist* view would tend to exaggerate the role of choice to the neglect of other motivating and even determining factors. It claims that all man's activity is voluntary, whereas a great deal of it may be reflex, instinctive, governed by sensory attraction or unconscious motivating factors.

Let us try to maintain a balanced view which takes into account all the facts, even though they may appear to be at variance with each other. In asserting that man's behavior is sometimes voluntary, we shall avoid the extreme voluntarist position and give full recognition to other factors. But before we can even begin a discussion of free choice, it is essential that we establish very clearly the nature of the will and the role of motivation in its activity.

THE EXISTENCE OF WILL

We have seen that human appetition can be of two kinds, depending on whether the cognition which evokes it is sensory or rational. Thus the attractive smell of a certain food may elicit a strong tendency of the sensory appetite, while at the same time my intellectual awareness that it will make me sick causes a rational tendency to avoid it. Conversely, the fireman may go into danger motivated by principle, while his senses elicit only repugnance. Not that sense and intellect always evoke contrary appetition: my intellect may tell me that this pleasant-tasting food is also nourishing, or that the intelligent thing to do is avoid this painful object. The important fact is that we can be motivated by non-sensory stimuli such as honor, freedom, or rights, and by intellectual knowledge of sensory objects, as when food is desired precisely because of its nutrition value, i.e., because of qualities known through universal principles. Thus we see evidence of two kinds of human appetition, which can be either antagonistic or complementary.

Will is the power of rational appetition, or the tendency regarding an intellectually known object. Reasoning from the above observations about sensory and rational tendencies, its existence is obvious: if it is a fact that man experiences these activities, he obviously has the power or ability to do so. This power may not always be in operation, and is in potency for many different acts. These facts give ground for concluding the existence of a distinct power whose act is volition, just as intellect is a power whose act is thinking,[1] though neither is a separate substance but only an ability of man. Hence it is not correct to say "the will chooses" but rather "man chooses by means of his will."

The will has a formal object (being as good) distinct from that of the intellect (being as true). Intellect and will are thus distinct potencies, but very intimately related. They also must enjoy the same level of immateriality: if the intellect is spiritual, so is the will. Why? Could not a spiritual intellect act on a material will? Can not a spiritual cause produce a material effect, as in the case of creation? The answer lies in the way that the intellect "acts" on the will. God creates by way of efficient causality, whereas the intellect does not act upon the will efficiently, but precisely by eliciting appetitive acts through motives, and is therefore in the realm of final causality. Their complementary roles flow from the nature of an elicited appetite.

NATURE OF VOLITION

Volition is the general name applied to all activity involving attraction-aversion tendency resulting from intellectual awareness. It may be defined as a conscious tendency regarding an intellectually known object.

Volition or will-activity can be of many different kinds. It may be the simple tending of any appetitive power toward an object known as good; St. Thomas called this simple tending which is the

[1] Factor analysis by R. B. Cattell reveals the existence of a β factor which seems to be will, just as Spearman's G appears to be general intelligence or intellect (Gannon, 1954, pp. 402–403). Snider (1954) also found mathematical evidence for the existence of will, using a different technique.

first act of the will by the name of love, and noted that it is not free but spontaneous. Volition is desire if it regards an object absent or not possessed; it is called enjoyment or complacency if the object is already present and possessed. (Note that the names of some of these states of will are taken from their accompanying emotions.) Volition is called intention if it regards the goal or end, resolution if it regards means, and interest if it is a general disposition to direct activity toward a specific goal. It is choice if it involves selection between various motives. Thus choice is seen to be only one of many acts of the will.

Far from being an uncaused act, choice is seen always to involve two causes: efficient and final. The will itself is an ability by which the human being (the ego or self) exerts efficient causality; but being an elicited appetite, of its very nature it demands also a final cause or purpose for which to act. It is of the nature of the will to act because of a motive.

Motive may be defined here as an object intellectually known as good, serving to attract the will. This is motive in the strict sense of the word as used in Scholastic philosophy, not motivating factors such as organic drives, habitual tendencies, or sensory attraction. The prime importance of motive as a key to understanding the operation of the will is brought out by Lindworsky (1929), and by studies of Communist brain-washing.[2] Without intellectual convictions there can be no decisiveness of will. Only by understanding the role of

---

[2] One authoritative nontechnical report on the subject of brain-washing is that by Maj. William E. Mayer, "Why Did Many GI Captives Cave In?" *U.S. News and World Report*, Feb. 24, 1956, pp. 56–72. An Army psychiatrist, Major Mayer spent four years interviewing brain-washed Americans from the Korean conflict. His report emphasizes that there was no question of physical torture, but rather points to serious weaknesses in Americans' character and shortcomings in their education. His whole report accords well with the Scholastic teaching on choice and the importance of motives. A similar view using different sources is presented by Eugene Kinkead, "A Reporter at Large: The Study of Something New in History," *The New Yorker*, Oct. 26, 1957, pp. 102–153. Like Mayer, he points out that steadfast choice requires intellectual convictions about the truths of democracy and ". . . adherence to religious beliefs. Many of the men said that in prison camps these intangibles were of greater help to them than anything else. Now, much more than in the past, such things bulk large in Army training" (p. 152).

motive in the will-act can one avoid needless misunderstanding when we come to the question of free choice.

OBJECT OF WILL

The technical terms material and formal object can apply to the motives which serve as objects of the will in a manner analogous to the way these terms were used with regard to the object of knowledge. Thus the material object is that which attracts the will, and the formal object is the particular aspect under which it attracts.

The *material* object of the will can be any being, since every being has some ontological good. This good may be material (physical) or spiritual, particular or universal. Thus the motive for the will may be the good of a dinner, a particular right, the democratic ideal of justice for all, or God Himself. It may be a pleasurable good such as smoking, a useful good such as coffee to keep me awake while studying, or it may be a good sought for its own proper and intrinsic worth (*bonum honestum*).

The *formal* object of the will is always some intellectually known aspect of goodness. The formal object of the will is goodness in general, regardless of how it is realized in the particular good of any of its material objects. It may be only negative, in that the object is "good to avoid." It may be only an apparent good, not a true or moral good: a person's motive for murder may be because it seemed good to him at the time, even though murder in itself may be bad. The object of the intellect is being as ontologically true; as long as it is true that this being contains at least apparent goodness, the intellect can present it to the will under its formal object of goodness in general.

It is quite clear from the foregoing that the will is never free with regard to the goodness in general, since its very nature is to tend toward the good. It is naturally determined to seek the good. Even the person who wants to be miserable is not seeking misery precisely in so far as it is not good, but because he mistakenly looks upon it as a means to happiness. Similarly, the suicide does not seek nonbeing as such, but rather avoidance of trouble, and this nonbeing appears to him as being-without-trouble.

ELICITED AND COMMANDED ACTS

Elicited acts or volitions are activities taking place in the will itself. They may be of many kinds, such as desire, complacency, choice. It is with these acts of the will itself that we are primarily concerned in this chapter.

Commanded acts are those voluntary acts which are commanded by the will but executed by some power other than the will. Thus if I choose to lift a 300-pound weight, I do not choose with my muscles nor lift with my will. Moreover, the will may command but the muscles be unable to obey. The execution is clearly a matter of physics and only my intention is a matter of choice. The will may command acts of almost any of our other operative powers: I may voluntarily conjure up certain images in my imagination, direct the attention of my special senses, willingly think about a certain topic, or move this pencil about the table. All of these are voluntary acts if done under the command of the will. As in the case of the 300-pound weight, the command is not always obeyed. I may choose to entertain only certain images, but be disappointed in the execution of this resolve because of the spontaneous activity of imagination not under my control.

This distinction between choice and execution is strikingly illustrated by some work in experimental neurosurgery done by Wilder Penfield at McGill University in Montreal. Keeping the patient conscious and using only a local anesthetic to enter the cranium, the surgeon was able to stimulate directly the motor centers of the cortex. Thus by touching a certain point he would cause the patient's left foot to rise. The patient, being fully conscious, was then instructed not to raise his foot. In spite of his best efforts, the foot would come up. But his insistence that he did not want it to brought out clearly the distinction between the voluntary choice and the involuntary movement. No stimulus made him *want* to.

Both elicited and commanded acts may be called *voluntary*, since this word refers to any act flowing from the will in any way. Note that the words "voluntary" and "willingly" are often used in popular speech as synonymous with "free." Actually, some volitions elicited in the will are quite spontaneous and not free, though technically voluntary since elicited by the will. Again, an act which is the result of a previous choice or voluntary habit may be called a voluntary act to the extent that it flows from the will, even though it is not free at the time. For example, the driver may not be actually choosing to speed at the moment of a crash, yet his fatal speed may be voluntary in virtue of a prior decision to speed or a culpable habit of speeding.

Voluntary acts must therefore be distinguished into those that are *actually* voluntary, *virtually* voluntary, and *habitually* voluntary. The first are those in which the operative power executes a choice under the present influence of an actual volition. For example, I choose to pick up this pencil and do so while choosing. An act is virtually voluntary if it happens in virtue of a previous act of choice which has ceased to exist in the will at the time it is being executed. For instance, if I am walking downtown to buy some shoes, my walking shows the influence of the previous decision, even though I may have long since ceased to be actually choosing to purchase shoes and am now thinking about something else entirely. Lastly, my motive may be habitual, and I may perform an act without any new act of choice, but it will still be a voluntary act to the extent that the habit was built up voluntarily.

Failure to make these necessary distinctions accounts for much of the confusion which arose over early attempts to study freedom of choice in the experimental psychology laboratory. Experimenters looked in vain for an act of choice during the experiment, but there was none. The choice was made at the time the person agreed to do the experiment or accepted the instructions; what happened during the experiment followed in virtue of this previous choice and did not involve a new act of the will. A great deal of what is discussed under the term "set" belongs in the category of the virtual or habitual voluntary.

THE WILL AND OTHER POWERS

Voluntary Control. The will can normally exercise some control over man's other activities, depending on their nature. The vegetative processes can be influenced only indirectly; for example, growth by regulating the intake of food, or heartbeat by controlling physical or emotional stimuli. Sensory and rational cognitive powers naturally tend to their acts, but will can often control the conditions of their operation, and direct their attention to this or that object. I can decide to look or not to look, to think of this or of that, since these are all good and hence within the formal object of the will. This voluntary attention becomes the key to what control we have over the sense appetites, which are quite spontaneous, as we saw when discussing emotion. I cannot control the fact that a certain object evokes desire, but I can usually conjure up other images, or direct my attention to opposing motives and thereby dominate its attraction.

Lastly, over voluntary musculature I normally have direct control, so that I can move my hand at will. This seems to be accomplished largely by the will's control over the imagination, wherein my decision is translated into motor images which being sensory have a neurological basis, apparently in the motor centers of the cerebral cortex. Some materialists have mistaken these for volition itself, just as the sensists confused thought and its accompanying images. Actually, motor images are not the initiators of all action, but merely the sense-level intermediary between choice and its execution through voluntary muscles. Others noted that choice involved slight movement of the muscles of the right arm, as if stretching out in an "I take this one" gesture, and concluded that this muscle twitch *is* choice, instead of its incipient execution.

Action of Other Powers on Will. Since the nature of the will as an elicited appetite means that it can be influenced only through final causality (motive), there is no question of any efficient cause (except God) moving the will. The question is whether other powers can influence the will through motivation, and how.

The influence of the intellect is plainly paramount. But since the rational intellect is so intimately bound up with sensory knowledge, it is not surprising that imagination and the other senses can thus indirectly affect the will by vivid presentation of attractive goods. Moreover, we stressed in Chapter 5 how subjective factors can distort or enhance perception and imagination. Drive and emotion can shift our attention to other aspects of a situation, as when hunger causes one to consider only the desirability of stealing, or pride gives us a false picture of our own importance as a motive. Since intellect originally sees the situation as a mixture of conflicting aspects, a person can usually determine whether or not he has allowed emotion so to channel his thought, which is why we speak of a man *yielding* to temptation.

Summary

In this chapter we have seen that there exists in man a power of rational appetency distinct from sensory appetite on the one hand and from intellect on the other. We have seen that its nature is to tend toward the intellectually known good and hence the presence of a motive is absolutely indispensible for its operation. We have seen that it is naturally determined toward the good in general, and that its first act regarding an object presented simply as good without qualification is a spontaneous tending which is not free. The next chapter will be devoted to the problem of whether all of man's acts are necessarily determined, or whether he is capable of self-determination or free choice.

REVIEW QUESTIONS

1. Define will, volition, motive.
2. How do you know that the will exists? Is it a "thing"?
3. Is a commanded act voluntary? Is it a volition?
4. Is volition without a motive possible?
5. Is an unconscious motive possible? Explain.
6. In cognition, we find cooperation between the sensory and intellectual levels; is this always true in appetition?
7. Is man the only irrational animal? Explain.

8. "Freedom is nonsense, as there are many things I am not free to do, such as running 100 miles an hour." (See Thomas Aquinas, *S. T.*, Ia, 81, 3 ad 2um; 83, 1 ad 4um; Ia IIae, 6, 4; 13, 5.)
9. "Will is the power of free choice." Is this a good definition? Why?
10. "Will is a power of tending with regard to a known good." Is this a good definition? Why?
11. "Harry was so drunk he didn't know what he was doing, so he was not responsible." Was he? Why? Was he free? Can one be responsible for an act even though not free at the time? How?
12. Are all acts of the will choices? Are all acts of the will voluntary? Is every volition a choice? Is every free act a volition?
13. "I just can't help disliking spinach; it nauseates me, in spite of myself. Obviously I have no free choice about it." Discuss. (See Thomas Aquinas, *S. T.*, Ia, 83, 1 ad 1um and ad 5um; Ia IIae, 6, 7 ad 2um; 10, 3; 77, 7.)
14. "If the will is free, then all education, training, and psychotherapy are in vain, since free will could go contrary to them. Either they are useless, or the will is not free." It this reasoning correct? (See *S. T.*, Ia IIae, 9, 2.)
15. Can desire be either sensory or rational? Can an impulse be either sensory or rational?

FOR FURTHER READING

AQUINAS, ST. THOMAS. *Summa Theol.*, Ia, 59, 1; 80, 2; esp. 82 entire; Ia IIae, 8–17. *Truth*, 22, 3–4; 24, 1.

AVELING, F. *Personality and Will.* New York: Appleton, 1931.

EYMIEU, ANTONIN, S.J. *Le Gouvernement de soi-même.* Vol. III. *L'Art de vouloir.* Paris: Perrin, 1935.

GILSON, ETIENNE. *The Spirit of Medieval Philosophy.* New York: Scribner, 1936. Chap. XIV.

LINDWORSKY, JOHANNES, S.J. *The Psychology of Asceticism.* London: Edwards, 1936.

LINDWORSKY, JOHANNES, S.J. *The Training of the Will.* Milwaukee: Bruce, 1929.

MCCARTHY, RAPHAEL C., S.J. *The Measurement of Conation.* Chicago: Loyola University Press, 1926.

MOORE, THOMAS VERNER. *The Driving Forces of Human Nature and Their Adjustment.* New York: Grune & Stratton, 1948. Part VI.

MOORE, THOMAS VERNER. *Dynamic Psychology.* Philadelphia: Lippincott, 1926. Parts IV, V.

O'CONNOR, WILLIAM R. *The Eternal Quest*. New York: Longmans, 1947.

O'CONNOR, WILLIAM R. *The Natural Desire for God*. Milwaukee: Marquette University Press, 1948.

SULLIVAN, ROBERT P., O.P. "Man's Thirst for Good," *Thomistic Stud.*, No. 4. Westminster, Md.: Newman, 1952.

SULLIVAN, ROBERT P., O.P. *The Thomistic Concept of the Natural Necessitation of the Human Will*. River Forest, Ill.: Pontifical Faculty of Philosophy, 1952.

12

FREE CHOICE AND ITS LIMITS

Three views: exaggerated indeterminism, determinism, and freedom of choice within limits. Kinds of freedom. Limits of freedom. Deliberation: roles of intellect and will. Three proofs of free choice. Freedom and scientific psychology. Objections against free choice.

Is man the hopeless and helpless victim of forces that surround him? The tail wagged by heredity, or the mirror of environment? This problem is one of the most crucial in all philosophy. Either man is to some extent the master of his own destiny, or he is a mere chip being tossed about on life's ocean. Either he is a responsible agent with the corresponding rights and duties, or our entire system of law must be reexamined. Because it is the crucial question with regard to the determinants of human behavior, it is of paramount interest to philosopher, psychologist, sociologist, and political theorist. Perhaps here more than on any other question the interests of philosophy and psychology overlap; certainly more so than on the question of the soul which is a purely philosophical one of no interest to the scientific psychologist as such.

186

THREE VIEWS

Because one finds some psychologists stating flatly that there is no such "thing" as "free will" while outstanding psychologists speak quite frankly of free choice and self-determination, one suspects immediately that the issue may be clouded by unfortunate historical developments and lack of agreement on the meaning of terms. We must be careful to dissect out the true issue and get at facts rather than mere words. Scholastic philosophers were probably overly suspicious of the new science of psychology and its talk of stimulus-response and unconscious motivation. Scientific psychologists were equally suspicious of talk about independence of motives and freedom from the laws of physical causality. Perhaps we can set the stage for an intelligent evaluation of the problem by first considering two extreme theoretical positions.

Exaggerated Indeterminism

Perhaps the worst enemies of free choice are those who insist too much on it—not the determinists but the exaggerated indeterminists, the adherents of the theory of unmotivated behavior. Though they would deny it formally, there have been men who talked as if they held that *all* men's actions are free, ignoring the fact that in one's ordinary waking day one may be carried along for some time by the force of habit, organic drives, natural preference, sensory attraction, and other determinants, without making an act of choice every minute. "Let us have faith in the wonderful powers of the will; but let us believe also that it is the part of wisdom to recognize well and appreciate the organic impulses," quotes Père Eymieu, S.J., approvingly (1925, I, p. 293). He warns that, though the soul which has this power of willing is spiritual, "whatever is received is received according to the manner of the recipient"—the soul is doing its work in a material body, so let us face the facts, he urges, without surprise or scandal (p. 295).

Again, there are those who seem to hold that at least in those deliberate acts which are free, *all* the motives are known to us. Now even in these acts, a certain portion of the motives are unknown to us, though we may be vaguely conscious of the influence they exert. We are not always as free as we think. This is not entirely the discovery of modern depth psychology. The Fathers of the Desert and medieval writers on asceticism certainly acknowledged the powerful pull which subconscious motivation and the lower appetites can have on the will, and were amazingly aware of the subtleties of compensation and rationalization. Tanquery (n. 781) in speaking of the mortification of our thoughts speaks of "a sort of psychological determinism." Full of pride in our intellect, we invent rational explanations for many actions which stem from baser motivation, just as the man who, under the influence of posthypnotic suggestion, picks up a chair and puts it in the middle of the table will explain, when asked why he did so, that he wanted to see something on the floor, and so moved the chair out of the way, being entirely unaware of the unconscious influence under which he acted. It is only by recognizing such facts that one can hope to defend free choice intelligently. To exaggerate the extent of our liberty is to make the doctrine untenable. It is to wield the battle-ax so strenuously that we cut our own throats.

Moreover, we have already seen that in some senses the will is naturally determined. Its nature is to tend toward the good in general, and it cannot be indifferent with regard to goodness itself. When we are presented with a good simply, without any alternatives (even the alternative of rejecting it), we have no choice.

The term "free will" has unfortunately come to mean this exaggerated indeterminism in the minds of many writers. They rightly criticize the tendency to ignore the important influence of factors which limit freedom: emotion, habit, the natural preference which comes from spontaneous likes and dislikes, external stimuli, organic drives, and physiological conditions. It is interesting to note that St. Thomas discussed these factors very thoroughly through many pages. This has been missed by some superficial modern critics, who looked in vain for such discussion in what they would call his "psychology" in Part I*a* of the *Summa*, when it actually appears in the I*a* II*ae*, which they would call his "ethics," though he, of course, knew nothing of such post-Wolffian divisions.

Another misconception which might be listed under this heading is that which makes the will out to be some supernatural force. Thus, we read in a discussion of the determinants of human behavior the misleading aside that "some believe in a causal sequence with an intervening supernatural power." [1] It is against this conception of will held by some psychologists that P. Mullahy reacts when he insists that "a naturalistic conception is possible in which these acts are as much a matter of observation as is anything else. They operate according to determined principles. Insofar as man lives in accordance with the natural conditions under which willing and choosing occur, he is free." [2] The question here is whether choice-making is a natural ability. Any appeal to an intervening supernatural power takes us outside the realm of both philosophy and science. Even though one's philosophy may leave open the possibility of the supernatural, we are concerned here precisely with the nature of man as revealed by analysis of his operations and abilities.

Lastly, free will symbolizes to many psychologists the doctrine of unmotivated and therefore uncaused behavior. This misinterpretation is illustrated, for instance, by the insistence of Fryer and Henry, (An Outline of General Psychology, p. 10), that "pyschological events have a cause. This statement may be made for all the sciences. It is called universal determinism. . . . Freedom of action in the sense of causelessness is an empty concept. . . . Uncaused action is a notion of the unthinking man. . . . There are as many varieties of beliefs in uncaused action as there are pickles. All are unscientific. . . . Every event has a cause."

Early experimenters asked the subject to choose between two colored liquids "for no reason." It is no wonder that D. O. Hebb states (1958, p. 63) that "free will for many workers meant that voluntary behavior was not subject to scientific law, not determined by cause

---

[1] Douglas Fryer & Edwin Henry, An Outline of General Psychology, 3d ed. (New York: Barnes and Noble, 1950), p. 10.
[2] Psychiatry, 1949, 12:379–386.

and effect." Again, a survey on free will in the light of experimental psychology and modern science is summed up by R. Piret: "From a general review of experimental works on the will, the author concludes that there is such a thing as physical freedom and moral liberty (freedom of low instincts and inferior tendencies), also psychological freedom (freedom of choice conditioned by motives and drives); but there is no metaphysical liberty or free will, that is to say choice independent of motives and drives. Will is, therefore, not independent of all causality. It is determinism that is right." [3] The unhappy inference in the last two sentences will be examined shortly.

It is important to realize that for some the word "will" has come to have this meaning of a magic, supernatural "thing" contrary to the laws of causality, if we are to understand why some psychologists object so strongly to the word. Otherwise it would seem ridiculous, for instance, that Boring, Langfeld, and Weld (1948, p. 50) can spend pages describing human activity involving choice, decisions and self-determination, and end with the statement that "there is a 'willing' but not a 'will.'" Presumably these learned gentlemen would not be guilty of the absurdity that man performs certain activities but does not have the power of doing so.

The validity of the principle of causality is established elsewhere. Even those scientists whose positivistic philosophy might lead them to consider causality a mere assumption do in actual practice base their scientific logic at least reductively on causality. Every activity of a creature demands a cause, either inside or outside himself. On this most philosophers and scientists agree.

It is preposterous to imagine that any Scholastic philosopher could have held action without cause or motive as a legitimate meaning of free will. If for no other reason, he could hardly deny the principle of causality here when he based his whole case from reason for the existence of God upon it. One will look in vain for any assertion of uncaused activity among the Scholastic philos-

---

[3] N. Braunshausen, "Le libre-arbitre à la lumière de la psychologie expérimentale et de la science moderne," *Revue des Sciences Pédagogiques*, 1947, 9:38–46 (*Psychol. Abstr.*, 1950, 24:1032).

ophers, who have been the principal systematic proponents of the doctrine of free choice.[4]

It even seems doubtful if any respectable proponent of free choice actually held for action without motive. We have already seen that the very nature of the will as an elicited appetite demands motive as a necessary condition for its operation. This motive is a final cause, and the will itself is not some mysterious entity but simply the ability or power man has to exercise efficient causality in response to such motivation. Thus, rather than a lack of causality, there is an abundance of it in the act of choice. If it is a fact that man makes choices, then it is a fact that he has the power or ability to do so. This is all that is meant by will.

Determinism

Determinism, too, is an ambiguous word. As opposed to the above doctrine of uncaused behavior, determinism can mean simply the assertion that every event has a cause. With this interpretation we have no quarrel.

Determinism, however, usually means something more. It is a denial that man has the power of self-determination or free choice. It means that all of his activity is determined by forces either outside or within himself over which he has no control. In brief, it holds not only that all human behavior requires an adequate cause but that every cause is a necessitating cause. According to this view, motives do not merely attract, they determine. It is not I who determine whether or not I yield to the attraction of this or that motive. Motivating forces not only influence us, they force us. It denies that the ego or self may be the efficient cause which selects or determines whether or not I yield to the attraction of this or that motive. Determinism takes several different forms.

1. *Physical determinism.* The first type of determinism claims that the only cause for activity is a physical stimulus evoking a

[4] D. O. Hebb, in a personal communication to the author, states that in the passage cited he "had in mind members of the English neurological school, who seem never to have recovered from the philosophy of the nineteenth century." These can hardly be considered representative exponents of the doctrine of free choice.

physical and automatic response. This notion appears in certain mechanistic philosophies and in the reflexology of early behaviorism, with its simple S–R formula. This formula would reduce psychology to physics or physiology.

2. *Psychological determinism.* Psychologists have long recognized that except in the case of the simple reflex there are "intervening variables" between stimulus and response. Hence the formula S-O-R, where O stands for something within the organism besides the stimulus which must be taken into account to explain a response. Psychic determinism says these intervening variables (images, thoughts, feelings, dispositions, and habits) wholly determine the course of our action. According to this theory, if one knew all the previous and present mental states, conscious and unconscious influences, one could predict with infallible certainty any behavior. One form of psychic determinism says that behavior is totally determined by motor images. Another form stresses unconscious motivating factors. According to this, we have the illusion of freedom but we are actually determined by forces of which we are unaware. Lastly, the most subtle form of psychic determinism is that which asserts that man always chooses what appears to be the greater good. This is ambiguous, for it can be simply another way of saying that the object of the will is good; we would never choose anything precisely because it is non-good or less good. The real question is not whether this appears to be a greater good, but whether it is a necessitating good. Otherwise the theory is simply a reassertion of the primacy of motives in volition, a commonplace in all theory of training, education, and psychotherapy.

3. *Theological determinism.* This view holds that God's cooperation determines the will-act.

Moderate Indeterminism

Faced with the dilemma of having only exaggerated indeterminism and determinism as alternatives, which side would one take? This seems to have been the situation for the psychologist of the early twentieth century. Knowing no third possibility, and rightly insisting on the necessity of a cause for every act, rejection of exaggerated indeterminism and acceptance of determinism seemed to be the only course holding scientific respectability. Unfortunately, he not only missed the possibility of a third alternative in this false dilemma, but he erroneously equated the first alternative with free will. If that is what the expression means, we too must reject free will. And if there is no alternative, "It is determinism that is right."

The theory proposed here is called moderate indeterminism, to distinguish it from the other two possibilities. It is called the doctrine of free choice rather than free will, since it is the act of choice which is free; still better, *man* is free in his act of choice. It is called self-determination because, in contrast to the theory of uncaused act, it insists that the self is a true cause, while in contrast to the determinists, it insists that under proper conditions man determines his own choice rather than being determined wholly by internal or external influences.

Moderate indeterminism recognizes the influence of motives, but they do not always determine. There must be adequate motive, but not every sufficient cause is a necessitating cause. The ego or self is the cause which determines which motive shall prevail. The question is not whether motives attract, or whether one motive is greater or weaker than another, but whether the motive necessitates me. In other words, do I have to do something just because I have sufficient reason for doing it? Recognizing the importance of both heredity and environment, moderate indeterminism holds that we can still determine to some extent what we do with heredity and how we react to environment. The adequate cause of human behavior must include the entire phenomenological field of the behaving organism, including the agent himself.[5]

Thus the dilemma of having to choose one or the other of the first two doctrines proposed above turns out to be a false one, solved by this third alternative. As we shall see later, this view is more and more being adopted by recent psychologists. The happy solution is well stated by Combs and Snygg:

[5] C. M. Louttit, *Psychol. Bull.*, 1950, 47:170–171.

This gives us a view of man neither so completely responsible for his behavior as the first view we have cited above, nor on the other hand so willy-nilly at the mercy of his environment as the second would lead us to believe. He is part controlled by and in part controlling of his destiny. It provides us with an understanding of man deeply and intimately affected by his environment but capable also of molding and shaping his destiny in important ways. Such a view fits more closely our own experience and is an understanding broadly significant in helping us find solutions to some of our great social problems. (1959, p. 310)

In summary, moderate indeterminism states that we must have an adequate cause, both final (motive) and efficient (ability to choose). It states that choice is always limited by the limitations of our knowledge, because of the need for motivation. The execution of choice is always limited by the laws of physics. Having cleared the ground of misunderstandings, we are now in a position to state the doctrine of free choice and examine the arguments for and against it.

NATURE AND KINDS OF FREEDOM

Freedom in general means the absence of coercion or necessitation. It does not mean lack of influences, but only that these influences do not force me.

But we must be careful not to define freedom only in a negative fashion, as if it were merely a lack of something. Free choice is self-in-action, a positive force rather than a mere absence of forces. Rather than lack of determination, it is self-determination. It is a positive power of selection between influences rather than the absence of all influences. Putting it metaphysically, freedom is the property of a being *in act*. Since whatever moves must be moved by something in act, self-determination demands that the self be in act to the extent that it determines its own conduct.

This is all-important because a common objection against free choice is based on the fact that we are not always aware of all of the influences at work upon us at a given time. The implication is that if we knew this or that unconscious or organic motivating factor, our conduct would be explainable by that cause and free choice would be negated. Actually, establishment of free choice does not depend upon the complete enumeration of all causal influences. Even the most astute psychiatrist might be unable to render account of all his likes and dislikes, his habits, organic tensions, memories, and vague desires. Free choice is not a denial that these things exist; it is a positive causal influence in addition. It is not necessary for the normal person to know all the various factors that might be impelling him in order for him to behave himself. I may not know why I feel like hitting the person, but normally I can choose not to hit him. The attraction is there, but I determine whether or not I yield to its influence, regardless of whether I understand it. I may resist the inclination in spite of not knowing its origin, its precise object, or its connection with previous experience. Otherwise the simplest act of self-control would demand a complete psychiatric history.[6]

Necessity

Freedom is the opposite of necessity. *Necessity* means that a being must be what it is and cannot be otherwise. Necessity is sometimes divided into antecedent and consequent. Consequent necessity is really just another way of saying that you cannot turn time backwards, or a restatement of the principle of noncontradiction. Once I have chosen, it is necessarily true as an historical fact that I have chosen. I may change my mind, but this is another choice, and does not alter the fact that the previous choice was made. This need not concern us here. Antecedent necessity is what must be eliminated if we are to establish freedom of choice.

Antecedent or predetermining necessity is subdivided into extrinsic and intrinsic. *Extrinsic* necessity, or coercion, is that imposed by an efficient cause. For instance, if the hammer drives the nail with sufficient force, it necessarily goes into the wood. Antecedent extrinsic necessity, or coercion, is the opposite of spontaneity. An action is spontaneous if it flows from the agent without being forced

⁶ Cf. Charles Odier, "Les Deux Sources, Consciente et Inconsciente, de la Vie Morale," *Cahiers de Philosophie*, November, 1943–February, 1947 (Neuchatel: Editions de la Baconnierc).

by an external efficient cause or constrained by external forces. The growth of organisms and the movement of animals enjoy this spontaneity, which is freedom only in an improper sense.

Intrinsic antecedent necessity means that something in the internal nature of a thing makes it act one way rather than another. This necessity may be metaphysical or absolute, as that a triangle must necessarily have three sides, or it may be physical or relative, as that acorns produce oak trees and not pine trees. Again, the mere lack of intrinsic necessity is not freedom in the full sense, but only contingence or passive possibility, since these terms do not exclude extrinsic necessity. Movement of subatomic particles or falling bodies may be contingent, but it is not free of extrinsic determination. Mere passive possibility is again freedom only improperly, as when we say that the billiard ball is free to move either right or left. What we mean is that it is free to *be* moved, and this is a far cry from the active power of self-determination which we attribute to the will. It implies lack of act. The difference might be summed up by saying that it is a matter of "not able to do" rather than "able not to do."

Freedom

Freedom in the proper sense means a lack of both extrinsic and intrinsic antecedent necessity. It means first that will enjoys the spontaneity of any elicited appetite, which cannot be coerced against its inclination by any external efficient cause. This does not mean that the will-act lacks cause, but simply that the will as an active operative power is the efficient cause of the act. As such, it is the property of a being in act, since whatever moves is moved by something in act. It is not a mere passive possibility for being moved.

Freedom of choice also means lack of intrinsic necessity. Besides not being subject to external coercion, in the act of choice the will is not necessitated by anything within itself. This is the opposite of psychological determinism. It means that choice is based upon indifferent motives, goods apprehended as adequate but nonnecessary final causes for action. Here again freedom does not consist in a lack of motives, but in a lack of necessity.

Freedom of choice, then, means self-determination in act, or that the ego has dominion over its own acts. This means that when confronted with a good seen as contingent or indifferent, and all other necessary conditions for action are fulfilled, I can determine whether or not I yield to the attraction of this motive. I am not determined by intrinsic or extrinsic necessity. (The expression "I am determined" is ambiguous, since it can mean either that I am necessitated by certain influences or that I have chosen firmly and intend to carry through.)

Other Kinds of Freedom. Freedom of choice or psychological freedom as just defined must be clearly distinguished from other kinds of freedom which are not the issue. (1) Physical freedom would mean immunity from the laws of physics. In the execution of his commanded voluntary act, man is obviously not free in this sense, as in the case of the 300-pound weight. A man bound in iron chains is not free to move about. (2) Moral freedom would mean that man was not under the obligation of moral law. Freedom of choice is neatly distinguished from this concept by the phrase, "I can (am able), but I may not (am not permitted)." (3) Political or social freedom refers to conditions within the framework of society in which we can exercise our human rights such as free speech, conscience, or property ownership.

Lastly, freedom of choice must be divided into freedom of exercise and freedom of specification. *Freedom of exercise* or contradiction refers to the power to do or not to do, i.e., the case in which the only alternative is not to act. *Freedom of specification* is the power of choosing one of two or more alternatives, i.e., between different objects. I am free to choose to go to Chicago or not (order of exercise), and I may choose to go by bus, plane, or train (order of specification). Freedom of exercise is the fundamental one, for at the very least I must be able not to act. If there is only one means to the end, I have no freedom of specification between alternative means, but am reduced to the order of exercise. Here choice of the end is necessarily bound up with this unique means, which I can reject by rejecting the end. It is irrelevant whether or not I am correct in seeing this as the only means: from the nature of an elicited appetite it is clear that I can only choose between known alternatives, so that the extent of my choice depends on my actual thinking regardless of its correctness.

If I am faced with the choice of specifying between objects which are opposed as moral good and evil, the possibility of choice is called *freedom of contrariety*. This is by no means essential to the notion of freedom; our examples have not involved moral choices. It is even a defect of freedom, or at least an imperfect freedom. Better than none at all, it puts man at the top of the visible universe, but places him at the lowest level of will, just as his rational intellect is lowest among intellects. Far from being the essence of freedom, to be faced with the need to choose between good and sin is an unfortunate consequence of our present condition, in which we are not free from the attractions of false goods and the danger of sensory factors swaying our judgment. True freedom means self-determination and mastery of one's acts, whereas freedom of contrariety always involves the possibility of acting contrary to reason and yielding to the attraction of false goods. God, and those souls and angels who enjoy the beatific vision, theologians tell us, are free from this dangerous kind of freedom. Freedom is the power of choosing between *eligible* goods: in the beatific vision one still has this power, but God is seen in such a way that nothing incompatible with His friendship is seen as an eligible good. Sin is impossible to such beings, not because they lack self-mastery, but because they know too much.[7]

LIMITS OF FREEDOM

Moderate indeterminism does not claim that man is free in all of his acts, nor fully free even in his choices. The limitations of free choice will be better understood if we consider four possible situations in which a good is presented by the intellect as an object for the will (see figure 10).

[7] Jacques Maritain, *Freedom in the Modern World* (New York: Scribner, 1936) develops this thought, at first shocking to the novice philosopher with his limited ideas of freedom. See Thomas Aquinas, *Truth*, 22, 6; S. T., Ia, 59, 3 ad 2um; 62, 8 ad 3um.

1. If any finite or limited good is presented by the intellect to the will correctly, this good obviously does not occupy the entire scope of the will, whose capacity extends to the universal good or good in general. Just as the object of the intellect is being as knowable, and the intellect is not limited to any particular truth, so the will has as its object being as desirable, and is not limited to any particular good. Nothing less than an infinite good can fill the entire horizon, so to speak, of will-activity. Any other good always has an aspect of non-good which leaves open the possibility that the will may divert

Figure 10

Four Possible Relations of Will and Object

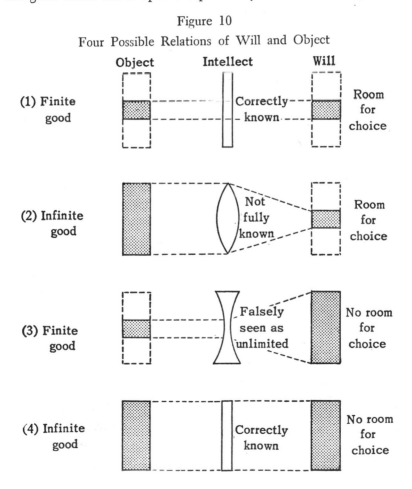

the attention of the intellect to some other good, or at least to the possibility that there are other goods and hence that this particular one is not necessary. Therefore the presentation of any particular good by the intellect always leaves room in the will for choice, for the intellect can always advert to the limitations of this good and consider the possibility of not choosing it. The function of the intellect is to discern truth; if one sees some finite good as unlimited in goodness and in no way rejectable, the intellect is not telling the truth about that object.

2. The second possibility is when the Infinite Good Itself is known, but in the indirect and imperfect way which we have described as natural for the rational intellect which must operate through sense. I may know *that* God is infinitely good, but in this life I do not see him *as* infinitely good. God as known in this life does not fill the whole horizon and leaves open the possibility of diverting our attention to some good incompatible with His friendship. This makes a choice possible and explains how sin can happen.

Sin is possible ultimately because the created intellect is objectively infinite, subjectively finite: capable of knowing God, but incapable (unaided by a supernatural gift) of knowing Him adequately. Without the objective capacity, there would be no sin but only ignorance or error; without the subjective limitations, we would not be left open to choices contrary to our best knowledge. Sin is an act of the whole man, not just of his will. The words "Ye shall be as Gods" and the name of Lucifer's conqueror Michael (which means "Who is like to God?") suggest that the sins of the angels and our first parents were due to their ability to conceive (and therefore "become") God. The angels sinned before they had the beatific vision.

3. A third possibility is that some finite good may be falsely seen by the intellect as unlimited, and hence filling the entire scope of the will. This would leave no room for choice. If something so distorts the picture that I cannot conceive of this good as rejectable in any way, and cannot even consider the possibility of rejecting it, I am not free. This could happen when the intellect

is clouded by strong emotion, sleep, alcohol or other drugs, certain mental disorders, brain injury, or perhaps sheer distraction or inadvertence. In any of these cases (though not always, e.g., not in every strong emotion) it may be that there are not two alternatives. The object is seen as unqualified good, with no room for any other consideration. In such a case there is no free choice.

It is obvious, however, that the intellect here is not functioning in accordance with its nature, which is to tell the truth about this object and present it to the will as finite, limited, and therefore rejectable. The will is not free because the intellect is impeded from doing its job. No deliberation between alternatives is possible, or at least freedom is diminished to the extent that such deliberation is impeded.

4. Lastly, we have the case of the beatific vision, in which the theologians tell us that the infinite goodness of God is known directly and intuitively as infinite. Here again there is no choice, for the scope of the will is completely occupied by the infinite object which fills its entire range. It cannot direct the attention of the intellect to any aspect of non-good.

Put technically, all this means that we have freedom of specification with regard to contingent means toward an end, but not with regard to happiness or the perfect good. Toward the latter I have freedom of exercise as long as I can abstain from considering it and consequently cease to will it.

DELIBERATION

From this it is clear that deliberation is a necessary prelude to choice. In the first presentation of any object to the will as good, before there is any question of whether or not it is limited and therefore rejectable, the natural and spontaneous inclination of the will is toward that good. But as a matter of fact we do not always choose everything which occurs to us. Normally, we can consider the possibility of an alternative, at least the alternative of rejecting it. In the third case given above, where various factors eliminated this possibility, it was because the intellect was not functioning properly. Hence a drug which "destroys free choice" really only eliminates the necessary condition for the exercise of choice, by interfering with the intellect's ability to consider alternatives.

The process may become extremely complex and involved, or on the other hand may not explicitly take even the complete form we have depicted in our analysis. Deliberation may demand in some instances no more than intuitive judgment, with implicit alternative.

Speculative and Practical Judgments. We must distinguish between judgments in the speculative order, where the intellect can sometimes achieve necessary truth, and practical judgments about a particular action. Once I understand that two plus two equal four, or that murder is wrong, I cannot judge otherwise. The intellect is forced by the evidence of the truth. But this is speculative; in the practical order, my intellect can never tell me that it is necessarily true that I must *say* two plus two equal four at this time, nor that I cannot murder this man. As long as I can see some aspect of goodness in the act, I can choose to say that two plus two equal five, or commit murder. The truth of the speculative judgments may be necessary, but when I get right down to the last practical judgment of what I am going to do here and now, the intellect can see alternative aspects of goodness and hence can only judge that this course of action is good but not necessary. ("Practical" here does not refer to practicality or feasibility, but merely to consent or the decision to put an idea into practice.)

Roles of Intellect and Will

Choice is seen as an activity of *man*, utilizing the powers both of intellect and will. Freedom resides formally in the act of choice, but we have seen that its foundation is in the unlimited scope of the intellect.[8] When functioning in accordance with its nature, it presents indifferent practical judgments which leave the will un-

---

[8] Thomas Aquinas, S. T., Ia IIae, 6, 2 ad 2um; 17, 1 ad 2um; C. G., II, 23, last argument. "Beings are free to the extent that, by their intellectuality, they escape from the determinism of matter," is Dom Lottin's conclusion (1929, p. 159). Again we insist that most difficulties in this matter stem from letting our imaginations make intellect and will out to be little persons rather than mere abilities of the same man.

determined, and free to determine selectively which motive shall prevail.

The intellect is not free, but necessarily knows what it knows. If it knows correctly, it knows the truth about finite goods. If an object is good, it is choosable; if it is finite, it is nonnecessary and rejectable. If the intellect sees the situation as it is, it is not free to judge otherwise, but its judgment leaves the will free.

In any case, the mutually complementary roles of intellect and will escape the charge of mutual causality sometimes brought: "The intellect causes the will to act and the will causes the intellect, so there is a vicious circle." The answer lies in the different kinds of causality exerted. It is true that the intellect causes the will to move by presenting motives or eligible goods. This is the realm of final causality. On the other hand, when these eligible goods are not seen as necessary, the will determines the intellect to the ultimate practical judgment that this one is to be chosen. This is the realm of efficient causality. The will directs the intellect, so to speak, to focus upon this aspect of goodness rather than that. Two efficient causes mutually causing each other would be a vicious circle; but this is not the present case. That would be as if one cripple said to another cripple, "You carry me and I'll carry you." The present situation could be compared to that in which a blind man says to the cripple, "I'll carry you and you tell me where to go." In this case each is a cause of the action, but in different ways: one providing the motion efficiently, the other supplying the goal or final cause.

The will cannot act until the intellect presents motives, but if it presents conflicting motives it leaves the will free to choose between them. The intellect can judge that "this is good to do," or, "I *could* do this," but with regard to a finite good this judgment is always indifferent or changeable by the will. Put differently, about a particular contingent good I never have absolute certainty, but only opinion. The intellect can never say absolutely, "I *will* do this," regarding any good in this life, for there is always the possibility of doing something else or not acting at all. Yet in these cases man does make a choice. The will actively settles this indifference.[9]

[9] Compare Thomas Aquinas in *S. T.*, Ia, 82, 4 and in Ia IIae, 9, 1.

PROOFS OF FREEDOM

Freedom from Extrinsic Necessity

That the will is not subject to coercion by an external efficient cause hardly needs proof. The act of the will is by its very nature an inclination, and coercion means that one is made to act contrary to his inclination. A forced act of will is a contradiction. The only thing which can move the will to act is a motive, and motive is not an efficient cause. The will cannot be forced to elicit its own act. (*S. T.*, Ia, 82, 1.)

Freedom from Internal Necessity

The real problem is the elimination of psychological determinism, or necessitation by the very motives which the intellect presents to the will. Ordinarily three proofs are given. The first is by far the most important, for it flows from an analysis of the relation of intellect and will, and the role of the indifferent judgment in the act of choice. Properly understood, it automatically answers most objections against moderate indeterminism.

1. *From Indifferent Judgments*[10]

(| Will is determined only to the extent that intellect determines it.

(| But intellect does not determine will with regard to finite goods seen as finite.

(| Therefore will is not determined with regard to finite goods seen as such.

The major premise of this proof flows from the fact that will follows intellect: appetition follows cognition, and the inclination of the will must correspond to the intellectual judgments which elicit it.

The minor premise simply examines the nature of the intellectual judgments which the will follows. Finite goods are seen as not good in every respect, and therefore rejectable. Since the intellect is capable of knowing the universal good, it recognizes any particular good as contingent or non-necessitating. I can have adequate reason

[10] Thomas Aquinas, *S. T.*, Ia, 83, 1; *Truth*, 24, 1.

(even God himself as now known) for doing something, but the reason does not tell me that I cannot do otherwise. Therefore I am free to determine whether or not I shall act because of this motive.

This indifferent or undetermined judgment regarding eligible goods is sometimes called changeable, but this is misleading. It suggests that the judgment is a determining motive right now, but that upon further information the judgment might change. This theory does not escape psychological determinism, for it could be argued that the further information then determines. Rather, right here and now with the information available I know that this good is nonnecessary, and that another alternative is possible. Again, the judgment is not free (active), since the intellect cannot help but know what it knows. But what it knows in this instance is that this act is choosable but rejectable; therefore the ultimate practical judgment to choose or reject it is determinable (passive) by the will.

2. *From Direct Experience.* Since powers are known only by their acts, we cannot observe the will introspectively. Moreover, since freedom is a property and a reasoned concept, it is not directly observable either. It would seem that freedom, at least in this sense, is beyond the methods of experimental psychology.[11]

But the act of choice seems to be as much a matter of phenomenological observation as any other psychological fact. Choices and decisions are as much a part of everyday experience as perceptions, images, or thinking. The capacity for freedom may be a matter of inference, but the experience of choice is an empirical datum to be observed and analyzed; the only alternative is the theory that this experience is a universal mass illusion, which in turn becomes a fact which must be explained. Whatever metaphysical implications are involved in its explanation, the fact seems inescapable.[12]

[11] John W. Stafford, C.S.V., "Freedom in Experimental Psychology," *Proc. Amer. Cath. Phil. Ass.*, 1940, 16:148–153; Louis J. A. Mercier, 'Freedom of the Will and Psychology, *New Scholasticism*, 1944, 18:252–261; H. Gruender, S.J., *Experimental Psychology*, 1932, p. 434ff. On the other hand, Ach, Michotte, Lindworsky, Prüm, Aveling, McCarthy, Barrett, and others in their laboratory experiments seem to have reached conclusions favoring free choice (cf. Lindworsky, 1929, pp. 32–38; Gannon, 1954, pp. 399–403).

[12] Nicholas Hobbs, "Science and Ethical Behavior," *Amer. Psychologist*, 1959, 5:221–223. O. H. Mowrer (1953) agrees that ethical responsibility is quite compatible with scientific psychology.

Before choice, I am conscious of the alternatives before me, and that I see them as non-necessitating. The whole process of deliberation is nonsense if the decision is already determined.

During choice, I am conscious that I actively determine the course to be taken. This experience of the actual domination we exercise over the act of choice has been called by psychologists "the active interposition of the ego." Although not open to quantitative measurement,[13] what we experience here is not a mere lack of necessitation or an ignorance of motivating factors, but a positive exertion of influence on the part of the self. Austin Farrer (1943, pp. 106–229) says that this is the only instance in which we really have direct experience of causality. In other instances causality may seem obvious, as when the hammer strikes a nail, but this is really only inference in comparison with the observation we have of ourselves when we settle an issue between conflicting motives. Recall the Montreal experiment related above where the patient reported the clear opposition between his choice and the movement of his foot under cortical stimulation.

After choice, we experience remorse, self-approval, and other evidences of a sense of responsibility. We are often clearly aware of the difference between hitting a person accidentally and deliberately. No matter how sorry we feel over the former, we do not feel responsible or guilty, as we would in the latter instance. We are quite conscious of whether or not the act flowed from a deliberate choice on our part, and this is reflected in such expressions as "I decided," "I made up my mind," "I made a choice," or "I yielded."

3. *From Moral and Legal Obligation.* Those who admit moral obligation or legal responsibility must logically admit that man is not completely the victim of determining forces. If a person cannot do otherwise, it is absurd to hold him responsible for what happens. Obligation involves both the possibility of my doing something and the fact that I am not forced to do it. Our entire legal system and administration of justice rests on this foundation. There would be no point in an elaborate trial to ascertain whether or not the alleged

[13] Raphael C. McCarthy, S.J., *The Measurement of Conation* (Chicago: Loyola University Press, 1926).

murderer were sane unless there was a difference between the normal man who can exercise free choice and the person in whom some abnormality prevents this. The same argument holds for the notion of merit and reward. Why praise a man for doing something unless he could have done otherwise?

It is true that criminologists are rightly more concerned with cure than with punishment, and tend to emphasize the various influences which caused him to be the kind of person who would commit a criminal act. But emphasis on rehabilitation does not deny responsibility. After a period of extreme "can't help it" theorizing in the 1920s and 1930s, the pendulum has swung back to a middle position among experts on crime and juvenile delinquency, partly because of evidence from the perpetrators themselves, who insist that no person or thing made them do anything they did not choose to do. As Sir Walter Moberly says, Christianity agrees with psychology in concern for the subjective factors in crime, in distinguishing guilt feelings from guilt, and in the primacy of treatment over punishment. But if no adults were responsible persons, who would treat or legislate? If we assume only a few are responsible, then society should be a vast mental hospital, a slave society where the majority were wards (non-responsible) of the few (responsible). Since we reject this, the law must assume most are responsible, and can afford to make special cases of the pathological, but they must remain the exception.[14]

It is interesting to note that for centuries only Catholic moral science considered factors which diminish freedom, and therefore guilt. Civil law looked only at the objective act, and took a "guilty or not guilty" attitude. Canon 2196 distinguishes the quality (abnormality) of an act from a quantity or degree of guilt. Although progress was gradual in developing the doctrine, the basic idea of diminished imputability was always clear in Catholic thinking, and received early and thorough refinement.[15] Civil law is still wrestling

[14] Sir Walter Moberly, *Responsibility: The Concept in Psychology, in the Law, and in the Christian Faith* (Greenwich, Conn.: Seabury Press, 1956).

[15] Alan Edward McCoy, O.F.M., *Force and Fear in Relation to Delictual Imputability and Penal Responsibility* (Washington: The Catholic University of America Press, 1944). Cf. Boganelli, 1937.

with the problem, partly because of the differences of terminology between the legal and psychiatric professions, and the narrowness of the M'Naghten rule ("know right from wrong and the consequences of his acts") which set a legal precedent only slowly being modified. Meanwhile, psychiatrists frankly state that a person can be quite responsible and free, even though there are psychiatric considerations in the case.[16]

FREE CHOICE AND NON-SCHOLASTIC PHILOSOPHY

Students often get the erroneous impression that only Scholastic philosophy defends such doctrines as free choice. But outside the historical stream of Scholasticism, itself composed of quite divergent views—such as those put forth by Plato, Aristotle, St. Augustine, St. Thomas, and Scotus, all of whom held for freedom—there have been many other philosophers and schools who maintained a doctrine of free choice. An examination of three contemporary survey textbooks in non-Scholastic philosophy taken at random reveals each devoting considerable space to the question, presenting valid arguments, and citing numerous philosophers favoring free choice. Yet of the many sources noted in the three textbooks, none is Scholastic.[17]

Kant holds freedom as a postulate of practical reason, at least. Descartes, Locke, C. E. M. Joad,[18] Henri Bergson,[19] Arthur H. Compton,[20] and the existentialists exemplify the wide variety of non-Scholastic philosophers holding with free choice. The existentialists are inclined to exaggerate it to an extreme. Oriental philosophies,

[16] F. Kennedy, H. R. Hoffman, & William H. Haines, "A Study of William Heirens," *Amer. J. Psychiatry*, 1947, 104:113–121; R. Allers, "Irresistible Impulses," *Amer. Eccles. Rev.*, 1939, 100:209–218.

[17] John Hospers, *An Introduction to Philosophical Analysis* (Englewood Cliffs, N.J.: Prentice-Hall, 1953), pp. 262–281. Excellent on the distinction between being caused and being compelled. Harold T. Titus, *Living Issues in Philosophy* (New York: American Book, 1953), pp. 172–189, presents the case for freedom. Philip Wheelwright, *The Way of Philosophy* (New York: Odyssey, 1954), pp. 299–321, gives both sides.

[18] *Guide to Philosophy* (New York: Dover, 1936), "Self and Freedom," pp. 229–250.

[19] *Time and Free Will* (New York: Macmillan, 1950).

[20] *The Freedom of Man* (New Haven: Yale University Press, 1935); "Science and Man's Freedom," *Atlantic Monthly*, 1957, 200, 4:71–74.

though tinged with varying degrees of fatalism, do not usually avow rank determinism.

P. Sorokin[21] of Harvard found that down through the centuries human thinking has dipped into determinism periodically but has always returned to the conviction that man has free choice. From history the environmental determinists would find it hard to explain how man could have been "conditioned" by Western culture to deny freedom—one is tempted to suggest that determinism could only arise because man freely chose to deny he can freely choose. In contrast to the preoccupation with the abnormal in modern drama, Shakespeare's plays, along with their shrewd insight into the subtleties of human emotion and mixed motivations, dramatize consistently the common human persuasion that the normal man is the protagonist on life's stage who ultimately determines his own destiny.

FREEDOM AND MODERN PSYCHOLOGY

Although this is predominantly a philosophical question, psychologists have always discussed the determinants of behavior and hence have a legitimate interest in the problem. During the first half of the twentieth century, psychology manifested an understandable anxiety to be a "grown-up" science and was very defensive in its avoidance of any term which might seem to smack of "uncaused activity," a meaning which had been erroneously attached to the term free will.

But the intervening variables between stimulus and response merited increasing use of such terms as "cortical control" or "ability of man to direct his drives" or "selective inhibition and facilitation" or "choice behavior" or "self-in-acton" or "the active interposition of the ego." John E. Anderson of the University of Minnesota, in his preface to The Psychology of Development and Personal Adjustment (1949, p. vii), stated frankly his hesitation between criticism from his superscientific colleagues and deprivation of his student

[21] Social and Cultural Dynamics (New York: American Book, 1937–1941), II:339–349.

readers of what he felt to be the truth; he solved the problem by giving the students a clear statement of human responsibility in choice behavior, even at the risk of unfavorable reviews.

Finally in 1950 Hadley Cantril of Princeton, then president of the Eastern Psychological Association, came out with an unabashed use of the term "free choice," and claimed that the scientific basis for a code of responsibility lies there. Since then, there has been an ever-increasing chorus of outstanding psychologists advocating the theory of free choice. Gardner Murphy, director of research at the Menninger Foundation, demonstrates how, by exercise of intel- ligence and conscious choice, man can actually transcend his bio- logical and cultural inheritances and open the way for a free expres- sion of his virtually unlimited potentialities (*Human Potentialities,* 1958). Herbert A. Simon of the Carnegie Institute of Technology speaks of "rational choice" (1957), and Edwin G. Boring of Harvard satirizes the psychologist who would deny it (1954, p. x).

Non-directive and existential therapies threw the responsibility squarely on the patient, implying that he had the power of free choice. When the psychiatrist helps the patient to face reality and understand his motivations, he considers the cooperation of the patient as free, not forced; were it forced, the psychiatrist would still claim that freedom for himself which he denies his patient. D. B. Klein (*Abnormal Psychology,* 1951, pp. 142, 143) of the Uni- versity of Southern California points out the inconsistency between theory and practice among those who still deny free choice verbally:

> As a matter of fact, even the staunchest psychiatric advocates of determinism are not hesitant to use the concept of freedom in their professional work. . . .
> What is more, even an ultradeterministic psychiatrist wants to be left free to choose the course of action he deems best for his patients, and sees no incongruity in talking about his responsibility for their welfare. In his professional role he wants to be regarded as a free agent capable of making free choices, and willing to as- sume responsibility for what he prescribes.

Speaking of the developing child, Stone and Church state that "he develops a species of *self-determination* (it is no longer fashionable to speak of a free will) and becomes able to accept or refuse the choices offered to him. . . . He becomes, within certain obvious limits, the master of his own destiny." (1957, p. 337. Italics and parentheses theirs.) Experiments receiving favorable review show the superiority of higher values as motives, of conscious ego over unconscious drives (e.g., using hypnosis), and of ego as power able to transform past experience rather than a mere product of it.[22] The list could go on indefinitely: Gordon W. Allport (1955), David Ausubel (1952), Percival M. Symonds (1956), Abraham H. Maslow (1954), J. McVicker Hunt (1952), Timothy Leary (1957). Robert W. White (1952, pp. 364–365), director of the psychological clinic at Harvard, states well the position of moderate indeterminism in a modern context:

> Thus far the scientific study of man has unwittingly contributed to the trend toward apprehension and uncertainty. All three views of man—the social, the biological, and the psychodynamic—display that one-sided determinism which selectively views the person as the hapless product of forces. . . . But equally we have insisted that some attempt should be made to examine the gap in the scientific account so that natural growth and the activity of the person can be put back into the story. . . . precisely here lie the very facts about human nature that offer man the hope of influencing his own destiny. . . . Even though he be a nexus of biological, psychodynamic, social and cultural forces, a person serves to some extent as a transforming and redistributing center, responding selectively to create a new synthesis. Under reasonably favorable circumstances personality tends to continue its growth, strengthen its individuality, and assert its power to change the surrounding world.

DIFFICULTIES AGAINST FREE CHOICE

Greater Seeming Good Always Prevails. Jonathan Edwards, a colonial American writer, claimed that man is not free because he always chooses what appears to be the greater good. This is am-

---

[22] David C. McClelland, "Conscience and the Will Rediscovered," review of Karl Mierke's *Wille und Leistung* (Gottingen: Verlag für Psychologie, 1955), *Contemp. Psychol.*, 1957, 2:177–179.

biguous, and could mean nothing more than that the object of the will is good: we never choose something precisely because it is *less* good. It also emphasizes the importance of motive in choice. But it is a tricky form of psychological determinism when it implies that the greater good determines choice. This is a problem at least as old as St. Thomas (*S. T.*, Ia, 82, 2).

The ambiguity is unmasked when we grant that the "greater" good always wins if by that is meant the good contained in the ultimate practical judgment. But just what makes this judgment ultimate? A finite good is seen as contingent or indifferent, be it greater, lesser, or equal to any other good. The will efficiently makes the intellect decide that this is to be chosen. It is irrelevant to freedom whether deliberation compares it to any other good or not: either this good is necessary or it is contingent. The question is not whether it seems greater, but whether I *must* choose it. The burden of the proof is on those who assert such necessity.

Suppose I am thirsty, have only one nickel, and am confronted with a vending machine which will dispense me either a large glass of milk or a small glass of orange juice. Which is greater? Under the aspect of quantity, the milk is. But since I prefer the taste of orange, this becomes the greater good under the aspect of quality. Each aspect is a good falling within the formal object of the will. Each is plainly superior in its own category. If intellect were restricted to only one aspect of goodness, there would be no choice. But when I see each has objectively greater good, only by active interposition of the will can I make one the greater subjective good by determining which aspect of goodness will prevail. The point is that I am not necessitated by the preferable taste of the orange any more than by the larger quantity of the milk; as a matter of fact, I can put my nickel in my pocket and choose to remain thirsty.

The false assumption behind this objection to free choice is that any finite good can somehow of itself become so great as to exclude the possibility of rejecting it. We have seen that certain factors can cause this, but only by eliminating the proper conditions for normal functioning of the intellect. The objection also falsely assumes that the attraction of motives renders choice impossible, or that it can occur only when goods are objectively equal. The facts are all to the contrary, for we act against natural attractions, and choose in spite of rarely, if ever, encountering objectivity equal motives. As long as there is an adequate cause (reason) for acting, I can choose it, regardless of whether it is greater, less, or equal. I *make* it seem greater by voluntarily directing my attention to the aspect of good which I choose.

What is this "greater good" which always prevails? There are five possibilities. Is it always sensory good? Then all men are hedonists, and nobody acts for motives which are intellectual, much less noble. Is it always rational good? Then no man yields to his passions, and there is no vice in the world. Is it always habitual inclination? Then no reform is possible, and no tragic fall. Is it always natural preference or *indeliberate* inclination? Then no heroes, no asceticism, no responsibility for good or evil. Or is it *deliberate* inclination? Then it is because of choice. Jonathan Edwards' dictum is thus either contrary to the facts or redundant. Actually, we all find ourselves at times acting contrary to sensory attraction, and confess having acted contrary to what we know was rational. We act against our old habits, and against our natural preferences. If the good contained in the ultimate practical judgment seems greater, it is only because "we ourselves by our own wilful act inclined the beam" of judgment, as William James puts it.[23]

Free Choice Is Unscientific. We have already shown at some length that this objection is baseless if it implies lack of causality. We have also noted that the execution of acts commanded by the will is strictly under the laws of physics. Choice is not contrary to the law of conservation of energy, for it does not create energy but merely directs it in this direction rather than that. The will is inorganic, but whatever energy is needed for the organic activities connected with volition is supplied by the body. An automobile obeys physical laws, but this does not mean that no driver directs its activity. This "law" is now being questioned and called a theory by physicists themselves (though they often resent a philosopher doing so). But there is really no need at all to discuss a metaphysical problem at the

[23] *Principles of Psychology* (1896), Vol. II, p. 534.

level of physical theory. The will-act is qualitative, and does not change the quantity of matter or energy.[24]

The elicited act of the will, being spiritual, is not subject to physical law. But "man is part of nature, and must follow nature's laws." True, but what is the nature of man? To assume the nature of the will-act without regard for factual evidence is unscientific. It is certainly caused, for the will is in the realm of being, and the principle of causality is a law of being. Will is outside the realm of physics, though not beyond metaphysics. It is not outside man, but man's nature is partly spiritual (not supernatural).

The scientist is most bothered about the fact that choice introduces a factor which he cannot include in a formula. When evidence of choice behavior clearly indicated active self-determination by the ego, some psychologists began using terms like Psi-factor. Others rebelled at this, and relegated it to the realm of goblins, gremlins, or the supernatural. Science, they said, aims to predict and control. But is the desire to predict and control more basic to science than the desire to understand? If the primary purpose of science is to discover what is knowable about the universe, it is unscientific to rule out fact which does not fit preconceived theory. Does science boast an open mind, or hide in a closed universe?

Determinism is not a conclusion from facts, but an assumption uncritically adopted during the heyday of mechanistic physics. There is positive evidence for free choice, and only theoretical opposition against it. Let the facts speak for themselves. If they are unique, and beyond the narrow bounds of classic physical theory, this does not make them any less true.

The breakthrough came when Heisenberg's principle of indeterminacy or uncertainty showed that physical science itself could not always hope to predict. Failing to distinguish between active indifference and passive contingent possibility, some rashly hailed this as evidence for freedom. Mere lack of predictability is not itself a positive power of self-determination. Variability does not choose. More correctly, Nobel prize-winning physicist A. H. Compton (1935, 1957) pointed out that although this principle indicates chance

[24] Thomas Aquinas, S. T., Ia, 82, 4; Ia IIae, 9, 1 and 3.

rather than free self-determination, it at least opened the way to the establishment of free choice by knocking the scientific props from under theoretical oppositon to it.

Paradoxically, "One may predict and logically systematize compulsive (neurotic) behavior, whereas the mentally healthy man is more spontaneous, free, and creative in his personal behavior—hence, in detail, less predictable or logically organizable. A science of clinical psychology seems more realizable (as to detailed prediction) than a science of the general healthy personality!" [25] Statistical predictability of the normal is actually possible to a high degree of accuracy, in spite of free choice. The reason for this is the fact that human nature is basically the same for everyone, and the same motives are going to appeal in about the same proportion to most people, in spite of the individual differences. These predictions apply to averages, not individuals. They do not *cause* anyone to choose, but simply indicate how many will probably choose because of the same motives. Psychologists are used to the concept of probable error,[26] and know that the formula for an individual would have to be n-dimensional, a most complex calculus of possibilities.[27]

Neurology. Perhaps the most genuine problem facing science here is to identify the precise manner by which volition is translated into action. We have already seen clear evidence that volition is not neurological, but the bridge between the two is baffling. The world-famous neurologist Sir Charles Sherrington (1940) seems to contradict himself on this point, for in Chapter 7 he equates cause with physical cause, then spends much of Chapters 9, 10, and 11 showing that mind is irreducible to physics or biology, that brain and mind are "phenomena of two different categories" (p. 318). Experiments show that will can evoke action in a muscle fatigued by electrical stimuli, while an electrical stimulus can move a muscle fatigued by wilful action. Eddington came closer to the real issue when he util-

[25] Carlton W. Berenda, "Is Clinical Psychology a Science?" *Amer. Psychologist*, 1957, 12:725–729. Cf. C. E. Moustakas (Ed.), *The Self* (New York:Harper, 1956).
[26] Edward G. Boring, A *History of Experimental Psychology* (1950), p. 467, describes McDougall's position on freedom in this way.
[27] Leona B. Tyler, "Toward a Workable Psychology of Individuality," *Amer. Psychologist*, 1959, 14:75–81.

ized the concept of indeterminacy in cortical nerve cells, and Eccles proposes a plausible neurological theory of how volition might influence action when he suggests that minute but not random influences could take advantage of indeterminacy in the cortex, showing how Eddington's worry about the amount of influence was needless if you consider the synaptic knob rather than the whole neuron.[28]

The philosopher is beholden for such details to the scientist. Motor images are sensory, and therefore have a material component proper to animal nature. Being quasi-immaterial, they share with will the realm of psychic reality. Thus the level of sense is the natural intermediary between the spiritual will and nerve action, since it has both psychic and physical components. This is especially significant when we remember that these are not two separate beings, since man is a substantial unit.

Hypnosis and Suggestion. A vast amount of experimentation with hypnotism over nearly a century has shown that it is a natural phenomenon: unusual, but not very mysterious or even abnormal. It seems to be largely a matter of narrowed attention plus heightened suggestibility, both of which are possible to all men in some degree. Consequently the power of the hypnotist over his subject differs only in degree and circumstance from the power of any persuader, salesman, or seducer. We all have varying degrees of sales resistance, and some are far more able to dominate than others.

This explanation seems borne out by the facts. Under hypnosis a person will do many silly or embarrassing things which he would not do otherwise. Usually the suggestion to do something contrary to his moral principles will shock the subject out of the hypnotic state. For example, in hypnotic experiments using a rubber dagger, an adult can be told to stab someone under the suggestion of hate. Given a real dagger, he will ordinarily wake up (the intended victim is protected by invisible plate glass). But if the person has weak moral convictions and is vulnerable to nonhypnotic persuasion or seduction anyway, he is understandably liable to act on immoral hypnotic suggestion. Similar results have been obtained

---

[28] John C. Eccles, *The Neurophysiological Basis of Mind* (New York: Oxford, 1953), pp. 272–279.

for posthypnotic suggestion; for example, the person will act on a given signal after waking, even though told that he would forget the instructions and only remember to act on signal, as in the case of the man moving the chair.

Does this contradict free choice? *Before* hypnosis the subject is usually free to choose whether or not he will consent to it. We say usually, for the same limitations of free choice which we have laid down earlier apply here. One may be tricked into it without knowing what is involved, or be otherwise unable to deliberate because of distraction or other factors. Here the person cannot choose, because he does not know; it is not the will but his knowledge that is affected.

During the hypnotic state, the person's knowledge is limited to what the hypnotist directs his attention toward. Deliberation is interfered with and hence the necessary conditions for choice. Acts may be virtually voluntary to the extent that he vaguely foresaw and consented to them when he agreed to undergo hypnosis. Habitual convictions may be strong enough to control important conduct, as noted above.

After hypnosis, the rationalization with which he defends his obedience to the posthypnotic suggestion indicates that the subject is not aware of what was told him under hypnosis. Knowledge is thus limited and freedom to that extent diminished. But as we said about unconscious motivation in general, it normally leaves the person free to resist the influence even without understanding it. He may feel uncomfortable and mystified by these impulses, but usually he can control them. He is in ignorance or error only as to *why* he feels impelled to act, but not about *what* he does. Hence if he has clear convictions about the object of his impulse he may resist it; if it is a nonmoral issue, like moving the chair, the suggestion may cause him to see it only as desirable.

The facts of hypnosis are thus seen to be quite compatible with moderate indeterminism. Although "cures" obtained by it are usually too superficial and transient for it to have much value as therapy, hypnosis is often useful in psychiatric diagnosis, in psychological research, and as anaesthetic. In the hands of a skilled and competent professional man it is quite legitimate. As parlor or vaudeville enter-tainment, or in the hands of the amateur or less conscientious, it is dangerous and unethical.

Subliminal Motivation. This is advertising which uses devices to impress the public without their being aware of it, such as flashes so quick as to be below the threshold (limen) of consciousness. "Mo-tivation research" attempts to discover and appeal to the public's unconscious desires. The question here is akin to that of hypnosis. Psychologists dispute the effectiveness of these means, but we incline to agree with Edgar H. Schein of M.I.T. that they leave free choice intact to the same degree as those other "techniques which have always been used implicitly by the competent manipulators, and which the man in the street has always been able to resist by an act of reason—if he chose to do so." [29]

Infinite Series. "If I am not determined (necessitated) to choose A rather than B, then I need a third motive C for choosing between them. But if this determines me to choose, I am not free; if it doesn't, then I cannot choose and need a further determiner D, etc." This argument is essentially the same as that which says, "If the will is not determined to choose, then it has no adequate reason for choosing, and therefore it would never choose."

The facts provide the best answer here. We do choose, and with-out an infinite series of motives. We do not even need a third mo-tive: since either A or B is good, I have adequate reason for choosing one. I have final cause and efficient cause (will).[30] The argu-ment implies that volition needs a motive for itself, other than the object. But tendency is movement; it is the act of a being in potency precisely in its aspect of potency, and it therefore indicates an im-perfection: will-act is not an end, but motion toward an end (*S. T.*, Ia IIae, 1, 1 ad 2um). Another fallacy implied is that every sufficient motive is a necessitating one.

Theological Determinism. "God surely knows what I am going to

---

[29] "The Id as Salesman," review of Vance Packard's *The Hidden Persuaders* (New York: McKay, 1957), *Contemp. Psychol.*, 1957, 2:308–309.
[30] *S. T.*, Ia, 84, 4 ad 3um; Ia IIae, 9, 3.

do, and must cooperate if I am to do it. But God's cooperation is irresistible, and to do otherwise than what He forsees would make the divine knowledge false, which cannot be. Therefore I am not free." This objection really belongs to the philosophy of God (theodicy) or to theology. Briefly, we must distinguish the facts from the explanation of the facts.

The *facts* are clear enough: God has the perfection of freedom, and can confer that perfection on man; if He does so, He sees perfectly all that this involves. Note the word *sees:* There is no time in God, and to speak of *fore*knowledge here is anthropomorphism (projecting human qualities on Him). It is not of the nature of knowledge to cause its object; the essence of knowledge is conformity between knower and object, however achieved. The fact that I see a man sit down does not make him sit. What does God see? He sees me choose freely, since that is the nature He has given me. If it is true that I freely choose A, He knows this. Hence it is non-sense to talk as if I would cross God up if I choose B, for that too is included in His eternal knowledge. He does not guess or predict; He knows.

As for His cooperation, it does not derogate from His omnipotence that creatures exercise their own efficient causality. The fact that He cooperates with the will does not force our choices any more than His cooperation with our intellect means that He thinks our thoughts: He is the ultimate cause of both, the proximate cause of neither. God does not have to share with any creatures the perfection of freedom; but once He does, He cannot contradict Himself by not leaving them free. (This is not because of any lack in God, who can do any*thing*; a contradiction is non-being, *nothing*.) "Just as by moving natural causes He does not prevent their acts from being natural, so by moving voluntary causes He does not prevent them from being voluntary, but rather is the cause of this very freedom in them, for He operates in each thing according to its proper nature." [31] In fact, "it would be more repugnant to the divine movement if the will were moved of necessity, which is not in ac-

[31] *S. T.*, Ia, 83, 1 ad 3um.

cordance with its nature, than for it to be moved freely in accordance with its nature." [32]

The *explanation* of just how God knows and cooperates with man's free choice constitutes one of the knottiest problems in philosophy. St. Thomas, in the two passages just quoted, seems to go as far as the human mind can go with certainty. His followers divided into two main camps for several centuries in attempts to probe further the workings of divine knowledge and cooperation. Both sides agree on the facts stated above. One group, predominantly Dominicans following Banez, O.P., emphasizes the supreme dominion of God and proposes a theory of predetermining decrees to safeguard it. The other group, predominantly Jesuits following Molina, S.J., emphasizes the freedom of man and proposes a special theory of divine knowledge. Both seem to follow St. Thomas in principle,[33] while going beyond him in their theories. The controversy has largely died, perhaps because of a growing suspicion on both sides that neither theory is adequate, and a new approach is possible even within the framework of St. Thomas's thought.[34] After all, if God's knowledge and action are identical with His infinite essence, they are beyond complete and adequate comprehension by our minds.

Since the question involves the supernatural aid of grace as well as the natural cooperation of God with creatures, the problem pertains also to theology, but the principles are the same. The question of whether original sin robbed man of freedom of choice is purely theological. The burden of positive proof is on those who assert that revelation teaches it has, and none seems forthcoming.

REVIEW QUESTIONS

1. Does physical freedom pertain to elicited or to commanded acts? To which does moral freedom pertain?
2. Could free choice be proved using only objective (behavioristic) methods of psychology, i.e., without using the experience of the ego?

[32] S. T., Ia IIae, 10, 4 ad 1um.
[33] William R. O'Connor, "Molina and Banez as Interpreters of St. Thomas Aquinas," *The New Scholasticism*, 1947, 21:243–259.
[34] Bernard Lonergan, S.J., "St. Thomas's Thought on Gratia Operans," *Theol. Studies*, 1941, 2:289–324; 1942, 3:69–88, 375–402, 533–578. Pages 387–402 and 541–553 are especially good on the basic problem and the facts.

3. Could it be proved from unpredictability? Is chance the same as freedom?
4. Could free choice be deduced from observation of human behavior in society, law procedures, etc.?
5. Eric Fromm (*Man for Himself*, 1947, pp. 231–235) seems to consider moderate indeterminism, reject it, then follow it in practice. Is this what he actually does? If so, how would you explain it?
6. Do I need explicit or reflex consciousness of my freedom in order to make a free choice? Implicit?
7. Several modern psychology texts (Karn & Weitz, Garrett) define freedom as the ability to do what I want. Is this sound? Why?
8. Suppose I am confronted with two goods, one which I see as choosable and the other I see as rejectable. Am I free?
9. Is the mere possession of the power of deliberation a sufficient condition for free choice, or must there be actual exercise (however brief) of this power?
10. Must choice always be between moral good and evil?
11. The foundation for free choice is said to be in the nature of the intellect. Why?
12. If sensism were true, could determinism be false? Why?
13. Does strong emotion always eliminate free choice? Can it?
14. Do habits eliminate free choice? Do they diminish it?
15. Can will, emotion, and imagination all influence what a man thinks?
16. Do I have freedom of exercise with regard to particular contingent goods? Freedom of specification?
17. Do I have freedom of specification with regard to happiness or the perfect good? Do I have freedom of exercise? (Hint: is thinking about happiness an infinite good?)
18. Is there freedom of exercise with regard to God directly and intuitively known as He is? Freedom of specification?
19. Contrast the teaching of Socrates with that of St. Thomas regarding the role of knowledge in human liberty: is there opposition? or development? Is Aristotle's position a transition step?
20. What is a liberal?
21. What is academic freedom?
22. Does freedom of speech mean that one may say anything he wishes? Have the U.S. courts ever ruled on this?
23. Analyze the argument for human freedom given by Nobel prize-winner Lecomte du Noüy in *Human Destiny* (New York: Longmans, 1947), pp. 47–51. Does it prove freedom of choice? What is the key point of his argument?
24. Why does our first proof (from indifferent judgments) eliminate the need to consider whether the object of choice is a *greater* good?

Answer the following objections:

25. If I am not determined (necessitated) to choose A rather than B, then I need a third motive C for choosing between them. But if this determines me to choose, I am not free; if it doesn't, then I cannot choose and need a further determiner D, etc.
26. The will-act of its very nature must follow upon intellection. But the intellect is not free; it necessarily knows what it knows. Therefore the will cannot be free either.
27. The will always tends toward its object under some aspect of goodness. Therefore there is no such thing as crime, only ignorance or error.
28. Scientists can predict how many people will commit suicide in New York next year. Therefore determinism is right.
29. One "proof" of free choice is from consciousness. But consciousness often testifies falsely: a drunk or insane person might say he is conscious of being free, or of many other things which he isn't. Hence this argument is worthless.
30. Is opposition to the notion of free choice based on factual evidence or philosophical considerations? What positive evidence is advanced against the fact of free choice? Is free choice simply a lack of other determining factors?

FOR FURTHER READING

Scholastic

AQUINAS, ST. THOMAS. *Summa Theol.*, Ia, 19, 10; 59, 3; 83 (entire); Ia IIae, 10, 2–4; 13, 1 and 6; 14. *Summa Contra Gent.*, I, 85; II, 47 ff., esp. 66.

American Catholic Philosophical Association. "The Problem of Liberty," *Proc.*, Vol. 16. 1940.

DE FINANCE, JOSEPH, S.J. *Être et agir dans la philosophie de S. Thomas.* Paris: Beauchesne, 1945.

FORD, JOHN C., S.J., & KELLY, GERALD, S.J. "Psychiatry and Moral Responsibility," *Theological Stud.*, 1954, 15:59–67.

GILL, HENRY V., S.J. *Fact and Fiction in Modern Science.* New York: Fordham University Press, 1944. Chap. 8, pp. 67–76.

GILSON, ETIENNE. *The Christian Philosophy of St. Thomas.* New York: Random House, 1956. Pp. 236–248.

GILSON, ETIENNE. *The Spirit of Medieval Philosophy.* New York: Scribner, 1936. Chap. XV.

GRUENDER, HUBERT, S.J. *Free Will, the Greatest of the Seven World Riddles.* St. Louis: Herder, 1916.
GRUENDER, HUBERT, S.J. *Problems of Psychology.* Milwaukee: Bruce, 1937. Probs. 3, 4.
LONERGAN, BERNARD J. F., S.J. "The Notion of Freedom," in *Insight: A Study of Human Understanding.* New York: Philosophical Library, 1956. Pp. 607–633.
LOTTIN, DOM ODON. *La Théorie du libre arbitre depuis S. Anselme jusqu'à S. Thomas D'Aquin.* Louvain: Mont-Cesar, 1929. (Extrait de la *Revue Thomiste,* 1927–1929.)
MAHER, MICHAEL, S.J. *Psychology.* (9th Ed.) New York: Longmans, 1933. Chaps. 18 and 19 give one of the best explanations of will and choice.
RICKABY, JOSEPH, S.J. *Free Will and Four English Philosophers.* London: Burns, 1905.
SHARPE, A. B. *The Freedom of the Will.* Vol. I. Westminster Lectures. St. Louis: Herder, 1906.
SIMON, YVES. *Traité du libre arbitre.* Liège: Sciences et Lettres, 1951.

Non-Scholastic

ADLER, MORTIMER J. *The Idea of Freedom.* New York: Doubleday, 1958.
BARTA, FRANK R. *The Moral Theory of Behavior.* Springfield, Ill.: Charles C Thomas, 1953.
BERGSON, HENRI. *Time and Free Will.* New York: Macmillan, 1950.
BERTOCCI, PETER A. *Free Will, Responsibility, and Grace.* Nashville, Tenn.: Abingdon, 1957.
DAVIDSON, M. *The Free Will Controversy.* London: Watts, 1942.
DAVIDSON, M. *Free Will or Determinism.* London: Watts, 1937.
FARRER, AUSTIN M. *Finite and Infinite.* Chicago: Allenson, 1943. Pp. 106–229.
FARRER, AUSTIN M. *The Freedom of the Will.* London: A. & C. Black, 1958.
HERRICK, C. JUDSON, *Fatalism or Freedom: A Biologist's Answer.* New York: Norton, 1926.
HOOK, SIDNEY (Ed.) *Determinism and Freedom in the Age of Modern Science.* New York: New York University Press, 1958. Proceedings of the New York University Institute of Philosophy.
HOSPERS, JOHN. *An Introduction to Philosophical Analysis.* Englewood Cliffs, N.J.: Prentice-Hall, 1953. Pp. 262–281.
JOAD, C. E. M. *Guide to Philosophy.* New York: Dover, 1936. Pp. 229–250.

LEWIS, C. S., *The Abolition of Man*. New York: Macmillan, 1947.

SPRINKLE, HENRY CALL. *Concerning the Philosophical Defensibility of a Limited Indeterminism*. New Haven: Yale University Press, 1957.

TITUS, HAROLD H. *Living Issues in Philosophy*. New York: American Book, 1953. Chap. XI, pp. 172–189.

WEISS, PAUL. *Man's Freedom*. New Haven: Yale University Press, 1950.

WHEELWRIGHT, PHILIP. "Freedom of Choice," in *The Way of Philosophy*. New York: Odyssey, 1954. Chap. X, pp. 299–321.

Psychologists

CANTRIL, HADLEY. *The "Why" of Man's Experience*. New York: Macmillan, 1950b. Esp. pp. 8, 160–168.

GANNON, TIMOTHY J. "Conscious Control," in *Psychology: The Unity of Human Behavior*. Boston: Ginn, 1954. Chap. 14, pp. 384–409. An excellent explanation of free choice in the light of modern psychology.

GRUENDER, HUBERT, S.J. *Experimental Psychology*. Milwaukee: Bruce, 1932. Chap. 17.

HARMON, FRANCIS L. "Volition," in *Principles of Psychology*. (Rev. Ed.). Milwaukee: Bruce, 1951. Chap. 18.

LINDWORSKY, JOHANNES, S.J. *Experimental Psychology*. Trans. by Harry DeSilva. New York: Macmillan, 1931. Pp. 316–344.

LINDWORSKY, JOHANNES, S.J. *The Training of the Will*. Milwaukee: Bruce, 1929. Pp. 25–153.

LUCE, R. DUNCAN. *Individual Choice Behavior*. New York: Wiley, 1959. Statistical probability approach.

McDOUGALL, WILLIAM. *An Outline of Psychology*. (3d Ed.) London: Methuen, 1926. Pp. 447–448 argues against psychological determinism.

MOORE, THOMAS VERNER. *The Driving Forces of Human Nature and Their Adjustment*. New York: Grune & Stratton, 1948. Chap. 27.

NUTTIN, JOSEPH. *Psychology, Morality and Education*. Springfield, Ill.: Templegate, 1959. The chapter "The Nature of Free Activity" shows how the current psychological data which invalidate extreme indeterminism are quite compatible with a correct concept of free choice.

RANK, OTTO. *Will Therapy*. New York: Knopf, 1936. (To this might be added the writings of other psychiatrists such as Viktor Frankl and Abraham Low.)

SNIDER, LOUIS B., S.J. "A Research Method of Validating Self-determination," in Magda B. Arnold & John A. Gasson, S.J., and others, *The Human Person: An Approach to an Integral Theory of Personality*. New York: Ronald, 1954. Pp. 222–263.

PART FOUR

HUMAN POWERS AND HABITS

13

OPERATIVE POWERS

*Existence of operative powers. Distinct from operation, from
one another, and from man's substance, but not separate.
Powers as essential properties. Nature of an operative power.
Powers and the unity of man.*

In Part 1 we distinguished between man and his abilities. In Parts
2 and 3 we have used this concept in relating the many operations
of man to his several powers. Now in Part 4 we return to the distinction for a more formal discussion of the existence and nature of
man's powers in this chapter,[1] and of their perfection through habit
in the next chapter.

Why bother with powers at all? Why not simply consider man
and his operations? This may be satisfactory at the level of science,
but the philosopher must ask some questions which take us deeper.
Can man be the immediate principle of his operations? It seems
that the proper act of a substance is to exist, not to digest or think.
Again, if there are only substance and activity, does one substance
cease to differ from another when activities cease? Then there is no

[1] This chapter may be taken up immediately after Chap. 2, if desired.

227

difference between man and brute animal when man is not actually thinking or willing. A sleeping man or an infant would have no rights. Again, if substance (nature) is the sole principle of operation, how can the same man have different *kinds* of operations simultaneously? These activities can even be in opposition, so that we seem to have a nature in conflict with itself. If operation is the act of substance, what happens to the unity of man? He would seem to be as many substances as he has activities, or kinds of activity.

THE EXISTENCE OF OPERATIVE POWERS

Distinct from Operation. Whatever man's ability to act may be, whether or not it turns out to be identical with his nature, it is immediately clear that at least it is not identical with his operation. For the activity can come and go, begin and cease, while the man remains. This fact that his operations are intermittent while he remains permanent is evidence for the basic distinction between potency and act. If they were identical, then man would begin and cease with the starting and stopping of his operations. He is still the kind of being that *can* think, even when he ceases thinking. He may still be a man even when his breathing and heart stop, as many medical reports show. Heart massage and artificial respiration do not work a substantial change, but simply restore activity in one capable of it.

Distinct from One Another. Secondly, the facts point clearly to a distinction between man's abilities, based on the different kinds of activity of which he is capable. Throughout the preceding chapters we have been examining different operations: cognitive and appetitive, sensory and rational, and even vegetative. Activities so diverse and even opposed must stem from different proximate principles of operation, even though ultimately rooted in the same one man.[2]

We have already seen in Chapter 3 that acts are specified (known to be different) by their proper formal objects. The material objects may be the same in each of several acts: a steak, for instance, which I should eat because I am anemic. It is the formality under

[2] Thomas Aquinas, *S. T.*, Ia, 77, 2.

which I relate to it which differentiates the various activities. Knowing is different from wanting it, wanting different from digesting. Knowledge in terms of universal principles (diet) is different from concrete sensory representation, animal appetite is different from choice based on intellectual conviction.

Now potencies are specified by their proper acts, just as acts are specified by their formal objects. We do not observe potency; we infer it from observable act. Irreducible formal objects, therefore, require distinct powers. In this sense we do not distinguish between potencies; they differentiate themselves by their acts. The act of running indicates a different ability from the act of seeing. We do not think with our imagination or hear with our appetite. These are distinct powers because they are abilities for different kinds of operation. There is always a proportion between a potency and its act; they must be in the same category. Diversity of operation indicates diversity of operative potency or power.[3] On the other hand, I may have visual percepts of various colored objects but need only one power of vision, since these are not different *kinds* of activity, but all come under the formal object of vision.

Distinct from Man's Substance. Since man's powers are distinct from his operations as potency from act, and distinct from one another as potencies for different and even opposed operations, it is not difficult to conclude that they are distinct from his substance (but not separate from it). The formal proof is as follows.[4]

The proper act of a substance is to exist. But existence is not the same as operation. Man does not "do" a man; he "is" a man, and does other things. If to be a man is the act of his substance, to operate must be the act of some other potency. Now potency and act must be in the same genus. Operation is obviously accident, not substance. Therefore the potency for operation must be in the genus of accident.

Again, were my substance identical with my potency for operation, then logically whenever I was in act (existing) I would be doing all of the things I can do, which is absurd. My substance can

[3] Thomas Aquinas, *S. T.*, Ia, 77, 3; 78, 1.
[4] Thomas Aquinas, *S. T.*, Ia 77, 1.

Figure 11

(A) Substance   (C) Powers

――――――― = ―――――――

(B) Existence   (D) Operation

be in act while I am also in potency to other acts: therefore I have other potencies besides my essential potency to be. These other potencies are my operative powers.

Figure 11 puts the argument schematically. Substance or essence is to existence or "to be" as operative power is to activity or operation: A is to B as C is to D. If I show that A is not D (man is not his operation), have I proved that A is not C (man is not his operative power)? If I show that B is not D, can A equal C? i.e., if existence is not operation, can the potency for operation be identical with substance?

Potency in Order of Operation. This argument seems to lead to a serious difficulty. Operative powers were said to be in potency, not in act, when a man was not exercising them. But above it was asserted that he still had such powers, i.e., was still the kind of being that could do these acts. Man still actually has the power, even though he is not using it. This would argue that the powers were still in act, namely, the act of existing. Now they cannot be both in potency and in act at the same time. Are they actual or potential?

To answer this we must recall that potency and act are analogous concepts. They correspond only in the same order: something may be in potency in one order, and in act in another. We must look at that to which a potency is essentially ordered. Power is essentially ordered to operation; substance is essentially ordered to existence, only secondarily to operation. Four orders of potency and act may be distinguished here (see Figure 12). (*a*) In the order of substance, matter is potency and form is act. (*b*) But in the order of accident, this substance composed of matter and form is in potency (as substance) to accidental forms as act. (*c*) In the order of existence, this substance with its accidental perfections may be still considered in potency (as essence) to the act of existence. Your discussion of the potential existence of a hypothetical triangle can include its essential properties. (*d*) Lastly, existing complete essence is in further potency (as nature) to the act of operation.

The operative powers are actual in the order of accident (*b*) and the order of existence (*c*). They are in act, not in potency, in so far as they are accidental forms or perfections of an existing substance. The fact that I have this ability is a real quality in me. But in the order of operation (*d*) they are in potency: even though actual existing powers, they are only in potency in the order of operation until they begin to function.

NATURE OF AN OPERATIVE POWER

Another difficulty suggested by the proof for the distinction of powers from substance is this. Accidents can come and go, while substance remains. Being in the genus of accident, can operative powers come and go? Am I still a man if I no longer even have the power of thinking or choosing, i.e., if I am not the kind of being that *can* think, regardless of whether I am actually thinking?

To answer this we must recall that there are two kinds of accidents: proper and contingent. *Proper* accidents or properties are accidents which always and naturally inhere in this substance, and make it to be this kind of substance. Thus matter is always quantified, so quantity is a property of matter. *Contingent* or adventitious accidents are those which can come and go without substantial change. An idea, an image, the act of running are all contingent

Figure 12

(a)	(b)	(c)	(d)
Order of Substance	Order of Accident	Order of Existence	Order of Operation

Matter (potency)
+ } = Substance (potency)
Form (act)   + } = Essence (potency)
         Accident (act)   + } = Nature (potency)
         [powers as forms]   Existence (act)   [substance with powers as potencies]

↓

Operation (act)

accidents: they come and go without changing our nature. But intellect, imagination, and being radically the kind of thing that can run are all properties of human nature, inseparable from it. If one lacks such basic powers, one is just not the kind of being we call man. The paralyzed man may not walk now, but he once did, or at least is the kind of being which could, if not impeded by abnormal circumstances; we would never say this of a desk or a tree.

This notion of property also answers some of the other questions raised at the beginning of this chapter. Can one say that man differs only accidentally from the brute animals, since intellect and will are accidents? Not if we realize that we differentiate one essence from another precisely by their properties. We do not know essences directly. But when certain properties manifest that man is in a different category of being, we say he differs essentially.

What is our nature when powers are not operative? We know powers from acts, so it is true that if we had no evidence, even inferential, of activity, we could conclude nothing about a nature. But it is often obvious that we have the power even when it is not in act. When sound asleep we are still the kind of being that can think; the mere act of awakening does not change our nature and give us a power that we did not possess. Similarly, the drunk or abnormal person is still basically rational, in the sense that he possesses the root power of thinking even though he does not have the exercise of the power at that time. Sobering up or medical treatment cannot change the nature so as to give it a power which it did not have; we do not pump intelligence through a hypodermic syringe or a pair of electrodes. The proof is that no amount of such treatment will make rational a being whose nature was not such to begin with. Try giving electroshock, insulin, thyroxin, or glutamic acid to a dog or a monkey. Again, the infant manifests no thought, but no one would claim that mere growth or the passage of time changes his nature and gives him a new power; maturation is only a condition for its exercise, providing the necessary materials for thought. Were not his basic potentialities determinate, we would never know whether to expect this infant to mature into a monkey, or this kitten to grow up a mathematician. Certain powers are properties of the nature of each being. This notion is important to ethics, when discussing rights of the mentally ill, the unborn baby, etc.

Operative potencies are thus in the realm of accidents, being the peculiar and special kind of accident we call properties. Accidental does not necessarily mean unimportant or incidental: it means inherence in substance as opposed to separate existence. These powers are an intimate part of our nature, but they are not substances. It is for this reason that we avoid the older term "faculty," which in the last two centuries has come to connote a little entity in man, a *homunculus* or little man in the head who sees and chooses.[5] This not only distorted the whole issue, but is unfortunate because a caricature of the original idea. Faculty comes from *facio* (meaning I do) and suggests action, not substance.

This very dynamic character of the abilities of man as Aristotle and St. Thomas conceived it is at once most in accord with the best in modern psychology and most opposed to the mechanical, substantive conception implied by the old faculty psychologists. Even Freud's id, ego, superego, and censor, though usually classed as highly dynamic concepts, smack more of the eighteenth and nineteenth century philosophers. "Self-actualization," "functional autonomy," and "operant learning"—whether the terms are used by the homeostatic (need-reduction) or the behavior-primacy (environment) theorists—are all more intelligible against the philosophical framework of these immanently active, fecund principles of operation. "Every doer is perfected by doing" (*omne agens operando perficitur*), says St. Thomas in many places, seven centuries before progressive education or dynamic theories of personality development. For him, there are two significant characteristics of a living being: the tendency to actualize potency from within, and the tendency of a partially actualized potency toward further actualization. And for him this is not determined wholly by random contact with environment or mere need to maintain the status quo, but by the whole scope of our unrealized capacities: by man's nature, if

[5] Cf. J. Card. Mercier *The Origins of Contemporary Psychology* (2d ed., London: R. & T. Washbourne, 1918), pp. 224–246; C. A. Hart, *The Thomistic Concept of Mental Faculty* (Washington: The Catholic University of America Press, 1930).

you will, but an open-end nature endowed with objectively un-limited capacities and goals as broad and deep as all being.

We have seen that a cognitive power is not purely passive, an inert receiver of impressions. It is actively passive, or reactive. A percept or idea is not a dead picture, but a vital operation, an act. We saw that will is the ability of man to exercise efficient causality in a most intimate way. This helps us to understand substance not as a mere substratum, on which hang accidents like clothes on a store-window dummy, but a dynamic reality operating through its powers which are simply qualities which make it the kind of being that can so act. It also answers the specious objection that the power of reproduction could never cause a new substance, since cause and effect must be proportionate. Powers do not act by themselves, because they do not exist by themselves, and action follows being. Substance causes another substance. It does so in the only way a created substance can act, namely through the quasi-instrumentality of its power of reproduction. Only that Being which is its own "to be" can have its power of acting identical with Itself.

POWERS AND THE UNITY OF MAN

An operative potency is the proximate principle *by which* man acts. Man is the ultimate principle *which* acts.

For example, the intellect is the proximate principle by which man thinks: thinking is the act, intellect is the ability to think, man is the thinker. (We shall see later that the soul is the *ultimate* principle *by which* man is a thinker, i.e., the substantial form which makes him the kind of being that can think; as opposed to the intellect which is an accidental form and the proximate principle by which he thinks.)

These distinctions are necessary if we are to understand correctly the notion of operative powers in the light of man's unity. Man is one substance or supposit. Substance considered precisely as the source of activity is called nature, which therefore includes those essential properties which make it capable of its various activities. But no multiplicity of accidents can give rise to a distinct substance, for accidents are qualities having no being except through inherence. Therefore man's nature remains one being.

The fact that the various powers are distinct from one another explains how man is capable of different and even conflicting activities. Since they are all accidents of the same substance, this conflict is all within the same person: there would be no true internal conflict if Joe's emotions were at odds with Pete's intellect! Though relatively simple to enumerate, man's powers are exceedingly complex in their interaction and combined multiple activities, as both the psychologist in his perception experiments and the psychiatrist in his office find when they try to isolate and disentangle them. Similarly, in the philosophical sense there is no such power as "speech" because speech involves complex activity of many powers at once.

The notion of powers helps us to understand individual differences which are in the powers rather than merely an activity or in substances. If in activity, men would not differ when asleep; if in substance, there would still be the question of how these substances differ. It also explains how man can share some aspects of his nature with brute animals and even with the vegetative level, since he has powers of all three kinds. Again, the activities of the different powers are related to different organs of the body, as we have seen. Diversity of organic structure and function thus corresponds to differences of powers, leaving man's substance as one.

Modern psychology, understandably afraid of the word "faculty" because of its connotation, just as it was of the term "free will" for similar reasons, nonetheless has provided interesting confirmation for the basic concept of operative potencies. Psychological testing has revealed that man's activities are not only intermittent but fall into different categories. Each different way of acting stems from some general tendency to act in this way. These tendencies seem to be inborn, but are developed and individualized by actual experience. Although capable of great modification by environmental influence, these tendencies to action seem to vary innately between individuals, usually in a bell-curve distribution.

Now all of these facts about natural tendencies or abilities in man coincide with the notion of operative potencies or powers. The difference is only in terminology, and in the technological manner by which the facts were acquired. Mention has already been made of the evidence from factor analysis by Spearman, Cattell, and others for intellect and will as distinct powers. The work of Thurstone seems also to verify the notion of diverse powers through factor analysis of test results.[6] We listed many different operations of intellect; this allows for the special or subgroup activities under the general heading of intelligence. To a lesser degree visual perception also involves diverse kinds of experiences, yet we logically group them as basically stemming from the same power. Always we must remember the interrelatedness of all man's powers, though distinct, as mere abilities of the same one man. Their distinction, and ultimate unity in man, account for the fact that factor analysis shows that no two human abilities are perfectly correlated or perfectly uncorrelated. Both the unity of man and the complexity of his operations are rooted in the fact that his several powers are but accidents of one substance.

REVIEW QUESTIONS

1. Show that operation is distinct from power.
2. Show that our operative powers are distinct from one another.
3. What do you mean by saying that acts are specified by their formal objects? Does this mean that man has as many powers as he has acts, or has kinds of acts?
4. Show that operative power is distinct from man's substance (a) from the separability of operations, (b) from the diversity of human activities, and (c) from the relation between essence and existence.
5. Power must belong to either the realm of substance or that of accident. But if substantial, man is many beings and his unity is destroyed; if not, then it is just accidental whether man has an intellect or not. Solve this dilemma.
6. a. In the order of essence, does power belong to the class of formal or efficient cause?
   b. In the order of operation, to which of these does it belong?
   c. As an instrumental cause, to which does it belong?

⁶ L. L. Thurstone, *Vectors of Mind* (Chicago: University of Chicago Press, 1935), pp. 45–53.

7. Contrast the Thomistic notion of operative potency with the extreme "faculty" theory.
8. What justification is there for saying that St. Thomas's picture of man is both more complex and more unified than that of the faculty theorists of a few centuries ago? Is it more in accord with modern dynamic psychology and psychiatry, or less?
9. "All men are created equal." In what sense is this true? In what sense not? Show how the notion of operative power is necessary for a correct interpretation.
10. Since intellect and will are accidents, is the difference between man and ape just accidental?
11. Is the difference between a worm and an elephant accidental or essential? What kind of difference is there between a dog and a living carrot?

FOR FURTHER READING

ADLER, MORTIMER J. *What Man Has Made of Man.* New York: Longmans, 1937. Pp. 79–81; Note 46, p. 205.

ALLERS, RUDOLF. "Functions, Factors, and Faculties," *The Thomist*, 1944, 7:323–362.

AQUINAS, ST. THOMAS. *Summa Theol.*, Ia, 54, 1; 77; 78, 1 and 2; 85, 7.

ARISTOTLE. *On the Soul.* I, 5.

BRENNAN, ROBERT E., O.P. *Thomistic Psychology.* New York: Macmillan, 1941. Chap. 9, and esp. pp. 250–257 on integration with modern psychology.

HART, CHARLES A. *The Thomistic Concept of Mental Faculty.* Washington: The Catholic University of America Press, 1930.

KLUBERTANZ, GEORGE P., S.J. "The Unity of Human Operation," *The Modern Schoolman*, 1950, 27:75–103.

MURPHY, GARDNER. *Human Potentialities.* New York: Basic Books, 1958.

PEGIS, ANTON C. "St. Thomas and the Unity of Man," in J. A. McWilliams, S.J. (Ed.), *Progress in Philosophy.* Milwaukee: Bruce, 1955. Pp. 153–173.

ROZWADOWSKI, A., S.J. "De distinctione potentiarum a substantia," *Gregorianum*, 1935, 16:272–281.

SPEARMAN, CHARLES. *Psychology down the Ages.* Vol. I. New York: St. Martin's, 1937. Chap. 11. See also his *The Abilities or Man and Human Ability.*

14

HABITS

The existence and need of habit. Nature and definition. Acquisition of habit. Varieties of habit. Habits and dynamic psychology. Habit and modern learning theory.

Emphasis on the rational nature of man may be a necessary antidote to the materialistic philosophy which threatened to dominate our Western culture a few decades ago, but the student is in danger of getting the impression that man consists of a reason and a will somehow stuck onto a substance, like arms on a crude scarecrow—and forming just about as much in the way of a person. Our description in the last chapter of the dynamic nature of operative power sets the stage for our agreeing that in practice he comes much closer to verifying the adage that "man is a bundle of habits".

As a matter of philosophical fact (and philosophy is much more factual than its critics realize), after infancy man's intellect and will by no means always pass directly from a state of pure operative potency to a state of act. Without going as far as psychological determinism, we must admit that a very large part of the activity of these powers is determined by the complex systems of habits which have been built up in them. This is a great advantage: it would be an intolerable burden if we had to start from scratch each time to think through our reasons for acting and to make a new choice. Habits, born of previous conviction and choice, rid us of much routine decision-making. This frees us for more creative achievement. More than that, we are carried through many difficult or tempting situations by the force of good habits, where otherwise weakness might cause us to abandon principle. The old member of Alcoholics Anonymous rejects a proffered drink automatically; habit is now his friend, and prevents each situation from being a crisis.

NATURE OF HABITS

But what is a habit? Most students will offer a definition which makes habit a repetition of acts. But if habit consists of acts, then no act means no habit. Suppose Professor Jones is asleep, and not even dreaming. Can I say he is a good man? That he knows a lot of chemistry? He is not doing any good acts, nor exercising any actual knowledge of chemistry. What reality in him justifies my attributing goodness and knowledge to him, even when asleep? Certainly it is not his acts, for he is not performing any. Is it his *power* of performing such acts? Then how does the professor differ from his grandson, who also has the powers of intellect and will? Both possess intellect, the potency for knowing chemistry; yet nobody attributes knowledge of chemistry to his grandson.

Comparing the two, sleeping professor and grandson, we can see no difference: both possess intellect, and neither is displaying actual knowledge of chemistry. Wake up the professor and ask questions about chemistry of each. Immediately we observe a difference in performance. The grandson may have only the potency for acquiring chemical knowledge, but the professor answers our questions with ease, without needing to acquire the answers because he somehow already possesses them. How? Not in act, for he is not always thinking of all the chemistry he knows. Not purely in potency, for he differs from his grandson precisely in not having to acquire the knowledge. But since potencies are known by their acts, it is clear from the ease of his performance that the professor's powers are not pure potency for learning chemistry, starting at zero, but powers already well disposed to think about chemistry with great facility. He has habitual knowledge. But it consists of impressed, not expressed, *species*—otherwise the knowledge would be actual (see section "Intellectual Memory" in Chapter 7). Similarly, his will is disposed to good acts, so that we call him a good man; for virtue is nothing more or less than a good habit of the will.

DEFINITION OF HABIT

Habit is *an acquired quality of an operative power which disposes that power to act with facility in a certain way.*[1] Let us examine the precise meanings of these words.

"Acquired"—we are born with powers as properties of our nature, but habits are always acquired. They are called second nature, since they enrich and further specify our nature as a source of operation.

"Quality"—habit is not a substance, nor even a distinct power; habits are simply a further perfection of our powers. They are more or less stable, or permanent, qualities modifying the basic abilities.

"Power"—since habit is the quality of a power, it resides in that power even when the power is not operating. Habits are in the realm of potency, not act. Hence they exist without our awareness, for we are conscious of acts, not powers. We know they exist only from the ease with which the powers act.

"Disposes"—not determines. If we define habit in terms of act, the difficulty arises that what is already in act cannot be otherwise than what it is; hence possession of habit would mean that I am determined to one act and have no choice. But if habit is a disposition of the potency, it means only that I am more likely to act that way. Being still in potency, I can complete the act or not. Being disposed, I am less free than if starting from zero, so habits do diminish freedom even though not eliminating it.

"Facility"—ease. Here is the advantage of habits, as explained above. The diminution of freedom is in the interest of efficiency.

[1] Thomas Aquinas, S. T., Ia IIae, 49 and 50.

Conversely, herein lies the danger of vices, or bad habits: bad action is made easy, which is why Aristotle says that vices render us "capable of doing evil well." (Note that facility is an attribute of the action, whereas the habit itself is a quality of the operative power.)

"Certain way"—where the power is originally rather indifferent as to how or toward what objects it would operate. Habit tends to channel activity along a definite line, but always we must consider the nature of the power it perfects, as will be clear when we consider the varieties of habit.

Potency or Act? The question of whether habit is potency or act is somewhat similar to the question we raised in the previous chapter about the powers themselves. The difference in this case is that here we are dealing with an additional perfection of the power, ordered not merely to operation but to facilitated operation. In the order of accident and in the order of existence, habit is act; it is a quality, an actual form perfecting and disposing a power. But in the order of operation it is still potency, ordered to facilitated operation as act. This is technically expressed by saying that habit is the first act of a power, and operation is the second act. This semiactualization places habit in a unique position midway between potency and act.[2] But the philosopher must take reality as he finds it, not try to force it into neat preconceived categories. It is this very aspect of habit which explains how habits dispose but do not determine, as was explained above.

Some writers use the term *entitative* habit to refer to dispositions like health and sanctifying grace, because they perfect the entity or nature rather than the operative power. This is permissible if we note that as perfections of nature, which is the ultimate principle of operation, such habits would be indirectly ordered to operation (vital operation and the beatific vision, respectively). But St. Thomas never seems to have called grace an entitative habit, apparently because for him habit is always directly ordered to operation.

[2] V. J. Bourke, "The Role of Habits in the Thomistic Metaphysics of Potency and Act," in R. Brennan (Ed.), *Essays in Thomism* (New York: Sheed, 1942), Pp. 103–109.

ACQUISITION OF HABITS

Our definition says only that habits are acquired; it does not state how. Since the philosopher is only interested in the nature of habits, he can rightly leave the conditions of their acquisition to the psychologists, whose investigations on the topic fill volumes.

Although repetition in some form is the usual way of acquiring habits, repetition is by no means necessary to the nature of habit itself. It is enough that habit be acquired, regardless of how. Sometimes a single act can engender a habit.[3] One clear explanation may cause me to understand something in geometry, let us say. There is no need for repetition: I have the idea, and twenty years later could use it with ease even though I have never thought about it since that day in high school. Obviously I was not born with knowledge of geometry or of anything else. It was acquired, but not by repetition. This way of acquiring knowledge holds chiefly for simple ideas which appeal directly to understanding; most knowledge is made habitual only by repeated use. Again, one intense emotional experience may implant a habit: a single great fright in childhood, for example, may leave a habitual emotional revulsion for similar objects. The child need not repeat the frightening experience many times to acquire this emotional habit. (Supernatural virtues are acquired and fit the definition of habit, but they are infused by God and belong to the order of grace, not to philosophy or psychology.)

VARIETIES OF HABIT

St. Thomas usually preferred to restrict the term habit to the rational level. For him the subrational powers are the subjects of habit in the strictest sense only to the extent that they are under the command of the will. Similarly, brute animals have no habits in this sense except to the extent that they are influenced by their trainers.

---

[3] Thomas Aquinas, *S. T.*, Ia IIae, 51, 3 (last half of the body of the article).

There is ample reason for so restricting the term, plus the force of tradition in Scholastic philosophy.

But even Aristotle, St. Thomas, and their most ardent followers are seen at times to use the word habit in a broader sense, to include habitual knowledge and the dispositions of other powers. Such a manner of speaking does not contradict St. Thomas and is certainly much more in accord with modern English usage.

Language being conventional, it seems practical to use the term habit in conformity with this broader meaning. The philosopher should feel at home with analogy, and this seems to be an analogy of proper proportionality. Granted the different degrees of indeterminacy, the definition still fits if we take into account the natures of the various operative potencies. By whatever name, the facts are there. Again, facility in thinking is admittedly different from thought content, but retained knowledge seems also to verify the definition of habit, even if in an analogous sense.

If the issue were more important than mere terminology, we would object to some of the arguments which restrict the term. The senses, at least the internal senses, do seem to acquire modifications which dispose them as subjects of *improved* action, rather than merely directing them to determinate objects. Recall the experiment of wearing inverted prisms for glasses, and the superior perceptions of the experienced woodsman. These and other lines of evidence point to perceptual habits in a true sense of the word, yet their development is not due to influence from the rational level.[4] The wearer of the prisms does not reason intellectually to the position of things; he acquires a perceptual habit of seeing them aright. Again, the dog learns to avoid the hot radiator grill through his own sad experience, and the cat improves her skill and accuracy in jumping by practice— both without the influence of a trainer.[5]

---

[4] Klubertanz (1953), p. 276, seems to hold differently. On the other hand, throughout Chap. 12 he speaks of motor habits, habits of the sensory appetites, of the estimate power, and of sense memory, and speaks of retained images in the imagination and retained intelligible species in the potential intellect as being in the "state of habit" (p. 276, 281).

[5] Klubertanz (*ibid.*) seems to admit this possibility when he says animals can acquire these determinations "by force of circumstances" (p. 295).

Habit in Any Power. To many, habit suggests activities at the very opposite end of the scale from rational: an automatism like scratching one's head, or alcoholism. We would like to emphasize the broad range of its application, and speak of habits as perfections of *any* of man's operative powers. Thus we have traits and skills or habits of acting, emotional complexes or habits of feeling, perceptual habits, association of images or habits of the imagination, retained or habitual knowledge both sensory and rational, attitudes and understanding or habits of thinking, and character or habits of will. We need only to remember that the term is analogous and depends on the power to be perfected. Throughout the whole scale of human activity, habit is an important medium between stimulus and response. Along with native equipment and self-determination, habits constitute the "O" in the S-O-R formula of psychology.

Groups and Systems of Habits. Rarely does a habit exist in reality as an isolated perfection. Usually, habits are combined in varying degrees of complexity. The good mechanic has motor dexterity, facility in picturing spatial relations, the urge to have things work right, and understanding of the principles of machinery—all so closely interwoven that it is difficult, if not impossible, to isolate the function of each in a given act. Smoking or drug addiction may involve appetitive habits, association of images, attitudinal thinking, motor habits, and physiological modification in organic tissues. These are not only habit systems but systems of systems, piling up and interacting. In the well-adjusted personality or virtuous man these habit systems are integrated and in an orderly, hierarchical fashion related to each other and the good of the whole man.

HABITS AND DYNAMIC PSYCHOLOGY

Personality is largely a matter of habits. Mere possession of basic potencies makes one a person, but how experience habituates these powers and how they are now disposed to act tells what kind of personality one has. Again, we judge personality not by what one happens to do at the moment, but by what is characteristic or typical because flowing from the more or less stable dispositions we call

Figure 13

Good act	Good habit	Pure potency	Bad act

$$A \leftarrow ----\ \overline{}\ ---0\ --------\rightarrow B$$

H BH

habits. They are always with one, awake or asleep, acting or not. Their all-pervasive influence on behavior is powerful, subtle, and often unconscious.

Habits and Free Choice. As mentioned previously, habits diminish freedom of choice by disposing the will to act in a certain way and thus removing some of its original indeterminacy. But habits do not determine, because as qualities of a power they belong to the realm of potency, leaving us free to determine whether we will bridge the gap from potency to act.

Referring to Figure 13, we may consider schematically the will without any habits at 0, or zero on the scale of act. Perfected by a good habit, it would be at H, still short of act but further along than originally and hence able to reach A with greater ease than before. Thus the good man finds it easy to perform good acts. (If habit placed it already at A, the will would be determined; but being in potency at H it still can determine whether or not to traverse the remaining distance $H \rightarrow A$.) But he can perform bad acts, as sad experience shows. Only to do so he must act against the disposition of his good habit, i.e., travel the whole distance $H \rightarrow B$. Conversely, the bad man can do a good act, since his bad habit still leaves him in potency; but he in turn must act against the disposition of habit and travel from BH to A.

This explanation leaves intact both freedom of choice and the value of character training.[6] It also gives sound philosophical basis for the practice of psychotherapy, and especially for the client-centered and existential therapies of Carl Rogers, L. Binswanger, Rollo May, Viktor Frankl, U. Sonneman, and others which throw the

---

[6] See J. Lindworsky, S.J., *The Training of the Will* (Milwaukee: Bruce, 1929), a classic treatise on motivation and free choice; and A. Eymieu, S.J., *Le Gouvernement de soi-même* (Paris: Perrin, 1935), esp. Vol. III, *L'Art de vouloir.*

responsibility on the client and enlist the cooperation of his free choice, while recognizing that his personality problems are largely a matter of faulty adjustive habits developed over the years.

Because these habits are unconscious and persistent, to detect and change the way they affect our feeling and acting may require time and skill on the part of the psychiatrist or clinical psychologist. It is precisely because it happens at the level of habit formation and therefore unconsciously in great part that the way in which emotion can distort the operation of our natural powers is so baffling. These are the dynamisms that Freud and others try to describe and explain.

Abnormal States. Although habits normally diminish but do not destroy freedom of choice, in certain pathological cases the force of habit may be so strong and so irrational that for practical purposes we can say that the person is not free. This of course is abnormal, and does not change our concept of man's essential nature. But it does constitute a difficult problem in both ethics and law.[7]

Nature of Will-Habits. Since the nature of the will is to act because of motives, "disposed to act in a certain way" in our definition of habit means "disposed to act because of certain motives." Hence there is no question of training the will like a muscle, which acts regardless of the value of what it lifts. The famous German experimental psychologist J. Lindworsky, S.J., (1929) refutes the muscle-training theory of will by showing that it can be habituated only by being disposed to respond habitually to certain values as effective motives. This position seems to be confirmed by Knight Dunlap (1932) whose "beta hypothesis" or negative practice advocates breaking habits by doing the very action not wanted, showing that the will does not gain strength from mere exercise but that the reason or motive for its action is cardinal. Experiments on transfer of habits of neatness, with and without stress on the *value* of neatness, lead to the same conclusion.

This primacy of motives explains how prudence is the connection between the intellectual virtues (wisdom, understanding, knowledge)

---

[7] See chap. 12, our third argument for free choice, based on the concept of responsibility. Cf. James E. Royce, S.J., *Personality and Mental Health* (Milwaukee: Bruce, 1955), pp. 226–231.

and the other moral virtues (justice, fortitude, temperance). Prudence is a moral virtue, but an intellectual one. It is the practical wisdom of choosing the right means to the end, actually applying values in a concrete situation.

HABITS AND LEARNING

The term *learning* has been likewise broadened so as to include the whole range of human activity. Rather than the mere acquisition of knowledge, learning or even conditioning has come to refer to any change in mode of response acquired through experience, and the result of this change is called habit.[8] Thus we have not only learning of school subjects, but emotional learning, volitional learning, perceptual learning, sensorimotor learning, and so forth.

We must keep in mind the analogical nature of knowledge: "trial and error" learning which is just random activity with chance success is at the sensory level, and is quite different from the inductive reasoning and testing of hypotheses typical of scientific inquiry. Again, "insight" may be intellectual intuition of the principles involved, or it may be merely a total sensory awareness of a situation with its concrete relations, the sudden recognition of a pattern (Gestalt) such as Kohler's ape had of the two pieces of bamboo and the banana outside the cage. We must distinguish between the process and the product: the learned response is not always the learning response. Even insight may involve some residue of habit-formation, though not in the process. Association, conditioning, trial and error, and insightful understanding may in practice all shade into one another in varying degrees.

With these distinctions in mind, and admitting the complexity of human activity involving the simultaneous and interrelated operations of many powers, we find little if anything in the experimental data to raise any serious problem. When honestly evaluated they are quite in accord with the concept of man presented here.

Experimental psychology has yielded a prodigious amount of

[8] Floyd L. Ruch, *Psychology and Life*, 3d ed. (Chicago: Scott, Foresman, 1948), pp. 318–320.

literature on the topic of learning. A welter of theories are still being tested in the laboratory and debated by their proponents. Pavlov's conditioning seemed to provide Watson with the answer as to how learning takes place; subsequent events have shown that it raises more questions than it answers. Rather than explaining, it needs to be explained. Patched up as it now is with drives, sets, secondary-reinforcement, operant behavior, it has lost its original physiological meaning and approaches more and more the notion of habit-formation.

Psychologists have long since ceased to speak of the conditioned reflex in connection with most learning, and prefer the broader term conditioned response.[9] The breakdown of attempts to explain learning as any process of connections in the nervous system really begins with the report of Karl S. Lashley on the results of his fifteen years of attempts to do just this. He systematically cut out every part of the cerebral cortex of white rats, without eliminating the possibility of learning. As an eminent neurophysiologist, he was elected president of the American Psychological Association in 1929, when behaviorism was perhaps at its peak in American psychology. In his presidential address to the Ninth International Congress of Psychology in December of that year, he said that it had been characteristic of American psychology to "explain psychological processes and functions in terms of correlated neural anatomy. In reading this, I have been impressed chiefly by its futility. The chapter on the nervous system seems to provide an excuse for pictures in an otherwise dry and monotonous text. That it has any other function is not clear. . . ." (*Psychol. Rev.*, 1930, 37:1). Although Halstead (1947) and others have corrected Lashley's work, showing that there is even less correlation between amount of brain damage and mental functions in humans than Lashley found in his rats, Lashley's frank confession tells the story graphically:

> I began life as an ardent advocate of muscle-twitch psychology. I became glib in formulating all problems of psychology in terms of

[9] Ruch (1948), p. 323; Munn (1946), pp. 100–101. Professors Horace B. English of Ohio State (1951, p. 147) and O. Hobart Mowrer of Illinois (1947, p. 107) might be quoted to the same effect.

stimulus-response and in explaining all things as conditioned reflexes. . . . I embarked enthusiastically upon a program of experiments to prove. . . . and the result is as though I had maliciously
planned an attack upon the whole system. . . . the conditioned
reflex turned out not to be a reflex (*J. Gen. Psychol.*, 1931, 5:14).

Decades later, Hilgard in his classic *Theories of Learning* made a
careful review of the experimental work aimed at explaining learning in terms of physiology and concluded that such experiments
"have not led to any significant generalizations about the precise
mechanisms of learning" and "new interest in neuro-physiological
theories of learning also has thus far led to little that is of genuine
explanatory value" (1956, p. 453). Physiological theories not only
do not explain, he goes on, but they are not even established.
"Despite all the attention commonly given to simple conditioning
in learning theory, the evidence for it is very fragmentary" (p. 462).
"There is some concealing of ignorance in attributing specific stimulus-response bases for psychological functions such as drives, sets,
images, and thoughts. If we are critical about accepting the results
of experiments, then stomach contractions are *not* the basis of
appetite, eye movements are *not* the cause of the Muller-Lyer
illusion, kinesthetic cues are *not* the preferred ones in maze learning,
tongue movements are *not* the basis for thinking. The burden of
proof is on those who believe otherwise" (p. 477).

Transfer. A similar situation appears when one surveys the trans-
fer-of-training controversy. Much of the difficulty arose from the
absurd connotations of the eighteenth-century "faculty" theory. Conversely, the opposing theory of identical elements suggests a post-
Cartesian concept of knowledge as atoms in a mental chemistry. As
the muddy water has gradually settled and the facts are seen in
clearer perspective,[10] neither position is entirely vindicated, but the
compromise position of modified transfer is strikingly in tune with
the notion of operative power as a vital, fecund potency perfectible

[10] E.g., Walter B. Kolesnik, *Mental Discipline in Modern Education* (Madison:
University of Wisconsin Press, 1958). See also recent texts on educational psy-
chology, such as the revised editions of that by William A. Kelly, and of that by
W. D. Commins & B. Fagin.

by habit. As in the case of conscious experience, free choice, operative powers, teleology, and other concepts rejected in earlier phases of modern psychology, the trend of scientific thought has come full circle on this point.[11] The swing is attested by J. P. Guilford in his presidential address to the American Psychological Association:

> A general theory to be seriously tested is that some primary abilities can be improved with practice of various kinds and that positive transfer effects will be evident in tasks depending on those abilities. At the present time some experiments are going on of this type. . . . In one sense, these investigations have returned to the idea of formal discipline. The new aspect of the disciplinary approach is that the presumed functions that are being "exercised" have been indicated by empirical research (1950, p. 449).

The facts of abnormal psychology give additional confirmation that our abilities can be trained. In cases of brain injury and hysteria, it is reported that the patient suffered total loss of mental content, sometimes not even being able to understand any language or recall any previous event. Yet the ability of these patients to reason and acquire knowledge was not that of an infant with corresponding lack of knowledge, but that of a mature adult with well-developed powers. The capacity for learning is evidently something other than the act of knowing or the acquired knowledge, and is perfected by previous use.[12]

CONCLUSION

Though we stretch the application of the term habit into conformity with modern usage, we have by no means abandoned thereby the richness of the traditional philosophical conception. Our concept of habit as perfectant of an operative power is dynamic. It connotes more than mere automatic routine of semiconscious repetition

[11] R. E. Brennan, *Thomistic Psychology* (New York: Macmillan, 1941), pp. 255–256 gives a clear summary of the confirmation from psychological testing and factor analysis. See also T. V. Moore's chapter on transfer in his *Cognitive Psychology* (1939), pp. 473–493.

[12] See for example the cases reported by William James, or by William Mc-Dougall, *An Outline of Abnormal Psychology* (New York: Scribner, 1926), cases 51, 52, pp. 483–485.

or neurological conditioning. Rather, it tells of a vital growth of originally indeterminate potencies. This is not organic or physical growth, but metaphysical growth in the order of potency for operation. Like the current renewed interest in motivation and existential relations, it implies finality: the developed ordering of all our powers toward their proper objects, for the good of the whole man.

REVIEW QUESTIONS

1. Is habit properly defined as a repetition of acts? Discuss.
2. Can you define habit without the notion of operative power?
3. Is habit the same as trait?
4. Why do habits belong to the realm of the unconscious?
5. Is a habit always acquired?
6. Why does not our definition of habit say anything about *how* habit is acquired?
7. Do you prefer the strict Thomistic tradition which confines the term habit to the rational level, or the text's conformity with modern usage?
8. Do you feel that the Thomistic tradition is altogether consistent on the point?
9. Do you feel that our extension of the term to qualities of any power is in basic disagreement with the metaphysical principles of St. Thomas?
10. If habit were act, what would the possession of will-habit do to freedom of choice?
11. Do you think that recent psychological theory on learning is approaching or departing from the Thomistic concept of habit?
12. Are habits proper or contingent accidents? Why?
13. "Learning consists in the establishment of functional connections between nerve cells in the cerebral cortex." Evaluate this statement now, in the light of the concluding section of Chapter 8.

FOR FURTHER READING

AQUINAS, ST. THOMAS. *Summa Theol.*, Ia IIae, 49–54; 57.
BOURKE, VERNON J. "The Role of Habitus in the Thomistic Metaphysics of Potency and Act," in R. Brennan (Ed.), *Essays in Thomism*. New York: Sheed, 1942. Pp. 103–109.
CASTIELLO, JAIMIE, S.J. *A Humane Psychology of Education*. New York: Sheed, 1936a.

CASTIELLO, JAIMIE, S.J. "The Psychology of Habit in St. Thomas," *The Modern Schoolman*, 1936b, 14:8–12.

CASTIELLO, JAIMIE, S.J. "The Psychology of Intellectual and Moral Habits," *Jesuit Educational Quart.*, 1941, 4:59–70.

ENGLISH, HORACE B. *Historical Roots of Learning Theory*. New York: Random House, 1954.

HULL, ERNEST R., S.J. *The Formation of Character*. St. Louis: Herder, 1921.

JAMES, WILLIAM. *Principles of Psychology*. New York: Holt, 1896. Vol. I, pp. 104–127. A classic description of habits; excellent treatment of psychology, but weak philosophically.

JAMES, WILLIAM. *Talks to Teachers*. New York: Holt, 1925.

KLUBERTANZ, G. P., S.J. "The Unity of Human Operation," *The Modern Schoolman*, 1950, 27:75–85.

LOTTIN, DOM ODON. *Principes de morale*. Louvain: Mont Cesar, 1946. I:173–175, 313–314. On habits.

MARITAIN, JACQUES. *Art and Scholasticism*. New York: Scribner, 1930. Chap. IV.

SERTILLANGES, A. D. *The Intellectual Life*. Westminster, Md.: Newman, 1948.

On the Nature of Learning

COMMINS, W. D., & FAGIN, BARRY. *Educational Psychology*. (Rev. Ed.) New York: Ronald, 1954.

DEESE, JAMES. *The Psychology of Learning*. (Rev. Ed.) New York: McGraw-Hill, 1958.

DUNLAP, KNIGHT. *Habits, Their Making and Unmaking*. New York: Liveright, 1932.

ESTES, WILLIAM K., and others. *Modern Learning Theory*. New York: Appleton-Century-Crofts, 1954.

HILGARD, ERNEST R. *Theories of Learning*. (Rev. Ed.) New York: Appleton-Century-Crofts, 1956. Pp. 452–485.

LASHLEY, KARL S. "Basic Neural Mechanisms in Behavior," *Psychol. Rev.*, 1930, 37:1–24.

LASHLEY, KARL S. "Cerebral Control versus Reflexology," *J. Gen. Psychol.*, 1931, 5:3–20.

McGEOCH, JOHN A., & IRION, A. L. *The Psychology of Human Learning*. New York: Longmans, 1952.

MAYER, MARY HELEN. *The Philosophy of Teaching of St. Thomas Aquinas*. Milwaukee: Bruce, 1929.

MOORE, THOMAS VERNER. *Cognitive Psychology*. Philadelphia: Lippincott, 1939. Chap. VII, "The Transfer of Training," pp. 473–493; Chap. IX, "The Memory Trace," pp. 513–525.

MOWRER, O. H. "On the Dual Nature of Learning: A Reinterpretation of 'Conditioning' and 'Problem-solving'," *Harv. Educ. Rev.*, 1947, 17:102–148.

SPEARMAN, CHARLES. *Psychology Down the Ages*. New York: St. Martin's, 1927. II:236–237.

PART FIVE

HUMAN SUBSTANCE

15

MAN A LIVING BEING

Life and life operations. Is man one being or many? The unity of the human organism. The nature of life: analysis of vital operations. Living beings essentially superior to non-living.

In Chapter 2 we asked some questions which could be answered only after we had examined the full panoply of man's activities, for we said that we can know a being only from its operations. Having seen the variety of man's acts, habits, and powers, we are at last in a position to make explicit from this evidence the nature of man as a living being.

"Life" is an abstract term. The existential approach of St. Thomas was more concrete; he frequently states that "to live" is simply the "to be" of living things. Life, for him, is the very being of a living thing. To ask the nature of human life is to bring us to the fulfillment of our investigation of human nature: it is to ask what sort of being man is.

Is life equivalent to the operations of a living thing? [1] We have

---

[1] Thomas Aquinas, S. T., Ia, 18, 2. Life operations are called vital operations, since vital in Latin means "of or pertaining to life." Unfortunately the word vital in English often connotes "necessary for life" and suggests only a certain few physiological operations such as heartbeat and respiration.

already seen that man is not always acting in all the ways he can. Is he then less alive? Moreover, since operations are in the realm of accident rather than substance, equating life with operation would mean that man's being is merely a group of accidents. But man is obviously a substance, and no accumulation of accidents can add up to substance. All these activities must be the operations of some thing which operates: one cannot conceive of just activity with nothing acting. Operations come and go, begin and cease, while man remains. What man *is* must be something other than what he does.

What, then, is the nature of this substance, the being which performs vital or life operations? Is it essentially a different kind of substance from nonliving being? This question will be the burden of the present chapter. Having established that man is substantially different from other beings, we shall in the next chapter examine what in man accounts for the difference.

UNITY OF HUMAN ORGANISM

First we must ask the question whether man is a substance at all, or merely a conglomeration of many substances. It would be fruitless to look for a principle of unity which makes man one being, if he were not first seen to be one.

Moreover, we must ask the question the right way, or risk coming up with a false concept of man. "Ask a foolish question and you get a foolish answer" almost summarizes the history of this problem. To add behaving organism to experiencing mind and come up with dualism is to confuse the orders of accident and substance: it is the kind of philosophical ineptness which plagued the beginnings of modern scientific psychology.

Kinds of Unity

In order to ask the right question, and without presuming to have proved anything about them, let us list the various kinds of unity or oneness:

1. Unity of simplicity: without parts
2. Unity of composition: with parts

a. Intrinsic: unity within the being

    (i) Substantial: of substantial principles forming one substance

    (ii) Accidental: of substance and the accidents inhering in it

b. Extrinsic: union of different beings

    (i) Unity of purpose or activity: horse and rider, or several men pushing a car

    (ii) Unity of aggregation or juxtaposition: a heap of stones

Unity of simplicity (1) and mere extrinsic unity (2*b*) are fairly obvious. The most difficult and the most important kind of unity for us is intrinsic unity (2*a*), whether substantial or accidental. Substantial unity is often called *per se*, meaning "of itself" or "in its very nature." This means that even though the being is composed of parts, it is still only one being. Intrinsic accidental unity is also important because accidents inhering in a substance do not destroy the substantial unity. For this reason such unity is also sometimes included under the term per se.[2]

We shall maintain that man is one. He is not a unity of simplicity, for he is obviously a composite. Nor is it merely the extrinsic unity of different beings, which is not real oneness at all. He has intrinsic unity or unity per se, both substantial (composed of two principles) and accidental (having diverse powers and operations). As usual, we proceed from operations to nature; we know whether man is one by examining whether he operates as one.

The Evidence against Unity

At first glance the evidence that man is not one being seems overwhelming. The philosopher, if he is honest, must take into account all the facts, or at least his explanation must be able to assimilate them. The facts pertinent here are gathered from many sources: our own experience, the clinical psychology of abnormal states, the biology of organism, biochemistry, and the arguments of some

[2] There are many different divisions of unity, and the above is not to be taken as exhaustive or the only possible division. Terminology will vary slightly, since "accidental" could properly apply both to the union of substance and accident (or of accidents within a substance), and also to the extrinsic unity of several substances.

notable philosophers. Let us list first some factual evidence which seems to indicate that man is not one being.

1. *Parts*. The very fact that man is composed of many parts might be cited as such evidence. We have seen that man has many operative parts: sensory and rational, cognitive and appetitive. The eye is not the hand. Are they both man? More important, biology tells us that man is composed of many individual cells and that growth takes place by division and multiplication of these cells. The theory has been proposed that man is simply a colony of cells, which are individuals much like the bees or ants which constitute the colony of insects.

2. *Chemical elements*. Moreover, spectroscopic analysis reveals properties of many different elements within the living body.

3. *Particles*. The nature of neural activity indicates electrochemical activities involving a flow of electrons, and perhaps of atoms in the case of other changes in the body.

4. *Fragmentary life*. Besides the well-known experiment in which Alexis Carrell kept a piece of chicken heart alive for years after the chicken had been dead, there is much evidence of various kinds of tissues being capable of separate existence as in skin grafts and organ transplants.

5. *Multiple personality*. Clinical psychology tells us of many cases where the person had two or even three "personalities," so that he was now Dr. Jekyll and now Mr. Hyde, or showed three different "faces of Eve." This is in addition to the splitting of personality manifested in schizophrenia, and the conflicts we all feel within ourselves at times.

Evidence for Unity: Direct Experience

What are we to make of all this? Are we not immediately conscious of the fact that it is the same ego or I who has all these parts and does all these things? Here we must be careful lest a purely subjective phenomenological approach lead us back to the quibbles that flowed from an excessive introspectionism at the beginning of this century. But both philosophers and psychologists today are recognizing that even subjective experiences are communicable.

When you say, "I have a toothache," I can know your toothache in a very real way. I am not merely aware of the words you are saying, but I actually have something of your experience within me, which I can share with you. These common experiences of mankind furnish direct evidence for unity.

1. Whatever I do or think, I am immediately and directly conscious of the fact that it is I who see, I who feel, I who think. I am aware of my own body, and have some idea of its parts and their location through what the psychologists call "propriosensation." Now the important thing about this bit of evidence is that I know myself as myself, not as something other. I am quite clear that if someone steps on my toe he is stepping on me.

2. Secondly, when I know anything else, in the very fact of knowing this other thing I am implicitly aware of myself as distinct from "other." This implicit awareness of self is, upon analysis, a clear indication of the unity that man has in opposition to all the rest of reality. Recent psychological experiments which have attempted to isolate a man from all external stimulation by suspending him in a vat of water at body temperature and excluding all sights and sounds (stimulus deprivation) have brought out the fact that all awareness of other somehow involves awareness of self.

3. Finally, by explicit or conscious acts of self-reflection, I can be directly aware of myself as the single source and term of my own activities. This of course is a special type of self-awareness and different from the above. (In older Scholastic philosophy it was called simply consciousness.)

From all this we conclude that man has direct evidence of himself as a single unit, in spite of the multiplicity of operations and parts which he observes in himself.

From External Observation

But we do not have to depend solely on this type of direct internal evidence. We can analyze man's operations objectively and conclude to his unity from the fact that all of his activities are for a common and internal end. We can argue from the unity of purpose to unity of nature, for the simple reason that a thing can act only in so far as it has being. For a thing to act primarily in such a way as not to be good (metaphysically) for itself would be to contradict its own being. If the various parts of man were indeed a mere colony of independent beings, they could not have the whole man as their primary end without losing their identity as supposits or substantial units. In order to prove that a being is one from the unity of its operations, we must show (1) that the parts are primarily and directly ordered to a common end; (2) that this common end is intrinsic, not something outside themselves; and (3) that they are ordered to this common end intrinsically, i.e., by the nature of the being itself.

1. *Primarily and directly.* We grant that a part may act secondarily for itself without destroying substantial unity. Thus the heart also supplies itself with blood; but the primary purpose of the heart is to pump blood for the whole body, not merely for itself. Conversely, we grant that separate units may indirectly work for the good of the whole without proving substantial unity. All the bees or ants share indirectly in the good of the whole colony. But the parts of man work primarily and directly for the good of the whole man; and this can only happen if man is a unit.

2. *Intrinsic end.* Nutrition, growth, scar tissue are all aimed at the good of the organism itself. If several men join to push a truck, or even to form a business corporation, this common end does not make them one (except metaphorically) because the end is outside themselves. The key to the unity of a living thing is *intrinsic* finality. The proper end of the business itself is extrinsic to the members; only indirectly and as a means does it relate to their own good. Similarly, the parts of a machine work for a common end, but it is an end outside the machine: garments are extrinsic to the sewing machine.

3. *Intrinsically ordered.* But take the case of an automatic oiling device, or the voltage regulator on your automobile: does not this work for the good of the whole? And is not the good to which it is ordered intrinsic to the machine? Yes, but this does not prove that the parts of the machine constitute a substantial unit rather than a mere aggregate. The reason is that these devices are so designed by an extrinsic agent: they show no intrinsic finality. Contrast the

autonomic or endocrine systems of the human body: it is their self-organizing and self-regulating aspects which point to the unity of a living thing. The most marvelous feed-back and self-correcting features of modern machines are but the products of the men who designed and built them; on this precise point they are essentially different from even simple organisms which develop and maintain themselves from within. Even the lowly amoeba is an organism in this sense (though not in biological terminology because it has only one cell).

Further evidence for the unity of man can be observed when we consider the dynamic unity of purpose between disparate functions. The circulatory, digestive, endocrine, and nervous systems not only maintain vegetative or biological life in themselves, each other, and throughout the body. They also develop and maintain the sense organs as instruments of conscious life. The fetus develops sense organs months before there is any question of using them. Of what use are eyes to a fetus? This shows an overall unity in organization from the beginning of development. And they are specifically *human* eyes and ears, not dog or "just animal" eyes and ears. These sense organs are to serve as channels for intellection, as we have seen. Human knowledge is characteristically intellectivo-sensitive, a perceptual judgment by which we know being in sensible things.

Man's sensory appetites and motor coordination unite physiological processes and mental activity to adjust man as a whole to his environment, utilizing everything from organic needs to scientific choices. Fainting, blushing, hysterical paralysis, hypnotically induced body changes, and even psychosomatic disorders like gastric ulcers from chronic worry—all point to the unified organization of man across all levels of operation.[3]

We must stress here that the unity is primarily that of intrinsic finality. All of these phenomena have meaning precisely because they are ordered for the good of the whole man, not merely because they

[3] Although commonly observable, the pertinent facts can be seen even more clearly in scientific investigation. The semipopular writings of doctors like Alexis Carrell (*Man the Unknown*), Sir Charles Sherrington (*Man on His Nature*), and Walter B. Cannon (*The Wisdom of the Body*) contain authentic and fascinating details.

are intricately connected. Otherwise we make a poor argument and prove only that they are closely interrelated beings, not that they are functions of one being. Even when they go awry and work against the good of the whole, as in the case of tumor or ulcers, this is an accidental disorder, the abuse of what normally works for the good of the whole. We judge a nature from its normal function, not the abnormal; from use, not abuse. It is suspected that the secret of cancer may lie in the failure of whatever normally stops cell multiplication when the body has finished a job of repair by scar tissue.

Reply to Difficulties

We grant that the application of these criteria to organisms below man is sometimes difficult. Sometimes it is hard to tell whether we have a cluster of individual organisms together, or a single organism. The fact that they are all alike often indicates a colony, as opposed to the different structure and functions of the cells of an organism. But as we said earlier about the distinction between plant and animal, or between animal and man, the mere fact that we find it hard to tell the difference in an individual case does not prove that there is no difference, any more than the fact that I could not tell counterfeit from real money means that they are of equal value. Again, there are cases of symbiosis, such as grafts on fruit trees, parasites, Siamese twins. Close association and even sharing of some parts may suggest unity, but it is usually clear that these are distinct living beings, manifesting different and even specifically distinct kinds of operations.

Let us now return to the five types of evidence mentioned above which seemed to point to the conclusion that man is not one. Here, the concern of the philosopher is not to question facts. Rather, it is the interpretation of the facts and the correctness of the ultimate conclusions drawn which fall within his competence. The trouble is usually not with facts asserted, but with the failure to consider other pertinent facts and maintain a balanced view. After all, the demonstration of man's unity from the evidence we have just considered cannot be brushed aside.

1. *Parts.* Possession of parts of various kinds does not prove any more than that man is a complex organized being rather than a simple homogeneous one (similar throughout). In fact, their very heterogeneity (dissimilarity) argues against the cell-colony theory. But the basic question is whether these parts themselves act *as independent beings.* The evidence says that they do not, but as parts of a unified whole, to whose good they are essentially subordinated and outside of which they have no existence, or have existence in an utterly different manner than when existing as parts. They do not operate for themselves, but for man.

2. *Chemical elements.* Here we must distinguish between chemical properties and substance in the philosophical sense. Certainly the elements which make up the body will produce their characteristic pattern of lines on the spectrograph, and some can be tagged and traced through the system. But do these chemical "substances" exhibit *all* and *only* the properties they have when not in the body? Nitrogen does not grow, water does not see and hear. They now do things that they were never capable of doing before. But this means they are a different kind of being. They are no longer nitrogen and water, but living human flesh. This is substance of a different nature, even though some of the chemical properties may be retained. The nitrogen *was* nitrogen before becoming part of the body, and it will be nitrogen again when the body decomposes. Right now it is human substance, a part of man's body; it does not act as an independent being. This is clear from our demonstration of intrinsic finality above. Conversely, man does not act like a chemical element or an electric current. Essentially different operation shows different kind of substance; even though elements enter into the composition of man, they do so precisely by being substantially changed into man.

This should cause no surprise. We have already remarked that heterogeneity of parts characterizes any complex organism. Tissue is of different kinds in different parts of the body, yet it is all human. So the elements retain some of their various properties, but this does not prevent their all being man. That man is not the same all over (homogeneous) is a commonly observable fact, not a discovery of modern chemistry. Since the elements which compose man do show *some* of their original characteristics while in the composite, and since they are obtainable when the body decomposes, whereas other elements are not, we say that they are there *virtually*. This means that although not present actually (since man as one being has only one act of existence), neither are they present in the merest potency, but rather in a state of potency somewhat disposed to becoming again actually what they were previously, before composition.

This notion of degrees of proximity to act is found in many cases of potency and explains what is otherwise quite unintelligible. How can a simple spark change hydrogen and oxygen into water, or explode a million tons of matter? How can a little child start an avalanche? There seems to be no proportion between cause and effect if we look only at the efficient cause. But if we look to the material cause, the matter upon which the efficient cause works, we find it well disposed, in ready potency to such act. Hence the old philosophical axiom, "The more disposed the material cause, the less is required of the efficient cause." Carving a likeness of Moses from a cube of marble is much harder than if the marble is already rough-hewn to the approximate shape. Both are in potency to look like Moses, but one is virtually a human figure already. The analogy here is of an accidental form, namely, shape, but the reasoning applies also to substantial form, as in the changes that take place when food is assimilated and waste products excreted. Man is virtually, though not actually, nitrogen and water and the rest. In man these chemical "substances" are not supposits, i.e. complete substantial units with their own proper acts of existing. Remember that in seeking to know whether these are beings or one being we are asking philosophical questions, and these cannot have chemical answers. The two approaches are not opposed, they are simply different.

3. *Particles.* The same reasoning as in (2) could apply to the evidence for subatomic particles like electrons, namely, that they are virtually present. There is considerable evidence for their activity, and enough evidence to show that they behave differently than when not in the human composite, for man does things that these particles

by themselves do not. Again, we are speaking of what is demonstrable fact; in so far as this involves theoretical constructs, it belongs to the realm of scientific theory. Theories may change, and in any case are outside the realm of philosophy.

4. *Fragmentary life.* The key answer again is that we must not look merely to the fact that these parts are capable of being kept alive after separation: the question is whether they have independent existence *before* they are severed from the whole.

Applying the notion of virtual presence, we see that even in the unified organism these parts exist in varying degrees of proximate potency to separate existence. Being already organized to that degree of perfection by its union with the organism, the matter is well disposed to operate as living when separated. It is not in mere potency to life, as food is before being digested and assimilated into human flesh. It is actually part of the one living being which is virtually many. Whether the part can live by itself depends on how nearly disposed its potency is to separate existence. This usually is a question of how complex the organism is.

In a simple one-celled organism mere division can result in two complete beings, yet nobody would argue that before the division it was two, except potentially. A worm is so simple in structure ("a digestive tract with a hole on each end") that again mere division can result in two worms: it is already disposed to such an actuality by its nature. A cutting or slip of a plant virtually contains the perfection of the whole plant, as all it lacks are roots. As functions and organs become more specialized, any part contains virtually less of the whole, and its chances of independent survival diminish. Organs and tissues in test tubes can exist for any length of time only when the other functions of the total organism are somehow artificially supplied in the laboratory by the ingenuity of the scientist. They lack that self-organization and self-maintenance we noted in the total living thing. Hair and fingernails are said to grow for a while after death. The cells which produce them are so specialized that even though organized for that function and virtually independent for it, they cannot supply other vital operations and so eventually cease. But they are capable of that function at any time only because organized to that level by the total organism, which contains the virtualities or potencies for many different kinds of operation.

Thus man is seen to be actually one, but virtually multiple by reason of his many parts and potencies. He is virtually an animal and virtually vegetative, for these powers are part of his nature. It is not surprising that some of these parts may have the potency for separate existence, but far from proving that they have independent being before separation, the evidence points to the conclusion that they have these potencies only in virtue of their existence as parts of the whole.

5. *Multiple personaltiy*. Here we must distinguish between *person* in the philosophical sense and *personality* in the psychological or psychiatric sense. Person is in the realm of substance, an individual supposit of rational nature (Boethius). It is a question of being: one *is*, not has, a person.

Personality belongs to the order of accident: the total of one's habit systems and conscious experiences at least potentially identifiable by this person as his own. We say "at least potentially identifiable" because actual recall and recognition may involve all degrees of difficulty, from a simple absent-mindedness or normal forgetting up to those abnormal states in which the different streams of experience and habits can be linked only by the use of extraordinary means like hypnosis or sodium pentothal. A hysterical case of multiple personality, then, is simply two sets of accidents inhering in one substance. The person is the same, but the psychological personality may change, as first one and then another set of habitual associations and emotions is operating. Psychiatrists like Morton Prince and William McDougall who reported on some of the classic cases claim that the person would always recognize the underlying identity when cured, or under hypnosis, or at least on his death bed.

Similarly, when a man says, "I wasn't myself today," he is not claiming to be a different person or substance, but merely that today's actions and feelings were not his usual personality pattern. The very expression implies a recognition of his identity, for if he were not the same person it would be pointless to remark that he is not acting as the same. The person also retains his identity in schizophrenic "splitting" of personality, or in other instances of personality conflict. Here thought and emotion do not correspond. Affect may be inappropriate, or lacking. Sense appetite may attract one way, reason the other. Does this destroy the unity of the person? Quite the contrary: there would be no true internal conflict were these not all the powers and operations of the same one man, as we noted in Chapter 13 when explaining the multiplicity of man's powers as proper accidents of one substance.

NATURE OF LIFE

Having established the unity of man as one living organism, we must now investigate further just what life is, and how a living being differs from nonliving things. We have already made considerable strides in this investigation by analyzing man's intrinsic finality, his self-organizaton for the good of the whole. For our first naïve impression of the difference between living and nonliving objects has to do with whether they exhibit self-initiated activity. Thus if a thing is inert and moves only when moved from outside, we judge it is dead; and primitive peoples may judge an automobile alive because it apparently moves itself.

Upon closer analysis, it is seen that the car does not truly move itself, for it depends upon designer, mechanic, and driver, and so is utterly different from a living thing, which, as we have seen is self-sufficient. Even its "self-starter" turns out not to be such in reality. More important, the "self" of the car is seen to be not one being, but an aggregate, a number of substances put in juxtaposition by an external agent and moving each other as distinct things. But for one thing to move another is not self-activity at all. On the other hand, some apparently inert glob of matter will upon further examination be found to exercise remarkable self-activity: it grows, nourishes and repairs itself, and reproduces its kind. We say it is alive, whereas the automobile is not.

Self-actualizing Independence

Examining all things which are said to live in contrast with those which do not, we find one characteristic appearing throughout: a living being exhibits a certain independence or self-sufficiency in

action. It is more a self-contained unit, less dependent upon outside help for preserving and exercising its nature. The most marvelous electronic computers not only do not grow by themselves, but
they need a host of technicians swarming over them to keep them
in operation. They cannot gather knowledge; it must be fed into
them. They cannot use the data creatively; what they do must be
programmed into them. In contrast, man grows, develops his mode
of operation, maintains life, "becomes" the whole universe through
his knowledge, and is a determining force in his environment—the
source of all this activity is within, and he utilizes and transforms
what he receives from outside with a power of self-actualization not
found in nonliving things.

Vital activity thus is seen to be fundamentally *that by which the
living thing perfects itself*. Some capacity for such operations seems
to be found in all living beings, and none found in nonliving things.[4]

"Living" Is Analogous

The term "living" covers a wide range of beings. Since to live is to
be a certain way, the term must be analogous, as being itself is.
Proportionately to the being of the thing and thus analogously, this
self-activity will be found to exist in all living beings from God down
to a fungus. (Extension of the term in metaphors like "living waters"
is, of course, an extrinsic and improper analogy.)

God is most independent and self-contained. Intellectual life
displays more initiative than sensory life, and so the analogy runs
down the hierarchy of living beings from God and angels through
men and down to brutes and vegetation. The lowest plants are somewhat at the mercy of their surroundings, but even here we see vegetative life go on, adapt, and reproduce, while machinery obsolesces,
mountains crumble, and that very symbol of stability, Gibraltar, is
being slowly torn asunder by apparently feeble plant life.

Within these main categories we see degrees in the analogy; for
instance, the genius with intuitive intellect is far less dependent
upon outside help than the moron, and the circus monkey exhibits far

---

[4] Aristotle, *De Anima*, I, 1 (412a, 14–15); II, 2 (413a, 23–413b, 2); Thomas
Aquinas, *S. T.*, Ia, 18, 1–3.

more self-movement than the shellfish. Life is by no means a univocal term, but there is an analogy of proper proportionality between each living being and the degree or manner in which it has the characteristics. Man is our most direct and primary example; other kinds of beings up and down the scale are known only by analogy with our own life. But man is a good one to have to start with, since he combines immaterial and organic operations and thus partakes of the characteristics of both spiritual and material living beings.

Man's Self-initiating and Self-perfective Activity

Let us now examine in greater detail the notion of life as we find it verified in the operations of the living things we know, especially man. The first two operations man shares with God and the angels; the last four with the organisms below him.

1. *Knowledge*. We have already seen that knowledge differs from just passively receiving an impression precisely in the power of the knower to enrich his own form by the addition of cognitive forms in act.

2. *Appetition*. Likewise, in appetition man perfects himself by responding to stimuli in ways which show a lack of proportion between stimulus and response, indicating how in varying degrees he initiates the response from within.

3. *Nutrition*. The self-perfective nature of a living being is clearly illustrated by the manner in which we take food from the outside and transform it by our own digestive powers so that it is assimilated into living human flesh. Contrast this with the way in which crystals are said to "grow" by the mere accretion of more of the same from the outside, not by taking foreign matter and actively transforming it within themselves as living beings do by intussusception. We "feed" a car gasoline, but nothing comparable to nourishment takes place, for the gasoline never becomes automobile. Nourishment continues even after a thing reaches maturity and stops growing.

4. *Growth*. Perhaps the most fascinating evidence for both the unity and self-perfectiveness of the human organism comes from embryology, where we see a simple one-celled structure evolve and

differentiate itself into two, then four cells, gradually into three general types of tissue, and eventually into the marvelous complexity of organs that make up the complete body. Who or what does it? No mother takes credit for the fashioning that goes on within her during those nine months. No anatomist would presume to construct a single organ like the cochlea of the ear, much less the interrelated regulatory system we call the endocrine glands. The nervous system alone comprises some twelve billion cells, all starting from one. And considering the permutations and combinations possible, it is statistically staggering that they should ever fit together correctly, never mind in the majority of cases. With so many trillions of chances of something going wrong, the fact that the human being ever comes out right attests to incredibly unified order. Here is internal finality at work, self-organization undeniable. Compare this process with the assembly line at the Ford plant where a car is "growing" as it moves along. How many external agents are at work, and how little does the car have to do with the whole process! Yet a fetus does not even take blood from the mother; it manufactures its own from materials it selects from the mother's blood stream. Even one-celled animals grow to full size by their own active assimilation of matter.

5. *Self-repair*. The pruning of vines and fruit trees, and the fact that some lower organisms will grow a whole new limb if one is amputated, are interesting illustrations of this power of living things, but they may cause us to overlook the importance of something so prosaic as the formation of scar tissue, without which all human recovery would be impossible and all surgery vain. As doctors never tire of reminding themselves, they do not "cure" anything really, but only help nature to help itself. The surgeon does not join tissues; he puts them in close proximity in the hope that nature will take over and do what he cannot. But if you "injure" your car or a computer, you can expect no self-perfecting powers to work a repair. (The rust that forms after damage is not analogous to scar tissue. Just the opposite: it is decomposition rather than growth.)

This ability for self-repair in living things is sometimes called irritability, but the term seems unfortunate. The "irritability" of dynamite is not for the good of the dynamite, but destroys it. The compass needle is stimulated or irritated by a magnet, but this reaction does not have as its purpose the preservation and perfection of the compass itself, as self-repair has. The expression "adaptation to environment" is similar: thermostatic controls "adapt" furnaces to temperature changes, but the lack of intrinsically unified finality is soon apparent. There is nothing here comparable to the way a heart or a kidney, for example, will double its capacity to accommodate an increased demand.

6. *Reproduction*. Lastly, we have machines which make other machines, but we have no machine capable of reproducing itself, as human beings can, and also other animals and plants. This indefinite reproduction of the species is one of the central marvels of the biological world, to which thousands of interesting phenomena pertain. Some are controversial and demand scientific investigation, but the one fact is clear. Nonliving substances may produce other nonliving substances, but only living things reproduce, i.e., make more of the same species, which in turn can reproduce themselves, and so on indefinitely.

An electronic computer might conceivably be programmed to produce other electronic computers so programmed, but besides their dependence on man not only in origin but also for repair, they would not in any true sense grow. Their production would be all by extrinsic accretion, not self-organization. They would also differ from living beings in the matter of nutrition, since man would have to supply materials. If this hypothetical self-reproducing "machine" were programmed to get its raw materials from, say, the atmosphere, in addition to having the power of true internal growth and self-repair, it would *be* a living thing. But could man make a living being? We must first ask what "makes" a living thing. That is the problem for our next chapter.[5]

Immanent Action

Those familiar with other textbooks in Scholastic philosophy may be surprised that no mention is made of immanent action as a criterion of life. The reason is twofold. First, neither St. Thomas nor

[5] The actual question of synthesizing a living being will be discussed toward the end of Chap. 19.

Aristotle uses the notion of immanent action at any time in defining life. They often distinguish between immanent and transient action, but never as a means of dividing living beings from nonliving. The Greek equivalent of "immanent activity" does not even appear in the entire text of Aristotle's *De Anima*. Secondly, the use of this term creates unnecessary difficulties which arise purely from the terminology and otherwise present no philosophical problem. The usual solution is to broaden and distort the meaning of "immanent" until it means "independently self-perfective," as we have explained vital operations to be. But this is not what the word means, either in modern English, medieval Latin, or Aristotle's Greek. Immanent means "remaining within" and could apply to the activity of even nonliving beings which have motion within themselves, be they Aristotle's fire or the modern physicist's atom. It is the opposite of transient (that which acts on another), whether the agent be living or not.

The question is not whether the orbital movement of subatomic particles is immanent; the question is whether it is self-initiating and self-organizing. The truth is that it depends wholly on an external cause for its origin, and shows no signs of true growth, self-repair, or species reproduction. Any change tends to make it something else, instead of perfecting. Aristotle's physics may have been inadequate, but his definition of life in terms of *self-perfective* activity (rather than *immanent* activity) is open to no more difficulties from nuclear physics than from his own concept of fire,[6] which also had its principle of operation within itself.

Some Difficulties

1. Could it be argued that the movement of the animal is given it by its parents, just as the movement in the atom is given it by its external cause? They would thus be equally lacking in self-initiated activity.

Answer: The difference is that when the atom is formed it has this

---

[6] *Physica*, VIII, 4, 254b, 7–256a, 3; Thomas Aquinas, *S. T.*, Ia, 18, 1 ad 2um. See James E. Royce, S.J., "Life and Living Beings," *The Modern Schoolman*, 1960, 37:213–232.

motion actually; it is formed as a moving substance. But when the animal is formed by its parents, it may have little activity at all; it is given not motion but a nature which can cause its own motion.

2. Does not a spring or a rubber band have self-action?

Answer: Not of its own nature, but only by reason of external agents: the manufacturer and the person who stretched it. Passive rather than active, it does not initiate the movement and exercises no control over it. Like electricity and unlike living beings, it depends wholly on external forces to cause its motion.

3. But is not the motion of self-initiated activity contrary to the principle of causality? To move or perfect oneself would seem to be pulling oneself up by his own bootstraps. After all, nothing gives what it hasn't got. If I already have the perfection, then I don't need so to perfect myself; if I do not, then I cannot give it to myself.

Answer: The budding philosopher who answered that the professor might not have a headache but still gave one to *him* was more accurate than perhaps he knew. The professor did not have the headache actually, but he did possess it virtually by possessing the power to give the student one. Recall our explanation of the very nature of an operative power. By it the living being possesses the perfection of a certain vital activity *virtually*. When not exercising the power, it has the formal perfection of this activity only in potency. But as an efficient (instrumental) cause the power actually exists. There is no circle of causality here, because the potency and act are in different orders. It is in potency in the realm of formal cause, but an actually existing efficient cause. Answering another way, one might say that it is precisely in the possession of this unique kind of self-perfective power that living beings differ from nonliving, and any attempt to explain life by reducing it to nonlife is begging the question at issue. Man is virtually multiple; even the amoeba or animals in the one-cell stage have powers of self-movement which require a stimulus as part cause at most, being themselves the principal cause of their own action.

4. But "movement" seems hardly to apply to higher vital activities such as intellection.

Answer: Movement here is taken in a broad sense of any transition from potency to act, not mere locomotion.

5. But in contemplation of truth already acquired, there seems to be no movement even in this wider sense; certainly in the case of God's knowledge there is no transition at all from potency to act.

Answer: True, and we include under the term any such perfection, which is operation only in an analogous sense.[7] The question is not of passage from potency to act, but independent self-sufficiency in having the perfection. And this is why our answer to question 3 above does not make all living beings independent of God, or self-sufficient in being. The difference between God and creature is one of dependence in being; the difference between living and nonliving is one of dependence in operation. God gives *being* to both dog and atom; but to the former He gives a nature capable of initiating its own activity; to the latter He gives only the activity which comes with the nature.

6. Certain seeds have been found fertile although kept for centuries, and frogs have likewise been kept in a state of suspended animation for alleged decades or more. Are they alive?

Answer: Remember that our definition speaks of being, not activity. The acid test is not whether the being is actually manifesting self-perfectivity, but whether it is the kind of being that can do so. Now the proof that these beings are capable of vital activities is the fact that they do grow when given an opportunity; mere opportunity will never evoke such activity in a rock or a machine. (There is some evidence that minute, infinitesimal activity may be going on in seeds, such as hardly measurable carbon dioxide exchange; this would not alter our position, which is based on kind of being, rather than on actual activity.)

REVIEW QUESTIONS

1. "Life is vital operations." Criticize on two counts.

[7] Aristotle, *De Anima*, II, 5 (417a, 28–417b, 9). Cf. Thomas Aquinas, *S. T.*, Ia, 18, 1; 79, 2; Marianne T. Miller, "The Problem of Action in the Commentary of St. Thomas Aquinas on the Physics of Aristotle," *Modern Schoolman*, 1946, 23:135–167, esp. p. 144.

2. What is the relation between the notion of life and the unity of man?
3. Why does our discussion of unity begin with the arguments against it?
4. "You have to say either that an automobile is one since all parts work for a common purpose, or that man is not one since he is made up of various parts, chemical elements, and powers." Solve this dilemma.
5. Do both man and auto have composite unity? Is it of the same kind?
6. "Chemical properties of the elements are manifested within the living organism; therefore the body is not one, but an aggregate of substances." Criticize.
7. Philosophy says man is one. Clinical psychology gives us cases of multiple personality. Do they therefore contradict?
8. Are living bodies essentially different from nonliving? Why?
9. Are living bodies essentially superior to nonliving? Why?
10. Is "life" a univocal or analogous concept? Why?
11. Explain how "life" could be an analogy of intrinsic (proper) proportionality.
12. What is the basic characteristic of all living beings?
13. Name four functions which distinguish organic life from all nonliving beings.

FOR FURTHER READING

AQUINAS, ST. THOMAS. *Summa Theol.*, Ia, 18, 1 and 2. *Summa Contra Gent.* I, 97–98.

BECK, WILLIAM S. *Modern Science and the Nature of Life.* New York: Harcourt, Brace, 1957.

VON BERTALANFFY, L. *Problems of Life: An Evaluation of Modern Biological Thought.* London: Watts, 1952.

DRIESCH, HANS. *Mind and Body.* London: Methuen, 1927.

DRIESCH, HANS. *The Science and Philosophy of the Organism.* London: Black, 1908. 2 vols. Seems to make the soul an efficient rather than formal cause.

GILBY, THOMAS, O.P. "Thought, Volition and the Organism," *The Thomist*, 1940, 2:1–13.

GILL, HENRY V., S.J. "Entropy, Life, and Evolution," in *Fact and Fiction in Modern Science.* New York: Fordham University Press, 1944.

GOLDSTEIN, KURT. *The Organism.* New York: American Book, 1939.

KLUBERTANZ, GEORGE P., S.J. *The Philosophy of Human Nature.* New York: Appleton-Century-Crofts, 1953. Pp. 12–49.

LILLIE, RALPH S. *General Biology and the Philosophy of Organism.* Chicago: University of Chicago Press, 1945. Chap. 2.

MOORE, THOMAS VERNER. *Cognitive Psychology.* Philadelphia: Lippincott, 1939. Pp. 45–73, 86–89, 550–559.

DU NUÖY, LECOMTE. *Human Destiny.* New York: Longmans, 1947.

SCHRODINGER, ERWIN. *What Is Life?* New York: Macmillan, 1945.

SINNOTT, E. W. *Cell and Psyche: The Biology of Purpose.* Chapel Hill: University of North Carolina Press, 1950.

WINDLE, SIR BERTRAM C. A. *Vitalism and Scholasticism.* St. Louis: Herder, 1920.

WINDLE, SIR BERTRAM C. A. *What Is Life? A Study of Vitalism and Neo-vitalism.* St. Louis: Herder, 1908.

16

THE SOUL AS FORM

Dualism unsatisfactory. Notion of formal cause; substantial form, hylomorphism. Definition of soul. Proof of soul's existence. The soul and vital operations. Three souls or one? The psychosomatic problem.

A fundamental contradiction now seems to rear its ugly head. We have insisted on the unity of man as one being, yet we hear talk of matter and soul as distinct, and therefore two. Which is man, one or two?

MONISM, DUALISM, OR NEITHER?

As in most problems which have occupied great minds, conflicting answers have been proposed. The most common are monism and dualism. Since each has been held by intelligent men, it behooves us to examine them for what truth they may contain. Yet they cannot both be right, and perhaps neither is satisfactory. Even this may suggest an answer for us.

Monism

From the Greek *monos*, meaning "one," this refers to any philosophy which teaches that there is *only one ultimate principle of*

279

reality in the universe, and therefore in man. Monism may be either frank or disguised.

Frank monism may be either of two extremes: (1) materialism holds that the only ultimate principle of reality in the universe is matter. Remember that this is not a mere assertion of the reality of matter: if so, most of us would be materialists. Rather, it is a denial of all else. It is a metaphysical position, not a scientific one, since pronouncements about the ultimate constituents of all being are beyond the scope of science. Some scientists hold this as their philosophy, many do not. (2) Idealism or spiritualism also holds for only one ultimate principle, but says the only reality is mind or spirit. This is less common than its opposite in modern America. But many contemporary Oriental philosophies, some schools of Western thought in recent centuries, and a few sects in America today emphasize the reality of the spiritual to the exclusion of the material, which is considered unimportant or even nonexistent. Some religious groups hold this as their philosophy; many do not.

Disguised monism is a softened expression of one of the above extremes, usually materialistic, since men do not like to be crude about a position when there is conflicting evidence. Thus we have double-aspect theories, epiphenomenalism, and certain forms of parallelism. In all of these a subtle materialism is couched in terms which speak of the conflicting evidence as merely pointing to two aspects of the same ultimate reality, like the concave and convex sides of the same curve. For them, brain and thought are "a matter of how you look at it."

Exaggerated Dualism

This holds that *man is two beings,* actually dual. If intelligent men have seen evidence which convinces them of the reality of matter, and others see equally impressive evidence for the reality of the spiritual, it is not surprising that still others should see good reason to accept both lines of evidence and reconcile them in some system which attempts to account for both instead of denying either. This has been done many times over the centuries in various ways, the most common being some form of either parallelism or interaction-ism.

Psychophysical parallelism says that man is two beings, only appar-ently united. Matter and spirit each function with varying degrees of independence of the other. Something is happening in the brain while thought goes on, but there may be no real connection. Certain forms of occasionalism also fit in this category.

Interactionism is by far the more common form of dualism. The union here is real and not merely apparent; but it is only accidental, the union of two complete substances. This position says man is two things, each acting on the other. In some books on psychosomatic medicine we have a "mind" which worries and a "body" which develops gastric ulcers, as if the psyche and the soma were two beings.

However poetically we may speak of the jockey and his horse becoming "as one" in a race, we are clear they remain two separate substances of different nature. Whether or not Plato actually com-pared the union of body and soul to that of a horse and rider, he seems to have held the ultimate duality of human nature. With Aristotle's works lost, it is doubly understandable that early Chris-tianity seized upon Platonic dualism. Not only was nothing better known, but Plato's notion lent itself readily to the antithesis be-tween pagan debauchery and the salvation of one's soul with which the early Christians were concerned. This conviction was perpe-tuated by the ascetical writers for similar reasons, with strong in-fluence from neo-Platonism. Even St. Ignatius of Loyola speaks of the soul as "imprisoned within the body."

Descartes imposed this dualism upon most of modern philosophy and psychology when he made man a body and a mind, hooked to-gether at the pineal gland. This is probably the most fateful error in the history of philosophy, for no matter how intimate and intricate the interaction of mental and bodily processes, dualism of this sort destroys the unity of man.

Precisely here is the crux of the problem: dualism reconciles the two streams of evidence, for material and for spiritual reality in man, only to run afoul of the evidence that man is one being. Dualism is a most unacceptable term to most modern psychologists and biologists, because they are too impressed with the unity of human nature. They are so determined to maintain it that they often prefer to adopt some disguised materialistic monism because they see no other answer, even though it means unsatisfactory explanation of the evidence for the immaterial.

Is there a way out of this dilemma? Apparently not, if we read the many books which present the above alternatives and then leave the student with the impression that they have exhausted the possibilities.[1] Culturally conditioned to think of Aristotle and the medieval Christian philosophers as sterile and unrealistic speculators, these modern writers are emotionally almost incapable of looking to them for a solution, or even of being aware that they held another alternative worth considering.

Matter and Form

The word "dualism" is so firmly entrenched in the modern mind as meaning Platonic or Cartesian exaggerated dualism that one hesitates to invite contamination by using it for Aristotle's system. At least it should never be so used without a modifier like "moderate" or "hylomorphic" to indicate that we repudiate any splitting of man into two beings.

To Aristotle and St. Thomas, man is neither two beings, as dualism asserts, nor composed of only one principle, as the monists say. For them, prime matter and substantial form unite as coprinciples to form one being. Man is thus composed of two principles, not one. But he is one being, not two. Lest this strike one as so much jabberwocky, we must review the whole notion of formal causality to insure a correct conception of the soul as form. Only thus can the matter-and-form dualism of Aristotle be understood as utterly different from the rank dualism which the term suggests to most moderns, even those well informed about other philosophies.

---

[1] E.g., Professor W. E. Hocking of Harvard, *Types of Philosophy*; Edna Heidbreder, *Seven Psychologies*; H. Flanders Dunbar, *Mind and Body*; Gardner Murphy, *An Historical Introduction to Modern Psychology*.

FORMAL CAUSALITY

In the last chapter we satisfied ourselves that man is essentially different from nonliving things. As inquirers we want to know what this difference is. Science gives us many wonderful details. Physiologists describe how the endocrine glands normally maintain just the right balance of inflammatory and anti-inflammatory hormones in the blood stream to enable the body to repair injury with maximum speed and minimum infection. Psychologists from Freud to Skinner have elaborate theories on the workings of human dynamics and the learning process. Embryologists tell us that during the nine months the skin covering the young retina becomes transparent and transforms itself into cornea and lens because of a substance set free by the optic vesicle in the cerebrum. Excellent, and ingeniously discovered.

But the philosopher in his search for ultimates finds these less an explanation than something to be explained. *Why* should the optic vesicle secrete a substance just at that time with the property of rendering the skin translucid? And why should it act thus on just the skin over the future retina? Why is man the kind of being that is capable of operant conditioning or ego-involvement, conformity or creativity? What makes him to *be* a man at all?

We say that a thing is the way it is be*cause* . . . and get many different answers, all true. The question "Why?" can be answered in as many different ways as there are kinds of cause. Some are easier to grasp than others. Cause in general is that which positively contributes to the being of the thing. Why is this statue what it is? Because the sculptor wanted money, or to honor Abraham Lincoln (final cause.) Why? Because the sculptor made it that way (efficient cause). These two are obvious. They are called extrinsic causes, because they are outside the statue.

Intrinsic Causes

But there are other causes to account for why the statue is what it is, causes within the statue itself and therefore called intrinsic.

Neither the sculptor's purpose (money) nor the sculptor himself and his instruments (efficient causes) enter into the internal constitution of the statue.[2]

Material. But if we ask why the nose has this particular shape at the bridge, we might get the answer, be*cause* the marble at this point had a peculiar soft grain in it. This is an intrinsic cause, the matter or *material* cause. It causes by giving itself to the effect, by allowing itself to be acted upon by the efficient cause in such a way that it can become this being. We may ask why the statue is heavy, enduring, or beautifully colored, and again the cause of these properties is the marble itself, the material cause. It is passive, but important because its potency sets the limits of the finished product: even the greatest sculptor cannot make a statue with no material at all to work on, nor out of something which does not have the potency to become statue.

Formal. Lastly, we may ask why this statue is what it is, i.e., a representation of Lincoln, and we will get the answer, be*cause* the marble has the form or figure of Lincoln. This answer does not deny that the sculptor made the statue, nor that he made it for the reason alleged. It points to what he produced in it, which makes it to be what it is. This is intrinsic to the statue, its *formal* cause.

Form is nothing more or less than the fact that the thing is the way it is: this kind of being, resulting from the adequate action of an efficient cause (or causes) upon a properly disposed material cause. It is not a thing separate from the being itself, like an extrinsic cause. Like a material cause, it causes not by doing anything, but just by being. Cause here is an analogous term. To cause by being desirable (final) is a different thing than to cause by mallet and chisel (efficient), and both are again different from intrinsic causes, which contribute to the existence of the statue internally, by giving themselves to constitute the very being of the thing.

To speak of internal cause as "it" is misleading, for that which has existence is neither the material cause nor the formal cause, but the

[2] If we say the image did, we are still speaking of an extrinsic (exemplary) cause; for as a cognitive form it exists in the sculptor's mind, and acts as a cause by directing his efficient activity. It even existed before the statue, so it could not be inside the statue. It is also called *extrinsic* formal cause.

composite being which results from matter being in this form. It even seems preferable to say *being*, rather than *having*, this form, because the latter suggests that matter is a thing which can have, and form something which can be had. Neither are things. The existing being is a thing; matter and form simply refer to the fact that this designated quantity of being (matter) is now existing as this kind (form) of being.[3]

Substantial Form

So far, our example has been of shape or figure, an accidental form. This was only to set the stage. What we are really concerned with is substantial form. Not the fact that the marble is this or that shape, but that the substance is marble at all [4] and not calcium chloride or U-235 or green cheese. Exactly the same reasoning applies, except that we move from the realm of accidental change to substantial change.

This is most clearly seen against the background of man's unity established in the previous chapter. Suppose a house collapses in a heap, or is exploded into bits (but not burned). It is no longer a house. But is there a substantial change? No, for the simple reason that the house was not *a* substance to begin with. The mass of rubble is still wood and plaster, steel and glass, exactly the same substances as before. The house was not one, but many beings, each with its substantial form. It is still the same beings, now arranged in a different accidental form or shape. Accidental means not having its own proper act of existence. The shape of the house had no existence other than the existences of the parts so arranged. The substantial forms of wood, glass, and the rest remain.

In contrast, examine a human corpse. The accidental forms of shape, size, structure, and arrangement of parts, color, and weight may all be exactly the same as they were in the living body. It looks

---

[3] We shall see that there is a problem here when we discuss the spirituality and immortality of the human soul. But we elect to establish the notion of soul as form first, and face the apparent contradictions later.

[4] We prescind from the question of whether marble is a unified substance or an accidental aggregate of particles. The facts of substantial change and the unity of the living body are true in either case, so it need not concern us.

more like a body than the ruins look like a house. But has there been a substantial change? Yes. This matter is no longer living human flesh. Regardless of accidental similarities, it is a different kind of being. There is no longer that by which it was human; there is only a heap of molecules temporarily arranged in the shape of a man. We say this matter has changed its substantial form.

In the collapse of the house, wood remained wood, glass remained glass. In the death of the body, matter ceased to be human and became nonliving matter. When the carpenter builds the house, he changes wood into different sizes and shapes, and arranges an accidental unity with other substances, but he does not make wood into some unified, different kind of substance we call house. But when man eats food, he actually transforms water, carbohydrates, and other substances into his own substance, so that this same matter which formerly existed by the substantial forms of these molecules (or whatever physical unit is postulated) now ceases to be that kind of being and begins to exist by the substantial form which makes matter to be man.

Form is cause in a very analogous sense. Produced in matter by the efficient cause, it strikes one as having more of the nature of effect than cause. It causes only by uniting with matter to form this being. Not being a thing, it does not come and go. It simply begins and ceases accordingly as the being is or is not this kind of being, just as the lap does not go anywhere when you stand up, nor the light when it goes out. To return to the comparison of the statue: when we say the sculptor "put" the form of Lincoln into the marble, we do not mean that he went out and got a form of Lincoln and somehow inserted it into the marble. No, he efficiently caused the marble to *be* this form. And when the statue crumbles into dust, we do not say that the form of Lincoln "went" anywhere, but simply that the marble ceases to be in this form. To ask whether the material being and its substantial form are one, says Aristotle, is as silly as to ask whether the wax and its shape are one.

Hylomorphism

This concept of form or formal cause is simple, yet absolutely fundamental to any understanding of man as a composite unit.

Descartes admitted that his brilliant mathematical mind was unable to grasp the notion correctly ("a formis abhorreo"), and he spread the philosophical bassinet into which modern psychology was born with a tradition of univocal, efficient causality which made even good minds, thus culturally conditioned, practically unable to conceive formal causality.[5] It is the key to Aristotle's conception of the ultimate nature of material beings, called *hylomorpism*, from Greek words for matter and form.[6]

Matter is seen to be subject to change. At one time it is food on a plate, later it becomes man, still later it is so much fertilizer. (And since this can become plant and therefore food again, we call the process the metabolic or nitrogen cycle.) Matter is actually only one thing at any one time, but it is potentially many. When actually cabbage, it is potentially cow. When actually beef, it is potentially man. When actually man, it is potentially fertilizer (or tiger, if there are man-eating tigers about).

From this we conclude that any material being is a composite of two substantial principles: one which makes it actually what it is, one which makes it potentially other things. If there were no substantial potency, there would be no change. We would have to say that in digestion food was annihilated and more human flesh created, and that in death the matter of the living body was annihilated and the matter of the corpse created. The only alternative is to say that man has two constituitive principles, one by which he is actually man and the other by which he is potentially corpse. If both were actual, he would be two things at once; if they were both only potential, he would not be what he is. There must be a principle (matter) common to man, food, and corpse; and a principle (form) specific to each.

These principles are not directly observable. They are the logical conclusion from the facts of change. But the process by which we

[5] Karl Buhler, William James, and Harvey Carr are among the eminent psychologists who have said that the matter-and-form unity of Scholastic philosophy is probably the best ultimate explanation of man, but that it was too difficult for them to think that way when not habituated to it from youth.

[6] *Hyle-* would be more correct than *hylo-*, and *eidos* would be really more appropriate in this context than *morphe*. But the term hylomorphism has crystallized now. The adjective hylomorphic is perhaps best translated as simply matter-and-form theory, union, etc.

arrive at them is a far simpler deduction from commonly observable facts than the findings of physics or chemistry. They are intelligible, but not picturable. Easily understood, they cause trouble if the student attempts to imagine them. This chapter is a task for intellect, not sense perception.

Matter and form are called incomplete substances, because each, of its nature, demands to be united with the complementary incomplete substance in order to constitute a complete substance. Since the potential principle is not any kind of matter by itself, but only because it is united with this or that substantial form, it is called *prime* matter, first matter, or substantial potency. It is passive, indeterminate but determinable. Since the form here is what determines this matter to be not merely in this shape or manner but this specific kind of being, it is called *substantial* form.

Prime matter has a relation to substantial form similar to that which second or informed matter (substance) has to accidental form. Thus the matter is actually marble because it has the substantial form[7] of marble. If we pour acid on it and make it something else, this is a change of substantial form. If we give it a different shape while it remains marble, this is a change of accidental form. Just as the marble cannot exist without being in some shape (perhaps irregular and nameless), so prime matter cannot exist without being some kind of matter.

Recent advances in chemistry and physics seem to confirm this notion, for it seems now that, theoretically, any material substance can become any other material substance, if we can just find the right way of changing it. "You can't make a silk purse out of a sow's ear" is an old adage aimed at emphasizing the impossibility of producing an effect which is not within the potentiality of the material cause. A sow's ear certainly does not seem very apt matter, and the task seems impossible until we learn a great deal more organic chemistry. But you *can* make a silk purse out of it now by feeding it to some silkworms or fertilizing their mulberry bushes with it!

[7] Or forms (see footnote 4).

THE SOUL

Returning to the notion of death, we can exemplify Aristotle's four chief kinds of cause in this way. Why is John Jones dead? (*a*) Because Smith murdered him: efficient cause. (*b*) Because Smith wanted revenge: final cause. (*c*) Because Jones was the kind of being that could die: material cause. (*d*) Because his matter has ceased to be united with the human substantial form by which it was this organized whole: formal cause.

Each is a true and legitimate answer to the question. Each is different, for it points to a different kind of cause. (*a*) and (*b*) are extrinsic causes, (*c*) and (*d*) are intrinsic. Each exerts causality in a different way and is irreducible to any of the others. The same electricity will run a waffle iron and a radio, but no amount of current increase will give you music instead of waffles. No amount of final causality will make an efficient cause. Likewise, no amount of efficient causality will make a formal cause.

This is important, for the most common error here is to think of the soul as an efficient cause, a gimmick or demiurge moving man from within. This is the error of certain vitalists, who oppose the mechanistic theory because of the manifest intrinsic teleology of the organism, yet attribute to the parts some kind of intelligence or otherwise hypostatize what are only constituents. The mechanists themselves, taking this view and thinking of the soul as an efficient cause or physical energy, are triumphant when investigation reveals no such entity. For this reason vitalism is a misleading term. It is nonmechanistic, but it is not always hylomorphic.

What is a soul? The soul is simply *the substantial form of a living thing,* or that by which we live. It is that which "makes" this matter living: not efficiently, for the parents did that; nor is it why the matter functions this way, for that is the final cause or purpose; nor why it is *able* to live, for that is material cause; but why it is actually living body, or that which unites with matter to make it be living body.

How do we know we have a soul? By reasoning from the facts.

There is a difference between living body and corpse. Not imaginary, but a real difference. Not accidental, but an essential difference. What makes the difference? It must be something real and essential. This essential difference is the soul. Being a principle and not a being, it is not empirically observable. Our knowledge of it is the result of a reasoning process. We can conclude to its existence just as surely as we can to any truth where the facts are clear and the logic inescapable. But it does not depend upon our reasoning for its existence: the difference between man and a corpse is a reality whether I am thinking about it or not.

Is it a difference in man's intrinsic nature? The efficient cause made the living body different to begin with. But the difference is not merely extrinsic. Life is not a constant succession of activities imposed upon living beings from outside by their maker, like so many ventriloquist's dummies being operated by a super-manipulator. Their efficient cause, either Ultimate (God) or proximate (parents), actually gave them an internal nature capable of doing these activities themselves. The dummy's wit is not his own, but that of the ventriloquist. But my thoughts and choices and growth are mine, not God's or my parents'. The difference then is within me, intrinsic to my nature.

As part of human nature, the soul is not supernatural. One way it can be known is by faith or theology, but being a natural constituent it is also discoverable from facts and reasoning, just as the area of a triangle might be revealed by God and taken on faith, but can also be demonstrated by geometry. To many of us the first notion of the soul was a religious concept. This is legitimate, but not our only source of knowledge about the soul. Darwin once said, "Linnaeus and Cuvier were my masters, but they were just schoolboys to old Aristotle," who is called the biologist's biologist. Firmly rooted in naturalistic observation, Aristotle derived the notion of the soul from factual observation, not religious sources.

The reason why the soul is apparently inescapable and always bobs up again after an occasional submersion by a wave of materialism is that it is the logical conclusion from the facts. Non-Scholastic writers as diversified as C. E. Joad, Henri Bergson, John Wild, Pitirim

Sorokin, Charles Spearman, and Carl Jung bring this out in their historical studies.[8] William James finally arrives at the soul "in which scholastic psychology and common-sense have always believed" (1896, Vol. I, p. 181). The imageless thought controversy uncovered much evidence leading in this direction. Eminent neurophysiologists like Wilder Penfield [9] and Karl S. Lashley have concluded that the brain is simply the instrument used by the soul. Just because it is contrary to the positivism and materialism which have been prevalent in Western culture until recently does not make the soul an exclusively Catholic concept.

But does this widespread conviction indicate that the soul is necessary? People once thought the existence of a substance called phlogiston was necessary to explain fire, and that something had to keep the stars from falling. People once thought the earth was flat and the sun moved around it. Perhaps this universal acceptance of soul is a similar error, to be corrected by the progress of science.

The above list was not intended as an argument from authority. Nor is truth settled by a majority vote. The last court of appeal in philosophy must always be evidence and logical reasoning. The point was simply that the soul is not a merely religious, much less Catholic, concept. In scientific matters involving facts not easily obtainable, error among nontechnical minds is quite understandable. Apart from the fact that the ancient Greeks knew the earth was round, and that St. Thomas said, long before Galileo, that it was just as possible that the earth went around the sun as vice versa, those errors can be detected and demonstrated by further scientific progress. But such technical problems are questions of efficient causality, and the soul must not be thought of as an efficient cause.

This problem is not one to be solved by the accumulation of more and more facts, as Gardner Murphy says (1949, p. 445). The necessary facts are commonly observable. The question is what kind of being man is, granted the facts about his operations. This is a philo-

[8] Other non-Catholic writers who attest to this constant recurrence of the soul include M. J. Adler, M. Black, J. H. Coffin, William Crashaw, H. Driesch, C. Sherrington, and R. Müller-Freienfels. (See the General Bibliography.)

[9] Statement at Johns Hopkins Hospital, Mar. 25, 1950. Lashley admits that this "sounds like a plunge into mysticism" (1930, p. 20).

sophical question. The solution is a correct conception of formal cause. The soul is not contrary to the laws of physics and chemistry; it is the reason why the organism obeys different laws and performs different activities than matter does when not united with the soul. Psychology has progressed not because the soul was discarded, but because of advances in scientific and quantitative methods of studying man's operations.

To discard the soul is to say that matter of itself is capable of life. Then every material being should be alive, and the difference disappears. Body is not body simply because it is matter. Pinch my arm and you pinch me only because this matter is substantially one with the rest of me. Amputate the arm, and this matter ceases to be mine; you would not pinch *me* now if it is lying discarded in a corner of the surgery. It is no longer that composite of soul and matter we call body.

Does the fact that the matter is organized explain life? Then all organized matter should be alive, and again, how account for the difference between man and a corpse? As we have seen, organized structure is precisely what needs to be explained, rather than being an explanation. For however much its structure may explain the activities of a machine, we can always fall back upon the machinist to explain the structure. But what explains the fact that a living body organizes its own structure by its own activity? Structure cannot explain itself, much less before it even exists, as in the one-cell stage from which we all start. But it contained within itself its own blueprint in the genes and chromosomes, you say, produced by its efficient cause. Very well, but blueprint is not structure: it is precisely this ability of an organism to implement its own blueprints which points to its being a different kind of nature from nonliving things. Now substantial form is simply the fact that this is a certain kind of being: it is the internal reality which accounts for the real, intrinsic difference between living and nonliving being (S. T., Ia, 75, 1).

Definition of Soul. As usual, we have proceeded inductively, examining the facts and drawing what conclusions we could from them. We do not make up a definition out of our heads and then look for it to be verified in nature. We are now ready to formulate the results of our investigation in a definition. We have seen that the soul is simply the reality in man which makes him different from a corpse: the substantial form which unites with prime matter to form man. Soul is *the ultimate internal formal principle by which we live.*

"Ultimate"—as Aristotle says,[10] it is the first act. It is prior to operation, which is second act; prior even to operative powers, which are actual perfections of substance even though in potency to operation. Substantial form is the first actuality, the most fundamental reality about a thing, the fact that it *is* this kind of being. By *ultimate* we mean just this—as opposed to proximate principles of vital operation, our operative powers. Powers are accidental forms, the proximate principles by which man exercises life. Soul is substantial form, the ultimate principle by which man is living being.

"Internal"—intrinsic to man's nature, as explained. Opposed to extrinsic causes, it is constitutive of man's essence. God may be the ultimate extrinsic cause, but we are looking here for the ultimate within the nature of man himself.

"Formal"—as distinct from an efficient cause. The soul must not be thought of as a "thing" inside man causing various activities. Rather, it refers to the fact that *man* is capable of causing these activities, and that man is not just matter, since matter of itself does not live. Neither is the soul alone the man, for our analysis of change has shown that, in addition to form which makes him actually what he is, there is another internal constituent, the material principle which makes him potentially other.

"Principle"—an incomplete substance or a contituent of being, rather than a complete being itself. It is a cause, a reality which contributes positively to the being of a thing. We saw that the concept is analogous: that formal causality is not like other contributions to being.

"By which"—not *that which* lives (the supposit, man), but *that by which* man is living. Man is the efficient cause of his activities, the soul is the formal cause of his being alive.

[10] *De Anima,* II, 1, 412a 28.

"We live"—all vital operations: vegetative, sensory, rational.

Proof. We can summarize our findings in these two chapters as follows:

⟨[Man operates as a unified being, essentially superior to nonliving beings.

⟨[But such operation requires an internal principle of unified vital operation, or soul.

⟨[Therefore man has a soul.

The major premise was established in Chapter 15. The minor is simply an application of the principle of causality, that operation follows being. A thing's nature is manifested by its operation, and substantial form determines the nature of a material being. Soul is simply the name used for the substantial form of a living organism. (The substantial form of a nonliving being has no special name.)

THE SOUL AND VITAL OPERATIONS

We have already seen that life is not the vital operations themselves, for *to live* is simply *to be* the kind of being that can have such activities, whether actually having them or not. Operation is not being.

Toward the end of World War II, a Russian soldier was pronounced dead by the attending surgeon. A team of progressive physicians went to work. Four and a half minutes later his heart began to beat. He breathed in three minutes, became conscious in an hour.[11] Many similar cases have been reported, and previous experiments had revived dogs which had been reported dead for as long as fifteen minutes. A letter to *Time* asked where his soul was during these four and a half minutes. To answer such a question, we must recall how we know there is a soul anywhere, at any time. We know it only if a being shows a capacity for vital operations. Suppose we give heart massage, artificial respiration, oxygen, blood transfusion, adrenalin injections, etc., to a corpse in the morgue. Nothing happens, because it is not the kind of being that can respond to such stimuli by spontaneous activity. The difference between the soldier

[11] "Medicine: 4½ Minutes of Death," *Time*, July 23, 1945, p. 75.

and the corpse is that he could and did respond, and therefore had that within him by which he was alive. His soul is precisely that which makes him capable of so reacting. Since the soldier did so, the only answer is that his soul was right there within him, that he was alive.

The fact that the stimulation in this case was extraordinary is irrelevant. The amount of help from the outside needed by the living body is a matter of degree: we all depend upon certain things, such as oxygen, food, water. These do not give life, but are used by a living body. No amount of such stimulation will make a corpse live, for it cannot itself take and use them.

But did not the surgeon certify that the soldier was dead? As the doctor who edits *Time's* "Medicine" column said in a footnote, medical men have never defined death. Those who fail to distinguish between operation and operative potency are often oblivious to the difference between real and apparent death.[12] The above comparison with the corpse brings out that real death is a substantial change, while apparent death is a cessation of activities which are only accidents.

Just as life cannot be vital operations, so the soul cannot be the operations. The soul is first act, substantial actuality; the operations are second act, accidental actualities. Vital operations are the effect, not the cause, of man's life. They show life is there, but they do not explain it. The composite substance acts, proximately through parts and powers. For instance, there is no doubt that the heart pumping blood is a part cause (efficient) of life activity. But what makes the heart live? What makes it to *be* the peculiar kind of thing which will pump, year in and year out, adapting itself to shifting demands and even doubling its size? Blood may be pumped mechanically, but the machine does not live. Why is this particular glob of matter a living organism, and not so much fertilizer (molecules) arranged in the shape of a heart? Only because it is substan-

---

[12] For this reason, the Catholic Church permits conditional administration of the last rites in cases of apparent death, on the possibility that real death has not yet occurred and the soul is still present. For the same reason, Christ delayed until Lazarus had been buried four days and putrefaction had set in, to insure that His raising him would testify divine power.

tially united with a substantial form which is a principle of life: the soul.

Blood. Could the blood be the cause of life? Blood won't help a dead body, as we have seen. The heart must already be able to use blood. Blood is caused by living beings, not living beings by blood. Those who argue the blood is the soul because of a passage in the book of Leviticus (17:11) forget that this is symbolic; Moses was giving ritual, not teaching either science or philosophy. Such a position would create insurmountable difficulties. Would blood transfusion mean transfer of life, or that part of the donor's soul is now in someone else? If the soul is form, this would mean that part of the receiver actually is the donor, which is absurd. We can now pump all the blood out of a dog or an Rh baby, and pump in a new supply. Have we made the dog a different living being, or the baby a different person? This would follow if blood is the soul or principle of life. And how explain that the corpse may be full of blood yet dead, while the dog or baby devoid of blood can live?

Animal and Vegetable "Souls." The implication that the dog also has a substantial form as principle of life brings up the question as to whether all living beings have souls. This causes no difficulty if we recall what we mean by soul and how we discover its existence. Since any living being must have a substantial form which makes it essentially different from the nonliving, it is clear that in this sense every live plant and animal has a soul.

This strikes the student as strange only because he is used to thinking of the term exclusively as applied to man's spiritual, immortal soul as known from religion. We have already laid the foundation for a distinction in kinds of soul when we drew its existence from vital operations. For just as man exhibits some operations which are immaterial and other organisms do not, so his ultimate formal principle of operation is immaterial whereas those of others are not. Likewise, a plant's substantial form is known to be inferior to that of the brute animal because the animal has sensory cognition and appetition, which plants lack. There are as many kinds of soul as there are kinds of living being, for soul is what makes the being live in this way.

The whole function of the brute or plant soul is to unite with matter as a coprinciple of material (or at best quasi-immaterial) operations. Such a soul is called a material form because it is a principle only of material operations and wholly involved in matter. It is thus very different from the human soul which is also the ultimate principle of the strictly spiritual operations of intellection and volition. It is only to this latter form that we are used to attaching the term soul, but the language of philosophy need not disturb us if we are clear about the realities discussed. It is strictly a question of evidence: if a being exhibits no incontestable signs of immaterial operation, we do not assert it has a spiritual principle. The contrast will be clear from the next two chapters, where only the human soul will be seen to be spiritual and therefore immortal. Meanwhile, the notion of an animal soul helps us grasp the concept of soul as substantial form.

Three Souls or One? If soul is the ultimate formal principle of vital operations, and man has three kinds of vital activity, viz., vegetative, sensory, and rational, one might argue that by our line of reasoning he must have three souls: a vegetative soul, an animal soul, and a rational soul.

Once we understand soul as the formal cause of our being, to ask if man has three souls makes as little sense as asking if man has to have three sets of parents. Just as one act of efficient causality gave him being, so only one formal cause gives his substance this kind of being. Three or three hundred operations and powers would still be accidental forms; soul is substantial form. To have three souls or substantial forms would make him three substances or beings. It would mean the same substantial potency (matter) was actuated by three acts of the same order, which is absurd. By the same token, there is no need to postulate a third something as a bond between soul and matter, once we understand that they are related as act and potency.

Man is virtually vegetable, animal, and rational. But virtually means powers, capacities. The powers are all inherent in the same substance. Man is actually one nature, potentially many. He is not actually a plant; he is a man, with vegetative powers.

Unity of Man. We have already seen in Chapter 15 that man is one being. Therefore whatever constitutes man must ultimately unite as coprinciples to form one being. One must be careful here not to use an argument which will only prove that man is a very intimately united number of substances. This type of argument occurs when we argue from the unity of the effect rather than from the unity of the operation. Thus when several people push a car, the effect is one: the motion of the car. But the operations are several: there are as many "pushings" as there are pushers.

The common finality whereby the embryo grows eyes and ears long before it can see or hear shows that all is under the control of one organizing principle. The fact that it is the same ego or I who am the ultimate subject of operations at all three levels shows that I am one substance with many actions. They may interact and even conflict, but they are all mine. It is the same person who worries, gets ulcers, chooses, grows, and dies. This unity is especially evident from the nature of human knowledge: my sensory perception and my intellectual judgment are both mine, in the same consciousness. How compare an idea with an image, if it were one being who had the idea and another who had the image? The comparison is possible only because both terms of the comparison are my operations. That is why St. Thomas uses the fact of human knowledge in this connection, because the operation itself exhibits unity of diverse principles. Neither matter nor soul can have a perceptual judgment, only man can.

PSYCHOSOMATICS: REAL OR PSEUDO PROBLEM?

Having understood (not perceived) the nature of formal cause, we are now able to appreciate Aristotle's solution to the dilemma between monism and dualism. His third alternative is indeed a unique position, combining the truth of the various other theories and avoiding their inadequacies. It is a sort of middle position, but it is not true merely because it is in the middle. Rather, it is in the middle because a true theory must accept all the facts, and not be content with viewing reality from just one standpoint.

False Dilemma. It is almost amusing to observe the mental squirming of the author in the preface or introductory chapter of nearly any text in psychosomatic medicine. On the one hand, he is trying to impress upon his biologically oriented medical colleagues the reality and importance of the psychological as distinct from the physical. Worry and imagination *can* cause organic harm. On the other hand, he is trying desperately to avoid letting his insistence on the distinction leave him open to the charge of dualism. The reason is that the only dualism either he or his readers know is a Cartesian split of man into two beings.

Unfortunately, this dualism is usually assumed to be what the followers of Aristotle and St. Thomas hold. Nothing could be more false. Perhaps the biggest problem Aquinas faced in the thirteenth century was trying to "sell" Aristotle's hylomorphism to a world steeped in the neo-Platonic tradition of Christian asceticism which emphasized so strongly the opposition of body and spirit. But as Chesterton points out, sin is a spiritual act. The body is good and incapable of moral evil. Sin must involve a choice, and we have seen that volition is spiritual.

Organic Unity. St. Thomas had two great masters: Aristotle, whom he calls simply The Philosopher, and his own teacher, St. Albert the Great. Each was the outstanding biologist of his day. Throughout our discussion of man's activities, we have followed this biological orientation and emphasized the importance of sense in human cognition, and of emotions in human dynamics. Man is an organism, but a special kind: one that thinks. When arguing about the unity of man's nature, St. Thomas constantly refers to two basic pieces of commonly observable evidence: the fact of human knowledge and the fact of human death.

We point to an organism and say, "This man knows." What we point to is obviously material, yet we have seen that his knowledge is also immaterial. He must be a composite of both material and spiritual principles to account for this nature. Matter alone cannot know, any more than a dead eye can see. Spirit alone cannot see or feel. Idea, image, metabolism are all acts of the same agent. The two principles are distinct, but they are not separate. They form one being. Again, "This man dies." What happens is a substantial change.

He ceases to be a knower, a dreamer, an organism. He has ceased to be a man.

In this organically based view, soul is so intimate to man as substantial form that there is no question of his unity. The antithesis of psyche and soma becomes a pseudo problem. The student is not worried by apparent contradiction when he passes from elementary biology or psychology courses to psychopathology and psychosomatics, if his philosophical conception of man is that presented here. Not that St. Thomas has said everything possible about human nature. We have much to learn about man from the behavioral sciences. But he and Aristotle did give us the broad, basic framework or outline into which the details as uncovered can fit in orderly perspective. Having facts is useless if we do not know what to do with them.

Substance versus Accident. "Mind" and "body" really refer to mental and bodily processes. These are operations, therefore in the realm of accident. Just because man has two (or ten) different sets of operations, is he two (or ten) beings? Soul and matter are substantial principles which constitute man, whatever powers or operations he may have. Both matter and soul are needed to have a man, before he can do either mental or bodily operations.

Matter by itself cannot digest; a dead stomach does not develop ulcers. Only the composite of matter and soul can perform even "bodily" functions. So true is this that it is not correct to say "soul and body," for matter is not body until substantially informed by the soul. A body is composed of soul and matter; a corpse *was*, not *is*, a human body. Similarly, soul alone cannot see and feel, for these "mental" processes are organic and demand matter as a coprinciple. Mind is not a substance, but is operations and habituated powers. These powers, habits, and acts all inhere in the substance of man without destroying his unity, for accidents do not multiply substance. On the other hand, neither matter nor soul is capable of existing or operating by itself (we shall see the exception with regard to the human soul in Chapter 18). The potencies reside in the composite, which alone is a being.

To equate "mind" with soul, and "body" with matter, is to confuse the orders of substance and accident. This has been a favorite indoor sport since Descartes. Mind for him was substance, and ideas for those who came later were bits of this substance associated in various ways. Body was just matter, to be studied as a machine (see Figure 14). But can there be "just matter"? The physicist studies the properties of material beings and the laws of their operation, but as scientist he never tries to say what matter is. We have seen that matter is always some *kind* of matter, i.e., it is always united with some substantial form. If it is living matter, the name for this form is soul.

Psychologists studying the laws of behavior and experience again stop short of the ultimate nature of man. That is why it is absurd to criticize psychology for not treating of the soul. Scholastics who do so betray a Cartesian influence, forgetting the distinction between substance and accident. For the same reason, the old dichotomy between "physical" and "mental" is misleading and metaphysically incorrect. Much of the controversy about psychogenesis (the psycho-

Figure 14

Plato and Descartes

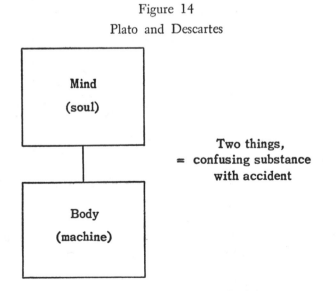

Figure 15

Aristotle and St. Thomas

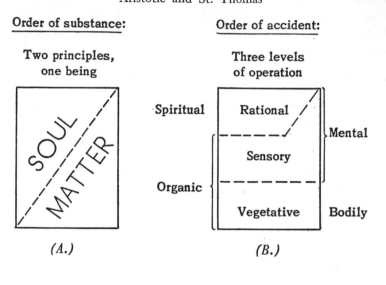

Order of substance:

Two principles,
one being

(A.)

Order of accident:

Three levels
of operation

·Spiritual

Organic

(B.)

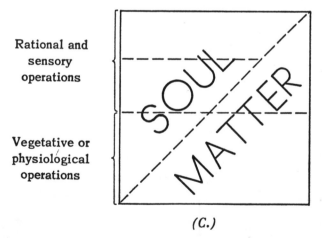

Rational and
sensory
operations

Vegetative or
physiological
operations

(C.)

logical rather than organic causation of mental illness)[13] is a tempest in a post-Cartesian teapot: the whole man is the patient, a psycho-

[13] Frederick H. Lund & Harry J. Glosser, "The Nature of Mental Illness: Diversity of Psychiatric Opinion," *Education*, 1957, 78:154–166.

biological unit. Water may be H₂O, but one does not ask whether a patient was scalded by the H or the O.

Figure 15 represents the hylomorphic view, first distinguishing (A) substantial principles on a diagonal axis, and (B) operative powers on the horizontal axis, then (C) combining the two diagrams below to give the total scheme. This composite diagram may appear complex, because it represents both accidental and substantial principles. But it will bear study, for it contains the solution to the pseudo problem created by Plato and Descartes. Note that "organic" and "mental" overlap at the level of sensory operations, for we have stressed the organic nature of perception and emotion. The diagonal line cuts across these, indicating that they demand both matter and soul (form) as substantial coprinciples. Herein lies the philosophical explanation of hysterical paralysis, brain waves, psychosomatic illness, shock therapy for even psychic disorders, motor-image theories of volition, and a host of other facts which are otherwise puzzling. The dotted line dividing rational and sensory operation cuts upward at the point where matter intersects, to illustrate that matter does not enter intrinsically into intellection and volition; but the diagonal continues, to indicate that matter does have a part (extrinsic) even here.

In the perceptual judgment, the intellectivo-sensitive act of knowing which is peculiar to man alone, we seem to intuit implicitly the relation of the intellective soul to matter as actuated to be my living body. In knowing myself as subject I experience my most intimate contact with matter, while at the same time I am aware that this very experience somehow involves immateriality.

REVIEW QUESTIONS

1. Is the soul a cause of man or of man's vital operations? Explain.
2. The soul is said to be the principle of vital operations. But in Chapter 13 we said that the principle of human operation was an operative power. Reconcile and explain.
3. Formulate your own definition of soul. Explain each important element in your definition.
4. Does every material being have a substantial form?
5. Does every material being have a soul?

6. Does every living organism have a soul?
7. Are there as many different kinds of souls as there are kinds of living beings?
8. Do a live man and a corpse have the same substantial form? the same accidental forms?
9. The soul is the principle of vital operations, and therefore prior to them; why is not this chapter prior to that on life-activities?
10. Is the soul directly observable? In what sense is its existence obvious? In what sense not?
11. Can the existence of soul be proved from the fact of substantial change occurring between living and nonliving things? Explain.
12. Can the existence of soul be proved from the fact of essential difference between living and nonliving things, even without the substantial change mentioned in the previous question? Explain.
13. Is it more correct to say that man is composed of body and soul, or that man's body is composed of soul and matter? Discuss.
14. Why were certain vitalists in error when they tried to discover scientific evidence of the soul as a cause or force in the organism?
15. If the soul is an efficient and not a formal cause, how many beings is man? Why?
16. Is it technically correct to refer to the resuscitation of the Russian soldier described in this chapter as a "miracle" of modern medicine? Why?
17. Is it correct to call the soul supernatural or divine?
18. Is an incomplete substance the same as a substantial principle?
19. Is it correct to refer to Thomistic hylomorphism as simply dualism?
20. When we say "body acts on mind, mind acts on body" (a) do the terms refer to the realm of substance or operation? (b) does the term body mean prime matter? Why? (c) does the term mind mean soul? Why?
21. In man, is spiritual coextensive with conscious (or mental)?
22. Is matter alone capable of digesting? Is soul alone capable of sensation?
23. Is matter coordinately or subordinately involved in digestion? in sensation? in intellection?
24. Is the so-called psychosomatic problem of interaction between body and mind a real problem or a pseudo problem (a) to the Thomist? (b) to the dualist? Explain.
25. If there is no dualism, then what constitutes internal conflict?
26. Can this problem be solved without the distinction between substance and accident?
27. Does a theory of three souls (one for each level of operation) solve the problem?

28. Show how one's theory of knowledge determines one's notion of man's nature and unity.
29. What is the difference between personality in psychology and person in philosophy?

FOR FURTHER READING

AQUINAS, ST. THOMAS. *Commentary on Aristotle's De Anima*. Books I and II. (Trans. by K. Foster & S. Humphries as "Aristotle. *De Anima* in the Version of William of Moerbeke and the Commentary of St. Thomas Aquinas," with an introduction by Ivo Thomas, O.P. New Haven: Yale University Press, 1951.)

AQUINAS, ST. THOMAS. *The Soul*. Trans. by John P. Rowan. St. Louis: Herder, 1949.

AQUINAS, ST. THOMAS. *Summa Theol.*, Ia, 75, 1–5; 76, 1, 3, 4 and 5. *Summa Contra Gent.*, II, 56–57; 68–69.

ARISTOTLE. *On the Soul*. I, 3; II, 1–4.

BRENNAN, ROBERT E., O.P. *Thomistic Psychology*. New York: Macmillan, 1941. Chaps. 3, 11.

CROWELL, DAVID H., & DOLE, A. A. "Animism and College Students," *J. Educ. Res.*, 1957, 50:391–395.

ENTRALGO, PEDRO LAIN. *Mind and Body, Psychosomatic Pathology*. New York: P. J. Kenedy & Sons, 1956. Gives history of the problem.

FEIGL, HERBERT, and others (Eds.) "Concepts, Theories, and the Mind-Body Problem," in *Minnesota Studies in the Philosophy of Science*. Vol. II. Minneapolis: University of Minnesota Press, 1958.

GANNON, TIMOTHY J. *Psychology: The Unity of Human Behavior*. Boston: Ginn, 1954. Chap. I.

GILBY, THOMAS, O.P. "Vienne and Vienna," *Thought*, 1946, 21:63–82.

GILSON, ETIENNE. *The Spirit of Medieval Philosophy*. New York: Scribner, 1936. Chap. 13.

GRUENDER, HUBERT, S.J. *Problems of Psychology*. Milwaukee: Bruce, 1937. Chaps. 1, 5, 6.

GRUENDER, HUBERT, S.J. *Psychology without a Soul*. (2d. Ed.) St. Louis: Herder, 1917.

HOENEN, PETER, S.J. *The Philosophical Nature of Physical Bodies*. Trans. by D. Hassel, S.J. West Baden Springs, Ind.: West Baden College, 1955.

McDOUGALL, WILLIAM. *Body and Mind: A History and Defense of Animism*. London: Methuen, 1915.

MAHER, MICHAEL, S.J. *Psychology: Empirical and Rational*. (9th Ed.) London: Longmans, 1921. Chap. 21–23 and 25–26 contain what is probably the most thorough treatment in English.

PEGIS, ANTON C. *The Problem of the Soul in the Thirteenth Century.* Toronto: Institute of Medieval Studies, 1934.

SIWEK, PAUL, S.J. *Aristotelis de anima libri tres.* (Edidit, versione auxit, notis illustravit.) Rome: Gregorian University, 1933.

SIWEK, PAUL, S.J. *La Psychophysique humaine d'après Aristote.* Paris: Alcan, 1930.

STRASSER, STEPHAN. *The Soul in Metaphysical and Empirical Psychology.* Pittsburgh: Duquesne University Press, 1957.

See also the pertinent chapters in the works by Gardeil, Gerrity, Olgiati, and Sertillanges in the list of *Readings* before Chap. 1.

17

NATURE OF THE HUMAN SOUL

Man more than mere organism. The human soul is substantial, with permanent identity. Soul is simple, inextended. Human soul is spiritual, essentially independent of matter but with some dependence. Presence of the soul in the body. Division, transplants. Differences in souls.

Human nature always presents "a difficulty which has been central in psychology: man, while a biological organism, is not merely that, but something more." This quotation might be from the biologist Aristotle, as he tries to reconcile hylomorphism with the clear evidence from the immateriality of intellection and volition that man's soul is spirtual. At the inorganic, plant, and animal levels, matter could not be without form, nor form without matter. The union was complementary and parallel, up to the point of the human form. Nobody likes to distort his own brain child, but honest acceptance of the facts forced Aristotle to make an exception of the human form, breaking the symmetry of his system. He concluded that, unlike

307

other forms, man's soul is somehow separable. It is spiritual and immortal.[1]

Or, the quotation might be from a disputation at a medieval university, where St. Thomas Aquinas is integrating the organic hylomorphism of Aristotle with the Christian tradition of the separability of man's spiritual soul. Had Aquinas been less daring, he would have taken the easy way and gone along with the prevalent neo-Platonic dualism, forgetting Aristotle. But he saw that the soundest course in the long run even for a theologian was to choose a philosophy which most accorded with experiential fact and rigorous logic, even though it did not come tailor-made to fit the needs of theology.

Aristotle, as a scientist-philosopher, was more concerned with universals, with essences. St. Thomas, as a philosopher-theologian, was more concerned with individuals, with existence. As a Christian he had even more reason than Aristotle to insist on the possibility of the soul's existence as an independent being after death; it was for these souls, he believed, that Christ lived and suffered. According to hylomorphism, the separated soul after death is not a complete human nature, a position not to the liking of some theologians. But this did not bother Aquinas as much as the apparent inconsistency in the dual role which the human soul plays in his doctrine, as form of the body yet spiritual and immortal. How could the soul be both a principle of being when it is the form of man, and a being after man's death? Is it a being and yet not a being? This is a metaphysical scandal.

That St. Thomas felt a real challenge in presenting Aristotle to his contemporaries is evident from the number of times he treats this problem, and the long dialectical approaches which precede his own solution. In these, he gives about twenty reasons why it seems that the human soul cannot be both a form and a thing.[2] If it is only a

---

[1] De Anima, II, 2, 413b 26–27; III, 4, 429b 5. χωριστός can be separate, separated, or separable, but the first two meanings are ruled out by our discussion in the two preceding chapters. He goes on in III, 5, 430a 22 to say that the soul is ἀθάνατον (immortal) and ἀίδιον (everlasting). Needless to say, much of Aristotle's thought here is difficult to interpret, and we are undoubtedly inclined to read our own meanings into his words.

[2] Qq. Disp. de Anima, q. 1; also C. G., II, 56–71; S. T., 76, 1 and 5.

form, a principle and not a being, then this individual's immortal destiny is a joke once the man dies. If it is capable of separate existence, then man before death seems to be two beings. His answer is that the soul is reductively in the genus of substance, but it is not a complete substance. As form it is incomplete substance and coprinciple with matter, but being spiritual it is capable of separate existence, independent of matter. It is not a nature or essence (second substance), but it belongs to the realm of substance rather than accident.

In the last analysis, his position seems to be this: The evidence all points to the soul being a coexisting form when united with matter, but an existing thing when man dies. It is both a being and a principle of being, but not at the same time. Since there is nothing absurd or contradictory in this, why not accept the logical consequences of the facts?

Actually, the quotation which opens this chapter is by the editor of a current symposium on personality.[3] History repeats itself, and the same facts keep demanding recognition in every century. In establishing that intellect is strictly immaterial in Chapter 6, we witnessed the breakdown of all attempts to explain thought by brain or sense. We noted that J. B. Rhine of Duke University felt he had evidence for spirituality from his work on extrasensory perception and telepathy. Not basing our case on such disputable grounds, we preferred to examine other facts which have convinced a host of philosophers and psychologists that man is more than merely a biological organism.

Why does the editor quoted say that what his eminent authors have hit upon is "a difficulty which has been central in psychology"? Partly for the same reason that it was a problem in the time of St. Thomas: they approach it from a historical background of Cartesian dualism, much as the early medievals did from a background of Platonic dualism. But whereas the Christian Middle Ages were vividly convinced of the reality of spirit, modern thought until recently has been dominated by materialism. The result is greater

---

[3] J. L. McCary (Ed.), *Psychology of Personality: Six Modern Approaches* (New York: Logos Press, 1956), p. xiii.

difficulty in accepting the spirituality of the human soul. Only recently have leading psychologists like Maslow, Mowrer, Cantril, G. Allport, and others begun to make it scientifically respectable to talk of man's spiritual aspects. Facts have a stubborn way of constantly reasserting themselves, however, even in the face of materialistic preconceptions.

Taking our cue from St. Thomas's bold devotion to truth, in the previous chapter we emphasized the unity of man, even though in so doing we might seem to play down the nature of the soul as a spiritual reality capable of separate existence after death. This was a calculated risk, necessary if our task is to provide a concept of human nature representative of all the pertinent facts. Only thus could it be adequate to the needs of the biological and social sciences.

Our opening quotation indicates that, like ourselves, others have discovered that man is "something more." We have already examined the nature of thought and choice, and found them strictly immaterial in themselves, even though extrinsically dependent on matter. The conclusion can now be drawn that the ultimate formal principle of such operations must itself be spiritual, and only extrinsically dependent on matter.

THE HUMAN SOUL IS SUBSTANTIAL

We have put the soul in the realm of substance. The nonphilosopher is inclined to think of substance as synonymous with material substance, as when he speaks of a very solid floor as substantial. But substance is opposed to accident, and means simply that which exists in itself and not in another by inherence. Substance can be either spiritual or material. God and angels (presuming they exist) are spiritual substances. They exist in themselves, not as accidents of something else.

Matter and form are called incomplete substances, because they require each other to form a complete nature. But no number of accidents would add up to a substance. Accidents may be material, like size, shape, and quantity. Or they may be spiritual, like ideas and volition. They can never exist by themselves; they are always the shape or idea of something. Since matter and form belong in the genus of substance rather than accident, we say that the soul is substantial even though not a complete substance. Powers, habits, and acts all require an ultimate subject in which they inhere. This is the material composite in the case of vegetative and sensory powers, but must be the soul alone for intellect and will.

The logical positivists who deny substance appear slightly less logical than positive at this point. These men are understandably reacting against the deductive essentialism of the rationalistic age which preceded them. Like some of the extreme semanticists, they seem inclined to say that because I cannot define "breakfast" to their satisfaction, they are justified in denying that I ate breakfast at all. But positivism is not the only alternative, as is clear even historically from the rise of existentialism and other realistic philosophies, and from the fact that several of the leaders of logical positivism in America have abandoned that position. Most of the difficulties of the positivists stem from a faulty concept of substance passed down from Locke and others, and the confusion of the proper realms of science and philosophy. Substance is not a static, unknowable substratum. It is existing reality, dynamic and changing, knowable by philosophical analysis which goes beyond the mere linking of words to individual sense experiences.

Soul Is Basis of Personal Identity. William James and others have proposed theories which would make the ultimate subject of our mental processes the stream of consciousness itself. In this hypothesis ideas would be accidents not inhering in any substance, thoughts without a thinker. This betrays a Cartesian concept of mind. It contradicts the very notion of an accident whose nature is to inhere in substance. And it fails to explain the enduring sense of personal identity we experience. They speak of a "brand" or "familiarity mark," but as James admits the crux of the whole explanation is a bald assumption: "the only point that is obscure is the act of appropriation itself." [4] If there is nothing to do the appropriating, nobody to recognize and claim the brand, I have no basis for assert-

---

[4] William James, *Principles of Psychology* (New York: Holt, 1896), I:340. He goes on to admit (p. 344) that he cannot prove it.

ing that these thoughts are all mine. The ultimate explanation of conscious identity throughout a stream of thoughts and memories is the fact that they are all acts of the same knower.

The metabolic cycle replaces all of the matter in our bodies regularly. Every seven years, it used to be said, but science and the monthly food bill tell us it is much sooner than that. Why am I still the same person? There must be some permanent element in man's nature which remains through all these changes. I am still responsible for acts committed when every molecule of matter was different. My lawyer could hardly get me off a murder charge on the grounds that I am not now the same person because my matter has been replaced since I committed the act. Chaucer or Dante might take twenty years to complete a masterwork; a scientist may pursue one line of research for even longer. The soul is what makes possible the continuity of their line of thought. We have seen in Chapter 15 that the abnormalities of amnesia and multiple personality do not invalidate this position, which is further confirmed by psychoanalytic and other studies of personality development from infancy through adulthood. Thanks to sodium pentothal and hypnosis, it now seems theoretically possible to recall any conscious experience we have ever had, given the right stimulus. If so, there must be an abiding substantial ego through all the interchanges of matter.

THE HUMAN SOUL IS SIMPLE

To be simple is to be undivided and indivisible, to lack parts. Since there are many different kinds of parts, there are many kinds of simplicity. *Spatial* parts are the result of extension. To have spatial parts is to be quantified. We can designate these parts in an extended being: this half, that third. Lack of spatial parts is called quantitative or integral simplicity. *Constituent* parts are the result of composition. To have constituent or entitative parts is to be compounded in the order of essence or substance, e.g., by matter and form. Lack of such parts is called essential simplicity.

The human soul has integral and essential simplicity; i.e., it lacks spatial and constituent parts. We do not claim lack of the metaphysical "parts," essence and existence, which would be *absolute* simplicity and proper only to God. Nor do we claim that the soul lacks virtual or *operative* parts. The soul is complex, not simple, in so far as it has many different powers. But these "parts" do not destroy its entitative simplicity, since they do not indicate substantial composition as constituent elements and spatial extension do.

Proof. As usual, we argue from operations to nature. Any simple, inextended operation could only come from and reside in an inextended subject. Quantified being can only give rise to extended operations. Extension is an infallible sign of composition, for it shows potential multiplicity. But where there is no sign of composition, we can only conclude that the agent is simple. Now an idea, a judgment, an act of choice, perfect reflection, the permanent identity of the conscious ego, all show inextension. Matter excludes other matter from occupying the same space; these acts show a compenetration, a disregard for the limitations imposed by quantity, which can only be due to the fact that they are not spatial. My concept of a triangle cannot be measured. I can have larger and smaller images, but the idea of what a triangle is applies equally well to all triangles, large and small, which could not be possible if the idea had size itself. My idea of an elephant is no bigger than my idea of a flea, for neither is quantified. Ideas do not occupy space: not having parts, they cannot extend over quantified matter. Nor does a simple idea occupy many parts of the brain at once, for then we would have many ideas, not one, of any one thing. A judgment means recognition of identity or nonidentity of two concepts; but if one concept is in one space, and the other in another part, I could never get the two together in a judgment. The only conclusion is that the ultimate subject of such simple operations is itself simple.

THE HUMAN SOUL IS SPIRITUAL

The above argument may not strike one as overwhelmingly conclusive. This is partly because our imagination gets in the way. We cannot picture these concepts, so the reasoning is hard to make very graphic. Another reason is that the attribute of simplicity itself is not very impressive. Any form, even that of beings below man, is simple per se, extended only by reason of its varying relation to matter. Spirituality is much more important, and peculiar to man's soul alone. The argument may well be considered after spirituality has been discussed, to appreciate its full significance.

What does spirituality add to simplicity? Independence of matter. A mathematical point, say the mid-point of this wooden table, is simple. It is inextended, has no spatial or constituent parts. But it is not spiritual, for it is wholly dependent on the table for its existence. Burn the table, and the mid-point vanishes. We do not destroy it by breaking it up into pieces, for it has no actual or potential parts. But we destroy it by destroying that upon whose existence it totally depends.

The same applies to the substantial form or "soul" of the plant or brute animal, though here is positive perfection beyond that of the mathematical point. These forms are simple, and cannot be broken into parts. But since they are wholly dependent upon the material composite for their existence, when the plant or animal dies the form simply ceases. Ceases what? To coexist, since the only existence it has is coexistence with matter in the being of the composite. But in the case of the human soul, its intellectual and volitional acts indicate a different relation to matter. Matter is the principle of individuation. If ideas are universal, they are without individuation and therefore without matter.[5]

Spiritual in the strict sense means *intrinsically independent of matter.* This does not exclude extrinsic dependence on matter, as the rational intellect of man differs from the angelic and divine precisely by its dependence on sense organs and phantasms. But matter does not enter intrinsically into the very nature of thought. Matter is intrinsic to sense knowledge, only extrinsic to thought.

Proof. If the human soul is intrinsically independent of matter for at least some of its operations, then it must be intrinsically independent of matter in its being, for being is known by its operations. An effect cannot be above its cause; spiritual operations can never flow from a material principle. We have already established the strictly

[5] S. T., Ia, 75, 2 and 3.

immaterial nature of thought and volition in earlier chapters. Now these operations cannot reside in a material being as their ultimate subject of inherence, for a spiritual accident cannot inhere in a material substance. Therefore the human soul is spiritual.

Spiritual does not mean supernatural, much less divine. We have insisted that the soul is a constituent of man's nature. But if it is the nature of man to think and choose, then an ultimate principle of such spiritual operations is natural to man. Immaterial does not mean unnatural, any more than metaphysical is the same as mystical or even mythical. Our thinking needs to be clear here, for not only do we naturally look for sensory images to accompany each concept; we also tend to think of real as synonymous with material.

The most powerful things in the world are things we cannot see or feel. Ideas start wars, and thinking can change a whole economy. Choices based on principle, or on love and hate, direct whatever is done by bulldozers or atom bombs. We yield to rights, or fight for them. None of these—idea, love, hate, principle, right—is something you can weigh or measure. The materialists themselves, by their elaborate hypotheses or appeals to unknown but discoverable factors, simply confirm the assertion that man can soar beyond the confines of sensory observation. If the facts argue that something is knowable in the realm of spirit, but unaccountable in material terms, logic demands that we accept the spiritual explanation rather than hold out blindly for a material one.

It is true that if you cut up a man, you will not find a soul. It is also true that if you cut into the man whose idea it is to deny the soul, you will not find an idea. Attempts to prove or disprove the soul by accurate weighing before and after death miss the point, as does photography at the moment of death. If the soul is spiritual, it can affect neither scale nor photographic plate. Discovery of more and more facts in physiology will never supplant the soul, for these facts will never explain spiritual operations. Biochemistry is continually revealing more marvels which call for soul as substantial form, but afford no explanation of universal ideas and lofty choices. If matter can think, you cannot explain why all material beings do not; if it cannot, then you cannot explain in material terms the beings that do. Thought and choice are irreducible to the laws of physical nature; above but not contrary to such laws, they remain within the metaphysical laws of being and causality.

Degree of Independence. We say that the soul is independent of matter "for at least some" of its operations, because we do not wish to imply for an instant that it is independent of matter for all. Distinct but not separate from soul, matter enters directly and necessarily into vegetative and sensory operations. For these the soul is *intrinsically dependent* on matter. Neither an angel nor a separated soul can digest or feel, because neither has bodily organs, which are essential for such processes. The subject of organic activity is the composite of which soul and matter are coordinate causes. St. Thomas acknowledged freely that fever, a blow on the head, or strong passion could diminish or even eliminate temporarily the exercise of free choice. He saw no contradiction between organic causation of mental disorder and the spirituality of the soul. The moderns have more in common with Aristotle and St. Thomas than they realize, and less with Plato and Descartes.

In contrast, soul alone is the principal cause of spiritual activities, with the organic (through sense) only a subordinate cause. Brain is only an extrinsic organ of the intellect. As seat of the internal senses, brain certainly has a relation to thought; but the relation is too indefinite and out of proportion for it to be intrinsic or essential. It is only extrinsic and instrumental.

PRESENCE OF SOUL IN BODY

If the soul is simple and spiritual, how is it located in an extended body? This question implies that body is matter alone, and misses the essential notion of soul as form. If soul is united to matter as act to potency, if it actualizes matter to form body, there is no question of body being a somatic container for some ghostlike psyche. It is really just as correct to say that matter is in the soul as to say that soul is in matter. Each unites with the other to form man, even man's body. The soul is wherever man is, for that is what makes matter to be man. Being simple, it is wholly there wherever it is.[6] When an arm is cut off, there is not less soul than before. The same soul is simply not united with as much matter. When a baby grows into a man, his soul is not bigger; it merely actualizes more matter.

But the soul does not actualize matter in exactly the same way throughout the body. Otherwise each part would be man, instead of just each part being human. Parts differ in structure and function. The soul exercises its various operative potencies through various organs. Thus the power of vision is in the eye, not the hand. St. Thomas saw no difficulty in localizing the activity of the internal senses in the brain. A blow on the head which leaves one unconscious has not eliminated the soul, but suspended the organic activity by which the soul exercises certain of its powers. The soul is virtually multiple even though essentially simple. It has only potestative or virtual "parts."

Virtual presence differs from spatial presence. It means to be in a given place by virtue of some power exerted, rather than by occupying any quantity of space. If an angel were to move a chair, we would say that the angel was virtually present at the particular place where the chair was. The angel could not be there quantitatively, for being simple and spiritual it occupies no space. But it exerts causality at this point of space, so it is there by its power. Similarly, the soul is present in the eye by virtue of its vegetative powers and its power of vision, and so with the other parts of the body. Again we emphasize that the soul is not an efficient cause. It is not an entity residing in the eye and looking through it. It is the form of the eye, making matter able to see; the composite does the seeing.

The soul as form is only present in those parts which are actually the unified substance of the living human body. It has no substantial union with food not yet assimilated, waste products not yet excreted, bacteria and other parasites, fillings in the teeth, nor perhaps other apparent parts of the body.

Indivisible. When discussing the unity of man in Chapter 15, we saw that an organism can be potentially many even though actually

[6] S. T., Ia, 75, 8.

one. Now the soul is the principle of actual unity; matter is the principle of potential multiplicity. The soul therefore cannot be divided; it is simple and indivisible. Living bodies can be divided, not by dividing their souls but by dividing the composite in such a way that the matter after division is still organized at the level of perfection of a living body. Being thus organized means that it has the substantial form (not mere shape) of a living thing. The act of division was sufficient to produce matter having this form, since the matter was already living and virtually, though not actually, a separate being. This is also what happens when an embryo is divided at the one-cell stage and grows into two complete individuals. Human identical twins present a slightly special case, and will be noted in Chapter 19.

Transplants. These notions are useful in understanding the relation of soul to such phenomena as skin grafts and organ transplants. As long as it was an integral part of the donor's body, the tissue was informed by the donor's soul. Being virtually capable of separate vegetative existence by reason of such information, when severed it becomes actually living with its own vegetative form. It may continue to live by this form after being implanted, either indefinitely, like the graft on a fruit tree, or until such time as the receiver's body gradually replaces all the cells of the new tissue with its own cells. In the case of skin grafts between identical twins, the new part seems to become directly informed by the soul of the receiver, losing its own form at the time the graft is made.

INDIVIDUAL DIFFERENCES

A disputed question among Scholastic philosophers is whether men differ only in their bodies, each having the same kind of soul, or whether human souls themselves differ from one another. This difference would be accidental, of course, for all are essentially human.

Some maintain that all individual differences are in the matter, every human soul being of the same kind and in itself of the same degree of perfection. This seems to suit a dualistic conception such as that of Plato or Descartes, where soul is a separate entity.

Others, including St. Thomas, hold that because of the intimate union of soul and matter there is a real though accidental difference in souls.[7] A soul is not just any human soul, but the unique form which unites with matter to form John Smith and no other. It corresponds to the perfection of the body, as act is limited by potency. This position is quite in accord with the interdependence of thought and brain described in Chapter 8. It also emphasizes the unity of man, wherein matter and soul are not separate but coprinciples of one being. Human nature is thus better understood as the source of the perceptual judgment, the knowledge characteristic of man, wherein the universal principles of being are seen in sensed objects.

REVIEW QUESTIONS

1. What relation do you see between the influence of Cartesian dualism and the prevalence of materialism in the beginnings of modern psychology?
2. Is the human soul a being or a principle of being or both? Explain.
3. Do you prefer to begin with the spirituality and independence of the soul and then discuss its hylomorphic union with matter, or vice versa?
4. What facts indicate that the soul is what gives continued identity to the person?
5. Are all spiritual substances simple?
6. How does spirituality differ from simplicity?
7. How do you show that the human soul is spiritual?
8. Is the human soul in this life entirely independent of matter for any operations?
9. Is it intrinsically independent of matter for some operations? Which?
10. Is it extrinsically dependent on matter even for these?
11. Is it intrinsically dependent on matter for some?
12. Is the entire soul present in one's finger?
13. When the finger is amputated, is the soul cut off? part of it?
14. Do you think that all human souls are alike, and individual differences are only in matter?

[7] Thomas Aquinas, S. T., Ia, 85, 7; C. G., II, 81; In Sent., d. 32, q. 2, a. 3. Cf. Slavin (1936); Koren (1955), p. 258. On the unique pattern of endocrine functioning proper to each individual, and other evidence on physiological basis for innate differences, see R. Williams, Biochemical Individuality (New York: Wiley, 1956).

FOR FURTHER READING

ADLER, MORTIMER J. *What Man Has Made of Man.* New York: Longmans, 1937.

AQUINAS, ST. THOMAS. *Summa Theol.* Ia, 75, 1, 2, 3 and 6; 85, 1.

ARISTOTLE. *On the Soul.* III, 4, 5.

FERM, VERGILIUS. *First Adventures in Philosophy.* New York: Scribner, 1936. Pp. 429–445 give an objective treatment of materialism versus spirituality by a non-Scholastic.

McCORMICK, JOHN F., S.J. "The Burden of the Body," *The New Scholasticism,* 1938, 12:392–400.

MAHER, MICHAEL, S.J. *Psychology: Empirical and Rational* (9th Ed.) LONDON: Longmans, 1921. Chaps. 21–23.

MARTIN, OLIVER. "An Examination of Contemporary Naturalism and Materialism," in John Wild (Ed.), *The Return to Reason.* Chicago: Regnery, 1953. Pp. 68–91.

WILD, JOHN. *Introduction to Realistic Philosophy.* New York: Harper, 1948.

St. Thomas and many Scholastic authors are very brief on the spirituality of the soul at this point, since they consider the groundwork has already been done in the arguments for the spirituality of the intellect. See Chap. 6 above, and the final section of the *Readings* therein: "Thought Not a Function of Brain." The growing rejection of materialism in the area of psychotherapy is attested by such writings as the following:

FRANKL, VIKTOR E. *From Death-camp to Existentialism.* Boston: Beacon Press, 1959.

FRANKL, VIKTOR E. *The Doctor and the Soul.* New York: Knopf, 1955.

MAY, ROLLO, & others (Eds.) *Existence: A New Dimension in Psychiatry and Psychology.* New York: Basic Books, 1958. Includes material by L. Binswanger.

SARTRE, JEAN-PAUL. *Existential Psychoanalysis.* Trans. by Hazel E. Barnes. New York: Philosophical Library, 1954.

SONNEMANN, ULRICH. *Existence and Therapy.* New York: Grune & Stratton, 1955.

18

IMMORTALITY OF THE HUMAN SOUL

Meaning of Immortality. The argument from spirituality.
From the natural capacities of men. From the moral order.
The separated soul. Individuality of souls, transmigration.

Quo vadis, where are you going? We pride ourselves on being reasonable, and have jokes about people who find themselves on trains or planes and don't know where they are going. Surely it is reasonable to expect a person to know whither he is headed, what direction or meaning there is to his going, even if he does not fully know what lies at the end of his journey. Even the vagrant hobo or wandering vacationer at least has some idea of what he wants: survival, independence, recreation, perhaps some other legitimate or intelligible goal.

What is the end of life itself? It would seem supremely unreasonable to live out our whole lives without knowing whether they have any meaning, any goal. If life here has a destiny and a purpose, one cannot live the same way as one would if there were nothing but

321

oblivion and annihilation after death. The answer to this question will affect radically the whole conduct of one's life. A man's scale of values, intermediate goals, criterion of success, and conception of happiness all hinge on the meaning he attaches to life on earth. If the grave is the end of everything for him, every moment and every decision will be different than if there is a life beyond. With the question of immortality our investigation of human nature reaches its climax.

Nearly Universal Conviction. The Judaeo-Christian tradition of Western civilization has always believed firmly in the immortal destiny of the human soul, as attested clearly in both the Old and New Testaments of the Bible. The conviction is deep in the teachings of all the major religions of the world, the classic literatures of both Oriental and Western cultures, and the folklore of pagan primitives around the globe. As philosophers we cannot appeal to religious faith, but this widespread agreement itself suggests that we are here at grips with something very fundamental to man's nature and able to be deduced from commonly observable facts.

Some Deny. There are some who teach that death is the end of everything for a man. They usually approach the problem with a preconceived materialism which does not allow for a spiritual soul capable of survival after the death of the body. Sometimes they are dissuaded by the ineffectual attempts to establish a life beyond the grave made by those who appeal to spiritism, mediums and séances, or other forms of occultism. These do the cause of the doctrine of immortality more harm than good with their illogical and unscientific ventures. One noted biologist[1] univocally makes life to be synonymous with organic life, adducing the incontestable but irrelevant argument that once a body is dead it is no longer alive. He misses the whole point that any life after death must be of man's spiritual soul and hence not life in the biological sense. Others speak of immortality only in a metaphorical sense, as when poets say that some-

[1] Dr. Selman A. Waksman, in a statement to the Associated Press, Dec. 4, 1957.

one will live forever in the admiration and memory of men. A few deny personal immortality by asserting that the soul comes back as another person or thing; this doctrine of transmigration of souls will be discussed later. Schopenhauer with his usual pessimism feels that "to desire immortality is to desire the perpetuation of a great mistake."

It seems incorrect to include the Buddhists among those who deny immortality, since the vast majority of them apparently understand nirvana to be not a return to absolute nothing, but an ecstatic state of peaceful contemplation, free of all passions. Kant, after rejecting the rational proofs for immortality, turns around and holds it as a postulate of practical reason; we prefer to base our position on more solid philosophical grounds than a blind *feeling* that the soul "just must be immortal."

Metaphysical Difficulties. Objections against immortality based on the positivist assumption that only what is observable and measurable is real are subject to the same criticisms under which positivism itself is now tottering. Science now deals in qualities as well as in quantities, and is more and more concerned with theories about things which cannot be directly observed. More serious are the philosophical arguments which St. Thomas himself lists in his dialectical approach to the problem. (*a*) The forms or souls of plants and brute animals, although simple and unable per se to corrupt into parts, cease when the plant or animal dies because such forms have no separate existence. But the generation of man is similar to the generation of animals, it is argued, and therefore their ends should be similar. (*b*) Again, man's soul is contingent being, not eternal or necessary. It once did not exist, so it seems logical that it should return to the nothing from which it came. (*c*) The operation proper to the rational soul of man is perceptual knowledge, understanding derived from sense. Now existence without operation is meaningless; if we cannot have our proper operation after the sense organs die, there is no point in asserting continued existence of the soul.[2]

[2] S. T., Ia, 75, 6 obj. 1–3.

MEANING OF IMMORTALITY

In the face of these varied arguments, and considering the extreme importance of the issue, it behooves us first to define precisely what is involved.

"Life after death" here certainly does not mean that the body will live when it is dead. To live is analogous, and we are speaking of the existence of the spiritual soul of man, not biological life. Nor do we mean some temporary revival after apparent death, or continuance of some functions for a short time. We mean that the soul will endure forever, after complete death of the body. (Resurrection of the body will be considered toward the end of the chapter.) We are not speaking metaphorically of immortality in memory or symbol, nor of identification with the external existence of God, but actual continued existence of the individual soul.

Immortality means *unceasing duration of life.* An immortal being has a beginning, but will not end; it thus differs from eternal, which has neither beginning nor end. Immortal means immune from corruption in any way.

Corruption in general means ceasing to be, breaking up into parts. It can be of several different kinds.

1. Proper or *intrinsic* corruption involves dissolution from within.

a. Of itself (per se) any material being can corrupt, because composed of spatial or constituent parts into which it can decompose.

b. Incidentally (*per accidens*) a thing corrupts with the destruction of that upon which it intrinsically depends. Recall the example of the mathematical point in the previous chapter. Material forms below man's corrupt in this way, by reason of their total dependence on the composite. Brute animal souls being simple cannot decompose, but they cease when the animal does.

A being which is not corruptible in either of these ways is said to be immortal by nature.

2. Improper or *extrinsic* corruption means annihilation, separation of essence and existence. Since any contingent being is not its own existence, it does not necessarily exist. A thing might be immortal

by nature, but not actually continue in existence. Regardless of its independence of matter or inability to decompose, it could cease to be if the First Cause did not conserve it in being. Annihilation removes existence absolutely. This is the only way a spiritual substance can cease to exist. A being which will not cease in this way is said to be immortal in fact.

All of these types of corruption must be excluded if we are to establish that the human soul is immortal. This is done most directly in the first or metaphysical proof. To this, two other arguments are added, less analytical and more popular in appeal.

PROOFS OF IMMORTALITY

Metaphysical or Ontological Argument

The human soul is not subject to intrinsic corruption. It cannot corrupt of itself (per se), for it is simple and inextended. Not being composed, it cannot break up into parts because it has none.

It is not subject to incidental corruption (*per accidens*), because it is spiritual and intrinsically independent of matter, as proven in the preceding chapter. Not depending wholly upon the body for its rational operations and therefore not for its being, it will not cease to exist when the body dies. The human soul is thus immortal by nature.

But for God to annihilate (extrinsic corruption) what is immortal by nature would be inconsistent and unreasonable, a contradiction of His own design. Such imperfection is impossible to God. Therefore the soul is immortal in fact.

It is not necessary to appeal to faith to know this much about God. As First Cause discoverable by natural reason in philosophy, He is all perfect and incapable of contradicting Himself. He cannot set up a nature and then go contrary to it. He is free to create or not, but He is not free to do the absurd. This is not because of any lack of power or self-determination in God, but because of His perfection and infinite wisdom. To the question, "How can we know what God will do or will not do?" we can answer that God manifests His plan not only through revelation but also through the nature of what

He makes. Without His telling us, we can see His design through an analysis of the soul, just as we can often figure out the manufacturer's idea just from the machine, even though we do not have any explanation from him. It is then an easy inference that He will not act like an inconsistent fool and contradict His own plan.

One might object that an artist could paint an "immortal" picture and then destroy it, for it is his and he can do what he wants with it; so could God annihilate the human soul, since He has supreme dominion. We reply that the picture is not truly immortal by nature, but only one we judge would deserve to be so because of its excellence. Also, the artist may be acting legally, since it is his own property, but one could question his wisdom if the picture were truly of such perennial worth. God's wisdom cannot be questioned. He cannot change His mind, nor could it be said that He did not know what He was doing when He freely made the soul immortal.

From Natural Capacities

An argument for the immortality of the human soul can be drawn from an analysis of the unlimited capacities of our intellect and will. It is sometimes called the argument from desire, but this suggests that the argument is reducible to "I desire to be immortal, therefore I am." This is hardly conclusive, for I might desire lots of things and not get them. Or one might not desire immortality, preferring extinction at death because of a faulty conception of the afterlife, or because of a guilty conscience. Our proof argues from the very nature of our two highest powers to the conclusion that we are made to live forever, whether we consciously desire it or not.

The formal object of *the intellect* is being. This means that it can know whatever is or can be, all that is intelligible. This unlimited capacity for truth sets up in man an insatiable curiosity. We all want to know more and more, whether it be Mrs. Grundy's gossip or the conditions in outer space. Instead of being satisfied that he knows enough, the more a man knows the greater is his desire to learn. The most brilliant men are most painfully aware of all there is yet to know. A thousand lifetimes would not suffice to fill up one's intellect completely.

The will has a corresponding capacity for unlimited goodness. Its object being goodness as such, there is nothing which it cannot desire. However much it may possess, it can always want more. True, we may rightly expect a reasonable amount of happiness in this life, but even those who claim to be quite content are capable of more. No matter how much we feel we are loved, we are all heart-hungry in the sense that we want fuller and more secure satisfaction of our desire to be loved and more adequate exploitation of our capacity to love. Our songs, our poetry, our world conquests all attest to the nature of the human will as made for unlimited good. Moreover, even the nicest finite things tire us after a while. True happiness demands an object which we can never exhaust, a never-ending fountain of new delights with which we can never become bored.

Now these unlimited capacities of intellect and will can never be fully satisfied in this life, nor with anything less than an eternity with God. Only when the intellect can feed upon the inexhaustible intelligibility of Him who is Infinite Truth will our curiosity be sated. Only when our wills possess the infinite goodness and beauty of Goodness Itself will they rest content. As the poet Browning says,

> Ah, but a man's reach should exceed his grasp,
> Or what's a Heaven for?

It is absurd to say that in a universe where other things reach their natural goals, for the most part and with admitted exceptions, only man should be necessarily and completely frustrated in achieving the end for which he was designed. Therefore the human soul must continue to a state where its two highest basic capacities are satisfied by an adequate object: Infinite Knowledge and Love.

This argument is teleological, not theological. Purpose is as undeniable a reality as efficient cause. Even the most antiteleological person finds it impossible to talk for five minutes about the kidney or hormones without implying design or function. A natural tendency, which is universal because based in the nature of man, could hardly be aimed at a nonexistent object. To postulate this is unintelligible, but it is the only alternative to our argument. Nor is it a valid objection that not all seeds become trees, for the existence of forests is proof enough that by and large the purpose of seeds is fulfilled. There is no difficulty about the fact that nature achieves its goal in this case by making millions more seeds than ever become trees. They have no intrinsic value, and this is one way of arranging things to guarantee the desired result. But if the human soul is not immortal, it means that no man achieves his end, that the entire species is essentially frustrated.

It is true that some people may not attain God, and thus they miss their end. This possibility is the inevitable consequence of free choice. But they do so by their own agency, not because their end was impossible of achievement or nonexistent. What we are arguing here is the absurdity of a world scheme in which *nobody* achieves his natural goal, and this by necessity.

Again, we say "necessarily and completely" frustrated, for we admit that minor accidental capacities of all men may not all be satisfied. At least our essential happiness is possible. Failure to grasp the essential nature of the future life indicated by this argument causes people to claim they do not desire heaven because they imagine it an eternity of playing the harp, instead of the enjoyment of God as Infinite Truth and Goodness. Any other objects or persons that might be desired are so minor a consideration as to be utterly negligible.

From the Moral Order

Lastly, we may argue to the logical necessity of a life after death from the experience we have of moral obligation.[3] To argue from moral obligation to immortality here, and then in ethics to argue from immortality to moral obligation would be a vicious circle. But quite apart from and prior to any ethical considerations, it is a fact that people generally *experience* moral obligation and a sense of responsibility. Our proof simply raises the question of whether this widespread phenomenological fact has any validity if the soul is not immortal.

Every investigation of the existing universe reveals order. The atomic table in chemistry made possible the prediction of the existence and properties of certain elements before they were dis-

[3] See A. E. Taylor, *The Faith of a Moralist*, Series I (New York: St. Martin's, 1951).

covered. Order underlies the classifications of zoology and botany. Astronomy finds indescribable order in the paths of the stars and allows very precise predictions. All physical laws attest the intelligible order of the observable world. Exceptions are recognizable as such only because there are laws to which they can be exceptions. Many apparent instances of disorder are found later to have meaning, as when the overenthusiastic followers of early evolutionary theory decided certain endocrine glands were vestigial because they could see no function for them. Cutting them out led to progress in our knowledge about hormones, but it was not the only time when nature embarrassed man because of his ignorance of her laws.

In such a universe, it is preposterous that disorder should reign only in the case of man. We see people trying to do what they see to be right, and receiving no reward in this life. Others literally get away with murder. Still others are punished unjustly for crimes they did not commit. What rationality is there in moral values? Why should anyone experience a sense of obligation and responsibility? There is certainly no adequate sanction in this life. Unless there is a life after death in which everything will be squared up and people will receive what they deserve, the whole notion of obligation makes no sense at all.

Some will argue that the sanction against bad conduct is that society will not approve. This makes no provision for the person whose attitude is "to hell with society." Appeals to the good of posterity are likely to be met with an equally cynical "What did posterity ever do for me?" Threats of punishment or physical force reduce morality to a question of adequate policing, and right to the matter of who has the biggest fists or atom bombs. None of these can be the ultimate sanction for the moral order. It must be beyond this life. Therefore the soul must be immortal, or there is no adequate foundation for our notions of good and evil, for responsibility and human dignity, for the very fabric of social and political structure.

Eternal Sanction. Some Scholastic philosophers claim that this last argument proves that there will be some future life, but not that it will last forever. This opinion does not seem sound, for the reason that a sanction which is not everlasting is not really adequate as an ultimate sanction. If the good knew that heaven would eventually cease, they would be tempted to feel that a virtuous life was not worth the effort.

Moreover, the thought that it was coming to an end would spoil their whole state of happiness. Happiness is the *stable* possession of the perfect good. Were we to achieve temporary satisfaction of our basic capacities either in this life or the next, but know that we were to lose out eventually, we would not be perfectly happy. In fact, the prospect of loss would sadden us all the more because the enjoyment was so intense. To enjoy perfect happiness, we must know that it is permanent. We can enjoy a party even though we know it will not last forever, because we implicitly accept that fact as part of the nature of things. But if we look to such temporary joys as sources of lasting happiness, we always find that sooner or later they turn to ashes in our mouths.

Likewise, if the bad knew that eventually they would be freed no matter what they did or how severe the punishment was, they could tell themselves they were willing to risk it. It would mean that in the long run everybody would end up the same way, so the difference between moral and immoral would become zero eventually, and mere expediency would be at least as reasonable as obligation. Only immortality provides an adequate sanction.

SOLUTION OF DIFFICULTIES

The first of the philosophical arguments against immortality mentioned above reasoned from a parallel with the brute form. But we have seen that the evidence shows a lack of parity, for men exhibit spiritual operations whereas brutes do not. The death of the body may be similar in the two cases, but man's spiritual operations do not involve the body intrinsically, as all brute activities do.

The second objection argued from the fact that even the human soul is contingent being, hence does not have existence necessarily. We admit that such a being is open to the absolute possibility of annihilation, looking only to its contingent nature. But since only

God can annihilate, we must look to His nature to see if it is also a possibility relative to His part. We found that this would be against His infinite wisdom.

The third objection presents some real problems, for it argued that the immortal soul after the death of the body could not know, because of the lack of sense knowledge from which to abstract ideas. Now the manner of operation of the separated soul cannot be studied through observed experience. As philosophers we may not appeal to revelation, and theology offers only speculation on this point, for the most part anyway. What faith does tell us for sure is that we shall enjoy the beatific vision, direct intuition of God Himself. This is not only beyond philosophical proof but a supernatural gift over and above (but not contrary to, as is clear from our second argument) our natural capacities. From unaided reason we can only conjecture that certain conditions will prevail, because of the nature of the soul and its separated state.[4]

Without some special supernatural aid we will be unable to know singular material objects or acquire further knowledge of the physical universe, for such operations demand sense experience and that is impossible without bodily organs. But there seems to be no intrinsic impossibility of our knowing spiritual realities, for they are intelligible and our intellect is immaterial. God, angels, our own and other human souls would thus be known without need to derive from sense. Again, we have impressed intelligible *species* stored in the potential intellect by way of habit, and this habitual knowledge need not cease with the body.

The use of this and the acquisition of other knowledge does seem to call for some extra help on the part of God, to supply the role played by sense knowledge when the soul is joined to matter. But although we do not know just how, there seems no absurdity in this possibility because matter has only an extrinsic and subordinate part in the human intellection. Even God could not supply for sense if matter entered intrinsically and essentially into the activity of the

[4] Thomas Aquinas, in *S. T.*, Ia, 89, combines philosophical and theological speculation through eight articles on the topic.

intellect. But we have seen that it does not. Therefore it seems legitimate to assume that He will somehow provide the necessary conditions for our intellect to function.

Resurrection of the Body. The separated soul is seen to be not a complete man in any case. (The Hebrew use of soul for person in the Old Testament is metonymy, a typical figure of speech with no pretense at philosophical precision.) Even if its highest powers are satisfied, and happiness therefore essentially achieved, the soul still seems to have a certain incompleteness. We shall be too absorbed in enjoying God to be distracted by any desire for bodily pleasures, for He contains them all equivalently and to a supereminent degree. But it is still true that the soul is not an angel; its nature is to be united with matter to form a man.

This, plus the fact that it seems proper that the whole man should share in the reward or punishment of the soul, seems to constitute an argument from natural reason for the resurrection of the body and its eventual reunion with the soul. But although St. Thomas seems to feel that the above reasons are quite compelling, we agree with Suarez that they are only suasive and show it is fitting. Faith tells us that the future resurrection is a fact; philosophy seems only to demonstrate that it ought to be. In either case, it seems that the conditions of bodily life after the resurrection would be quite different from the present state. We would have all of the advantages and none of the disadvantages of a body: all the pleasure of eating without the need to depend on food, all of the beauty of full maturity with none of the defects of old age or failure to develop properly, and so of all other aspects of organic life.

INDIVIDUALITY OF SOULS

Personal Identity of the Soul. But before the resurrection of the body, or if this does not occur, how can the soul retain its individual identity after death? Matter is the principle of individuation. Separated from matter, will all souls coalesce into one confused mass of spiritual substance?

When we say that matter is the principle of individuation, this does not mean that prime matter confers some perfection. Being passive and of itself indeterminate, it cannot contribute individuality as a characteristic. The soul as a simple, spiritual substance has its own identity, and is not subject to any change by which its identity could be lost. Matter is the principle of individuation in the sense that it makes possible the plurality of individuals within the same species.

One soul is not another soul, even though both are human, because each is united with different matter. This soul is not just any human soul, but is identifiable as the soul which united with matter to form John Q. Jones in a certain place at a certain time. This is true only of the soul of John Q. Jones, even though he have an "identical" twin. And it is historically and irrevocably true. Even after separation by death, for all eternity his soul retains this transcendental relation to the composite it formed with matter, that is, this man and no other.

Matter Is Indifferent. This conception finds no particular difficulty in the fact that the soul is united with different matter at various times, through the metabolic cycle. It is only necessary that it actualize *some* matter in order for it to form Jones' body. The soul is the subject of actual permanent identity, matter only the principle of potential multiplicity. For instance, matter which was once Jones may become fertilizer, then vegetable, then Smith (or may become Smith directly, if Smith is a cannibal and eats Jones). What makes this matter to be any of these is the fact that it is informed at the time by one substantial form rather than another.

Hence we see little problem in questions about the resurrection which vex those who apparently have not fully grasped hylomorphism. If this same matter once belonged to Smith and at another time to Jones, to whom will it belong at the resurrection? Our answer is that it makes no difference. As Shakespeare said about money, " 'twas mine, 'tis his, and has been slave to thousands." Smith's body will be *any* matter substantially united to his soul as potency to act, regardless of whether it had ever been previously his or not. One suspects some lurking Platonic dualism in those theologians who feel the dogma that each will be reunited with "his" body means that the same identical matter must be involved. If it means all matter in the resurrected body must be the same as in the previous life, the above facts of the metabolic cycle and cannibalism present difficult problems, which are no problem at all in hylomorphism. And if it means that all the matter previously used must now be united, then one who had eaten normally for a lifetime would be mountainous in size at the resurrection. If it means only that some matter must be the same, we are back at the question of why any matter is my body at all; according to this view, some of the resurrected body would be mine and some would not.

We have digressed only in the hope that this discussion may help toward a fuller understanding of the hylomorphic union. For the same reason, we might consider the frequent question of why the corpse should be given a Christian burial if it is only so much fertilizer in the shape of a man. The reason is twofold. First, it is out of reverence for the fact that this matter was once substantially united with the soul to form a human person, the object of our honor and remembrance—and, in the Christian scheme, the recipient of the sacraments, which are bodily signs of grace, conferred on the whole man. Secondly, it is a mark of belief in the eventual resurrection of the body, and hence of the future life of the soul. Cremation has been generally accepted in most cultures as a symbolic denial of immortality, a gesture which says that all is finished when the ashes are scattered to the wind. It is precisely for this reason that the Catholic Church forbids cremation, as shown from the fact that it is allowed where demanded by public health or other compelling reasons, and it is then clear that there is no symbolic denial of immortality.

Reincarnation. With this fuller appreciation of the manner in which the individual human soul actuates matter to form this man's body, we should find little difficulty in refuting the theory sometimes proposed that souls could lose their personal identity and return to life on earth in a different body. This is called metempsychosis, transmigration of souls, or reincarnation.[5] The very notion of

[5] See Paul Siwek, S.J., *The Enigma of the Hereafter: The Reincarnation of Souls* (New York: Philosophical Library, 1952). The notion enjoyed a brief revival when Morey Bernstein published *The Search for Bridey Murphy* (New York: Doubleday, 1956; and in *True* magazine, February, 1956). The vogue quickly subsided when many factual discrepancies were pointed out between the Ireland which Ruth Simmons described and the actual conditions in Ireland at the time when Bridey Murphy was supposed to have lived. Moreover, Bern-

hylomorphism seems to rule out the possibility. For if Napoleon's soul were to return, any matter with which it would substantially unite would by that very fact be Napoleon's body. It might be necessary to appeal to theology for absolute proof that such a return cannot happen. But philosophically we can take the position that the burden of the proof lies with the affirmative, and examine any assertion very critically for evidence. None has been offered to date.

This individual cannot be somebody else, regardless of change of material conditions. The senile psychotic may not look, speak, or act anything like himself at the age of twenty, much less at birth. But he is the same person. Even more preposterous is the theory that the soul could return as the form of a dog or other animal, for if the human soul actuated matter it could only be the formal cause of a human being, not any other kind. It is impossible for the same form to be the act of two potencies, differing either individually or specifically. If a lion eats Napoleon, his body becomes lion. If Napoleon eats the lion, the lion becomes Napoleon. But Napoleon's soul retains its individual identity in either case.

REVIEW QUESTIONS

1. Is incorruptibility the same as immortality?
2. Is immortality the same as eternity?
3. What are the chief reasons why some deny immortality?
4. Would you say that the majority of peoples on the earth believe in immortality?
5. Prove from its nature that the human soul is immortal.
6. Does this proof exclude the possibility of annihilation?
7. Prove immortality from the soul's natural capacities.
8. Show why this proof is not merely a matter of wishful thinking.
9. Does the argument from the moral order have any force with those who deny moral obligation?
10. What fact remains for these people to explain?
11. Which of the three arguments for immortality do you feel is the most conclusive? Why?
12. What do you consider the hardest difficulty against immortality?

---

stein's statement that Ruth Simmons was a good hypnotic subject immediately tells us that being highly suggestible she could readily come up to the hypnotist's expectations.

13. How do you answer it?
14. If matter is the principle of individuation, what is the basis for the soul's identity as an individual after death?
15. Why is metempsychosis more compatible with a Platonic than a Thomistic notion of soul?
16. Since the soul can exist by itself, is it not a complete substance?

FOR FURTHER READING

AQUINAS, ST. THOMAS. *Summa Theol.* Ia, 75, 2 and 6; 89; Ia IIae, 85, 6. *Summa Contra Gent.*, II, 55, and 79–82. *On the Soul*, 14.

ARISTOTLE. *On the Soul.* II, 2, 413b 24–27; III, 4, 429b 22; 5, 430a 22–25.

AVELING, FRANCIS. *The Immortality of the Soul.* Vol. I. Westminster Lectures. St. Louis: Herder, 1906.

D'ARCY, MARTIN C., S.J. *Death and Life.* London: Longmans, 1942.

FELL, GEORGE, S.J. *The Immortality of the Human Soul.* St. Louis: Herder, 1908.

HOCKING, WILLIAM E. *The Meaning of Immortality in Human Experience.* New York: Harper, 1957.

LAMONT, CORLISS. *The Illusion of Immortality.* (3d Ed.) New York: Philosophical Library, 1959. Presents a strong, but often confused and unscientific, case against immortality.

McCORMICK, JOHN F., S.J. "The Burden of Intellect," *The Modern Schoolman*, 1935, 12:79–81.

MAHER, MICHAEL, S.V. *Psychology: Empirical and Rational.* (9th Ed.) London: Longmans, 1921. Chap. 24.

MARITAIN, JACQUES. *The Range of Reason.* New York: Scribner, 1952. Pp. 54–65.

MONTAGU, ASHLEY. *Immortality.* New York: Grove Press, 1955. Dismisses personal immortality as wishful thinking. Takes advantage of the fact that the Scholastic arguments are sometimes poorly expressed.

PLATO. *Phaedo: The Apology of Socrates; Alcibiades I.*

ROHDE, ERWIN. *Psyche: the Cult of Souls and Belief in Immortality among the Greeks.* Trans. by W. B. Willis. New York: Harcourt, Brace, 1925.

TAYLOR, A. E. *The Christian Hope of Immortality.* New York: Macmillan, 1947.

TAYLOR, A. E. *The Faith of a Moralist.* Series I. New York: St. Martin's, 1951.

ZEDLER, BEATRICE H. "Averroës and Immortality," *The New Scholasticism*, 1954, 28:436–453.

19

THE ORIGIN OF MAN

The cause of the human soul: not generated by parents but created by God. The soul does not exist before the body, but is created when infused, which seems to be at the moment of conception. Origin of man's body: evolution. Could man synthesize a living body? Conclusion.

Where did I come from? This is the final question in our investigation of human nature. The origin of the human soul is more readily understood now that we have considered its spiritual nature and immortal destiny. Although the origin of other animals is a matter of biology, the cause of the human soul presents some rather knotty problems for the philosopher. We shall consider first the cause of the human soul, then the time of its origin, and lastly the evolution of man's body.

THE CAUSE OF THE HUMAN SOUL

Since being is a continuation of becoming, a thing's existence tells us of its beginning. Now the substantial forms of other animals, having no existence apart from the composite, have no cause other than the cause of the animal itself. We saw in Chapter 16 how the substantial form is the result of the sum of efficient causes working on an apt material cause and making it become this kind of material being. Two parent dogs, disposing the matter of the germ plasm in their reproductive organs, are the proximate efficient cause of matter passing from potentially to actually puppy, and hence of the new dog form or soul.[1] Human parents prepare matter in a similar way to become a new human body; the question is whether this is adequate to cause the human substantial form.

Not Educed from Matter. A thing can be made actually to be something else only if it potentially is the other thing to begin with. Hydrogen and oxygen become water, one worm can become two, food can become man, animal germ plasm can become a new animal, because in each case the terminal product is within the potency of matter and all that is required is an adequate efficient cause.

The human soul is spiritual, and not within the potentialities of matter. No efficient cause, even God, can produce a spiritual effect from a material cause. Matter is in potency to become any other kind of matter, and hence any material form may be educed from it by a proper cause. But the spiritual human soul cannot arise by eduction from matter. The act of generation is a biological process, and therefore material.

Not Generated by Parents' Souls. One might argue that there is no need to postulate the origin of the human spiritual soul by a material process of generation. The parents' souls are also spiritual; could not they act as a spiritual cause producing a spiritual effect? Here there would be no violation of the principle of causality.

[1] For this reason "be kind to the birds because God created their souls" is sentimental nonsense, as is much antivivisection propaganda. God is, of course, ultimately the First Cause of all being, but not in any special sense of plant or animal souls. The reason why we should avoid wanton cruelty to animals is not because of their dignity, but our own. Animals have no personal rights, and are for man to use. When a man abuses them, it is wrong because he is acting in a manner unworthy of his own rational nature, which is the norm of morality. Coleman (1956, p. 93) quotes an interesting pathological instance of the lack of logic which occurs here: an antivivisectionist advocates kindness to brute animals and proposes savage cruelty toward any fellow man who disagrees with his view.

The difficulties arise when we attempt to explain precisely how this would happen. By composition? The soul is simple and could not be compounded from something received from each parent. There is no evidence that it arises from just one parent, to say nothing of the problems arising if we attempted to designate which one. By division? The parent's soul is simple and spiritual, so there is no possibility of dividing off a piece of it for the child's soul. By eduction? The new soul could not be educed from the potency of spiritual substance, for spirit does not contain a principle of substantial change: there is no potency in spirit for becoming other, analogous to prime matter in material being. The parents' souls would have nothing to work on, nothing out of which to make the soul. By production? One might consider whether it is necessary to talk of the parents' souls making the new soul "out of" any preexisting subject, i.e., whether they could simply produce it by their sheer reproductive activity.

Aside from the fact that the parental reproductive activity is entirely biological, this solution is rejected because no created cause gives being absolutely. Any efficient cause we know operates only by making something which already exists to be this way rather than that; never does it make something simply to be rather than not be. (Even in spiritual activity the idea, for example, is the actuation of the potential intellect and not creation from nothing.) The reason for this is that no creature has being of itself, and nothing gives what it has not. Contingent being is participated being, over which the recipient has no dominion. Act is limited only by the potency into which it is received; if "to be" were mine to give, it would be unlimited as act; and I could cause all finite existence including my own, which is absurd.

Origin by Creation. Since only the First Cause has being of Itself and hence dominion over existence, only God can give being absolutely. He alone can make a thing simply be, rather than cause what already exists to be in another way. By a process of elimination, then, we arrive at the conclusion that the human soul can originate only through creation by God.[2] This can be put more positively as follows.

[2] Thomas Aquinas, *S. T.*, Ia, 90; *C. G.*, II, 87.

⟮ What is independent of matter in its being must be independent of matter in its becoming.

⟮ But the human soul is intrinsically independent of matter in its being.

⟮ Therefore it is intrinsically independent of matter in its becoming, i.e., the generative act of the parents is only the extrinsic cause setting the time and place for the origin of the soul, which must be created by God.

Creation. Creation can be defined as *production in being by an efficient cause without any preexisting subject.* This definition is preferable to saying that to create is to "make out of nothing," because such an expression implies that God takes an already existing blob of "nothing" and makes something of it. The difficulty is really one of letting our imagination interfere with what must be a purely intellectual understanding. Since efficient cause is always distinct from its effect, there is no question of the soul being God, or a part of God. Creation is the antithesis of pantheism.

It is interesting that even the pagan Aristotle seems to have come to some awareness of this difference in the origin of the human soul,[3] although it is usually said that he had no clear idea of creation. Note that although we assume throughout this chapter the existence of a Creator as proved elsewhere in philosophy, we are not moving in a vicious circle, because the demonstration of God's existence through philosophy in no way presumes anything about the soul.

One might object that the body is in potency to the soul, and therefore the soul must be educed from the potency of matter. This does not follow, for to be in potency to a form is not necessarily to have that form in potency. Matter is in potency to any form which can actuate it, and we have seen that the human soul does this. But only material forms can be educed from the potency of matter.

Again, this doctrine of creation might seem to detract from the fullness of parenthood, since the parents do not generate the soul. But their offspring are truly theirs nonetheless, for it is not necessary that one produce all the component parts in order to be the true cause of a thing. Thus the artist is the real author of the picture, even

[3] *On the Generation of Animals,* II, chap. 3.

though he does not make the canvas or oils. Relations like father and son are said of the *person*, not of the part: we do not say that John, Sr., is the father of John's body, but of John. On the contrary, the doctrine proposed here rather enhances the human reproductive act, since it depicts the joint action of God and parent in producing the child. It is the very opposite of puritanism, since it exalts sex to the sacred role of an invitation of the Creator for His most intimate co-operation. No act in the natural order involves God so directly.

TIME OF SOUL'S ORIGIN

Although not the direct cause of the soul's existence, the parents are the occasion of its origin in that they set the time and place for God to create it. The question arises as to just when this occurs.

No Preexistence. In discussing the individuality of souls in the previous chapter, we saw that, unlike an angel whose nature it is to exist by itself as a complete substance, the human soul has as its proper role to unite with matter to form this man and no other. Hence any existence previous to the man is contrary to the very meaning of soul as substantial form. We saw that the separate existence of the soul after death does not contradict this, since it retains previously acquired knowledge, a transcendental relation to the body, and even a certain exigency to be united with matter. But *before* actual union with body it can have no such relation. The notion that God has a supply of souls which are not anybody's in particular until He infuses them into human embryos is entirely unwarranted and lacks any evidence. They would have no individuality, no personal human identity, and would be in an unnatural state because unable to acquire any knowledge in the way proper to man. At the beginning of Chapter 7, we saw that the theory that we are born with ideas carried over from a previous life has nothing to support it, and much evidence against it.

Created When Infused. From this it appears quite certain that the soul is created by God at the time it is infused into matter, i.e., when it is substantially united with the embryo to form a complete living human being. The human parents produce germ cells (sperm and ovum) which unite to form a single cell (zygote). The soul is created and infused when this matter is appropriately disposed to receive it and form a man.

Exactly when this happens is more controversial, and still an open question, with Scholastic philosophers of high standing on both sides. It is worth examining because among other things it illustrates some aspects of the relation between philosophy and science. The major premise of the argument is a philosophical principle, and hence perennially valid. The minor premise is one of fact, and on this modern biology can supply details not known to the medieval philosophers. Hence the conclusion could differ, even though there is no philosophical disagreement. The difference will not be about the essential nature of man, for this is not dependent on scientific minutiae; it can only be on an accidental point, namely, the precise time of the soul's origin. This shows how philosophy is independent of science for its fundamental conclusions, yet can profit from scientific particulars on occasion.

At the Moment of Conception. We shall propose our argument as follows:

⟨ Since the soul is the principle of vital operations, the human soul is present when there is specifically human operation.

⟨ But there is evidence of specifically human operation from the first moment of conception.

⟨ Therefore the human soul is present from the first moment of conception.

The major premise is simply a restatement of the principle of causality. How do we know that there is a soul at all? As a necessary explanation to account for the facts. All the philosophers involved agree on this.

The minor is a question of evidence. St. Thomas was not a biologist. Aristotle, although he held epigenesis rather than preformation centuries before the microscope was invented, did not have the technological devices necessary to uncover any evidence of specifically human organization and operation in the embryo during its first stages. He thought that he was unjustified in asserting true human life before the male embryo was 40 days old, and before 80 to 90 days in the female. St. Thomas was equally honest in following this scientific unwillingness to go beyond the evidence. They taught a succession of forms, the embryo having first a vegetative soul and later a sensitive one, before the human soul finally arrives. Aquinas postulates an exception by way of miracle to account for Christ's soul being present from the moment of conception, as he is apparently unwilling to let theological convenience dictate a systematic position which would go contrary to scientific evidence as he knew it at the time.

Some modern Scholastics seem reluctant to depart from this position, possibly because of an unconscious emotional repugnance against asserting that St. Thomas was wrong. But if St. Thomas were alive today, he would be the first to insist that factual evidence and not his say-so should determine the issue. The above argument seems to be not only within the framework of his general philosophical principles but actually more in accordance with his spirit.[4]

What are the facts? The zygote is so tiny that a dozen could rest on the head of a pin, so we are not surprised that modern microscopes have revealed facts which were utterly inaccessible to the ancients. At the moment sperm and ovum unite and the two pronuclei fuse, an orderly process of development begins, with a definiteness compared by one professor of embryology to the action of a stop watch when you press the release. The new individual is characterized by the resulting unique constellation of genes and chromosomes before the zygote divides for the first time.

This organization is not only intricate and vital; it is specifically human. The chromosomes contain determiners for specifically human eyes and ears, not just animals eyes and ears in general. The offspring of all vertebrates may go through the same stages of embryological development, and in similar ways. But careful study on guinea pigs, rhesus monkeys, and other vertebrates has shown that each goes through those stages in ways which are characteristic and peculiar to its own species. The guinea pig goes through the stage when it superficially resembles a tadpole in a way that is proper to guinea pigs and different from the way the rhesus monkey goes

[4] Donceel (1955, p. 271) and Klubertanz (1953, p. 410, no. 4) both state that the majority of Scholastics today hold our opinion.

through the tadpole stage. This has been observed even at the earliest levels of development, and could hardly be different in the case of the human. Embryologists make it quite clear from the way they write and speak that they consider the living body from the one-cell stage on to be a human individual, not some general plant or animal which will become human in 40 or 80 days.

If one were to wait until one had clear evidence of *rational* activity before concluding to the eixstence of a human soul, it would not be a matter of days, but of years. As long as the embryo is clearly the product of human generation, it has a human nature, even if severe organic defect prevents it from ever exercising any rational activities, as in the case of some idiots. Nobody doubts that the child at birth has a human soul, yet mere passage down the birth canal does not change his essential nature and make human what was not before. Examination of the fetus back through earlier stages gives no clue as to when one can draw the line. The available evidence seems to force us back to the very moment of conception.[5]

In confirmation, it is interesting to note that our law courts concur in this, for they have held that a child *in utero* can inherit, and only a human person can have rights. For the believing Catholic there are also some interesting suasive theological arguments from the doctrine on the Immaculate Conception[6] and the fact that the Church changed her law so as to excommunicate all who deliberately procure an abortion, not only after 40 or 80 days. But as a philosophical question it must be settled on its own merits, which means facts and reasoning.

Koren (1955, p. 268) says that for our doctrine the "main argument would seem to be that any other solution gets involved in all kinds of unnecessary complications." This criticism certainly does not apply to the above proof, which is based on positive evidence. One might

---

[5] C. Sherrington, *Man on His Nature*, 2d ed. (Garden City, N.Y.: Doubleday-Anchor, 1953), p. 74.

[6] The decree itself does not pretend to pronounce on this point. Theologians who are reluctant to abandon St. Thomas's position explain away this implication of the decree by terms like "second instant" and "passive conception" but the latter seems to stem from outmoded notions of the role of the wife in conception, and of the true nature of the ovum. The liturgy (Dec. 8 to Sept. 8) clearly implies our position.

retort that some opponents seem to base their adherence to the old doctrine on a desire to avoid complications, for example, in explaining human identical twins. Now we admit that this point is less neatly handled from our position. But we prefer to build our case on the ordinary situation and see if the exception can be fitted in without destroying it—this is the original meaning of "the exception proves (tests) the rule." There is no good reason to suppose that, in cases where the original fecundated ovum divides into two human beings, any insurmountable difficulty is encountered. Before division there can be only one soul; at the time of division a second soul is created for the second twin (it is irrelevant as well as impossible to say which one). This seems no greater a difficulty than to say that the intermediate vegetative soul is an instrument (Koren, p. 270), when in fact the embryo does not act as an instrument but as a nature.

ORIGIN OF MAN'S BODY

The origin of the individual human body is today a fairly well understood biological process, and the general outlines of genetics and embryology are not a matter of controversy. Whether a body could be produced artificially will be discussed shortly. The origin of the whole human species, or of the first human body, could have been either by a process of evolution or by direct creation.

Evolution. Around the beginning of this century, after Darwin's theories had received wide notice, it was a burning question whether man's body could have originally arisen by biological evolution from lower forms of life. Opposition came chiefly from formalistic Catholics who did not know the remote history of Catholic thought on the point, and from Protestants whose rejection of a teaching authority to guide their private interpretation of the Bible engendered a tendency toward a defensive literalness about Bible texts as their only stronghold against rising materialism. When the first book of Genesis says that God made Adam out of the slime of the earth, many felt constrained to take this as meaning that He did so by a direct and separate act of creation.

Today there is a much more relaxed attitude toward evolution.

Formerly thought to represent a clash between science and religion, it is now looked upon by many Catholic thinkers as an instance of science simply discovering more about how God does things.

This change has taken place for a variety of reasons. First, advanced scriptural studies have convinced scholars that the Bible is quite open to evolutionary interpretation, or at least contains nothing contrary to it. Secondly, lest this seem to be an instance of jumping on the evolutionary bandwagon in a purely opportunist manner, it must be emphasized that a good look at Christian tradition shows evolution to be no novel idea dating from the time of Darwin. Six centuries before him, St. Thomas Aquinas had admitted the possibility,[7] and it accords with his Aristotelian doctrine of change by disposing matter. St. Augustine anticipated the modern discussions by nearly fifteen centuries in proposing the doctrine that evolution shows the glory of God even more clearly than separate acts of direct creation. Thirdly, as the dust of controversy has settled we see that much of the dispute involved false issues which have been eliminated by a careful philosophical analysis of what is really at stake. Scientific evolution as such, for example, is neither theistic nor atheistic; it has no concern with whether God as First Cause started the process or not, but only with the process.

Finally, the theory of evolution itself has gained scientific respectability by abandoning the dogmatism adopted by some of its earlier proponents, partly, no doubt, as a reaction to the opposition they encountered. It has good explanatory value, which is the criterion of a scientific theory. Gaps in our knowledge are admitted, and opinions vary as to the manner in which certain changes may have occurred. Nonetheless, evolution seems to afford the best explanation for the most facts, and is thus a useful, interesting, and legitimate hypothesis.[8]

Acceptable Theory of Evolution. For these reasons many philosophers and theologians now favor evolution as the preferred theory for the origin of man's body. Atheistic evolution would be contrary

---

[7] *Qq. Disp. de Potentia Dei,* 3, 4 ad 7um.
[8] See George P. Klubertanz, S.J., *The Philosophy of Human Nature* (New York: Appleton-Century-Crofts, 1953), appendixes G and N for an excellent delineation of the issues.

to the principle of causality, upon which scientific demonstration itself ultimately rests. But there would seem to be nothing amiss if God had wished to make man's body out of the slime of the earth by putting into matter the potentialities of evolving through various stages until, under His Divine Providence, gene mutations in some anthropoid primate produced a zygote into which He could infuse a human soul. This theory seems preferable to the anthropomorphism which pictures God on the banks of the Euphrates molding Adam's body by hand. Theologians agree that the Bible is not a scientific document, nor even a profane history as such; it teaches us that God made man, with no pretense of telling us precisely how.[9] In our theory, there is no question of God making a man out of an ape, but of His making a human zygote from previously evolved animal matter.

We have seen that the first and every human soul must be created by God, regardless of the natural causes by which matter was disposed to the point of being apt for its infusion. To try to explain the origin of intellect and will from animal life by postulating a new "emergent," derived from lower forms but not contained in them, still ignores the essential difference between material and immaterial and violates the logic of science itself. Even God could not put into matter the potency of evolving a spiritual soul. We know there was a special intervention on the part of God in the production of the first man.

The need for God as First Cause and the special creation of the human soul are known from philosophy. One further point is demanded by theology. The whole economy of redemption in the Judaeo-Christian tradition is based on the unity of all mankind in the fall of the first Adam through original sin, and on its sharing in the restoration through the Messiah, the second Adam.[10] For this to occur, all men must be lineal descendants of the first man and blood brothers of the Redeemer. This cannot be demonstrated either philosophically or scientifically, but we note that nothing here is

[9] See Charles Hauret, *Beginnings: Genesis and Modern Science* (Dubuque: Priory Press, 1955). Also John L. McKenzie, S.J., *The Two-edged Sword: An Interpretation of the Old Testament* (Milwaukee: Bruce, 1956), pp. 104–108.
[10] See Genesis I, and St. Paul's Epistles to the Romans and to the Hebrews.

contradictory. Gene mutations, either spontaneous or caused by cosmic rays and other natural radiations, could explain the different appearances of the various "races"—brown, white, black, yellow, red —just as we can change a strain of brown-eyed fruit flies to blue-eyed by gamma rays. Recent trips (e.g., Kon-Tiki) have demonstrated the possibility of world-wide migration of all peoples by primitive rafts from a common point of origin on the globe. The different so-called missing links are separated not only in space but in time; if truly human, they could easily be descendants of one progenitor. (If not, there is no proof that the offspring of more than one actually became man.)

As for the six days mentioned in Genesis I, neither the Hebrew nor the Greek word means only a day of twenty-four hours, but can mean any period of time. The six "days" could have been six billion years of evolutionary process, and may not refer to chronological sequence at all. The point of the enumeration is that God is the author of every being. The Biblical account of the origin of the first woman has never been satisfactorily explained, but this is a problem for Scripture scholars. The language of the Old Testament is often metaphorical. Here it is at least expressing some dependence in origin of the first woman on the first man; precisely what that dependence was we do not know, but we need not be so literal-minded as to assume that God necessarily performed thoracic surgery in the Garden of Eden.

Could Man Synthesize Living Body? A final question allied to evolution is the possibility that scientists in a laboratory could produce living protoplasm. One reason for considering it in this connection is because it helps clarify our thinking on the question, "Can life come from nonlife?"

When this issue is raised in discussions on evolution, it is assumed that nonliving matter is the total and adequate cause. Now life from nonlife in this sense is impossible. But neither does it happen in this way in evolution, for in addition to nonliving matter as a material cause we also have God as the efficient cause. Thus the effect is not above the total cause, for God is living and is quite adequate to produce living beings. He is the ultimate cause, and the problem is how he might use secondary causes as His instruments. These instrumental causes need not be alive, any more than the painter's brush needs to be artistic. The artist must be, or there will be no work of art; but the brush is never an adequate cause.[11]

The same distinction must be made with regard to the artificial synthesis of living matter. By itself, nonliving matter is not an adequate cause. But the total cause here includes the scientist, who is not only alive but intelligent, and thus well above the minimum level of perfection demanded by the principle of causality. After all, we turn nonliving matter into living matter every day, when we digest the food we eat. There is no philosophical reason why science cannot understand the process well enough, in time, to duplicate it. We are certain that matter itself will never do so alone. But the scientist is more than mere matter.

If two parent dogs dispose matter so as to produce a new puppy dog, why cannot a scientist? It seems to be a question of how much biochemistry we can learn. Apparently the Russians have synthesized a protein-like substance which produces amino acid; California chemists have reconstructed the components back into an active virus; and it seems quite clear that we can synthesize artificial nucleotide chains in DNA (or nucleic acid).[12] There would be little point in speculating about the possibility of what has already occurred.

Lest this again should seem like trimming our philosophical sails to the shift in scientific wind, we should recall that the ancient and medieval philosophers, including St. Thomas, held a similar position. Before Reddi and Pasteur, *omne vivum ex vivo* was not the accepted formula, for it was supposed that maggots were spontaneously generated in decaying flesh, under the influence of the sun or other bodies. Our knowledge of the sun's action and cosmic rays has increased prodigiously since then, but the scientist in his laboratory

[11] See Klubertanz (1953), appendix L, "Efficient Causality in Material Things," for a good discussion of the nature of change by disposition, and appendix N for its application to the question of evolution.
[12] See William S. Beck, *Modern Science and the Nature of Life* (New York: Harcourt, Brace, 1957), and more recent journals.

may well accomplish things which the ancients attributed to heavenly bodies.[13] The basic philosophical principles still hold. Recall our discussion of substantial change in explaining the nature of formal cause (Chapter 16).

Could this synthetic living matter be human? It is at this point that the problem becomes real for the philosopher (it is already a staggering one for the scientist, still struggling with the molecular structure of some of the proteins). Since we have seen that not even God, much less the scientist, could dispose matter so as to produce in it the spiritual form of man, there is no question of man producing a human soul in the laboratory. Plant and animal souls are within the potency of matter, and are caused by causing the composite plant or animal. For man, the most we could do would be to dispose matter so that it would be apt matter into which God could infuse a soul. The question is whether He would create one for this occasion. Philosophically, it seems that all we can say is that this is not His plan; the normal way of human reproduction is by the generative act of the parents, and He would probably not cooperate with any other means. The short-lived embryos produced in the laboratory by artificially fecundating a human ovum with a human sperm could conceivably have a human soul, but not in our present understanding of the working of Divine Providence. They are probably animated by some infrahuman animal form.

CONCLUSION

Men have speculated for decades about the possibility of a man-made human being, a robot which would be a mechanical imitation of man. Between electronics and biochemistry we now have basis in fact for some of the fantasy one reads in science fiction. But so far we are more impressed by the essential superiority of living beings over nonliving, and that even the simplest plants have powers of self-repair, internal growth, and reproduction of their species which surpass the most fantastic electronic computers, not so much in degree as in kind.

[13] Modern scholastic philosophers agree. See Koren (1955), pp. 294–295.

This qualitative superiority becomes even more evident when we enter the realm of human experience. We may anthropomorphically attribute loyalty, excitement, perfectionism, and other reactions to a computer, but we have no evidence that it actually experiences such emotions or has any sense of values. Quite the contrary: we know that it reacts only in accordance with the way we built it. Man's spirit shows a contrasting independence of what others may try to make him. He is an individual, not a product. His creativity and appreciation of beauty far transcend the artificial poetry or music a computer might crank out.

Most important, he has a sense of his own dignity and responsibility, his historical roots and immortal destiny, which no machine can experience because it has neither these to know nor the means of knowing them. With this comes the fact that man is a social being. Because of the dignity of others and what he can share with them, he becomes committed to others: he cares about them, communicates with them, expects response from them. Man's nature makes him capable of unique relationships with other men, with the meaning of the universe, and with its Author.

REVIEW QUESTIONS

1. Are the parents the cause or the occasion for the origin of the human soul?
2. In what sense are they the occasion?
3. Why cannot the human soul arise from the act of generation?
4. Why cannot the spiritual souls of the parents produce the child's soul?
5. Why is creation the act of God alone?
6. What reasons can you give against the existence of the human soul prior to its union with matter in the embryo?
7. Can you give any reasons for it?
8. Do you feel the argument that the soul is present from the moment of conception is conclusive or merely suasive?
9. Would its rejection alter our understanding of the nature of man?
10. What practical consequences would its rejection have?
11. Do you know of any other evidence for or against it?
12. Is all evolution atheistic?

13. What factors have contributed to a shift in the attitude toward evolution?
14. Could the human soul be a product of evolution?
15. Supposing evolution, was Adam ever a subhuman animal if the human soul is infused at the zygote stage?
16. Distinguish between the two senses of the expression "Can life come from nonlife?"
17. In terms of adequate causality, how does the theory of atheistic evolution differ from the theory that man could synthesize living protoplasm?

FOR FURTHER READING

AQUINAS, ST. THOMAS. *Summa Theol.*, Ia, 90, 118. *Summa Contra Gent.*, II, 83–89.

BRENNAN, ROBERT E., O.P. *Thomistic Psychology.* New York: Macmillan, 1941. Pp. 313–320, on the origin of the soul; pp. 327–328 on the origin of man's body.

DONCEEL, JOSEPH F. *Philosophical Psychology.* New York: Sheed, 1955. Pp. 269–271.

HUDECZEK, METH. M., O.P. "De tempore animationis foetus humani secundum embryologiam hodiernam," *Angelicum*, 1952, 29:162–181.

KLUBERTANZ, GEORGE P., S.J. *Philosophy of Human Nature.* New York: Appleton-Century-Crofts, 1953. Pp. 311–312, 410.

LaCROIX, ROBERT. *L'Origine de l'âme humaine.* Ottawa: Les Editions de l'Université, 1945. (Appendice: Le moment de l'infusion de l'âme raisonnable.)

MESSENGER, E. C. (Ed.) "The Soul of the Unborn Babe," in *Theology and Evolution.* London: Sands, 1949. Pp. 217–332. Opposes our position, as does LaCroix, Cardinal Mercier, and Canon Dordolot.

REANY, WILLIAM. *The Creation of the Human Soul.* New York: Benziger, 1932.

On Evolution:

DE CHARDIN, PIERRE TEILHARD, S.J. *The Phenomenon of Man.* New York: Harper, 1959.

EWING, J. FRANKLIN, S.J. "Human Evolution—1956," *Anthrop. Quart.*, 1956, 29:91–139.

FOTHERGILL, PHILIP G. "Towards an Interpretation of Evolution—the Teaching of 'Humani Generis,'" *The Tablet* (London), 1955, 205: 543–544.

GILL, HENRY V., S.J. *Fact and Fiction in Modern Science*. New York: Fordham University Press, 1944. Chap. 6, "The Origin of Life," pp. 50–57; Chap. 7, "Entropy, Life, and Evolution," pp. 58–66.

HAURET, CHARLES. *Beginnings: Genesis and Modern Science*. Trans. by E. P. Emmans, O.P. Dubuque: The Priory Press, 1955.

KLUBERTANZ, GEORGE P., S.J. *The Philosophy of Human Nature*. New York: Appleton-Century-Crofts, 1953. Appendices G, N.

KOREN, HENRY J., C.S.Sp. *An Introduction to the Philosophy of Animate Nature*. St. Louis: Herder, 1955. Chaps. 22, 23.

MESSENGER, E. C. *Evolution and Theology*. New York: Macmillan, 1932.

MESSENGER, E. C. (Ed.) *Theology and Evolution*. Westminster, Md.: Newman, 1950.

MORRISON, JOHN L. "American Catholics and the Crusade Against Evolution," *Rec. of the Amer. Catholic Historical Soc. of Philadelphia*, 1953, 44:59–71.

MURRAY, RAYMOND W., C.S.C. *Man's Unknown Ancestors*. (2d Ed.) Milwaukee: Bruce, 1948.

ROE, ANNE, & SIMPSON, GEORGE G. (Eds.) *Behavior and Evolution*. New Haven: Yale University Press, 1958.

RUFFINI, ERNESTO CARDINAL. *The Theory of Evolution Judged by Reason and Faith*. Trans. by Rev. Francis O'Hanlon. New York: J. F. Wagner, 1959. Unfortunately, this has been misrepresented as an official Church position.

VOLLERT, CYRIL, S.J. "Evolution of the Human Body," *The Catholic Mind*, March, 1952, No. 1071, 135–154.

Appendix

DO ANIMALS HAVE INTELLECT?

To expatiate upon the importance of thought would be absurd. The traditional definition of man as "the thinking animal" fixes thought as the essential difference between man and the brutes—surely an important matter. (John Dewey, How We Think, p. 14.)

Whether brute animals think is really of no direct concern to the philosophy of human nature. One legitimate reaction to the question is that we simply do not care whether they do or not. As long as we are satisfied that analysis of our operations affords conclusive evidence that man thinks, our concept of the nature of man remains unchanged, regardless of what we decide may be the nature of other animals. If someone feels that intellect is necessary to explain animal activities, this does not invalidate the evidence for human intellect. At most, it would mean that such a person should be logically consistent and give animals the rights and responsibilities proper to an intelligent being.

The question can contribute indirectly to our study of man because it is sometimes said that man is not by nature a rational animal, but *acquires* rationality from his environmental experiences. This is an assertion which should be open to testing by empirical evidence. The facts which have been accumulated in the study of animals thus become pertinent. If man is just a high type of vertebrate who acquires rationality by social conditioning, others of the higher vertebrates should be able to acquire rationality if given similar environmental opportunities. And conversely, if other animals fail to develop rationality under identical social conditions, the difference would seem to be in the very nature of man and brute respectively.

Condition for Rational Development

Our account of the formation of ideas in Chapter 7 and our delineation of the subjective factors in perception in Chapter 5 both indicate the importance of environmental sensory experience in the development of even intellectual knowledge. Language is a sensory, social means of communicating thought, and its importance for rational development cannot be ignored. Evidence which confirms these assertions is available from the study of people like Helen Keller who are born deaf, and from instances where children have been deprived of normal human environment.

It is always difficult to get accurate information on the latter cases, for if psychologists and social workers were around to record the data then there would not have been the complete lack of human social contact which is precisely the variable in question. But a few cases seem to be well enough authenticated to be considered. Two children, apparently abandoned in the jungle by their parents, were reported to have been raised by wolves in India. When found, they walked on all fours and were in a state of great mental retardation. One died shortly and the other lived only a few years after being brought into human society. Neither developed to any high degree of rationality. The French physician Itard studied and tried to help a wild boy found in the forest of Aveyron in similar circumstances. He likewise made some progress but never fully overcame the effects of early stultification. From these cases it seems that human social contact is an important condition for the development of rationality.

But a condition is not a cause. Having the wheels greased may be a necessary condition for having the car run, but it does not cause the car to move. Lack of proper environment may retard human development, just as failure to grease the wheels may mean that the car will not move. But in neither case will merely applying the condition produce the effect if the cause is not at work. Therefore, we cannot logically conclude from the low mentality of these children that environment is anything more than a condition for the normal actuation of man's rational nature.

Experiments with Animals

We are not lacking in evidence for the other aspect of our problem. Many brute animals have been given educational opportunities vastly superior to those afforded with unfortunate children mentioned above. Yet even these children showed some evidence of true rational response in spite of severely retarded beginnings, whereas the animals never do, even when given ideal conditions right from the start. At least two experiments have involved human parents "adopting" a baby ape and raising it exactly the same as a human baby.[1] In both cases, careful scientific records were kept, and in both cases the early sensory and motor development of the ape was ahead of the child at the same age. This is to be expected, for the ape has a shorter life span and would be further developed when maturing at a proportionate rate. In both cases the experiment was abandoned when it became quite clear that the ape showed no signs of true intellect long after a human child had far surpassed it.

Robert M. Yerkes of Yale University studied primates for about half a century, and his colony of apes were given every advantage of civilization. Among other things, they showed signs of a crude barter, a sort of prostitution, and an ability to play slot machines. His reports of these superficial semblances to human behavior have often been appealed to in attempts to reduce man to mere animal. But Yerkes himself seems from his lifelong study to have drawn just the opposite conclusion: that as our knowledge and understanding of anthropoid life increases, so also does our thankfulness that we are man.[2]

[1] W. N. Kellogg & Luella Kellogg, *The Ape and the Child* (New York: Mc-Graw-Hill, 1933); Cathy H. (Mrs. Keith J.) Hayes, *Ape in Our House* (New York: Harper, 1951).
[2] Cf. Brennan (1945), p. 185.

Köhler's report of the chimpanzee who put the two sticks together
to get the banana outside his cage is another instance of frequent distortion in secondary sources. Köhler's own report makes it clear
that the ape put the sticks together accidentally after an hour or so
of aimless play in which he apparently forgot all about the banana,
and only later saw the new Gestalt in which the combined stick was
long enough. Köhler himself does not claim perceptual insight to be
an act of intellect.[3]

T. V. Moore made a comprehensive survey of the experimental
data available and found that higher vertebrates manifest a grasp
of concrete spatial configurations, to about the degree attained by a
high-grade human idiot. This he attributes to the activity of the
central or synthetic sense. "But when we attempt to measure their
power of abstract thought and their ability to see and form general
principles in the logical order, we obtain zero scores, for such abilities
are simply not present."[4]

Why Don't Animals Talk?

There is no doubt about the fact that animals can communicate.
Bees can transmit to other bees both the direction and the distance of
a find. Most animals can make their wants known in some way. But
the question is not whether they communicate, but whether they
do so by the conventional symbols of conceptual language or by
concrete natural signs. All of the evidence points to the latter. To
suggest that maybe they have a true conceptual language which we
do not understand is an unwarranted assumption. To postulate that
they have ideas and simply do not communicate is not only a gra-
tuitous assertion but quite contrary to everything we know about the
nature of knowledge as communicable. Moreover, to argue "Why
should the animals manifest their thought to us?" admits that they
do not. Since we can only go on the manifestations of evidence, this
is tantamount to saying that for our purpose the issue is settled.

[3] W. Köhler, *Gestalt Psychology* (New York: Liveright, 1947), p. 341. See
F. L. Harmon, *Principles of Psychology* (Rev. ed., Milwaukee: Bruce, 1951),
pp. 399–403 for a good discussion of Köhler's work.
[4] T. V. Moore, "Human and Animal Intelligence," in H. S. Jennings et al.,
Scientific Aspects of the Race Problem (New York: Longmans, 1941), p. 152.

It is sometimes asserted (Garrett, 1955, p. 69) that the reason animals do not talk is because they do not have the equipment. But parrots and other animals do talk. Some species of apes possess vocal apparatus capable of modulating sounds. Parrots and any animals having lips, tongue, and larynx are far better equipped than many paralyzed or otherwise handicapped persons. Yet the latter somehow manage to communicate ideas, whereas the former never do. Yerkes says, "It may not be asserted that any of the anthropoid types speaks" (1929, p. 546; also p. 569). Garrett seems to contradict himself here, for on the same page he reports that Vicki, an ape raised as a child, was able to say three words, *mamma, papa,* and *cup*—quite impossible if she lacked the necessary equipment! The only conclusion is that the reason animals do not talk is that they have nothing to say, i.e., no concepts to express but only concrete sensory experiences.

Negative Evidence

It is good to remind ourselves that we cannot expect to have the same kind of positive evidence as would be forthcoming if the conclusion were a positive one. What evidence do you have that there is not a live alligator in the corner of the room as you read this? Only negative evidence; the burden of the proof is on him who asserts its presence. The closest you can come to positive evidence is to walk over to the corner and give the alligator a chance to snap at you if he is there. Similarly, we can only report on those experiments where conditions are created in which brute animals should manifest thought if they have any.

Note that this is a different matter from asserting that animals do stupid things, and that men do not. The question is whether animals *ever* show intellect; whereas man's has already been established, without implying that he always uses it. Neither does this involve a denial that animals do many extremely ingenious things. The explanation of how they do them will be discussed shortly. The question now is whether they manifest intellect when conditions warrant it.

Naturalists have set up many experiments to test whether animals understand why they are doing what they do. For instance, an elaborate series of seven steps is observed in the laying of an egg and storing it; at step four the experimenter removes the egg in full sight of the insect, who proceeds to go right on and complete the remaining steps even though the whole process is now pointless. Birds will continue to collect food for their young even when they have seen them killed.[5] Again, the animal fails to modify his behavior when it would be logical to do so if he understood its purpose. It is proverbial that horses will follow their self-protective pattern even when it means burning to death in the stable.

Monkeys are great imitators. For centuries they have watched birds fly in the jungle. Yet they have never shown any evidence of abstracting out the principles of flight and applying them as did the Wright brothers. Nothing approaching the construction of machinery or mass production is ever observed in animals, nor the invention of any tool which shows more than concrete perception of spatial relations. Their language has no transposable signs, normative grammar, or abstract symbols. All these are signs of universal ideas.

Progress of some sort is almost infallibly a sign of intellect. Yet naturalists of ancient times observed exactly the same activities that we see animals doing today. It is incredible that the animals would have even rudimentary intellect and show no real accomplishment or transmission of anything they learn to their followers. Even the crudest primitives have some tradition. This is even more striking in the case of domesticated animals, where selective breeding and constant opportunities to learn from their association with man would be most conducive to progress. Yet even under these conditions we see no unequivocal evidence of genuine intellectual progress.

Akin to this is the animal's lack of any awareness of personal identity, and hence of self-reflectiveness or historicity. Man is the only animal that blushes; he alone seems to have a true sense of responsibility. Other animals show no appreciation of beauty, nor any attempts at art. Humor is completely lacking, even in the "laughing" hyena; it takes intellect to recognize incongruity and thus appreciate the ridiculous.

---

[5] Reports of such experiments were recounted for many years in the *Reader's Digest* under the running head "Fooling the Animals."

Ambiguous Terms

We have already noted that such terms as intelligence, learning, trial and error, insight, and ability to adjust or solve problems are all ambiguous. Thus *insight* may mean a total perceptual awareness (Gestalt) in which concrete relations are seen, as in the case of the ape with the two sticks and the banana, or it may mean true intellectual understanding in terms of universal principles. *Trial and error* may mean chance connection in one of a series of random movements which is then associated with success, or it may mean an elaborate inductive reasoning process which involves the testing of hypotheses by a series of experiments. Even *concept* now often refers merely to concrete associations and generalized stimuli, perhaps associated with abstract symbol or satisfying experience. But a true intellectual concept is an understanding of what a thing *is*, not merely what it is *for*. These other uses of the term concept are analogous, and involve generalized association of sense experience rather than abstraction. The fact that a monkey can learn to associate concrete reactions with the general shape of a triangle is not evidence that it understands the nature of triangularity, i.e., has a true concept. *Intelligence* may mean any ability to learn or adjust such as most animals manifest, or it may be the capacity for abstract thought such as we analyzed in Chapter 6. To say that an animal is more or less intelligent simply refers to the degree to which his internal senses are developed.

Internal Sense Powers Ignored

It is the failure to appreciate the marvelous versatility of the internal senses which deludes most people into concluding that animals have intellect. They see animals do many wonderful things, which obviously surpass the power of mere reflex or sensation. Therefore they immediately conclude that intellect must be at work. The solution is not to deny that animals act in a very clever manner. Fuller study of the powers of synthetic or central sense, imagination, memory, and estimative power will satisfy us that the most ingenious animal accomplishments can be explained by the activity of these internal senses. Imagination, for instance, is capable of forming an image of three-dimensional space wherein we can visualize generalized relations.[6] Associations and memories can pile up with incredible richness; sensory discrimination can be very acute. ("Kluger Hans," the counting horse, sensed when to stop counting out the answer from subtle cues which even his master was unaware of giving him. Controlled experimentation showed he was helpless outside his master's presence.) Yet all these operations are possible at least to animals with well-developed brain and nervous systems, such as most higher vertebrates have. Such operations are quite adequate to explain the facts, without appealing to intellect. (See Chapter 5.)

True Intelligence Involved

Lastly, we readily concede that the activities of brute animals, including insects such as bees and ants, show definitely that there is intelligence in the strict sense of true understanding somewhere in the total picture. The leaf-roller beetle who cuts a perfect parabola may know no analytic geometry; the bee who constructs his honeycomb according to the best principles of structural design may not be a mechanical engineer. Like the navigation ability of homing pigeons and the built-in radar of bats, these manifest true intellect at work. The question here is, whose intellect is it?

Masterful understanding on just one point is contrary to the nature of intellect, which has being as its object. The intellect should be able to make some progress on other things. But these animals show no ability to generalize over into even allied areas. They do the same thing the same way for centuries, with no improvement and no application of their ability to other problems. This suggests that there is no real grasp of what is applied, but that they simply are following a concrete behavior pattern. They could hardly be so brilliant in one tiny area without it showing elsewhere. If they truly understand the solution to the problem, why do they always use the same solution

---

[6] Klubertanz (1953, p. 132) calls this an "abstract" image, but this seems a bit misleading. "General" image might be better. Similarly, the concrete associations obtained by the rhesus monkey can include the general image of "threeness" without this necessarily being a true concept of number as implied by Hicks (1956).

when there are others? Why do they always solve it perfectly the first time, if it is really the result of their understanding? Man usually takes time to work things out, and is rarely as proficient in the beginning of his life as later on. All this indicates that it is not the animal's own intellect which is responsible for the wonders he performs.

The automatic pilot in a modern airplane certainly manifests intelligence at work, yet nobody argues that the device itself understands why it functions. The intellect of the designer is given full credit. A similar argument could lead to the conclusion that, if the animal does not have an intellect, the Designer of the animal does. But this would take us beyond the philosophy of human nature.

FOR FURTHER READING

FABRE, JEAN HENRI C. *Fabre's Book of Insects*, retold from Alexander Teixeira de Mattos' translation of Fabre's "*Souvenirs entomologiques*" by Mrs. Rudolph Stowell. New York: Tudor, 1937.

FABRE, JEAN HENRI C. *The Hunting Wasps*. Trans. by Alexander Teixeira de Mattos. New York: Dodd, Mead, 1915.

FRISCH, JOHN A. "Did the Peckhams Witness the Invention of a Tool by *Ammophila Urnaria?*" *The Amer. Midland Naturalist*, September, 1940.

GRUENDER, HUBERT, S.J. *Experimental Psychology*. Milwaukee: Bruce, 1932. Pp. 245–252, 286–300.

KATZ, DAVID. *Animals and Men*. New York: Longmans, 1937.

KÖHLER, WOLFGANG. *The Mentality of Apes*. New York: Harcourt, Brace, 1925.

LORENZ, K. Z. *King Solomon's Ring*. New York: Crowell, 1952.

MOORE, THOMAS VERNER. "Human and Animal Intelligence," in H. S. Jennings and others, *Scientific Aspects of the Race Problem*. New York: Longmans, 1941. Pp. 95–158.

MUCKERMANN, HENRY, S.J. *Humanizing the Brute*. St. Louis: Herder, 1906.

ROMANES, GEORGE JOHN. *Mental Evolution in Animals* (with a posthumous essay "Instinct" by Charles Darwin). London: Kegan Paul, Trench, Trubner & Co., 1883.

SCHILLER, CLAIRE H. (Ed.) *Instinctive Behavior: The Development of a Modern Concept*. New York: International Universities Press, 1957.

TEALE, E. W. *The Insect World of J. Henri Fabre*. New York: Dodd, Mead, 1949.

THORPE, W. H. *Learning and Instinct in Animals*. Cambridge, Mass.: Harvard University Press, 1956.

TINBERGEN, N. *The Study of Instinct*. New York: Oxford, 1951.

VON FRISCH, K. *Bees: Their Vision, Chemical Senses, and Language*. Ithaca, N.Y.: Cornell University Press, 1950.

WASMANN, ERIC, S.J. *Instinct and Intelligence in the Animal Kingdom*. St. Louis: Herder, 1903.

WILM, E. C. *Theories of Instinct*. New Haven: Yale University Press, 1925.

YERKES, ROBERT M., & YERKES, ADA W. *The Great Apes*. New Haven: Yale University Press, 1929.

GENERAL BIBLIOGRAPHY

ADLER, MORTIMER J. *God and the Professors*. New York: Conference of Science, Philosophy, and Religion, 1940.

ADLER, MORTIMER J. "Introduction," in Robert E. Brennan, O.P., *Thomistic Psychology*. New York: Macmillan, 1941. Pp. vii–xiv.

ADLER, MORTIMER J. *What Man Has Made of Man*. New York: Longmans, 1937.

ADRIAN, EDGAR D. *The Physical Background of Perception*. New York: Oxford, 1947.

ALFORD, LELAND B. "Cerebral Localization: Outline of a Revision," *J. Nerv. & Ment. Dis. Monogr.*, 1948, No. 77.

ALLERS, RUDOLF. "Abnormality: A Chapter in Moral Psychology," *Homilectic and Pastoral Rev.*, December, 1941–August, 1942, 42, Nos. 2–10.

ALLERS, RUDOLF. "Functions, Factors, and Faculties," *The Thomist*, 1944, 7:323–362.

ALLERS, RUDOLF. "Intellectual Cognition," in R. E. Brennan (Ed.), *Essays in Thomism*. New York: Sheed, 1942b. Pp. 41–62.

ALLERS, RUDOLF. "The Intellectual Cognition of Particulars," *The Thomist*, 1941, 3:95–163.

ALLERS, RUDOLF. "Irresistible Impulses," *Amer. Eccles. Rev.*, 1939, 100: 209–218.

ALLERS, RUDOLF. *The Psychology of Character*. Trans. by E. B. Strauss. London: Sheed, 1931.

ALLERS, RUDOLF. "The Vis Cogitativa and Evaluation," *The New Scholasticism*, 1941, 15:195–221.

ALLPORT, FLOYD H. *Theories of Perception and the Concept of Structure.* New York: Wiley, 1955.

ALLPORT, GORDON W. *Becoming: Basic Considerations for a Psychology of Personality.* New Haven: Yale University Press, 1955.

ALLPORT, GORDON W. *The Nature of Personality: Selected Papers.* Cambridge, Mass.: Addison-Wesley, 1950.

AMERICAN CATHOLIC PHILOSOPHICAL ASSOCIATION. "The Problem of Liberty," *Proc.*, Vol. 16, 1940.

AMES, A., JR. "Reconsideration of the Origin and Nature of Perception," in S. Ratner, *Vision and Action.* New Brunswick, N.J.: Rutgers University Press, 1953. Pp. 251–274.

AMES, A., JR. "Visual Perception and the Rotating Trapezoidal Window," *Psychol. Monogr.*, 1951, Vol. 65, No. 7 (Whole No. 324).

ANABLE, RAYMOND J., S.J. *Philosophical Psychology.* New York: Fordham University Press, 1941.

ANDERSON, JOHN E., *The Psychology of Development and Personal Adjustment.* New York: Holt, 1949.

ANDREWS, T. G. (Ed.) *Methods of Psychology.* New York: Wiley, 1948.

ANGYAL, ANDERS. *Foundations for a Science of Personality.* New York: Commonwealth Fund, 1941.

AQUINAS, ST. THOMAS. *Basic Writings of St. Thomas Aquinas.* Ed. by Anton C. Pegis. New York: Random House, 1945.

AQUINAS, ST. THOMAS. *Commentary on Aristotle's De Anima.* Books I and II. Trans. by K. Foster & S. Humphries as *Aristotle. De Anima* (in the version of William of Moerbeke and the commentary of St. Thomas Aquinas), with Introduction by Thomas Ivo, O.P. New Haven: Yale University Press, 1951.

AQUINAS, ST. THOMAS. *Introduction to St. Thomas Aquinas.* Ed. by Anton C. Pegis. New York: Modern Library, 1948.

AQUINAS, ST. THOMAS. *On the Truth of the Catholic Faith (Summa Contra Gentiles.)* Trans. by James F. Anderson. Garden City, N.Y.: Doubleday (Image), 1955.

AQUINAS, ST. THOMAS. *The Soul.* Trans. by John P. Rowan. St. Louis: Herder, 1949.

AQUINAS, ST. THOMAS. *Summa Theologiae.* Ottawa: Studium Generale, O.P., 1941–1944.

AQUINAS, ST. THOMAS. *The Summa Theologica.* Trans. by the fathers of the English Dominican Province. New York: Benziger, 1947.

AQUINAS, ST. THOMAS. *Truth.* Trans. by Robert W. Mulligan, S.J., James V. McGlynn, S.J., & Robert W. Schmidt, S.J. Chicago: Regnery, 1952–1954. 3 vols.

ARISTOTLE. *De Anima.* (in the version of William of Moerbeke and the commentary of St. Thomas Aquinas). Trans. by K. Foster & Silvester Humphries, with an introduction by Ivo Thomas, O.P. New Haven: Yale University Press, 1951.

ARISTOTLE. *On the Soul.* (Rev. Ed.) The Loeb Classical Library. Ed. and trans. by W. S. Hett. Cambridge, Mass.: Harvard University Press, 1957.

ARNOLD, MAGDA B. "The Status of Emotion in Contemporary Psychology," in A. A. Roback (Ed.), *Present-day Psychology.* New York: Philosophical Library, 1955. Pp. 135–188.

ARNOLD, MAGDA B., & GASSON, JOHN A. *The Human Person: An Approach to an Integral Theory of Personality.* New York: Ronald, 1954.

AUSUBEL, DAVID P. *Ego Development and the Personality Disorders: A Developmental Approach to Psychopathology.* New York: Grune & Stratton, 1952.

AVELING, FRANCIS. *The Immortality of the Soul.* Vol. I. Westminster Lectures. St. Louis: Herder, 1906.

AVELING, FRANCIS. *Personality and Will.* New York: Appleton-Century-Crofts, 1931.

BARTA, FRANK R. *The Moral Theory of Behavior.* Springfield, Ill.: Charles C Thomas, 1953.

BARTLETT, SIR FREDERIC. *Thinking: An Experimental and Social Study.* London: G. Allen, 1958.

BARTLEY, J. HOWARD. *Principles of Perception.* New York: Harper, 1958.

BARUK, H. "Personality: Psychological and Metaphysical Problem," *Phil. Today,* 1957, 1:122–127.

BATESON, G. "Cultural Determinants of Personality," in J. McV. Hunt (Ed.), *Personality and the Behavior Disorders.* Vol. 2. New York: Ronald, 1944. Pp. 714–735.

BEARDSLEE, DAVID C., & WERTHEIMER, M. (Eds.) *Readings in Perception.* New York: Van Nostrand, 1958.

BECK, WILLIAM S. *Modern Science and the Nature of Life.* New York: Harcourt, Brace, 1957.

BERENDA, CARLTON W. "Is Clinical Psychology A Science?" *Amer. Psychologist,* 1957, 12:725–729.

BERGSON, HENRI. *Matter and Memory.* Trans. by N. M. Paul & W. S. Palmer. New York: Macmillan, 1950a.

BERGSON, HENRI. *Time and Free Will.* New York: Macmillan, 1950b.

BERNARD, L. L. *Instinct: A Study in Social Psychology.* New York: Holt, 1924.

BERNSTEIN, MOREY. *The Search for Bridey Murphy.* New York: Doubleday, 1956.

VON BERTALANFFY, L. *Problems of Life: An Evaluation of Modern Biological Thought*. London: Watts, 1952.

BERTOCCI, PETER A. *Free Will, Responsibility, and Grace*. Nashville, Tenn.: Abingdon, 1957.

BIER, WILLIAM C., S.J. *Perception in Present-day Psychology: A Symposium*. New York: American Catholic Psychological Association (Fordham University), 1956.

BINET, ALFRED. *L'Étude expérimentale de l'intelligence*. Paris: Schleicher Frères, 1903.

BINET, ALFRED, & SIMON, TH. "Langage et pensé," *Année Psychol.*, 1908, 14:284–339.

BLACK, MARVIN M. *The Pendulum Swings Back*. London: Cokesbury Press, 1937.

BLAKE, ROBERT R., & RAMSEY, GLENN V. (Eds.) *Perception: An Approach to Personality*. New York: Ronald, 1950.

BOGANELLI, ELEUTHERIUS. "De Personalitate Psycho-physio-pathologica Delinquentis Enixe Expendenda in Judicio Ferendo de Culpabilitate Delicti," *Apollinaris*, 1937, 10:408-430.

BORING, EDWARD G., "CP Speaks," *Contemporary Psychol.*, 1958, 3: 361–362.

BORING, EDWARD G. *A History of Experimental Psychology*. (2d Ed.) New York: Appleton-Century-Crofts, 1950.

BORING, EDWARD G. "Preface," in H. Misiak & V. Staudt, *Catholics in Psychology*. New York: McGraw-Hill, 1954. Pp. ix–xi.

BORING, EDWARD G. Review of James J. Gibson, *The Perception of the Visual World*, *Psychol. Bull.*, 1951, 48:360–363.

BORING, EDWARD G. *Sensation and Perception in the History of Experimental Psychology*. New York: Appleton-Century-Crofts, 1942.

BORING, EDWARD G., LANGFELD, H. S., & WELD, H. P. *Foundations of Psychology*. New York: Wiley, 1948.

BOULOGNE, CHARLES-DAMIAN, O.P. *My Friends the Senses*. New York: P. J. Kenedy & Sons, 1953.

BOURKE, VERNON J. "Habitus as a Perfectant of Potency in the Philosophy of St. Thomas Aquinas." Unpublished doctoral dissertation, University of Toronto, 1938.

BOURKE, VERNON J. "The Role of Habitus in the Thomistic Metaphysics of Potency and Act," in R. Brennan (Ed.), *Essays in Thomism*, New York: Sheed, 1942. Pp. 103–109.

BOUTROUX, ÉMILE. *Historical Studies in Philosophy*. Trans. by Fred Rothwell. London: Macmillan, 1912.

BRACELAND, FRANCIS J. (Ed.) *Faith, Reason, and Modern Psychiatry: Sources for a Synthesis*. New York: P. J. Kenedy & Sons, 1955.

BRAUNSHAUSEN, N. "Le Libre-arbitre à la lumière de la psychologie expérimentale et de la science moderne," *Rev. des Sci. Pédag.*, 1947, 9:38–46 (*Psychol. Abstr.*, 1950, 24:1032).

BRENNAN, ROBERT E., O.P. *General Psychology.* (Rev. Ed.) New York: Macmillan, 1952.

BRENNAN, ROBERT E., O.P. *History of Psychology from the Standpoint of a Thomist.* New York: Macmillan, 1945.

BRENNAN, ROBERT E., O.P. *Thomistic Psychology.* New York: Macmillan, 1941.

BRIDGES, KATHERINE M. "A Genetic Theory of Emotions," *J. Genet. Psychol.*, 1930, 37:514–527.

BROWN, C. W., & GHISELLI, E. E. *Scientific Method in Psychology.* New York: McGraw-Hill, 1955.

BROWN, ROGER. *Words and Things.* Glencoe, Ill.: Free Press, 1958.

BRUNER, J. S. & GOODMAN, C. D. "Value and Need as Organizing Factors in Perception," *J. Abnorm. Soc. Psychol.*, 1947, 42:33–44.

BRUNER, J. S., GOODNOW, J. J., & AUSTIN, G. A. *A Study of Thinking.* New York: Wiley, 1956.

BRUNSWIK, EGON. *The Concept and Framework of Psychology.* Chicago: University of Chicago Press, 1952.

BUDDENBROCK, WOLFGANG VON. *The Senses.* Ann Arbor: University of Michigan Press, 1958.

BUXTON, C. E., and others. *Improving Undergraduate Instruction in Psychology.* New York: Macmillan, 1952.

CALDIN, E. F. *The Power and Limits of Science.* London: Chapman & Hall, 1949.

CAMERON, NORMAN. *The Psychology of Behavior Disorders.* Boston: Houghton Mifflin, 1947.

CAMMACK, J. S., S.J. *Moral Problems of Mental Defect.* London: Burns, 1938.

CANNON, WALTER B. *Bodily Changes in Pain, Hunger, Fear and Rage.* (2d Ed.) New York: Appleton-Century-Crofts, 1929.

CANNON, WALTER B. *The Wisdom of the Body.* (2d Ed.) New York: Norton, 1939.

CANTRIL, HADLEY. "An Inquiry into the Characteristics of Man," *J. Abnorm. Soc. Psychol.*, 1950a, 45:490–503.

CANTRIL, HADLEY. *The "Why" of Man's Experience.* New York: Macmillan, 1950b.

CARNAP, R. "The Methodological Character of Theoretical Concepts," in *Minnesota Studies in the Philosophy of Science.* Vol. I. Minneapolis: University of Minnesota Press, 1956. Pp. 38–76.

CARRELL, ALEXIS. *Man the Unknown.* New York: Harper, 1939.

CARTWRIGHT, DARWIN. Review of Roy R. Grinker (Ed.) *Toward a Unified Theory of Human Behavior, Contemporary Psychol.*, 1957, 2:121–123.

CASSIRER, ERNST. *An Essay on Man.* New Haven: Yale University Press, 1944.

CASTIELLO, JAIMIE, S.J. *A Humane Psychology of Education.* New York: Sheed, 1936a.

CASTIELLO, JAIMIE, S.J. "The Psychology of Habit in St. Thomas," *The Modern Schoolman*, 1936b, 14:8–12.

CASTIELLO, JAIMIE, S.J. "The Psychology of Intellectual and Moral Habits," *Jesuit Educ. Quart.*, 1941, 4:59–70.

CATTELL, RAYMOND B. "The Discovery of Ergic Structures in Man in Terms of Common Attitudes," *J. Abnorm. Soc. Psychol.*, 1950, 45: 598–618.

CHANT, S. N. F., & SIGNORI, E. I. *Interpretive Psychology.* New York: McGraw-Hill, 1957.

CHAPIN, MARY V., & WASHBURN, MARGARET FLOY. "Study of the Images Representing the Concept of Meaning," *Amer. J. Psychol.*, 1912, 23:109–114.

DE CHARDIN, PIERRE TEILHARD, S.J. *The Phenomenon of Man.* New York: Harper, 1959.

COADY, SR. MARY ANASTASIA. *The Phantasm According to the Teaching of St. Thomas.* Washington: The Catholic University of America Press, 1932.

COFFIN, JOSEPH H. *The Soul Comes Back.* New York: Macmillan, 1929.

COLE, LAWRENCE E. *Human Behavior: Psychology as a Bio-social Science.* New York: World, 1953.

COLEMAN, JAMES C. *Abnormal Psychology and Modern Life.* Chicago: Scott, Foresman, 1956.

COMBS, ARTHUR W., & SNYGG, DONALD. *Individual Behavior: A Perceptual Approach to Behavior.* (Rev. Ed.) New York: Harper, 1959.

COMMINS, W. D., & FAGIN, BARRY. *Educational Psychology.* (Rev. Ed.) New York: Ronald, 1954.

COMPTON, ARTHUR G. *The Freedom of Man.* New Haven: Yale University Press, 1935.

COMPTON, ARTHUR G. "Science and Man's Freedom," *Atlantic Monthly*, 1957, 200 (4):71–74.

COPLESTON, F. C. *Aquinas.* Baltimore: Penguin, 1955.

COPLESTON, FREDERICK, S.J. *Contemporary Philosophy: Studies of Logical Positivism and Existentialism.* Westminster, Md.: Newman, 1956.

CROWELL, DAVID H., & DOLE, A. A. "Animism and College Students," *J. Educ. Res.*, 1957, 50:391–395.

D'ARCY, MARTIN C., S.J. *Death and Life*. London: Longmans, 1942.

DAVID, HENRY P., & VON BRACKEN, HELMUT. (Eds.) *Perspectives in Personality Theory*. New York: Basic Books, 1957.

DAVIDSON, M. *The Free Will Controversy*. London: Watts, 1942.

DAVIDSON, M. *Free Will or Determinism*. London: Watts, 1937.

DAVIS, R. C. Review of Warner Brown & H. C. Gilhousen, *College Psychology*, *Psychol. Bull.*, 1951, 48:366–367.

DAY, SEBASTIAN J., O.F.M. *Intuitive Cognition: A Key to the Significance of the Later Scholastics*. St. Bonaventure, N.Y.: Franciscan Institute, 1947.

DEESE, JAMES. *The Psychology of Learning*. (Rev. Ed.) New York: Mc-Graw-Hill, 1958.

DEWEY, JOHN. *How We Think*. Boston: Heath, 1910.

DIEMERT, F. JEROME, S.J. "Thomistic Psychology and the Social Dimension of Man," *Proc. Jesuit Phil. Ass.*, 1959.

DOLLARD, J., & MILLER, N. E. *Personality and Psychotherapy*. New York: McGraw-Hill, 1950.

DONCEEL, JOSEPH F., S.J. *Philosophical Psychology*. New York: Sheed, 1955.

DONCEEL, JOSEPH F., S.J. "What Kind of Science is Psychology?" *The New Scholasticism*, 1945, 19:117–135.

DRESSLER, ALWIN. "Can One Live without a Brain?" *Magazine Dig.*, 1934, 8:18–19. [Condensed from (Berlin) *Illustrierte Beobachter*, Sept. 9, 1933.]

DRIESCH, HANS. *Mind and Body*. London: Methuen, 1927.

DRIESCH, HANS. *The Science and Philosophy of the Organism*. London: Black, 1908. 2 vols.

DUNBAR, H. FLANDERS. *Emotions and Bodily Changes*. New York: Columbia University Press, 1954.

DUNBAR, H. FLANDERS, *Mind and Body: Psychosomatic Medicine*. (2d Ed.) New York: Random House, 1955.

DUNCKER, KARL. On Problem Solving. *Psychol. Monogr.*, 1945, No. 270.

DUNLAP, KNIGHT. *Habits, Their Making and Unmaking*. New York: Liveright, 1932.

DUNN, MIRIAM F. "The Psychology of Reasoning," *Catholic Univ. Stud. in Psychol. and Psychiat.*, 1926, Vol. I, No. 1.

DUNNE, PETER. "The Production of the Intelligible Species," *The New Scholasticism*, 1953, 27:176–197.

ECCLES, JOHN C. *The Neurophysiological Basis of Mind*. New York: Oxford, 1953.

ENGLISH, HORACE B. *Child Psychology*. New York: Holt, 1951.

ENGLISH, HORACE B. *Historical Roots of Learning Theory*. New York: Random House, 1954.

ENTRALGO, PEDRO LAIN. *Mind and Body: Psychosomatic Pathology.* New York: P. J. Kenedy & Sons, 1956.

ESTABROOKS, G. H. "Your Brain," *Sci. Amer.*, July, 1936, 155:20–22.

ESTES, WILLIAM K., and others. *Modern Learning Theory.* New York: Appleton-Century-Crofts, 1954.

EWING, J. FRANKLIN, S.J. "Human Evolution—1956," *Anthrop. Quart.*, 1956, 29:91–139.

EYMIEU, ANTONIN, S.J. *Le Gouvernement de soi-même.* Vol. I. *Les Grandes lois.* Vol. II, *L'Obsession et le scrupule.* Vol. III, *L'Art de vouloir.* Vol. IV, *La Loi de la vie.* Paris: Perrin, 1925–1936. 4 vols.

FABRE, JEAN HENRI C. *Fabre's Book of Insects*, retold from Alexander Teixeira de Mattos' translation of Fabre's *Souvenirs entomologiques* by Mrs. Rudolph Stowell. New York: Tudor, 1937.

FABRE, JEAN HENRI C. *The Hunting Wasps.* Trans. by Alexander Teixeira de Mattos. New York: Dodd, Mead, 1915.

FARRELL, WALTER, O.P. *Companion to the Summa.* New York: Sheed, 1942.

FARRER, AUSTIN M. *Finite and Infinite.* Chicago: Allenson, 1943.

FARRER, AUSTIN M. *The Freedom of the Will.* London: A. & C. Black, 1958.

FEIGL, HERBERT. "Philosophical Embarrassments of Psychology" (invited address to the 1958 convention of the American Psychological Association), *Amer. Psychologist*, 1959, 14:115–128.

FEIGL, HERBERT, and others (Eds.) *Minnesota Studies in the Philosophy of Science.* Vol I, "The Foundations of Science and the Concepts of Psychology and Psychoanalysis," 1956. Vol. II, "Concepts, Theories, and the Mind-Body Problem," 1958. Minneapolis: University of Minnesota Press.

FELL, GEORGE, S.J. *The Immortality of the Human Soul.* St. Louis: Herder, 1908.

FERM, VERGILIUS. *First Adventures in Philosophy.* New York: Scribner, 1936.

DE FINANCE, JOSEPH, S.J. "Being and Subjectivity," trans. by W. Norris Clarke, S.J., *Cross Currents*, 1956, 6:163–178.

DE FINANCE, JOSEPH, S.J. "Cogita cartesien et réflexion thomiste," *Arch. de Phil.*, 1946, Vol. XVI, No. 2.

DE FINANCE, JOSEPH, S.J. *Être et agir dans la philosophie de S. Thomas.* Paris: Beauchesne, 1945.

FINGER, F. W. "Textbooks and General Psychology," *Psychol. Bull.*, 1954, 51:82–90.

FLETCHER, RONALD. *Instinct in Man: In the Light of Recent Work in Comparative Psychology.* New York: International Universities Press, 1957.

FLYNN, THOMAS V., S.J. "The Cogitative Power," *The Thomist*, 1953, 16:542–563.

FORD, JOHN C., S.J. *Depth Psychology, Morality and Alcoholism.* Weston, Mass.: Weston College, 1951.

FORD, JOHN C., S.J., & KELLY, GERALD, S.J. "Psychiatry and Moral Responsibility," *Theological Stud.*, 1954, 15:59–67.

FOREST, AIMÉ. *La Structure métaphysique du concret selon Saint Thomas d'Aquin.* Paris: Vrin, 1931.

FOTHERGILL, PHILIP G. "Towards an Interpretation of Evolution: The Teaching of 'Humani Generis,'" *The Tablet* (London), 1955, 205: 543–544.

FRANK, LAWRENCE K., *Feelings and Emotions.* New York: Doubleday, 1953.

FRANKL, VIKTOR E. *The Doctor and the Soul.* New York: Knopf, 1955.

FRANKL, VIKTOR E. *From Death-camp to Existentialism.* Boston: Beacon Press, 1959.

FRISCH, JOHN A. "Did the Peckhams Witness the Invention of a Tool by *Ammophila Urnaria?*" *The Amer. Midland Naturalist*, September, 1940.

FROMM, ERIC. *Man for Himself: An Inquiry into the Psychology of Ethics.* New York: Rinehart, 1947.

GAFFNEY, MARK A., S.J. *Psychology of the Interior Senses.* St. Louis: Herder, 1942.

GANNON, TIMOTHY J. *Psychology: The Unity of Human Behavior.* Boston: Ginn, 1954.

GARDEIL, H. D., O.P. *Introduction to the Philosophy of St. Thomas.* Vol. III, *Psychology.* Trans. by John A Otto St. Louis: Herder, 1956.

GARRETT, HENRY E. *General Psychology* New York American Book, 1955.

GEACH, PETER. *Mental Acts: Their Content and Their Objects.* New York: Humanities Press, 1957.

GELDARD, F. A. *The Human Senses.* New York: Wiley, 1953.

GEMELLI, AGOSTINO. "Orienting Concepts in the Study of Affective States," *J. Nerv. Ment. Dis.*, 1949, 110:198–214, 299–314.

GERRITY, BRO. BENIGNUS, F.S.C. *Nature, Knowledge, and God.* Milwaukee: Bruce, 1947.

GIBSON, J. J. *The Perception of the Visual World.* Boston: Houghton Mifflin, 1940.

GILBY, THOMAS, O.P. "Thought, Volition and the Organism," *The Thomist*, 1940, 2:1–13.

GILBY, THOMAS, O.P. "Vienne and Vienna," *Thought*, 1946, 21:63–82.

GILL, HENRY V., S.J. *Fact and Fiction in Modern Science*. New York: Fordham University Press, 1944.

GILSON, ETIENNE. *The Christian Philosophy of St. Thomas*. New York: Random House, 1956.

GILSON, ETIENNE. *The Philosophy of St. Thomas*. St. Louis: Herder, 1925.

GILSON, ETIENNE. *Réalisme thomiste et critique de la connaissance*. Paris: Vrin, 1939.

GILSON, ETIENNE. *The Spirit of Medieval Philosophy*. New York: Scribner, 1936.

GILSON, ETIENNE. *The Unity of Philosophical Experience*. New York: Scribner, 1937.

GOLDSTEIN, KURT. *Human Nature in the Light of Psychopathology*. Cambridge: Harvard University Press, 1940.

GOLDSTEIN, KURT. *The Organism*. New York: American Book, 1939.

GRAHAM, C. H. "Behavior, Perception, and the Psychophysical Methods," *Psychol. Rev.*, 1950, 57:108–120.

GRINKER, ROY R. (Ed.) *Toward a Unified Theory of Behavior*. New York: Basic Books, 1956.

GRUENDER, HUBERT, S.J. *Experimental Psychology*. Milwaukee: Bruce, 1932.

GRUENDER, HUBERT, S.J. *Free Will, the Greatest of the Seven World Riddles*. St. Louis: Herder, 1916.

GRUENDER, HUBERT, S.J. *Problems of Psychology*. Milwaukee: Bruce, 1937.

GRUENDER, HUBERT, S.J. *Psychology without a Soul*. (2d Ed.) St. Louis: Herder, 1917.

GUILFORD, J.P. "Creativity," *Amer. Psychologist*, 1950, 5:444–454.

GUILFORD, J. P. *Personality*. New York: McGraw-Hill, 1959.

GURR, JOHN E., S.J. "Genesis and Function of Principles in Philosophy," *Proc. Amer. Cath. Phil. Ass.*, 1955, 29:121–133.

GURR, JOHN E., S.J. *The Principle of Sufficient Reason in Some Scholastic Systems, 1750–1900*. Milwaukee: Marquette University Press, 1959.

GURR, JOHN E., S.J. "Some Historical Origins of Rationalism in Catholic Philosophy Manuals," *Proc. Amer. Cath. Phil. Ass.*, 1956, 30:17–180.

HALL, CALVIN S., LINDZEY, GARDNER. *Theories of Personality*. New York: Wiley, 1957.

HALSTEAD, W. C. *Brain and Intelligence*. Chicago: University of Chicago Press, 1947.

HAMLYN, D. W. *The Psychology of Perception: A Philosophical Ex-

amination of Gestalt Theory and Derivative Theories of Perception. New York: Humanities Press, 1957.

HARMON, FRANCIS L. *Principles of Psychology.* (Rev. Ed.) Milwaukee: Bruce, 1951.

HARMON, FRANCIS L. *Understanding Personality.* Milwaukee: Bruce, 1948.

HARRELL, W., & HARRISON, R. "The Rise and Fall of Behaviorism," *J. Gen. Psychol.*, 1938, 18:401–402.

HART, CHARLES A. *The Thomistic Concept of Mental Faculty.* Washington: The Catholic University of America Press, 1930.

HAURET, CHARLES. *Beginnings: Genesis and Modern Science.* Trans. by E. P. Emmans, O.P. Dubuque: The Priory Press, 1955.

HAYES, CATHY H. *Ape in Our House.* New York: Harper, 1951.

HEBB, D. O. *A Textbook of Psychology.* Philadelphia: Saunders, 1958.

HEIDBREDER, EDNA. *Seven Psychologies.* New York: Century, 1933.

HELSON, H. (Ed.) *Theoretical Foundations of Psychology.* New York: Van Nostrand, 1951.

HERR, VINCENT V., S.J. "Gestalt Psychology: Empirical or Rational?" in Anton C. Pegis (Ed.), *Essays in Modern Scholasticism.* Westminster, Md.: Newman, 1944. Pp. 222–243.

HERRICK, C. JUDSON. *Fatalism or Freedom: A Biologist's Answer.* New York: Norton, 1926.

HICKS, LESLIE H. "An Analysis of Number-concept Formation in the Rhesus Monkey," *J. Comp. Physiol. Psychol.*, 1956, 49:212–218.

HILGARD, ERNEST R. *Introduction to Psychology.* New York: Harcourt, Brace, 1953; 2d Ed., 1957.

HILGARD, ERNEST R. *Theories of Learning.* (Rev. Ed.) New York: Appleton-Century-Crofts, 1956.

HOBAN, JAMES H. *The Thomistic Concept of Person and Some of Its Social Implications.* Washington: The Catholic University of America Press, 1939.

HOBBS, NICHOLAS. "Science and Ethical Behavior," *Amer. Psychologist,* 1959, 5:217–225.

HOCKING, WILLIAM E. *The Meaning of Immortality in Human Experience.* New York: Harper, 1957.

HOCKING, WILLIAM E. *Types of Philosophy.* New York: Scribner, 1929.

HOENEN, PETRUS, S.J. *Cosmologia.* (4th Ed.) Rome: Gregorian University, 1949.

HOENEN, PETER, S.J. *The Philosophical Nature of Physical Bodies.* West Baden Springs, Ind.: West Baden College, 1955.

HOENEN, PETER, S.J. *Reality and Judgment According to St. Thomas.* Trans. by H. F. Tiblier, S.J. Chicago: Regnery, 1952.

HOOK, SIDNEY (Ed.) *Determinism and Freedom in the Age of Modern Science.* New York: New York University Press, 1958.

HOOK, SIDNEY (Ed.) *Psychoanalysis, Scientific Method and Philosophy.* New York: New York University Press, 1959.

HOSPERS, JOHN. *An Introduction to Philosophical Analysis.* Englewood Cliffs, N.J.: Prentice-Hall, 1953.

HUDECZEK, METH. M., O.P. "De tempore animationis foetus humani secundum embryologiam hodiernam," *Angelicum,* 1952, 29:162–181.

HULL, ERNEST R., S.J. *The Formation of Character.* St. Louis: Herder, 1921.

HUMPHREY, G. *Thinking: An Introduction to Its Experimental Psychology.* New York: Wiley, 1951.

HUNT, J. McVICKER. "Psychological Services in the Tactics of Psychological Science" (presidential address to American Psychological Association convention, Sept. 1, 1952), *Amer. Psychologist,* 1952, 7:608–622.

ITTLESON, W. H., & CANTRIL, H. *Perception: A Transactional Approach.* New York: Doubleday, 1954.

JAMES, WILLIAM. *The Principles of Psychology.* New York: Holt, 1896. 2 vols.

JOAD, C. E. M. *A Critique of Logical Positivism.* Chicago: University of Chicago Press, 1950.

JOAD, C. E. M. *Guide to Philosophy.* New York: Dover, 1936.

JOAD, C. E. M. *How Our Minds Work.* London: Westhouse, 1946.

JOHANN, ROBERT O., S.J. "Toward a Philosophy of Subjectivity," *Proc. Jesuit Phil. Ass.,* 1958, pp. 35–75.

JOHNSON, DONALD M. *The Psychology of Thought and Judgment.* New York: Harper, 1955.

JUNG, CARL G. *Modern Man in Search of a Soul.* New York: Harcourt, Brace, 1933.

KANE, WILLIAM H., O.P., and others. *Science in Synthesis: A Dialectical Approach to the Integration of the Physical and Natural Sciences.* River Forest, Ill.: Dominican College, 1953.

KAPP, ERNEST. *The Greek Foundations of Traditional Logic.* New York: Columbia University Press, 1942.

KARN, HARRY W., & WEITZ, JOSEPH. *An Introduction to Psychology.* New York: Wiley, 1955.

KASNER, E., & NEWMAN, J. *Mathematics and the Imagination.* New York: Simon and Schuster, 1940.

KATZ, DAVID. *Animals and Men.* New York: Longmans, 1937.

KATZ, DAVID. *Gestalt Psychology.* New York: Ronald, 1950.

KEELER, LEO W., S.J. *The Problem of Error from Plato to Kant.* Rome: Gregorian University, 1934.

KELLER, HELEN. *The Story of My Life.* New York: Grosset, 1904.

KELLOGG W. N., & KELLOGG, LUELLA. *The Ape and the Child.* New York: McGraw-Hill, 1933.

KENNEDY, F., HOFFMAN, H. R., & HAINES, WILLIAM H. "A Study of William Heirens," *Amer. J. Psychiat.*, 1947, 104:113–121.

KLEIN, D. B., *Abnormal Psychology.* New York: Holt, 1951.

KLEITMAN, N. *Sleep and Wakefulness.* University of Chicago Press, 1939.

KLUBERTANZ, GEORGE P., S.J. *The Discursive Power.* St. Louis: *The Modern Schoolman,* 1952.

KLUBERTANZ, GEORGE P., S.J. *The Philosophy of Human Nature.* New York: Appleton-Century-Crofts, 1953.

KLUBERTANZ, GEORGE P., S.J. "St. Thomas and the Knowledge of the Singular," *The New Scholasticism,* 1952, 26:135–166.

KLUBERTANZ, GEORGE P., S.J. "The Unity of Operation," *The Modern Schoolman,* 1950, 27:75–103.

KLUCKHOHN, CLYDE, & MURRAY, HENRY, A. (Eds.) *Personality in Nature, Society, and Culture.* New York: Knopf, 1948.

KOFFKA, KURT. *Principles of Gestalt Psychology.* New York: Harcourt, Brace, 1935.

KÖHLER, WOLFGANG. *Gestalt Psychology.* New York: Liveright, 1929.

KÖHLER, WOLFGANG. *The Mentality of Apes.* New York: Harcourt, Brace, 1925.

KOLESNIK, WALTER B. *Mental Discipline in Modern Education.* Madison: University of Wisconsin Press, 1958.

KOREN, HENRY J., C.S.Sp. *An Introduction to the Philosophy of Animate Nature.* St. Louis: Herder, 1955.

KRECH, DAVID, & CRUTCHFIELD, RICHARD S. *Elements of Psychology.* New York: Knopf, 1958.

LACROIX, ROBERT. *L'Origine de l'âme humaine.* Ottawa: Les Editions de l'Université, 1945.

LAMONT, CORLISS. *The Illusion of Immortality.* (3d Ed.) New York: Philosophical Library, 1959.

LASHLEY, KARL S. "Basic Neural Mechanisms in Behavior" (presidential address), *Psychol. Rev.*, 1930, 37:1–24.

LASHLEY, KARL S. *Brain Mechanisms and Intelligence.* Chicago: University of Chicago Press, 1929.

LASHLEY, KARL S. "Cerebral Control versus Reflexology," *J. Gen. Psychol.*, 1931, 5:3–20.

LEARY, TIMOTHY. *Interpersonal Diagnosis of Personality.* New York: Ronald, 1957.

378   APPENDIX

Ledvina, J. P. *Philosophy and Psychology of Sensation.* Washington: The Catholic University of America Press, 1941.

Lee, Otis. *Existence and Inquiry.* Chicago: University of Chicago Press, 1949.

Lewin, Kurt. *A Dynamic Theory of Personality: Selected Papers.* New York: McGraw-Hill, 1935.

Lewis, C. S. *The Abolition of Man.* New York: Macmillan, 1947.

Lillie, Ralph S. *General Biology and the Philosophy of Organism.* Chicago: University of Chicago Press, 1945.

Lindworsky, Johannes, S.J. *Experimental Psychology.* New York: Macmillan, 1931.

Lindworsky, Johannes, S.J. *The Psychology of Asceticism.* London: Edwards, 1936.

Lindworsky, Johannes, S.J. *The Training of the Will.* Milwaukee: Bruce, 1929.

Lonergan, Bernard J. F., S.J. *Insight: A Study of Human Understanding.* New York: Philosophical Library, 1956.

Lonergan, Bernard J. F., S.J. "St. Thomas' Thought on *Gratia Operans,*" *Theol. Stud.* 1941, 2:289–324; 1942, 3:69–88, 375–402, 533–578.

Lorenz, K. Z. *King Solomon's Ring.* New York: Crowell, 1952.

Lottin, Dom Odon. *La Théorie du libre arbitre depuis S. Anselme jusqu'à S. Thomas d'Aquin.* Louvain: Mont-Cesar, 1299, (Extrait de la *Rev. Thomiste,* 1927–1929.)

Lottin, Dom Odon. *Principes de morale.* Louvain: Mont-Cesar, 1946.

Luce, R. Duncan. *Individual Choice Behavior.* New York: Wiley, 1959.

Lund, F. H., & Glosser, H. J. "The Nature of Mental Illness: Diversity of Psychiatric Opinion," *Educ.,* 1957, 78:154–166.

McAndrew, Sr. M. Bernardina. "An Experimental Investigation of Young Children's Ideas of Causality," *Catholic Univer. Stud. in Psychol. and Psychiat.,* 1943, Vol. VI, No. 2.

McCall, Raymond J. *Preface to Psychology.* Milwaukee: Bruce, 1959.

McCarthy, Raphael C., S.J. *The Measurement of Conation.* Chicago: Loyola University Press, 1926.

McCary, J. L. (Ed.) *Psychology of Personality: Six Modern Approaches.* New York: Logos Press, 1956.

McClelland, David C. "Conscience and the Will Rediscovered," review of Karl Mierke's *Wille und Leistung* (Göttingen: Verlag für Psychologie, 1955), *Contemporary Psychol.,* 1957, 2:177–179.

McClelland, David C. (Ed.) *Studies in Motivation.* New York: Appleton-Century-Crofts, 1955.

McClelland, David C., & Atkinson, J. W. "The Projective Expression of Needs: The Effect of Different Intensities of the Hunger Drive on Perception," *J. Psychol.*, 1948, 25:205–222.

McCLELLAND, DAVID C., and others. *The Achievement Motive.* New York: Appleton-Century-Crofts, 1953.

McCORMICK, JOHN F., S.J. "The Burden of the Body," *The New Scholasticism*, 1938, 12:392–400.

McCORMICK, JOHN F., S.J. "The Burden of Intellect," *The Modern Schoolman*, 1935, 12:79–81.

McCOY, ALAN EDWARD, O.F.M. *Force and Fear in Relation to Delictual Imputability and Penal Responsibility.* Washington: The Catholic University of America Press, 1944.

McDOUGALL, WILLIAM. *Body and Mind: A History and Defense of Animism.* London: Methuen, 1915.

McDOUGALL, WILLIAM. *The Energies of Men.* (4th Ed.) London: Methuen, 1939.

McDOUGALL, WILLIAM. *Outline of Abnormal Psychology.* New York: Scribner, 1926a.

McDOUGALL, WILLIAM. *An Outline of Psychology.* (3d Ed.) London: Methuen, 1926b.

McGEOCH, JOHN A., & IRION, A. L. *The Psychology of Human Learning.* (2d Ed.) New York: Longmans, 1952.

McKENZIE, JOHN L., S.J. *The Two-edged Sword: An Interpretation of the Old Testament.* Milwaukee: Bruce, 1956.

McKIAN, J. D. "The Metaphysics of Introspection According to St. Thomas Aquinas," *The New Scholasticism*, 1941, 15:89–117.

McMULLIN, ERNAN. "Realism in Modern Cosmology," *Proc. Amer. Cath. Phil. Ass.*, 1955, 29:137–150.

MacPARTLAND, JOHN. *The March Toward Matter.* New York: Philosophical Library, 1952.

MAHER, MICHAEL, S.J. *Psychology: Empirical and Rational.* (9th ed.) London: Longmans, 1921.

MARC, ANDRÉ, S.J. *Psychologie réflexive.* Brussels: L'Edition Universelle, 1949. 2 vols.

MARITAIN, JACQUES. *Art and Scholasticism.* New York: Scribner, 1930.

MARITAIN, JACQUES. *Distinguish to Unite: The Degrees of Knowledge.* New York: Scribner, 1959.

MARITAIN, JACQUES. *Freedom in the Modern World.* New York: Scribner, 1936.

MARITAIN, JACQUES. *The Range of Reason.* New York: Scribner, 1952.

MARITAIN, JACQUES. *True Humanism.* New York: Scribner, 1938.

MARTIN, OLIVER. "An Examination of Contemporary Naturalism and Materialism," in John Wild (Ed.), *The Return to Reason.* Chicago: Regnery, 1953. Pp. 68–91.

MARTIN, OLIVER. *The Order and Integration of Knowledge.* Ann Arbor: University of Michigan Press, 1956.

MASLOW, ABRAHAM A. *Motivation and Personality.* New York: Harper, 1954.

MAURER, ARMAND, C.S.B. "Introduction," in *St. Thomas Aquinas: The Division and Methods of the Sciences.* (2d Rev. Ed.) Toronto: Pontifical Institute, 1958.

MAY, ROLLO, and others (Eds.) *Existence: A New Dimension in Psychiatry and Psychology.* New York: Basic Books, 1958.

MAYER, MARY HELEN. *The Philosophy of Teaching of St. Thomas Aquinas.* Milwaukee: Bruce, 1929.

MAYER, MAJOR WILLIAM E. "Why Did Many G.I. Captives Cave In?" *U.S. News and World Report,* Feb. 24, 1956, Pp. 56–72.

MERCIER, J. CARDINAL. *The Origins of Contemporary Psychology.* (2d Ed.) London: R. & T. Washbourne, 1918.

MESSENGER, E. C. *Evolution and Theology.* New York: Macmillan, 1932.

MESSENGER, E. C. (Ed.) *Theology and Evolution.* London: Sands, 1949.

MEYER, HANS. *The Philosophy of St. Thomas Aquinas.* Trans. by Rev. F. Eckhoff. St. Louis: Herder, 1944.

MICHAELS, PETER. "A Christian Abnormal Psychology," *Integrity,* I:2–44, 1947.

MICHEL, VIRGIL. "Psychological Data," *The New Scholasticism,* 1929, 3:185–188.

MICHOTTE, ALBERT E. "The Emotions Regarded as Functional Connections," in Martin L. Reymert (Ed.), *Feelings and Emotions.* New York: McGraw-Hill, 1950.

MILLER, MARIANNE T. "The Problem of Action in the Commentary of St. Thomas Aquinas on the Physics of Aristotle," *The Modern Schoolman,* 1946, 23:135–167.

MISIAK, HENRYK, & STAUDT, VIRGINIA M. *Catholics in Psychology.* New York: McGraw-Hill, 1954.

MOBERLY, SIR WALTER. *Responsibility: The Concept in Psychology, in the Law, and in the Christian Faith.* Greenwich, Conn.: Seabury Press, 1956.

MONAGHAN, EDWARD A. "Major Factors in Cognition," *Catholic Univer. Stud. in Psychol. and Psychiat.,* 1935, Vol. III, No. 5.

MONTAGU, ASHLEY. *Immortality.* New York: Grove Press, 1955.

MOORE, THOMAS VERNER. *Cognitive Psychology.* Philadelphia: Lippincott, 1939.

MOORE, THOMAS VERNER. "Consciousness and the Nervous System," *Catholic Univer. Stud. in Psychol. and Psychiat.,* 1938, Vol. IV, No. 3.

MOORE, THOMAS VERNER. *The Driving Forces of Human Nature and Their Adjustment.* New York: Grune & Stratton, 1948.

MOORE, THOMAS VERNER. *Dynamic Psychology.* Philadelphia: Lippincott, 1926.

MOORE, THOMAS VERNER. "Human and Animal Intelligence," in H. S. Jennings and others, *Scientific Aspects of the Race Problem.* New York: Longmans, 1941. Pp. 95–158.

MOORE, THOMAS VERNER. "Image and Meaning in Memory and Perception," *Psychol. Monogr.*, 1919, 27(119):67–296.

MOORE, THOMAS VERNER. "The Process of Abstraction," *University of California Publications in Psychology,* 1910, I:73–197.

MOORE, THOMAS VERNER. "Reasoning Ability of Children in the First Years of School Life," *Catholic Univer. Stud. in Psychol. and Psychiat.,* 1929, Vol. II, No. 2.

MOORE, THOMAS VERNER. "A Scholastic Theory of Perception," *The New Scholasticism,* 1933, VII:222–238.

MOORE, THOMAS VERNER. "The Temporal Relations of Meaning and Imagery," *Psychol. Rev.,* 1915, 22:177–225.

MORGAN, CLIFFORD T. *Introduction to Psychology.* New York: McGraw-Hill, 1956.

MORRISON, JOHN L. "American Catholics and the Crusade against Evolution," *Rec. Amer. Catholic Historical Soc. of Philadelphia,* 1953, 44:59–71.

MOUNIER, EMMANUEL. *The Character of Man.* Trans. by Cynthia Rowland. New York: Harper, 1956.

MOUROUX, J. *The Meaning of Man.* Trans. by A. H. C. Downes. New York: Sheed, 1948.

MOWRER, O. H. *Learning Theory and Personality Dynamics: Selected Papers.* New York: Ronald, 1950.

MOWRER, O. H. "On the Dual Nature of Learning: A Reinterpretation of 'Conditioning' and 'Problem-solving'," *Harvard Educ. Rev.,* 1947, 17:102–148.

MOWRER, O. H. "The Psychologist Looks at Language," (presidential address), *Amer. Psychologist,* 1954, 9:660–694.

MOWRER, O. H. "Some Philosophical Problems in Mental Disorder and Its Treatment," *Harvard Educ. Rev.,* 1953, 23:117–127.

MUCKERMANN, HENRY, S.J. *Humanizing the Brute.* St. Louis: Herder, 1906.

MÜLLER-FREIENFELS, RICHARD. *The Evolution of Modern Psychology.* Trans. by W. B. Wolfe. New Haven, Conn.: Yale University Press, 1935.

MUNN, NORMAN L. *Psychology: The Fundamentals of Human Adjustment.* (3d Ed.), Boston: Houghton Mifflin, 1956.

MURPHY, GARDNER. *An Historical Introduction to Modern Psychology.* (Rev. Ed.) New York: Harcourt, Brace, 1949.

MURPHY, GARDNER. *Human Potentialities.* New York: Basic Books, 1958.

MURRAY, RAYMOND W., C.S.C. *Man's Unknown Ancestors.* (2d Ed.) Milwaukee: Bruce, 1948.

Nebraska Symposium on Motivation. Lincoln: University of Nebraska Press. Published annually since 1953.

DU NOÜY, LECOMTE. *Human Destiny.* New York: Longmans, 1947.

NUTTIN, JOSEPH. *Psychoanalysis and Personality: A Dynamic Theory of Normal Personality.* New York: Sheed, 1953.

NUTTIN, JOSEPH. *Psychology, Morality and Education.* Springfield, Ill.: Templegate, 1959.

O'CONNOR, WILLIAM R. *The Eternal Quest.* New York: Longmans, 1947.

O'CONNOR, WILLIAM R. "Molina and Bañez as Interpreters of St. Thomas Aquinas," *The New Scholasticism,* 1947, 21:243–259.

O'CONNOR, WILLIAM R. *The Natural Desire for God.* Milwaukee: Marquette University Press, 1948.

ODIER, CHARLES. "Les Deux sources, consciente et inconsciente, de la vie morale," *Cahiers de Philosophie,* November, 1943–February, 1947, 4–5.

OLGIATI, FRANCESCO. *The Key to the Study of St. Thomas.* Trans. by J. S. Zybura. St. Louis: Herder, 1925.

O'NEILL, REGINALD F., S.J. *Theories of Knowledge.* Englewood Cliffs, N.J.: Prentice-Hall, 1960.

OSGOOD, CHARLES E. *Method and Theory in Experimental Psychology.* New York: Oxford, 1953.

OSGOOD, CHARLES E. Review of J. P. van de Geer, *A Psychological Study of Problem Solving* (Haarlem: Uitgeverij de Toorts, 1957), *Contemporary Psychol.,* 1958, 3:197–198.

OSGOOD, CHARLES E., and others. *The Measurement of Meaning.* Urbana, Ill.: University of Illinois Press, 1957.

PEGHAIRE, JULIEN. "A Forgotten Sense, the Cogitative, According to St. Thomas Aquinas," *The Modern Schoolman,* 1943, 20:123–140, 210–229.

PEGIS, ANTON C. *The Problem of the Soul in the Thirteenth Century.* Toronto: Institute of Medieval Studies, 1934.

PEGIS, ANTON C. "St. Thomas and the Unity of Man," in J. A. McWilliams, S.J. (Ed.), *Progress in Philosophy.* Milwaukee: Bruce, 1955. Pp. 153–173.

PENFIELD, WILDER. "The Permanent Record of the Stream of Consciousness," *Proc. 14th Int. Congr. Psychol.,* Montreal, 1954.

PHILLIPS, R. P., O.P. *Modern Thomistic Philosophy*. Westminster, Md.: Newman, 1950.

PIAGET, JEAN. *Logic and Psychology*. New York: Basic Books, 1957.

PIAGET, JEAN. *The Moral Judgment of the Child*. Glencoe, Ill.: Free Press, 1948.

PIAGET, JEAN. *The Origins of Intelligence in Children*. New York: International Universities Press, 1952.

PIAGET, JEAN. *The Psychology of Intelligence*. New York: Harcourt, Brace, 1950.

PLATO. *Phaedo; The Apology of Socrates; Alcibiades I*. New York: Random House, 1941.

POSTMAN, L., BRUNER, J. S., & McGINNIES, E. "Personal Values as Selective Factors in Perception," *J. Abnorm. Soc. Psychol.*, 1948, 43:142–154.

PROTHRO, TERRY E., & TESKA, P. T. *Psychology: A Biosocial Study of Behavior*. Boston: Ginn, 1950.

RANK, OTTO. *Will Therapy*. New York: Knopf, 1936.

RAPAPORT, DAVID. *Emotions and Memory*. New York: International Universities Press, 1957.

REANY, WILLIAM. *The Creation of the Human Soul*. New York: Benziger, 1932.

REGIS, L. M., O.P. *Epistemology*. Trans. by I. C. Byrne. New York: Macmillan, 1959.

REGIS, L. M., O.P. *St. Thomas and Epistemology*. Milwaukee: Marquette University Press, 1946.

REINHARDT, KURT F. *A Realistic Philosophy*. Milwaukee: Bruce, 1944.

REITH, HERMAN, C.S.C. *An Introduction to Philosophical Psychology*. Englewood Cliffs, N.J.: Prentice-Hall, 1956.

RENARD, HENRI, S.J., & VASKE, MARTIN O., S.J. *The Philosophy of Man*. (Rev. Ed.) Milwaukee: Bruce, 1956.

REYMERT, MARTIN L. (Ed.) *Feelings and Emotions: The Mooseheart Symposium*. New York: McGraw-Hill, 1950.

REYMERT, MARTIN L. (Ed.) *Feelings and Emotions: The Wittenburg Symposium*. Worcester: Clark University Press, 1928.

RICKABY, JOSEPH, S.J. *Free Will and Four English Philosophers*. London: Burns, 1905.

RIMAUD, JEAN. "Les Psychologues contre la morale," *Etudes*, 1949, 263:3–22.

ROE, ANNE, & SIMPSON, GEORGE G. (Eds.) *Behavior and Evolution*. New Haven: Yale University Press, 1958.

ROHDE, ERWIN. *Psyche: The Cult of Souls and Belief in Immortality among the Greeks*. Trans. by W. B. Willis. New York: Harcourt, Brace, 1925.

ROMANES, GEORGE JOHN. *Mental Evolution in Animals* (with a posthumous essay "Instinct" by Charles Darwin). London: Kegan Paul, Trench, Tubner & Co., 1883.

ROUSSELOT, PIERRE, S.J. *The Intellectualism of St. Thomas*. Trans. by James E. O'Mahony, O.M.Cap. London: Sheed, 1935.

ROYCE, JAMES E., S.J. "Life and Living Beings," *The Modern Schoolman*, 1960, 37:213–232.

ROYCE, JAMES E., S.J. *Personality and Mental Health*. Milwaukee: Bruce, 1955.

ROYCE, JAMES E., S.J. "St. Thomas and the Definition of Active Potency," *The New Scholasticism*, 1960, 34(4):431–437.

ROZWADOWSKI, A., S.J. "De distinctione potentiarum a substantia," *Gregorianum*, 1935, 16:272–281.

RUCH, FLOYD L. *Psychology and Life*. (5th Ed.) Chicago: Scott, Foresman, 1958.

RUFFINI, ERNESTO, CARDINAL. *The Theory of Evolution Judged by Reason and Faith*. Trans. by Rev. Francis O'Hanlon. New York: J. F. Wagner, 1959.

RYAN, EDMUND J., C.Pp.S. *The Role of the Sensus Communis in the Philosophy of St. Thomas Aquinas*. Carthagena, Ohio: Messenger Press, 1951.

SANFORD, R. N. "The Effects of Abstinence from Food upon Imaginal Processes: A Preliminary Experiment," *J. Psychol.*, 1936, 2:129–136.

SARTRE, JEAN-PAUL. *Existential Psychoanalysis*. Trans. by Hazel E. Barnes. New York: Philosophical Library, 1954.

SCHEIN, EDGAR H. "The Id as Salesman," review of Vance Packard's *The Hidden Persuaders* (New York: McKay, 1957), *Contemporary Psychol.*, 1957, 2:308–309.

SCHILLER, CLAIRE H. (Ed.) *Instinctive Behavior: The Development of a Modern Concept*. New York: International Universities Press, 1957.

SCHNEIDERS, ALEXANDER A. *Introductory Psychology*. New York: Rinehart, 1951.

SCHNEIDERS, ALEXANDER A., "Psychology as a Normative Science," in Magda B. Arnold & John A. Gasson, S.J., and others, *The Human Person: An Approach to an Integral Theory of Personality*. New York: Ronald, 1954. Pp. 373–394.

SCHRODINGER, ERWIN, *What Is Life?* New York: Macmillan, 1945.

SERTILLANGES, A. D. *The Intellectual Life*. Westminster, Md.: Newman, 1948.

SHARPE, A. B. *The Freedom of the Will*. Vol. I. Westminster Lectures. St. Louis: Herder, 1906.

SHERRINGTON, CHARLES S. Man on His Nature. (2d Ed.) Cambridge, 1940. Garden City, N.Y.: Doubleday (Anchor), 1953.

SIMON, HERBERT A. Models of Man. New York: Wiley, 1957.

SIMON, YVES. Traité du libre arbitre. Liège: Sciences et Lettres, 1951.

SIMON, YVES, & PEGHAIRE, JULIEN. "The Philosophical Study of Sensation," The Modern Schoolman, 1945, 23:111–119.

SINNOTT, E. W. Cell and Psyche: The Biology of Purpose. Chapel Hill: University of North Carolina Press, 1950.

SIWEK, PAUL, S.J. Aristotelis de anima libri tres. (Edidit, versione auxit, notis illustravit.) Rome: Gregorian University, 1933.

SIWEK, PAUL, S.J. The Enigma of the Hereafter: The Reincarnation of Souls. New York: Philosophical Library, 1952.

SIWEK, PAUL, S.J. Experimental Psychology. New York: J. F. Wagner, 1959.

SIWEK, PAUL, S.J. Psychologia metaphysica. (5th Ed.) Rome: Gregorian University, 1956.

SIWEK, PAUL, S.J. La Psychophysique humaine d'après Aristote. Paris: Alcan, 1930.

SLAVIN, ROBERT J. The Philosophical Basis of Individual Differences. Washington: The Catholic University of America Press, 1936.

SMITH, GERARD B., S.J. "A Date in the History of Epistemology," The Thomist (Maritain Volume), 1943, 5:246–255.

SMITH, VINCENT EDWARD. Idea-Men of Today. Milwaukee: Bruce, 1950.

SNIDER, LOUIS B., S.J. "A Research Method of Validating Self-determination," in Magda B. Arnold & John A. Gasson, S.J., and others, The Human Person: An Approach to an Integral Theory of Personality. New York: Ronald, 1954. Pp. 222–263.

SOLOMON, HARRY C., COBB, STANLEY, & PENFIELD, WILDER (Eds.) The Brain and Human Behavior. Baltimore: Williams & Wilkins, 1958.

SONNEMANN, ULRICH. Existence and Therapy. New York: Grune & Stratton, 1955.

SOROKIN, P. Social and Cultural Dynamics. New York: American Book, 1937–1941. 4 vols.

SPEARMAN, CHARLES. The Abilities of Man. New York: St. Martin's, 1927a.

SPEARMAN, CHARLES. The Nature of "Intelligence" and the Principles of Cognition. (2d Ed.) New York: St. Martin's, 1927b.

SPEARMAN, CHARLES. Psychology down the Ages. New York: St. Martin's, 1937.

SPEARMAN, CHARLES, & JONES, L. W. Human Ability. New York: St. Martin's, 1950.

SPRINKLE, HENRY CALL. Concerning the Philosophical Defensibility of *a Limited Indeterminism*. New Haven: Yale University Press, 1933.

STAFFORD, JOHN W., C.S.V. "Freedom in Experimental Psychology," *Proc. Amer. Cath. Phil. Ass.*, 1940, 16:148–153.

STEVENS, S. S. (Ed.) *Handbook of Experimental Psychology*. New York: Wiley, 1951.

STEVENS, S., & DAVIS, H. *Hearing: Its Psychology and Physiology*. New York: Wiley, 1938.

STONE, L. JOSEPH, & CHURCH, JOSEPH. *Childhood and Adolescence: A Psychology of the Growing Person*. New York: Random House, 1957.

STRASSER, STEPHAN. *The Soul in Metaphysical and Empirical Psychology*. Pittsburgh: Duquesne University Press, 1957.

STRATTON, G. M. "Vision without Inversion of the Retinal Image," *Psychol. Rev.*, 1897, 4:341–360, 463–481.

SULLIVAN, DANIEL J. *An Introduction to Philosophy*, Milwaukee: Bruce, 1957.

SULLIVAN, ROBERT P., O.P. "Man's Thirst for Good," *Thomistic Stud.* No. 4. Westminster, Md.: Newman, 1952.

SULLIVAN, ROBERT P., O.P. *The Thomistic Concept of the Natural Necessitation of the Human Will*. River Forest, Ill.: Pontifical Faculty of Philosophy, 1952.

SYMONDS, PERCIVAL M. *Dynamics of Psychotherapy*. Vol. I, *Principles*. Vol. II, *Process*. New York: Grune & Stratton, 1956–1957.

SYMONDS, PERCIVAL M. *The Ego and the Self*. New York: Appleton-Century-Crofts, 1951.

TANQUEREY, A. *The Spiritual Life*. (2d Ed.) Trans. by H. Branders. Tournai, Belgium: Desclee, 1930.

TAYLOR, A. E. *The Christian Hope of Immortality*. New York: Macmillan, 1947.

TAYLOR, A. E. *The Faith of a Moralist*. Series I. New York: St. Martin's, 1951.

TEALE, E. W. *The Insect World of J. Henri Fabre*. New York: Dodd, Mead, 1949.

TERRUWE, A. A. A. *Psychopathic Personality and Neurosis*. Trans. by Conrad W. Baars, M.D. Ed. by Jordan Aumann, O.P. New York: P. J. Kenedy & Sons, 1958.

THORPE, W. H. *Learning and Instinct in Animals*. Cambridge, Mass.: Harvard University Press, 1956.

THURSTONE, LOUIS L. *Vectors of Mind*. Chicago: University of Chicago Press, 1935.

THURSTONE, LOUIS L., and others. *The Measurement of Values*. Chicago: University of Chicago Press, 1959.

TINBERGEN, N. *The Study of Instinct.* New York: Oxford, 1951.

TITCHENER, EDWARD B. "Description versus Statement of Meaning," *Am. J. Psychol.,* 1912, 23:164–182.

TITCHENER, EDWARD B. *Experimental Psychology. Part I, Qualitative Experiments.* Part II, *Teacher's Manual.* New York: Macmillan, 1918.

TITCHENER, EDWARD B. *Lectures on the Experimental Psychology of the Thought Processes.* New York: Macmillan, 1927.

TITCHENER, EDWARD B. *Systematic Psychology: Prolegomena.* New York: Macmillan, 1929.

TITCHENER, EDWARD B. *A Text-Book of Psychology.* New York: Macmillan, 1912.

TITUS, HAROLD H. *Living Issues in Philosophy.* New York: American Book, 1953.

DE TONQUÉDEC, JOSEPH. *La Critique de la connaissance.* Paris: Beauchesne, 1929.

TOURNIER, PAUL. *The Meaning of Persons.* New York: Harper, 1957.

TRAVIS, L. E. "Brain Potentials and the Temporal Course of Consciousness," *J. Exp. Psychol.,* 1937, 21:302–309.

TYLER, LEONA B. "Toward a Workable Psychology of Individuality," *Amer. Psychologist,* 1959, 14:75–81.

VERCORS (pscud.) *You Shall Know Them.* New York: Little, Brown, 1953.

VINACKE, W. EDGAR. *The Psychology of Thinking.* New York: McGraw-Hill, 1952.

VOLLERT, CYRIL, S.J. "Evolution of the Human Body," *The Catholic Mind,* 1952, No. 1071. Pp. 135–154.

VON FRISCH, K. *Bees: Their Vision, Chemical Senses, and Language.* Ithaca, N.Y.: Cornell University Press, 1950.

WALKER, LESLIE J., S.J. *Theories of Knowledge.* (2d Ed.) New York: Longmans, 1924.

WASMANN, ERIC, S.J. *Instinct and Intelligence in the Animal Kingdom.* St. Louis: Herder, 1903.

WEISS, PAUL. *Man's Freedom.* New Haven: Yale University Press, 1950.

WEISS, PAUL. *Nature and Man.* New York: Holt, 1947.

WELLMUTH, JOHN J. *The Nature and Origins of Scientism.* Milwaukee: Marquette University Press, 1944.

WHEELWRIGHT, PHILIP. *The Way of Philosophy.* New York: Odyssey, 1954.

WHITE, ROBERT W. *Lives in Progress.* New York: Dryden, 1952.

WHITEHEAD, ALFRED N. *Science and the Modern World.* New York: Macmillan, 1925.

WHORF, B. L. *Language, Thought, and Reality: Selected Writings of Benjamin Lee Whorf.* Ed. by John B. Carroll. Cambridge, Mass.: Massachusetts Institute of Technology Press, 1956.

WILD, JOHN. *Introduction to Realistic Philosophy.* New York: Harper, 1948.

WILD, JOHN (Ed.) *The Return to Reason: Essays in Realistic Philosophy.* Chicago: Regnery, 1953.

WILHELMSEN, FREDERICK S. *Man's Knowledge of Reality.* Englewood Cliffs, N.J.: Prentice-Hall, 1956.

WILLIAMS, ROGER J. *Biochemical Individuality.* New York: Wiley, 1956.

WILM, E. C. *Theories of Instinct.* New Haven: Yale University Press, 1925.

WINDLE, SIR BERTRAM C. A. *Vitalism and Scholasticism.* St. Louis: Herder, 1920.

WINDLE, SIR BERTRAM C. A. *What is Life? A Study of Vitalism and Neo-vitalism.* St. Louis: Herder, 1908.

WITKIN, H. A., and others. *Personality Through Perception: An Experimental and Clinical Study.* New York: Harper, 1954.

WOODWORTH, ROBERT S. *Contemporary Schools of Psychology.* (Rev. Ed.) New York: Ronald, 1948.

WOODWORTH, ROBERT S., *Dynamics of Behavior.* New York: Holt, 1958.

WOODWORTH, ROBERT S. *Experimental Psychology.* (1st Ed.) New York: Holt, 1938.

WOODWORTH, ROBERT S., & SCHLOSBERG, H. *Experimental Psychology.* (Rev. Ed.) New York: Holt, 1954.

WOODWORTH, ROBERT S. "Non-sensory Components of Sense Perception," in *Psychological Issues.* New York: Columbia University Press, 1939. Pp. 80–88.

WOODWORTH, ROBERT S. "A Revision of Imageless Thought," *Psychol. Rev.,* 1915, 22:1–27.

WUELLNER, BERNARD, S.J. *A Christian Philosophy of Life.* Milwaukee: Bruce, 1957.

WUNDT, WILHELM. *Introduction to Psychology.* Trans. by R. Pitner. London: G. Allen, 1912.

YERKES, ROBERT M. *Chimpanzees: A Laboratory Colony.* New Haven: Yale University Press, 1943.

YERKES, ROBERT M., & YERKES, ADA W. *The Great Apes.* New Haven: Yale University Press, 1929.

YOUNG, P. T. "Auditory Localization with Acoustical Transposition of the Ears," *J. Exp. Psychol.,* 1928, 11:399–429.

YOUNG, P. T. "The Role of Hedonic Processes in Motivation," in *Ne-*

braska Symposium on Motivation, 1955. Lincoln: University of Nebraska Press, 1955. Pp. 193–238.

ZEDLER, BEATRICE G. "Averroës and Immortality," *The New Scholasticism*, 1954, 28:436–453.

Index

Abilities (see Powers)
Abstract idea, 92
Abstraction, 117
Accident and substance, 27, 32, 230, 233–234, 300–303
Acts of will, elicited, 180
Adaptation, 61, 66, 273
Affective states, 166
Agent intellect, 117–120
Ambiguous figures, 74
Animal intelligence, 83–84, 90, 358, 361
Animal soul, 296–297, 330, 338
Animals differ from plants, 42–43
Annihilation of soul, 324–326
Ape and child, 357
Appetite, 33–34, 155–159
  elicited, 34, 157
  kinds of, 157
  rational, 157–159, 176–177
  sensory, divisions of, 166
    organic nature of, 172
Appetition follows cognition, 156
Artificial life, 348–350

Banez, 220
Behaviorism, 28, 44–47, 175
  and thought, 102
  and will, 182
Bernard of Chartres, 15
Binet, Alfred, 98
Blood and life, 296
Body, 292
  and mind, 300
Boring, E. G., 19, 47, 210
Brain, and free choice, 180, 215
  and learning, 248–251
  and thought, 101–103, 146–148, 316
  bibliography, 114
Brain-washing, 178
Brain waves, 102–103
Bridgman, P., 13
Burial, Christian, 334

Cantril, H., 46, 104, 210, 310
Carnap, R., 13, 57
Carrell, A., 260, 267
Cartwright, D., vi

391

Cell colony, 264
Central sense, 72
Change, intentional, 133–134
  physical, 133
  substantial, 285–287
Chemical elements, 260, 265
Choice (see Free choice)
Cognition (see Knowledge)
Cognitive power, 82
Cognitive powers, summary of, 54
Cole, L. E., 12
Colony theory, 264
Combs, Arthur W., 46, 193–194
Commanded acts, 180
Common object, 53
Common sense, 72
Comparative sense, 82
Compton, A. H., 214
Conation, 155
Concept, 91, 143, 361
  formation, bibliography, 130
Conception of embryo, 342
Conceptual language, 105–109
Conceptualism, 116
Concrete idea, 91
Concupiscible appetite, 167
Conditioning, 83, 248–249
Conflict, 235, 268, 298
Conscience, 121
Consciousness, 28–29, 43, 48, 261
  and central sense, 73
  and modern psychology, 43–48
  stream of, 311–312
Constancy, 77
Contrast, 75
Control, of emotion, 170
  voluntary, 182
Copy theory of knowledge, 51
Creation of soul, 339–341
Creative imagination, 80
Cremation, 334
Criminology, 207
Crutchfield, Richard S., 67
Cues, perceptual, 67, 77
Cutaneous senses, 63

Darwin, Charles, 346
Death, 287, 289, 294–295, 299–300
Deliberation, 201
Delusion, 77
Democritus, 115
Descartes, René, 32, 43, 281, 301
Desire, 162
Determinism, 191–192
  physical, 213–216
  psychological, 211–213
  theological, 218–220
Differences, individual, 235, 318–319
Discursive power, 82
Distinct versus separate, 31
Division of living things, 318
Double-aspect theories, 280
Dreams, 80
Drive, 161
Drugs and choice, 202
Dualism, 32, 258, 282, 309
  exaggerated, 280–282, 299–303
Dunlap, K., 246
Dynamics, 33–34, 155–159

Eccles, J., 216
Edwards, Jonathan, 211
EEG (electroencephalography), 102
Ego, 29
Elements in substance, 260, 265
Elicited acts of will, 180
Elicited appetite, 34, 157
Emotion, 165–172
  control of, 170
  definition of, 166
  nature of, 168
Engrams, 145–146, 248–249
Entitative habit, 241
Epiphenomenalism, 280
Epistemology, 50
Equilibrium, 64
ESP (extrasensory perception), 127
Essentialism, 12, 51, 311
Estimative power, 82
  bibliography, 87

Evolution, 345–348
 bibliography, 352–353
Exaggerated dualism, 280–282, 299–303
Exaggerated indeterminism, 187
Exemplary cause, 284n.
Existential therapy, 245, 320
Existentialism, 14, 29, 208
Experience, 28–30, 44, 47
Expressed *species*, 141n.
External senses, 58–59

Faculty, 31, 233
Fantasy, 80
Feeling, 166
Feigl, H., 21
Final cause (*see* Teleology)
Fly-catcher plant, 42
Formal causality, 283–288
Formal object, 52
 of intellect, 124
Fragmentary life, 260, 267
Free choice, 186–222
 and abnormality, 207, 246
 definition of, 197
 difficulties against, 211
 and emotion, 170
 and God, 218–220
 and habit, 240, 245
 and hypnosis, 216
 limits of, 188, 195, 198, 245–246
 and neurology, 215
 and nonscholastics, 208
 proofs of, 204–208
 and psychology, 205, 209
 bibliography, 224
 and science, 213–215
 and unconscious, 194–195
"Free will," 188–190
Freedom, of contrariety, 198
 of exercise, 197
 kinds of, 194

Freedom, of specification, 197
Future life, 331–335

General image, 362
Generation of souls, 338
Genesis, 345–348
Gestalt psychology, 27, 74
 bibliography, 86–87
Gibson, J. J., 47
Gilson, Etienne, 14, 50
Good, 156–160, 177, 198–201, 327
Greater seeming good, 211
Growth, 271–272
Guilford, J. P., 46, 250

Habit, 35, 239–241
 acquisition of, 242
 definition of, 240
 and free choice, 240, 245
 in subrational powers, 242–244
Habitual knowledge, 123, 240
Habitually voluntary acts, 181
Hallucination, 77
Happiness, 327–328
Hearing, 62
Hebb, D. O., 146, 189, 191n.
Hedonism, 175
Heisenberg, 214
Heredity and intelligence, 110
Hierarchy of tendencies, 158–159
Hilgard, Ernest R., on brain and learning, 249
 on consciousness, 28, 47
 on ideas, 104–105
 on language, 109
 on operationism, 30
 on physiology, 35
 on reliability of perception, 79
 on teleology of special senses, 65
 on thinking, 93
History, importance of, 14
Hunt, J. McV., 16, 211

Hylomorphism, 286–294
  diagram of, 302
Hypnosis and free choice, 216

Idea, 91, 143
  formation of, 117
  diagram of, 143
Idealism, 116, 280
Ideas, origin of, 115–120
Identity, personal, 311–312, 332–335
Illusion, 75
Imageless thought, 98–100
  bibliography, 113
Imagination, 80
Immanent action, 273–276
Immaterial intellection, 135–136
Immaterial judgment, 97
Immateriality, degrees of, 134
  of intellect, 91–105
  of knowledge, 133–134
  of soul, 313–316
Immortality, definition of, 324
  false notions, 322–324
  objections against, 323, 330–334
  proofs of, 325
Impressed species, 141
Impulse, 162
Incentive, 160
Incidental object, 53
Incomplete substances, 310–311
Indeterminancy, 214
Indeterminism, 187
Individual differences, 235, 318–319
Individuality of souls, 332
Innatism, 116
Insight, 90, 247, 361
Instinctive behavior, 82, 162, 175, 361–363
Intellect, acts of, 120–124
  agent, 117–120
  definition of, 109
  immateriality of, 91–105
  object of, 124–126
  passive, 117
  potential, 117–120

Intellect, and will in choice, 202
Intellection, diagram of, 143
Intellectual process, summary of, 142
Intelligence, 90, 104
  animal, 358–361
  definition of, 109
  measurement of, 109
Intentional being, 132
Interactionism, 281
Internal senses, and animal behavior, 361–362
  definition of, 71
Interoceptive sensations, 64
Intraorganic sensations, 64
Introspection, 43, 45
IQ, 109
Irascible appetite, 167

James, William, on free choice, 213
  on soul, 287n., 311–312, 332–335
Judgment, 120
  immaterial, 97

Kapp, Ernest, 121
Kinesthesis, 63
Klein, D. B., on free choice, 210
Knowing versus wanting, 33–34
Knowledge, cause of, 137–139
  definition of, 137
  diagram of, 143
  habitual, 123, 240
  nature of, 131–133
  and non-knowers, 42–43
  objects of, 52
  powers, summary of, 54
Köhler, Wolfgang, 358
Krech, David, 67

Language, 105–109
  animal, 101, 105–106, 358–359
Lashley, K. S., 83n., 147, 248
  on soul, 291n.
Law, 207

Learning, 35, 247
  bibliography, 252
Levels of tendency, 158–159
Life, 257, 294
  nature of, 269–276
  synthetic, 348–350
Limen, 65
Lindworsky, J., 178, 246
Living versus nonliving, 259–260, 294
Logical positivism, 12–13, 311
  bibliography, 57

McCary, J. L., 18, 309
McMullin, Ernan, 13
M'Naghten rule, 208
Man, superiority of, 100, 296
Maslow, A. A., 8, 104, 205n., 211, 310
Material cause, 284
Material object, 52
Materialism, 89–90, 280, 290–291,
    309–310, 315
  and psychotherapy, 320
Matter, 301
  and form, 282–288
  principle of individuation, 333
Maurer, Armand, 26n.
Meaning, 105–108
Memory, intellectual, 122
  sense, 81
Mental word, 143–144
Metempsychosis, 334
Mind, 48–49
  and body, 300
"Mind stuff," 43, 49, 301
Moderate dualism, 282
Moderate indeterminism, 192
Molina, 220
Monism, 279
Mowrer, O. H., 310
Mood, 166
Moral freedom, 197
Moral obligation, 206
Morgan, Clifford T., on experiment, 8
  on reliability of perception, 79
  on skin receptors, 63

Morgan, Clifford T., on thought, 100
Motivation, 155
  complex, 163
  in perception, 78
Motive, 160
  and will, 178
Motor images, 216
Murphy, Gardner, 24, 104, 210

Nature, 32
Natural appetite, 157
Necessity, 195
Need, 157, 161
Negative practice, 246
Nominalism, 107

Objective versus subjective, 28–30, 45–
    48
Objects of knowledge, 52–53
Ontologism, 116
Operation follows being, 25
Operationism, 27, 30, 47, 51
  and St. Thomas, 31
Operative powers (see Powers)
Orexis, 155–156
Organ, 34–35, 50, 60, 71, 291
  and emotion, 172
  (See also Brain)
Organic sensations, 64
Organism, 34–35
Origin, of ideas, 115–120
  of man's body, 345
Osgood, Charles E., 107

Particular reason, 82
Passion, 170
Passive intellect, 117
Pavlov, Ivan P., 248
Penfield, Wilder, 81n., 180
  on soul, 291
Per se, definition of, 259
Perception, 73–74
  bibliography, 85

Perception, subjective factors in, 74–79
and thought, 96
Perceptual cues, 77
Perceptual judgment, 26, 50
Person, 268
Personal identity, 311
Personality, 244, 268
multiple, 260, 268
Phantasm, 118, 143
Phenomenology, 29, 50
Phi phenomenon, 77
Philosophy, 5–14
history of, 14–17
Physiology, 34–35, 263
Plants differ from animals, 42–43
Plato, 32, 116, 281, 301
Positivism, 12–13, 311
bibliography, 57
Posthypnotic suggestion, 188
Powers, 30–32, 227–234
distinct from man, 229
and modern psychology, 235
nature of, 231
perfected by habits, 249–251
specified by object, 53, 228, 229
Preexistence of soul, 341
Presence of soul in body, 316–318
Proper object, 52
Propriosensation, 261
Protoplasm, 270–273, 292
synthesis of, 348–350
Pseudophone, 66
Psi-factor, 214
Psyche, 6, 289–294
Psychology, difference from philosophy, 6
relation to philosophy, 17
Psychophysical parallelism, 281
Psychosomatic medicine, 172, 299
Psychosomatic problem, 298–303

Quasi-immaterial intellection, 135
Quiddity, 91

Rational animal, 90, 355–357
Rational psychology, 28n.
Realism, 50–52, 79
bibliography, 56
Reasoning, 121
Reflection, 94
Reflex, 83, 162, 248–249
Reincarnation, 334
Reminiscence, 82
Repressed desire, 162
Repression, 167
Reproduction, 273
Resurrection, 332
Rogers, C. L., 245

Science, and free choice, 213–215
and man, bibliography, 21
nature of, 6–14
Secondary perceptual cues, 77
Selectivity in perception, 78
Self-determination, 193
(See also Free choice)
Self-repair, 272
Semantic differentials, 107
Sensation, three phases, 60
Senses, internal, 70
number of, 62
special, 59
Sensism, 89, 115
Sentiment, 166
Set, 78, 181
Sherrington, C., 146, 215, 291n., 344
Simplicity of soul, 312–313
Singulars, knowledge of, 125
Skin senses, 63
Smell, 63
Smith, G., 50n.
Snygg, Donald, 46, 193–194
Soul, 289–294
as being, 308–309
creation, 339–341
after death, 331–335
definition of, 292–294
knowledge of, 26
presence in body, 316–318

Soul, proof, 294
  simple, 312–313
  spiritual, 313–316
  substantial, 310
  time of origin, 341–345
  and vital operations, 294–302
Spatial relations, 66
Spearman, C., 15, 31, 90, 104, 236
Special sense, definition of, 59
Special senses, outline, 58
Species, 139–143
Speculative judgments, 202
Speech, in animals, 101, 105–106,
  358–359
  power of, 235
Spiritual, definition of, 135–136
  soul as, 313–316
Spiritualism, 280
Spirituality of soul, 313–316
Stimulus and response, 158, 244, 247–
  249
Stream of consciousness, 311–312
Subconscious, 49n.
Subconscious motivation, 188
Subject-object relation, 50–52
Subjective versus objective, 28–30, 45–
  48
Subjective factors in perception, 74–79
Subliminal motivation, 218
Subliminal stimuli, 66
Substance and accident, 27, 32, 230,
  233–234, 300–303
Substantial form, 285–294
Substantiality of soul, 310–311
Subvocal speech, 102
Summary of intellectual process, 142
Suspended animation, 276
Synthesis of living body, 348–350
Synthetic sense, 72

Taste, 62
Teleology, vii, 65, 158–160
  intrinsic, 262, 264
Temperament, 166
Tendency, levels of, 158–159

Terman, L., 104
Terruwe, A. A. A., 167
Thinking, 109
Thought, 89–91
  and brain, 101–103, 146–148, 316
Threshold, 65
Time of soul's origin, 341–345
Titchener, Edward B., 44, 115
Training of will, 246
Transfer of training, 249
Transient action, 273–276
Transmigration of souls, 334
Transplants, 318
Trial and error, 90, 247, 361
Tropisms, 42

Unconscious, 36, 49, 167, 188
  and free choice, 194–195, 246
  motivation, 176
Unifying sense, 72
Unity, kinds of, 258
  of man, 24, 234, 258, 268, 297–303
  and powers, 317–318
Universal ideas, 91–93
Unlimited capacity of intellect, 94–97

Values and recent psychology, 104
Vercors, 4
Vestibular sense, 64
Vices, 241
Virtual presence, 234–235, 265–267,
  275, 317
Virtually voluntary acts, 181
Visceral sensations, 64
Vision, 62
Vital operations, nature of, 270
  scope of term, 257n.
  and soul, 294–302
Vitalism, 289
Volition, 177
Voluntarism, 176
Voluntary acts, 180
Voluntary attention, 97

Watson, J., 44
Weber-Fechner law, 61
White, R. W., on free choice, 211
Whole or parts, 24–28
Whorf, B., 107
Wild boy of Aveyron, 356
Will, 33, 157, 176–177
   habits of, 245–247
   objects of, 179
Will training, 246

Wolf-children of India, 356
Word, and concept, 108
   mental, 144
Wurzburg controversy, 44, 97–100

Yerkes, R. M., 357

Zygote, 343

IMPRIMI POTEST

Alexander F. McDonald, S.J.
Praep. Prov. Oregon.

NIHIL OBSTAT

Ioannes McCorkle, S.S.
Censor Librorum

IMPRIMATUR

✠ Thomas A. Connolly
Archiepiscopus Seattlensis

Die 6a ianuarii 1960